Praise for The Tales of Alvin Maker

"[*Prentice Alvin* is] another thoughtful, involving, im-
mensely appealing yarn, bubbling with folksy charm;
Alvin shows no sign of running out of steam."
                    —*Kirkus Reviews* (starred review)

"The best fantasy series now in progress, Card's Tales of
Alvin Maker record the life of a secular messiah in an
early nineteenth-century America where folk magic
really works. . . . Card continues to surprise and delight
with the new perspectives of light and shadow that his
alternate history throws on the young country's growing
pains."   —*Publishers Weekly*

"At long last, Card returns to what promises to be his most
notable creation, the Tales of Alvin Maker. . . . From
beginning to end, this novel is full of riches that include
Card's command of language (dialect, too!), sense of
history, and vivid portraits of alternate versions of Napoleon, William Henry Harrison, Honoré de Balzac, and
others. This superb and welcome book continues the
saga at the same high level as before and is most highly
recommended."
          —Booklist (starred review) on *Alvin Journeyman*

BY ORSON SCOTT CARD
FROM TOM DOHERTY ASSOCIATES

ENDER UNIVERSE

ENDER SERIES
Ender's Game
Ender in Exile
Speaker for the Dead
Xenocide
Children of the Mind

ENDER'S SHADOW SERIES
Ender's Shadow
Shadow of the Hegemon
Shadow Puppets
Shadow of the Giant
Shadows in Flight

THE FIRST FORMIC WAR
(with Aaron Johnston)
Earth Unaware
Earth Afire
Earth Awakens

THE SECOND FORMIC WAR
(with Aaron Johnston)
The Swarm

ENDER NOVELLAS
A War of Gifts
First Meetings

THE MITHERMAGES
The Lost Gate
The Gate Thief
Gatefather

THE TALES OF ALVIN
MAKER
Seventh Son
Red Prophet
Prentice Alvin

Alvin Journeyman
Heartfire
The Crystal City

HOMECOMING
The Memory of Earth
The Call of Earth
The Ships of Earth
Earthfall
Earthborn

WOMEN OF GENESIS
Sarah
Rebekah
Rachel & Leah

THE COLLECTED SHORT
FICTION OF ORSON SCOTT
CARD
*Maps in a Mirror: The Short
    Fiction of Orson Scott Card*
Keeper of Dreams

STAND-ALONE FICTION
Invasive Procedures
    (with Aaron Johnston)
Empire
Hidden Empire
The Folk of the Fringe
Hart's Hope
*Pastwatch: The Redemption of
    Christopher Columbus*
Saints
Songmaster
Treason
The Worthing Saga
Wyrms
Zanna's Gift

PRENTICE ALVIN

· AND ·

ALVIN JOURNEYMAN

ORSON SCOTT CARD

A TOM DOHERTY ASSOCIATES BOOK | NEW YORK

This is a work of fiction. All of the characters, organizations, and events portrayed in these novels are either products of the author's imagination or are used fictitiously.

PRENTICE ALVIN AND ALVIN JOURNEYMAN

Prentice Alvin copyright © 1989 by Orson Scott Card

Alvin Journeyman copyright © 1995 by Orson Scott Card

Maps by Alan McKnight

All rights reserved.

A Tor Book
Published by Tom Doherty Associates
175 Fifth Avenue
New York, NY 10010

www.tor-forge.com

Tor® is a registered trademark of Macmillan Publishing Group, LLC.

ISBN 978-0-7653-9360-9

Our books may be purchased in bulk for promotional, educational, or business use. Please contact your local bookseller or the Macmillan Corporate and Premium Sales Department at 1-800-221-7945, extension 5442, or by e-mail at MacmillanSpecialMarkets@macmillan.com.

First Mass Market Edition: April 2017

Printed in the United States of America

0 9 8 7 6 5 4 3 2 1

Contents

MAPS   vi, vii

PRENTICE ALVIN   1

ALVIN JOURNEYMAN   389

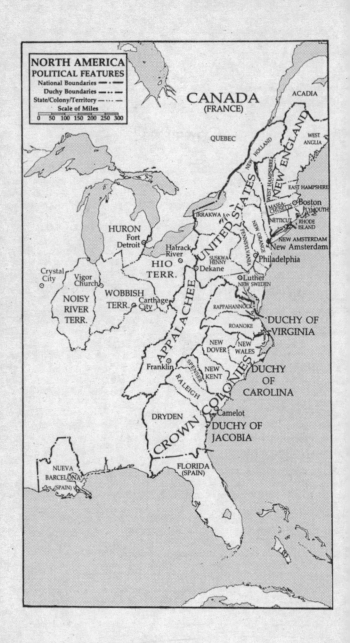

NORTH AMERICA
POLITICAL FEATURES
National Boundaries
Duchy Boundaries
State/Colony/Territory
Scale of Miles
0 50 100 150 200 250 300

CANADA
(FRANCE)

ACADIA

QUEBEC

NEW HOLLAND

WEST HAMPSHIRE

WEST ANGLIA

EAST HAMPSHIRE

HURON

Fort Detroit

IRRAKWA

MASSA-CHUSETTS

Boston
PLYMOUTH

Crystal City

Vigor Church

Hatrack River

HIO TERR.

Dekane

SUSKWA HENRY

NETICUT

RHODE ISLAND

NEW AMSTERDAM

New Amsterdam

NOISY RIVER TERR.

WOBBISH TERR.

Carthage City

UNITED STATES

NEW ORANGE

PENNSYLVANIA

Philadelphia

Luther

NEW SWEDEN

RAPPAHANNOCK

DUCHY OF VIRGINIA

ROANOKE

Franklin

APPALACHEE

NEW DOVER

NEW WALES

SPENSER

NEW KENT

DUCHY OF CAROLINA

RALEIGH

DRYDEN

CROWN COLONIES

Camelot

DUCHY OF JACOBIA

NUEVA BARCELONA
(SPAIN)

FLORIDA
(SPAIN)

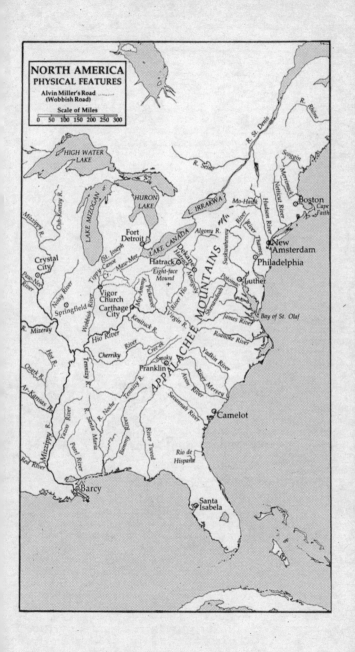

NORTH AMERICA
PHYSICAL FEATURES

Alvin Miller's Road
(Wobbish Road)

Scale of Miles

0 50 100 150 200 250 300

HIGH WATER LAKE

R. Seine

R. St. Denis

R. Rhone

Scoggin

Merrimac

Nettisal

HURON LAKE

LAKE MIZOGAN

L. IRRAKWA

Mo-Hawk

Boston

Cape Faith

Fort Detroit

Algony R.

St. Joseph

Mano-Mee

LAKE CANADA

Irrakwa River

Hudson River

Thames

New Amsterdam

Crystal City

Osh-Kontisy R.

Tippy-Canoe

Cr.

Hatrack

Dekane

Dutch River

Morango

Suskwahenny

Philadelphia

Mizzipy R.

Pease-Nee-Mah River

Noisy River

Springfield

Eight-face Mound

Wobbish River

My-Ammon

Picka-wee

River Hio

Virgin R.

Potomac

Luther

Vigor Church

Carthage City

Shenandoah

Bay of St. Olaf

Kenituck R.

Hio River

Virgin R.

James River

R. Mizeray

Hot R.

Tennizy R.

Cherriky

River

Crik-it

Roanoke River

Ozark R.

Smoky

Yadkin River

Franklin

Aron River

APPALACHEE MOUNTAINS

Ar-Kansas R.

R. Noche

Tennizy R.

River Mersey

Mizzipy R.

R. Santa Maria

Savannah River

Camelot

Yazoo River

Banny

Pearl River

River Tweed

Rio de Hispani

Red River

Barcy

Santa Isabela

PRENTICE
ALVIN

For all my good teachers, especially:

Fran Schroeder,
fourth grade, Millikin Elementary, Santa Clara, California,
for whom I wrote my first poems.

Ida Huber,
tenth-grade English, Mesa High School, Arizona,
who believed in my future more than I did.

Charles Whitman,
playwriting, Brigham Young University,
who made my scripts look better than they deserved.

Norman Council,
literature, University of Utah,
for Spenser and Milton, alive.

Edward Vasta,
literature, University of Notre Dame,
for Chaucer and for friendship.

And always François.

ACKNOWLEDGMENTS

In the preparation of this volume of the Tales of Alvin Maker I have, as always, depended on others for help. For immeasurable help on the opening chapters of this book, my thanks go to the gentlefolk of the second Sycamore Hill Writers Workshop, to wit: Carol Emshwiller, Karen Joy Fowler, Gregg Keizer, James Patrick Kelly, John Kessel, Nancy Kress, Shariann Lewitt, Jack Massa, Rebecca Brown Ore, Susan Palwick, Bruce Sterling, Mark L. Van Name, Connie Willis, and Allen Wold.

Thanks also to the Utah State Institute of Fine Arts for awarding a prize to my narrative poem "Prentice Alvin and the No-Good Plow." That encouragement led to my developing the story in prose and at greater length; this is the first volume to include part of the story recounted in that poem.

For details of frontier life and crafts, I have used John Seymour's wonderful book *The Forgotten Crafts* (New York City: Knopf, 1984) and Douglass L. Brownstone's *A Field Guide to America's History* (New York City: Facts On File, Inc., 1984).

I'm grateful that Gardner Dozois has kindly allowed pieces of the Tales of Alvin Maker to appear in the pages of *Isaac Asimov's Science Fiction Magazine,* allowing it to find an audience before the books appeared.

Beth Meacham at Tor is one of that vanishing breed of

editors with a golden touch; her advice is never intrusive, always wise; and (rarest editorial trait of all) she returns my telephone calls. For that alone she may be sainted.

Thanks to my writing class in Greensboro in the winter and spring of 1988 for suggestions that led to important improvements in the book; and to my sister, friend, and editorial assistant, Janice, for her work on keeping story details fresh in mind.

Thanks most of all to Kristine A. Card, who listens to me ramble through the many versions of each as-yet-unwritten book, reads the dot-matrix printouts of the early drafts, and is my second self through every page of everything I write.

I

THE OVERSEER

Let me start my history of Alvin's prenticeship where things first began to go wrong. It was a long way south, a man that Alvin had never met nor never would meet in all his life. Yet he it was who started things moving down the path that would lead to Alvin doing what the law called murder—on the very day that his prenticeship ended and he rightly became a man.

It was a place in Appalachee, in 1811, before Appalachee signed the Fugitive Slave Treaty and joined the United States. It was near the borders where Appalachee and the Crown Colonies meet, so there wasn't a White man but aspired to own a passel of Black slaves to do his work for him.

Slavery, that was a kind of alchemy for such White folk, or so they reckoned. They calculated a way of turning each bead of a Black man's sweat into gold and each moan of despair from a Black woman's throat into the sweet clear sound of a silver coin ringing on the money-changer's table. There was buying and selling of souls in that place. Yet there was nary a one of them who understood the whole price they paid for owning other folk.

Listen tight, and I'll tell you how the world looked from inside Cavil Planter's heart. But make sure the children are asleep, for this is a part of my tale that children ought not to hear, for it deals with hungers they don't understand too well, and I don't aim for this story to teach them.

CAVIL PLANTER WAS a godly man, a church-going man, a tithepayer. All his slaves were baptized and given Christian names as soon as they understood enough English to be taught the gospel. He forbade them to practice their dark arts—he never allowed them to slaughter so much as a chicken themselves, lest they convert such an innocent act into a sacrifice to some hideous god. In all ways Cavil Planter served the Lord as best he could.

So, how was the poor man rewarded for his righteousness? His wife, Dolores, she was beset with terrible aches and pains, her wrists and fingers twisting like an old woman's. By the time she was twenty-five she went to sleep most nights crying, so that Cavil could not bear to share the room with her.

He tried to help her. Packs of cold water, soaks of hot water, powders and potions, spending more than he could afford on those charlatan doctors with their degrees from the University of Camelot, and bringing in an endless parade of preachers with their eternal prayers and priests with their hocum pocus incantations. All of it accomplished nigh onto nothing. Every night he had to lie there listening to her cry until she whimpered, whimper until her breath became a steady in and out, whining just a little on the out-breath, a faint little wisp of pain.

It like to drove Cavil mad with pity and rage and despair. For months on end it seemed to him that he never slept at all. Work all day, then at night lie there praying for relief. If not for her, then for him.

It was Dolores herself who gave him peace at night. "You have work to do each day, Cavil, and can't do it unless you sleep. I can't keep silent, and you can't bear to hear me. Please—sleep in another room."

Cavil offered to stay anyway. "I'm your husband, I belong here"—he said it, but she knew better.

"Go," she said. She even raised her voice. "Go!"

So he went, feeling ashamed of how relieved he felt. He slept that night without interruption, a whole five hours until dawn, slept well for the first time in months, perhaps years—and arose in the morning consumed with guilt for not keeping his proper place beside his wife.

In due time, though, Cavil Planter became accustomed to sleeping alone. He visited his wife often, morning and night. They took meals together, Cavil sitting on a chair in her room, his food on a small side table, Dolores lying in bed as a Black woman carefully spooned food into her mouth while her hands sprawled on the bedsheets like dead crabs.

Even sleeping in another room, Cavil wasn't free of torment. There would be no babies. There would be no sons to raise up to inherit Cavil's fine plantation. There would be no daughters to give away in magnificent weddings. The ballroom downstairs—when he brought Dolores into the fine new house he had built for her, he had said, "Our daughters will meet their beaux in this ballroom, and first touch their hands, the way our hands first touched in your father's house." Now Dolores never saw the ballroom. She came downstairs only on Sundays to go to church and on those rare days when new slaves were purchased, so she could see to their baptism.

Everyone saw her on such occasions, and admired them both for their courage and faith in adversity. But the admiration of his neighbors was scant comfort when Cavil surveyed the ruins of his dreams. All that he prayed for—it's as if the Lord wrote down the list and then in the margin noted "no, no, no" on every line.

The disappointments might have embittered a man of

weaker faith. But Cavil Planter was a godly, upright man, and whenever he had the faintest thought that God might have treated him badly, he stopped whatever he was doing and pulled the small psaltery from his pocket and whispered aloud the words of the wise man.

> *In thee, O Lord, do I put my trust;*
> *Bow down thine ear to me;*
> *Be thou my strong rock.*

He concentrated his mind firmly, and the doubts and resentments quickly fled. The Lord was with Cavil Planter, even in his tribulations.

Until the morning he was reading in Genesis and he came upon the first two verses of chapter 16.

> *Now Sarai Abram's wife bare him no children: and she had an handmaid, an Egyptian, whose name was Hagar. And Sarai said unto Abram, Behold now, the Lord hath restrained me from bearing: I pray thee, go in unto my maid: it may be that I may obtain children by her.*

At that moment the thought came into his mind, Abraham was a righteous man, and so am I. Abraham's wife bore him no children, and mine likewise has no hope. There was an African slavewoman in their household, as there are such women in mine. Why shouldn't I do as Abraham did, and father children by one of these?

The moment the thought came into his head, he shuddered in horror. He'd heard gossip of White Spaniards and French and Portuguese in the jungle islands to the south who lived openly with Black women—truly they were the lowest kind of creature, like men who do with beasts. Besides, how could a child of a Black woman ever be an heir

to him? A mix-up boy could no more take possession of an
Appalachee plantation than fly. Cavil just put the thought
right out of his mind.

But as he sat at breakfast with his wife, the thought came
back. He found himself watching the Black woman who fed
his wife. Like Hagar, this woman is Egyptian, isn't she? He
noticed how her body twisted lithely at the waist as she bore
the spoon from tray to mouth. Noticed how as she leaned
forward to hold the cup to the frail woman's lips, the servant's breasts swung down to press against her blouse. Noticed how her gentle fingers brushed crumbs and drops from
Dolores's lips. He thought of those fingers touching *him,* and
trembled slightly. Yet it felt like an earthquake inside him.

He rushed from the room with hardly a word. Outside the
house, he clutched his psaltery.

> *Wash me thoroughly from mine iniquity,*
> *And cleanse me from my sin.*
> *For I acknowledge my transgressions:*
> *And my sin is ever before me.*

Yet even as he whispered these words, he looked up and
saw the field women washing themselves at the trough.
There was the young girl he had bought only a few days before, six hundred dollars even though she was small, since
she was probably breeding stock. So fresh from the boat she
was that she hadn't learned a speck of Christian modesty.
She stood there naked as a snake, leaning over the trough,
pouring cups of water over her head and down her back.

Cavil stood transfixed, watching her. What had only been
a brief thought of evil in his wife's bedroom now became a
trance of lust. He had never seen anything so graceful as
her blue-black thighs sliding against each other, so inviting
as her shiver when the water ran down her body.

Was this the answer to his fervent psalm? Was the Lord telling him that it was indeed with him as it had been with Abraham?

Just as likely it was witchery. Who knew what knacks these fresh-from-Africa Blacks might have? She knows I'm here a-watching, and she's tempting me. These Blacks are truly the devil's own children, to excite such evil thoughts in me.

He tore his gaze from the new girl and turned away, hiding his burning eyes in the words of the book. Only somehow the page had turned—when did he turn it?—and he found himself reading in the Song of Solomon.

> *Thy two breasts are like two young roes*
> *That are twins, which feed among the lilies.*

"God help me," he whispered. "Take this spell from me."

Day after day he whispered the same prayer, yet day after day he found himself watching his slavewomen with desire, particularly that newbought girl. Why was it God seemed to be paying him no mind? Hadn't he always been a righteous man? Wasn't he good to his wife? Wasn't he honest in business? Didn't he pay tithes and offerings? Didn't he treat his slaves and horses well? Why didn't the Lord God of Heaven protect him and take this Black spell from him?

Yet even when he prayed, his very confessions became evil imaginings. O Lord, forgive me for thinking of my newbought girl standing in the door of my bedroom, weeping at the caning she got from the overseer. Forgive me for imagining myself laying her on my own bed and lifting her skirts to anoint them with a balm so powerful the welts on her thighs and buttocks disappear before my eyes and she begins to giggle softly and writhe slowly on the sheets and look over her shoulder at me, smiling, and then she turns over and reaches out to me and—O Lord, forgive me, save me!

Whenever this happened, though, he couldn't help but wonder—why do such thoughts come to me even when I pray? Maybe I'm as righteous as Abraham; maybe it's the Lord who sent these desires to me. Didn't I first think of this while I was reading scripture? The Lord can work miracles—what if I went in unto the newbought girl and she conceived, and the Lord worked a miracle and the baby was born White? All things are possible to God.

This thought was both wonderful and terrible. If only it were true! Yet Abraham heard the voice of God, so he never had to wonder about what God might want of him. God never said a word to Cavil Planter.

And why not? Why didn't God just tell him right out? Take the girl, she's yours! Or, Touch her not, she is forbidden! Just let me hear your voice, Lord, so I'll know what to do!

> *O Lord my rock;*
> *Unto thee will I cry,*
> *Be not silent to me:*
> *Lest, if thou be silent to me,*
> *I become like them*
> *That go down into the pit.*

On a certain day in 1810 that prayer was answered.

Cavil was kneeling in the curing shed, which was mostly empty, seeing how last year's burly crop was long since sold and this year's was still a-greening in the field. He'd been wrestling in prayer and confession and dark imaginings until at last he cried out, "Is there no one to hear my prayer?"

"Oh, I hear you right enough," said a stern voice.

Cavil was terrified at first, fearing that some stranger—his overseer, or a neighbor—had overheard some terrible confession. But when he looked, he saw that it wasn't anyone he knew. Still, he knew at once *what* the man was. From the strength in his arms, his sun-browned face, and his open shirt—no jacket at all—he knew the man was no gentleman. But he was no White trash, either, nor a tradesman. The stern look in his face, the coldness of his eye, the tension in his muscles like a spring tight-bound in a steel trap: He was plainly one of those men whose whip and iron will keep discipline among the Black fieldworkers. An overseer. Only he was stronger and more dangerous than any overseer Cavil had ever seen. He knew at once that *this* overseer would get every ounce of work from the lazy apes who tried to avoid work in the fields. He knew that whoever's plantation was run by *this* overseer would surely prosper. But Cavil also knew that he would never dare to hire such a man, for this overseer was so strong that Cavil would soon forget who was man and who was master.

"Many have called me their master," said the stranger. "I knew that you would recognize me at once for what I am."

How had the man known the words that Cavil thought in the hidden reaches of his mind? "Then you *are* an overseer?"

"Just as there was one who was once called, not *a* master, but simply Master, so am I not *an* overseer, but *the* Overseer."

"Why did you come here?"

"Because you called for me."

"How could I call for you, when I never saw you before in my life?"

"If you call for the unseen, Cavil Planter, then of course you will see what you never saw before."

Only now did Cavil fully understand what sort of vision it was he saw, there in his own burly curing shed. A man whom many called their master, come in answer to his prayer.

"Lord Jesus!" cried Cavil.

At once the Overseer recoiled, putting up his hand as if to fend off Cavil's words. "It is forbidden for any man to call me by that name!" he cried.

In terror, Cavil bowed his head to the dirt. "Forgive me, Overseer! But if I am unworthy to say your name, how is it I can look upon your face? Or am I doomed to die today, unforgiven for my sins?"

"Woe unto you, fool," said the Overseer. "Do you really believe that you have looked upon my *face?*"

Cavil lifted his head and looked at the man. "I see your eyes even now, looking down at me."

"You see the face that you invented for me in your own mind, the body conjured out of your own imagination. Your feeble wits could never comprehend what you saw, if you saw what I truly am. So your sanity protects itself by devising its own mask to put upon me. If you see me as an Overseer, it is because that is the guise you recognize as having the greatness and power I possess. It is the form that you at once love and fear, the shape that makes you worship and recoil. I have been called by many names. Angel of Light and Walking Man, Sudden Stranger and Bright Visitor, Hidden One and Lion of War, Unmaker of Iron and Water-bearer. Today you have called me Overseer, and so, to you, that is my name."

"Can I ever know your true name, or see your true face, Overseer?"

The Overseer's face became dark and terrible, and he opened his mouth as if to howl. "Only one soul alive in all the world has ever seen my true shape, and that one will surely die!"

The mighty words came like dry thunder and shook Cavil Planter to his very root, so that he gripped the dirt of the shed floor lest he fly off into the air like dust whipped away in the wind before the storm. "Do not strike me dead for my impertinence!" cried Cavil.

The Overseer's answer came gentle as morning sunlight. "Strike you dead? How could I, when you are a man I have chosen to receive my most secret teachings, a gospel unknown to priest or minister."

"Me?"

"Already I have been teaching you, and you understood. I know you desire to do as I command. But you lack faith. You are not yet completely mine."

Cavil's heart leapt within him. Could it be that the Overseer meant to give him what he gave to Abraham? "Overseer, I am unworthy."

"Of course you are unworthy. None is worthy of me, no, not one soul upon this earth. But still, if you obey, you may find favor in my eyes."

Oh, he will! cried Cavil in his heart, yes, he will give me the woman! "Whatever you command, Overseer."

"Do you think I would give you Hagar because of your foolish lust and your hunger for a child? There is a greater purpose. These Black people are surely the sons and daughters of God, but in Africa they lived under the power of the devil. That terrible destroyer has polluted their blood—why else do you think they are Black? I can never save them as long as each generation is born pure Black, for then the devil owns them. How can I reclaim them as my own, unless you help me?"

"Will my child be born White then, if I take the girl?"

"What matters to me is that the child will not be born pure Black. Do you understand what I desire of you? Not one Ishmael, but many children; not one Hagar, but many women."

Cavil hardly dared to name the secretest desire of his heart. "All of them?"

"I give them to you, Cavil Planter. This evil generation is your property. With diligence, you can prepare another generation that will belong to me."

"I will, Overseer!"

"You must tell no one that you saw me. I speak only to those whose desires already turn toward me and my works, the ones who already thirst for the water I bring."

"I'll speak no word to any man, Overseer!"

"Obey me, Cavil Planter, and I promise that at the end of your life you will meet me again and know me for what I truly am. In that moment I will say to you, You are mine, Cavil Planter. Come and be my true slave forever."

"Gladly!" cried Cavil. "Gladly! Gladly!"

He flung out his arms and embraced the Overseer's legs. But where he should have touched the visitor, there was nothing. He had vanished.

From that night on, Cavil Planter's slavewomen had no peace. As Cavil had them brought to him by night, he tried to treat them with the strength and mastery he had seen in the face of the fearful Overseer. They must look at me and see His face, thought Cavil, and it's sure they did.

The first one he took unto himself was a certain new-bought slavegirl who had scarce a word of English. She cried out in terror until he raised the welts upon her that he had seen in his dreams. Then, whimpering, she permitted him to do as the Overseer had commanded. For a moment, that first time, he thought her whimpering was like Dolores's voice when she wept so quietly in bed, and he felt the same deep pity that he had felt for his beloved wife. Almost he reached out tenderly to the girl as he had once reached out to comfort Dolores. But then he remembered the face of the Overseer and thought, this Black girl is His enemy; she is my property. As surely as a man must plow and plant the land God gave to him, I must not let this Black womb lie fallow.

Hagar, he called her that first night. You do not understand how I am blessing you.

In the morning he looked in the mirror and saw something new in his face. A kind of fierceness. A kind of terrible hidden strength. Ah, thought Cavil, no one ever saw what I truly am, not even me. Only now do I discover that what the Overseer is, I also am.

He never felt another moment's pity as he went about his nightly work. Ashen cane in hand, he went to the women's cabin and pointed at the one who was to come with him. If any hung back, she learned from the cane how much reluctance cost. If any other Black, man or woman, spoke in protest, the next day Cavil saw to it that the overseer took it out of them in blood. No White guessed and no Black dared accuse him.

The newbought girl, his Hagar, was first to conceive. He watched her with pride as her belly began to grow. Cavil knew then that the Overseer had truly chosen him, and he took fierce joy in having such mastery. There would be a child, *his* child. And already the next step was clear to him. If his White blood was to save as many Black souls as possible, then he could not keep his mix-up babes at home, could he? He would sell them south, each to a different buyer, to a different city, and then trust the Overseer to see that they in turn grew up and spread his seed throughout all the unfortunate Black race.

And each morning he watched his wife eat her breakfast. "Cavil, my love," she said one day, "is something wrong? There's something darker in your face, a look of—rage, perhaps, or cruelty. Have you quarreled with someone? I would not speak except you—you frighten me."

Tenderly he patted his wife's twisted hand as the Black

woman watched him under heavy-lidded eyes. "I have no anger against any man or woman," said Cavil gently. "And what you call cruelty is nothing more than mastery. Ah, Dolores, how can you look in my face and call me cruel?"

She wept. "Forgive me," she cried. "I imagined it. You, the kindest man I've ever heard of—the devil put such a vision in my mind, I know it. The devil can give false visions, you know, but only the wicked are deceived. Forgive me for my wickedness, Husband!"

He forgave her, but she wouldn't stop her weeping until he had sent for the priest. No wonder the Lord chose only men to be his prophets. Women were too weak and compassionate to do the work of the Overseer.

THAT'S HOW IT began. That was the first footfall on this dark and terrible path. Nor Alvin nor Peggy ever knew this tale until I found it out and told them both long after, and they recognized at once that it was the start of all.

But I don't want you to think this was the whole cause of all the evil that befell, for it wasn't. There were other choices made, other mistakes, other lies and other willing cruelties done. A man might have plenty of help finding the short path to hell, but no one else can make him set foot upon it.

2

RUNAWAY

Peggy woke up in the morning with a dream of Alvin Miller filling her heart with all kinds of terrible desires. She wanted to run from that boy, and to stay and wait for him; to forget she knew him, and to watch him always.

She lay there on her bed with her eyes almost closed, watching the grey dawnlight steal into the attic room where she slept. *I'm holding something,* she noticed. The corners of it clenched into her hands so tight that when she let go her palm hurt like she been stung. But she wasn't stung. It was just the box where she kept Alvin's birth caul. Or maybe, thought Peggy, maybe she *had* been stung, stung deep, and only just now did she feel the pain of it.

Peggy wanted to throw that box just as far from her as she could, bury it deep and forget where she buried it, drown it underwater and pile rocks on so it wouldn't float.

Oh, but I don't mean that, she said silently, *I'm sorry for thinking such a thing, I'm plain sorry, but he's coming now, after all these years he's coming to Hatrack River and he won't be the boy I seen in all the paths of his future, he won't be the man I see him turning into. No, he's still just a boy, just eleven years old. He's seen him enough of life that somewise maybe he's a man inside, he's seen grief and pain enough for someone five times his age, but it's still an eleven-year-old boy he'll be when he walks into this town.*

And I don't want to see no eleven-year-old Alvin come here. He'll be looking for me, right enough. He knows who I am, though he never saw me since he was two weeks old. He knows I saw his future on the rainy dark day when he was born, and so he'll come, and he'll say to me, "Peggy, I know you're a torch, and I know you wrote in Taleswapper's book that I'm to be a Maker. So tell me what I'm supposed to be." *Peggy knew just what he'd say, and every way he might choose to say it—hadn't she seen it a hundred times, a thousand times? And she'd teach him and he'd become a great man, a true Maker, and—*

And then one day, when he's a handsome figure of twenty-one and I'm a sharp-tongued spinster of twenty-six he'll feel so grateful *to me, so* obligated, *that he'll propose him-*

self for marriage to me as his bounden duty. And I, being lovesick all these years, full of dreams of what he'll do and what we'll be together, I'll say yes, and saddle him with a wife he wished he didn't have to marry, and his eyes will hunger for other women all the days of our lives together—

Peggy wished, oh she wished so deep, that she didn't know for certain things would be that way. But Peggy was a torch right enough, the strongest torch she'd ever heard of, stronger even than the folk hereabouts in Hatrack River ever guessed.

She sat up in bed and did not throw the box or hide it or break it or bury it. She opened it. Inside lay the last scrap of Alvin's birth caul, as dry and white as paper ash in a cold hearth. Eleven years ago when Peggy's mama served as midwife to pull baby Alvin out of the well of life, and Alvin first sucked for breath in the damp air of Papa's Hatrack River roadhouse, Peggy peeled that thin and bloody caul from the baby's face so he could breathe. Alvin, the seventh son of a seventh son, and the thirteenth child—Peggy saw at once what the paths of his life would be. Death, that was where he was headed, death from a hundred different accidents in a world that seemed bent on killing him even before he was hardly alive.

She was Little Peggy then, a girl of five, but she'd been torching for two years already, and in that time she never did a seeing on a birthing child who had so many paths to death. Peggy searched up all the paths of his life, and found in all of them but one single way that boy could live to be a man.

That was if she kept that birth caul, and watched him from afar off, and whenever she saw death reaching out to take him, she'd use that caul. Take just a pinch of it and grind it between her fingers and whisper what had to happen, see it in her mind. And it would happen just the way she said. Hadn't she held him up from drowning? Saved him from a wallowing buffalo? Caught him from sliding off a roof? She even split a roof beam once, when it was like to fall from fifty feet up and squash him on the floor of a half-built church; she split that beam neat as you please, so it fell on one side of him and the other, with just a space for him to stand there in between. And a hundred other times when she acted so early that nobody ever even guessed his life had been saved, even those times she saved him, using the caul.

How did it work? She hardly knew. Except that it was his own power she was using, the gift born right in him. Over the years he'd learned somewhat about his knack for making things and shaping them and holding them together and splitting them apart. Finally this last year, all caught up in the wars between Red men and White, he'd taken charge of saving his own life, so she hardly had to do a thing to save him anymore. Good thing, too. There wasn't much of that caul left.

She closed the lid of the box. I don't want to see him, thought Peggy. I don't want to know any more about him.

But her fingers opened that lid right back up, cause of course she had to know. She'd lived half her life, it seemed like, touching that caul and searching for his heartfire away far off in the northwest Wobbish country, in the town of Vigor Church, seeing how he was doing, looking up the paths of his future to see what danger lay in ambush. And when she was sure he was safe, she'd look farther ahead, and see him coming back one day to Hatrack River, where he was born, coming back and looking into her face and saying, It was you who saved me all those times, you who saw I was a Maker back afore a living soul thought such a thing was possible. And then she'd watch him learn the great depths of his power, the work he had to do, the crystal city he had to build; she saw him sire babies on her, and saw him

touch the nursing infants she held in her arms; she saw the
ones they buried and the ones that lived; and last of all she
saw him—

Tears came down her face. I don't want to know, she said.
I don't want to know all the roads of the future. Other girls
can dream of love, the joys of marriage, of being mothers
to strong healthy babes; but all my dreams have dying in
them, too, and pain, and fear, because my dreams are true
dreams, I know more than a body can know and still have
any hope inside her soul.

Yet Peggy *did* hope. Yes sir, you can be sure of it—she
still clung to a kind of desperate hope, because even knowing what's likely to come down the pathways of a body's
life, she still caught her some glimpses, some clear plain
visions of certain days, certain hours, certain passing moments of joy so great it was worth the grief just to get there.

Trouble was those glimpses were so rare and small in the
spreading futures of Alvin's life that she couldn't find a road
that led there. All the pathways she could find easily, the
plain ones, the ones most likely to become real, those all
led to Alvin wedding her without love, out of gratitude and
duty, a miserable marriage. Like the story of Leah in the
Bible, whose beautiful husband Jacob hated her even though
she loved him dear and bore him more babies than his other
wives and would've died for him if he'd as much as asked
her.

It's an evil thing God did to women, thought Peggy, to
make us hanker after husband and children till it leads us
to a life of sacrifice and misery and grief. Was Eve's sin so
terrible, that God should curse all women with that mighty
curse? You will groan and bear children, said Almighty
Merciful God. You will be eager for your husband, and he
will rule over you.

That was what was burning in her—eagerness for her

husband. Even though he was only an eleven-year-old boy who was looking, not for a wife, but for a teacher. He may be just a boy, thought Peggy, but I'm a woman, and I've seen the man he'll be, and I yearn for him. She pressed one hand against her breast; it felt so large and soft, still somewhat out of place on her body, which used to be all sticks and corners like a shanty cabin, and now was softening, like a calf being fattened up for the return of the prodigal.

She shuddered, thinking what happened to the fatted calf, and once again touched the caul, and *looked:*

In the distant town of Vigor Church, young Alvin was breakfasting his last morning at his mother's table. The pack he was to carry on his journey to Hatrack River lay on the floor beside the table. His mother's tears flowed undisguised across her cheeks. The boy loved his mother, but never for a moment did he feel sorry to be leaving. His home was a dark place now, stained with too much innocent blood for him to hanker to stay. He was eager to be off, to start his life as a prentice boy to the blacksmith of Hatrack River, and to find the torch girl who saved his life when he was born. He couldn't eat another bite. He pushed back from the table, stood up, kissed his mama—

Peggy let go the caul and closed the lid of the box as tight and quick as if she was trying to catch a fly inside.

Coming to find me. Coming to start a life of misery together. Go ahead and cry, Faith Miller, but not because your little boy Alvin's on his way east. You cry for me, the woman whose life your boy will wreck. You shed your tears for one more woman's lonely pain.

Peggy shuddered, shook off the bleak mood of the grey dawn, and dressed herself quickly, ducking her head to avoid the low sloping crossbeams of the attic roof. Over the years she'd learned ways to push thoughts of Alvin Miller Junior clean out of her mind, long enough to do her duty as daughter in her parents' household and as torch for the people of the country hereabouts. She could go hours without thinking about that boy, when she set her mind to it. And though it was harder now, knowing he was about to set his foot on the road toward her that very morning, she still put thoughts of him aside.

Peggy opened the curtain of the south-facing window and sat before it, leaning on the sill. She looked out over the forest that still stretched from the roadhouse, down the Hatrack River and on to the Hio, with only a few pig farms here and there to block the way. Of course she couldn't *see* the Hio, not that many miles from here, not even in the clear cool air of springtime. But what her natural eyes couldn't see, the burning torch in her could find easy enough. To see the Hio, she had only to search for a far-off heartfire, then slip herself inside that fellow's flame, and see out of his eyes as easy as she could see out of her own. And once there, once she had ahold of someone's heartfire, she could see other things, too, not just what he saw, but what he thought and felt and wished for. And even more: Flickering away in the brightest parts of the flame, often hidden by all the noise of the fellow's present thought and wishes, she could see the paths ahead of him, the choices coming to him, the life he'd make for himself if he chose this or that or another way in the hours and days to come.

Peggy could see so much in other people's heartfires that she hardly was acquainted with her own.

She thought of herself sometimes like that lone lookout boy at the tip-top of a ship's mast. Not that she ever saw her a ship in her whole life, except the rafts on the Hio and one time a canal boat on the Irrakwa Canal. But she read some books, as many as ever she could get Doctor Whitley Physicker to bring back to her from his visits to Dekane. So she knew about the lookout on the mast. Clinging to the rigging, arms half-wrapped in the lines so he didn't fall if there was a sudden roll or pitch of the boat, or a gust of wind unlooked-for; froze blue in winter, burnt red in summer; and nothing to do all day, all the long long hours of his watch, but look out onto the empty blue ocean. If it was a pirate ship, the lookout watched for victims' sails. If it was a whaler, he looked for blows and breaches. Most ships, he just looked for land, for shoals, for hidden sand bars; looked for pirates or some sworn enemy of his nation's flag.

Most days he never saw a thing, not a thing, just waves and dipping sea birds and fluffy clouds.

I am on a lookout perch, thought Peggy. Sent up aloft some sixteen years ago the day I was born, and kept here ever since, never once let down below, never once allowed to rest within the narrow bunkspace of the lowest deck, never once allowed to so much as close a hatch over my head or a door behind my back. Always, always I'm on watch, looking far and near. And because it isn't my natural eyes I look through, I can't shut them, not even in sleep.

No escape from it at all. Sitting here in the attic, she could see without trying:

Mother, known to others as Old Peg Guester, known to herself as Margaret, cooking in the kitchen for the slew of guests due in for one of her suppers. Not like she has any particular knack for cooking, either, so kitchen work is hard, she isn't like Gertie Smith who can make salt pork taste a hundred different ways on a hundred different days. Peg Guester's knack is in womenstuff, midwifery and house hexes, but to make a good inn takes good food and now Old-pappy's gone she has to cook, so she thinks only of the kitchen and couldn't hardly stand interruption, least of all from her daughter who mopes around the house and hardly speaks at all and by and large that girl is the most unpleas-

ant, ill-favored child even though she started out so sweet
and promising, everything in life turns sour somehow. . . .

Oh, that was such a joy, to know how little your own
mama cared for you. Never mind that Peggy also knew the
fierce devotion that her mama had. Knowing that a portion
of love abides in your mama's heart doesn't take away but
half the sting of knowing her dislike for you as well.

And Papa, known to others as Horace Guester, keeper of
the Hatrack River Roadhouse. A jolly fellow, Papa was, even
now out in the dooryard telling tales to a guest who was having trouble getting away from the inn. He and Papa always
seemed to have something more to talk about, and oh, that
guest, a circuit lawyer from up Cleveland way, he fancied
Horace Guester was just about the finest most upstanding
citizen he ever met, if all folks was as good-hearted as old
Horace there'd be no more crime and no more lawyering in
the upriver Hio country. Everybody felt that way. Everybody
loved old Horace Guester.

But his daughter, Peggy the torch, she saw into his heartfire and knew how he felt about it. He saw those folks
a-smiling at him and he said to himself, If they knew what
I really was they'd spit in the road at my feet and walk away
and forget they ever saw my face or knew my name.

Peggy sat there in her attic room and all the heartfires
glowed, all of them in town. Her parents' most, cause she
knew them best; the lodgers who stayed in the roadhouse;
and then the people of the town.

Makepeace Smith and his wife Gertie and their three
snot-nose children planning devilment when they weren't
puking or piddling—Peggy saw Makepeace's pleasure in
the shaping of iron, his loathing for his own children, his
disappointment as his wife changed from a fascinating un-
attainable vision of beauty into a stringy-haired hag who

screamed at the children first and then came to use the same voice to scream at Makepeace.

Pauley Wiseman, the sheriff, loving to make folks a-scared of him; Whitley Physicker, angry at himself because his medicine didn't work more than half the time, and every week he saw death he couldn't do a thing about. New folks, old folks, farmers and professionals, she saw through their eyes and into their hearts. She saw the marriage beds that were cold at night and the adulteries kept secret in guilty hearts. She saw the thievery of trusted clerks and friends and servants, and the honorable hearts inside many who were despised and looked down on.

She saw it all, and said nothing. Kept her mouth shut. Talked to no one. Cause she wasn't going to lie. She promised years before that she'd never lie, and kept her word by keeping still.

Other folks didn't have her problem. They could talk and tell the truth. But Peggy couldn't tell the truth. She knew these folks too well. She knew what they all were scared of, what they all wanted, what they all had done that they'd kill her or theirself if they once got a notion that she knew. Even the ones who never done a bad thing, they'd be so ashamed to think she knew their secret dreams or private craziness. So she never could speak frankly to these folks, or something would slip out, not even a word maybe, it might be just the way she turned her head, the way she side-stepped some line of talk, and they'd know that she knew, or just fear that she knew, or just fear. Just fear alone, without even naming what it was, and it could undo them, some of them, the weakest of them.

She was a lookout all the time, alone atop the mast, hanging to the lines, seeing more than she ever wanted to, and never getting even a minute to herself.

When it wasn't some baby being born, so she had to go

and do a seeing, then it was some folks in trouble somewhere that had to be helped. It didn't do her no good to sleep,
neither. She never slept all the way. Always a part of her
was looking, and saw the fire burning, saw it flash.

Like now. Now this very moment, as she looked out over
the forest, there it was. A heartfire burning ever so far off.

She swung herself close in—not her body, of course, her
flesh stayed right there in the attic—but being a torch she
knew how to look *close* at far-off heartfires.

It was a young woman. No, a girl, even younger than herself. And strange inside, so she knew right off this girl first
spoke a language that wasn't English, even though she spoke
and thought in English now. It made her thoughts all twisty
and queer. But some things run deeper than the tracks that
words leave in your brain; Little Peggy didn't need no help
understanding that baby the girl held in her arms, and the
way she stood at the riverbank knowing she would die, and
what a horror waited for her back at the plantation, and what
she'd done last night to get away.

SEE THE SUN there, three fingers over the trees. This runaway Black slave girl and her little bastard half-White boy-
baby, see them standing on the shore of the Hio, half hid up
in trees and bushes, watching as the White men pole them
rafts on down. She a-scared, she know them dogs can't find
her but very soon they get them the runaway finder, very
worse thing, and how she ever cross that river with this
boy-baby?

She cotch her a terrible thought: I leave this boy-baby, I
hide him in this rotten log, I swim and steal the boat and I
come back to here. That do the job, yes sir.

But then this Black girl who nobody never teach how to
be a mama, she know a good mama don't leave this baby
who still gots to suck two-hand times a day. She whisper,

Good mama don't leave a little boy-baby where old fox or weasel or badger come and nibble off little parts and kill him dead. No ma'am not me.

So she just set down here a-hold of this baby, and watch the river flow on, might as well be the seashore cause she never get across.

Maybe some White folks help her? Here on the Appalachee shore the White folk hang them as help a slavegirl run away. But this runaway Black slavegirl hear stories on the plantation, about Whites who say nobody better be own by nobody else. Who say this Black girl better have that same right like the White lady, she say no to any man be not her true husband. Who say this Black girl better can keep her baby, not let them White boss promise he sell it on weaning day, they send this boy-baby to grow up into a house slave in Drydenshire, kiss a White man's feet if he say boo.

"Oh, your baby is so *lucky*," they say to this slavegirl. "He'll grow up in a fine lord's mansion in the Crown Colonies, where they still have a king—he might even *see* the King someday."

She don't say nothing, but she laugh inside. She don't set no store to see a king. Her pa a king back in Africa, and they shoot him dead. Them Portuguese slavers show her what it mean to be a king—it mean you die quick like everybody, and spill blood red like everybody, and cry out loud in pain and scared—oh, *fine* to be a king, and *fine* to see one. Do them White folk believe this lie?

I don't believe them. I say I believe them but I lie. I never let them take him my boy-baby. A king grandson him, and I tell him every day he growing up. When he the tall king, ain't nobody hit him with the stick or he hit them back, and nobody take his woman, spread her like a slaughterpig and stick this half-White baby in her but he can't do nothing, he sit in his cabin and cry. No ma'am, no sir.

So she do the forbidden evil ugly bad thing. She steal two candles and hot them all soft by the cookfire. She mash them like dough, she mash in milk from her own teat after boy-baby suck, and she mash some of her spit in the wax too, and then she push it and poke it and roll it in ash till she see a poppet shape like Black slavegirl. Her very own self.

Then she hide this Black slavegirl poppet and she go to Fat Fox and beg him feathers off that big old blackbird he cotch him.

"Black slavegirl don't need her no feathers," say Fat Fox.

"I make a boogy for my boy-baby," she say.

Fat Fox laugh, he know she lie. "Ain't no blackfeather boogy. I never heared of such a thing."

Black slavegirl, she say, "My papa king in Umbawana. I know all secret thing."

Fat Fox shake his head, he laugh, he laugh. "What do you know, anyway? You can't even talk English. I'll give you all the blackbird feathers you want, but when that baby stops sucking you come to me and I'll give you another one, all Black this time."

She hate Fat Fox like White Boss, but he got him black-bird feathers so she say, "Yes sir."

Two hands she fill up with feathers. She laugh inside. She far away and dead before Fat Fox never put him no baby in her.

She cover Black slavegirl poppet with feathers till she little girl-shape bird. Very strong thing, this poppet with her own milk and spit in it, blackbird feathers on. Very strong, suck all her life out, but boy-baby, he never kiss no White Boss feet, White Boss never lay no lash on him.

Dark night, moon not showing yet. She slip out her cabin.

Boy-baby suck so he make no sound. She tie that baby to her teat so he don't fall. She toss that poppet on the fire. Then all the power of the feather come out, burning, burning, burning. She feel this fire pour into her. She spread her wings, oh so wide, spread them, flap like she see that big old blackbird flap. She rise up into the air, high up in that dark night, she rise and fly, far away north she fly, and when that moon he come up, she keep him at her right hand so she get this boy-baby to land where White say Black girl never slave, half-White boy-baby never slave.

Come morning and the sun and she don't fly no more. Oh, like dying, like dying she think, walking her feet on the ground. That bird with her wing broke, she pray for Fat Fox to find her, she know that now. After you fly, make you sad to walk, hurt you bad to walk, like a slave with chains, that dirt under your feet.

But she walk with that boy-baby all morning and now she come to this wide river. This close I come, say runaway Black slavegirl. I fly this far, yes I fly this river across. But that sun come up and I come down before this river. Now I never cross, old finder find me somehow, whup me half dead, take my boy-baby, sell him south.

Not me. I trick them. I die first.

No, I die second.

OTHER FOLKS COULD argue about whether slavery was a mortal sin or just a quaint custom. Other folks could bicker on about how Emancipationists were too crazy to put up with even though slavery was a real bad thing. Other folks could look at Blacks and feel sorry for them but still be somewhat glad they were mostly in Africa or in the Crown Colonies or in Canada or somewhere else far and gone. Peggy couldn't afford the luxury of having opinions on the subject. All she knew was that no heartfire ever was in such pain as the soul of a Black who lived in the thin dark shadow of the lash.

Peggy leaned out the attic window, called out: "Papa!"

He strode out from the front of the house, walked into the road, where he could look up and see her window. "You call me, Peggy?"

She just looked at him, said naught, and that was all the signal that he needed. He good-byed and fare-thee-welled that guest so fast the poor old coot was halfway into the main part of town before he knew what hit him. Pa was already inside and up the stairs.

"A girl with a babe," she told him. "On the far side of the Hio, scared and thinking of killing herself if she's caught."

"How far along the Hio?"

"Just down from the Hatrack Mouth, near as I can guess. Papa, I'm coming with you."

"No you're not."

"Yes I am, Papa. You'll never find her, not you nor ten more like you. She's too scared of White men, and she's got cause."

Papa looked at her, unsure what to do. He'd never let her come before, but usually it was Black men what ran off. But then, usually she found them this side the Hio, lost and scared, so it was safer. Crossing into Appalachee, it was prison for sure if they were caught helping a Black escape. Prison if it wasn't a quick rope on a tree. Emancipationists didn't fare well south of the Hio, and still less the kind of Emancipationist who helped run-off bucks and ewes and pickaninnies get north to French country up in Canada.

"Too dangerous across the river," he said.

"All the more reason you need me. To find her, and to spot if anyone else happens along."

"Your mother would kill me if she knew I was taking you."

"Then I'll leave now, out the back."

"Tell her you're going to visit Mrs. Smith—"

"I'll tell her nothing or I'll tell the truth, Papa."

"Then I'll stay up here and pray the good Lord saves my life by not letting her notice you leaving. We'll meet up at Hatrack Mouth come sundown."

"Can't we—"

"No we can't, not a minute sooner," he said. "Can't cross the river till dark. If they catch her or she dies afore we get there then it's just too bad, cause we can't cross the Hio in the daylight, bet your life on that."

NOISE IN THE forest, this scare Black slavegirl very bad. Trees grab her, owls screech out telling where they find her, this river just laugh at her all along. She can't move cause she fall in the dark, she hurt this baby. She can't stay cause they find her sure. Flying don't fool them finders, they look far and see her even a hand of hands away off.

A step for sure. Oh, Lord God Jesus save me from this devil in the dark.

A step, and breathing, and branches they brush aside. But no lantern! Whatever come it see me in the dark! Oh, Lord God Moses Savior Abraham.

"Girl."

That voice, I hear that voice, I can't breathe. Can you hear it, little boy-baby? Or do I dream this voice? This lady voice, very soft lady voice. Devil got no lady voice, everybody know, ain't that so?

"Girl, I come to take you across the river and help you and your baby get north and free."

I don't find no words no more, not slave words or Umbawa talk. When I put on feathers do I lose my words?

"We got a good stout rowboat and two strong men to row. I know you understand me and I know you trust me and I know you want to come. So you just set there, girl, you hold my hand, there, that's my hand, you don't have to say a word, you just hold my hand. There's some White men but they're my friends and they won't touch you. Nobody's going to touch you except me, you believe that, girl, you just believe it."

Her hand it touch my skin very cool and soft like this lady voice. This lady angel, this Holy Virgin Mother of God.

Lots of steps, heavy steps, and now lanterns and lights and big old White men but this lady she just hold on my hand.

"Scared plumb to death."

"Look at this girl. She's most wasted away to nothing."

"How many days she been without eating?"

Big men's voices like White Boss who give her this baby.

"She only left her plantation last night," said the Lady.

How this White lady know? She know everything, Eve the mama of all babies. No time to talk, no time to pray, move very quick, lean on this White lady, walk and walk and walk to this boat it lie waiting in the water just like I dream, O! here the boat little boy baby, boat lift us cross the Jordan to the Promise Land.

THEY WERE HALFWAY across the river when the Black girl started shaking and crying and chattering.

"Hush her up," said Horace Guester.

"There's nobody near us," answered Peggy. "No one to hear."

"What's she babbling about?" asked Po Doggly. He was a pig farmer from near Hatrack mouth and for a moment Peggy thought he was talking about *her*. But no, it was the Black girl he meant.

"She's talking in her African tongue, I reckon," said Peggy. "This girl is really something, how she got away."

"With a baby and all," agreed Po.

"Oh, the baby," said Peggy. "I've got to hold the baby."

"Why's that?" asked Papa.

"Because you're both going to have to carry her," she said. "From shore to the wagon, at least. There's no way this child can walk another step."

When they got to shore, they did just that. Po's old wagon was no great shakes for comfort—one old horseblanket was about as soft as it was going to get—but they laid her out and if she minded she didn't say so. Horace held the lantern high and looked at her. "You're plumb right, Peggy."

"What about?" she asked.

"Calling her a child. I swear she couldn't be thirteen. I swear it. And her with a baby. You sure this baby's hers?"

"I'm sure," said Peggy.

Po Doggly chuckled. "Oh, you know them guineas, just like bunny rabbits, the minute they can they do." Then he remembered that Peggy was there. "Begging your pardon, ma'am. We don't never have ladies along till tonight."

"It's *her* pardon you have to beg," said Peggy coldly. "This child is a mixup. Her owner sired this boy without a by-your-leave. I reckon you understand me."

"I won't have you discussing such things," said Horace Guester. His temper was hot, all right. "Bad enough you coming along on this without you knowing all this kind of thing about this poor girl, it ain't right telling her secrets like that."

Peggy fell silent and stayed that way all the ride home. That was what happened whenever she spoke frankly which is why she almost never did. The girl's suffering made her forget herself and talk too much. Now Papa was thinking on about how much his daughter knew about this Black girl in just a few minutes, and worrying how much she knew about *him*.

Do you want to know what I know, Papa? I know why you do this. You're not like Po Doggly, Papa, who doesn't think much of Blacks but hates seeing any wild thing cooped up. He does this, helping slaves make their way to Canada, cause he's just got that need in him to set them free. But you, Papa, you do it to pay back your secret sin. Your pretty little secret who smiled at you like heartbreak in person and you could've said no but you didn't, you said yes oh yes. While Mama was expecting me, it was, and you were off in Dekane buying supplies, you stayed there a week and had that woman must be ten times in six days, I remember every one of those times as clear as you do, I can feel you dreaming about her in the night. Hot with shame, hotter with desire, I know just how a man feels when he wants a woman so bad his skin itches and he can't hold still. All these years you've hated yourself for what you did and hated yourself all the more for loving that memory, and so you pay for it. You risk going to jail or getting hung up in a tree some- where for the crows to pick, not because you love the Black man but because you hope maybe doing good for God's children might just set you free of your own secret love of evil.

And here's the funny thing, Papa. If you knew I knew your secret you would probably die, it might just kill you on the spot. And yet if I could tell you, just tell you that I know, then I could tell you something else on top of that, I could say, Papa, don't you see that it's your knack? You who thinks he never had no knack, but you got one. It's the knack for making folks feel loved. They come to your inn and they feel right to home. Well you saw her, and she was hungry, that woman in Dekane, she needed to feel the way you make folks feel, needed you so bad. And it's hard, Papa, hard not to love a body who loves you so powerful, who hangs onto you like clouds hanging onto the moon, knowing you're go- ing to go on, knowing you'll never stay, but hungering, Papa. I looked for that woman, looked for her heartfire, far and wide I searched for her, and I found her. I know where she is. She ain't young now like you remember. But she's still pretty, pretty as you recall her, Papa. And she's a good woman, and you done her no harm. She remembers you fondly, Papa. She knows God forgave her and you both. It's you who won't forgive, Papa.

Such a sad thing, Peggy thought, coming home in that wagon. Papa's doing something that would make him a hero in any other daughter's eyes. A great man. But because I'm a torch, I know the truth. He doesn't come out here like Hector afore the gates of Troy, risking death to save other folks. He comes slinking like a whipped dog, cause he *is* a whipped dog inside. He runs out here to hide from a sin that the good Lord would have forgave long ago if he just allowed forgiveness to be possible.

Soon enough, though, Peggy stopped thinking it was sad about her Papa. It was sad about most *everybody,* wasn't it? But most sad people just kept right on being sad, hanging onto misery like the last keg of water in a drouth. Like the way Peggy kept waiting here for Alvin even though she knew he'd bring no joy to her.

It was that girl in the back of the wagon who was different. She had a terrible misery coming on her, going to lose her boy-baby, but she didn't just set and wait for it to happen so she could grieve. She said no. Plain no, just like that, I won't let you sell this boy south on me, even to a good rich family. A rich man's slave is still a slave, ain't he? And down south means he'll be even farther away from where he can run off and make it north. Peggy could feel those feelings in that girl, even as she tossed and moaned in the back of the wagon.

Something more, though. That girl was more a hero than Papa or Po Doggly either one. Because the only way she could think to get away was to use a witchery so strong that Peggy never even heard of it before. Never dreamed that

Black folks had such lore. But it was no lie, it was no dream neither. That girl flew. Made a wax poppet and feathered it and burnt it up. Burnt it right up. It let her fly all this way, this long hard way till the sun came up, far enough that Peggy saw her and they took her across the Hio. But what a price that runaway had paid for it.

When they got back to the roadhouse, Mama was just as angry as Peggy ever saw her. "It's a crime you should have a whipping for, taking your sixteen-year-old daughter out to commit a crime in the darkness."

But Papa didn't answer. He didn't have to, once he carried that girl inside and laid her on the floor before the fire.

"She can't have ate a thing for days. For weeks!" cried Mama. "And her brow is like to burn my hand off just to touch her. Fetch me a pan of water, Horace, to mop her brow, while I het up the broth for her to sip—"

"No, Mama," said Peggy. "Best you find some milk for the baby."

"The baby won't die, and this girl's likely to, don't you tell me my business, I know physicking for *this,* anyway—"

"No, Mama," said Peggy. "She did a witchery with a wax poppet. It's a Black sort of witchery, but she had the know-how and she had the power, being the daughter of a king in Africa. She knew the price and now she can't help but pay."

"Are you saying this girl's bound to die?" asked Mama.

"She made a poppet of herself, Mama, and put it on the fire. It gave her the wings to fly one whole night. But the cost of it is the rest of her life."

Papa looked sick at heart. "Peggy, that's plain crazy. What good would it do her to escape from slavery if she was just going to die? Why not kill herself there and save the trouble?"

Peggy didn't have to answer. The baby she was a-holding started to cry right then, and that was all the answer there was.

"I'll get milk," said Papa. "Christian Larsson's bound to have a gill or so to spare even this time of the night."

Mama stopped him, though. "Think again, Horace," she said. "It's near midnight now. What'll you tell him you need the milk *for?*"

Horace sighed, laughed at his own foolishness. "For a runaway slavegirl's little pickaninny baby." But then he turned red, getting hot with anger. "What a crazy thing this Black girl done," he said. "She came all this way, knowing that she'd die, and now what does she reckon we'll do with a little pickaninny like that? We sure can't take it north and lay it across the Canadian border and let it bawl till some Frenchman comes to take it."

"I reckon she just figures it's better to die free than live slave," said Peggy. "I reckon she just knew that whatever life that baby found here had to be better than what it was there."

The girl lay there before the fire, breathing soft, her eyes closed.

"She's asleep, isn't she?" asked Mama.

"Not dead yet," said Peggy, "but not hearing us."

"Then I'll tell you plain, this is a bad piece of trouble," said Mama. "We can't have people knowing you bring runaway slaves through here. Word of that would spread so fast we'd have two dozen finders camped here every week of the year, and one of them'd be bound to take a shot at you sometime from ambush."

"Nobody has to know," said Papa.

"What are you going to do, tell folks you happened to trip over her dead body in the woods?"

Peggy wanted to shout at them, She ain't dead yet, so mind how you talk! But the truth was they had to get some things planned, and quick. What if one of the guests woke up in the night and came downstairs? There'd be no keeping this secret then.

"How soon will she die?" Papa asked. "By morning?"

"She'll be dead before sunrise, Papa."

Papa nodded. "Then I better get busy. The girl I can take care of. You women can think of something to do with that pickaninny, I hope."

"Oh, we can, can we?" said Mama.

"Well I know I can't, so you'd better."

"Well then maybe I'll just tell folks it's my own babe."

Papa didn't get mad. Just grinned, he did, and said, "Folks ain't going to believe that even if you dip that boy in cream three times a day."

He went outside and got Po Doggly to help him dig a grave.

"Passing this baby off as born around here ain't such a bad idea," said Mama. "That Black family that lives down in that boggy land—you remember two years back when some slaveowner tried to prove he used to own them? What's their name, Peggy?"

Peggy knew them far better than any other White folks in Hatrack River did; she watched over them the same as everyone else, knew all their children, knew all their names. "They call their name Berry," she said. "Like a noble house, they just keep that family name no matter what job each one of them does."

"Why couldn't we pass this baby off as theirs?"

"They're poor, Mama," said Peggy. "They can't feed another mouth."

"We could help with that," said Mama. "We have extra."

"Just think a minute, Mama, how that'd look. Suddenly the Berrys get them a light-colored baby like this, you *know* he's half-White just to look at him. And then Horace Guester starts bringing gifts down to the Berry house."

Mama's face went red. "What do you know about such things?" she demanded.

"Oh, for heaven's sake, Mama, I'm a torch. And you know people would start to talk, you know they would."

Mama looked at the Black girl lying there. "You got us into a whole lot of trouble, little girl."

The baby started fussing.

Mama stood up and walked to the window, as if she could see out into the night and find some answer writ on the sky. Then, abruptly, she headed for the door, opened it.

"Mama," said Peggy.

"There's more than one way to pluck a goose," said Mama.

Peggy saw what Mama had thought of. If they couldn't take the baby down to the Berry place, they could maybe keep the baby here at the roadhouse and say they were taking care of it for the Berrys cause they were so poor. As long as the Berry family went along with the tale, it would account for a half-Black baby showing up one day. And nobody'd think the baby was Horace's bastard—not if his wife brought it right into the house.

"You realize what you're asking them, don't you?" said Peggy. "Everybody's going to think somebody else has been plowing with Mr. Berry's heifer."

Mama looked so surprised Peggy almost laughed out loud. "I didn't think Blacks cared about such things," she said.

Peggy shook her head. "Mama, the Berrys are just about the best Christians in Hatrack River. They have to be, to keep forgiving the way White folks treat them and their children."

Mama closed the door again and stood inside, leaning on it. "How *do* folks treat their children?"

It was a pertinent question, Peggy knew, and Mama had thought of it only just in time. It was one thing to look at that scrawny fussing little Black baby and say, I'm going to take care of this child and save his life. It was something else again to think of him being five and seven and ten and seventeen years old, a young buck living right there in the house.

"I don't think you have to fret about that," said Little Peggy, "not half so much as how *you* plan to treat this boy. Do you plan to raise him up to be your servant, a lowborn child in your big fine house? If that's so, then this girl died for nothing, she might as well have let them sell him south."

"I never hankered for no slave," said Mama. "Don't you go saying that I did."

"Well, what then? Are you going to treat him as your own son, and stand with him against all comers, the way you would if you'd ever borne a son of your own?"

Peggy watched as Mama thought of that, and suddenly she saw all kinds of new paths open up in Mama's heart-fire. A son—that's what this half-White boy could be. And if folks around here looked cross-eyed at him on account of him not being all White, they'd have to reckon with Margaret Guester, they would, and it'd be a fearsome day for them, they'd have no terror at the thought of hell, not after what she'd put them through.

Mama hadn't felt such a powerful grim determination in all the years Peggy'd been looking into her heart. It was one of those times when somebody's whole future changed right before her eyes. All the old paths had been pretty much the same; Mama had no choices that would change her life. But now, this dying girl had brought a transformation. Now there were hundreds of new paths open, and all of them had a little boy-child in them, needing her the way her daughter'd never needed her. Set upon by strangers, cruelly treated by the boys of the town, he'd come to her again and again for protection, for teaching, for toughening, the kind of thing that Peggy'd never done.

That's why I disappointed you, wasn't it, Mama? Cause I

knew too much, too young. You wanted me to come to you in my confusion, with my questions. But I never had no questions, Mama, cause I knew from childhood up. I knew what it meant to be a woman from the memories in your own head. I knew about married love without you telling me. I never had a tearful night pressed up against your shoulder, crying cause some boy I longed for wouldn't look at me; I never longed for any boy around here. I never did a thing you dreamed your little girl would do, cause I had a torch's knack, and I knew everything and needed nothing that you wanted to give me.

But this half-Black boy, he'll need you no matter what his knack might be. I see down all those paths, that if you take him in, if you raise him up, he'll be more son to you than I ever was your daughter, though your blood is half of mine.

"Daughter," said Mama, "if I go through this door, will it turn out well for the boy? And for us, too?"

"Are you asking me to See for you, Mama?"

"I am, Little Peggy, and I never asked for that before, never on my own behalf."

"Then I'll tell you." Peggy hardly needed to look far down the paths of Mama's life to find how much pleasure she'd have in the boy. "If you take him in, and treat him like your own son, you'll never regret doing it."

"What about your papa? Will he treat him right?"

"Don't you know your own husband?" asked Peggy.

Mama walked a step toward her, her hand all clenched up even though she never laid a hand on Peggy. "Don't get fresh with me," she said.

"I'm talking the way I talk when I See," said Peggy. "You come to me as a torch, I talk as a torch to you."

"Then say what you have to say."

"It's easy enough. If you don't know how your husband will treat this boy, you don't know that man at all."

"So maybe I don't," said Mama. "Maybe I don't know him at all. Or maybe I do, and I want you to tell me if I'm right."

"You're right," said Peggy. "He'll treat him fair, and make him feel loved all the days of his life."

"But will he really love him?"

There wasn't no chance that Peggy'd answer that question. Love wasn't even in the picture for Papa. He'd take care of the boy because he ought to, because he felt a bounden duty, but the boy'd never know the difference, it'd feel like love to him, and it'd be a lot more dependable than love ever was. But to explain that to Mama would mean telling her how Papa did so many things because he felt so bad about his ancient sins, and there'd never be a time in Mama's life when she was ready to hear *that* tale.

So Peggy just looked at Mama and answered her the way she answered other folks who pried too deep into things they didn't really want to know. "That's for him to answer," Peggy said. "All you need to know is that the choice you already made in your heart is a good one. Already just deciding that has changed your life."

"But I haven't even decided yet," said Mama.

In Mama's heart there wasn't a single path left, not a single one, in which she didn't get the Berrys to say it was their boy, and leave him with her to raise.

"Yes you have," said Peggy. "And you're glad of it."

Mama turned and left, closing the door gentle behind her, so as not to wake the traveling preacher who was sleeping in the room upstairs of the door.

Peggy had just one moment's unease, and she wasn't even sure why. If she'd thought about it a minute, she'd have known it was on account of how she cheated her Mama without even knowing it. When Peggy did a Seeing for anybody else, she always took care to look far down the paths of their life, looking for darkness from causes not even guessed at. But Peggy was so sure she knew her Mama and Papa, she didn't even bother looking except at what was coming up right away. That's how it goes within a family. You think you know each other so well, and so you don't bother hardly getting to know each other at all. It wouldn't be years yet till Peggy would think back on this day, and try to figure why she didn't See what was coming. Sometimes she'd even imagine that her knack failed her. But it didn't. She failed her own knack. She wasn't the first to do so, nor the last, nor even the worst, but there's few ever lived to regret it more.

The moment of unease passed, and Peggy forgot it as her thoughts turned to the Black girl on the common-room floor. She was awake, her eyes open. The baby was still mewling. Without the girl saying a thing, Peggy knew she was willing for the babe to suckle, if she had anything in her breasts to suck on out. The girl hadn't even strength to open up her faded cotton shirt. Peggy had to sit beside her, cradling the child against her own thighs while she fumbled the girl's buttons open with her free hand. The girl's chest was so skinny, her ribs so stark and bare, that her breasts looked to be saddlebags tossed onto a rail fence. But the nipple still stood up for the baby to suck, and a white froth soon appeared around the baby's lips, so there was something there, even now, even at the very end of his mama's life.

The girl was far too weak to talk, but she didn't need to; Peggy heard what she wanted to say, and answered her. "My own mama's going to keep your boy," said Peggy. "And no wise is she going to let any man make a slave of him."

That was what the girl wanted most to hear—that and the sound of her greedy boy-baby slurping and humming and squealing at her breast.

But Peggy wanted her to know more than that before she died. "Your boy-baby's going to know about you," she told the girl. "He's going to hear how you gave your life so you could fly away and take him here to freedom. Don't you think he'll ever forget you, cause he won't."

Then Peggy looked into the child's heartfire, searched there for what he'd be. Oh, that was a painful thing, because the life of a half-White boy in a White town was hard no matter which of the paths of his life he chose. Still, she saw enough to know the nature of the babe whose fingers scratched and clutched at his mama's naked chest. "And he'll be a man worth dying for, too, I promise you that."

The girl was glad to hear it. It brought her peace enough that she could sleep again. After a time the babe, satisfied, also fell asleep. Peggy picked him up, wrapped him in a blanket, and laid him in the crook of his mama's arm. Every last moment of your mama's life you'll be with her, she told the boychild silently. We'll tell you that, too, that she held you in her arms when she died.

When she died. Papa was out with Po Doggly, digging her grave; Mama was off at the Berrys, to persuade them to help her save the baby's life and freedom; and here was Peggy, thinking as if the girl was already dead.

But she wasn't dead, not yet. And all of a sudden it came to Peggy, with a flash of anger that she was too stupid to think of it before, that there was one soul she knew of who had the knack in him to heal the sick. Hadn't he knelt by Ta-Kumsaw at the battle of Detroit, that great Red man's body riddled with bullet holes, hadn't Alvin knelt there and healed him up? Alvin could save this girl, if he was here.

She cast off in the darkness, searching for the heartfire that burned so bright, the heartfire she knew better than any in the world, better even than her own. And there he was, running in the darkness, traveling the way Red men did, like he was asleep, and the land around him was his soul. He was coming faster than any White could ever come, even with the fastest horse on the best road between the Wobbish and the Hatrack, but he wouldn't be here till noon tomorrow, and by then this runaway slavegirl would be dead and in the ground up in the family graveyard. By twelve hours at most she'd miss the one man in this country who could have saved her life.

Wasn't that the way of it? Alvin could save her, but he'd never know she needed saving. While Peggy, who couldn't do a thing, she knew all that was happening, knew all the things that might happen, knew the one thing that *should* happen if the world was good. It wasn't good. It wouldn't happen.

What a terrible gift it was, to be a torch, to know all these things a-coming, and have so little power to change them. The only power she'd ever had was just the words of her mouth, telling folks, and even then she couldn't be sure what they'd choose to do. Always there'd be some choice they could make that would set them down a path even worse than the one she wanted to save them from—and so many times in their wickedness or cantankerousness or just plain bad luck, they'd make that terrible choice and then things'd be worse for them than if Peggy'd just kept still and never said a thing. I wish I didn't know. I wish I had some hope that Alvin would come in time. I wish I had some hope this girl would live. I wish that I could save her life myself.

And then she thought of the many times she *had* saved a life. Alvin's life, using Alvin's caul. At that moment hope *did* spark up in her heart, for surely, just this once, she could use a bit of the last scrap of Alvin's caul to save this girl, to restore her.

Peggy leapt up and ran clumsily to the stairs, her legs so numb from sitting on the floor that she couldn't hardly feel her own footsteps on the bare wood. She tripped on the stairs and made some noise, but none of the guests woke up, as far as she noticed right off like that. Up the stairs,

then up the attic ladderway that Oldpappy made into a
proper stairway not three months afore he died. She threaded
her way among the trunks and old furniture until she
reached her room up against the west end of the house.
Moonlight came in through her south-facing window, making a squared-off pattern on the floor. She pried up the
floorboard and took the box from the place where she hid it
whenever she left the room.

She walked too heavy or this one guest slept too light, but
as she came down the ladderway, there he stood, skinny
white legs sticking out from under his longshirt, a-gazing
down the stairs, then back toward his room, like as if he
couldn't make up his mind whether to go in or out, up or
down. Peggy looked into his heartfire, just to find out whether
he'd been downstairs and seen the girl and her baby—if he
had, then all their thought and caution had been in vain.

But he hadn't—it was still possible.

"Why are you still dressed for going out?" he asked. "At
this time of the morning, too?"

She gently laid her finger against his lips. To silence him,
or at least that's how the gesture began. But she knew right
away that she was the first woman ever to touch this man
upon the face since his mama all those many years ago. She
saw that in that moment his heart filled, not with lust, but
with the vague longings of a lonely man. He was the minister who'd come day before yesterday morning, a traveling
preacher—from Scotland, he said. She'd hardly paid him no
mind, her being so preoccupied with knowing Alvin was on
his way back. But now all that mattered was to send him
back into his room, quick as could be, and she knew one
sure way to do it. She put her hands on his shoulders, getting a strong grip behind his neck, and pulled him down to
where she could kiss him fair on the lips. A good long buss,
like he never had from a woman in all his days.

Just like she expected, he was back into his room almost before she let go of him. She might've laughed at that, except she knew from his heartfire it wasn't her kiss sent him back, like she planned. It was the box she still held in one hand, which she had pressed up against the back of his neck when she held him. The box with Alvin's caul inside.

The moment it touched him, he felt what was inside. It wasn't no knack of his, it was something else—just being so near something of Alvin's done it to him. She saw the vision of Alvin's face loom up inside his mind, with such fear and hatred like she never seen before. Only then did she realize that he wasn't just any minister. He was Reverend Philadelphia Thrower, who once had been a preacher back in Vigor Church. Reverend Thrower, who once had tried to kill the boy, except Alvin's pa prevented him.

The fear of a woman's kiss was nothing to him compared to his fear of Alvin Junior. The trouble was that now he was *so* afraid he was already thinking of leaving right this minute and getting out of this roadhouse. If he did that, he'd have to come downstairs and then he'd see all, just what she meant to fend off. This was how it went so often—she tried to stave off a bad thing and it turned out worse, something so unlikely she didn't see it. How could she not have reckonized who he was? Hadn't she seen him through Alvin's eyes all those many times in years past? But he'd changed this last year, he looked thin and haunted and older. Besides, she wasn't looking for him here, and anyhow it was too late to undo what she already done. All that mattered now was to keep him in his room.

So she opened his door and followed him inside and looked him square in the face and said, "He was born here."

"Who?" he said. His face was white as if he'd just seen the devil himself. He knew who she meant.

"And he's coming back. Right now he's on his way. You're

only safe if you stay in your room tonight, and leave in the morning at first light."

"I don't know—know what you're talking about."

Did he really think he could fool a torch? Maybe he didn't know she was—no, he knew, he knew, he just didn't believe in torching and hexing and knacks and suchlike. He was a man of science and higher religion. A blamed fool. So she'd have to prove to him that what he feared most was so. She knew him, and she knew his secrets. "You tried to kill Alvin Junior with a butchery knife," she said.

That did it, right enough. He fell to his knees. "I'm not afraid to die," he said. Then he began to murmur the Lord's prayer.

"Pray all night, if you like," she said, "but stay in your room to do it."

Then she stepped through the door and closed it. She was halfway down the stairs when she heard the bar fall into place across the door. Peggy didn't even have time to care whether she caused him undue misery—he wasn't really a murderer in his heart. All she cared for now was to get the caul down to where she could use it to help the runaway, if by any chance Alvin's power was really hers to use. So much time that minister had cost her. So many of the slavegirl's precious breaths.

She was still breathing, wasn't she? Yes. No. The babe lay sleeping beside her, but her chest didn't move even as much as him, her lips didn't make even so much as a baby's breath on Peggy's hand. But her heartfire still burned! Peggy could see that plain enough, still burned bright because she was so strong-hearted, that slavegirl was. So Peggy opened up the box, took out the scrap of caul, and rubbed a dry corner of it to dust between her fingers, whispering to her, "Live, get strong." She tried to do what Alvin did when he healed, the way he could feel the small broken places in a person's body, set them right. Hadn't she watched him as he did it so many times before? But it was different, doing it herself. It was strange to her, she didn't have the vision for it, and she could feel the life ebbing away from the girl's body, the heart stilled, the lungs slack, the eyes open but unlighted, and at last the heartfire flashed like a shooting star, all sudden and bright, and it was gone.

Too late. If I hadn't stopped in the hall upstairs, hadn't had to deal with the minister—

But no, no, she couldn't blame herself, it wasn't her power anyway, it was too late before she began. The girl had been dying all through her body. Even Alvin himself, if he was here, even he couldn't have done it. It was never more than a slim hope. Never even hope enough that she could see a single pathway where it worked. So she wouldn't do like so many did, she wouldn't endlessly blame herself when after all she'd done her best at a task that had little hope in it from the start.

Now that the girl was dead, she couldn't leave the baby there to feel his mama's arm grow cold. She picked him up. He stirred, but slept on in the way that babies do. Your mama's dead, little half-White boy, but you'll have *my* mama, and my papa too. They got love enough for a little one; you won't starve for it like some children I seen. So you make the best of it, boy-baby. Your mama died to bring you here—you make the best of it, and you'll be something, right enough.

You'll be something, she heard herself whispering. You'll be something, and so will I.

She made her decision even before she realized there was even a decision to be made. She could feel her own future changing even though she couldn't see rightly what it was going to be.

That slave girl guessed at the likeliest future—you don't have to be a torch to see *some* things plain. It was an ugly life ahead, losing her baby, living as a slave till the day she dropped. Yet she saw just the faintest glimmer of hope for her baby, and once she saw it, she didn't hold back, no sir, that glimmer was worth paying her life for.

And now look at me, thought Peggy. Here I look down the paths of Alvin's life and see misery for myself—nowhere near as bad as that slavegirl's, but bad enough. Now and then I catch the shine of a bright chance for happiness, a strange and backward way to have Alvin and have him love me, too. Once I seen it, am I going to sit on my hands and watch that bright hope die, just because I'm not sure how to get to it from here?

If that beat-down child can make her own hope out of wax and ash and feathers and a bit of herself, then I can make my own life, too. Somewhere there's a thread that if I just lay hold on it, it'll lead me to happiness. And even if I never find that particular thread, it'll be better than the despair waiting for me if I stay. Even if I never become a part of Alvin's life when he comes to manhood, well, that's still not as steep a price as that slavegirl paid for freedom.

When Alvin comes tomorrow, I won't be here.

That was her decision, just like that. Why, she could hardly believe she never thought of it before. Of all people in the whole of Hatrack River, she ought to have knowed that there's *always* another choice. Folks talked on about how they were forced into misery and woe, they didn't have no choice at all—but that runaway girl showed that there's always a way out, long as you remember even death can be a straight smooth road sometimes.

I don't even have to get no blackbird feathers to fly, neither.

Peggy sat there holding the baby, making bold and fearsome plans for how she'd leave in the morning afore Alvin could arrive. Whenever she felt a-scared of what she'd set herself to do, she cast her gaze down on that girl, and the sight of her was comfort, it truly was. I might someday end up like you, runaway girl, dead in some stranger's house. But better that unknown future than one I knew all along I'd hate, and then did nothing to avoid.

Will I do it, will I really do it in the morning, when the time's come and no turning back? She touched Alvin's caul with her free hand, just snaking her fingers into the box, and what she saw in Alvin's future made her feel like singing. Used to be most paths showed them meeting up and starting out her life of misery. Now only a few of those paths were there—in most of Alvin's futures, she saw him come to Hatrack River and search for the torch girl and find her gone. Just changing her mind tonight had closed down most of the roads to misery.

Mama came back with the Berrys before Papa came in from gravedigging. Anga Berry was a heavyset woman with laughter lines outnumbering the lines of worry on her face, though both kinds were plain enough. Peggy knew her well and liked her better than most folks in Hatrack River. She had a temper but she also had compassion, and Peggy wasn't surprised at all to see her rush to the body of the girl and take up that cold limp hand and press it to her bosom. She murmured words almost like a lullaby, her voice was so low and sweet and kind.

"She's dead," said Mock Berry. "But that baby's strong I see."

Peggy stood up and let Mock see the baby in her arms. She didn't like him half so well as she liked his wife. He was the kind of man who'd slap a child so hard blood flowed, just cause he didn't like what was said or done. It was almost worse cause he didn't rage when he did it. Like he felt nothing at all, to hurt somebody or not hurt somebody made no powerful difference in his mind. But he worked hard, and even though he was poor his family got by; and nobody who knew Mock paid heed to them crude folks what said there wasn't a buck who wouldn't steal or a ewe you couldn't tup.

"Healthy," said Mock. Then he turned to Mama. "When he grow up to be a big old buck, ma'am, you still aim to call him your boy? Or you make him sleep out back in the shed with the animals?"

Well, he wasn't one to pussyfoot around the issue, Peggy saw.

"Shut your mouth, Mock," said his wife. "And you give me that baby, Miss. I just wish I'd knowed he was coming or I'd've kept my youngest on the tit to keep the milk in. Weaned that boy two months back and he's been nothing but trouble since, but you ain't no trouble, baby, you ain't no trouble at all." She cooed to the baby just like she cooed to his dead mama, and he didn't wake up either.

"I told you. I'll raise him as my son," said Mama.

"I'm sorry, ma'am, but I just never heard of no White woman doing such a thing," said Mock.

"What I say," said Mama, "that's what I do."

Mock thought on that a moment. Then he nodded. "I reckon so," he said. "I reckon I never heard you break your word, not even to Black folks." He grinned. "Most White folk allow as how lying to a buck ain't the same as *lying*."

"We'll do like you asked," said Anga Berry. "I'll tell anybody who ask me this is my boy, only we gave him to you cause we was too poor."

"But don't you ever go forgetting that it's a lie," said Mock. "Don't you ever go thinking that if it really was our own baby, we'd ever give him up. And don't you ever go thinking that my wife here ever would let some White man put a baby in her, and her being married to me."

Mama studied Mock for a minute, taking his measure in

the way she had. "Mock Berry, I hope you come and visit me any day you like while this boy is in my house, and I'll show you how one White woman keeps her word."

Mock laughed. "I reckon you a regular Mancipationist."

Papa came in then, covered with sweat and dirt. He shook hands with the Berrys, and in a minute they told him the tale they all would tell. He made his promises too, to raise the boy like his own son. He even thought of what never entered Mama's head—he said a few words to Peggy, to promise her that they wouldn't give no preference to the boy, neither. Peggy nodded. She didn't want to say much, cause anything she said would either be a lie or give her plans away; she knew she had no intention to be in this house for even a single day of this baby's future here.

"We go on home now, Goody Guester," said Anga. She handed the baby to Mama. "If one of my children wake up with a boogly dream I best be there or you hear them screams clear up here on the high road."

"Ain't you going have no preacher say words at her grave?" said Mock.

Papa hadn't thought of it. "We do have a minister upstairs," he said.

But Peggy didn't let him hold that thought for even a moment. "No," she said, sharp as she could.

Papa looked at her, and knew that she was talking as a torch. Wasn't no arguing that point. He just nodded. "Not this time, Mock," he said. "Wouldn't be safe."

Mama fretted Anga Berry clear to the door. "Is there anything I ought to know?" said Mama. "Is there anything different about Black babies?"

"Oh, powerful different," said Anga. "But that baby, he half-White I reckon, so you just take care of that White half, and I reckon the Black half take care of hisself."

"Cow's milk from a pig bladder?" Mama insisted.

"You know all them things," said Anga. "I learnt everything I know from you, Mrs. Guester. All the women round here do. How come you asking me now? Don't you know I need my sleep?"

Once the Berrys were gone, Papa picked up the girl's body and carried her outside. Not even a coffin, though they would overlay the corpse with stones to keep the dogs off. "Light as a feather," he said when first he hoisted her. "Like the charred carcass of a burnt log."

Which was apt enough, Peggy had to admit. That's what she was now. Just ashes. She'd burnt herself right up.

Mama held the pickaninny boy while Peggy went up into the attic and fetched down the cradle. Nobody woke up this time, except that minister. He was *wide* awake behind his door, but he wasn't coming out for any reason. Mama and Peggy made up that little bed in Mama's and Papa's room, and laid the baby in it. "Tell me if this poor orphan baby's got him a name," said Mama.

"She never gave him one," said Peggy. "In her tribe, a woman never got her a name till she married, and a man had no name till he killed him his first animal."

"That's just awful," said Mama. "That ain't even Christian. Why, she died unbaptized."

"No," said Peggy. "She was baptized right enough. Her owner's wife saw to that—all the Blacks on their plantation were baptized."

Mama's face went sour. "I reckon she thought that made her a Christian. Well, I'll have a name for you, little boy." She grinned wickedly. "What do you think your papa would do if I named this baby Horace Guester Junior?"

"Die," said Peggy.

"I reckon so," said Mama. "I ain't ready to be a widow

yet. So for now we'll name him—oh, I can't think, Peggy. What's a Black man's name? Or should I just name him like any White child?"

"Only Black man's name I know is Othello," said Peggy.

"That's a queer name if I ever heard one," said Mama. "You must've got that out of one of Whitley Physicker's books."

Peggy said nothing.

"I know," said Mama. "I know his name. Cromwell. The Lord Protector's name."

"You might better name him Arthur, after the King," said Peggy.

Mama just cackled and laughed at that. "That's your name, little boy. Arthur Stuart! And if the King don't like such a namesake, let him send an army and I still won't change it. His Majesty will have to change his own name first."

EVEN THOUGH SHE got to bed so late, Peggy woke early next morning. It was hoofbeats woke her—she didn't have to go to the window to recognize his heartfire as the minister rode away. Ride on, Thrower, she said silently. You won't be the last to run away this morning, fleeing from that eleven-year-old boy.

It was the north-facing window she looked out of. She could see between the trees to the graveyard up the hill. She tried to see where the grave was dug last night, but there wasn't no sign her natural eyes could see, and in a graveyard there wasn't no heartfires neither, nothing to help her. Alvin will see it though, she knew that sure. He'd head for that graveyard first thing he did, cause his oldest brother's body lay there, the boy Vigor, who got swept away in the Hatrack River saving Alvin's mother's life in the last hour before she gave birth to her seventh son. But Vigor hung on to life just long enough, in spite of the river's strongest pulling at him, hung on just long enough that when Alvin was born he was the seventh of seven living sons. Peggy herself had watched his heartfire flicker and die right after the babe was born. He would've heard that story a thousand times. So he'd come to that graveyard, and *he* could feel his way through the earth and find what lay hidden there. He'd find that unmarked grave, that wasted body so fresh buried there.

Peggy took the box with the caul in it, put it deep in a cloth bag along with her second dress, a petticoat, and the most recent books Whitley Physicker had brought. Just because she didn't want to meet him face to face didn't mean she could forget that boy. She'd touch the caul again tonight, or maybe not till morning, and then she'd stand with him in memory and use his senses to find that nameless Black girl's grave.

Her bag packed, she went downstairs.

Mama had drug the cradle into the kitchen and she was singing to the baby while she kneaded bread, rocking the cradle with one foot, even though Arthur Stuart was fast asleep. Peggy set her bag outside the kitchen door, walked in and touched her Mama's shoulder. She hoped a little that she'd see her Mama grieving something awful when she found out Peggy'd gone off. But it wasn't so. Oh, she'd carry on and rage at first, but in the times to come she'd miss Peggy less than she might've guessed. It was the baby'd take her mind off worrying about her daughter. Besides, Mama knew Peggy could take care of herself. Mama knew Peggy wasn't a one to need to hold a body's hand. While Arthur Stuart needed her.

If this was the first time Peggy noticed how her Mama felt about her, she'd have been hurt deep. But it was the hundredth time, and she was used to it, and looked behind it to the reason, and loved her Mama for being a better soul than most, and forgave her for not loving Peggy more.

"I love you, Mama," said Peggy.

"I love you too, baby," said Mama. She didn't even look up nor guess what Peggy had in mind.

Papa was still asleep. After all, he dug a grave last night and filled it too.

Peggy wrote a note. Sometimes she took care to put in a lot of extra letters in the fancy way they did in books, but this time she wanted to make sure Papa could read it for himself. That meant putting in no more letters than it took to make the sounds for reading out loud.

I lov you Papa and Mama but I got to leav I no its rong to lev Hatrak with out no torch but I bin torch sixtn yr. I seen my fewchr and ile be saf donte you fret on my acown.

She walked out the front door, carried her bag to the road, and waited only ten minutes before Doctor Whitley Physicker came along in his carriage, bound on the first leg of a trip to Philadelphia.

"You didn't wait on the road like this just to hand me back that Milton I lent you," said Whitley Physicker.

She smiled and shook her head. "No sir, I'd like you take me with you to Dekane. I plan to visit with a friend of my father's, but if you don't mind the company I'd rather not spend the money for a coach."

Peggy watched him consider for a minute, but she knew he'd let her come, and without asking her folks, neither. He was the kind of man thought a girl had as much worth as any boy, and more than that, he plain liked Peggy, thought of her as something like a niece. And he knew that Peggy never lied, so he had no need to check with her folks.

And she hadn't lied to him, no more than she ever lied when she left off without telling all she knew. Papa's old lover, the woman he dreamed of and suffered for, she lived there in Dekane—widowed for the last few years, but her mourning time over so she wouldn't have to turn away company. Peggy knew that lady well, from watching far off for all these years. If I knock on her door, thought Peggy, I don't even have to tell her I'm Horace Guester's girl, she'd take me in as a stranger, she would, and care for me, and help me on my way. But maybe I *will* tell her whose daughter I am, and how I knew to come to her, and how Papa still lives with the aching memory of his love for her.

The carriage rattled over the covered bridge that Alvin's father and older brothers had built eleven years before, after the river drowned the oldest son. Birds nested in the rafters. It was a mad, musical, happy sound they made, at least to her ears, chirping so loud inside the bridge that it sounded like she imagined grand opera ought to be. They had opera in Camelot, down south. Maybe someday she'd go and hear it, and see the King himself in his box.

Or maybe not. Because someday she might just find the path that led to that brief but lovely dream, and then she'd have more important things to do than look at kings or hear the music of the Austrian court played by lacy Virginia musicians in the fancy opera hall in Camelot. Alvin was more important than any of these, if he could only find his way to all his power and what he ought to do with it. And she was born to be part of it. That's how easily she slipped into her dreams of him. Yet why not? Her dreams of him, however brief and hard to find, were true visions of the future, and the greatest joy and the greatest grief she could find for herself both touched this boy who wasn't even a man yet, who had never seen her face to face.

But sitting there in the carriage beside Doctor Whitley Physicker, she forced those thoughts, those visions from her mind. What comes will come, she thought. If I find that path

I find it, and if not, then not. For now, at least, I'm free. Free of my watch aloft for the town of Hatrack, and free of building all my plans around that little boy. And what if I end up free of him forever? What if I find another future that doesn't even have him in it? That's the likeliest end of things. Give me time enough, I'll even forget that scrap of a dream I had, and find my own good road to a peaceful end, instead of bending myself to fit his troubled path.

The dancing horses pulled the carriage along so brisk that the wind caught and tossed her hair. She closed her eyes and pretended she was flying, a runaway just learning to be free.

Let him find his path to greatness now without me. Let me have a happy life far from him. Let some other woman stand beside him in his glory. Let another woman kneel a-weeping at his grave.

3

LIES

Eleven-year-old Alvin lost half his name when he came to Hatrack River. Back home in the town of Vigor Church, not far from where the Tippy-Canoe poured its waters into the Wobbish, everybody knowed his father was Alvin, miller for the town and the country round about. Alvin Miller. Which made his namesake, his seventh son, Alvin *Junior*. Now, though, he was going to live in a place where there wasn't six folks who so much as ever met his pa. No need for names like Miller and Junior. He was just Alvin, plain Alvin, but hearing that lone name made him feel like only half hisself.

He came to Hatrack River on foot, hundreds of miles

across Wobbish and Hio territories. When he set out from home it was with a pair of sturdy broke-in boots on and a pack of supplies on his back. He did five miles that way, before he stopped up at a poor cabin and gave his food to the folk there. After another mile or so he met a poor traveling family, heading on west to the new lands in the Noisy River country. He gave them the tent and blanket in his pack, and because they had a thirteen-year-old boy about Alvin's size, he pulled off them new boots and gave them straight out, just like that, socks too. He kept only his clothes and the empty pack on his back.

Why, them folks were wide-eyed and silly-faced over it, worrying that Alvin's pa might be mad, him giving stuff away like that, but he allowed as how it was his to give.

"You sure I won't be meeting up with your pa with a musket and a possy-come-and-take-us?" asked the poor man.

"I'm sure you won't, sir," said young Alvin, "on account of I'm from the town of Vigor Church, and the folks there won't see you at all unless you force them."

It took them near ten seconds to realize where they'd heard the name of Vigor Church before. "Them's the folk of the Tippy-Canoe massacre," they said. "Them's the folk what got blood on their hands."

Alvin just nodded. "So you see they'll leave you be."

"Is it true they make every traveler listen to them tell that terrible gory tale of how they killed all them Reds in cold blood?"

"Their blood wasn't cold," said Alvin, "and they only tell travelers who come right on into town. So just stay on the road, leave them be, ride on through. Once you cross the Wobbish, you'll be in open land again, where you'll be glad to meet up with settled folk. Not ten mile on."

Well, they didn't argue no more, nor even ask him how he came not to have to tell the tale hisself. The name of the

Massacre of Tippy-Canoe was enough to put a silence on folks like setting in a church, a kind of holy, shameful, reverent attitude. Cause even though most Whites shunned the bloody-handed folk who shed Red men's blood at Tippy-Canoe, they still knew that if they'd stood in the same place, they'd've done the same thing, and it'd be their hands dripping red till they told a stranger about the wretched deed they done. That guilty knowledge didn't make many travelers too keen on stopping in Vigor Church, or any homes in the upper Wobbish country. Them poor folks just took Alvin's boots and gear and moved on down the road, glad of a stretch of canvas over their heads and a slice of leather on their big boy's feet.

Alvin betook him off the road soon after, and plunged into woodland, into the deepest places. If he'd been wearing boots, he would've stumbled and crunched and made more noise than a rutting buffalo in the woods—which is about what most White folks did in the natural forest. But because he was barefoot, his skin touching the forest floor, he was like a different person. He had run behind Ta-Kumsaw through the forests of this whole land, north and south, and in that running young Alvin learned him how the Red man ran, hearing the greensong of the living woodland, moving in perfect harmony to that sweet silent music. When he ran that way, not thinking about where to step, the ground became soft under young Alvin's feet, and he was guided along, no sticks breaking when he stepped, no bushes swishing or twigs snapping off with his onward push. Behind him he left nary a footprint or a broken branch.

Just like a Red man, that was how he moved. And pretty soon his White man's clothing chafed on him, and he stopped and took it off, stuffed it into the pack on his back, and then ran naked as a jaybird, feeling the leaves of the bushes against his body. Soon he was caught up in the rhythm of his own running, forgetting anything about his own body, just part of the living forest, moving onward, faster and stronger, not eating, not drinking. Like a Red man, who could run forever through the deep forest, never needing rest, covering hundreds of miles in a single day.

This was the natural way to travel, Alvin knew it. Not in creaking wooden wagons, rattling over dry ground, sucking along on muddy roads. And not on horseback, a beast sweating and heaving under you, slave to your hurry, not on any errand of its own. Just a man in the woods, bare feet on the ground, bare face in the wind, dreaming as he ran.

All that day and all that night he ran, and well into the morning. How did he find his way? He could feel the slash of the well-traveled road off on his left, like a prickle or an itch, and even though that road led through many a village and many a town, he knew that after a while it'd fetch him up at the town of Hatrack. After all, that was the road his own folks followed, bridging every stream and creek and river on the way, carrying him as a newborn babe in the wagon. Even though he never traveled it before, and wasn't looking at it now, he knew where it led.

So on the second morning he fetched up at the edge of the wood, on the verge of a field of new green maize billowing over rolling ground. There was so many farms in this settled country that the forest was too weak to hold him in his dream much longer anyhow.

It took a while, just standing there, to remember who he was and where he was bound. The music of the greenwood was strong behind him, weak afore. All he could know for sure was a town ahead, and a river maybe five mile on, that's all he could *feel* for sure. But he knew it was the Hatrack River yonder, and so the town could be no other than the one he was bound for.

He had figured to run the forest right up to the edge of

town. Now, though, he had no choice but to walk those last miles on White man's feet or not go at all. That was a thought he had never thought of—that there might be places in the world so settled that one farm butted right against the next, with only a row of trees or a rail fence to mark the boundary, farm after farm. Was this what the Prophet saw in his visions of the land? All the forest killed back and these fields put in their place, so a Red man couldn't run no more, nor a deer find cover, nor a bear find him where to sleep come wintertime? If that was so, no wonder he took all the Reds who'd follow him out west, across the Mizzipy. There was no living for a Red man here.

That made Alvin a little sad and a little scared, to leave behind the living lands he'd come to know as well as a man knows his own body. But he wasn't no philosopher. He was a boy of eleven, and he also hankered to see an eastern town, all settled up and civilized. Besides, he had business here, business he'd waited a year to take up, ever since he first learned there was such a body as the torch girl, and how she looked for him to be a Maker.

He pulled his clothes out of his pack and put them on. He walked the edge of the farmland till he came to a road. First time the road crossed a stream, there was proof it was the right road: a covered bridge stood over that little one-jump brooklet. His own pa and older brothers built that bridge, and others like it all the way along that road from Hatrack to Vigor Church. Eleven years ago they built it, when Alvin was a baby sucking on his mama while the wagon rattled west.

He followed the road, and it wasn't awful far. He'd just run hundreds of miles through virgin forest without harm to his feet, but the White man's road had no part of the greensong and it didn't yield to Alvin's feet. Within a couple of miles he was footsore and dusty and thirsty and hungry. Alvin hoped it wasn't too many miles on White man's road, or he'd sure be wishing he'd kept his boots.

The sign beside the road said, Town of Hatrack, Hio.

It was a good-sized town, compared to frontier villages. Of course it didn't compare to the French city of Detroit, but that was a foreign place, and this town was, well, American. The houses and buildings were like the few rough structures in Vigor Church and other new settlements, only smoothed out and growed up to full size. There was four streets that crossed the main road, with a bank and a couple of shops and churches and even a county courthouse and some places with shingles saying Lawyer and Doctor and Alchemist. Why, if there was professional folk here, it was a town *proper,* not just a hopeful place like Vigor Church before the massacre.

Less than a year ago he'd seen a vision of the town of Hatrack. It was when the Prophet, Lolla-Wossiky, caught him up in the tornado that he called down onto Lake Mizogan. The walls of the whirlwind turned to crystal that time, and in the crystal Alvin had seen many things. One of them was the town of Hatrack the way it was when Alvin was born. It was plain that things hadn't stayed the same in these eleven years. He didn't recognize a thing, walking through the town. Why, this place was so big now that not a soul even seemed to notice he was a stranger to give him howdy-do.

He was most of the way through the built-up part of town before he realized that it wasn't the town's bigness that made folks pay him no mind. It was the dust on his face, his bare feet, the empty pack on his back. They looked, they took him in at a glance, and then they looked away, like as if they were halfway scared he'd come up and ask them for bread or a place to stay. It was something Alvin never met up with before, but he knowed it right away for what it was. In the last eleven years, the town of Hatrack, Hio, had learned the difference between rich and poor.

The built-up part was over. He was through the town, and he hadn't seen a single blacksmith's shop, which was what he was supposed to be looking for, nor had he seen the road-house where he was born, which was what he was really looking for. All he saw right now was a couple of pig farms, stinking the way pig farms do, and then the road bent a bit south and he couldn't see more.

The smithy had to still be there, didn't it? It was only a year and a half ago that Taleswapper had carried the pren-tice contract Pa wrote up for Makepeace, the blacksmith of Hatrack River. And less than a year ago that Taleswapper hisself told Alvin that he delivered that letter, and Make-peace Smith was amenable—that was the word he used, *amenable*. Since Taleswapper talked in his halfway English manner, with the *R*s dropped off the ends of words, it sounded to Alvin like old Taleswapper said Makepeace Smith was "a meaner bull," till Taleswapper wrote it down for him. Anyway, the smith was here a year ago. And the torch girl in the roadhouse, the one he visioned in Lolla-Wossiky's crystal tower, she *must* be here. Hadn't she writ-ten in Taleswapper's book, "A Maker is born"? When he looked at those words the letters burned with light like as if they been conjured, like the message writ by the hand of God on the wall in that Bible story: "Mean, mean, take all apart, son," and sure enough, it came to pass, Babylon was took all apart. Words of prophecy was what turned letters bright like that. So if that Maker was Alvin himself, and he knowed it was, then she must see more in her torchy way. She must know what a Maker really *is* and how to be one.

Maker. A name folks said with a hush. Or spoke of wist-ful, saying that the world had done with Makers, there'd be no more. Oh, some said Old Ben Franklin was a Maker, but he denied being so much as a wizard till the day he died. Taleswapper, who knew Old Ben like a father, he said Ben only made one thing in his life, and that was the American Compact, that piece of paper that bound the Dutch and Swedish colonies with the English and German settlements of Pennsylvania and Suskwahenny and, most important of all, the Red nation of Irrakwa, altogether forming the United States of America, where Red and White, Dutchman, Swede and Englishman, rich and poor, merchant and laborer, all could vote and all could speak and no one could say, I'm a better man than you. Some folks allowed as how that made Ben as true a Maker as ever lived, but no, said Taleswapper, that made Ben a binder, a knotter, but not a Maker.

I am the Maker that torch girl wrote about. She touched me as I was a-borning, and when she did she saw that I had Maker-stuff in me. I've got to find that girl, growed up to be sixteen years old by now, and she's got to tell me what she saw. Cause the powers I've found inside me, the things that I can do, I know they've got a purpose bigger than just cutting stone without hands and healing the sick and running through the woods like any Red man can but no White man ever could. I've got a work to do in my life and I don't have the first spark of an idea how to get ready for it.

Standing there in the road, with a pig farm on either hand, Alvin heard the sharp *ching ching* of iron striking iron. The smith might as well have called out to him by name. Here I am, said the hammer, find me up ahead along the road.

Before he ever got to the smithy, though, he rounded the bend and saw the very roadhouse where he was born, just as plain as ever in the vision in the crystal tower. White-washed shiny and new with only the dust of this summer on it, so it didn't look quite the same, but it was as welcome a sight as any weary traveler could hope for.

Twice welcome, cause inside it, with any decent luck, the torch girl could tell him what his life was supposed to be.

Alvin knocked at the door cause that's what you do, he thought. He'd never stayed in a roadhouse before, and had no notion of a public room. So he knocked once, and then twice, and then hallooed till finally the door opened. It was a woman with flour on her hands and her checked apron, a big woman who looked annoyed beyond belief—but he knew her face. This was the woman in his crystal tower vision, the one what pulled him out of the womb with her own fingers around his neck.

"What in the world are you thinking of, boy, to knock my door like that and start hullaballooing like there was a fire! Why can't you just come on in and set like any other folk, or are you so powerful important that you got to have a servant come and open doors for you?"

"Sorry, ma'am," said Alvin, about as respectful as could be.

"Now what business could you have with us? If you're a beggar then I got to tell you we'll have no scraps till after dinner, but you're welcome to wait till then, and if you got a conscience, why, you can chop some wood for us. Except for look at you, I can't believe you're more than fourteen years old—"

"Eleven, ma'am."

"Well, then, you're right big for your age, but I still can't figure what business you got here. I won't serve you no liquor even if you got money, which I doubt. This is a Christian house, in fact more than mere Christian because we're true-blue Methodist and that means we don't touch a drop nor serve it neither, and even if we did we wouldn't serve children. And I'd stake ten pound of porkfat on a wager that you don't have the price of a night's lodging."

"No ma'am," said Alvin, "but—"

"Well then here you are, dragging me out of my kitchen with the bread half-kneaded and a baby who's bound to cry for milk any minute, and I reckon you don't plan to stand at the head of the table and explain to all my boarders why their dinner is late, on account of a boy who can't open a door his own self, no, you'll leave me to make apologies myself as best I can, which is right uncivil of you if you don't mind my saying, or even if you do."

"Ma'am," said Alvin, "I don't want food and I don't want a room." He knew enough courtesy *not* to add that travelers had always been welcome to stay in his father's house whether they had money or not, and a hungry man didn't get afternoon scraps, he set down at Pa's own table and ate with the family. He was catching on to the idea that things were different here in civilized country.

"Well, all we deal in here is food and rooms," said the roadhouse lady.

"I come here, ma'am, cause I was born in this house almost twelve years ago."

Her whole demeanor changed at once. She wasn't a roadhouse mistress now, she was a midwife. "Born in this house?"

"Born on the day my oldest brother Vigor died in the Hatrack River. I thought as how you might even remember that day, and maybe you could show me the place where my brother lies buried."

Her face changed again. "You," she said. "You're the boy who was born to that family—the seventh son of—"

"Of a seventh son," said Alvin.

"Well what's become of you, tell me! Oh, it was a portentous thing. My daughter stood there and looked afar off and saw that your big brother was still alive as you came out of the womb—"

"Your daughter," said Alvin, forgetting himself so much

that he interrupted her clean in the middle of a sentence. "She's a torch."

The lady turned cold as ice. *"Was,"* she said. "She don't torch no more."

But Alvin hardly noticed how the lady changed. "You mean she lost her knack for it? I never heard of a body losing their knack. But if she's here, I'd like to talk to her."

"She ain't here no more," said the lady. Now Alvin finally caught on that she didn't much care to talk about it. "There ain't no torch now in Hatrack River. Babies will be born here without a body touching them to see how they lie in the womb. That's the end of it. I won't say another word about such a girl as that who'd run off, just run right off—"

Something caught in the lady's voice and she turned her back to him.

"I got to finish my bread," said the lady. "The graveyard is up the hill there." She turned around again to face him, with nary a sign of the anger or grief or what-all that she felt a second before. "If my Horace was here I'd have him show you the way, but you'll see it anyhow, there's a kind of path. It's just a family graveyard, with a picket fence around it." Her stern manner softened. "When you're done up there you come on back and I'll serve you better than scraps." She hurried on into the kitchen. Alvin followed her.

There was a cradle by the kitchen table, with a babe asleep in it but wiggling somewhat. Something funny about the baby but Alvin couldn't say right off what it was.

"Thank you for your kindness, ma'am, but I don't ask for no handouts. I'll work to pay for anything I eat."

"That's rightly said, and like a true man—your father was the same, and the bridge he built over the Hatrack is still there, strong as ever. But you just go now, see the graveyard, and then come back by and by."

She bent over the huge wad of dough on the kneading

PRENTICE ALVIN • 73

table. Alvin got the notion for just a moment that she was crying, and maybe he did and maybe he didn't see tears drop from her eyes straight down into the dough. It was plain she wanted to be alone.

He looked again at the baby and realized what was different. "That's a pickaninny baby, isn't it?" he said.

She stopped kneading, but left her hands buried to the wrist in dough. "It's a baby," she said, "and it's *my* baby. I adopted him and he's mine, and if you call him a pickaninny I'll knead your face like dough."

"Sorry, ma'am, I meant no harm. He just had a sort of cast to his face that gave me that idea, I reckon—"

"Oh, he's half-Black all right. But it's the White half of him I'm raising up, just as if he was my own son. We named him Arthur Stuart."

Alvin got the joke of that right off. "Ain't nobody can call the King a pickaninny, I reckon."

She smiled. "I reckon not. Now get, boy. You owe a debt to your dead brother, and you best pay it now."

The graveyard was easy to find, and Alvin was gratified to see that his brother Vigor had a stone, and his grave was as well-tended as any other. Only a few graves here. Two stones with the same name—"Baby Missy"—and dates that told of children dying young. Another stone that said "Old-pappy" and then his real name, and dates that told of a long life. And Vigor.

He knelt by his brother's grave and tried to picture what he might have been like. The best he could do was imagine his brother Measure, who was his favorite brother, the one who was captured by Reds along with Alvin. Vigor must have been like Measure. Or maybe Measure was like Vigor. Both willing to die if need be, for their family's sake. Vigor's death saved my life before I was born, thought Alvin, and yet he hung on to the last breath so that when I was born I was still the seventh son of a seventh son, with all my brothers ahead of me alive. The same kind of sacrifice and courage and strength that it took when Measure, who hadn't killed a single Red man, who near died just trying to stop the Tippy-Canoe massacre from happening, took on himself the same curse as his father and his brothers, to have blood on his hands if he failed to tell any stranger the true story of the killing of all them innocent Reds. So when he knelt there at Vigor's grave, it was like he was kneeling at Measure's grave, even though he knew Measure wasn't dead.

Wasn't wholly dead, anyway. But like the rest of the folk of Vigor Church, he'd never leave that place again. He'd live out all his days where he wouldn't have to meet too many strangers, so that for days on end he could forget the slaughter on that day last summer. The whole family, staying together there, with all the folks in the country roundabout, living out their days of life until them as had the curse all died, sharing each other's shame and each other's loneliness like they was all kin, every one of them.

All them together, except for me. I didn't take no curse on me. I left them all behind.

Kneeling there, Alvin felt like an orphan. He might as well be. Sent off to be a prentice here, knowing that whatever he did, whatever he made, his kin could never come on out to see. He could go home to that bleak sad town from time to time, but that was more like a graveyard than this grassy living place, because even with dead folks buried here, there was hope and life in the town nearby, people looking forward instead of back.

Alvin had to look forward, too. Had to find his way to what he was born to be. You died for me, Vigor, my brother that I never met. I just haven't figured out yet why it was so important for me to be alive. When I find out, I hope to make you proud of me. I hope you'll think that I was worth dying for.

When his thoughts was all spent and gone, when his heart had filled up and then emptied out again, Alvin did something he never thought to do. He looked under the ground.

Not by digging, mind you. Alvin's knack was such that he could get the feel of underground without using his eyes. Like the way he looked into stone. Now it might seem to some folk like a kind of grave-robbing, for Al to peek inside the earth where his brother's body lay. But to Al it was the only way he'd ever see the man who died to save him.

So he closed his eyes and gazed under the soil and found the bones inside the rotted wooden box. The size of him— Vigor was a big boy, which is about what it would take to roll and yaw a full-sized tree in a river's current. But the soul of him, that wasn't there, and even though he knowed it wouldn't be Al was somewhat disappointed.

His hidden gaze wandered to the small bodies barely clinging to their own dust, and then to the gnarled old corpse of Oldpappy, whoever that was, fresh in the earth, only a year or so buried.

But not so fresh as the other body. The unmarked body. One day dead at most, she was, all her flesh still on her and the worms hardly working at her yet.

He cried out in the surprise of it, and the grief at the next thought that came to mind. Could it be the torch girl buried there? Her mother said that she run off, but when folks run off it ain't unusual for them to come back dead. Why else was the mother grieving so? The innkeeper's own daughter, buried without a marker—oh, that spoke of terrible bad things. Did she run off and get herself shamed so bad her own folks wouldn't mark her burying place? Why else leave her there without a stone?

"What's wrong with you, boy?"

Alvin stood, turned, faced the man. A stout fellow who was right comfortable to look upon; but his face wasn't too easy right now.

"What are you doing here in this graveyard, boy?"

"Sir," said Alvin, "my brother's buried here."

The man thought a moment, his face easing. "You're one of that family. But I recall all their boys was as old as you even back then—"

"I'm the one what was born here that night."

At that news the man just opened up his arms and folded Alvin up inside. "They named you Alvin, didn't they," said the man, "just like your father. We call him Alvin Bridger around here, he's something of legend. Let me see you, see what you've become. Seventh son of a seventh son, come home to see your birthplace and your brother's grave. Of course you'll stay in my roadhouse. I'm Horace Guester, as you might guess, I'm pleased to meet you, but ain't you somewhat big for—what, ten, eleven years old?"

"Almost twelve. Folks say I'm tall."

"I hope you're proud of the marker we made for your brother. He was admired here, even though we all met him in death and never in life."

"I'm suited," said Alvin. "It's a good stone." And then, because he couldn't help himself, though it wasn't a particularly wise thing to do, he up and asked the question most burning in him. "But I wonder, sir, why one girl got herself buried here yesterday, and no stone nor marker tells her name."

Horace Guester's face turned ashen. "Of course you'd see," he whispered. "Doodlebug or something. Seventh son. God help us all."

"Did she do something shameful, sir, not to have no marker?" asked Alvin.

"Not shame," said Horace. "As God is my witness, boy,

this girl was noble in life and died a virtuous death. She stays unmarked so this house can be a shelter to others like her. But oh, lad, say you'll never tell what you found buried here. You'd cause pain to dozens and hundreds of lost souls along the road from slavery to freedom. Can you believe me that much, trust me and be my friend in this? It'd be too much grief, to lose my daughter and have this secret out, all in the same day. Since I can't keep the secret from you, you have to keep it with me, Alvin, lad. Say you will."

"I'll keep a secret if it's honorable, sir," said Alvin, "but what honorable secret leads a man to bury his own daughter without a stone?"

Horace's eyes went wide, and then he laughed like he was calling loony birds. When he got control of hisself, he clapped Alvin on the shoulder. "That ain't my daughter in the ground there, boy, what made you think it was? It's a Black girl, a runaway slave, who died last night on her way north."

Now Alvin realized for the first time that the body was way too small to be no sixteen-year-old, anyhow. It was a child-size body. "That baby in your kitchen, it's her brother?"

"Her son," said Horace.

"But she's so small," said Alvin.

"That didn't stop her White owner from getting her with child, boy. I don't know how you stand on the question of slavery, or if you even thought about it, but I beg you do some thinking now. Think about how slavery lets a White man steal a girl's virtue and still go to church on Sunday while she groans in shame and bears his bastard child."

"You're a Mancipationist, ain't you?" said Alvin.

"Reckon I am," said the innkeeper, "but I reckon all good Christian folk are Mancipationists in their hearts."

"I reckon so," said Alvin.

"I hope *you* are, cause if word gets out that I was helping a slavegirl run off to Canada, there'll be finders and cotchers from Appalachee and the Crown Colonies a-spying on me so I can't help no others get away."

Alvin looked back at the grave and thought about the babe in the kitchen. "You going to tell that baby where his mama's grave is?"

"When he's old enough to know, and not to tell it," said the man.

"Then I'll keep your secret, if you keep mine."

The man raised his eyebrows and studied Alvin. "What secret *you* got, Alvin, a boy as young as you?"

"I don't have no partickler wish to have it known I'm a seventh son. I'm here to prentice with Makepeace Smith, which I reckon is the man I hear a-hammering at the forge down yonder."

"And you don't want folks knowing you can see a body lying in an unmarked grave."

"You caught my drift right enough," said Alvin. "I won't tell your secret, and you won't tell mine."

"You have my word on it," said the man. Then he held out his hand.

Took that hand and shook it, gladly. Most grownup folk wouldn't think of making a bargain like that with a mere child like him. But this man even offered his hand, like they were equals. "You'll see I know how to keep my word, sir," said Alvin.

"And anyone around here can tell you Horace Guester keeps a promise, too." Then Horace told him the story that they were letting out about the baby, how it was the Berrys' youngest, and they gave it up for Old Peg Guester to raise, cause they didn't need another child and she'd always hankered to have her a son. "And that part is true enough," said Horace Guester. "All the more, with Peggy running off."

"Your daughter," said Alvin.

Suddenly Horace Guester's eyes filled up with tears and he shuddered with a sob like Alvin never heard from a growed man in his life. "Just ran off this morning," said Horace Guester.

"Maybe she's just a-calling on somebody in town or something," said Alvin.

Horace shook his head. "I beg your pardon, crying like that, I just beg your pardon, I'm awful tired, truth to tell, up all night last night, and then this morning, her gone like that. She left us a note. She's gone all right."

"Don't you know the man she run off with?" asked Alvin. "Maybe they'll get married, that happened once to a Swede girl out in the Noisy River country—"

Horace turned a bit red with anger. "I reckon you're just a boy so you don't know better than to say such a thing. So I'll tell you now, she didn't run off with no *man*. She's a woman of pure virtue, and no one ever said otherwise. No, she run off alone, boy."

Alvin thought he'd seen all kinds of strange things in his life—a tornado turned into a crystal tower, a bolt of cloth with all the souls of men and women woven in it, murders and tortures, tales and miracles. Alvin knew more of life than most boys at eleven years of age. But this was the strangest thing of all, to think of a girl of sixteen just up and leaving her father's house, without no husband or nothing. In all his life he never saw a woman go *nowhere* by herself beyond her own dooryard.

"Is she—is she *safe?*"

Horace laughed bitterly. "Safe? Of course she's safe. She's a torch, Alvin, the best torch I ever heard of. She can see folks miles off, she knows their hearts, ain't a man born can come near her with evil on his mind without she knows exactly what he's planning and just how to get away. No, I ain't *worried* about her. She can take care of herself better than any man. I just—"

"Miss her," said Alvin.

"I guess it don't take no torch to guess that, am I right, lad? I miss her. And it hurt my feelings somewhat that she up and left with no warning. I could've given her God bless to send her on her way. Her mama could've worked up some good hex, not that Little Peggy'd need it, or anyhow just pack her a cold dinner for on the road. But none of that, no fare-thee-well nor God-be-with-you. It was like as if she was running from some awful boogly monster and had no time to take but one spare dress in a cloth bag and rush on out the door."

Running from some monster—those words stung right to Alvin's soul. She was such a torch that it might well be she saw Alvin coming. Up and ran away the morning he arrived. If she wasn't no torch then maybe it was just chance that took her off the same day he come. But she *was* a torch. She saw him coming. She knew he came all this way a-hoping to meet her and beg her to help him find his way into becoming whatever it was that he was born to be. She saw all that, and ran away.

"I'm right sorry that she's gone," said Alvin.

"I thank you for your pity, friend, it's good of you. I just hope it won't be for long. I just hope she'll do whatever she left to do and come on back in a few days or maybe a couple of weeks." He laughed again, or maybe sobbed, it was about the same sound. "I can't even go ask the Hatrack torch to tell a fortune about her, cause the Hatrack River torch is gone."

Horace cried outright again, for just a minute. Then he took Alvin by the shoulders and looked him in the eye, not even hiding the tears on his cheeks. "Alvin, you just remember how you seen me crying all unmanlike, and you remember that's how fathers feel about their children when they're gone. That's how your own pa feels right now, having you so far away."

"I know he does," said Alvin.

"Now if you don't mind," said Horace Guester, "I need to be alone here."

Alvin touched his arm just a moment and then he went away. Not down to the house to have his noon meal like Old Peg Guester offered. He was too upset to sit and eat with them. How could he explain that he was nigh on to being as heartbroke as them, to have that torch girl gone? No, he'd have to keep silence. The answers he was looking for in Hatrack, they were gone off with a sixteen-year-old girl who didn't want to meet him when he came.

Maybe she seen my future and she hates me. Maybe I'm as bad a boogly monster as anybody ever dreamed of on an evil night.

He followed the sound of the blacksmith's hammer. It led him along a faint path to a springhouse straddling a brook that came straight out of a hillside. And down the stream, along a clear meadow slope, he walked until he came to the smithy. Hot smoke rose from the forge. Around front he walked, and saw the blacksmith inside the big sliding door, hammering a hot iron bar into a curving shape across the throat of his anvil.

Alvin stood and watched him work. He could feel the heat from the forge clear outside; inside must be like the fires of hell. His muscles were like fifty different ropes holding his arm on under the skin. They shifted and rolled across each other as the hammer rose into the air, then bunched all at once as the hammer came down. Close as he was now, Alvin could hardly bear the bell-like crash of iron on iron, with the anvil like a sounding fork to make the sound ring on and on. Sweat dripped off the blacksmith's body, and he was naked to the waist, his white skin ruddy from the heat, streaked with soot from the forge and sweat from his pores. I've been sent here to be prentice to the devil, thought Alvin.

But he knew that was a silly idea even as he thought it. This was a hardworking man, that's all, earning his living with a skill that every town needed if it hoped to thrive. Judging from the size of the corrals for horses waiting to be shod, and the heaps of iron bars waiting to be made into plows and sickles, axes and cleavers, he did a good business, too. If I learn this trade, I'll never be hungry, thought Alvin, and folks will always be glad to have me.

And something more. Something about the hot fire and the ruddy iron. What happened in this place was akin somehow to making. Alvin knew from the way he'd worked with stone in the granite quarry, when he carved the millstone for his father's mill, he knew that with his knack he could probably reach inside the iron and make it go the way he wanted it to go. But he had something to learn from the forge and the hammer, the bellows and the fire and the water in the cooling tubs, something that would help him become what he was born to become.

So now he looked at the blacksmith, not as a powerful stranger, but as Alvin's future self. He saw how the muscles grew on the smith's shoulders and back. Alvin's body was strong from chopping wood and splitting rails and all the hoisting and lifting that he did earning pennies and nickels on neighbors' farms. But in that kind of work, your whole body went into every movement. You rared back with the axe and when it swung it was like your whole body was part of the axhandle, so that legs and hips and back all moved into the chop. But the smith, he held the hot iron in the tongs, held it so smooth and exact against the anvil that while his right arm swung the hammer, the rest of his body couldn't move a twitch, that left arm stayed as smooth and steady as a rock. It shaped the smith's body differently, forced the arms to be much stronger by themselves, muscles rooted to the neck and breastbone standing out in a way they never did on a farmboy's body.

Alvin felt inside himself, the way his own muscles grew, and knew already where the changes would have to come. It was part of his knack, to find his way within living flesh most as easily as he could chart the inner shapes of living stone. So even now he was hunkering down inside, teaching his body to change itself to make way for the new work.

"Boy," said the smith.

"Sir," said Alvin.

"Have you got business for me? I don't know you, do I?"

Alvin stepped forward, held out the note his father writ.

"Read it to me, boy, my eyes are none too good."

Alvin unfolded the paper. "From Alvin Miller of Vigor Church. To Makepeace, Blacksmith of Hatrack River. Here is my boy Alvin what you said could be your prentice till he be seventeen. He'll work hard and do what all you say, and you teach him what all a man needs to be a good smith, like in the articles I signed. He is a good boy."

The smith reached for the paper, held it close to his eyes. His lips moved as he repeated a few phrases. Then he slapped the paper down on the anvil. "This is a fine turn," said the smith. "Don't you know you're about a year late, boy? You was supposed to come last spring. I turned away three offers for prentice cause I had your pa's word you was coming, and here I've been without help this whole year cause he *didn't* keep his word. Now I'm supposed to take you in with a year less on your contract, and not even a by-your-leave or beg-your-pardon."

"I'm sorry, sir," said Alvin. "But we had the war last year. I was on my way here but I got captured by Choc-Taw."

"Captured by—oh, come now, boy, don't tell me tales like that. If the Choc-Taw caught you, you wouldn't have such a dandy head of hair now, would you! And like as not you'd be missing a few fingers."

"Ta-Kumsaw rescued me," said Alvin.

"Oh, and no doubt you met the Prophet hisself and walked on water with him."

As a matter of fact, Alvin done just that. But from the smith's tone of voice, he reckoned that it wouldn't be wise to say so. So Alvin said nothing.

"Where's your horse?" asked the smith.

"Don't have one," said Alvin.

"Your father wrote the date on this letter boy, two days ago! You must've rode a horse."

"I ran." As soon as Alvin said it, he knew it was a mistake.

"*Ran?*" said the smith. "With *bare feet?* It must be nigh four hundred mile or more to the Wobbish from here! Your feet ought to be ripped to rags clear up to your knees! Don't tell me tales, boy! I won't have no liars around me!"

Alvin had a choice, and he knew it. He could explain about how he could run like a Red man. Makepeace Smith wouldn't believe him, and so Alvin would have to show him some of what he could do. It would be easy enough. Bend a bar of iron just by stroking it. Make two stones mash together to form one. But Alvin already made up his mind he didn't want to show his knacks here. How could he be a proper prentice, if folks kept coming around for him to cut them hearthstones or fix a broken wheel or all the other fixing things he had a knack for? Besides, he never done such a thing, showing off just for the sake of proving what he could do. Back home he only used his knack when there was need.

So he stuck with his decision to keep his knack to himself, pretty much. Not tell what he could do. Just learn like any normal boy, working the iron the way the smith himself did, letting the muscles grow slowly on his arms and shoulders, chest and back.

"I was joking," Alvin said. "A man gave me a ride on his spare mount."

"I don't like that kind of joke," said the smith. "I don't like it that you lied to me so easy like that."

What could Alvin say? He couldn't even claim that he hadn't lied—he had, when he told about a man letting him ride. So he was as much a liar as the smith thought. The only confusion was about *which* statement was a lie.

"I'm sorry," said Alvin.

"I'm not taking you, boy. I don't have to take you anyway, a year late. And here you come lying to me the first thing. I won't have it."

"Sir, I'm sorry," said Alvin. "It won't happen again. I'm not known for a liar back home, and you'll see I'll be known for square dealing here, if you give me a chance. Catch me lying or not giving fair work all the time, and you can chuck me, no questions asked. Just give me a chance to prove it, sir."

"You don't look like you're eleven, neither, boy."

"But I am, sir. You know I am. You yourself with your own arms pulled my brother Vigor's body from the river on the night that I was born, or so my pa told me."

The smith's face went distant, as if he was remembering. "Yes, he told you true, I was the one who pulled him out. Clinging to the roots of that tree even in death, so I thought I'd have to cut him free. Come here, boy."

Alvin walked closer. The smith poked and pushed the muscles of his arms.

"Well, I can see you're not a lazy boy. Lazy boys get soft, but you're strong like a hardworking farmer. Can't lie about *that,* I reckon. Still, you haven't seen what real work is."

"I'm ready to learn."

"Oh, I'm sure of that. Many a boy would be glad to learn from me. Other work might come and go, but there's always a need for a blacksmith. That'll never change. Well, you're strong enough in body, I reckon. Let's see about your brain. Look at this anvil. This here's the bick, on the point, you see. Say that."

"Bick."

"And then the throat here. And this is the table—it ain't faced with blister steel, so when you ram a cold chisel into it the chisel don't blunt. Then up a notch onto the steel face, where you work the hot metal. And this is the hardie hole, where I rest the butt of the fuller and the flatter and the swage. And this here's the pricking hole, for when I punch holes in strap iron—the hot punch shoots right through into this space. You got all that?"

"I think so, sir."

"Then name me the parts of the anvil."

Alvin named them as best he could. Couldn't remember the job each one did, not all of them, anyways, but what he did was good enough, cause the blacksmith nodded and grinned. "Reckon you ain't a half-wit, anyhow, you'll learn quick enough. And big for your age is good. I won't have to keep you on a broom and the bellows for the first four years, the way I do with smaller boys. But your age, that's a sticking point. A term of prentice work is seven year, but my written-up articles with your pa, they only say till you're seventeen."

"I'm almost twelve now, sir."

"So what I'm saying is, I want to be able to hold you the full seven years, if need be. I don't want you whining off just when I finally get you trained enough to be useful."

"Seven years, sir. The spring when I'm nigh on nineteen, then my time is up."

"Seven years is a long time, boy, and I mean to hold you to it. Most boys start when they're nine or ten, or even seven years old, so they can make a living, start looking for a wife at sixteen or seventeen years old. I won't have none of that. I expect you to live like a Christian, and no fooling with any of the girls in town, you understand me?"

"Yes sir."

"All right then. My prentices sleep in the loft over the kitchen, and you eat at table with my wife and children and me, though I'll thank you not to speak until spoken to inside the house—I won't have my prentices thinking they have the same rights as my own children, cause you don't."

"Yes sir."

"And as for now, I need to het up this strap again. So you start to work the bellows there."

Alvin walked to the bellows handle. It was T-shaped, for two-handed working. But Alvin twisted the end piece so it was at the same angle as the hammer handle when the smith lifted it into the air. Then he started to work the bellows with one arm.

"What are you doing, boy!" shouted Alvin's new master. "You won't last ten minutes working the bellows with one arm."

"Then in ten minutes I'll switch to my left arm," said Alvin. "But I won't get myself ready for the hammer if I bend over every time I work the bellows."

The smith looked at him angrily. Then he laughed. "You got a fresh mouth, boy, but you also got sense. Do it your way as long as you can, but see to it you don't slack on wind—I need a hot fire, and that's more important than you working up strength in your arms right now."

Alvin set to pumping. Soon he could feel the pain of this unaccustomed movement gnawing at his neck and chest and back. But he kept going, never breaking the rhythm of the bellows, forcing his body to endure. He could have made the muscles grow right now, teaching them the pattern with his hidden power. But that wasn't what Alvin was here for, he was pretty sure of that. So he let the pain come as it would, and his body change as it would, each new muscle earned by his own effort.

Alvin lasted fifteen minutes with his right hand, ten minutes with his left. He felt the muscles aching and liked the way it felt. Makepeace Smith seemed pleased enough with what he did. Alvin knew that he'd be changed here, that his work would make a strong and skillful man of him.

A man, but not a Maker. Not yet fully on the road to what he was born to be. But since there hadn't been a Maker in the world in a thousand years or more, or so folks said, who was he going to prentice himself to in order to learn *that* trade?

4

MODESTY

Whitley Physicker helped Peggy down from the carriage in front of a fine-looking house in one of the best neighborhoods of Dekane. "I'd like to see you to the door, Peggy Guester, just to make sure they're home to greet you," said he, but she knew he didn't expect her to allow him to do that. If anybody knew how little she liked to have folks fussing over her, it was Doctor Whitley Physicker. So she thanked him kindly and bid him farewell.

She heard his carriage rolling off, the horse clopping on the cobblestones, as she rapped the knocker on the door. A maid opened the door, a German girl so fresh off the boat she couldn't even speak enough English to ask Peggy's name. She invited her in with a gesture, seated her on a bench in the hall, and then held out a silver plate.

What was the plate *for?* Peggy couldn't hardly make sense at all of what she saw inside this foreign girl's mind. She was expecting something—what? A little slip of paper, but Peggy didn't have a notion why. The girl thrust the salver closer to her, insisting. Peggy couldn't do a thing but shrug.

Finally the German girl gave up and went away. Peggy sat on the bench and waited. She searched for heartfires in the house, and found the one she looked for. Only then did she realize what the plate was for—her calling card. Folks in the city, rich folks anyway, they had little cards they put their name on, to announce theirself when they came to visit. Peggy even remembered reading about it in a book, but it was a book from the Crown Colonies and she never thought folks in free lands kept such formality.

Soon the lady of the house came, the German girl shadowing her, peering from behind her fine day gown. Peggy knew from the lady's heartfire that she didn't think herself dressed in any partickler finery today, but to Peggy she was like the Queen herself.

Peggy looked into her heartfire and found what she had hoped for. The lady wasn't annoyed a bit at seeing Peggy there, merely curious. Oh, the lady was judging her, of course—Peggy never met a soul, least of all herself, what didn't make some judgment of every stranger—but the judgment was kind. When the lady looked at Peggy's plain clothes, she saw a country girl, not a pauper; when the lady looked at Peggy's stern, expressionless face, she saw a child who had known pain, not an ugly girl. And when the lady imagined Peggy's pain, her first thought was to try to heal her. All in all, the lady was *good.* Peggy made no mistake in coming here.

"I don't believe I've had the pleasure to meet you," said the lady. Her voice was sweet and soft and beautiful.

"I reckon not, Mistress Modesty," said Peggy. "My name is Peggy. I think you had some acquaintance with my papa, years ago."

"Perhaps if you told me his name?"

"Horace," said Peggy. "Horace Guester, of Hatrack, Hio."

Peggy saw the turmoil in her heartfire at the very sound of his name—glad memory, and yet a glimmer of fear of what this strange girl might intend. Yet the fear quickly subsided—her husband had died several years ago, and so was beyond hurt. And none of these emotions showed in the lady's face, which held its sweet and friendly expression with perfect grace. Modesty turned to the maid and spoke a few words of fluent German. The maid curtsied and was gone.

"Did your father send you?" asked the lady. Her unspoken question was: Did your father tell you what I meant to him, and he to me?

"No," said Peggy. "I come here on my own. He'd die if he found out I knew your name. You see I'm a torch, Mistress Modesty. He has no secrets, not from me. Nobody does."

It didn't surprise Peggy one bit how Modesty took that news. Most folks would've thought right off about all the secrets they hoped she wouldn't guess. Instead, the lady thought at once how awful it must be for Peggy, to know things that didn't bear knowing. "How long has it been that way?" she said softly. "Surely not when you were just a little girl. The Lord is too merciful to let such knowledge fill a child's mind."

"I reckon the Lord didn't concern himself much with me," said Peggy.

The lady reached out and touched Peggy's cheek. Peggy knew the lady had noticed she was somewhat dirty from the dust of the road. But what the lady mostly thought of wasn't clothes or cleanliness. A torch, she was thinking. That's why a girl so young wears such a cold, forbidding face. Too much knowledge has made this girl so hard.

"Why have you come to me?" asked Modesty. "Surely you don't mean harm to me or your father, for such an ancient transgression."

"Oh, no ma'am," said Peggy. Never in her life did her own voice sound so harsh to her, but compared to this lady she was squawking like a crow. "If I'm torch enough to know your secret, I'm torch enough to know there was some good in it as well as sin, and as far as the sin goes, Papa's paying for it still, paying double and treble every year of his life."

Tears came into Modesty's eyes. "I had hoped," she murmured, "I had hoped that time would ease the shame of it, and he'd remember it now with joy. Like one of the ancient faded tapestries in England, whose colors are no longer bright, but whose image is the very shadow of beauty itself."

Peggy might've told her that he felt more than joy, that he relived all his feelings for her like it happened yesterday. But that was Papa's secret, and not hers to tell.

Modesty touched a kerchief to her eyes, to take away the tears that trembled there. "All these years I've never spoken to a mortal soul of this. I've poured out my heart only to the Lord, and he's forgiven me; yet I find it somehow exhilarating to speak of this to someone whose face I can see with my eyes, and not just my imagination. Tell me, child, if you didn't come as the avenging angel, have you come perhaps as a forgiving one?"

Mistress Modesty spoke with such elegance that Peggy found herself reaching for the language of the books she read, instead of her natural talking voice. "I'm a—a supplicant," said Peggy. "I come for help. I come to change my life, and I thought, being how you loved my father, you might be willing to do a kindness for his daughter."

The lady smiled at her. "And if you're half the torch you

claim to be, you already know my answer. What kind of help do you need? My husband left me a good deal of money when he died, but I think it isn't money that you need."

"No ma'am," said Peggy. But what was it that she wanted, now that she was here? How could she explain why she had come? "I didn't like the life I saw for myself back in Hatrack. I wanted to—"

"Escape?"

"Somewhat like that, I reckon, but not exactly."

"You want to become something other than what you are," said the lady.

"Yes, Mistress Modesty."

"What is it that you wish to be?"

Peggy had never thought of words to describe what she dreamed of, but now, with Mistress Modesty before her, Peggy saw how simply those dreams might be expressed. "You, ma'am."

The lady smiled and touched her own face, her own hair. "Oh, my child, you must have higher aims than that. Much of what is best in me, your father gave me. The way he loved me taught me that perhaps—no, not *perhaps*—that I *was* worth loving. I have learned much more since then, more of what a woman is and ought to be. What a lovely symmetry, if I can give back to his daughter some of the wisdom he brought to me." She laughed gently. "I never imagined myself taking a pupil."

"More like a disciple, I think, Mistress Modesty."

"Neither pupil nor disciple. Will you stay here as a guest in my home? Will you let me be your friend?"

Even though Peggy couldn't rightly see the paths of her own life, she still felt them open up inside her, all the futures she could hope for, waiting for her in this place. "Oh, ma'am," she whispered, "if you will."

5

DOWSER

Hank Dowser'd seen him prentice boys a-plenty over the years, but never a one as fresh as this. Here was Makepeace Smith bent over old Picklewing's left forehoof, all set to drive in the nail, and up spoke his boy.

"Not that nail," said the blacksmith's prentice boy. "Not there."

Well, that was as fine a moment as Hank ever saw for the master to give his prentice boy a sharp cuff on the ear and send him bawling into the house. But Makepeace Smith just nodded, then looked at the boy.

"You think you can nail this shoe, Alvin?" asked the master. "She's a big one, this mare, but I see you got you some inches since last I looked."

"I can," said the boy.

"Now just hold your horses," said Hank Dowser. "Picklewing's my only animal, and I can't just up and buy me another. I don't want your prentice boy learning to be a farrier and making his mistakes at my poor old nag's expense." And since he was already speaking his mind so frank like, Hank just rattled right on like a plain fool. "Who's the master here, anyway?" said he.

Well, that was the wrong thing to say. Hank knew it the second the words slipped out of his mouth. You don't say Who's the master, not in front of the prentice. And sure enough, Makepeace Smith's ears turned red and he stood up, all six feet of him, with arms like oxlegs and hands that could crush a bear's face, and he said, "I'm the master here, and when I say my prentice is good enough for the job, then he's good enough, or you can take your custom to another smith."

"Now just hold your horses," said Hank Dowser.

"I *am* holding your horse," said Makepeace Smith. "Or at least your horse's leg. In fact, your horse is leaning over on me something heavy. And now you start asking if I'm master of my own smithy."

Anybody whose head don't leak knows that riling the smith who's shoeing your horse is about as smart as provoking the bees on your way in for the honey. Hank Dowser just hoped Makepeace would be somewhat easier to calm down. "Course you are," said Hank. "I meant nothing by it, except I was surprised when your prentice spoke up so smart and all."

"Well that's cause he's got him a knack," said Makepeace Smith. "This boy Alvin, he can tell things about the inside of a horse's hoof—where a nail's going to hold, where it's going into soft hurting flesh, that kind of thing. He's a natural farrier. And if he says to me, Don't drive that nail, well I know by now that's a nail I don't want to drive, cause it'll make the horse crazy or lame."

Hank Dowser grinned and backed off. It was a hot day, that's all, that's why tempers were so high. "I have respect for every man's knack," said Hank. "Just like I expect them to have respect for mine."

"In that case, I've held up your horse long enough," said the smith. "Here, Alvin, nail this shoe."

If the boy had swaggered or simpered or sneered, Hank would've had a reason to be so mad. But Prentice Alvin just hunkered down with nails in his mouth and hooked up the left forehoof. Picklewing leaned on him, but the boy was right tall, even though his face had no sign of beard yet, and he was like a twin of his master, when it come to muscle under his skin. It wasn't one minute, the horse leaning that way, before the shoe was nailed in place. Picklewing didn't so much as shiver, let alone dance the way he usually did when the nails went in. And now that Hank thought about it a little, Picklewing always *did* seem to favor that leg just a little, as if something was a mite sore inside the hoof. But he'd been that way so long Hank hardly noticed it no more.

The prentice boy stepped back out of the way, still not showing any brag at all. He wasn't doing a thing that was the tiniest bit benoctious, but Hank still felt an unreasonable anger at the boy. "How old is he?" asked Hank.

"Fourteen," said Makepeace Smith. "He come to me when he was eleven."

"A mite old for a prentice, wouldn't you say?" asked Hank.

"A year late in arriving, he was, because of the war with the Reds and the French—he's from out in the Wobbish country."

"Them was hard years," said Hank. "Lucky me I was in Irrakwa the whole time. Dowsing wells for windmills the whole way along the railroad they were building. Fourteen, eh? Tall as he is, I reckon he lied about his age even so."

If the boy disliked being named a liar, he didn't show no sign of it. Which made Hank Dowser all the more annoyed. That boy was like a burr under his saddle, just made him mad whatever the boy did.

"No," said the smith. "We know his age well enough. He was born right here in Hatrack River, fourteen years ago, when his folks were passing through on their way west. We buried his oldest brother up on the hill. Big for his age though, ain't he?"

They might've been discussing a horse instead of a boy. But Prentice Alvin didn't seem to mind. He just stood there, staring right through them as if they were made of glass.

"You got four years left of his contract, then?" asked Hank.

"Bit more. Till he's near nineteen."

"Well, if he's already this good, I reckon he'll be buying out early and going journeyman." Hank looked, but the boy didn't brighten up at this idea, neither.

"I reckon not," said Makepeace Smith. "He's good with the horses, but he gets careless with the forge. Any smith can do shoes, but it takes a *real* smith to do a plow blade or a wheel tire, and a knack with horses don't help a bit with that. Why, for my masterpiece I done me an anchor! I was in Netticut at the time, mind you. There ain't much call for anchors *here,* I reckon."

Picklewing snorted and stamped—but he didn't dance lively, the way horses do when their new shoes are troublesome. It was a good set of shoes, well shod. Even *that* made Hank mad at the prentice boy. His own anger made sense to him. The boy had put on Picklewing's last shoe, on a leg that might have been lamed in another farrier's hands. The boy had done him *good.* So why this wrath burning just under the surface, getting worse whatever the boy did or said?

Hank shrugged off his feelings. "Well, that's work well done," he said. "And so it's time for me to do my part."

"Now, we both know a dowsing's worth more than a shoeing," said the smith. "So if you need any more work done, you know I owe it to you, free and clear."

"I *will* come back, Makepeace Smith, next time my nag needs shoes." And because Hank Dowser was a Christian man and felt ashamed of how he disliked the boy, he added praise for the lad. "I reckon I'll be sure to come back while this boy's still under prentice bond to you, him having the knack he's got."

The boy might as well not've heard the good words, and

the master smith just chuckled. "You ain't the only one who feels like that," he said.

At that moment Hank Dowser understood something that he might've missed otherwise. This boy's knack with hooves was good for trade, and Makepeace Smith was just the kind of man who'd hold that boy to every day of his contract, to profit from the boy's name for clean shoeing with no horses lost by laming. All a greedy master had to do was claim the boy wasn't good at forgework or something like, then use that as a pretext to hold him fast. In the meantime the boy'd make a name for this place as the best farriery in eastern Hio. Money in Makepeace Smith's pocket, and nothing for the boy at all, not money nor freedom.

The law was the law, and the smith wasn't breaking it—he had the right to every day of that boy's service. But the custom was to let a prentice go as soon as he had the skill and had sense enough to make his way in the world. Otherwise, if a boy couldn't hope for early freedom, why should he work hard to learn as quick as he could, work as hard as he could? They said even the slaveowners in the Crown Colonies let their best slaves earn a little pocket money on the side, so's they could buy their freedom sometime before they died.

No, Makepeace Smith wasn't breaking no law, but he was breaking the custom of masters with their prentice boys, and Hank thought ill of him for it; it was a mean sort of master who'd keep a boy who'd already learned everything the master had to teach.

And yet, even knowing that it was the boy who was in the right, and his master in the wrong—even knowing that, he looked at that boy and felt a cold wet hatred in his heart. Hank shuddered, tried to shake it off.

"You say you need a well," said Hank Dowser. "You want it for drinking or for washing or for the smithy?"

"Does it make a difference?" asked the smith.

"Well, I think so," said Hank. "For drinking you need pure water, and for washing you want water that got no disease in it. But for your work in the smithy, I reckon the iron don't give no never mind whether it cools in clear or murky water, am I right?"

"The spring up the hill is giving out, slacking off year by year," said the smith. "I need me a well I can count on. Deep and clean and pure."

"You know why the stream's going slack," said Hank. "Everybody else is digging wells, and sucking out the water before it can seep out the spring. Your well is going to be about the last straw."

"I wouldn't be surprised," said the smith. "But I can't undig their wells, and I got to have my water, too. Reason I settled here was because of the stream, and now they've dried it up on me. I reckon I could move on, but I got me a wife and three brats up at the house, and I like it here, like it well enough. So I figure I'd rather draw water than move."

Hank went on down to the stand of willows by the stream, near where it came out from under an old springhouse, which had fallen into disrepair. "Yours?" asked Hank.

"No, it belongs to old Horace Guester, him who owns the roadhouse up yonder."

Hank found him a thin willow wand that forked just right, and started cutting it out with his knife. "Springhouse doesn't get much use now, I see."

"Stream's dying, like I said. Half the time in summer there ain't enough water in it to keep the cream jars cool. Springhouse ain't no good if you can't count on it all summer."

Hank made the last slice and the willow rod pulled free. He shaved the thick end to a point and whittled off all the leaf nubs, making it as smooth as ever he could. There was some dowsers who didn't care how smooth the rod was, just broke off the leaves and left the ends all raggedy, but Hank knew that the water didn't always want to be found, and then you needed a good smooth willow wand to find it. There was others used a clean wand, but always the same one, year after year, place after place, but that wasn't no good neither, Hank knew, cause the wand had to be from willow or, sometimes, hickory that grew up sucking the water you were hoping to find. Them other dowsers were mountebanks, though it didn't do no good to say so. They found water most times because in most places if you dig down far enough there's *bound* to be water. But Hank did it right, Hank had the true knack. He could feel the willow wand trembling in his hands, could feel the water singing to him under the ground. He didn't just pick the first sign of water, either. He was looking for clear water, high water, close to the surface and easy to pull. He took *pride* in his work.

But it wasn't like that prentice boy—what was his name?—Alvin. Wasn't like him. Either a man could nail horseshoes without ever laming the horse, or he couldn't. If he *ever* lamed a horse, folks thought twice before they went to that farrier again. But with a dowser, it didn't seem to make no difference if you found water every time or not. If you called yourself a dowser and had you a forked stick, folks would pay you for dowsing wells, without bothering to find out if you had any knack for it at all.

Thinking that, Hank wondered if maybe that was why he hated this boy so much—because the boy already had a name for his good work, while Hank got no fame at all even though he was the only true dowser likely to pass through these parts in a month of Sundays.

Hank set down on the grassy bank of the stream and pulled off his boots. When he leaned to set the second boot on a dry rock where it wouldn't be so like to fill up with bugs, he saw two eyes blinking in the shadows inside a thick stand of bushes. It gave him such a start, cause he thought to see a bear, and then he thought to see a Red man hankering after dowser's scalp, even though both such was gone from these parts for years. No, it was just a little light-skinned pickaninny hiding in the bushes. The boy was a mixup, half-White, half-Black, that was plain to see once Hank got over the surprise. "What're you looking at?" demanded Hank.

The eyes closed and the face was gone. The bushes wiggled and whispered from something crawling fast.

"Never you mind him," said Makepeace Smith. "That's just Arthur Stuart."

Arthur Stuart! Not a soul in New England or the United States but knew that name as sure as if they lived in the Crown Colonies. "Then you'll be glad to hear that I'm the Lord Protector," said Hank Dowser. "Cause if the King be that partickler shade of skin, I got some news that'll get me three free dinners a day in any town in Hio and Suskwahenny till the day I die."

Makepeace laughed brisk at that idea. "No, that's Horace Guester's joke, naming him that way. Horace and Old Peg Guester, they're raising that boy, seeing how his natural ma's too poor to raise him. Course I don't think that's the whole reason. Him being so light-skinned, her husband, Mock Berry, you can't blame him if he don't like seeing that child eat at table with his coal-black children."

Hank Dowser started pulling off his stockings. "You don't suppose old Horace Guester took him in on account of he's the party responsible for causing the boy's skin to be so light."

"Hush your mouth with a pumpkin, Hank, before you say such a thing," said Makepeace. "Horace ain't that kind of a man."

"You'd be surprised who I've known turn out to be that kind of a man," said Hank. "Though I don't think it of Horace Guester, mind."

"Do you think Old Peg Guester'd let a half-Black bastard son of her husband into the house?"

"What if she didn't know?"

"She'd know. Her daughter Peggy used to be torch here in Hatrack River. And everybody knowed that Little Peggy Guester never told a lie."

"I used to hear tell about the Hatrack River torch, afore I ever come here. How come I never seen her?"

"She's gone, that's why," said Makepeace. "Left three years ago. Just run off. You'd be wise never to ask about her up to Guester's roadhouse. They're a mite ticklish on the subject."

Barefoot now, Hank Dowser stood up on the bank of the stream. He happened to glance up, and there off in the trees, just a-watching him, stood that Arthur Stuart boy again. Well, what harm could a little pickaninny do? Not a bit.

Hank stepped into the stream and let the ice-cold water pour over his feet. He spoke silently to the water: I don't mean to block your flow, or slack you down even further. The well I dig ain't meant to do you no harm. It's like giving you another place to flow through, like giving you another face, more hands, another eye. So don't you hide from me, Water. Show me where you're rising up, pushing to reach the sky, and I'll tell them to dig there, and set you free to wash over the earth, you just see if I don't.

"This water pure enough?" Hank asked the smith.

"Pure as it can be," said Makepeace. "Never heard of nobody taking sick from it."

Hank dipped the sharp end of the wand into the water, upstream of his feet. Taste it, he told the wand. Catch the flavor of it, and remember, and find me more just this sweet.

The wand started to buck in his hands. It was ready. He lifted it from the stream; it settled down, calmer, but still shaking just the least bit, to let him know it was alive, alive and searching.

Now there was no more talking, no more thinking. Hank just walked, eyes near closed because he didn't want his vision to distract from the tingling in his hands. The wand never led him astray; to *look* where he was going would be as much as to admit the wand had no power to find.

It took near half an hour. Oh, he found a few places right off, but not good enough, not for Hank Dowser. He could tell by how sharp the wand bucked and dropped whether the water was close enough to the surface to do much good. He was so good at it now that most folks couldn't make no difference between him and a doodlebug, which was about as fine a knack as a dowser could ever have. And since doodlebugs were right scarce, mostly being found among seventh sons or thirteenth children, Hank never wished anymore that he was a doodlebug instead of just a dowser, or not often, anyway.

The wand dropped so hard it buried itself three inches deep in the earth. Couldn't do much better than that. Hank smiled and opened his eyes. He wasn't thirty feet back of the smithy. Couldn't have found a better spot with his eyes open. No doodlebug could've done a nicer job.

The smith thought so, too. "Why, if you'd asked me where I wished the well would be, this is the spot I'd pick."

Hank nodded, accepting the praise without a smile, his eyes half-closed, his whole body still a-tingle with the strength of the water's call to him. "I don't want to lift this wand," said Hank, "till you've dug a trench all round this spot to mark it off."

"Fetch a spade!" cried the smith.

Prentice Alvin jogged off in search of the tool. Hank noticed Arthur Stuart toddling after, running full tilt on them short legs so awkward he was bound to fall. And fall he did, flat down on his face in the grass, moving so fast he slid a yard at least, and came up soaking wet with dew. Didn't pause him none. Just waddled on around the smithy building where Prentice Alvin went.

Hank turned back to Makepeace Smith and kicked at the soil just underfoot. "I can't be sure, not being a doodlebug," said Hank, as modest as he could manage, "but I'd say you won't have to dig ten feet till you strike water here. It's fresh and lively as I ever seen."

"No skin off my nose either way," said Makepeace. "I don't aim to dig it."

"That prentice of yours looks strong enough to dig it hisself, if he doesn't lazy off and sleep when your back is turned."

"He ain't the lazying kind," said Makepeace. "You'll be staying the night at the roadhouse, I reckon."

"I reckon not," said Hank. "I got some folks about six mile west who want me to find them some *dry* ground to dig a good deep cellar."

"Ain't that kind of *anti*-dowsing?"

"It is, Makepeace, and it's a whole lot harder, too, in wettish country like this."

"Well, come back this way, then," said Makepeace, "and I'll save you a sip of the first water pulled up from your well."

"I'll do that," said Hank, "and gladly." That was an honor he wasn't often offered, that first sip from a well. There was power in that, but only if it was freely given, and Hank couldn't keep from smiling now. "I'll be back in a couple of days, sure as shooting."

The prentice boy come back with the spade and set right to digging. Just a shallow trench, but Hank noticed that the boy squared it off without measuring, each side of the hole equal, and as near as Hank could guess, it was true to the compass points as well. Standing there with the wand still rooted into the ground, Hank felt a sudden sickness in his stomach, having the boy so close. Only it wasn't the kind of sickness where you hanker to chuck up what you ate for breakfast. It was the kind of sickness that turns to pain, the sickness that turns to violence; Hank felt himself yearning to snatch the spade out of the boy's hands and smack him across the head with the sharp side of the blade.

Till finally it dawned on him, standing there with the wand a-trembling in his hand. It wasn't *Hank* who hated this boy, no sir. It was the *water* that Hank served so well, the *water* that wanted this boy dead.

The moment that thought entered Hank's head, he fought it down, swallowed back the sickness inside him. It was the plain craziest idea that ever entered his head. Water was water. All it wanted was to come up out of the ground or down out of the clouds and race over the face of the earth. It didn't have no malice in it. No desire to kill. And anyway, Hank Dowser was a Christian, and a Baptist to boot—a natural dowser's religion if there ever was one. When he put folks under the water, it was to baptize them and bring them to Jesus, not to drownd them. Hank didn't have murder in his heart, he had his Savior there, teaching him to love his enemies, teaching him that even to hate a man was like murder.

Hank said a silent prayer to Jesus to take this rage out of his heart and make him stop wishing for this innocent boy's death.

As if in answer, the wand leapt right out of the ground, flew clear out of his hands and landed in the bushes most of two rods off.

That never happened to Hank in all his days of dowsing.

A wand taking off like that! Why, it was as if the water had spurned him as sharp as a fine lady spurns a cussing man.

"Trench is all dug," said the boy.

Hank looked sharp at him, to see if he noticed anything funny about the way the wand took off like that. But the boy wasn't even looking at him. Just looking at the ground inside the square he'd just ditched off.

"Good work," said Hank. He tried not to let his voice show the loathing that he felt.

"Won't do no good to dig here," said the boy.

Hank couldn't hardly believe his ears. Bad enough the boy sassing his own master, in the trade he knew, but what in tarnation did this boy know about dowsing?

"What did you say, boy?" asked Hank.

The boy must have seen the menace in Hank's face, or caught the tone of fury in his voice, because he backed right down. "Nothing, sir," he said. "None of my business anyhow."

Such was Hank's built-up anger, though, that he wasn't letting the boy off so easy. "You think you can do my job too, is that it? Maybe your master lets you think you're as good as he is cause you got your knack with *hooves,* but let me tell you, boy, I am a true dowser and my wand tells me there's water here!"

"That's right," said the boy. He spoke mildly, so that Hank didn't really notice that the boy had four inches on him in height and probably more than that in reach. Prentice Alvin wasn't so big you'd call him a giant, but you wouldn't call him no dwarf, neither.

"That's *right?* It ain't for you to say right or wrong to what my wand tells me!"

"I know it, sir, I was out of turn."

The smith came back with a wheelbarrow, a pick, and two stout iron levers. "What's all this?" he asked.

"Your boy here got smart with me," said Hank. He knew as he said it that it wasn't quite fair—the boy had already apologized, hadn't he?

Now at last Makepeace's hand lashed out and caught the boy a blow like a bear's paw alongside his head. Alvin staggered under the cuffing, but he didn't fall. "I'm sorry, sir," said Alvin.

"He said there wasn't no water here, where I said the well should be." Hank just couldn't stop himself. "I had respect for *his* knack. You'd think he'd have respect for mine."

"Knack or no knack," said the smith, "he'll have respect for my customers or he'll learn how long it takes to be a smith, oh sir! he'll learn."

Now the smith had one of the heavy iron levers in his hand, as if he meant to cane the boy across the back with it. That would be sheer murder, and Hank hadn't the heart for it. He held out his hand and caught the end of the lever. "No, Makepeace, wait, it's all right. He did tell me he was sorry."

"And is that enough for you?"

"That and knowing you'll listen to me and not to him," said Hank. "I'm not so old I'm ready to hear boys with hoof-knacks tell me I can't dowse no more."

"Oh, the well's going to be dug right here, you can bet your life. And this boy's going to dig it all himself, and not have a bite to eat until he strikes water."

Hank smiled. "Well, then, he'll be glad to discover that I know what I'm doing—he won't have to dig far, that's for sure."

Makepeace rounded on the boy, who now stood a few yards off, his hands slack at his side, showing no anger on his face, nothing at all, really. "I'm going to escort Mr. Dowser back to his new-shod mare, Alvin. And this is the last I want to see of you until you can bring me a bucket of clean water from this well. You won't eat a bite or have a sip of water until you drink it from here!"

"Oh, now," said Hank, "have a heart. You know it takes a couple of days sometimes for the dirt to settle out of a new well."

"Bring me a bucket of water from the new well, anyway," said Makepeace. "Even if you work all night."

They headed back for the smithy then, to the corral where Picklewing waited. There was some chat, some work at saddling up, and then Hank Dowser was on his way, his nag riding smoother and easier under him, just as happy as a clam. He could see the boy working as he rode off. There wasn't no flurry of dirt, just methodical lifting and dumping, lifting and dumping. The boy didn't seem to stop to rest, either. There wasn't a single break in the sound of his labor as Hank rode off. The *shuck* sound of the spade dipping into the soil, then the *swish-thump* as the dirt slid off onto the pile.

Hank didn't calm down his anger till he couldn't hear a sound of the boy, or even remember what the sound was like. Whatever power Hank had as a dowser, this boy was the enemy of his knack, that much Hank knew. He had thought his rage was unreasonable before, but now that the boy had spoke up, Hank knew he had been right all along. The boy thought he was a master of water, maybe even a doodlebug, and that made him Hank's enemy.

Jesus said to give your enemy your own cloak, to turn the other cheek—but what about when your enemy aims to take away your livelihood, what then? Do you let him ruin you? Not this Christian, thought Hank. I learned that boy something this time, and if it doesn't take, I'll learn him more later.

6

MASQUERADE

Peggy wasn't the belle of the Governor's Ball, but that was fine with her. Mistress Modesty had long since taught her that it was a mistake for women to compete with each other. "There is no single prize to be won, which, if one woman attains it, must remain out of reach for all the others."

No one else seemed to understand this, however. The other women eyed each other with jealous eyes, measuring the probable expense of gowns, guessing at the cost of whatever amulet of beauty the other woman wore; keeping track of who danced with whom, how many men arranged to be presented.

Few of them turned a jealous eye toward Peggy—at least not when she first entered the room in mid-afternoon. Peggy knew the impression she was making. Instead of an elegant coiffure, her hair was brushed and shining, pulled up in a style that looked well-tended, but prone to straying locks here and there. Her gown was simple, almost plain—but this was by calculation. "You have a sweet young body, so your gown must not distract from the natural litheness of youth." Moreover, the gown was unusually modest, showing less bare flesh than any other woman's dress; yet, more than most, it revealed the free movement of the body underneath it.

She could almost hear Mistress Modesty's voice, saying, "So many girls misunderstand. The corset is not an end in itself. It is meant to allow old and sagging bodies to imitate the body that a healthy young woman naturally has. A corset on *you* must be lightly laced, the stays only for comfort, not containment. Then your body can move freely, and you can breathe. Other girls will marvel that you have the courage to appear in public with a natural waistline. But men don't measure the cut of a woman's clothes. Instead they pleasure in the naturalness of a lady who is comfortable, sure of herself, enjoying life on this day, in this place, in his company."

Most important, though, was the fact that she wore no jewelry. The other ladies all depended on beseemings whenever they went out in public. Unless a girl had a knack for beseemings herself, she had to buy—or her parents or husband had to buy—a hex engraven on a ring or amulet. Amulets were preferred, since they were worn nearer the face, and so one could get by with a much weaker—and therefore cheaper—hex. Such beseemings had no effect from far off, but the closer you came to a woman with a beseeming of beauty, the more you began to feel that her face was particularly beautiful. None of her features was transformed; you still saw what was actually there. It was your judgment that changed. Mistress Modesty laughed at such hexes. "What good does it do to fool someone, when he knows that he's being fooled?" So Peggy wore no such hex.

All the other women at the ball were in disguise. Though no one's face was hidden, this ball was a masquerade. Only Peggy and Mistress Modesty, of all the women here, were not in costume, were not pretending to some unnatural ideal.

She could guess at the other girls' thoughts as they watched her enter the room: Poor thing. How plain. No competition there. And their estimation was true enough—at least at first. No one took particular notice of Peggy.

But Mistress Modesty carefully selected a few of the men who approached her. "I'd like you to meet my young friend Margaret," she would say, and then Peggy would smile the fresh and open smile that was not artificial at all—her natural smile, the one that spoke of her honest gladness at meeting a friend of Mistress Modesty's. They would touch her hand and bow, and her gentle echoing courtesy was graceful and unmeasured, an honest gesture; her hand squeezed his as a friendly reflex, the way one greets a hoped-for friend. "The art of beauty is the art of truth," said Mistress Modesty. "Other women pretend to be someone else; you will be your loveliest self, with the same natural exuberant grace as a bounding deer or a circling hawk." The man would lead her onto the floor, and she would dance with him, not worrying about correct steps or keeping time or showing off her dress, but rather enjoying the dance, their symmetrical movement, the way the music flowed through their bodies together.

The man who met her, who danced with her, remembered. Afterward the other girls seemed stilted, awkward, unfree, artificial. Many men, themselves as artificial as most of the ladies, did not know themselves well enough to know they enjoyed Peggy's company more than any other young lady's. But then, Mistress Modesty did not introduce Peggy to such men. Rather she only allowed Peggy to dance with the kind of man who could respond to her; and Mistress Modesty knew which men *they* were because they were genuinely fond of Mistress Modesty.

So as the hours passed by at the ball, hazy afternoon giving way to bright evening, more and more men were circling Peggy, filling up her dance card, eagerly conversing with her during the lulls, bringing her refreshment—which she ate if she was hungry or thirsty, and kindly refused if she was not—until the other girls began to take note of her. There were plenty of men who took no notice of Peggy, of course; no other girl lacked because of Peggy's plenty. But they didn't see it that way. What they saw was that Peggy was always surrounded, and Peggy could guess at their whispered conversations.

"What kind of spell does she have?"

"She wears an amulet under her bodice—I'm sure I saw its shape pressing against that cheap fabric."

"Why don't they see how thick-waisted she is?"

"Look how her hair is awry, as if she had just come in from the barnyard."

"She must flatter them dreadfully."

"Only a certain *kind* of man is attracted to her, I hope you notice."

Poor things, poor things. Peggy had no power that was not already born within any of these girls. She used no artifice that they would have to buy.

Most important to her was the fact that she did not even use her own knack here. All of Mistress Modesty's other teachings had come easily to her over the years, for they were nothing more than the extension of her natural honesty. The one difficult barrier was Peggy's knack. By habit, the moment she met someone she had always looked into his heartfire to see who he was; and, knowing more about him than she knew about herself, she then had to conceal her knowledge of his darkest secrets. It was this that had made her so reserved, even haughty-seeming.

Mistress Modesty and Peggy both agreed—she could not tell others how much she knew about them. Yet Mistress Modesty assured her that as long as she was concealing something so important, she could not become her most beautiful self—could not become the woman that Alvin would love for herself, and not out of pity.

The answer was simple enough. Since Peggy could not tell what she knew, and could not hide what she knew, the only solution was not to know it in the first place. That was the real struggle of these past three years—to train herself *not* to look into the heartfires around her. Yet by hard work, after many tears of frustration and a thousand different tricks to try to fool herself, she had achieved it. She could enter a crowded ballroom and remain oblivious to the heart-fires around her. Oh, she *saw* the heartfires—she could not blind herself—but she paid no attention to them. She did not find herself drawing close to see deeply. And now she was getting skilled enough that she didn't even have to *try* not to see into the heartfire. She could stand this close to some-one, conversing, paying attention to their words, and yet see no more of his inner thoughts than any other person would.

Of course, years of torchery had taught her more about human nature—the kinds of thoughts that go behind cer-tain words or tones of voice or expressions or gestures—that she was very good at guessing others' present thoughts. But good people never minded when she seemed to know what was on their mind right at the moment. She did not have to hide that knowledge. It was only their deepest se-crets that she could not know—and those secrets were now invisible to her unless she chose to see.

She did not choose to see. For in her new detachment she found a kind of freedom she had never known before in all her life. She could take other people at face value now. She could rejoice in their company, not knowing and therefore not feeling responsible for their hidden hungers or, most ter-ribly, their dangerous futures. It gave a kind of exhilarating madness to her dancing, her laughter, her conversation; no one else at the ball felt so free as Modesty's young friend Margaret, because no one else had ever known such des-perate confinement as she had known all her life till now.

So it was that Peggy's evening at the Governor's Ball was glorious. Not a *triumph,* actually, since she vanquished no one—whatever man won her friendship was not conquered, but liberated, even victorious. What she felt was pure joy, and so those who were with her also rejoiced in her company. Such good feelings could not be contained. Even those who gossiped nastily about her behind their fans nevertheless caught the joy of the evening; many told the governor's wife that this was the best ball ever held in Dekane, or for that matter in the whole state of Suskwahenny.

Some even realized who it was who brought such gladness to the evening. Among them were the governor's wife and Mistress Modesty. Peggy saw them talking once, as she turned gracefully on the floor, returning to her partner with a smile that made him laugh with joy to be dancing with her. The governor's wife was smiling and nodding, and she pointed with her fan toward the dance floor, and for a moment Peggy's eyes met hers. Peggy smiled in warm greeting; the governor's wife smiled and nodded back. The gesture did not go unremarked. Peggy would be welcome at any party she wanted to attend in Dekane—two or three a night, if she desired, every night of the year.

Yet Peggy did not glory in this achievement, for she recognized how small it really was. She had won her way into the finest events in Dekane—but Dekane was merely the capital of a state on the edge of the American frontier. If she longed for social victories, she would have to make her way to Camelot, to win the accolades of royalty—and from there to Europe, to be received in Vienna, Paris, Warsaw, or Madrid. Even then, though, even if she had danced with every crowned head, it would mean nothing. She would die, they would die, and how would the world be any better because she had danced?

She had seen true greatness in the heartfire of a newborn baby fourteen years ago. She had protected the child because she loved his future; she had also come to love the boy because of who he was, the kind of soul he had. Most of all, though, more important than her feelings for Prentice Alvin, most of all she loved the work that lay ahead of him. Kings and queens built kingdoms, or lost them; merchants made fortunes, or squandered them; artists made works that time faded or forgot. Only Prentice Alvin had in him the seeds of Making that would stand against time, against the endless wasting of the Unmaker. So as she danced tonight, she danced for him, knowing that if she could win the love of these strangers, she might also win Alvin's love, and earn a place beside him on his pathway to the Crystal City, that place in which all the citizens can see like torches, build like makers, and love with the purity of Christ.

With the thought of Alvin, she cast her attention to his distant heartfire. Though she had schooled herself not to see into nearby heartfires, she never gave up looking into his. Perhaps this made it harder for her to control her knack, but what purpose was it to learn anything, if by learning she lost her connection to that boy? So she did not have to search for him; she knew always, in the back of her mind, where his heartfire burned. In these years she had learned not to see him constantly before her, but still she could see him in an instant. She did so now.

He was digging in the ground behind his smithy. But she hardly noticed the work, for neither did he. What burned strongest in his heartfire was anger. Someone had treated him unfairly—but that could hardly be new, could it? Make-peace, once the most fair-minded of masters, had become steadily more envious of Alvin's skill at ironwork, and in his jealousy he had become unjust, denying Alvin's ability more fervently the further his prentice boy surpassed him. Alvin lived with injustice every day, yet never had Peggy seen such rage in him.

"Is something wrong, Mistress Margaret?" The man who danced with her spoke in concern. Peggy had stopped, there in the middle of the floor. The music still played, and couples still moved through the dance, but near her the dancers had stopped, were watching her.

"I can't—continue," she said. It surprised her to find that she was out of breath with fear. What was she afraid of?

"Would you like to leave the ballroom?" he asked. What was his name? There was only one name in her mind: Alvin.

"Please," she said. She leaned on him as they walked toward the open doors leading onto the porch. The crowd parted; she didn't see them.

It was as if all the anger Alvin had stored up in his years of working under Makepeace Smith now was coming out, and every dig of his shovel was a deep cut of revenge. A dowser, an itinerant water-seeker, that's who had angered him, that's the one he meant to harm. But the dowser was none of Peggy's concern; nor was his provocation, however mean or terrible. It was Alvin. Couldn't he see that when he dug so deep in hatred it was an act of destruction? And didn't he know that when you work to destroy, you invite the Destroyer? When your labor is unmaking, the Unmaker can claim you.

The air outside was cooler in the gathering dusk, the last shred of the sun throwing a ruddy light across the lawns of the Governor's mansion. "Mistress Margaret, I hope I did nothing to cause you to faint."

"No, I'm not even fainting. Will you forgive me? I had a thought, that's all. One that I must think about."

He looked at her strangely. Any time a woman needed to part with a man, she always claimed to be near fainting. But not Mistress Margaret—Peggy knew that he was puzzled, uncertain. The etiquette of fainting was clear. But what was a gentleman's proper manner toward a woman who "had a thought"?

She laid her hand on his arm. "I assure you, my friend— I'm quite well, and I delighted in dancing with you. I hope we'll dance again. But for now, for the moment, I need to be alone."

She could see how her words eased his concern. Calling him "my friend" was a promise to remember him; her hope to dance with him again was so sincere that he could not help but believe her. He took her words at face value, and bowed with a smile. After that she didn't even see him leave.

Her attention was far away, in Hatrack River, where Prentice Alvin was calling to the Unmaker, not guessing what he was doing. Peggy searched and searched in his heartfire, trying to find something she might do to keep him safe. But there was nothing. Now that Alvin was being driven by anger, all paths led to one place, and that place terrified her, for she couldn't see what was there, couldn't see what would happen. And there were no paths out.

What was I doing at this foolish ball, when Alvin needed me? If I had been paying proper attention, I would have seen this coming, would have found some way to help him. Instead I was dancing with these men who mean less than nothing to the future of this world. Yes, they delight in me. But what is that worth, if Alvin falls, if Prentice Alvin is destroyed, if the Crystal City is unmade before its Maker begins to build it?

7

WELLS

Alvin didn't need to look up when the dowser left. He could feel where the man was as he moved along, his anger like a black noise in the midst of the sweet green music of the wood. That was the curse of being the only

White, man or boy, who could feel the life of the green-wood—it meant that he was also the only White who knew how the land was dying.

Not that the soil wasn't rich—years of forest growth had made the earth so fertile that they said the *shadow* of a seed could take root and grow. There was life in the fields, life in the towns even. But it wasn't part of the land's own song. It was just noise, whispering noise, and the green of the wood, the life of the Red man, the animal, the plant, the soil all living together in harmony, that song was quiet now, intermittent, sad. Alvin heard it dying and he mourned.

Vain little dowser. Why was he so mad? Alvin couldn't figure. But he didn't press it, didn't argue, because almost as soon as the dowser came along, Al could see the Unmaker shadowing the edges of his vision, as if Hank Dowser'd brought him along.

Alvin first saw the Unmaker in his nightmares as a child, a vast nothingness that rolled invisibly toward him, trying to crush him, to get inside him, to grind him into pieces. It was old Taleswapper who first helped Alvin give his empty enemy a name. The Unmaker, which longs to undo the universe, break it all down until everything is flat and cold and smooth and dead.

As soon as he had a name for it and some notion what it *was,* he started seeing the Unmaker in daylight, wide awake. Not right out in the open, of course. Look *at* the Unmaker and most times you can't see him. He goes all invisible behind all the life and growth and up-building in the world. But at the edges of your sight, as if he was sneaking up behind, that's where the sly old snake awaited, that's where Alvin saw him.

When Alvin was a boy he learned a way to make that Unmaker step back a ways and leave him be. All he had to do was use his hands to build something. It could be as simple as weaving grass into a basket, and he'd have some peace. So when the Unmaker showed up around the blacksmith's shop not long after Alvin got there, he wasn't too worried. There was plenty of chance for making things in the smithy. Besides, the smithy was full of fire—fire and iron, the hardest earth. Alvin knew from childhood on that the Unmaker hankered after water. Water was its servant, did most of its work, tearing things down. So it was no wonder that when a water man like Hank Dowser came along, the Unmaker freshened up and got lively.

Now, though, Hank Dowser was on his way, taking his anger and his unfairness with him, but the Unmaker was still there, hiding out in the meadow and the bushes, lurking in the long shadows of the evening.

Dig with the shovel, lever up the earth, hoist it to the lip of the well, dump it aside. A steady rhythm, a careful building of the pile, shaping the sides of the hole. Square the first three feet of the hole, to set the shape of the well house. Then round and gently tapered inward for the stonework of the finished well. Even though you know this well will never draw water, do it careful, dig as if you thought that it would last. Build smooth, as near to perfect as you can, and it'll be enough to hold that sly old spy at bay.

So why didn't Alvin feel a speck more brave about it?

Alvin knew it was getting on toward evening, sure as if he had him a watch in his pocket, cause here came Arthur Stuart, his face just scrubbed after supper, sucking on a horehound and saying not a word. Alvin was used to him by now. Almost ever since the boy could walk, he'd been like Alvin's little shadow, coming every day it didn't rain. Never had much to say, and when he did it wasn't too easy to understand his baby talk—he had trouble with his *R*s and *S*s. Didn't matter. Arthur never wanted nothing and never did no harm, and Alvin usually half-forgot the boy was around.

Digging there with the evening flies out, buzzing in his face, Alvin had nothing to do with his brain but think. Three years he been in Hatrack, and all that time he hadn't got him one inch closer to knowing what his knack was for. He hardly used it, except for the bit he done with the horses, and that was cause he couldn't bear to know how bad they suffered when it was so easy a thing for him to make the shoeing go right. That was a good thing to do, but it didn't amount to much up-building, compared to the ruination of the land all around him.

The White man was the Unmaker's tool in this forest land, Alvin knew that, better even than water at tearing things down. Every tree that fell, every badger, coon, deer, and beaver that got used up without consent, each death was part of the killing of the land. Used to be the Reds kept the balance of things, but now they were gone, either dead or moved west of the Mizzipy—or, like the Irrakwa and the Cherriky, turned White at heart, sleeves rolled up and working hard to unmake the land even faster than the White. No one left to try to keep things whole.

Sometimes Alvin thought he was the only one left who hated the Unmaker and wanted to build against him. And he didn't know how to do it, didn't have any idea what the next step ought to be. The torch who touched him at his birthing, she was the only one who might've taught him how to be a true Maker, but she was gone, run off the very morning that he came. Couldn't be no accident. She just didn't want to teach him aught. He had a destiny, he knew it, and not a soul to help him find the way.

I'm willing, thought Alvin. I got the power in me, when I can figure how to use it straight, and I got the desire to be whatever it is I'm meant to be, but somebody's got to teach me.

Not the blacksmith, that was sure. Profiteering old coot. Alvin knew that Makepeace Smith tried to teach him as little as he could. Even now Alvin reckoned Makepeace didn't know half how much Alvin had learned himself just by watching when his master didn't guess that he was alert. Old Makepeace never meant to let him go if he could help it. Here I got a destiny, a real honest-to-goodness Work to do in my life, just like the old boys in the Bible or Ulysses or Hector, and the only teacher I got is a smith so greedy I have to *steal* learning from him, even though it's mine by right.

Sometimes it burned Alvin up inside, and he got a hankering to do something spetackler to show Makepeace Smith that his prentice wasn't just a boy who didn't know he was being cheated. What would Makepeace Smith do if he saw Alvin split iron with his fingers? What if he saw that Al could straighten a bent nail as strong as before, or heal up brittle iron that shattered under the hammer? What if he saw that Al could beat iron so thin you could see sunlight through it, and yet so strong you couldn't break it?

But that was plain dumb when Alvin thought that way, and he knowed it. Makepeace Smith might gasp the first time, he might even faint dead away, but inside ten minutes he'd be figuring an angle how to make money from it, and Alvin'd be less likely than ever to get free ahead of time. And his fame would spread, yes sir, so that by the time he turned nineteen and Makepeace Smith had to let him go, Alvin would already have too much notice. Folks'd keep him busy healing and doodlebugging and fixing and stone shaping, work that wasn't even halfway toward what he was born for. If they brought him the sick and lame to heal, how would he ever have time to be aught but a physicker? Time enough for healing when he learned the whole way to be a Maker.

The Prophet Lolla-Wossiky showed him a vision of the Crystal City only a week before the massacre at Tippy-Canoe. Alvin knew that someday in the future it was up to him to build them towers of ice and light. That was his destiny, not to be a country fixit man. As long as he was bound to Makepeace Smith's service, he had to keep his real knack secret.

That's why he never ran off, even though he was big enough now that nobody'd take him for a runaway prentice. What good would freedom do? He had to learn first how to be a Maker, or it wouldn't make no difference if he went or stayed.

So he never spoke of what he could do, and scarce used his gifts more than to shoe horses and feel the death of the land around him. But all the time in the back of his brain he recollected what he really was. A Maker. Whatever that is, I'm it, which is why the Unmaker tried to kill me before I was born and in a hundred accidents and almost-murders in my childhood back in Vigor Church. That's why he lurks around now, watching me, waiting for a chance to get me, waiting maybe for a time like tonight, all alone out here in the darkness, just me and the spade and my anger at having to do work that won't amount to nothing.

Hank Dowser. What kind of man won't listen to a good idea from somebody else? Sure the wand went down hard—the water was like to bust up through the earth at that place. But the reason it *hadn't* busted through was on account of a shelf of rock along there, not four feet under the soil. Why else did they think this was a natural meadow here? The big trees couldn't root, because the water that fell here flowed right off the stone, while the roots couldn't punch through the shelf of rock to get to the water underneath it. Hank Dowser could find water, but he sure couldn't find what lay *between* the water and the surface. It wasn't Hank's fault he couldn't see it, but it sure was his fault he wouldn't entertain no notion it might be there.

So here was Alvin, digging as neat a well as you please, and sure enough, no sooner did he have the round side wall of the well defined than *clink, clank, clunk,* the spade rang against stone.

At the new sound, Arthur Stuart ran right up to the edge of the hole and looked in. "Donk donk," he said. Then he clapped his hands.

"Donk donk is right," said Alvin. "I'll be donking on solid rock the whole width of this hole. And I ain't going in to tell Makepeace Smith about it, neither, you can bet on that, Arthur Stuart. He told me I couldn't eat nor drink till I got water, and I ain't about to go in afore dark and start pleading for supper just cause I hit rock, no sir."

"Donk," said the little boy.

"I'm digging every scrap of dirt out of this hole till the rock is bare."

He carefully dug out all the dirt he could, scraping the spade along the bumpy face of the rock. Even so, it was still brown and earthy, and Alvin wasn't satisfied. He wanted that stone to shine white. Nobody was watching but Arthur Stuart, and he was just a baby anyhow. So Alvin used his knack in a way he hadn't done since leaving Vigor Church. He made all the soil flow away from the bare rock, slide right across the stone and fetch up tight against the smooth-edge earthen walls of the hole.

It took almost no time till the stone was so shiny and white you could think it was a pool reflecting the last sunlight of the day. The evening birds sang in the trees. Sweat dripped off Alvin so fast it left little black spots when it fell on the rock.

Arthur stood at the edge of the hole. "Water," he said.

"Now you stand back, Arthur Stuart. Even if this ain't all

that deep, you just stand back from holes like this. You can get killed falling in, you know."

A bird flew by, its wings rattling loud as could be. Somewhere another bird gave a frantic cry.

"Snow," said Arthur Stuart.

"It ain't snow, it's rock," said Alvin. Then he clambered up out of the hole and stood there, laughing to himself. "There's your well, Hank Dowser," Alvin said. "You ride on back here and see where your stick drove into the dirt."

He'd be sorry he got Al a blow from his master's hand. It wasn't no joke when a blacksmith hit you, specially one like his master, who didn't go easy even on a little boy, and sure not on a man-size prentice like Alvin.

Now he could go on up to the house and tell Makepeace Smith the well was dug. Then he'd lead his master back down here and show him this hole, with the stone looking up from the bottom, as solid as the heart of the world. Alvin heard himself saying to his master, "You show me how to drink that and I'll drink it." It'd be pure pleasure to hear how Makepeace'd cuss himself blue at the sight of it.

Except now that he could show them how wrong they were to treat him like they did, Alvin knew it didn't matter in the long run whether he taught them a lesson or not. What mattered was Makepeace Smith really did need this well. Needed it bad enough to pay out a dowser's cost in free ironwork. Whether it was dug where Hank Dowser said or somewhere else, Alvin knew he had to dig it.

That would suit Alvin's pride even better, now he thought of it. He'd come in with a bucket, just like Makepeace ordered him to—but from a well of his own choosing.

He looked around in the ruddy evening light, thinking where to start looking for a diggable spot. He heard Arthur Stuart pulling at the meadow grass, and the sound of birds having a church choir practice, they were so loud tonight.

Or maybe they were plain scared. Cause now he was looking around, Alvin could see that the Unmaker was lively tonight. By rights digging the first hole should've been enough to send it headlong, keep it off for days. Instead it followed him just out of sight, ever step he took as he hunted for the place to dig the true well. It was getting more and more like one of his nightmares, where nothing he did could make the Unmaker go away. It was enough to send a thrill of fear right through him, make him shiver in the warm spring air.

Alvin just shrugged off that scare. He knew the Unmaker wasn't going to touch him. For all the years of his life till now, the Unmaker'd tried to kill him by setting up accidents, like water icing up where he was bound to step, or eating away at a riverbank so he slipped in. Now and then the Unmaker even got some man or other to take a few swipes at Alvin, like Reverend Thrower or them Choc-Taw Reds. In all his life, outside his dreams, that Unmaker never did anything direct.

And he won't now either, Alvin told hisself. Just keep searching, so you can dig the *real* well. The false one didn't drive that old deceiver off, but the real one's bound to, and I won't see him shimmering at the edges of my vision for three months after that.

With that thought in mind, Alvin hunkered down and kept his mind on searching for a break in the hidden shelf of stone.

How Alvin searched things out underground wasn't like *seeing*. It was more like he had another hand that skittered through the soil and rock as fast as a waterdrop on a hot griddle. Even though he'd never met him a doodlebug, he figured doodling couldn't be much different than how he done it, sending his bug scouting along under the earth, feeling things out all the way. And if he *was* doodlebugging, then he had to wonder if folks was right who allowed as how it was the doodlebug's very *soul* that slithered under the ground, and there was tales about doodlebugs whose souls got lost and the doodler never said another word or moved a muscle till he finally died. But Alvin didn't let such tales scare him off from doing what he ought to. If there was a need for stone, he'd find him the natural breaks to make it come away without hardly chipping at it. If there was a need for water, he'd find him a way to dig on down to get it.

Finally he found him a place where the shelf of stone was thin and crumbled. The ground was higher here, the water deeper down, but what counted was he could get through the stone to it.

This new spot was halfway between the house and the smithy—which would be less convenient for Makepeace, but better for his wife Gertie, who had to use the same water. Alvin set to with a will, because it was getting on to dark, and he was determined to take no rest tonight until his work was done. Without even thinking about it he made up his mind to use his power like he used to back on his father's land. He never struck stone with his spade; it was like the earth turned to flour and fair to jumped out of the hole instead of him having to heft it. If any grownup happened to see him right then they'd think they was likkered up or having a conniption fit, he dug so fast. But nobody was looking, except for Arthur Stuart. It was getting nightward, after all, and Al had no lantern, so nobody'd ever even notice he was there. He could use his knack tonight without fear of being found out.

From the house came the sound of shouting, loud but not clear enough for Alvin to make out the words.

"Mad," said Arthur Stuart. He was looking straight at the house, as steady as a dog on point.

"Can you hear what they're saying?" said Alvin. "Old Peg

Guester always says you got ears like a dog, perk up at everything."

Arthur Stuart closed his eyes. "You got no right to starve that boy," he said.

Alvin like to laughed outright. Arthur was doing as perfect an imitation of Gertie Smith's voice as he ever heard.

"He's too big to thrash and I got to learn him," said Arthur Stuart.

This time he sounded just like Alvin's master. "I'll be," murmured Alvin.

Little Arthur went right on. "Either Alvin eats this plate of supper Makepeace Smith or you'll wear it on your head. I'd like to see you try it you old hag I'll break your arms."

Alvin couldn't help himself, he just laughed outright. "Consarn it if you ain't a perfect mockingbird, Arthur Stuart."

The little boy looked up at Alvin and a grin stole across his face. Down from the house come the sound of breaking crockery. Arthur Stuart started to laugh and run around in circles. "Break a dish, break a dish, break a dish!" he cried.

"If you don't beat all," said Alvin. "Now you tell me, Arthur, you didn't really understand all them things you just said, did you? I mean, you were just repeating what you heard, ain't that so?"

"Break a dish on his *head!*" Arthur screamed with laughter and fell over backward in the grass. Alvin laughed right along, but he couldn't take his eyes off the little boy. More to him than meets the eye, thought Alvin. Or else he's plain crazy.

From the other direction came another woman's voice, a full-throated call that floated over the moist darkening air. "Ar*thur!* Arthur *Stuart!*"

Arthur sat right up. "Mama," he said.

"That's right, that's Old Peg Guester calling," said Alvin.

"Go to bed," said Arthur.

"Just be careful she don't give you a bath first, boy, you're a mite grimy."

Arthur got up and started trotting off across the meadow, up to the path that led from the springhouse to the road-house where he lived. Alvin watched him out of sight, the little boy flapping his arms as he ran, like as if he was flying. Some bird, probably an owl, flew right alongside the boy halfway across the meadow, skimming along the ground like as if to keep him company. Not till Arthur was out of sight behind the springhouse did Alvin turn back to his labor.

In a few more minutes it was full dark, and the deep silence of night came quick after that. Even the dogs were quiet all through town. It'd be hours before the moon came up. Alvin worked on. He didn't have to see; he could feel how the well was going, the earth under his feet. Nor was it the Red man's seeing now, their gift for hearing the green-wood song. It was his own knack he was using, helping him feel his way deeper into the earth.

He knew he'd strike rock twice as deep this time. But when the spade caught up on big chunks of rock, it wasn't a smooth plate like it was at the spot Hank Dowser chose. The stones were crumbly and broke up, and with his knack Al hardly had to press his lever afore the stones flipped up easy as you please, and he tossed them out the well like clods.

Once he dug through that layer, though, the ground got oozy underfoot. If he wasn't who he was, he'd've had to set the work aside and get help to dredge it out in the morning. But for Alvin it was easy enough. He tightened up the earth around the walls of the hole, so water couldn't seep in so fast. It wasn't spadework now. Alvin used a dredge to scoop up the mucky soil, and he didn't need no partner to hoist it out on a rope, either, he just heaved it up and his knack was such that each scoop of ooze clung together and landed neat as you please outside the well, just like he was flinging bunny rabbits out the hole.

Alvin was master here, that was sure, working miracles in this hole in the ground. You tell me I can't eat or drink till the well is dug, thinking you'll have me begging for a cup of water and pleading for you to let me go to bed. Well, you won't see such a thing. You'll have your well, with walls so solid they'll be drawing water here after your house and smithy have crumbled into dust.

But even as he felt the sweet taste of victory, he saw that the Unmaker was closer than it had ever come in years. It flickered and danced, and not just at the edges of his vision anymore. He could see it right in front of him, even in the darkness, he could see it clearer than ever in daylight, cause now he couldn't see nothing real to distract him.

It was scary, all of a sudden, just like the nightmares of his childhood, and for a while Alvin stood in the hole, all froze with fear, as water oozed up from below, making the ground under him turn to slime. Thick slime a hundred feet deep, he was sinking down, and the walls of the well were getting soft, too, they'd cave in on him and bury him, he'd drown trying to breathe muck into his lungs, he knew it, he could feel it cold and wet around his thighs, his crotch; he clenched his fists and felt mud ooze between his fingers, just like the nothingness in all his nightmares—

And then he came to himself, got control. Sure, he was up to his waist in mud, and if he was any other boy in such a case he might have wiggled himself down deeper and smothered hisself, trying to struggle out. But this was Alvin, not some ordinary boy, and he was safe as long as he wasn't booglied up by fear like a child caught in a bad

dream. He just made the slime under his feet harden enough
to hold his weight, then made the hard place float upward,
lifting him out of the mud until he was standing on grav-
elly mud at the bottom of the well.

Easy as breaking a rat's neck. If that was all the Unmaker
could think of doing, it might as well go on home. Alvin
was a match for him, just like he was a match for Makepeace Smith and Hank Dowser both. He dug on, dredged
up, hoisted, flung, then bent to dredge again.

He was pretty near deep enough now, a good six feet
lower than the stone shelf. Why, if he hadn't firmed up the
earthen sides of the well, it'd be full of water over his head
already. Alvin took hold of the knotted rope he left dangling
and walked up the wall, pulling himself hand over hand up
the rope.

The moon was rising now, but the hole was so deep it
wouldn't shine into the well until near moon-noon. Never
mind. Into the pit Alvin dumped a barrowload of the stones
he'd levered out only an hour before. Then he clambered
down after it.

He'd been working rock with his knack since he was
little, and he was never more sure-handed with it than tonight. With his bare hands he shaped the stone like soft clay,
making it into smooth square blocks that he placed all
around the walls of the well from the bottom up, braced firm
against each other so that the pushing of soil and water
wouldn't cave it in. Water would seep easily through the
cracks between stones, but the soil wouldn't, so the well
would be clean almost from the start.

There wasn't enough stone from the well itself, of course;
Alvin made three trips to the stream to load the barrow with
water-smoothed rocks. Even though he was using his knack
to make the work easier, it was late at night and weariness
was coming on him. But he refused to pay attention. Hadn't

he learned the Red man's knack for running on long after weariness should have claimed him? A boy who followed Ta-Kumsaw, running without a rest from Detroit to Eight-Face Mound, such a boy had no need to give in to a single night of well-digging, and never mind his thirst or the pain in his back and thighs and shoulders, the ache of his elbows and his knees.

At last, at last, it was done. The moon past zenith, his mouth tasting like a horsehair blanket, but it was done. He climbed on out of the hole, bracing himself against the stone walls he'd just finished building. As he climbed he let go of his hold on the earth around the well, unsealed it, and the water, now tame, began to trickle noisily into the deep stone basin he'd built to hold it.

Still Alvin didn't go inside the house, didn't so much as walk to the stream and drink. His first taste of water would be from this well, just like Makepeace Smith had said. He'd stay here and wait until the well had reached its natural level, and then clear the water and draw up a bucket and carry it inside the house and drink a cup of it in front of his master. Afterward he'd take Makepeace Smith outside and show him the well Hank Dowser called for, the one Makepeace Smith had cuffed him for, and then point out the one where you could drop a bucket and it was splash, not clatter.

He stood there at the lip of the well, imagining how Makepeace Smith would sputter, how he'd cuss. Then he sat down, just to ease his feet, picturing Hank Dowser's face when he saw what Al had done. Then he lay right down to ease his aching back, and closed his eyes for just a minute, so he didn't have to pay no heed to the fluttering shadows of unmaking that kept pestering him out the corners of his eyes.

8

UNMAKER

Mistress Modesty was stirring. Peggy heard her breathing change rhythm. Then she came awake and sat up abruptly on her couch. At once Mistress Modesty looked for Peggy in the darkness of the room.

"Here I am," Peggy murmured.

"What has happened, my dear? Haven't you slept at all?"

"I dare not," said Peggy.

Mistress Modesty stepped onto the portico beside her. The breeze from the southwest billowed the damask curtains behind them. The moon was flirting with a cloud; the city of Dekane was a shifting pattern of roofs down the hill below them. "Can you see him?" asked Mistress Modesty.

"Not him," said Peggy. "I see his heartfire; I can see through his eyes, as he sees; I can see his futures. But himself, no, I can't see him."

"My poor dear. On such a marvelous night, to have to leave the Governor's Ball and watch over this faraway child in grave danger." It was Mistress Modesty's way of asking what the danger was without actually *asking*. This way Peggy could answer or not, and neither way would any offense be given or taken.

"I wish I could explain," said Peggy. "It's his enemy, the one with no face—"

Mistress Modesty shuddered. "No face! How ghastly."

"Oh, he has a face for *other* men. There was a minister once, a man who fancied himself a scientist. He saw the Unmaker, but could not see him truly, not as Alvin does. Instead he made up a manshape for him in his mind, and a name—called him 'the Visitor,' and thought he was an angel."

"An angel!"

"I believe that when most of us see the Unmaker, we can't comprehend him, we haven't the strength of intellect for that. So our minds come as close as they can. Whatever shape represents naked destructive power, terrible and irresistible force, that is what we see. Those who *love* such evil power, they make themselves see the Unmaker as beautiful. Others, who hate and fear it, they see the worst thing in the world."

"What does your Alvin see?"

"I could never see it myself, it's so subtle; even looking through his eyes I wouldn't have noticed it, if *he* hadn't noticed it. I saw that he was seeing something, and only then did I understand what it was he saw. Think of it as—the feeling when you think you saw some movement out of the corner of your eye, only when you turn there's nothing there."

"Like someone always sneaking up behind you," said Mistress Modesty.

"Yes, exactly."

"And it's sneaking up on Alvin?"

"Poor boy, he doesn't realize that he's calling to it. He has dug a deep black pit in his heart, just the sort of place where the Unmaker flows."

Mistress Modesty sighed. "Ah, my child, these things are all beyond me. I never had a knack; I can barely comprehend the things you do."

"You? No knack?" Peggy was amazed.

"I know—hardly anyone ever admits to not having one, but surely I'm not the only one."

"You misunderstand me, Mistress Modesty," said Peggy. "I was startled, not that you had no knack, but that you *thought* you had no knack. Of course you have one."

"Oh, but I don't mind not having one, my dear—"

"You have the knack of seeing potential beauty as if it were already there, and by seeing, you let it come to be."

"What a lovely idea," said Mistress Modesty.

"Do you doubt me?"

"I don't doubt that you believe what you say."

There was no point in arguing. Mistress Modesty believed her, but was afraid to believe. It didn't matter, though. What mattered was Alvin, finishing his second well. He had saved himself once; he thought the danger was over. Now he sat at the edge of the well, just to rest a moment; now he lay down. Didn't he see the Unmaker moving close to him? Didn't he realize that his very sleepiness opened himself wide for the Unmaker to enter him?

"No!" whispered Peggy. "Don't sleep!"

"Ah," said Mistress Modesty. "You speak to him. Can he hear you?"

"Never," said Peggy. "Never a word."

"Then what can you do?"

"Nothing. Nothing I can think of."

"You told me you used his caul—"

"It's a part of his power, that's what I use. But even his knack can't send away what came at his own call. I never had the knowledge to fend off the Unmaker itself, anyway, even if I had a yard of his caulflesh, and not just a scrap of it."

Peggy watched in desperate silence as Alvin's eyes closed. "He sleeps."

"If the Unmaker wins, will he die?"

"I don't know. Perhaps. Perhaps he'll disappear, eaten away to nothing. Or perhaps the Unmaker will own him—"

"Can't you see the future, torch girl?"

"All paths lead into darkness, and I see no path emerging."

"Then it's over," whispered Mistress Modesty.

Peggy could feel something cold on her cheeks. Ah, of course: her own tears drying in the cool breeze.

"But if Alvin were awake, *he* could fend off this invisible enemy?" Mistress Modesty asked. "Sorry to bother you with questions, but if I know how it works, perhaps I can help you think of something."

"No, no, it's beyond us, we can only watch—" Yet even as Peggy rejected Mistress Modesty's suggestion, her mind leapt ahead to ways of using it. I must waken him. I don't have to fight the Unmaker, but if I waken him, then he can do his fighting for himself. Weak and weary though he is, he might still find a way to victory. At once Peggy turned and rushed back into her room, scrabbled through her top drawer until she found the carven box that held the caul.

"Should I leave?" Mistress Modesty had followed her.

"Stay with me," said Peggy. "Please, for company. For comfort, if I fail."

"You won't fail," said Mistress Modesty. "*He* won't fail, if he's the man you say he is."

Peggy barely heard her. She sat on the edge of her bed, searching in Alvin's heartfire for some way to waken him. Normally she could use his senses even when he slept, hearing what he heard, seeing his memory of the place around him. But now, with the Unmaker seeping in, his senses were fading. She could not trust them. Desperately she cast about for some other plan. A loud noise? Using what little was left of Alvin's sense of the life around him, she found a tree, then rubbed a tiny bit of the caul and tried—as she had seen Alvin do it—to picture in her mind how the wood in the branch would come apart. It was painfully slow—Alvin did it so quickly!—but at last she made it fall. Too late. He barely heard it. The Unmaker had undone so much of the air around him that the trembling of sound could not pass through it. Perhaps Alvin noticed; perhaps he came a bit closer to wakefulness. Perhaps not.

How can I waken him, when he is so insensible that nothing can disturb him? Once I held this caul as a ridgebeam tumbled toward him; I burned a childsize gap in it, so that the hair of his head wasn't even touched. Once a millstone fell toward his leg; I split it in half. Once his own father stood in a loft, pitchfork in hand, driven by the Unmaker's madness until he had decided to murder his own most-beloved son; I brought Taleswapper down the hill to him, distracting the father from his dark purpose and driving off the Unmaker.

How? How did Taleswapper's coming drive off the Destroyer? Because he would have seen the hateful beast and given the cry against it, that's why the Unmaker left when Taleswapper arrived. Taleswapper isn't anywhere near Alvin now, but surely there's someone I can waken and draw down the hill; someone filled with love and goodness, so that the Unmaker must flee before him.

With agonizing fear she withdrew from Alvin's heartfire even as the blackness of the Unmaker threatened to drown it, and searched in the night for another heartfire, someone she could waken and send to him in time. Yet even as she searched, she could sense in Alvin's heartfire a certain lightening, a hint of shadows within shadows, not the utter emptiness she had seen before where his future ought to be. If Alvin had any chance, it was from her searching. Even if she found someone, she had no notion how to waken them. But she would find a way, or the Crystal City would be swallowed up in the flood that came because of Alvin's foolish, childish rage.

9

REDBIRD

Alvin woke up hours later, the moon low in the west, the first scant light appearing in the east. He hadn't meant to sleep. But he was tired, after all, and his work was done, so of course he couldn't close his eyes and hope to stay awake. There was still time to take a bucketful of water and carry it inside.

Were his eyes open even now? The sky he could see, light grey to the left, light grey to the right. But where were the trees? Shouldn't they have been moving gently in the morning breeze, just at the fringes of his vision? For that matter, there was no breeze; and beyond the sight of his eyes, and touch on his skin, there were other things he could not feel. The green music of the living forest. It was gone; no murmur of life from the sleeping insects in the grass, no rhythm of the heartbeats of the dawn-browsing deer. No birds roosting in the trees, waiting for the sun's heat to bring out the insects.

Dead. Unmade. The forest was gone.

Alvin opened his eyes.

Hadn't they already been open?

Alvin opened his eyes again, and still he couldn't see; without closing them, he opened them still again, and each time the sky seemed darker. No, not darker, simply farther away, rushing up and away from him, like as if he was falling into a pit so deep that the sky itself got lost.

Alvin cried out in fear, and opened his already-open eyes, and saw:

The quivering air of the Unmaker, pressing down on him, poking itself into his nostrils, between his fingers, into his ears.

He couldn't feel it, no sir, except that he knew what *wasn't* there now; the outermost layers of his skin, wherever the Unmaker touched, his own body was breaking apart, the tiniest bits of him dying, drying, flaking away.

"No!" he shouted. The shout didn't make a sound. Instead, the Unmaker whipped inside his mouth, down into his lungs, and he couldn't close his teeth hard enough, his lips tight enough to keep that slimy uncreator from slithering on inside him, eating him away from the inside out.

He tried to heal himself the way he done with his leg that time the millstone broke it clean in half. But it was like the old story Taleswapper told him. He couldn't build things up half so fast as the Unmaker could tear them down. For every place he healed, there was a thousand places wrecked and lost. He was a-going to die, he was half-gone already, and it wouldn't be just death, just losing his flesh and living on in the spirit, the Unmaker meant to eat him body and spirit both alike, his mind and his flesh together.

A splash. He heard a splashing sound. It was the most welcome thing he ever heard in his life, to hear a sound at all. It meant that there *was* something beyond the Unmaker that surrounded and filled him.

Alvin heard the sound echo and ring inside his own memory, and with that to cling to, with that touch of the real world there to hang on to, Alvin opened his eyes.

This time for real, he knew, cause he saw the sky again with its proper fringe of trees. And there was Gertie Smith, Makepeace's missus, standing over him with a bucket in her hands.

"I reckon this is the first water from this well," she said.

Alvin opened his mouth, and felt cool moist air come inside. "Reckon so," he whispered.

"I never would've thought you could dig it all out and line it proper with stones, all in one night," she said. "That mixup boy, Arthur Stuart, he come to the kitchen where I was making breakfast biscuits, and he told me your well was done. I had to come and see."

"He gets up powerful early," said Alvin.

"And you stay up powerful late," said Gertie. "If I was a man your size I'd give my husband a proper licking, Al, prentice or no."

"I just did what he asked."

"I'm certain you did, just like I'm certain he wanted you to excavate that there circle of stone off by the smithy, am I right?" She cackled with delight. "That'll show the old coot. Sets such a store by that dowser, but his own prentice has a better dowsing knack than that old fraud—"

For the first time Alvin realized that the hole he dug in anger was like a signboard telling folks he had more than a hoof-knack in him. "Please, ma'am," he said.

"Please what?"

"My knack ain't dowsing, ma'am, and if you start saying so, I'll never get no peace."

She eyed him cool and steady. "If you ain't got the dowser's knack, boy, tell me how come there's clear water in this well you dug."

Alvin calculated his lie. "The dowser's stick dipped here, too, I saw it, and so when the first well struck stone, I tried here."

Gertie had a suspicious nature. "Do you reckon you'd say the same if Jesus was standing here judging your eternal soul depending on the truth of what you say?"

"Ma'am, I reckon if Jesus was here, I'd be asking forgiveness for my sins, and I wouldn't care two hoots about any old well."

She laughed again, cuffed him lightly on the shoulder. "I like your dowsing story. You just happened to be watching old Hank Dowser. Oh, that's a good one. I'll tell that tale to everybody, see if I don't."

"Thank you, ma'am."

"Here. Drink. You deserve first swallow from the first bucket of clear water from this well."

Alvin knew that the custom was for the owner to get first drinks. But she was offering, and he was so dry he couldn't have spit two bits' worth even if you paid him five bucks an ounce. So he set the bucket to his lips and drank, letting it splash out onto his shirt.

"I'd wager you're hungry, too," she said.

"More tired than hungry, I think," said Alvin.

"Then come inside to sleep."

He knew he should, but he could see the Unmaker not far off, and he was afeared to sleep again, that was the truth. "Thank you kindly, Ma'am, but anyhow, I'd like to be off by myself a few minutes."

"Suit yourself," she said, and went on inside.

The morning breeze chilled him as it dried off the water he spilled on his shirt. Was his ravishment by the Unmaker only a dream? He didn't think so. He was awake right enough, and it was real, and if Gertie Smith hadn't come along and dunked that bucket in the well, he would've been unmade. The Unmaker wasn't hiding out no more. He wasn't sneaking in backways nor roundabout. No matter where he looked, there it was, shimmering in the greyish morning light.

For some reason the Unmaker picked this morning for a face-to-face. Only Alvin didn't know how he was supposed to fight. If digging a well and building it up so fine wasn't making enough to drive off his enemy, he didn't know what else to do. The Unmaker wasn't like the men he wrestled with in town. The Unmaker had nothing he could take ahold of.

One thing was sure. Alvin'd never have a night of sleep again if he didn't take this Unmaker down somehow and wrestle him into the dirt.

I'm supposed to be your master, Alvin said to the Unmaker. So tell me, Unmaker, how do I undo *you,* when all you are is Undoing? Who's going to teach me how to win this battle, when you can sneak up on me in my sleep, and I don't have the faintest idea how to get to you?

As he spoke these words inside his head, Alvin walked to the edge of the woods. The Unmaker backed away from him, always out of reach. Al knew without looking that it also closed up behind him, so it had him on all sides.

This is the middle of the uncut wood where I ought to feel most at home, but the greensong, it's gone silent here, and all around me is my enemy from birth, and me here with no plan at all.

The Unmaker, though, he had a plan. He didn't need to waste no time a-dithering about what to do, Alvin found that out real quick.

Cause while Alvin was a-standing there in the cool heavy breeze of a summer morning, the air suddenly went chill, and blamed if snowflakes didn't start to fall. Right down on the green-leaf trees they came, settling on the tall thick grass between them. Thick and cold it piled up, not the wet heavy flakes of a warm snow, but the tiny icy crystals of a deep winter blizzard blow. Alvin shivered.

"You can't do this," he said.

But his eyes weren't closed *now,* he knew that. This wasn't no half-asleep dream. This was real snow, and it was so thick and cold that the branches of summer-green trees were snapping, the leaves were tearing off and falling to the ground in a tinkle of broken ice. And Alvin himself was like to freeze himself clear to death if he didn't get out of there somehow.

He started to walk back the way he came, but the snow was coming down so thick he couldn't see more than five or six feet ahead of him, and he couldn't feel his way because the Unmaker had deadened the greensong of the living woods. Pretty soon he wasn't walking, he was running. Only he didn't run surefooted like Ta-Kumsaw taught him; he ran as noisy and stupid as any oaf of a White man, and like most Whites would've, he slipped on a patch of ice-covered stone and sprawled out face down across a reach of snow.

Snow that caught up in his mouth and nose and into his ears, snow that clung between his fingers, just like the slime last night, just like the Unmaker in his dream, and he choked and sputtered and cried out—

"I know it's a lie!"

His voice was swallowed up in the wall of snow.

"It's summer!" he shouted.

His jaw ached from the cold and he knew it'd hurt too much to speak again, but still he screamed through numb lips, "I'll make you stop!"

And then he realized that he could never make anything out of the Unmaker, could never make the Unmaker do or be anything because it was only Undoing and Unbeing. It wasn't the Unmaker he needed to call to, it was all the living things around him, the trees, the grass, the earth, the air itself. It was the greensong that he needed to restore.

He grabbed ahold of that idea and used it, spoke again, his voice scarce more than a whisper now, but he called to them, and not in anger.

"Summer," he whispered.

"Warm air!" he said.

"Leaves green!" he shouted. "Hot wind out of the southwest. Thunderheads in the afternoon, mist in the morning, sunlight hotting it up, burning off the fog!"

Did it change, just a little? Did the snowfall slacken? Did

the drifts on the ground melt lower, the heaps on the tree-limbs tumble off, baring more of the branch?

"It's a hot morning, dry!" he cried. "Rain may drift in later like the gift of the Wise Men, coming from a long way off, but for now sunlight beating on the leaves, waking you up, you're *growing,* putting out leaves, that's right! That's right!"

There was gladness in his voice because the snowfall was just a spatter of rain now, the snow on the ground was melted back to patches here and there, the broke-off leaves were sprouting on the branch again as quick as militia in a doubletime march.

And in the silence after his last shout, he heard birdsong.

Song like he'd never heard before. He didn't know this bird, this sweet melody that changed with every whistle and never played the same tune again. It was a weaving song, but one whose pattern you couldn't find, so you couldn't ever sing it again, but you also couldn't ravel it, spin it out and break it down. It was all of one piece, all of one single Making, and Alvin knew that if he could just find the bird with that song in his throat he'd be safe. His victory would be complete.

He ran, and now the greensong of the forest was with him, and his feet found the right places to step without him looking. He followed that song until he came to the clearing where the singing was.

Perched on an old log with a patch of snow still in the northwest shadow—a redbird. And sitting in front of that log, almost nose to nose as he listened to it sing—Arthur Stuart.

Alvin walked around the two of them real slow, walking a clean circle before he come much closer. Arthur Stuart like to never noticed he was there, he never took his eyes off that bird. The sunlight dazzled on the two of them, but neither bird nor boy so much as blinked. Alvin didn't say nothing, either. Just like Arthur Stuart, he was all caught up in the redbird song.

It wasn't no different from all the other redbirds, the thousand scarlet songbirds Alvin had seen since he was little. Except that from its throat came music that no other bird had ever sung before. This wasn't *a* redbird. Nor was it *the* redbird. There was no single bird had some gift the other redbirds lacked. It was just Redbird, the one picked for this moment to speak in the voice of all the birds, to sing the song of all the singers, so that this boy could hear.

Alvin knelt down on the new-grown grass not three feet from Redbird, and listened to its song. He knew from what Lolla-Wossiky once told him that Redbird's song was all the stories of the Red man, everything they ever done that was worth doing. Alvin halfway hoped to understand that ancient tale, or at least to hear how Redbird told of things that he took part in. The Prophet Lolla-Wossiky walking on water; Tippy-Canoe River all scarlet with Red folks' blood; Ta-Kumsaw standing with a dozen musketballs in him, still crying out for his men to stand, to fight, to drive the White thieves back.

But the sense of the song eluded him no matter how he listened. He might run the forest with a Red man's legs and hear the greensong with a Red man's ears, but Redbird's song wasn't meant for him. The saying told the truth: No girl gets all the suitors, and no boy gets all the knacks. There was much that Alvin could do already, and much ahead of him to learn, but there'd be far more that was always out of his ken, and Redbird's song was part of that.

Yet Alvin was sure as shucks that Redbird wasn't here by accident. Come like this at the end of his first face-to-face with the Unmaker, Redbird had to have some purpose. He had to get some answers out of Redbird's song.

Alvin was just about to speak, just about to ask the question burning in him ever since he first learned what his destiny might be. But it wasn't his voice that broke into Redbird's song. It was Arthur Stuart's.

"I don't know days coming up," said the mixup boy. His voice was like music and the words were clearer than any Alvin ever heard that three-year-old say before. "I only know days gone."

It took a second for Alvin to hitch himself to what was going on here. What Arthur said was the answer to Alvin's question. Will I ever be a Maker like the torch girl said? That was what Alvin would've asked, and Arthur's words were the answer.

But not Arthur Stuart's own answer, that was plain. The little boy no more understood what he was saying than he did when he was mimicking Makepeace's and Gertie's quarrel last night. He was giving Redbird's answer. Translating from birdsong into speech that Alvin's ears were fit to understand.

Alvin knew now that he'd asked the wrong question. He didn't need Redbird to tell him he was supposed to be a Maker—he knowed that firm and sure years ago, and knew it still in spite of all doubts. The real question wasn't whether, it was *how* to be a Maker.

Tell me how.

Redbird changed his song to a soft and simple tune, more like normal birdsong, quite different from the thousand-year-old Red man's tale that he'd been singing up to now. Alvin didn't understand the sense of it, but he knew all the same what it was about. It was the song of Making. Over and over, the same tune repeating, only a few moments of it—but they were blinding in their brightness, a song so true that Alvin saw it with his eyes, felt it from his lips to his groin, tasted it and smelled it. The song of Making, and it was his own song, he knew it from how sweet it tasted on his tongue.

And when the song was at its peak, Arthur Stuart spoke again in a voice that was hardly human it piped so sharp, it sang so clear.

"The Maker is the one who is part of what he makes," said the mixup boy.

Alvin wrote the words in his heart, even though he didn't understand them. Because he knew that someday he *would* understand them, and when he did, he would have the power of the ancient Makers who built the Crystal City. He would understand, and use his power, and find the Crystal City and build it once again.

The Maker is the one who is part of what he makes.

Redbird fell silent. Stood still, head cocked; and then became, not Redbird, but any old bird with scarlet feathers. Off it flew.

Arthur Stuart watched the bird out of sight. Then he called out after it in his own true childish voice, "Bird! Fly bird!" Alvin knelt beside the boy, weak from the night's work, the grey dawn's fear, this bright day's birdsong.

"I flied," said Arthur Stuart. For the first time, it seemed, he took notice Alvin was there, and turned to him.

"Did you now?" whispered Alvin, reluctant to destroy the child's dream by telling him that folks don't fly.

"Big blackbird tote me," said Arthur. "Fly and fly." Then Arthur reached up his hands and pressed in on Alvin's cheeks. "Maker," he said. Then he laughed and laughed with joy.

So Arthur wasn't just a mimic. He really understood Redbird's song, some of it, at least. Enough to know the name of Alvin's destiny.

"Don't you tell nobody," Alvin said. "I won't tell nobody you can talk to birds, and you don't tell nobody I'm a Maker. Promise?"

Arthur's face grew serious. "Don't talk birds," he said. "Birds talk *me*." And then: "I *flied*."

"I believe you," Alvin said.

"I beeve *you*," said Arthur. Then he laughed again.

Alvin stood up and so did Arthur. Al took him by the hand. "Let's go on home," he said.

He took Arthur to the roadhouse, where Old Peg Guester was full of scold at the mixup boy for running off and bothering folks all morning. But it was a loving scold, and Arthur grinned like an idiot at the voice of the woman he called Mama. As the door closed with Arthur Stuart on the other side, Alvin told himself, I'm going to tell that boy what he done for me. Someday I'll tell him what this meant.

Alvin came home by way of the springhouse path and headed on down toward the smithy, where Makepeace was no doubt angry at him for not being ready for work, even though he dug a well all night.

The well. Alvin found himself standing by the hole that he had dug as a monument to Hank Dowser, with the white stone bright in the sunlight, bright and cruel as scornful laughter.

In that moment Alvin knew why the Unmaker came to him that night. Not because of the true well that he dug. Not because he had used his knack to hold the water back, not because he had softened the stone and bent it to his need. It was because he had dug that first hole down to the stone for one reason only—to make Hank Dowser look the fool.

To punish him? Yes sir, to make him a laughingstock to any man who saw the stone-bottomed well on the spot that Hank had marked. It would destroy him, take away his name as a dowser—and unfairly so, because he *was* a good dowser who got hisself fooled by the lay of the land. Hank made an honest mistake, and Al had got all set to punish him as if he was a fool, which surely he was not.

Tired as he was, weak from labor and the battle with the Unmaker, Alvin didn't waste a minute. He fetched the spade from where it lay by the working well, then stripped off his shirt and set to work. When he dug this false well, it was a work of evil, to unmake an honest man for no reason better than spite. Filling it in, though, was a Maker's work. Since it was daylight, Alvin couldn't even use his knack to help—he did full labor on it till he thought he was so tired he might just die.

It was noon, and him without supper or breakfast either one, but the well was filled right up, the turves set back on so they'd grow back, and if you didn't look close you'd never know there'd been a hole at all. Alvin *did* use his knack a little, since no one was about, to weave the grassroots back together, knit them into the ground, so there'd be no dead patches to mark the spot.

All the time, though, what burned worse than the sun on his back or the hunger in his belly was his own shame. He was so busy last night being angry and thinking how to make a fool of Hank Dowser that it never once occurred to him to do the right thing and use his knack to break right through the shelf of stone in the very spot Hank picked. No one ever would've known save Alvin hisself that there'd been aught wrong with the place. That would've been the Christian thing, the charitable thing to do. When a man slaps your face, you answer by shaking his hand, that's what Jesus said to do, and Alvin just plain wasn't listening, Alvin was too cussed proud.

That's what called the Unmaker to me, thought Alvin. I could've used my knack to build up, and I used it to tear down. Well, never again, never again, never again. He made that promise three times, and even though it was a silent promise and no one'd ever know, he'd keep it better than any oath he might take before a judge or even a minister.

Well, too late now. If he'd thought of this before Gertie ever saw the false well or drew water from the true, he might've filled up the other well and made this one good after all. But now she'd seen the stone, and if he dug through it then all his secrets would be out. And once you've drunk water from a good new well, you can't never fill it up till it runs dry on its own. To fill up a living well is to beg for drouth and cholera to dog you all the days of your life.

He'd undone all he could. You can be sorry, and you can be forgiven, but you can't call back the futures that your bad decisions lost. He didn't need no philosopher to tell him that.

Makepeace wasn't a-hammering in the forge, and there wasn't no smoke from the smithy chimney, either. Must be Makepeace was up at the house, doing some chores there, Alvin figured. So he put the spade away back in the smithy and then headed on toward the house.

Halfway there, he come to the good well, and there was Makepeace Smith setting on the low wall of footing stones Al had laid down to be foundation for the wellhouse.

"Morning, Alvin," said the master.

"Morning, sir," said Alvin.

"Dropped me the tin and copper bucket right down to the bottom here. You must've dug like the devil hisself, boy, to get it so deep."

"Didn't want it to run dry."

"And lined it with stone already," said the smith. "It's a wonderment, I say."

"I worked hard and fast."

"You also dug in the right place, I see."

Alvin took a deep breath. "The way I figure, sir, I dug right where the dowser said to dig."

"I saw another hole just yonder," said Makepeace Smith. "Stone as thick and hard as the devil's hoof all along the bottom. You telling me you don't aim for folks to guess why you dug there?"

"I filled that old hole up," said Alvin. "I wish I'd never dug such a well. I don't want nobody telling stories on Hank Dowser. There was water there, right enough, and no dowser in the world could've guessed about the stone."

"Except you," said Makepeace.

"I ain't no dowser, sir," said Alvin. And he told the lie again: "I just saw that his wand dipped over here, too."

Makepeace Smith shook his head, a grin just creeping out across his face. "My wife told me that tale already, and I like to died a-laughing at it. I cuffed your head for saying he was wrong. You telling me now you want him to get the credit?"

"He's a true dowser," said Alvin. "And I *ain't* no dowser, sir, so I reckon since he *is* one, he ought to get the name for it."

Makepeace Smith drew up the copper bucket, put it to his lips, and drank a few swallows. Then he tipped back his head and poured the rest of the water straight onto his face and laughed out loud. "That's the sweetest water I ever drunk in my life, I swear."

It wasn't the same as promising to go along with his story and let Hank Dowser think it was his well, but Al knew it was the best he'd get from his master. "If it's all right, sir," said Al, "I'm a mite hungry."

"Yes, go eat, you've earned it."

Alvin walked by him. The smell of new water rose up from the well as he passed.

Makepeace Smith spoke again behind him. "Gertie tells me you took first swallow from the well."

Al turned around, fearing trouble now. "I did, sir, but not till she give it to me."

Makepeace studied on that notion awhile, as if he was

deciding whether to make it reason for punishing Al or not. "Well," he finally said, "well, that's just like her, but I don't mind. There's still enough of that first dip in the wooden bucket for me to save a few swallows for Hank Dowser. I promised him a drink from the first bucket, and I'll keep my word when he comes back around."

"When he comes, sir," said Alvin, "and I hope you won't mind, but I think I'd like it best and so would he if I just didn't happen to be at home, if you see what I mean. I don't think he cottoned to me much."

The smith eyed him narrowly. "If this is just a way for you to get a few hours off work when that dowser comes on back, why"—he broke into a grin—"why, I reckon that you've earned it with last night's labor."

"Thank you sir," said Alvin.

"You heading back to the house?"

"Yes sir."

"Well, I'll take those tools and put them away—you carry this bucket to the missus. She's expecting it. A lot less way to tote the water than the stream. I got to thank Hank Dowser special for choosing this very exact spot." The smith was still chuckling to himself at his wit when Alvin reached the house.

Gertie Smith took the bucket, set Alvin down, and near filled him to the brim with hot fried bacon and good greasy biscuits. It was so much food that Al had to beg her to stop. "We've already finished one pig," said Alvin. "No need to kill another just for my breakfast."

"Pigs are just corn on the hoof," said Gertie Smith, "and you worked two hogs' worth last night, I'll say that."

Belly full and belching, Alvin climbed the ladder into the loft over the kitchen, stripped off his clothes, and burrowed into the blankets on his bed.

The Maker is the one who is part of what he makes.

Over and over he whispered the words to himself as he went to sleep. He had no dreams or troubles, and slept clear through till suppertime, and then again all night till dawn.

When he woke up in the morning, just before dawn, there was a faint grey scarce brighter than moonlight sifting into the house through the windows. Hardly none of it got up into the loft where Alvin lay, and instead of springing up bright like he did most mornings, he felt logey from sleep and a little sore from his labors. So he lay there quiet, a faint sort of birdsong chirping in the back of his mind. He didn't think on the phrase Arthur Stuart told him from Redbird's song. Instead he got to wondering how things happened yesterday. Why did hard winter turn to summertime again, just from him shouting?

"Summer," he whispered. "Warm air, leaves green." What was it about Alvin that when he said *summer,* summer came? Didn't always work that way, for sure—never when he was a-working the iron or slipping through stone to mend or break it. Then he had to hold the shape of it firm in his mind, understand the way things lined up, find the natural cracks and creases, the threads of the metal or the grain of the rock. And when he was a-healing, that was so hard it took his whole mind to find how the body ought to be, and mend it. Things were so small, so hard to see—well, not *see,* but whatever it was he did. Sometimes he had to work so hard to understand the way things were inside.

Inside, down deep, so small and fine, and always the deepest secrets of the way things worked skittered away like roaches when you bring a lamp into the room, always getting smaller, forming themselves up in strange new ways. Was there some particle that was smallest of all? Some place

at the heart of things where what he saw was real, instead
of just being made up out of lots of smaller pieces, and them
out of smaller pieces still?

Yet he hadn't understood how the Unmaker made winter. So how did his desperate cries make the summer come
back?

How can I be a Maker if I can't even guess how I do what
I do?

The light came stronger from outside, shining through
the wavering glass of the windows, and for a moment Alvin thought he saw the light like little balls flying so *fast,*
like they was hit with a stick or shot from a gun, only even
faster than that, bouncing around, most of them getting
stuck in the tiny cracks of the wooden walls or the floor or
the ceiling, so only a precious few got up into the loft where
they got captured by Alvin's eyes.

Then that moment passed, and the light was just fire, pure
fire, drifting into the room like the gentle waves washing
against the shore of Lake Mizogan, and wherever they
passed, the waves turned things warm—the wood of the
walls, the massive kitchen table, the iron of the stove—so
that they all quivered, they all danced with life. Only Alvin
could see it, only Alvin knew how the whole room awoke
with the day.

That fire from the sun, that's what the Unmaker hates
most. The life it makes. Put that fire out, that's what the Unmaker says inside himself. Put all fires out, turn all water
into ice, the whole world smooth with ice, the whole sky
black and cold like night. And to oppose the Unmaker's desire, one lone Maker who can't do right even when he's
digging a well.

The Maker is the one who is part of—part of what? What
do I make? How am I part of it? When I work the iron, am I

part of the iron? When I shiver stone, am I part of the stone? It makes no sense, but I got to make sense of it or I'll lose my war with the Unmaker. I could fight him all my days, every way I know how, and when I died the world would be farther along his downhill road than it was when I got born. There's got to be some secret, some key to everything, so I can build it all at once. Got to find that key, that's all, find the secret, and then I can speak a word and the Unmaker will shy back and cower and give up and die, maybe even die, so that life and light go on forever and don't fade.

Alvin heard Gertie begin to stir in the bedroom, and one of the children uttered a soft cry, the last noise before waking. Alvin flexed and stretched and felt the sweet delicious pain of sore muscles waking up, getting set for a day at the forge, a day at the fire.

10

GOODWIFE

Peggy did not sleep as long or as well as Alvin. His battle was over; he could sleep a victor's sleep. For her, though, it was the end of peace.

It was still midafternoon when Peggy tossed herself awake on the smooth linen sheets of her bed in Mistress Modesty's house. She felt exhausted; her head hurt. She wore only her shift, though she didn't remember undressing. She remembered hearing Redbird singing, watching Arthur Stuart interpret the song. She remembered looking into Alvin's heartfire, seeing all his futures restored to him—but still did not find herself in any of them. Then her memory stopped. Mistress Modesty must have undressed her, put her to bed with the sun already nearing noon.

She rolled over; the sheet clung to her, and then her back went cold from sweat. Alvin's victory was won; the lesson was learned; the Unmaker would not find another such opening again. She saw no danger in Alvin's future, not soon. The Unmaker would doubtless lie in wait for another time, or return to working through his human servants. Perhaps the Visitor would return to Reverend Thrower, or some other soul with a secret hunger for evil would receive the Unmaker as a welcome teacher. But that wasn't the danger, not the immediate danger, Peggy knew.

For as long as Alvin had no notion how to be a Maker or what to do with his power, then it made no difference how long they kept the Unmaker at bay. The Crystal City would never be built. And it must be built, or Alvin's life—and Peggy's life, devoted to helping him—both would be in vain.

It seemed so clear now to Peggy, coming out of a feverish exhausted sleep. Alvin's labor was to prepare himself, to master his own human frailties. If there was some knowledge somewhere in the world about the art of Making, or the science of it, Alvin would have no chance to learn it. The smithy was his school, the forge his master, teaching him—what?—to change other men only by persuasion and long-suffering, gentleness and meekness, unfeigned love and kindness. Someone else, then, would have to acquire that pure knowledge which would raise Alvin up to greatness.

I am done with all my schooling in Dekane.

So many lessons, and I have learned them all, Mistress Modesty. All so I would be ready to bear the title you taught me was the finest any lady could aspire to.

Goodwife.

As her mother had been called Goody Guester all these years, and other women Goody this or Goody that, any woman could have the name. But few deserved it. Few there were who inspired others to call her by the name in full: Goodwife, not just Goody; the way that Mistress Modesty was never called Missus. It would demean her name to be touched by a diminished, a common title.

Peggy got up from the bed. Her head swam for a moment; she waited, then got up. Her feet padded on the wooden floor. She walked softly, but she knew she would be heard; already Mistress Modesty would be coming up the stairs.

Peggy stopped at the mirror and looked at herself. Her hair was tousled by sleep, stringy with sweat. Her face was imprinted, red and white, with the creases in the pillowcase. Yet she saw there the face that Mistress Modesty had taught her how to see.

"Our handiwork," said Mistress Modesty.

Peggy did not turn. She knew her mentor would be there.

"A woman should know that she is beautiful," said Mistress Modesty. "Surely God gave Eve a single piece of glass, or flat polished silver, or at least a still pool to show her what it was that Adam saw."

Peggy turned and kissed Mistress Modesty on the cheek. "I love what you've made of me," she said.

Mistress Modesty kissed her in return, but when they drew apart, there were tears in the older woman's eyes. "And now I shall lose your company."

Peggy wasn't used to others guessing what *she* felt, especially when she didn't realize that she had already made the decision.

"Will you?" asked Peggy.

"I've taught you all I can," said Mistress Modesty, "but I know after last night that you need things that I never dreamed of, because you have work to do that I never thought that anyone could do."

"I meant only to be Goodwife to Alvin's Goodman."

"For me that was the beginning and the end," said Mistress Modesty.

Peggy chose her words to be true, and therefore beautiful, and therefore good. "Perhaps all that some men need from a woman is for her to be loving and wise and careful, like a field of flowers where he can play the butterfly, drawing sweetness from her blossoms."

Mistress Modesty smiled. "How kindly you describe me."

"But Alvin has a sturdier work to do, and what he needs is not a beautiful woman to be fresh and loving for him when his work is done. What he needs is a woman who can heft the other end of his burden."

"Where will you go?"

Peggy answered before she realized that she knew the answer. "Philadelphia, I think."

Mistress Modesty looked at her in surprise, as if to say, You've already decided? Tears welled in her eyes.

Peggy rushed to explain. "The best universities are there— free ones, that teach all there is to know, not the crabbed religious schools of New England or the effete schools for lordlings in the South."

"This isn't sudden," said Mistress Modesty. "You've been planning this for long enough to find out where to go."

"It *is* sudden, but perhaps I *was* planning, without knowing it. I've listened to others talk, and now there it is already in my mind, all sorted out, the decision made. There's a school for women there, but what matters is the libraries. I have no formal schooling, but somehow I'll persuade them to let me in."

"It won't take much persuasion," Mistress Modesty said, "if you arrive with a letter from the governor of Suskwahenny. And letters from other men who trust my judgment well enough."

Peggy was not surprised that Mistress Modesty still intended to help her, even though Peggy had determined so suddenly, so ungracefully to leave. And Peggy had no foolish notion of pridefully trying to do without such help. "Thank you, Mistress Modesty!"

"I've never known a woman—or a man, for that matter—with such ability as yours. Not your knack, remarkable as it is; I don't measure a person by such things. But I fear that you are wasting yourself on this boy in Hatrack River. How could any man deserve all that you've sacrificed for him?"

"Deserving it—that's his labor. Mine is to have the knowledge when he's ready to learn it."

Mistress Modesty was crying in earnest now. She still smiled—for she had taught herself that love must always smile, even in grief—but the tears flowed down her cheeks. "Oh, Peggy, how could you have learned so well, and yet make such a mistake?"

A mistake? Didn't Mistress Modesty trust her judgment, even now? " 'A woman's wisdom is her gift to women,' " Peggy quoted. " 'Her beauty is her gift to men. Her love is her gift to God.' "

Mistress Modesty shook her head as she listened to her own maxim from Peggy's lips. "So why do you intend to inflict your wisdom on this poor unfortunate man you say you love?"

"Because some men are great enough that they can love a whole woman, and not just a part of her."

"Is *he* such a man?"

How could Peggy answer? "He will be, or he won't have me."

Mistress Modesty paused for a moment, as if trying to find a beautiful way to tell a painful truth. "I always taught you that if you become completely and perfectly yourself, then good men will be drawn to you and love you. Peggy, let us say this man has great needs—but if you must become something that is *not* you in order to supply him, then you will not be perfectly yourself, and he will *not* love you. Isn't that why you left Hatrack River in the first place, so he would love you for yourself, and not for what you did for him?"

"Mistress Modesty, I want him to love me, yes. But I love the work he must accomplish even more than that. What I am today would be enough for the man. What I will go and do tomorrow is not for the man, it is for his work."

"But—" began Mistress Modesty.

Peggy raised an eyebrow and smiled slightly. Mistress Modesty nodded and did not interrupt.

"If I love his work more than I love the man, then to be perfectly myself, I must do what his work requires of me. Won't I, then, be even more beautiful?"

"To me, perhaps," said Mistress Modesty. "Few men have vision clear enough for *that* subtle beauty."

"He loves his work more than he loves his life. Won't he, then, love the woman who shares in it more than a woman who is merely beautiful?"

"You may be right," said Mistress Modesty, "for I have never loved work more than I have loved the person doing it, and I have never known a man who truly loved his work more than his own life. All that I have taught you is true in the world I know. If you pass from my world into another one, I can no longer teach you anything."

"Maybe I can't be a perfect woman and also live my life as it must be lived."

"Or perhaps, Mistress Margaret, even the best of the world is not fit to recognize a perfect woman, and so will accept me as a fair counterfeit, while you pass by unknown."

That was more than Peggy could bear. She cast aside decorum and threw her arms around Mistress Modesty and kissed her and cried, assuring her that there was nothing counterfeit about her. But when all the weeping was done, nothing had changed. Peggy was finished in Dekane, and by next morning her trunk was packed.

Everything she had in the world was a gift from Mistress Modesty, except for the box Oldpappy gave her long ago. Yet what was in that box was a heavier burden by far than any other thing that Peggy carried.

She sat in the northbound train, watching the mountains drift by outside her east-facing window. It wasn't all that long ago that Whitley Physicker had brought her to Dekane in his carriage. Dekane had seemed the grandest place at first; at the time it seemed to her that she was discovering the world by coming here. Now she knew that the world was far too large for one person to discover it. She was leaving a very small place and going to another very small place, and perhaps from there to other small places. The same size heartfires blazed in every city, no brighter for having so much company.

I left Hatrack River to be free of you, Prentice Alvin. Instead I found a larger, far more entangling net outside. Your work is larger than yourself, larger than me, and because I know of it I'm bound to help. If I didn't, I'd be a vile person in my own eyes.

So if you end up loving me or not, that doesn't matter all that much. Oh, yes, to *me* it matters, but the course of the world won't change one way or the other. What matters is that we both prepare you to do your work. Then if love comes, then if you can play Goodman to my Goodwife, we'll take that as an unlooked-for blessing and be glad of it as long as we can.

11

WAND

It was a week before Hank Dowser found his way back to Hatrack River. A miserable week with no profit in it, because try as he would he couldn't find decent dry ground for them folks west of town to dig their cellar. "It's all wet ground," he said. "I can't help it if it's all watery."

But they held him responsible just the same. Folks are like that. They act like they thought the dowser *put* the water where it sets, instead of just pointing to it. Same way with torches—blamed them half the time for *causing* what they saw, when all they did was see it. There was no gratitude or even simple understanding in most folks.

So it was a relief to be back with somebody half-decent like Makepeace Smith. Even if Hank wasn't too proud of the way Makepeace was dealing with his prentice boy. How could Hank criticize him? He himself hadn't done much better—oh, he was pure embarrassed now to think how he railed on that boy and got him a cuffing, and for nothing, really, just a little affront to Hank Dowser's pride. Jesus stood and took whippings and a crown of thorns in silence, but I lash out when a prentice mumbles a few silly words. Oh, thoughts like that put Hank Dowser in a dark mood, and he was aching for a chance to apologize to the boy.

But the boy wasn't there, which was too bad, though Hank didn't have long to brood about it. Gertie Smith took Hank Dowser up to the house and near jammed the food down his throat with a ramrod, just to get in an extra half-loaf of bread, it felt like. "I can't hardly walk," said Hank, which was true; but it was also true that Gertie Smith cooked just as good as her husband forged and that prentice boy shod and Hank dowsed, which is to say, with a true knack. Everybody has his talent, everybody has his gift from God, and we go about sharing gifts with each other, that's the way of the world, the best way.

So it was with pleasure and pride that Hank drank the swallows of water from the first clear bucket drawn from the well. Oh, it was fine water, sweet water, and he loved the way they thanked him from their hearts. It wasn't till he was out getting mounted on his Picklewing again that he realized he hadn't seen the well. Surely he should've seen the well—

He rounded the smithy on horseback and looked where he thought he had dowsed the spot, but the ground didn't appear like it had been troubled in a hundred years. Not even the trench the prentice dug while he was standing there. It took him a minute to find where the well actually was, sort of halfway between smithy and house, a fine little roof over the windlass, the whole thing finished with smooth-worked stone. But surely he hadn't been so near the house when the wand dipped—

"Oh, Hank!" called Makepeace Smith. "Hank, I'm glad you ain't gone yet!"

Where was the man? Oh, there, back in the meadow just up from the smithy, near where Hank had first looked for the well. Waving a stick in his hand—a forked stick—

"Your wand, the one you used to dowse this well—you want it back?"

"No, Makepeace, no thanks. I never use the same wand twice. Doesn't work proper when it isn't fresh."

Makepeace Smith pitched the wand back over his head, walked back down the slope and stood exactly in the place where Hank *thought* he had dowsed the well to be. "What do you think of the well house we built?"

Hank glanced back toward the well. "Fine stonework. If

you ever give up the forge, I bet there's a living for you in stonecutting."

"Why, thank you, Hank! But it was my prentice boy did it all."

"That's some boy you got," said Hank. But it left a bad taste in his mouth, to say those words. There was something made him uneasy about this whole conversation. Makepeace Smith meant something sly, and Hank didn't know rightly what it was. Never mind. Time to be on his way. "Good-bye, Makepeace!" he said, walking his nag back toward the road. "I'll be back for shoes, remember!"

Makepeace laughed and waved. "I'll be glad to see your ugly old face when you come!"

With that, Hank nudged old Picklewing and headed off right brisk for the road that led to the covered bridge over the river. That was one of the nicest things about the westbound road out of Hatrack. From there to the Wobbish the track was as sweet as you please, with covered bridges over every river, every stream, every rush and every rivulet. Folks were known to camp at night on the bridges, they were so tight and dry.

There must've been three dozen redbird nests in the eaves of the Hatrack Bridge. The birds were making such a racket that Hank allowed as how it was a miracle they didn't wake the dead. Too bad redbirds were too scrawny for eating. There'd be a banquet on that bridge, if it was worth the trouble.

"Ho there, Picklewing, my girl, ho," he said. He sat astride his horse, a-standing in the middle of the bridge, listening to the redbird song. Remembering now as clear as could be how the wand had leapt clean out of his hands and flung itself up into the meadow grass. Flung itself northeast of the spot he dowsed. And that's just where Makepeace Smith picked it up when he was saying good-bye.

Their fine new well wasn't on the spot he dowsed at all. The whole time he was there, they all were lying to him, pretending he dowsed them a well, but the water they drank was from another place.

Hank knew, oh yes, he knew who chose the spot they used. Hadn't the wand as much as told him when it flew off like that? Flew off because the boy spoke up, that smart-mouth prentice. And now they made mock of him behind his back, not saying a thing to his face, of course, but he knew that Makepeace was laughing the whole time, figuring he wasn't even smart enough to notice the switch.

Well, I noticed, yes sir. You made a fool of me, Make-peace Smith, you and that prentice boy of yours. But I noticed. A man can forgive seven times, or even seven times seven. But then there comes the fiftieth time, and even a good Christian can't forget.

"Gee-ap," he said angrily. Picklewing's ears twitched and she started forward in a gentle walk, new shoes clopping loud on the floorboards of the bridge, echoing from the walls and ceiling. "Alvin," whispered Hank Dowser. "Prentice Alvin. Got no respect for any man's knack except his own."

12

SCHOOL BOARD

When the carriage pulled up in front of the inn, Old Peg Guester was upstairs hanging mattresses half out the windows to let them air, so she saw. She recognized Whitley Physicker's rig, a new-fangled closed car that kept the weather and most of the dust out; Physicker could use a carriage like that, now that he could afford to pay a man just to drive for him. It was things like that carriage that had most folks calling him *Dr. Physicker* now, instead of just Whitley.

The driver was Po Doggly, who used to have a farm of his own till he got to likkering up after his wife died. It was a good thing, Physicker hiring him when other folks just thought of old Po as a drunk. Things like that made most plain folks think well of Dr. Physicker, even if he did show off his money more than was seemly among Christians.

Anyway, Po hopped down from his seat and swung around to open the door of the carriage. But it wasn't Whitley Physicker got out first—it was Pauley Wiseman, the sheriff. If ever a man didn't deserve his last name, it was Pauley Wiseman. Old Peg felt herself wrinkle up inside just seeing him. It was like her husband Horace always said— any man who *wants* the job of sheriff is plainly unfit for the office. Pauley Wiseman wanted his job, wanted it more than most folks wanted to breathe. You could see it in the way he wore his stupid silver star right out in the open, on the outside of his coat, so nobody'd forget they was talking to the man who had the keys to the town jail. As if Hatrack River needed a jail!

Then Whitley Physicker got out of the carriage, and Old Peg knew exactly what business they were here for. The school board had made its decision, and these two were come to make sure she settled for it without making any noise about it in public. Old Peg tossed the mattress she was holding, tossed it so hard it near to flew clean out the window; she caught it by a corner and pulled it back so it'd hang proper and get a good airing. Then she ran down the stairs— she wasn't so old yet she couldn't run a flight of stairs when she wanted. Downward, anyways.

She looked around a bit for Arthur Stuart, but of course he wasn't in the house. He was just old enough for chores, and he did them, right enough, but after that he was always off by himself, over in town sometimes, or sometimes bothering around that blacksmith boy, Prentice Alvin. "What you do that for, boy?" Old Peg asked him once. "What you always have to be with Prentice Alvin for?" Arthur just grinned and then put his arms out like a street rassler all set to grab and said, "Got to learn how to throw a man twice my size." What made it funny was he said it just exactly in Alvin's own voice, complete with the way Alvin would've said it—with a joke in his voice, so you'd know he didn't take himself all that serious. Arthur had that knack, to mimic folks like as if he knew them right to the soul. Sometimes it made her wonder if he didn't have something of the torchy knack, like her runaway daughter Little Peggy; but no, it didn't seem like Arthur actually understood what he was doing. He was just a mimic. Still, he was smart as a whip, and that's why Old Peg knew the boy deserved to be in school, probably more than any other child in Hatrack River.

She got to the front door just as they started in to knock. She stood there, panting a little from her run down the stairs, waiting to open it even though she saw their shadows through the lace-curtain windows on the door. They were kind of shifting their weight back and forth, like they was nervous—as well they should be. Let 'em sweat.

It was just like them folks on the school board, to send Whitley Physicker of all people. It made Old Peg Guester mad just to see his shadow at her door. Wasn't he the one who took Little Peggy off six years ago, and then wouldn't tell her where the girl went? Dekane was all he said, to folks she seemed to know. And then Peg's husband Horace reading the note over and over, saying, If a torch can't see her own future safe, none of us can look out for her any better. Why, if it hadn't been for Arthur Stuart needing her so bad, Old Peg would have up and left. Just up and left, and see how they liked that! Take her daughter away and tell her it's all for the best—such a thing to tell a mother! Let's see what they think when *I* leave. If she hadn't had Arthur to look after, she would have gone so fast her shadow would've been stuck in the door.

And now they send Whitley Physicker to do it again, to set her grieving over another child, just like before. Only worse this time, because Little Peggy really *could* take care of herself, while Arthur Stuart couldn't, he was just a six-year-old boy, a boy with no future at all unless Old Peg fought for it tooth and nail.

They knocked again. She opened the door. There was Whitley Physicker, looking all cheerful and dignified, and behind him Pauley Wiseman, looking all important and dignified. Like two masts on the same ship, with sails all puffed out and bossy-looking. All full of wind. Coming to tell me what's right and proper, are you? We'll see.

"Goody Guester," said Dr. Physicker. He doffed his hat proper, like a gentleman. That's what's wrong with Hatrack River these days, thought Old Peg. Too many folks putting on like gentlemen and ladies. Don't they know this is Hio? All the high-toned folks are down in the Crown Colonies with His Majesty, the other Arthur Stuart. The long-haired White king, as opposed to her own short-haired Black boy Arthur. Anybody in the state of Hio who thinks he's a gentleman is just fooling himself and nobody but the other fools.

"I suppose you want to come in," said Old Peg.

"I hoped you'd invite us," said Physicker. "We come from the school board."

"You can turn me down on the porch as easy as you can inside my house."

"Now see here," said Sheriff Pauley. He wasn't used to folks leaving him standing on porches.

"We didn't come to turn you down, Goody Guester," said the doctor.

Old Peg didn't believe it for a minute. "You telling me that stiff-necked bunch of high-collar hypocrites is going to let a Black child into the new school?"

That set Sheriff Pauley off like gunpowder in a bucket. "Well, if you're so all-fired sure you know the answer, Old Peg, why'd you bother asking the question?"

"Cause I wanted you all down on record as being Black-hating slavers in your hearts! Then someday when the Emancipationists have their way and Black people have all their rights everywhere, you'll have to wear your shame in public like you deserve."

Old Peg didn't even hear her husband coming up behind her, she was talking so loud.

"Margaret," said Horace Guester. "No man stands on my porch without a welcome."

"*You* welcome them yourself, then," said Old Peg. She turned her back on Dr. Physicker and Sheriff Pauley and walked on into the kitchen. "I wash my hands of it," she shouted over her shoulder.

But once she was in the kitchen she realized that she wasn't cooking yet this morning, she was doing the upstairs beds. And as she stood there, kind of confused for a second, she got to thinking it was Pontius Pilate who did that first famous hand-washing. Why, she'd confessed herself unrighteous with her own words. God wouldn't look kindly on her if she once started in imitating someone as killed the Lord Jesus, like Pilate did. So she turned around and walked back into the common room and sat down near the hearth. It being August there wasn't no fire in it, which made it a cool place to sit. Not like the kitchen hearth, which was hot as the devil's privy on summer days like this. No reason she should sweat her heart out in the kitchen while these two decided the fate of Arthur Stuart in the coolest spot in the house.

Her husband and the two visitors looked at her but didn't say a thing about her storming out and then storming back in. Old Peg knew what was said behind her back—that you might as well try to set a trap for a cyclone as to tangle with Old Peg Guester—but she didn't mind a bit if men like Whitley Physicker and Pauley Wiseman walked a little wary around her. After a second or two, waiting for her to settle down, they went right on with their talk.

"As I was saying, Horace, we looked at your proposal seriously," Physicker said. "It would be a great convenience to us if the new teacher could be housed in your roadhouse instead of being boarded here and there the way it usually happens. But we wouldn't consider having you do it for free. We have enough students enrolled and enough basis in the property tax to pay you a small stipend for the service."

"How much does a sty pen come to in money?" asked Horace.

"The details remain to be worked out, but the sum of twenty dollars for the year was mentioned."

"Well," said Horace, "that's a mite low, if you're thinking you're paying the actual cost."

"On the contrary, Horace, we know that we're underpaying you by considerable. But since you offered to do it free, we hoped this would be an improvement on the original offer."

Horace was all set to agree, but Peg wouldn't stand for all this pretending. "I know what it is, Dr. Physicker, and it's no improvement. We didn't offer to put up the schoolteacher for *free*. We offered to put up *Arthur Stuart*'s teacher for free. And if you figure twenty dollars is going to make me change my mind about that, you better go back and do your figuring again."

Dr. Physicker got a pained look on his face. "Now, Goody Guester. Don't get ahead of yourself on this. There was not a man on the school board who had any personal objection to having Arthur Stuart attend the new school."

When Physicker said that, Old Peg took a sharp look at Pauley Wiseman. Sure enough, he squirmed in his chair like he had a bad itch in a place where a gentleman doesn't scratch. That's right, Pauley Wiseman. Dr. Physicker can say what he likes, but *I* know *you*, and there was one, at least, who had all kinds of objections to Arthur Stuart.

Whitley Physicker went on talking, of course. Since he was pretending that everybody loved Arthur Stuart dearly, he couldn't very well take notice of how uncomfortable Sheriff Pauley was. "We know Arthur has been raised by the two oldest settlers and finest citizens of Hatrack River, and the whole town loves him for his own self. We just can't think what benefit a school education would give the boy."

"It'll give him the same benefit it gives any other boy or girl," said Old Peg.

"Will it? Will his knowing how to read and write get him a place in a counting house? Can you imagine that even if they let him take the bar, any jury would listen to a Black lawyer plead? Society has decreed that a Black child will grow up to be a Black man, and a Black man, like ancient Adam, will earn his bread by the sweat of his body, not by the labors of his mind."

"Arthur Stuart is smarter than any child who'll be in that school and you know it."

"All the more reason we shouldn't build up young Arthur's hopes, only to have them dashed when he's older. I'm talking about the way of the world, Goody Guester, not the way of the heart."

"Well why don't you wise men of the school board just say, To hell with the way of the world, we'll do what's right!

I can't make you do what you don't want to do, but I'll be damned if I let you pretend it's for Arthur's own good!"

Horace winced. He didn't like it to hear Old Peg swear. She'd only taken it up lately, beginning with the time she cussed Millicent Mercher right in public for insisting on being called "Mistress Mercher" instead of "Goody Mercher." It didn't sit well with Horace, her using those words, especially since she didn't seem to ken the time and place for it like a man would, or at least so he said. But Old Peg figured if you can't cuss at a lying hypocrite, then what was cussing invented for?

Pauley Wiseman started turning red, barely controlling a stream of his own favorite cusswords. But Whitley Physicker was now a gentleman, so he merely bowed his head for a moment, like as if he was saying a prayer—but Old Peg figured it was more likely he was waiting till he calmed down enough for his words to come out civil. "Goody Guester, you're right. We didn't think up that story about it being for Arthur's own good till after the decision was made."

His frankness left her without a word, at least for the moment. Even Sheriff Pauley could only give out a kind of squeak. Whitley Physicker wasn't sticking to what they all agreed to say; he sounded espiciously close to telling the truth, and Sheriff Pauley didn't know what to do when people started throwing the truth around loose and dangerous. Old Peg enjoyed watching Pauley Wiseman look like a fool, it being something for which old Pauley had a particular knack.

"You see, Goody Guester, we want this school to work proper, we truly do," said Dr. Physicker. "The whole idea of public schools is a little strange. The way they do schools in the Crown Colonies, it's all the people with titles and money who get to attend, so that the poor have no chance to learn or rise. In New England all the schools are religious, so you don't come out with bright minds, you come out with perfect little Puritans who all stay in their place like God meant them to. But the public schools in the Dutch states and Pennsylvania are making people see that in America we can do it different. We can teach every child in every wildwood cabin to read and write and cipher, so that we have a whole population educated enough to be fit to vote and hold office and govern ourselves."

"All this is well and good," said Old Peg, "and I recollect hearing you give this exact speech in our common room not three months ago before we voted on the school tax. What I can't figure, Whitley Physicker, is why you figure my son should be the exception."

At this, Sheriff Pauley decided it was time to put an oar in. And since the truth was being used so recklessly, he lost control of himself and spoke truthfully himself. It was a new experience, and it went to his head a little. "Begging your pardon, Old Peg, but there isn't a drop of your blood in that boy, so he's no-wise your son, and if Horace here has some part of him, it isn't enough to turn him White."

Horace slowly got to his feet, as if he was preparing to invite Sheriff Pauley outside to punch some caution into him. Pauley Wiseman must have known he was in trouble the second he accused Horace of maybe being the father of a half-Black bastard. And when Horace stood up so tall like that, Pauley remembered he wasn't no match for Horace Guester. Horace wasn't exactly a small man and Pauley wasn't exactly a large one. So old Pauley did what he always did when things got out of hand. He turned kind of sideways so his badge was facing straight at Horace Guester. Take a lick at me, that badge said, and you'll be facing a trial for assaulting an officer of the law.

Still, Old Peg knew that Horace wouldn't hit a man over a word; he hadn't even knocked down that river rat who accused Horace of unspeakable crimes with barnyard animals.

Horace just wasn't the kind to lose control of himself in anger. In fact, Old Peg could see that as Horace stood there, he'd already forgotten about his anger at Pauley Wiseman and was thinking over an idea.

Sure enough, Horace turned to Old Peg as if Wiseman didn't even exist. "Maybe we should give it up, Peg. It was fine when Arthur was a sweet little baby, but . . ."

Horace, who was looking right at Old Peg's face, he knew better than to finish his sentence. Sheriff Pauley wasn't half so bright. "He just gets blacker every day, Goody Guester."

Well, what do you say to that kind of thing, anyway? At least now it was plain what was going on—that it was Arthur Stuart's color and nothing else that was keeping him out of the new Hatrack River School.

Whitley Physicker sighed into the silence. Nothing that happened with Sheriff Pauley there ever went according to plan. "Don't you see?" said Physicker. He sounded mild and reasonable, which he was good at. "There's some ignorant and backward folks"—and at this he took a cool look at Sheriff Pauley—"who can't abide the thought of a Black child getting the same education as their own boys and girls. What's the advantage of schooling, they figure, if a Black has it the same as a White? Why, the next thing you know, Blacks would be wanting to vote or hold office."

Old Peg hadn't thought of that. It just never entered her mind. She tried to imagine Mock Berry being governor, and trying to give orders to the militia. There wasn't a soldier in Hio who'd take orders from a Black man. It'd be as unnatural as a fish jumping out of the river to kill him a bear.

But Old Peg wasn't going to give up so easy, just because Whitley Physicker made one point like that. "Arthur Stuart's a good boy," she said. "He wouldn't no more try to vote than I would."

"I know that," said Physicker. "The whole school board

knows that. But it's the backwoods people who won't know it. They're the ones who'll hear there's a Black child in the school and they'll keep their children home. And here we'll be paying for a school that won't be doing its job of educating the citizenry of our republic. We're asking Arthur to forgo an education that will do him no good anyway, in order to allow others to receive an education that will do them and our nation a great deal of good."

It all sounded so logical. After all, Whitley Physicker was a doctor, wasn't he? He'd even been to college back in Philadelphia, so he had a deeper understanding than Old Peg would ever have. Why did she think even for a moment that she could disagree with a man like Physicker and not be wrong?

Yet even though she couldn't think of a single argument against him, she couldn't get rid of a feeling deep in her guts that if she said yes to Whitley Physicker, she'd be stabbing a knife right into little Arthur's heart. She could imagine him asking her, "Mama, why can't I go to school like all my friends?" And then all these fine words from Dr. Physicker would fly away like she'd never heard them, and she'd just sit there and say, "It's because you're Black, Arthur Stuart Guester."

Whitley Physicker seemed to take her silence as surrender, which it nearly was. "You'll see," said Physicker. "Arthur won't mind not going to school. Why, the White boys'll all be jealous of *him,* when he can be outside in the sun while they're cooped up in a classroom."

Old Peg Guester knew there was something wrong with all this, that it wasn't as sensible as it sounded, but she couldn't think what it was.

"And someday things might be different," said Physicker. "Someday maybe society will change. Maybe they'll stop keeping Blacks as slaves in the Crown Colonies and

Appalachee. Maybe there'll be a time when . . ." His voice trailed off. Then he shook himself. "I get to wondering sometimes, that's all," he said. "Silly things. The world is the way the world is. It just isn't natural for a Black man to grow up like a White."

Old Peg felt a bitter hatred inside her when he said those words. But it wasn't a hot rage, to make her shout at him. It was a cold, despairing hate, that said, Maybe I *am* unnatural, but Arthur Stuart is my true son, and I won't betray him. No I won't.

Again, though, her silence was taken to mean consent. The men all got up, looking relieved, Horace most of all. It was plain they never figured Old Peg would listen to reason so fast. The visitors' relief was to be expected, but why was Horace looking so happy? Old Peg had a nasty suspicion and she knew at once that it had to be the truth— Horace Guester and Dr. Physicker and Sheriff Pauley had already worked things out between them before they ever come a-calling today. This whole conversation was pretend. Just a show put on to make Old Peg Guester happy.

Horace didn't want Arthur Stuart in school any more than Whitley Physicker or anybody else in Hatrack River.

Old Peg's anger turned hot, but now it was too late. Physicker and Pauley was out the door, Horace following on out after them. No doubt they'd all pat each other on the back and share a smile out of Old Peg's sight. But Old Peg wasn't smiling. She remembered all too clear how Little Peggy had done a Seeing for her that last night before she run off, a Seeing about Arthur Stuart's future. Old Peg had asked Little Peggy if Horace would ever love little Arthur, and the girl refused to answer. That *was* an answer, sure enough. Horace might go through the motions of treating Arthur like his own son, but in fact he thought of him as just a Black boy that his wife had taken a notion to care for. Horace was no papa to Arthur Stuart.

So Arthur's an orphan all over again. Lost his father. Or, rightly speaking, never had a father. Well, so be it. He's got two mothers: the one who died for him when he was born, and me. I can't get him in the school. I knew I couldn't, knew it from the start. But I can get him an education all the same. A plan for it sprung into her head all at once. It all depended on the schoolmistress they hired, this teacher lady from Philadelphia. With luck she'd be a Quaker, with no hate for Blacks and so the plan would work out just fine. But even if the schoolmistress hated Blacks as bad as a finder watching a slave stand free on the Canadian shore, it wouldn't make a bit of difference. Old Peg would find a way. Arthur Stuart was the only family she had left in the world, the only person she loved who didn't lie to her or fool her or do things behind her back. She wasn't going to let him be cheated out of anything that might do him good.

13

SPRINGHOUSE

Alvin first knew something was up when he heard Horace and Old Peg Guester yelling at each other up at the old springhouse. It was so loud for a minute there that he could hear them clear over the sound of the forge-fire and his own hammering. Then they quietened themselves down a mite, but by then Alvin was so curious he kind of laid off the hammer. Laid it right down, in fact, and stepped outside to hear better.

No, no, he wasn't *listening*. He was just going to the well to fetch more water, some to drink and some for the cooling barrel. If he happened to hear them somewhat, he couldn't be blamed, now, could he?

"Folks'll say I'm a bad innkeeper, making the teacher live in the springhouse instead of putting her up proper."

"It's just an empty building, Horace, and we'll put it to use. And it'll leave us the rooms in the inn for paying customers."

"I won't have that schoolmistress living off alone by herself. It ain't decent!"

"Why, Horace? Are you planning to make advances?"

Alvin could hardly believe his ears. Married people just didn't say such things to each other. Alvin half expected to hear the sound of a slap. But instead Horace must've just took it. Everybody said he was henpecked, and this was about all the proof a body'd need, to have his wife accuse him of hankering after adultery and him not hit her or even say boo.

"It doesn't matter, anyway," said Old Peg. "Maybe you'll have your way and she'll say no. But we'll fix it up, anyway, and offer it to her."

Horace mumbled something that Alvin couldn't hear.

"I don't care if Little Peggy *built* this springhouse. She's gone of her own free will, left without so much as a word to me, and I'm not about to keep this springhouse like a monument just because she used to come here when she was little. Do you hear me?"

Again Alvin couldn't hear what Horace said.

On the other hand, he could hear Old Peg right fine. Her voice just sailed right out like a crack of thunder. "You're telling *me* who loved who? Well let me tell you, Horace Guester, all your love for Little Peggy didn't keep her here, *did* it? But my love for Arthur Stuart is going to get him an education, do you understand me? And when it's all said and done, Horace Guester, we'll just see who does better at loving their children!"

There wasn't exactly a slap or nothing, but there was a slammed door which like to took the door of the springhouse off its hinges. Alvin couldn't help craning his neck a little to see who did the slamming. Sure enough, it was Old Peg stalking away.

A minute later, maybe even more, the door opened real slow. Alvin could barely make it out through the brush and leaves that had grown up between the well and the springhouse. Horace Guester came out even slower, his face downcast in a way Alvin had never seen him before. He stood there awhile, his hand on the door. Then he pushed it closed, as gentle as if he was tucking a baby into bed. Alvin always wondered why they hadn't tore down that springhouse years ago, when Alvin dug the well that finally killed the stream that used to go through it. Or at least why they never put it to some use. But now Alvin knew it had something to do with Peggy, that torch girl who left right before Alvin showed up in Hatrack River. The way Horace touched that door, the way he closed it, it made Alvin see for the first time how much a man might dote on a child of his, so that even when she was gone, the places that she loved were like holy ground to her old dad. For the first time Alvin wondered if he'd ever love a child of his own like that. And then he wondered who the mother of that child might be, and if she'd ever scream at him the way Old Peg screamed at Horace, and if he'd ever have at her the way Makepeace Smith had at his wife Gertie, him flailing with his belt and her throwing the crockery.

"Alvin," said Horace.

Well, Alvin like to died with embarrassment, to be caught staring at Horace like that. "I beg pardon, sir," said Alvin. "I shouldn't ought to've been listening."

Horace smiled wanly. "I reckon as you'd have to be a deaf mute not to hear that last bit."

"It got a mite loud," said Alvin, "but I didn't exactly go out of my way not to hear, neither."

"Well, I know you're a good boy, and I never heard of no one carrying tales from you."

The words "good boy" rankled a bit. Alvin was eighteen now, less than a year to being nineteen, long since ready to be a journeyman smith out on his own. Just because Makepeace Smith wouldn't release him early from his prenticeship didn't make it right for Horace Guester to call him a *boy*. I may be Prentice Alvin, and not a man yet afore the law, but no woman yells *me* to shame.

"Alvin," said Horace, "you might tell your master we'll be needing new hinges and fittings for the springhouse doors. I reckon we're fixing it up for the new schoolteacher to live here, if she wants."

So that was the way of it. Horace had lost the battle with Old Peg. He was giving in. Was that the way of marriage, then? A man either had to be willing to hit his wife, like Makepeace Smith, or he'd be bossed around like poor Horace Guester. Well, if that's the choices, I'll have none of it, thought Alvin. Oh, Alvin had an eye for girls in town. He'd see them flouncing along the street, their breasts all pushed up high by their corsets and stays, their waists so small he could wrap his great strong hands right around and toss them every which way, only he never thought of tossing or grabbing, they just made him feel shy and hot at the same time, so he looked down when they happened to look at him, or got busy loading or unloading or whatever business brought him into town.

Alvin knew what they saw when they looked at him, those town girls. They saw a man with no coat on, just in his shirt-sleeves, stained and wet from his labor. They saw a poor man who'd never keep them in a fine white clapboard house like their papa, who was no doubt a lawyer or a judge or a merchant. They saw him *low,* a mere prentice still, and him already more than eighteen years old. If by some miracle he ever married one such girl, he knew how it would be, her always looking down at him, always expecting him to give way for her because she was a lady.

And if he married a girl who was as low as himself, it would be like Gertie Smith or Old Peg Guester, a good cook or a hard worker or whatever, but a hellion when she didn't get her way. There was no woman in Alvin Smith's life, that was sure. He'd never let himself be showed up like Horace Guester.

"Did you hear me, Alvin?"

"I did, Mr. Horace, and I'll tell Makepeace Smith first off when I see him. All the fittings for the springhouse."

"And nice work, too," said Horace. "It's for the schoolmistress to live there." But Horace wasn't so whipped that he couldn't get a curl to his lip and a nasty tone to his voice as he said, "So she can give *private* lessons."

The way he said "private lessons" made it sound like it'd be a whorehouse or something, but Alvin knew right off, by putting things together, exactly who would be getting private lessons. Didn't everybody know how Old Peg had asked to have Arthur Stuart accepted at the school?

"Well, so long," said Horace.

Alvin waved him good-bye, and Horace ambled away along the path to the inn.

Makepeace Smith didn't come in that afternoon. Alvin wasn't surprised. Now that Alvin had his full mansize on him, he could do the whole work of the smithy, and faster and better than Makepeace. Nobody said aught about it, but Alvin noticed back last year that folks took to dropping in during the times when Makepeace *wasn't* at the forge.

They'd ask Alvin to do their ironwork quick-like, while they was there waiting. "Just a little job," they'd say, only sometimes the job wasn't all that little. And pretty soon Alvin realized that it wasn't just chance brought them by. They wanted *Alvin* to do the work they needed.

It wasn't because Alvin did anything peculiar to the iron, either, except a hex or two where it was called for, and every smith did that. Alvin knew it wouldn't be right to best his master using some secret knack—it'd be like slipping a knife into a rassling match. It'd just bring him trouble anyway, if he used his knack to give *his* iron any peculiar strength. So he did his work natural, with his own strong arm and good eye. He'd earned every inch of muscle in his back and shoulders and arms. And if people liked his work better than Makepeace Smith's, why, it was because Alvin was a better blacksmith, not because his knack gave him the advantage.

Anyhow, Makepeace must've caught on to what was happening, and he took to staying away from the forge more and more. Maybe it was because he knew it was better for business, and Makepeace was humble enough to give way before his prentice's skill—but Alvin never quite believed that. More likely Makepeace stayed away so folks wouldn't see how he snuck a look over Alvin's shoulder now and then, trying to figure out what Al did better than his master. Or maybe Makepeace was plain jealous, and couldn't bear to watch his prentice at work. Could be, though, that Makepeace was just lazy, and since his prentice boy was doing the work just fine, why *shouldn't* Makepeace go out to drink himself silly with the river rats down at Hatrack Mouth?

Or perhaps, by some strange twist of chance, Makepeace was actually ashamed of how he kept Alvin to his prentice contract even though Alvin was plainly ready to take to the road as a journeyman. It was a low thing for a master to hold a prentice after he knew his trade, just to get the benefit of his labor without having to pay him a fair wage. Alvin brought good money into Makepeace Smith's household, everybody knew that, and all the while Alvin stayed dirt poor, sleeping in a loft and never two coins in his pocket to make a jingle when he walked to town. Sure, Gertie fed him proper—best food in town, Al knew well, having eaten a bite now and then with one of the town boys. But good food wasn't the same thing as a good wage. Food you ate and it was gone. Money you could use to buy things, or to do things—to have *freedom.* That contract Makepeace Smith kept in the cupboard up to the house, the one signed by Alvin's father, it made Alvin a slave as sure any Black in the Crown Colonies.

Except for one difference. Alvin could count the days till freedom. It was August. Not even a year left. Next spring he'd be free. No slave in the South ever knew such a thing; nary such a hope would ever enter their heads. Alvin had thought on that often enough over the years, when he was feeling most put upon; he'd think, if they can keep on living and working, having no hope of freedom, then I can hold out for another five years, three years, one year, knowing that it'll come to an end someday.

Anyway, Makepeace Smith didn't show up that afternoon, and when Alvin finished his assigned work, instead of doing chores and cleaning up, instead of getting ahead, he went on up to the springhouse and took the measure of the doors and windows. It was a place built to keep in the cool of the stream, so the windows didn't open, but the schoolmistress wouldn't cotton to *that,* never having a breath of air, so Alvin took the measure there, too. Not that he exactly decided to make the new window frames himself, seeing how he wasn't no carpenter particularly, except what woodworking skill any man learns. He was just taking the measure of the place, and when he got to the windows he kept going.

He took the measure of a lot of things. Where a little pot-bellied stove would have to go, if the place was going to be warm in the winter; and figuring that, he also figured how to lay in the right foundation under the heavy stove, and how to put the flaring around the chimney, all the things it'd take to make the springhouse into a tight little cabin, fit for a lady to live in.

Alvin didn't write down the measures. He never did. He just knew them, now that he'd put his fingers and hands and arms into all the places; and if he forgot, and took the measure wrong somehow, he knew that in a pinch he could make it fit even so. It was a kind of laziness, he knew, but he got precious little advantage from his knack these days, and there was no shame in such small fidging.

Arthur Stuart wandered along when Al was just about done at the springhouse. Alvin didn't say nothing, nor did Arthur; you don't greet somebody who belongs where you are, you hardly notice them. But when Alvin needed to get the measure of the roof, he just said so and then tossed Arthur up onto the roof as easy as Peg Guester tossed the feather mattresses from the inn beds.

Arthur walked like a cat on top of the roof, paying no heed to being up so high. He paced off the roof and kept his own count, and when he was done he didn't even wait to make sure Alvin was ready to catch him, he just took a leap into the air. It was like Arthur believed he could fly. And with Alvin there to catch him below, why, it might as well be true, since Alvin had such arms on him that he could catch Arthur easy and let him down as gentle as a mallard settling onto a pond.

When Al and Arthur was done with measuring, they went back to the smithy. Alvin took a few bars of iron from the pile, het up the forge, and set to work. Arthur set in to pumping the bellows and fetching tools—they'd been doing this so long that it was like Arthur was Alvin's own prentice, and it never occurred to either of them that there was anything wrong with it. They just did this together, so smooth that to other folks it looked like a kind of dance.

A couple of hours later, Alvin had all the fittings. It should've taken less time by half, only for some reason Alvin got it into his head that he ought to make a lock for the door, and then he got it into his head that it ought to be a real lock, the kind that a few rich folks in town ordered from back east in Philadelphia—with a proper key and all, and a catch that shut all by itself when you closed the door, so you'd never forget to lock the door behind you.

What's more, he put secret hexes on all the fittings, perfect six-point figures that spoke of safety, and no one with harm in his heart being about to turn the lock. Once the lock was closed and fastened in place on the door, nobody'd see those hexes, but they'd do the work sure, since when Alvin made a hex the measure was so perfect it cast a network of hexes like a wall for many yards on every side.

It occurred to Alvin to wonder why a hex should work at all. Of course he knew why it was such a magical shape, being twice three; and he knew how you could lay hexes down on a table and they'd fit snug together, as perfect as squares, only stronger, woven not with warp and weft, but with warp and weft and hax. It wasn't like squares, which were hardly ever found in nature, being too simple and weak; there was hexes in snowflakes and crystals and honey-combs. Making a single hex was the same as making a whole fabric of hexes, so that the perfect hexes he hid up inside the lock would wrap all the way around the house, sealing it from outside harm as surely as if he forged a net of iron and wove it right in place.

But that didn't answer the question *why* it worked. Why his hidden hexes should bar a man's hand, turn a man's mind away from entering. Why the hex should invisibly repeat itself as far as it could, and the more perfect the hex, the farther the net it threw. All these years of puzzling things out, and he still knew so little. Knew so near to nothing that he despaired, and even now, holding the springhouse fittings in his hands, he wondered if in fact he shouldn't content himself to be a good smith and forget these tales of Makering.

With all his wondering and questioning, Alvin never did ask himself what should have been the plainest question of all. Why would a schoolmistress need such a perfectly hexed, powerful lock? Alvin didn't even try to guess. He wasn't thinking like that. Instead he just knew that such a lock was something fine, and this little house had to be as fine as he could make it. Later on he'd wonder about it, wonder if he knew even then, before he met her, what this schoolmistress would mean to him. Maybe he already had a plan in the back of his mind, just like Old Peg Guester did. But he sure didn't know about it yet, and that was the truth. When he made all those fancy fittings, with patterns cut in them so the door would look pretty, he most likely was doing it for Arthur Stuart; maybe he was halfway thinking that if the schoolmistress had a right pretty little place to live, she'd be more inclined to give Arthur Stuart his private lessons.

It was time to quit for the day, but Alvin didn't quit. He pushed all the fittings up to the springhouse in a wheelbarrow, along with a couple of other tools he figured to need, and some scrap tin for the flaring of the chimney. He worked fast, and without quite meaning to, he used his knack to smooth the labor. Everything fit first time; the doors rehung as nice as could be, and the lock fitted exactly to the inside face of the door, bolted on so tight that it'd never come off.

This was a door no man could force—easier to chop through the split-log wall than attack this door. And with the hexes inside, a man wouldn't dare to lift his axe against the house, or if he did, he'd be too weak to strike a telling blow—these were hexes that even a Red might not laugh at.

Al took another trip back to the shed outside the smithy and chose the best of the old broke-down pot-belly stoves that Makepeace had bought for the iron in them. Carrying a whole stove wasn't easy even for a man strong as a black-smith, but it was sure the wheelbarrow couldn't handle such a load. So Alvin hefted it up the hill by main strength. He left it outside while he brought stones from the old stream-bed to make a foundation under the floor at the place where the stove would go. The floor of the springhouse was set on beams running the length of the house inside, but they hadn't planked over the strip where the stream used to go—it wouldn't have been much of a springhouse if they covered over the cold water. Anyway he put a tight stone foundation under an upstream corner where the floor was done but not too high off the ground, and then bolted sheets of thin-beat iron on top of the planks to make a fireproof floor. Then he hefted the stove into place and piped it up to the hole he knocked in the roof.

He set Arthur Stuart to work with a rasp, tearing the dead moss off the inside of the walls. It came off easy, but it mostly kept Arthur distracted so he didn't notice that Alvin was fixing things on that brokedown stove that couldn't be fixed by a natural man. Good as new, and all fittings tight.

"I'm hungry," said Arthur Stuart.

"Get on up to Gertie and tell her I'm working late and please send food down for both of us, since you're helping."

Arthur Stuart took off running. Alvin knew that he'd deliver the message word for word, and in Alvin's own voice, so that Gertie'd laugh out loud and give him a good supper in a basket. Probably such a good supper that Arthur'd have to stop and rest three or four times on the way back, it'd be so heavy.

All this time Makepeace Smith never so much as showed his face.

When Arthur Stuart finally got back, Alvin was on the roof putting the final touch on the flaring, and fixing some of the shingles while he was up there. The flaring fit so tight water'd never get into the house, he saw to that. Arthur Stuart stood below, waiting and watching, not asking if he could go ahead and eat, not even asking how long till Alvin'd come down; he wasn't the type of child to whine or complain. When Alvin was done, he dropped over the edge of the roof, caught himself on the lip of the eaves, then dropped to the ground.

"Cold chicken be mighty good after a hot day's work," said Arthur Stuart, in a voice that was exactly Gertie Smith's, except pitched in a child's high voice.

Alvin grinned at him and opened the basket. They fell to eating like sailors who'd been on short rations for half the voyage, and in no time they was both lying there on their backs, bellies packed full, belching now and then, watching the white clouds move like placid cattle grazing across the sky.

The sun was getting low toward the west now. Definitely time to pack in for the day, but Alvin just couldn't feel good about that. "Best you get home," he said. "Maybe if you just run that empty basket back up to Gertie Smith's, you can get in without your Ma gets too upset at you."

"What you doing now?"

"Got windows to frame and re-hang."

"Well I got walls to finish rasping down," said Arthur Stuart.

Alvin grinned, but he also knew that what he planned to do to the windows wasn't a thing he wanted witnesses for. He had no intention of actually doing a lot of carpentry, and he didn't ever let anybody watch him do something *obvious* with his knack. "Best you go home now," said Alvin.

Arthur sighed.

"You been a good help to me, but I don't want you getting in trouble."

To Alvin's surprise, Arthur just returned his own words back to him in his own voice. "You been a good help to me, but I don't want you getting in trouble."

"I mean it," said Alvin.

Arthur Stuart rolled over, got up, came over and sat down astride of Alvin's belly—which Arthur often did, but it didn't feel none too comfortable at the moment, there being about a chicken and a half inside that belly.

"Come on, Arthur Stuart," said Alvin.

"I never told nobody bout no redbird," said Arthur Stuart.

Well, that just sent a chill right through Alvin. Somehow he'd figured that Arthur Stuart was just too young that day more than three years ago to even remember that anything happened. But Alvin should've knowed that just because Arthur Stuart didn't talk about something didn't mean that he forgot. Arthur never forgot so much as a caterpillar crawling on a leaf.

If Arthur Stuart remembered the redbird, then he no doubt remembered that day when it was winter out of season, when Alvin's knack dug a well and made the stone come clean of dirt without using his hands. And if Arthur Stuart knew all about Alvin's knack, then what point was there in trying to sneak around and make it secret?

"All right then," said Alvin. "Help me hang the windows."

Alvin almost added, "as long as you don't tell a soul what you see." But Arthur Stuart already understood that. It was just one of the things that Arthur Stuart understood.

They finished before dark, Alvin cutting into the wood of the window frames with his bare fingers, shaping what was just wood nailed into wood until it was windows that could slide free, up and down. He made little holes in the sides of the window frames and whittled plugs of wood to fit them, so the window would stay up as far as a body might want. Of course, he didn't quite whittle like a natural man, since each stroke of the knife took off a perfect arc. Each plug was done in about six passes of the knife.

Meantime Arthur Stuart finished the rasping, and then they swept out the house, using a broom of course, but Alvin helped with his knack so that every scrap of sawdust and iron filings and flakes of moss and ancient dust ended up outside the house. Only thing they didn't do was try to cover the strip of open dirt down the middle of the springhouse, where once the stream flowed. That'd take felling a tree to get the planks, and anyway Alvin was starting to get a little scared, seeing how much he'd done and how fast he'd done it. What if somebody came *tonight* and realized that all this work was done in a single long afternoon? There'd be questions. There'd be guesses.

"Don't tell anybody that we did this all in a day," said Alvin.

Arthur Stuart just grinned. He'd lost one of his front teeth recently, so there was a spot where his pink gums showed up. Pink as a White person's gums, Alvin thought. Inside his mouth he's no different from a White. Then Alvin had this crazy idea of God taking all the people in the world who ever died and flaying them and hanging up their bodies like pigs in the butcher's shop, just meat and bones hanging there by the heel, even the guts and the head gone, just meat. And then God would ask folks like the Hatrack River School Board to come in and pick out which was Black folks and which was Red and which was White. They couldn't do it. Then God would say, "Well why in hell did you say that this one and this one and this one couldn't go to school with this one and this one and this one?" What answer would they have then? Then God would say, "You people, you're all the same rare meat under the skin. But I tell you, I don't like your flavor. I'm going to toss your beefsteaks to the dogs."

Well, that was such a funny idea that Alvin couldn't help but tell it to Arthur Stuart, and Arthur Stuart laughed just as hard as Alvin. Only after it was all said and the laughing was done did Alvin remember that maybe nobody'd told Arthur Stuart about how his ma tried to get him into the school and the school board said no. "You know what this is all about?"

Arthur Stuart didn't understand the question, or maybe he understood it even better than Alvin did. Anyways, he answered, "Ma's hoping the teacher lady'll learn me to read and write here in this springhouse."

"Right," said Alvin. No point in explaining about the school, then. Either Arthur Stuart already knew how some White folks felt about Blacks, or else he'd find out soon enough without Alvin telling him now.

"We're all the same rare meat," said Arthur Stuart. He used a funny voice that Alvin had never heard before.

"Whose voice was that?" asked Alvin.

"God, of course," said Arthur Stuart.

"Good imitation," said Alvin. He was being funny.

"Sure is," said Arthur Stuart. He wasn't.

TURNED OUT NOBODY came to the springhouse for a couple of days and more. It was Monday of the next week when Horace ambled into the smithy. He came early in the morning, at a time when Makepeace was most likely to be there, ostentatiously "teaching" Alvin to do something that Alvin already knew how to do.

"*My* masterpiece was a ship's anchor," said Makepeace. "Course, that was back in Newport, afore I come west. Them ships, them whaling ships, they weren't like little bitty houses and wagons. They needed *real* ironwork. A boy like you, you do well enough out here where they don't know better, but you'd never make a go of it *there,* where a smith has to be a *man.*"

Alvin was used to such talk. He let it roll right off him. But he was grateful anyway when Horace came in, putting an end to Makepeace's brag.

After all the *good-mornings* and *howdy-dos,* Horace got right to business. "I just come by to see when you'll have a chance to get started on the springhouse."

Makepeace raised an eyebrow and looked at Alvin. Only then did Alvin realize that he'd never mentioned the job to Makepeace.

"It's already done, sir," Alvin said to Makepeace—for all the world as if Makepeace's unspoken question had been, "Are you finished yet?" and not, "What is this springhouse job the man's talking about?"

"Done?" said Horace.

Alvin turned to him. "I thought you must've noticed. I thought you were in a hurry, so I did it right off in my free time."

"Well, let's go see it," said Horace. "I didn't even think to look on my way down here."

"Yes, I'm dying to look at it myself," said the smith.

"I'll just stay here and keep working," said Alvin.

"No," said Makepeace. "You come along and show off this work you done in your *free time.*" Alvin didn't hardly notice how Makepeace emphasized the last two words, he was so nervous to show off what he done at the springhouse. He only barely had sense enough to drop the keys he made into his pocket.

They made their way up the hill to the springhouse. Horace was the kind of man who could tell when somebody did real good work, and wasn't shy to say so. He fingered the fancy new hingework and admired the lock afore he put in the key. To Alvin's pride it turned smooth and easy. The door swung open quiet as a leaf in autumn. If Horace noticed the hexes, he didn't let on. It was other things he noticed, not hexery.

"Why, you cleaned off the walls," said Horace.

"Arthur Stuart did that," said Alvin. "Rasped it off neat as you please."

"And this stove—I tell you, Makepeace, I didn't figure the price of a new stove in this."

"It isn't a new stove," said Alvin. "I mean, begging your pardon, but it was a brokedown stove we kept for the scrap, only when I looked it over I saw we could fix it up, so why not put it here?"

Makepeace gave Alvin a cool look, then turned back to Horace. "That don't mean it's free, of course."

"Course not," said Horace. "If you bought it for scrap, though . . ."

"Oh, the price won't be too terrible high."

Horace admired how it joined to the roof. "Perfect work," he said. He turned around. To Alvin he looked a little sad, or maybe just resigned. "Have to cover the rest of the floor, of course."

"Not our line of work," said Makepeace Smith.

"Just talking to myself, don't mind me." Horace went over to the east window, pushed against it with his fingers, then raised it. He found the pegs on the sill and put them into the third hole on each side, then let the window fall back down to rest against the pegs. He looked at the pegs, then out the window, then back at the pegs, for a long time. Alvin dreaded having to explain how he, not trained as a fine carpenter, managed to hang such a fine window. Worse yet, what if Horace guessed that this was the original window, not a new one? That could only be explained by Alvin's knack—no carpenter could get inside the wood to cut out a sliding window like that.

But all Horace said was, "You did some extra work."

"Just figured it needed doing," said Alvin. If Horace wasn't going to ask about how he did it, Alvin was just as happy not to explain.

"I didn't reckon to have it done so fast," said Horace. "Nor to have so much done. The lock looks to be an expensive one, and the stove—I hope I don't have to pay for all at once."

Alvin almost said, You don't have to pay for any of it, but of course that wouldn't do. It was up to Makepeace Smith to decide things like that.

But when Horace turned around, looking for an answer, he didn't face Makepeace Smith, he stood square on to Alvin. "Makepeace Smith here's been charging full price for your work, so I reckon I shouldn't pay you any less."

Only then did Alvin realize that he made a mistake when he said he did the work in his free time, since work a prentice did in his official free time was paid for direct to the prentice, and not the master. Makepeace Smith never gave Alvin free time—whatever work anyone wanted done, Makepeace would hire Alvin out to do, which was his right under the prentice contract. By calling it free time, Alvin seemed to be saying that Makepeace had given him time off to earn money for himself.

"Sir, I—"

Makepeace spoke up before Alvin could explain the mistake. "Full price wouldn't be right," said Makepeace. "Alvin getting so close to the end of his contract, I thought he should start trying things on his own, see how to handle money. But even though the work looks right to you, to me it definitely looks second rate. So half price is right. I figure it took at least twenty hours to do all this—right, Alvin?"

It was more like ten, but Alvin just nodded. He didn't know what to say, anyway, since his master was obviously not committed to telling the plain truth about this job. And the job he did would have been at least twenty hours—two full days' labor—for a smith without Alvin's knack.

"So," said Makepeace, "between Al's labor at half price and the cost of the stove and the iron and all, it comes to fifteen dollars."

Horace whistled and rocked back on his heels.

"You can have my labor free, for the experience," Alvin said.

Makepeace glared at him.

"Wouldn't dream of it," said Horace. "The Savior said the laborer is worthy of his hire. It's the sudden high price of iron I'm a little skeptical about."

"It's a *stove,*" said Makepeace Smith.

Wasn't till I fixed it, Alvin said silently.

"You bought it as scrap iron," said Horace. "As you said about Al's labor, full price wouldn't be right."

Makepeace sighed. "For old times' sake, Horace, cause you brought me here and helped set me up on my own when I came west eighteen years ago. Nine dollars."

Horace didn't smile, but he nodded. "Fair enough. And since you usually charge four dollars a day for Alvin's hire, I guess his twenty hours at *half* price comes to four bucks. You come by the house this afternoon, Alvin, I'll have it for you. And Makepeace, I'll pay you the rest when the inn fills up at harvest time."

"Fair enough," said Makepeace.

"Glad to see that you're giving Alvin free time now," said Horace. "There's been a lot of folks criticizing you for being so tight with a good prentice, but I always told them, Makepeace is just biding his time, you'll see."

"That's right," said Makepeace. "I was biding my time."

"You don't mind if I tell other folks that the biding's done?"

"Alvin still has to do his work for me," said Makepeace.

Horace nodded wisely. "Reckon so," he said. "He works for you mornings, for himself afternoons—is that right? That's the way most fair-minded masters do it, when a prentice gets so near to journeyman."

Makepeace began to turn a little red. Alvin wasn't surprised. He could see what was happening—Horace Guester was being like a lawyer for him, seizing on this chance to shame Makepeace into treating Alvin fair for the first time in more than six years of prenticing. When Makepeace decided to pretend that Alvin really *did* have free time, why, that was a crack in the door, and Horace was muscling his way through by main force. Pushing Makepeace to give Alvin half days, no less! That was surely too much for Makepeace to swallow.

But Makepeace swallowed. "Half days is fine with me. Been meaning to do that for some time."

"So you'll be working afternoons yourself now, right, Makepeace?"

Oh, Alvin had to gaze at Horace with pure admiration. He wasn't going to let Makepeace get away with lazing around and forcing Alvin to do all the work at the smithy.

"When I work's my own business, Horace."

"Just want to tell folks when they can be sure to find the master in, and when the prentice."

"I'll be in *all day*."

"Why, glad to hear it," said Horace. "Well, fine work, I must say, Alvin. Your master done a good job teaching you, and you been carefuler than I ever seen before. You make sure to come by this evening for your four dollars."

"Yes sir. Thank you, sir."

"I'll just let you two get back to work now," said Horace. "Are these the only two keys to the door?"

"Yes sir," said Alvin. "I oiled them up so they won't rust."

"I'll keep them oiled myself. Thanks for the reminder."

Horace opened the door and pointedly held it open till Makepeace and Alvin came on out. Horace carefully locked the door, as they watched. He turned and grinned at Alvin. "Maybe first thing I'll have you do is make a lock this fine for *my* front door." Then he laughed out loud and shook his head. "No, I reckon not. I'm an innkeeper. My business is to let people in, not lock them out. But there's others in town who'll like the look of this lock."

"Hope so, sir. Thank you."

Horace nodded again, then took a cool gaze at Makepeace as if to say, Don't forget all you promised to do here today. Then he ambled off up the path to the roadhouse.

Alvin started down the hill to the smithy. He could hear Makepeace following him, but Alvin wasn't exactly hoping for a conversation with his master just now. As long as Makepeace said nothing, that was good enough for Alvin.

That lasted only till they were both inside the smithy.

"That stove was broke to hell and back," said Makepeace.

That was the last thing Alvin expected to hear, and the most fearful. No chewing-out for claiming free time; no attempt to take back what he'd promised in the way of work schedule. Makepeace Smith had remembered that stove better than Alvin expected.

"Looked real bad, all right," said Alvin.

"No way to fix it without recasting," said Makepeace. "If I didn't know it was impossible, I would've fixed it myself."

"I thought so, too," said Alvin. "But when I looked it over—"

The look on Makepeace Smith's face silenced him. He knew. There was no doubt in Alvin's mind. The master knew what his prentice boy could do. Alvin felt the fear of being found out right down to his bones; it felt just like hide-and-go-find with his brothers and sisters when he was little, back in Vigor Church. The worst was when you were the last one still hid and unfound, all the waiting and waiting, and then you hear the footsteps coming, and you tingle all over, you feel it in every part of your body, like as if your whole self was awake and itching to move. It gets so bad you want to jump out and scream, "Here I am! I'm here!" and then run like a rabbit, not to the haven tree, but just anywhere, just run full out until every muscle of your body was wore out and you fell down on the earth. It was crazy—no good came of such craziness. But that's how it felt playing with his brothers and sisters, and that's how it felt now on the verge of being found out.

To Alvin's surprise, a slow smile spread across his master's face. "So that's it," said Makepeace. "That's it. Ain't you full of surprises. I see it now. Your pa said when you was born, he's the seventh son of a seventh son. Your way with horses, sure, I knew about that. And what you done finding that well, sense like a doodlebug, I could see *that,* too. But now." Makepeace grinned. "Here I thought you were a smith like never was born, and all the time you was fiddling with it like an alchemist."

"No sir," said Alvin.

"Oh, I'll keep your secret," said Makepeace. "I won't tell a soul." But he was laughing in the way he had, and Alvin knew that while Makepeace wouldn't tell straight out, he'd be dropping hints from here to the Hio. But that wasn't what bothered Alvin most.

"Sir," said Alvin, "all the work I ever done for *you*, I done honest, with my own arms and skill."

Makepeace nodded wisely, like he understood some secret meaning in Alvin's words. "I get it," he said. "Secret's safe with me. But I knew it all along. Knew you couldn't be as good a smith as you seemed."

Makepeace Smith had no idea how close he was to death. Alvin wasn't a murderous soul—any lust for blood that might have been born in him was driven out of him on a certain day inside Eight-Face Mound near seven years ago. But during all the years of his prenticeship, he had never heard one word of praise from this man, nothing but complaints about how lazy Alvin was, and how second-rate his work was, and all the time Makepeace Smith was lying, all the time he knew Alvin was good. Not till Makepeace was convinced Alvin had used hidden knackery to do his smithwork, not till now did Makepeace ever let Alvin know that he was, in fact, a good smith. Better than good. Alvin knew it, of course, knew he was a natural smith, but never having it said out loud hurt him deeper than he guessed. Didn't his master know how much a word might have meant, even half an hour ago, just a word like, "You've got some skill at this, boy," or, "You have a right good hand with that sort of work"? But Makepeace couldn't do it, had to lie and pretend Alvin had no skill until now, when Makepeace believed that he didn't have a smith's skill after all.

Alvin wanted to reach out and take hold of Makepeace's head and ram it into the anvil, ram it so hard that the truth would be driven right through Makepeace's skull and into his brain. I never used my Maker's knack in any of my smithwork, not since I got strong enough to do it with my own strength and skill, so don't smirk at me like I'm just a trickster, and no real smith. Besides, even if I used my

Maker's art, do you think that's easy, either? Do you think I haven't paid a price for that as well?

All the fury of Alvin's life, all these years of slavery, all these years of rage at the unfairness of his master, all these years of secrecy and disguise, all his desperate longing to know what to do with his life and having no one in the world to ask, all this was burning inside Alvin hotter than the forge fire. Now the itching and tingling inside him wasn't a longing to run. No, it was a longing to do violence, to stop that smile on Makepeace Smith's face, to stop it forever against the anvil's beak.

But somehow Alvin held himself motionless, speechless, as still as an animal trying to be invisible, trying not to be where he is. And in that stillness Alvin heard the greensong all around him, and he let the life of the woodland come into him, fill his heart, bring him peace. The greensong wasn't loud as it used to be, farther west in wilder times, when the Red man still sang along with the greenwood music. It was weak, and sometimes got near drowned out by the unharmonious noise of town life or the monotones of well-tended fields. But Alvin could still find the song at need, and sing silently along with it, and let it take over and calm his heart.

Did Makepeace Smith know how close he came to death? For it was sure he'd be no match for Alvin rassling, not with Al so young and tall and so much terrible righteous fire in his heart. Whether he guessed or not, the smile faded from Makepeace Smith's face, and he nodded solemnly. "I'll keep all I said, up there, when Horace pushed me so hard. I know you probably put him up to it, but I'm a fair man, so I'll forgive you, long as you still pull some weight here for me, till your contract's up."

Makepeace's accusation that Alvin conspired with Horace should have made Alvin angrier, but by now the green-song owned him, and Alvin wasn't hardly even in the smithy. He was in the kind of trance he learned when he ran with Ta-Kumsaw's Reds, where you forget who and where you are, and your body's just a far-off creature running through the woods.

Makepeace waited for an answer, but it didn't come. So he just nodded wisely and turned to leave. "I got business in town," he said. "Keep at it." He stopped at the wide doorway and turned back into the smithy. "While you're at it, you might as well fix those other brokedown stoves in the shed."

Then he was gone.

Alvin stood there a long time, not moving, not hardly even knowing he had a body to move. It was full noon before he came to himself and took a step. His heart was utterly at peace then, with not a spot of rage left in it. If he'd thought about it, he probably would've knowed that the anger was sure to come back, that he wasn't so much healed as soothed. But soothing was enough for now, it'd do. His contract would be up this spring, and then he'd be out of this place, a free man at last.

One thing, though. It never did occur to him to do what Makepeace Smith asked, and fix those other brokedown stoves. And as for Makepeace, he never brought it up again, neither. Alvin's knack wasn't a part of his prenticeship, and Makepeace Smith must've knowed that, deep down, must've knowed he didn't have the right to tell young Al what to do when he was a-Making.

A FEW DAYS later Alvin was one of the men who helped lay the new floor in the springhouse. Horace took him aside and asked him why he never came by for his four dollars.

Alvin couldn't very well tell him the truth, that he'd never take money for work he did as a Maker. "Call it my share of the teacher's salary," said Alvin.

"You got no property to pay tax on," said Horace, "nor any children to go to the school, neither."

"Then say I'm paying you for my share of the land my brother's body sleeps in up behind the roadhouse," said Alvin.

Horace nodded solemnly. "That debt, if there *was* a debt, was paid in full by your father's and brothers' labor seventeen year gone, young Alvin, but I respect your wish to pay your share. So this time I'll consider you paid in full. But any other work you do for me, you take full wages, you hear me?"

"I will, sir," said Alvin. "Thank you sir."

"Call me Horace, boy. When a growed man calls me sir it just makes me feel old."

They went back to work then, and said nary another word about Alvin's work on the springhouse. But something stuck in Alvin's mind all the same: what Horace said when Alvin offered to let his wages be a share of the teacher's salary. "You got no property, nor any children to go to the school." There it was, right there, in just a few words. That was why even though Alvin had his full growth on him, even though Horace called him a growed man, he wasn't really a man yet, not even in his own eyes. Because he had no family. Because he had no property. Till he had those, he was just a big old boy. Just a child like Arthur Stuart, only taller, with some beard showing when he didn't shave.

And just like Arthur Stuart, he had no share in the school. He was too old. It wasn't built for the likes of him. So why did he wait so anxious for the schoolmistress to come? Why did he think of her with so all-fired much hope? She wasn't coming here for him, and yet he knew that he had done his work on the springhouse for her, as if to put her in his debt, or perhaps to thank her in advance for what he wanted her, so desperately, to do for him.

Teach me, he said silently. I got a Work to do in this world, but nobody knows what it is or how it's done. Teach me. That's what I want from you, Lady, to help me find my way to the root of the world or the root of myself or the throne of God or the Unmaker's heart, wherever the secret of Making lies, so that I can build against the snow of winter, or make a light to shine against the fall of night.

14

RIVER RAT

Alvin was in Hatrack Mouth the afternoon the teacher came. Makepeace had sent him with the wagon, to fetch a load of new iron that come down the Hio. Hatrack Mouth used to be just a single wharf, a stop for riverboats unloading stuff for the town of Hatrack River. Now, though, as river traffic got thicker and more folks were settling out in the western lands on both sides of the Hio, there was a need for a couple of inns and shops, where farmers could sell provender to passing boats, and river travelers could stay the night. Hatrack Mouth and the town of Hatrack River were getting more important all the time, since this was the last place where the Hio was close to the great Wobbish Road—the very road that Al's own father and brothers cut through the wilderness west to Vigor Church. Folks would come downriver and unship their wagons and horses here, and then move west overland.

There was also things that folks wouldn't tolerate in Hatrack River itself: gaming houses, where poker and other games got played and money changed hands, the law not being inclined to venture much into the dens of river rats and other such scum. And upstairs of such houses, it was said there was women who wasn't ladies, plying a trade that decent folks scarcely whispered about and boys of Alvin's age talked of in low voices with lots of nervous laughter.

It wasn't the thought of raised skirts and naked thighs that made Alvin look forward to his trips to Hatrack Mouth. Alvin scarce noticed those buildings, knowing he had no business there. It was the wharf that drew him, and the porthouse, and the river itself, with boats and rafts going by all the time, ten going downstream for every one coming up. His favorite boats were the steamboats, whistling and spitting their way along at unnatural speeds. With heavy engines built in Irrakwa, these riverboats were wide and long, and yet they moved upstream against the current faster than rafts could float downstream. There was eight of them on the Hio now, going from Dekane down to Sphinx and back again. No farther than Sphinx, though, since the Mizzipy was thick with fog, and nary a boat dared navigate there.

Someday, thought Alvin, someday a body could get on such a boat as *Pride of the Hio* and just float away. Out to the West, to the wild lands, and maybe catch a glimpse of the place where Ta-Kumsaw and Tenskwa-Tawa live now. Or upriver to Dekane, and thence by the new steam train that rode on rails up to Irrakwa and the canal. From there a body could travel the whole world, oceans across. Or maybe he could stand on this bank and the whole world would someday pass him by.

But Alvin wasn't lazy. He didn't linger long at riverside, though he might want to. Soon enough he went into the porthouse and turned in Makepeace Smith's chit to redeem the iron packed in nine crates on the dock.

"Don't want you using my hand trucks to tote those, now," said the portmaster. Alvin nodded—it was always the same. Folks wanted iron bad enough, the portmaster included, and he'd be up to the smithy soon enough asking for this or that. But in the meantime, he'd let Alvin heft the iron all himself, and not let him wear out the portmaster's trucks moving such a heavy load. Nor did Makepeace ever give Alvin money enough to hire one of the river rats to help with the toting. Truth to tell, Alvin was glad enough of that. He didn't much like the sort of man who lived the river life. Even though the day of brigands and pirates was pretty much over, there being too much traffic on the water now for much to happen in secret, still there was thievery enough, and crooked dealing, and Alvin looked down hard on the men who did such things. To his way of thinking, such men counted on the trust of honest folks, and then betrayed them; and what could that do, except make it so folks would stop trusting each other at all? I'd rather face a man with raw fighting in him, and match him arm for arm, than face a man who's full of lies.

So wouldn't you know it, Alvin met the new teacher and matched himself with a river rat all in the same hour.

The river rat he fought was one of a gang of them lolling under the eaves of the porthouse, probably waiting for a gaming house to open. Each time Alvin came out of the porthouse with a crate of iron bars, they'd call out to him, taunting him. At first it was sort of good-natured, saying things like, "Why are you taking so many trips, boy? Just tuck one of those crates under each arm!" Alvin just grinned at remarks like that, since he knew that they knew just how heavy a load of iron was. Why, when they unloaded the iron from the boat yesterday, the boatmen no doubt hefted two men to a crate. So in a way, teasing him about being lazy or weak was a kind of compliment, since it was only a joke because the iron was heavy and Alvin was really very strong.

Then Alvin went on to the grocer's, to buy the spices Gertie had asked him to bring home for her kitchen, along with a couple of Irrakwa and New England kitchen tools whose purpose Al could only half guess at.

When he came back, both arms full, he found the river rats still loitering in the shade, only they had somebody new to taunt, and their mockery was a little ugly now. It was a middle-aged woman, some forty years old by Alvin's guess, her hair tied up severe in a bun and a plain hat atop it, her dark dress right up to the neck and down the wrist as if she was afraid sunlight on her skin might kill her. She was staring stonily ahead while the river rats had words at her.

"You reckon that dress is sewed on, boys?"

They reckoned so.

"Probably never comes up for no man."

"Why no, boys, there's nothing *under* that skirt, she's just a doll's head and hands sewed onto a stuffed dress, don't you think?"

"No way could she be a *real* woman."

"I can tell a real woman when I see one, anyway. The minute they lay eyes on me, *real* women just naturally start spreading their legs and raising their skirts."

"Maybe if you helped her out a little, you could turn her into a real woman."

"This one? This one's carved out of wood. I'd get splinters in my oar, trying to row in such waters."

Well, that was about all Alvin could stand to hear. It was bad enough for a man to think such thoughts about a woman who invited it—the girls from the gaming houses, who opened their necklines down to where you could count their breasts as plain as a cow's teats and flounced along the streets kicking up their skirts till you could see their knees. But this woman was plainly a lady, and by rights oughtn't to have to hear the dirty thoughts of these low men. Alvin figured she must be waiting for somebody to fetch her—the stagecoach to Hatrack River was due, but not for a couple of hours yet. She didn't look fearful—she probably knew these men was more brag than action, so her virtue was safe enough. And from her face Alvin couldn't guess whether she was even listening, her expression was so cold and faraway. But the river rats' words embarrassed *him* so much he couldn't stand it, and couldn't feel right about just driving his wagon off and leaving her there. So he put the parcels he got from the port grocer into the wagon and then walked up to the river rats and spoke to the loudest and crudest talker among them.

"Maybe you'd best speak to her like a lady," said Alvin. "Or perhaps not speak to her at all."

Alvin wasn't surprised to see the glint these boys all got in their eyes the minute he spoke. Provoking a lady was one kind of fun, but he knew they were sizing him up now to see how easy he'd be to whup. They always loved a chance to teach a lesson to a town boy, even one built up as strong as Alvin was, him being a blacksmith.

"Maybe you'd best not speak to us at all," said the loud one. "Maybe you already said more than you ought."

One of the river rats didn't understand, and thought the game was still talking dirty about the lady. "He's just jealous. He wants to pole her muddy river himself."

"I haven't said enough," said Alvin, "not while you still don't have the manners to know how to speak to a lady."

Only now did the lady speak for the first time. "I don't need protection, young man," she said. "Just go along, please." Her voice was strange-sounding. Cultured, like

Reverend Thrower, with all the words clear. Like people who went to school in the East.

It would have been better for her not to speak, since the sound of her voice only encouraged the river rats.

"Oh, she's sweet on this boy!"

"She's making a move on him!"

"He wants to row our boat!"

"Let's show her who the real man is!"

"If she wants his little mast, let's cut it off and give it to him."

A knife appeared, then another. Didn't she know enough to keep her mouth shut? If they dealt with Alvin alone, they'd set up to have a single fight, one to one. But if they got to showing off for her, they'd be happy enough to gang up on him and cut him bad, maybe kill him, certainly take an ear or his nose or, like they said, geld him.

Alvin glared at her for a moment, silently telling her to shut her mouth. Whether she understood his look or just figured things out for herself or got plain scared to say more, she didn't offer any more conversation, and Alvin set to turning things in a direction he could handle.

"Knives," said Alvin, with all the contempt he could muster. "So you're afraid to face a blacksmith with bare hands?"

They laughed at him, but the knives got pulled back and put away.

"Blacksmith's *nothing* compared to the muscles we get poling the river."

"You don't pole the river no more, boys, and everybody knows that," said Alvin. "You just set back and get fat, watching the paddlewheel push the boat along."

The loudest talker got up and stepped out, pulling his filthy shirt off over his head. He was strongly muscled, all right, with more than a few scars making white and red marks here and there on his chest and arms. He was also missing an ear.

"From the look of you," said Alvin, "you've fought a lot of men."

"Damn straight," said the river rat.

"And from the look of you, I'd say most of them was better than you."

The man turned red, blushing under his tan clear down to his chest.

"Can't you give me somebody who's worth rassling? Somebody who mostly *wins* his fights?"

"I win my fights!" shouted the man—getting mad, so he'd be easy to lick, which was Al's plan. But the others, they started pulling him back.

"The blacksmith boy's right, you're no great shakes at rassling."

"Give him what he wants."

"Mike, you take this boy."

"He's yours, Mike."

From the back—the shadiest spot, where he'd been sitting on the only chair with a back to it—a man stood up and stepped forward.

"I'll take this boy," he said.

At once the loud one backed off and got out of the way. This wasn't what Alvin wanted at all. The man they called Mike was bigger and stronger than any of the others, and as he stripped his shirt off, Al saw that while he had a scar or two, he was mostly clean, and he had both his ears, a sure sign that if he ever lost a rassling match, he sure never lost *bad*.

He had muscles like a buffalo.

"My name is Mike Fink!" he bellowed. "And I'm the meanest, toughest son-of-a-bitch ever to walk on the water!

I can orphan baby alligators with my bare hands! I can throw a live buffalo up onto a wagon and slap him upside the head until he's dead! If I don't like the bend of a river, I grab ahold of the end of it and give it a shake to straighten it out! Every woman I ever put down come up with triplets, if she come up at all! When I'm done with you, boy, your hair will hang down straight on both sides cause you won't have no more ears. You'll have to sit down to piss, and you'll never have to shave again!"

All the time Mike Fink was making his brag, Alvin was taking off his shirt and his knife belt and laying them on the wagon seat. Then he marked a big circle in the dirt, making sure he looked as calm and relaxed as if Mike Fink was a spunky seven-year-old boy, and not a man with murder in his eyes.

So when Fink was shut of boasting, the circle was marked. Fink walked to the circle, then rubbed it out with his foot, raising a dust. He walked all around the circle, rubbing it out. "I don't know who taught you how to rassle, boy," he said, "but when you rassle *me,* there ain't no lines and there ain't no rules."

Once again the lady spoke up. "Obviously there are no rules when you speak, either, or you'd know that the word *ain't* is a sure sign of ignorance and stupidity."

Fink turned to the woman and made as if to speak. But it was like he knew he had nothing to say, or maybe he figured that whatever he said would make him sound more ignorant. The contempt in her voice enraged him, but it also made him doubt himself. At first Alvin thought the lady was making it more dangerous for him, meddling again. But then he realized that she was doing to Fink what Alvin had tried to do to the loudmouth—make him mad enough to fight stupid. Trouble was, as Alvin sized up the river man, he suspected that Fink didn't fight stupid when he was mad—it just made him fight meaner. Fight to kill. Act out his brag about taking off parts of Alvin's body. This wasn't going to be a friendly match like the ones Alvin had in town, where the game was just to throw the other man, or if they was fighting on grass, to pin him down.

"You're not so much," Alvin said, "and you know it, or you wouldn't have a knife hid in your boot."

Fink looked startled, then grinned. He pulled up his pantleg and took a long knife out of his boot, tossed it to the men behind him. "I won't need a knife to fight *you*," he said.

"Then why don't you take the knife out of the *other* boot?" asked Alvin.

Fink frowned and raised the other pantleg. "Ain't no knife here," he said.

Alvin knew better, of course, and it pleased him that Fink was worried enough about this fight not to part with his most secret knife. Besides which, probably nobody else knew about that knife but Alvin, with his ability to see what others couldn't see. Fink didn't want to let on to the others that he had such a knife, or word would spread fast along the river and he'd get no advantage from it.

Still, Alvin couldn't afford to let Fink fight with the knife on him. "Then take off the boots and we'll fight barefoot," Alvin said. It was a good idea anyway, knife or no knife. Alvin knew that when the river rats fought, they kicked like mules with their boots. Fighting barefoot might take some of the spunk out of Mike Fink.

But if Fink lost any spunk, he didn't show it. Just sat down in the dust of the road and pulled off his boots. Alvin did the same, and his socks too—Fink didn't wear socks. So now the two of them had on nothing but their trousers, and already out in the sunlight there was enough dust and sweat that their bodies were looking a little streaked and cakey with clay.

Not so caked up, though, that Alvin couldn't feel a hex of protection drawn over Mike Fink's whole body. How could such a thing be? Did he have a hex on some amulet in his pocket? The pattern was strongest near his backside, but when Alvin sent his bug to search that pocket, there was nothing but the rough cotton canvas of Fink's trousers. He wasn't carrying so much as a coin.

By now a crowd was gathered. Not just the river rats who'd been resting in the porthouse shade, but a whole slew of others, and it was plain they all expected Mike Fink to win. He must be something of a legend on the river, Alvin realized, and no surprise, with this mysterious hex he had. Alvin could imagine folks poking a knife at Fink, only to twist at the last moment, or lose their grip, or somehow keep the knife from doing harm. It was a lot easier to win all your wrassling if no man's teeth could bite into you, and if a knife couldn't do much more than graze your skin.

Fink tried all the obvious stuff first, of course, because it made the best show: Roaring, rushing at Alvin like a buffalo, trying to get a bear hug on him, trying to grab onto Alvin and give him a swing like a rock on a string. But Alvin wouldn't have none of that. He didn't even have to use knackery to get away, neither. He was younger and quicker than Fink, and the river man hardly so much as laid a hand on him, Al dodged away so sudden. At first the crowd hooted and called Alvin coward. But after a while of this, they began to laugh at Fink, since he looked so silly, rushing and roaring and coming up empty all the time.

In the meantime, Alvin was exploring to find the source of Fink's hex, for there was no hope of winning this fight if he couldn't get rid of that strong web. He found it soon enough—a pattern of dye embedded deep in the skin of Fink's buttock. It wasn't a perfect hex anymore, since the skin had changed shape somewhat as Fink grew over the years, but it was a clever pattern, with strong locks and links—good enough to cast a strong net over him, even if it was misshapen.

If he hadn't been in the middle of a rassling match with Fink, Alvin might have been more subtle, might have just weakened the hex a little, for he had no will to deprive Fink of the hex that had protected him for so long. Why, Fink might die of it, losing his hex, especially if he had let himself get careless, counting on it to protect him. But what choice did Alvin have? So he made the dyes in Fink's skin start to flow, seeping into his bloodstream and getting carried away. Alvin could do without full concentration—just set it to happening and let it glide on, while he worked on dodging out of Fink's way.

Soon enough Al could sense the hex weakening, fading, finally collapsing completely. Fink wouldn't know it, but Alvin did—he could now be hurt like any other man.

By this time, though, Fink was no longer making those rough and stupid rushes at him. He was circling, feinting, looking to grapple in a square, then use his greater bulk to throw Alvin. But Alvin had a longer reach, and there was no doubt his arms were stronger, so whenever Fink reached to grab, Alvin batted the river man's arms out of the way.

With the hex gone, however, Alvin didn't slap him away. Instead, he reached inside Fink's arms, so that as Fink grasped his arms, Alvin got his hands hooked behind Fink's neck.

Alvin pulled down hard, bowing Fink down so his head was even with Alvin's chest. It was too easy—Fink was letting him, and Alvin guessed why. Sure enough, Fink pulled Alvin closer and brought his head up fast, expecting to catch Alvin on the chin with the back of his head. He was so strong he might've broke Alvin's neck doing that—only Alvin's chin wasn't where Fink thought it would be. In fact, Alvin had already rared his own head back, and when Fink came up hard and out of control, Alvin rammed forward and smashed his forehead into Fink's face. He could feel Fink's nose crumple under the blow, and blood erupted down both their faces.

It wasn't all that surprising, for a man's nose to get broke during a rassle like this. It hurt like blazes, of course, and it would've stopped a friendly match—though of course a friendly match wouldn't have included head butts. Any other river rat would've shook his head, roared a couple of times, and charged back into the fight.

Instead, Fink backed away, a look of real surprise on his face, his hands gripping his nose. Then he let out a howl like a whupped dog.

Everybody else fell silent. It was such a funny thing to happen, a river rat like Mike Fink howling at a broke-up nose. No, it wasn't rightly funny, but it was strange. It wasn't how a river rat was supposed to act.

"Come on, Mike," somebody murmured.

"You can take him, Mike."

But it was a half-hearted sort of encouragement. They'd never seen Mike Fink act hurt or scared before. He wasn't good at hiding it, either. Only Al knew why. Only Al knew that Mike Fink had never in his life felt such a pain, that Fink had never once shed his own blood in a fight. So many times he'd broke the other fellow's nose and laughed at the pain—it was easy to laugh, because he didn't know how it felt. Now he knew. Trouble was, he was learning what others learned at six years old, and so he was acting like a six-year-old. Not crying, exactly, but howling.

For a minute Alvin thought that maybe the match was over. But Fink's fear and pain soon turned to rage, and he waded back into the fight. Maybe he'd learned pain, but he hadn't learned caution from it.

So it took a few more holds, a few more wrenches and

PRENTICE ALVIN • 213

twists, before Alvin got Fink down onto the ground. Even as frightened and surprised as Fink was, he was the strongest man Alvin had ever rassled. Till this fight with Fink, Alvin had never really had occasion to find out just how strong he was; he'd never been pushed to his limit. Now he was, and he found himself rolling over and over in the dust, hardly able to breathe it was so thick, Fink's own hot panting breath now above him, now below, knees ramming, arms pounding and gripping, feet scrabbling in the dust, searching for purchase enough to get leverage.

In the end it came down to Fink's inexperience with weakness. Since no man could ever break a bone of his, Fink had never learned to tuck his legs, never learned not to expose them to where a man could stomp them. When Alvin broke free and scrambled to his feet, Fink rolled over quick and, for just a moment, lying there on the ground, he drew one leg across the other like a pure invitation. Alvin didn't even think, he just jumped into the air and came down with both feet onto Fink's top leg, jamming downward with all his weight, so the bones of the top leg were bowed over the lower one. So sharp and hard was the blow that it wasn't just the top leg that shattered, but the bottom one, too. Fink screamed like a child in the fire.

Only now did Alvin realize what he'd done. Oh, yes, of course he'd ended the fight—nobody's tough enough to fight on with two broken legs. But Alvin could tell at once, without looking—or at least without looking with his *eyes*—that these were not clean breaks, not the kind that can heal easy. Besides, Fink wasn't a young man now, and sure he wasn't a boy. If these breaks healed at all, they'd leave him lame at best, outright crippled at the worst. His livelihood would be gone. Besides, he must have made a lot of enemies over the years. What would they do now, with him broken and halt? How long would he live?

So Alvin knelt on the ground beside where Mike Fink writhed—or rather, the upper half of him writhed, while he tried to keep his legs from moving at all—and touched the legs. With his hands in contact with Fink's body, even through the cloth of his pants, Alvin could find his way easier, work faster, and in just a few moments, he had knitted the bones together. That was all he tried to do, no more— the bruise, the torn muscle, the bleeding, he had to leave that or Fink might get up and attack him again.

He pulled his hands away, and stepped back from Fink. At once the river rats gathered around their fallen hero.

"Is his legs broke?" asked the loudmouth river rat.

"No," said Alvin.

"They're broke to pieces!" howled Fink.

By then, another man had slit right up the pantleg. Sure enough he found the bruise, but as he felt along the bone, Fink screeched and pulled away. "Don't touch it!"

"Didn't feel broke to me," said the man.

"Look how he's moving his legs. They ain't broke."

It was true enough—Fink was no longer writhing with just the top half of his body, his legs were wiggling now as much as any other part of him.

One man helped Fink to his feet. Fink staggered, almost fell, caught himself by leaning against the loudmouth, smearing blood from his nose on the man's shirt. The others pulled away from him.

"Just a boy," muttered one.

"Howling like a puppydog."

"Big old baby."

"Mike *Fink*." And then a chuckle.

Alvin stood by the wagon, putting on his shirt, then sat up on the wagon seat to pull on his shoes and socks. He glanced up to find the lady watching him. She stood not six feet off, since the smith's wagon was pulled right up against the loading dock. She had a look of sour distaste. Alvin realized she was probably disgusted at how dirty he was. Maybe he shouldn't have put his shirt right back on, but then, it was also impolite to go shirtless in front of a lady. In fact, the town men, especially the doctors and lawyers, they acted ashamed to be out in public without a proper coat and waistcoat and cravat. Poor folks usually didn't have such clothes, and a prentice would be putting on airs to dress like that. But a shirt—he had to have his shirt on, whether he was filthy with dust or not.

"Beg pardon, Ma'am," he said. "I'll wash when I get home."

"Wash?" she asked. "And when you do, will your brutality also wash away?"

"I reckon I don't know, since I never heard that word."

"I daresay you haven't," she said. "Brutality. From the word *brute*. Meaning beast."

Alvin felt himself redden with anger. "Maybe so. Maybe I should've let them go on talking to you however they liked."

"I paid no attention to them. They didn't bother me. You had no need to protect me, especially not that way. Stripping naked and rolling around in the dirt. You're covered with blood."

Alvin hardly knew what to answer, she was so snooty and bone-headed. "I wasn't naked," Alvin said. Then he grinned. "And it was *his* blood."

"And are you proud of that?"

Yes, he was. But he knew that if he said so, it would diminish him in her sight. Well, what of that? What did he care what she thought of him? Still, he said nothing.

In the silence between them, he could hear the river rats behind him, hooting at Fink, who wasn't howling anymore, but wasn't saying much, either. It wasn't just Fink they were thinking about now, though.

"Town boy thinks he's tough."

"Maybe we ought to show him a *real* fight."

"Then we'll see how uppity his ladyfriend is."

Alvin couldn't rightly tell the future, but it didn't take no torch to guess at what was going to happen. Al's boots were on, his horse was full-hitched, and it was time to go. But snooty as she was, he couldn't leave the lady behind. He knew she'd be the river rats' target now, and however little she thought she needed protection, he knew that these river men had just watched their best man get whupped and humbled, and all on account of her, which meant she'd likely end up lying in the dirt with her bags all dumped in the river, if not worse.

"Best you get in," Alvin said.

"I wonder that you dare to give me instructions like a common—What are you doing?"

Alvin was tossing her trunk and bags into the back of the wagon. It seemed so obvious to him that he didn't bother answering her.

"I think you're robbing me, sir!"

"I am if you don't get in," said Alvin.

By now the river rats were gathering near the wagon, and one of them had hold of the horse's harness. She glanced around, and her angry expression changed. Just a little. She stepped from the dock onto the wagon seat. Alvin took her hand and helped her arrange herself on the seat. By now, the loudmouth river rat was standing beside him, leaning on the wagon, grinning wickedly. "You beat one of us, blacksmith, but can you beat us all?"

Alvin just stared at him. He was concentrating on the man holding the horse, making his hand suddenly tingle with pain, like he was being punctured with a hundred pins. The man cried out and let go the horse. The loudmouth looked away from Alvin, toward the sound of the cry, and in the moment Alvin kicked him in the ear with his boot. It wasn't much of a kick, but then, it wasn't much of an ear, either, and the man ended up sitting in the dirt, holding his head.

"Gee-yap!" shouted Alvin.

The horse obediently lunged forward—and the wagon moved about an inch. Then another inch. Hard to get a wagonload of iron moving fast, at least all of a sudden. Alvin made the wheels turn smooth and easy, but he couldn't do a thing about the weight of the wagon or the strength of the horse. By the time the horse got moving, the wagon was a good deal heavier, with the weight of river rats hanging on it, pulling back, climbing aboard.

Alvin turned around and swung his whip at them. The whip was for show—it didn't hit a one. Still, they all fell off or let go of the wagon as if it *had* hit them, or scared them anyway. What really happened was that all of a sudden the wood of the wagon got as slick as if it was greased. There was no way for them to hold onto it. So the wagon lurched forward as they collapsed back into the dust of the road.

They weren't done, though. After all, Alvin had to turn around and head back *up* the road right past them in order to get to Hatrack River. He was trying to figure what to do next when he heard a musket go off, loud as a cannonshot, the sound hanging on in the heavy summer air. When he got the wagon turned around, he saw the portmaster standing on the dock, his wife behind him. He was holding one musket, and she was reloading the one he had just fired.

"I reckon we get along well enough most of the time, boys," said the portmaster. "But today you just don't seem to know when you been beat fair and square. So I guess it's about time you settled down in the shade, cause if you make another move toward that wagon, them as don't die from buckshot'll be standing trial in Hatrack River, and if you think you won't pay dear for assaulting a local boy and the new schoolteacher, then you really are as dumb as you look."

It was quite a little speech, and it worked better than most speeches Alvin had heard in his life. Those river rats just settled right down in the shade, taking a couple of long pulls from a jug and watching Al and the lady with a real sullen look. The portmaster went back inside before the wagon even turned the corner onto the town road.

"You don't suppose the portmaster is in danger from having helped us, do you?" asked the lady. Alvin was pleased to hear that the arrogance was gone from her voice, though she still spoke as clear and even as the ringing of a hammer on iron.

"No," said Alvin. "They all know that if ever a portmaster got harmed, them as did it would never work again on the river, or if they did, they wouldn't live through a night ashore."

"What about you?"

"Oh, I got no such guarantee. So I reckon I won't come back to Hatrack Mouth for a couple of weeks. By then all those boys'll have jobs and be a hundred miles up or downstream from here." Then he remembered what the portmaster had said. "You're the new schoolteacher?"

She didn't answer. Not directly, anyway. "I suppose there are men like that in the East, but one doesn't meet them in the open like this."

"Well, it's a whole lot better to meet them in the open than it is to meet them in private!" Al said, laughing.

She didn't laugh.

"I was waiting for Dr. Whitley Physicker to meet me. He expected my boat later in the afternoon, but he may be on his way."

"This is the only road, Ma'am," Alvin said.

"Miss," she said. "Not madame. That title is properly reserved for married women."

"Like I said, it's the only road. So if he's on his way, we won't *miss* him. Miss."

This time Alvin didn't laugh at his own joke. On the other hand, he thought, looking out of the corner of his eye, that he just might have caught a glimpse of her smiling. So maybe she wasn't as hoity-toity as she seemed, Alvin thought. Maybe she's almost human. Maybe she'll even consent to give private schooling to a certain little half-Black boy. Maybe she'll be worth the work I went to fixing up the springhouse.

Because he was facing forward, driving the wagon, it wouldn't be natural, let alone good manners, for him to turn and stare right at her like he wanted to. So he sent out his bug, his spark, that part of him that "saw" what no man or woman could rightly with their own eyes see. For Alvin this was near second nature by now, to explore people under the skin so to speak. Keep in mind, though, that it wasn't like he could see with his eyes. Sure enough he could tell what was under a body's clothes, but he still didn't see folks naked. Instead he just got a close-in experience of the surface of their skin, almost like he'd took up residence in one of their pores. So he didn't think of it like he was peeping in windows or nothing. It was just another way of looking at folks and understanding them; he wouldn't see a body's shape or color, but he'd see whether they was sweating or hot or healthy or tensed-up. He'd see bruises and old healed-up injuries. He'd see hidden money or secret papers—but if he was to read the papers, he had to discover the feel of the ink on the surface and then trace it until he could build up a picture of the letters in his mind. It was very slow. Not like seeing, no sir.

Anyhow, he sent his bug to "see" this high-toned lady that

he couldn't exactly look at. And what he found caught him by surprise. Cause she was every bit as hexed-up as Mike Fink had been.

No, more. She was layers deep in it, from hexy amulets hanging around her neck to hexes stitched into her clothes, even a wire hex embedded in the bun of her hair. Only one of them was for protection, and it wasn't half so strong as Mike Fink's had been. The rest were all—for what? Alvin hadn't seen such work before, and it took some thought and exploration to figure out what these hex-work webs that covered her were doing. The best he could get, riding along in the wagon, keeping his eyes on the road ahead, was that somehow these hexes were doing a powerful beseeming, making her look to be something that she wasn't.

The first thought he had, as I suppose was natural, was to try to discover what she really was, under her disguise. The clothes she wore were real enough—the hexery was only changing the sound of her voice, the hue and texture of the surface of her skin. But Alvin had little practice with beseemings, and none at all with beseemings wove from hexes. Most folks did a beseeming with a word and a gesture, tied up with a drawing of what they wanted to seem to be. It was a working on other folks' minds, and once you saw through it, it didn't fool you at all. Since Alvin always saw through it, such beseemings had no hold on him.

But hers was different. The hex changed the way light hit her and bounced off, so that you weren't fooled into thinking you saw what wasn't there. Instead you really saw her different, the light actually struck your eyes that way. Since it wasn't a change made on Alvin's mind, knowing the trickery didn't help him see the truth. And using his bug, he couldn't tell much about what was hidden away behind the hexes, except that she wasn't quite so wrinkled-up and bony as she looked, which made him guess she might be younger.

It was only when he gave up trying to guess at what lay under the disguise that he came to the real question: Why, if a woman had the power to disguise herself and seem to be anything she wanted, why would she choose to look like *that?* Cold, severe, getting old, bony, unsmiling, pinched-up, angry, aloof. All the things a woman ought to hope she never was, this teacher lady *chose* to be.

Maybe she was a fugitive in disguise. But she was definitely a woman underneath the hexes, and Alvin never heard of a woman outlaw, so it couldn't be that. Maybe she was just young, and figured other folks wouldn't take her serious if she didn't look older. Alvin knew about *that* right enough. Or maybe she was pretty, and men kept thinking of her the wrong way—Alvin tried to conjure up in his mind what might've happened with those river rats if she'd been real beautiful. But truth to tell, the rivermen probably would've been polite as they knew how, if she was pretty. It was only ugly women they felt free to taunt, since ugly women probably reminded them of their mothers. So her plainness wasn't exactly protection. And it wasn't designed to hide a scar, neither, cause Alvin could see her skin wasn't pocked or blemished or marred.

Truth was he couldn't guess at why she was all hid up under so many layers of lies. She could be anything or anybody. He couldn't even ask her, since to tell her he saw through her disguise was the same as to tell her of his knack, and how could he know she could be trusted with such a secret as *that,* when he didn't even know who she really was or why she chose to live inside a lie?

He wondered if he ought to tell somebody. Shouldn't the school board know, before putting the town's children into her care, that she wasn't exactly what she seemed to be? But he couldn't tell them, either, without giving himself away; and besides, maybe her secret was her own business and no harm to anyone. Then if he told the truth on her, it would ruin both him and her, with no good done for anybody.

No, best to watch her, real careful, and learn who she was the only way a body can ever truly know other folks: by seeing what they do. That's the best plan Alvin could think of, and the truth is, now that he knew she had such a secret, how could he *keep* from paying special attention to her? Using his bug to explore around him was such a habit for him that he'd have to work *not* to check up on her, especially if she was living up at the springhouse. He half hoped she wouldn't, so he wouldn't be bothered so much by this mystery; but he just as much hoped she would, so he could keep watch and make sure she was a rightful sort of person.

And I could watch her even better if I studied from her. I could watch her with her own eyes, ask her questions, listen to her answers, and judge what kind of person she might be. Maybe if she taught me long enough, she'd come to trust me, and I her, and then I'd tell her I'm to be a Maker and she'd tell her deep secrets to me and we'd help each other, we'd be true friends the way I haven't had no true friend since I left my brother Measure behind me in Vigor Church.

He wasn't pushing the horse too hard, the load being so heavy, what with her trunk and bags on top of the iron—and herself, to boot. So after all their talk, and then all this silence as he tried to figure out who she really was, they were still only about a half a mile out of Hatrack Mouth when Dr. Physicker's fancy carriage came along. Alvin recognized the carriage right off, and hailed Po Doggly, who was driving. It took all of a couple of minutes to move the teacher and her things from wagon to carriage. Po and Alvin did all the lifting—Dr. Physicker used all his efforts to help the teacher lady into the carriage. Alvin had never seen the doctor act so elegant.

"I'm terribly sorry you had to suffer the discomforts of a ride in that wagon," said the doctor. "I didn't think that I was late."

"In fact you're early," she said. And then, turning graciously to Alvin, she added, "And the wagon ride was surprisingly pleasant."

Since Alvin hadn't said a word for most of the journey, he didn't rightly know whether she meant it as a compliment for him being good company, or as gratitude that he kept his mouth shut and didn't bother her. Either way, though, it made him feel a kind of burning in his face, and not from anger.

As Dr. Physicker was climbing into the carriage, the teacher asked him, "What is this young man's name?" Since she spoke to the doctor, Alvin didn't answer.

"Alvin," said the doctor, settling into his seat. "He was born here. He's the smith's apprentice."

"Alvin," she said, now directing herself to him through the carriage window. "I thank you for your gallantry today, and I hope you'll forgive the ungraciousness of my first response. I had underestimated the villainous nature of our unwelcome companions."

Her words were so elegant-sounding it was like music hearing her talk, even though Alvin could only half-guess what she was saying. Her expression, though, was about as kindly as her forbidding face could look, he reckoned. He wondered what her real visage might look like underneath.

"My pleasure, Ma'am," he said. "I mean Miss."

From the driver's bench, Po Doggly gee-ed the pair of mares and the carriage took off, still heading toward Hatrack Mouth, of course. It wasn't easy for Po to find a place on that road to turn around, either, so Alvin was well on his way before the carriage came back and passed him. Po slowed the carriage, and Dr. Physicker leaned over and tossed a dollar coin into the air. Alvin caught it, more by reflex than by thought.

"For your help for Miss Larner," said Dr. Physicker. Then Po gee-ed the horses again and they went on, leaving Alvin to chew on the dust in the road.

He felt the weight of the coin in his hand, and for a moment he wanted to throw it after the carriage. But that wouldn't do no good at all. No, he'd give it back to Physicker some other time, in some way that wouldn't get nobody riled up. But still it hurt, it stung deep, to be paid for helping a lady, like as if he was a servant or a child or something. And what hurt worst was wondering if maybe it was her idea to pay him. As if she thought he had earned a quarter-day's wages when he fought for her honor. It was sure that if he'd been wearing a coat and cravat instead of one filthy shirt, she'd have thought he done the service due a lady from any Christian gentleman, and she'd know she owed him gratitude instead of payment.

Payment. The coin burned in his hand. Why, for a few minutes there he'd almost thought she liked him. Almost he had hoped that maybe she'd agree to teach him, to help him work out some understanding of how the world works, of what he could do to be a true Maker and tame the Unmaker's terrible power. But now that it was plain she despised him, how could he even ask? How could he even pretend to be worthy of teaching, when he knew that all she saw about him was filth and blood and stupid poverty? She knew he meant well, but he was still a brute in her eyes, like she said first off. It was still in her heart. Brutality.

Miss Larner. That's what the doctor called her. He tasted the name as he said it. Dust in his mouth. You don't take animals to school.

TEACHER

Miss Larner had no intention of giving an inch to these people. She had heard enough horror stories about frontier school boards to know that they would try to get out of keeping most of the promises they made in their letters. It was beginning already.

"In your letters you represented to me that I would have a residence provided as part of my salary. I do not regard an inn as a private residence."

"You'll have you own private room," said Dr. Physicker.

"And take all my meals at a common table? This is not acceptable. If I stay, I will be spending all my days in the company of the children of this town, and when that day's work is over, I expect to be able to prepare my own meals in private and eat them in solitude, and then spend the evening in the company of books, without distraction or annoyance. That is not possible in a roadhouse, gentlemen, and so a room in a roadhouse does *not* constitute a private residence."

She could see them sizing her up. Some were abashed by the mere precision of her speech—she knew perfectly well that country lawyers put on airs in their own towns, but they were no match for someone of real education. The only real trouble was going to come from the sheriff, Pauley Wiseman. How absurd, for a grown man still to use a child's nickname.

"Now see here, young lady," said the sheriff.

She raised an eyebrow. It was typical of such a man that, even though Miss Larner seemed to be on the greying side of forty, he would assume that her unmarried status gave him the right to call her "young lady," as one addresses a recalcitrant girlchild.

"What is 'here' that I am failing to see?"

"Well, Horace and Peg Guester *did* plan to offer you a small house off by yourself, but we said no to it, plain and simple, we said no to them, and we say no to you."

"Very well, then. I see that you do not, after all, intend to keep your word to me. Fortunately, gentlemen, I am not a common schoolteacher, grateful to take whatever is offered. I had a good position at the Penn School, and I assure you that I can return there at will. Good day."

She rose to her feet. So did all the men except the sheriff—but they weren't rising out of courtesy.

"Please."

"Sit down."

"Let's talk about this."

"Don't be hasty."

It was Dr. Physicker, the perfect conciliator, who took the floor now, after giving the sheriff a steady look to quell him. The sheriff, however, did not seem particularly quelled.

"Miss Larner, our decision on the private house was not an irrevocable one. But please consider the problems that worried us. First, we were concerned that the house would not be suitable. It's not really a house at all, but a mere room, made out of an abandoned springhouse—"

The old springhouse. "Is it heated?"

"Yes."

"Has it windows? A door that can be secured? A bed and table and chair?"

"All of that, yes."

"Has it a wooden floor?"

"A nice one."

"Then I doubt that its former service as a springhouse will bother me. Had you any other objections?"

"We damn well do!" cried Sheriff Wiseman. Then, seeing the horrified looks around the room, he added, "Begging the lady's pardon for my rough language."

"I am interested in hearing those objections," said Miss Larner.

"A woman alone, in a solitary house in the woods! It ain't proper!"

"It is the word *ain't* which is not proper, Mr. Wiseman," said Miss Larner. "As to the propriety of my living in a house to myself, I assure you that I have done so for many years, and have managed to pass that entire time quite unmolested. Is there another house within hailing distance?"

"The roadhouse to one side and the smith's place to the other," said Dr. Physicker.

"Then if I am under some duress or provocation, I can assure you that I will make myself heard, and I expect those who hear will come to my aid. Or are you afraid, Mr. Wiseman, that I may enter into some improper activity *voluntarily?*"

Of course that was exactly what he was thinking, and his reddening face showed it.

"I believe you have adequate references concerning my moral character," said Miss Larner. "But if you have any doubts on that score, it would be better for me to return to Philadelphia at once, for if at my age I cannot be trusted to live an upright life without supervision, how can you possibly trust me to supervise your young children?"

"It just ain't decent!" cried the sheriff. "Aren't."

"Isn't." She smiled benignly at Pauley Wiseman. "It has been my experience, Mr. Wiseman, that when a person assumes that others are eager to commit indecent acts whenever given the opportunity, he is merely confessing his own private struggle."

Pauley Wiseman didn't understand that she had just

accused him, not until several of the lawyers started in laughing behind their hands.

"As I see it, gentlemen of the school board, you have only two alternatives. First, you can pay my boat passage back to Dekane and my overland passage to Philadelphia, plus the salary for the month that I will have expended in traveling."

"If you don't teach, you get no salary," said the sheriff.

"You speak hastily, Mr. Wiseman," said Miss Larner. "I believe the lawyers present will inform you that the school board's letters constitute a contract, of which you are in breach, and that I would therefore be entitled to collect, not just a month's salary, but the entire year's."

"Well, that's not *certain,* Miss Larner," began one of the lawyers.

"Hio is one of the United States now, sir," she answered, "and there is ample precedent in other state courts, precedent which is binding until and unless the government of Hio makes specific legislation to the contrary."

"Is she a schoolteacher or a lawyer?" asked another lawyer, and they all laughed.

"Your second alternative is to allow me to inspect this— this springhouse—and determine whether I find it acceptable, and if I do, to allow me to live there. If you ever find me engaging in morally reprehensible behavior, it is within the terms of our contract that you may discharge me forthwith."

"We can put you in *jail,* that's what we can do," said Wiseman.

"Why, Mr. Wiseman, aren't we getting ahead of ourselves, talking of jail when I have yet to select which morally hideous act I shall perform?"

"Shut up, Pauley," said one of the lawyers.

"Which alternative do you choose, gentlemen?" she asked.

Dr. Physicker was not about to let Pauley Wiseman have

at the more weak-willed members of the board. He'd see to it there was no further debate. "We don't need to retire to consider this, do we, gentlemen? We may not be Quakers here in Hatrack River, so we aren't used to thinking of ladies as wanting to live by themselves and engage in business and preach and whatnot, but we're open-minded and willing to learn new ways. We want your services, and we'll keep to the contract. All in favor?"

"Aye."

"Opposed? The ayes have it."

"Nay," said Wiseman.

"The voting's over, Pauley."

"You called it too damn fast!"

"Your negative vote has been recorded, Pauley."

Miss Larner smiled coldly. "You may be sure *I* won't forget it, Sheriff Wiseman."

Dr. Physicker tapped the table with his gavel. "This meeting is adjourned until next Tuesday afternoon at three. And now, Miss Larner, I'd be delighted to escort you to the Guesters' springhouse, if this is a convenient hour. Not knowing when you would arrive, they have given me the key and asked me to open the cottage for you; they'll greet you later."

Miss Larner was aware, as they all were, that it was odd, to say the least, for the landlord not to greet his guest in person.

"You see, Miss Larner, it wasn't certain whether you'd accept the cottage. They wanted you to make your decision when you saw the place—and not in their presence, lest you feel embarrassed to decline it."

"Then they have acted graciously," said Miss Larner, "and I will thank them when I meet them."

IT WAS HUMILIATING, Old Peg having to walk out to the springhouse all by herself to plead with this stuck-up snooty old Philadelphia spinster. Horace ought to be going out there with her. Talk man to man with her—that's what this woman seemed to think she was, not a lady but a lord. Might as well come from Camelot, she might, thinks she's a princess giving orders to the common folk. Well, they took care of it in France, old Napoleon did, put old Louis the Seventeenth right in his place. But lordly women like this teacher lady, Miss Larner, they never got their comeuppance, just went on through life thinking folks what didn't talk perfect was too low to take much account of.

So where was Horace, to put this teacher lady in her place? Setting by the fire. Pouting. Just like a four-year-old. Even Arthur Stuart never got such a pout on him.

"I don't like her," says Horace.

"Well like her or not, if Arthur's to get an education it's going to be from her or nobody," says Old Peg, talking plain sense as usual, but does Horace listen? I should laugh.

"She can live there and she can teach Arthur if she pleases, or not if she don't please, but I don't like her and I don't think she belongs in that springhouse."

"Why, is it holy ground?" says Old Peg. "Is there some curse on it? Should we have built a palace for her royal highness?" Oh, when Horace gets a notion on him it's no use talking, so why did she keep on trying?

"None of that, Peg," said Horace.

"Then what? Or don't you need reasons anymore? Do you just decide and then other folks better make way?"

"Because it's Little Peggy's place, that's why, and I don't like having that benoctious woman living there!"

Wouldn't you know? It was just like Horace, to bring up their runaway daughter, the one who never so much as wrote to them once she ran away, leaving Hatrack River without a torch and Horace without the love of his life. Yes ma'am, that's what Little Peggy was to him, the love of his life. If I ran off, Horace, or, God forbid, if I died, would you treasure my memory and not let no other woman take my place? I reckon not. I reckon there wouldn't be time for my spot on the sheet to get cold afore you'd have some other woman lying there. Me you could replace in a hot minute, but Little Peggy, we have to treat the springhouse as a *shrine* and make me come out here all by myself to face this high-falutin old maid and beg her to teach a little Black child. Why, I'll be lucky if she doesn't try to buy him from me.

Miss Larner took her time about answering the door, too, and when she did, she had a handkerchief to her face— probably a perfumed one, so she wouldn't have to smell the odor of honest country folks.

"If you don't mind I've got a thing or two I'd like to discuss with you," said Old Peg.

Miss Larner looked away, off over Old Peg's head, as if studying some bird in a far-off tree. "If it's about the school, I was told I'd have a week to prepare before we actually registered students and began the autumn session."

From down below, Old Peg could hear the *ching-ching-ching* of one of the smiths a-working at the forge. Against her will she couldn't help thinking of Little Peggy, who purely hated that sound. Maybe Horace was right in his foolishness. Maybe Little Peggy haunted this springhouse.

Still, it was Miss Larner standing in the doorway now, and Miss Larner that Old Peg had to deal with. "Miss Larner, I'm Margaret Guester. My husband and I own this springhouse."

"Oh. I beg your pardon. You're my landlady, and I'm being ungracious. Please come in."

That was a bit more like it. Old Peg stepped up through the open door and stood there a moment to take in the room. Only yesterday it had seemed bare but clean, a place full of promise. Now it was almost homey, what with a doily and a dozen books on the armoire, a small woven rug on the floor, and two dresses hanging from hooks on the wall. The trunks and bags filled a corner. It looked a bit like somebody lived there. Old Peg didn't know what she'd expected. Of course Miss Larner had more dresses than this dark traveling outfit. It's just Old Peg hadn't thought of her doing something so ordinary as changing clothes. Why, when she's got one dress off and before she puts on another, she probably stands there in her underwear, just like anybody.

"Do sit down, Mrs. Guester."

"Around here we ain't much with Mr. and Mrs., except them lawyers, Miss Larner. I'm Goody Guester, mostly, except when folks call me Old Peg."

"Old Peg. What a—what an interesting name."

She thought of spelling out why she was called "Old" Peg—how she had a daughter what run off, that sort of thing. But it was going to be hard enough to explain to this teacher lady how she come to have a Black son. Why make her family life seem even more strange?

"Miss Larner, I won't beat around the bush. You got something that I need."

"Oh?"

"That is, not me, to say it proper, but my son, Arthur Stuart."

If she recognized that it was the King's proper name, she gave no sign. "And what might he need from me, Goody Guester?"

"Book-learning."

"That's what I've come to provide to all the children in Hatrack River, Goody Guester."

"Not Arthur Stuart. Not if those pin-headed cowards on the school board have their way."

"Why should they exclude your son? Is he over-age, perhaps?"

"He's the right age, Miss Larner. What he ain't is the right color."

Miss Larner waited, no expression on her face.

"He's Black, Miss Larner."

"Half-Black, surely," offered the teacher.

Naturally the teacher was trying to figure how the inn-keeper's wife came to have her a half-Black boy-baby. Old Peg got some pleasure out of watching the teacher act polite while she must surely be cringing in horror inside herself. But it wouldn't do to let such a thought linger too long, would it? "He's adopted, Miss Larner," said Old Peg. "Let's just say that his Black mama got herself embar-rassed with a half-White baby."

"And you, out of the goodness of your heart—"

Was there a nasty edge to Miss Larner's voice? "I wanted me a child. I ain't taking care of Arthur Stuart for pity. He's *my* boy now."

"I see," said Miss Larner. "And the good people of Ha-track River have determined that their children's education will suffer if half-Black ears should hear my words at the same time as pure White ears."

Miss Larner sounded nasty again, only now Old Peg dared to let herself rejoice inside, hearing the way Miss Larner said those words. "Will you teach him, Miss Larner?"

"I confess, Goody Guester, that I have lived in the City of Quakers too long. I had forgotten that there were places in this world where people of small minds would be so shameless as to punish a mere child for the sin of being born with skin of a tropical hue. I can assure you that I will re-fuse to open school at all if your adopted son is not one of my pupils."

"No!" cried Old Peg. "No, Miss Larner, that's going too far."

"I am a committed Emancipationist, Goody Guester. I will not join in a conspiracy to deprive any Black child of his or her intellectual heritage."

Old Peg didn't know what in the world an intellectual heritage was, but she knew that Miss Larner was in too much sympathy. If she kept up this way, she'd be like to ruin everything. "You got to hear me out, Miss Larner. They'll just get another teacher, and I'll be worse off, and so will Arthur Stuart. No, I just ask that you give him an hour in the evening, a few days a week. I'll make him study somewhat in the daytime, to learn proper what you teach him quick. He's a bright boy, you'll see that. He already knows his letters—he can *A* it and *Z* it better than my Horace. That's my husband, Horace Guester. So I'm not asking more than a few hours a week, if you can spare it. That's why we worked up this springhouse, so you could do it and none the wiser."

Miss Larner arose from where she sat on the edge of her bed, and walked to the window. "This is not what I ever imagined—to teach a child in secret, as if I were committing a crime."

"In *some* folks' eyes, Miss Larner—"

"Oh, I have no doubt of that."

"Don't you Quakers have silent meetings? All I ask is a kind of quiet meeting, don't you know—"

"I am not a Quaker, Goody Guester. I am merely a human being who refuses to deny the humanity of others, unless their own acts prove them unworthy of that noble kinship."

"Then you'll teach him?"

"After hours, yes. Here in my home, which you and your husband so kindly provided, yes. But in secret? Never! I shall proclaim to all in this place that I am teaching Arthur Stuart, and not just a few nights a week, but daily. I am free to tutor such pupils as I desire—my contract is quite specific on that point—and as long as I do not violate the contract, they must endure me for at least a year. Will that do?"

Old Peg looked at the woman in pure admiration. "I'll

be jiggered," she said, "you're mean as a cat with a burr in its behind."

"I regret that I've never seen a cat in such an unfortunate situation, Goody Guester, so that I cannot estimate the accuracy of your simile."

Old Peg couldn't make no sense of the words Miss Larner said, but she caught something like a twinkle in the lady's eye, so it was all right.

"When should I send Arthur to you?" she asked.

"As I said when I first opened the door, I'll need a week to prepare. When school opens for the White children, it opens for Arthur Stuart as well. There remains only the question of payment."

Old Peg was taken aback for a moment. She'd come here prepared to offer money, but after the way Miss Larner talked, she thought there'd be no cost after all. Still, teaching was Miss Larner's livelihood, so it was only fair. "We thought to offer you a dollar a month, that being most convenient for us, Miss Larner, but if you need more—"

"Oh, not cash, Goody Guester. I merely thought to ask if you might indulge me by allowing me to hold a weekly reading of poetry in your roadhouse on Sunday evenings, inviting all in Hatrack River who aspire to improve their acquaintance with the best literature in the English language."

"I don't know as how there's all that many who hanker after poetry, Miss Larner, but you're welcome to have a go of it."

"I think you'll be pleasantly surprised at the number of people who wish to be thought educated, Goody Guester. We shall have difficulty finding seats for all the ladies of Hatrack River who compel their husbands to bring them to hear the immortal words of Pope and Dryden, Donne and Milton, Shakespeare and Gray and—oh, I shall be daring—Wordsworth and Coleridge, and perhaps even an

American poet, a wandering spinner of strange tales named Blake."

"You don't mean old Taleswapper, do you?"

"I believe that is his most common sobriquet."

"You've got some of his poems wrote down?"

"Written? Hardly necessary, for that dear friend of mine. I have committed many of his verses to memory."

"Well, don't that old boy get around. Philadelphia, no less."

"He has brightened many a parlor in that city, Goody Guester. Shall we hold our first soiree this Sunday?"

"What's a swore raid?"

"Soiree. An evening gathering, perhaps with ginger punch—"

"Oh, you don't have to teach me nothing about hospitality, Miss Larner. And if that's the price for Arthur Stuart's education, Miss Larner, I'm sore afraid I'm cheating you, because it seems to me you're doing *us* the favor both ways."

"You're most kind, Goody Guester. But I must ask you one question."

"Ask away. Can't promise I'm too good at answers."

"Goody Guester," said Miss Larner. "Are you aware of the Fugitive Slave Treaty?"

Fear and anger stabbed right through Old Peg's heart, even to hear it mentioned. "A devilish piece of work!"

"Slavery is a devilish work indeed, but the treaty was signed to bring Appalachee into the Compact, and to keep our fragile nation from war with the Crown Colonies. Peace is hardly to be labeled devilish."

"It is when it's a peace that says they can send their damned finders into the free states and bring back captive Black people to be slaves!"

"Perhaps you're right, Goody Guester. Indeed, one could say that the Fugitive Slave Treaty is not so much a treaty of peace as it is an article of surrender. Nevertheless, it is the law of the land."

Only now did Old Peg realize what this teacher just done. What could it mean, her bringing up the Fugitive Slave Treaty, excepting to make sure Old Peg knew that Arthur Stuart wasn't safe here, that finders could still come from the Crown Colonies and claim him as the property of some family of White so-called Christians? And that also meant that Miss Larner didn't believe a speck of her story about where Arthur Stuart come from. And if she saw through the lie so easy-like, why was Old Peg fool enough to think everybody else believed it? Why, as far as Old Peg knew, the whole town of Hatrack River had long since guessed that Arthur Stuart was a slave boy what somehow run off and got hisself a White mama.

And if everybody knew, what was to stop somebody from giving report on Arthur Stuart, sending word to the Crown Colonies about a runaway slavechild living in a certain roadhouse near the Hatrack River? The Fugitive Slave Treaty made her adoption of Arthur Stuart plain illegal. They could take the boy right out of her arms and she'd never have the right to see him again. In fact, if she ever went south they could arrest her and hang her under the slave-poaching laws of King Arthur. And thinking of that monstrous King in his lair in Camelot made her remember the unkindest thing of all—that if they ever took Arthur Stuart south, they'd change his name. Why, it'd be high treason in the Crown Colonies, having a slavechild named with the same name as the King. So all of a sudden poor Arthur would find hisself with some other name he never heard of afore. She couldn't help thinking of the boy all confused, somebody calling him and calling him, and whipping him for not coming, but how could he know to come, since nobody called him by his right name?

Her face must've painted a plain picture of all the thoughts going through her head, because Miss Larner walked behind her and put her hands on Old Peg's shoulders.

"You've nought to fear from me, Goody Guester. I come from Philadelphia, where people speak openly of defying that treaty. A young New Englander named Thoreau has made quite a nuisance of himself, preaching that a bad law must be defied, that good citizens must be prepared to go to jail themselves rather than submit to it. It would do your heart good to hear him speak."

Old Peg doubted that. It only froze her to the heart to think of the treaty at all. Go to jail? What good would that do, if Arthur was being whipped south in chains? No matter what, it was none of Miss Larner's business. "I don't know why you're saying all this, Miss Larner. Arthur Stuart is the freeborn son of a free Black woman, even if she got him on the wrong side of the sheets. The Fugitive Slave Treaty means nothing to me."

"Then I shall think no more of it, Goody Guester. And now, if you'll forgive me, I'm somewhat weary from traveling, and I had hoped to retire early, though it's still light outside."

Old Peg sprang to her feet, mighty relieved at not talking anymore about Arthur and the Treaty. "Why, of course. But you ain't hopping into bed without taking a bath, are you? Nothing like a bath for a traveler."

"I quite agree, Goody Guester. However, I fear my luggage was not copious enough for me to bring my tub along."

"I'll send Horace over with my spare tub the second I get back, and if you don't mind hotting up your stove there, we can get water from Gertie's well yonder and set it to steaming in no time."

"Oh, Goody Guester, I fear you'll convince me before the evening's out that I'm in Philadelphia after all. It shall be almost disappointing, for I had steeled myself to endure the rigors of primitive life in the wilderness, and now I find that you are prepared to offer all the convivial blessings of civilization."

"I'll take it that what you said mostly means thank you, and so I say you're welcome, and I'll be back in no time with Horace and the tub. And don't you dare fetch your own water, at least not today. You just set there and read or philosophate or whatever an educated person does instead of dozing off."

With that Old Peg was out of the springhouse. She like to flew along the path to the inn. Why, this teacher lady wasn't half so bad as she seemed at first. She might talk a language that Old Peg couldn't hardly understand half the time, but at least she was willing to talk to folks—and she'd teach Arthur at no cost and hold poetry readings in the roadhouse to boot. Best of all, though, best of all she might even be willing to talk to Old Peg sometimes and maybe some of that smartness might rub off on her. Not that smartness was all that much good to a woman like Old Peg, but then, what good was a jewel on a rich lady's finger, either? And if being around this educated eastern spinster gave Old Peg even a jigger more understanding of the great world outside Hatrack River, it was more than Old Peg had dared to hope for in her life. Like daubing just a spot of color on a drab moth's wing. It don't make the moth into a butterfly, but maybe now the moth won't despair and fly into the fire.

MISS LARNER WATCHED Old Peg walk away. Mother, she whispered. No, didn't even whisper. Didn't even open her mouth. But her lips pressed together a bit tighter with the *M,* and her tongue shaped the other sounds inside her mouth.

It hurt her, to deceive. She had promised never to lie, and in a sense she wasn't lying even now. The name she had taken, *Larner,* meant nothing more than *teacher,* and since she *was* a teacher, it was as truly her name as Father's name was Guester and Makepeace's name was Smith. And when people asked her questions, she never lied to them, though she did refuse to answer questions that might tell them more than they ought to know, that might set them wondering.

Still, despite her elaborate avoidance of an open lie, she feared that she merely deceived herself. How could she believe that her presence here, so disguised, was anything but a lie?

And yet surely even that deception was the truth, at its root. She was no longer the same person she had been when she was torch of Hatrack River. She was no longer connected to these people in the former ways. If she claimed to be Little Peggy, that would be a deeper lie than her disguise, for they would suppose that she was the girl they once knew, and treat her accordingly. In that sense, her disguise was a reflection of who she really was, at least here and now—educated, aloof, a deliberate spinster, and sexually unavailable to men.

So her disguise was not a lie, surely it was not; it was merely a way to keep a secret, the secret of who she used to be, but was no longer. Her vow was still unbroken.

Mother was long since out of sight in the woods between the springhouse and the inn, but still Peggy looked after her. And if she wanted, Peggy could have seen her even yet, not with her eyes, but with her torch sight, finding Mother's heartfire and moving close, looking tight. Mother, don't you know you have no secrets from your daughter Peggy?

But the fact was that Mother could keep all the secrets she desired. Peggy would not look into her heart. Peggy hadn't come home to be the torch of Hatrack River again. After all these years of study, in which Peggy had read so many books so rapidly that she feared once that she might run out, that there might not be books enough in America to satisfy her—after all these years, there was only one skill she was certain of. She had finally mastered the ability *not* to see inside the hearts of other people unless she wanted to. She had finally tamed her torchy sight.

Oh, she still looked inside other people when she needed to, but she rarely did. Even with the school board, when she had to tame them, it took no more than her knowledge of human nature to guess their present thoughts and deal with them. And as for the futures revealed in the heartfire, she no longer noticed them.

I am not responsible for your futures, none of you. Least of all you, Mother. I have meddled enough in your life, in everyone's lives. If I know all your futures, all you people in Hatrack River, then I have a moral imperative to shape my own actions to help you achieve the happiest possible tomorrow. Yet in so doing, I cease to exist myself. My own future becomes the only one with no hope, and why should that be? By shutting my eyes to what *will* happen, I become like you, able to live my life according to my guesses at what *may* happen. I couldn't guarantee you happiness anyway, and this way at least I also have a chance of it myself.

Even as she justified herself, she felt the same sour guilt well up inside her. By rejecting her knack, she was sinning against the God that gave it to her. That great magister Erasmus, he had taught as much: Your knack is your destiny. You'll never know joy except through following the path laid out before you by what is inside you. But Peggy refused to submit to that cruel discipline. Her childhood had already been stolen from her, and to what end? Her mother disliked her, the people of Hatrack River feared her, often hated her, even as they came to her again and again, seeking answers to their selfish, petty questions, blaming her if any seeming ill came into their lives, but never thanking her for saving them from dire events, for they never knew how she had saved them because the evils never happened.

It wasn't gratitude she wanted. It was freedom. It was a lightening of her burden. She had started bearing it too young, and they had shown her no mercy in their exploitation. Their own fears always outweighed her need for a care-free girlhood. Did any of them understand that? Did any of them know how gratefully she left them all behind?

Now Peggy the torch was back, but they'd never know it. I did not come back for *you,* people of Hatrack River, nor did I come to serve your children. I came back for one pupil only, the man who stands even now at the forge, his heartfire burning so brightly that I can see it even in my sleep, even in my dreams. I came back having learned all that the world can teach, so I in turn can help that young man achieve a labor that means more than any one of us. *That* is my destiny, if I have one.

Along the way I'll do what other good I can—I'll teach Arthur Stuart, I'll try to fulfill the dreams his brave young mother died for; I'll teach all the other children as much as they're willing to learn, during those certain hours of the day that I've contracted for; I'll bring such poetry and learning into the town of Hatrack River as you're willing to receive.

Perhaps you don't desire poetry as much as you would like to have my torchy knowledge of your possible futures, but I daresay poetry will do you far more good. For knowing the future only makes you timid and complacent by turns, while poetry can shape you into the kind of souls who can face any future with boldness and wisdom and nobility, so that you need not know the future at all, so that any future will be an opportunity for greatness, if you have greatness in you. Can I teach you to see in yourselves what Gray saw?

> *Some heart once pregnant with celestial fire,*
> *Hands that the rod of empire might have swayed,*
> *Or waked to ecstasy the living lyre.*

But she doubted that any of these ordinary souls in Hatrack River were really mute, inglorious Miltons. Pauley Wiseman was no secret Caesar. He might wish for it, but he lacked the wit and self-control. Whitley Physicker was no Hippocrates, however much he tried to be a healer and conciliator—his love of luxury undid him, and like many other well-meaning physician he had come to work for what the fee could buy, and not for joy of the work itself.

She picked up the water bucket that stood by the door. Weary as she was, she would not allow herself to seem helpless even for a moment. Father and Mother would come and find Miss Larner had already done for herself all that she could do before the tub arrived.

Ching-ching-ching. Didn't Alvin rest? Didn't he know the sun was boiling the western sky, turning it red before sinking out of sight behind the trees? As she walked down the hill toward the smithy, she felt as if she might suddenly begin to run, to fly down the hill to the smithy as she had flown the day that Alvin was born. It was raining that day, and Alvin's mother was stuck in a wagon in the river. It was Peggy who saw them all, their heartfires off in the blackness of the rain and the flooding river. It was Peggy who gave alarm, and then Peggy who stood watch over the birthing, seeing Alvin's futures in his heartfire, the brightest heartfire she had ever seen or would ever see in all her life. It was Peggy who saved his life then by peeling the caul away from his face; and, by using bits of that caul, Peggy who had saved his life so many times over the years. She might turn her back on being torch of Hatrack River, but she'd never turn her back on *him.*

But she stopped herself halfway down the hill. What was she thinking of? She could not go to him, not now, not yet. He had to come to *her*. Only that way could she become his teacher; only that way was there a chance of becoming anything more than that.

She turned and walked across the face of the hill, slanting down and eastward toward the well. She had watched Alvin dig the well—both wells—and for once she was helpless to help him when the Unmaker came. Alvin's own anger and destructiveness had called his enemy, and there was nothing Peggy could do with the caul to save him that time. She could only watch as he purged the unmaking that was inside himself, and so defeated, for a time, the Unmaker who stalked him on the outside. Now this well stood as a monument both to Alvin's power and to his frailty.

She dropped the copper bucket into the well, and the windlass clattered as the rope unwound. A muffled splash. She waited a moment for the bucket to fill, then wound it upward. It arrived brimming. She meant to pour it out into the wooden bucket she brought with her, but instead she brought the copper bucket to her lips and drank from the cold heavy load of water that it bore. So many years she had waited to taste that water, the water that Alvin tamed the night he tamed himself. She had been so afraid, watching him all night, and when at last in the morning he filled up the first vengeful hole he dug, she wept in relief. This water wasn't salty, but still it tasted to her like her own tears.

The hammer was silent. As always, she found Alvin's heartfire at once, without even trying. He was leaving the smithy, coming outside. Did he know she was there? No. He always came for water when he finished his work for the day. Of course she could not turn to him, not yet, not until she actually heard his step. Yet, though she knew he was coming and listened for him, she couldn't hear him; he moved as silently as a squirrel on a limb. Not until he spoke did he make a sound.

"Pretty good water, ain't it?"

She turned around to face him. Turned too quickly, too eagerly—the rope still held the bucket, so it lurched out of her hands, splashed her with water, and clattered back down into the well.

"I'm Alvin, you remember? Didn't mean to frighten you, Ma'am. Miss Larner."

"I foolishly forgot the bucket was tied," she said. "I'm used to pumps and taps, I'm afraid. Open wells are not common in Philadelphia."

She turned back to the well to draw the bucket up again.

"Here, let me," he said.

"There's no need. I can wind it well enough."

"But why should you, Miss Larner, when I'm glad to do it for you?"

She stepped aside and watched as he cranked the windlass with one hand, as easily as a child might swing a rope. The bucket fairly flew to the top of the well. She looked into his heartfire, just dipped in, to see if he was showing off for her. He was not. He could not see how massive his own shoulders were, how his muscles danced under the skin as his arm moved. He could not even see the peacefulness of his own face, the same quiet repose that one might see in the face of a fearless stag. There was no watchfulness in him. Some people had darting eyes, as if they had to be alert for danger, or perhaps for prey. Others looked intently at the task at hand, concentrating on what they were doing. But Alvin had a quiet distance, as if he had no particular concern about what anyone else or he himself might be doing, but instead dwelt on inward thoughts that no one else could hear. Again the words of Gray's *Elegy* played out in her mind.

> *Far from the madding crowd's ignoble strife,*
> *Their sober wishes never learned to stray;*
> *Along the cool, sequestered vale of life*
> *They kept the noiseless tenor of their way.*

Poor Alvin. When I'm done with you, there'll be no cool sequestered vale. You'll look back on your prenticeship as the last peaceful days of your life.

He gripped the full, heavy bucket with one hand on the rim, and easily tipped it to pour it out into the bucket she had brought, which he held in his other hand; he did it as lightly and easily as a housewife pours cream from one cup into another. What if those hands as lightly and easily held my arms? Would he break me without meaning to, being so strong? Would I feel manacled in his irresistible grasp? Or would he burn me up in the white heat of his heartfire?

She reached out for her bucket.

"Please let me carry it, Ma'am. Miss Larner."

"There's no need."

"I know I'm dirtied up, Miss Larner, but I can carry it to your door and set it inside without messing anything."

Is my disguise so monstrously aloof that you think I refuse your help out of excessive cleanliness? "I only meant that I didn't want to make you work anymore today. You've helped me enough already for one day."

He looked straight into her eyes, and now he lost that peaceful expression. There was even a bit of anger in his eyes. "If you're afraid I'll want you to pay me, you needn't have no fear of that. If this is your dollar, you can have it back. I never wanted it." He held out to her the coin that Whitley Physicker had tossed him from the carriage.

"I reproved Dr. Physicker at the time. I thought it insulting that *he* should presume to pay you for the service you did me out of pure gallantry. It cheapened both of us, I thought, for him to act as if the events of this morning were worth exactly one dollar."

His eyes had softened now.

Peggy went on in her Miss Larner voice. "But you must forgive Dr. Physicker. He is uncomfortable with wealth, and looks for opportunities to share it with others. He has not yet learned how to do it with perfect tact."

"Oh, it's no never mind now, Miss Larner, seeing how it didn't come from you." He put the coin back in his pocket and started to carry the full bucket up the hill toward the house.

It was plain he was unaccustomed to walking with a lady. His strides were far too long, his pace too quick, for her to keep up with him. She couldn't even walk the same route he took—he seemed oblivious to the degree of slope. He was like a child, not an adult, taking the most direct route even if it meant unnecessary clambering over obstacles.

And yet I'm barely five years older than he is. Have I come to believe my own disguise? At twenty-three, am I already thinking and acting and living like a woman of twice that age? Didn't I once love to walk just as he does, over the most difficult ground, for the sheer love of the exertion and accomplishment?

Nevertheless, she walked the easier path, skirting the hill and then climbing up where the slope was longer and gentler. He was already there, waiting at the door.

"Why didn't you open the door and set the bucket inside? The door isn't locked," she said.

"Begging your pardon, Miss Larner, but this is a door that asks not to be opened, whether it's locked or not."

So, she thought, he wants to make sure I know about the hidden hexes he put in the locks. Not many people could see a hidden hex—nor could she, for that matter. She wouldn't have known about them if she hadn't watched him put the hexes in the lock. But of course she couldn't very well tell him *that*. So she asked, "Oh, is there some protection here that I can't see?"

"I just put a couple of hexes into the lock. Nothing much, but it should make it fairly safe here. And there's a hex in the top of the stove, so I don't think you have to worry much about sparks getting free."

"You have a great deal of confidence in your hexery, Alvin."

"I do them pretty good. Most folks knows a few hexes, anyway, Miss Larner. But not many smiths can put them into the iron. I just wanted you to know."

He wanted her to know more than that, of course. So she gave him the response he hoped for. "I take it, then, that you did some of the work on this springhouse."

"I done the windows, Miss Larner. They glide up and down sweet as you please, and there's pegs to hold them in place. And the stove, and the locks, and all the iron fittings. And my helper, Arthur Stuart, he scraped down the walls."

For a young man who seemed artless, he was steering the conversation rather well. For a moment she thought of toying with him, of pretending not to make the connections he was counting on, just to see how he handled it. But no—he was only planning to ask her to do what she came here to do. There was no reason to make it hard for him. The teaching itself would be hard enough. "Arthur Stuart," she said. "He must be the same boy that Goody Guester asked me to teach privately."

"Oh, did she already ask you? Or shouldn't I ask?"

"I have no intention of keeping it a secret, Alvin. Yes, I'll be teaching Arthur Stuart."

"I'm glad of that, Miss Larner. He's the smartest boy you ever knew. And a mimic! Why, he can hear anything once and say it back to you in your own voice. You'll hardly believe it even when he's a-doing it."

"I only hope he doesn't choose to play such a game when I'm teaching him."

Alvin frowned. "Well, it isn't rightly a game, Miss Larner. It's just something he does without meaning to in particular. I mean to say, if he starts talking back to you in your own voice, he isn't making fun or nothing. It's just that when he hears something he remembers it voice and all, if you know what I mean. He can't split them up and remember the words without the voice that gave them."

"I'll keep that in mind."

In the distance, Peggy heard a door slam closed. She cast out and looked, finding Father's and Mother's heartfires coming toward her. They were quarreling, of course, but if Alvin was to ask her, he'd have to do it quickly.

"Was there something else you wanted to say to me, Alvin?"

This was the moment he'd been leading up to, but now he was turning shy on her. "Well, I had some idea of asking you—but you got to understand, I didn't carry the water for you so you'd feel obliged or nothing. I would've done that anyway, for anybody, and as for what happened today, I didn't rightly know that you were the teacher. I mean maybe I might've guessed, but I just didn't think of it. So what I done was just itself, and you don't owe me nothing."

"I think I'll decide how much gratitude I owe, Alvin. What did you want to ask me?"

"Of course you'll be busy with Arthur Stuart, so I can't expect you to have much time free, maybe just one day a week, just an hour even. It could be on Saturdays, and you could charge whatever you want, my master's been giving me free time and I've saved up some of my own earnings, and—"

"Are you asking me to tutor you, Alvin?"

Alvin didn't know what the word meant.

"Tutor you. Teach you privately."

"Yes, Miss Larner."

"The charge is fifty cents a week, Alvin. And I wish you to come at the same time as Arthur Stuart. Arrive when he does, and leave when he does."

"But how can you teach us both at once?"

"I daresay you could benefit from some of the lessons I'll be giving him, Alvin. And when I have him writing or ciphering, I can converse with you."

"I just don't want to cheat him out of his lesson time."

"Think clearly, Alvin. It would not be proper for you to take lessons with me alone. I may be somewhat older than you, but there are those who will search for fault in me, and giving private instruction to a young bachelor would certainly give cause for tongues to wag. Arthur Stuart will be present at all your lessons, and the door of the springhouse will stand open."

"We could go up and you could teach me at the roadhouse."

"Alvin. I have told you the terms. Do you wish to engage me as your tutor?"

"Yes, Miss Larner." He dug into his pocket and pulled out a coin. "Here's a dollar for the first two weeks."

Peggy looked at the coin. "I thought you meant to give this dollar back to Dr. Physicker."

"I wouldn't want to make him uncomfortable about having so much money, Miss Larner." He grinned.

Shy he may be, but he can't stay serious for long. There'll always be a tease in him, just below the surface, and eventually it will always come out.

"No, I imagine not," said Miss Larner. "Lessons will begin next week. Thank you for your help."

At that moment, Father and Mother came up the path. Father carried a large tub over his head, and he staggered under the weight. Alvin immediately ran to help—or, rather, to simply take the tub and carry it himself.

That was how Peggy saw her father's face for the first time in more than six years—red, sweating, as he puffed from the labor of carrying the tub. And angry, too, or at least sullen. Even though Mother had no doubt assured him that the teacher lady wasn't half so arrogant as she seemed at first, still Father was resentful of this stranger living in the springhouse, a place that belonged only to his long-lost daughter.

Peggy longed to call out to him, call him Father, and assure him that it *was* his daughter who dwelt here now, that all his labor to make a home of this old place was really a gift of love to her. How it comforted her to know how much he loved her, that he had not forgotten her after all these years; yet it also made her heart break for him, that she couldn't name herself to him truly, not yet, not if she was to accomplish all she needed to. She would have to do with him what she was already trying to do with Alvin and with Mother—not reclaim old loves and debts, but win new love and friendship.

She could not come home as a daughter of this place, not even to Father, who alone would purely rejoice at her coming. She had to come home as a stranger. For surely that's what she was, even if she had no disguise, for after three years of one kind of learning in Dekane and another three of schooling and study, she was no longer Little Peggy, the quiet, sharp-tongued torch; she had long since become something else. She had learned many graces under the tutelage of Mistress Modesty; she had learned many other things from books and teachers. She was not who she had been. It would be as much a lie to say, Father, I am your daughter Little Peggy, as it was to say what she said now: "Mr. Guester, I am your new tenant, Miss Larner. I'm very glad to meet you."

He huffed up to her and put out his hand. Despite his misgivings, despite the way he had avoided meeting her when first she arrived at the roadhouse an hour or so past, he was too much the consummate innkeeper to refuse to greet her with courtesy—or at least the rough country manners that passed for courtesy in this frontier town.

"Pleased to meet you, Miss Larner. I trust your accommodation is satisfactory?"

It made her a little sad, to hear him trying fancy language on her, the way he talked to those customers he thought of as "dignitaries," meaning that he believed their station in life to be above his. I've learned much, Father, and this above all: that no station in life is above any other, if it's occupied by someone with a good heart.

As to whether Father's heart was good, Peggy believed it but refused to look. She had known his heartfire far too well in years past. If she looked too closely now, she might find things a daughter had no right to see. She'd been too young to control herself when she explored his heartfire all those years ago; in the innocence of childhood she had learned things that made both innocence and childhood impossible. Now, though, with her knack better tamed, she could at last give him privacy in his own heart. She owed him and Mother that.

Not to mention that she owed it to herself not to know *exactly* what they thought and felt about everything.

They set up the tub in her little house. Mother had brought another bucket and a kettle, and now Father and Alvin both set to toting water up from the well, while Mother boiled some on the stove. When the bath was ready, she sent the men away; then Peggy sent Mother away as well, though not without considerable argument. "I am grateful for your solicitude," Peggy said, "but it is my custom to bathe in utter privacy. You have been exceptionally kind, and as I now take my bath, alone, you may be sure I will think of you gratefully every moment."

The stream of high-sounding language was more than even Mother could resist. At last the door was closed and locked, the curtains drawn. Peggy removed her traveling gown, which was heavy with dust and sweat, and then peeled away her chemise and her pantalets, which clung hotly to her skin. It was one of the benefits of her disguise, that she need not trouble herself with corsetry. No one expected a spinster of her supposed age to have the perversely slender waist of those poor young victims of fashion who bound themselves until they could not breathe.

Last of all she removed her amulets, the three that hung around her neck and the one enwrapped with her hair. The amulets were hard-won, and not just because they were the new, expensive ones that acted on what others actually saw, and not just on their opinion of it. It had taken four visits before the hexman believed that she really did want to appear ugly. "A girl so lovely as you, you don't need my art," he said it over and over again, until she finally took him by the shoulders and said, "That's why I need it! To make me *stop* being beautiful." He gave in, but kept muttering that it was a sin to cover what God created well.

God or Mistress Modesty, thought Peggy. I *was* beautiful in Mistress Modesty's house. Am I beautiful now, when no one sees me but myself, I who am least likely to admire?

Naked at last, herself at last, she knelt beside the tub and ducked her head to begin the washing of her hair. Immersed in water, hot as it was, she felt the same old freedom she had felt so long ago in the springhouse, the wet isolation in which no heartfires intruded, so she was truly herself alone, and had a chance of knowing what her self might actually be.

There was no mirror in the springhouse. Nor had she

brought one. Nevertheless, she knew when her bath was done and she toweled herself before the stove, already sweating in the steamy room, in the early August evening— she knew that she *was* beautiful, as Mistress Modesty had taught her how to be; knew that if Alvin could see her as she really was, he would desire her, not for wisdom, but for the more casual and shallow love that any man feels for a woman who delights his eyes. So, just as she had once hidden from him so he wouldn't marry her for pity, now she hid from him so he wouldn't marry her for boyish love. This self, the smooth and youthful body, would remain invisible to him, so that her truer self, the sharp and well-filled mind, might entice the finest man in him, the man that would be, not a lover, but a Maker.

If only she could somehow disguise his body from her own eyes, so that she would not have to imagine his touch, as gentle as the touch of air on her skin as she moved across the room.

16

PROPERTY

The Blacks started in a-howling before the roosters got up. Cavil Planter didn't get up right away; the sound of it sort of fit into his dream. Howling Blacks figured in his dreams pretty common these days. Anyway it finally woke him, and he bounded up out of bed. Barely light outside; he had to open the curtain to get light enough to find his trousers. He could make out shadows moving down near the slave quarters, but couldn't see what all was going on. He thought the worst, of course, and pulled his shotgun down from the rack on his bedroom wall. Slaveowners, in case you didn't guess, always keep their firearms in the same room where they sleep.

Out in the hall, he nearly bumped into somebody. She screeched. It took Cavil a moment to realize it was his wife, Dolores. Sometimes he forgot she knew how to walk, seeing how she only left her room at certain times. He just wasn't used to seeing her out of bed, moving around the house without a slave or two to lean on.

"Hush now, Dolores, it's me, Cavil."

"Oh, what is it, Cavil! What's happening out there!" She was clinging to his arm, so he couldn't move on.

"Don't you think I can tell you better if you let me go find out?"

She hung on tighter. "Don't do it, Cavil! Don't go out there alone! They might kill you!"

"Why would they kill me? Am I not a righteous master? Will the Lord not protect me?" All the same, he felt a thrill of fear. Could this be the slave revolt that every master feared but none spoke of? He realized now that this very thought had been lingering at the back of his mind since he first woke up. Now Dolores had put it into words. "I have my shotgun," said Cavil. "Don't worry about me."

"I'm afraid," said Dolores.

"You know what *I'm* afraid of? That you'll stumble in the dark and really hurt yourself. Go back to bed, so I don't have to worry about you while I'm outside."

Somebody started pounding at the door.

"Master! Master!" cried a slave. "We need you, Master!"

"Now see? That's Fat Fox," said Cavil. "If it was a revolt, my love, they'd strangle him first off, before they ever came after me."

"Is that supposed to make me feel better?" she asked.

"Master! Master!"

"To bed," said Cavil.

For a moment her hand rested on the hard cold barrel of the shotgun. Then she turned and, like a pale grey ghost in the darkness of the hall, she disappeared into the shadows toward her room.

Fat Fox was near to jumping up and down he was so agitated. Cavil looked at him, as always, with disgust. Even though Cavil depended on Fat Fox to let him know which slaves talked ugly behind his back, Cavil didn't have to like him. There wasn't a hope in heaven of saving the soul of any full-blood Black. They were all born in deep corruption, like as if they embraced original sin and sucked more of it with their mother's milk. It's a wonder their milk wasn't black with all the foulness that must be in it. I wish it wasn't such a slow process, turning the Black race White enough to be worth trying to save their souls.

"It's that Salamandy girl, Master," said Fat Fox.

"Is her baby coming early?" said Cavil.

"Oh no," said Fat Fox. "No, no, it ain't coming, no Master. Oh please come on down. It ain't that gun you needing, Master. It's your big old buck knife I think."

"I'll decide that," said Cavil. If a Black suggests you ought to put your gun away, that's when you hang onto it tightest of all.

He strode toward the slave women's quarters. It was getting light enough by now that he could see the ground, could see the Blacks all slinking here and there in the dark, watching him, white eyes watching. That was a mercy from the Lord God, making their eyes white, else you couldn't see them at all in the shadows.

There was a passel of women all outside the door to the cabin where Salamandy slept. Her being so close to her time, she didn't have to do any field work these days, and she got a bed with a fine mattress. Nobody could say Cavil Planter didn't take care of his breeding stock.

One of the women—in the darkness he couldn't tell who, but from the voice he thought it was maybe Coppy, the one baptized as Agnes but who chose to call herself after the copperhead rattler—anyway she cried out, "Oh, Master, you got to let us bleed a chicken on this one!"

"No heathen abominations shall be practiced on my plantation," said Cavil sternly. But he knew now that Salamandy was dead. Only a month from delivery, and she was dead. It stabbed his heart deep. One child less. One breeding ewe gone. O God have mercy on me! How can I serve thee aright if you take away my best concubine?

It smelled like a sick horse in the room, from her bowel opening up as she died. She'd hung herself with the bedsheet. Cavil damned himself for a fool, giving her such a thing. Here he meant it as a sign of special favor, her being on her sixth half-White baby, to let her have a sheet on her mattress, and now she turned around and answered him like this.

Her feet dangled not three inches from the floor. She must have stood on the bed and then stepped off. Even now, as she swayed slightly in the breeze of his movement in the room, her feet bumped into the bedstead. It took a second or two for Cavil to realize what that meant. Since her neck wasn't broke, she must have been a long time strangling, and the whole time the bed was inches away, and she *knew* it. The whole time, she could have stopped strangling at any time. Could have changed her mind. This was a woman who wanted to die. No, wanted to *kill*. Murder that baby she was carrying.

Proof again how strong these Blacks were in their wickedness. Rather than give birth to a half-White child with a hope of salvation, she'd strangle to death herself. Was there no limit to their perversity? How could a godly man save such creatures?

"She kill herself, Master!" cried the woman who had spoke before. He turned to look at her, and now it was light enough to see for sure that it was Coppy talking. "She waiting for tomorrow night to kill somebody else, less we bleed a chicken on her!"

"It makes me ill, to think you'd use this poor woman's death as an excuse to roast a chicken out of turn. She'll have a decent burial, and her soul will *not* hurt anyone, though as a suicide she will surely burn in hell forever."

At his words Coppy wailed in grief. The other women joined in her keening. Cavil had Fat Fox set a group of young bucks digging a grave—not in the regular slaveyard, of course, since as a suicide she couldn't lie in consecrated ground. Out among the trees, with no marker, as befit a beast that took the life of her own young.

She was in the ground before nightfall. Since she was a suicide, Cavil couldn't very well ask the Baptist preacher or the Catholic priest to come help with it. In fact, he figured to say the words himself, only it happened that tonight was the night he'd already invited a traveling preacher to supper. That preacher showed up early, and the house slaves sent him around back where he found the burial in progress and offered to help.

"Oh, you don't need to do that," said Cavil.

"Let it never be said that Reverend Philadelphia Thrower did not extend Christian love to all the children of God—White or Black, male or female, saint or sinner."

The slaves perked up at that, and so did Cavil—for the opposite reason. That was Emancipationist talk, and Cavil felt a sudden fear that he had invited the devil into his own house by bringing this Presbyterian preacher. Nevertheless, it would probably do much to quiet the Blacks' superstitious fears if he allowed the rites to be administered by a real preacher. And sure enough, when the words were said and the grave was covered, they all seemed right quiet—none of that ghastly howling.

At dinner, the preacher—Thrower, that was his name—eased Cavil's fears considerably. "I believe that it is part of God's great plan for the Black people to be brought to America in chains. Like the children of Israel, who had to suffer years of bondage to the Egyptians, these Blacks' souls are under the Lord's own lash, shaping them to His own purposes. The Emancipationists understand one truth—that God loves his Black children—but they misunderstand everything else. Why, if they had their way and freed all the slaves at once, it would accomplish the devil's purpose, not God's, for without slavery the Blacks have no hope of rising out of their savagery."

"Now, that sounds downright theological," said Cavil.

"Don't the Emancipationists understand that every Black who escapes from his rightful master into the North is doomed to eternal damnation, him and all his children? Why, they might as well have remained in Africa as go north. The Whites up north hate Blacks, as well they should, since only the most evil and proud and stiff-necked dare to offend God by leaving their masters. But you here in Appalachee and in the Crown Colonies, you are the ones who truly love the Black man, for only you are willing to take responsibility for these wayward children and help them progress on the road to full humanity."

"You may be a Presbyterian, Reverend Thrower, but you know the true religion."

"I'm glad to know I'm in the home of a godly man, Brother Cavil."

"I hope I am your brother, Reverend Thrower."

And that's how the talk went on, the two of them liking each other better and better as the evening wore. By nightfall, when they sat on the porch cooling off, Cavil began to think he had met the first man to whom he might tell some part of his great secret.

Cavil tried to bring it up casual. "Reverend Thrower, do you think the Lord God speaks to any men today?"

Thrower's voice got all solemn. "I know He does."

"Do you think He might even speak to a common man like me?"

"You mustn't hope for it, Brother Cavil," said Thrower, "for the Lord goes where He will, and not where we wish. Yet I do know that it's possible for even the humblest man to have a—visitor."

Cavil felt a trembling in his belly. Why, Thrower sounded like he already knew Cavil's secret. But still he didn't blurt it out all at once. "You know what I think?" said Cavil. "I think that the Lord God can't appear in his true form, because his glory would kill a natural man."

"Oh, indeed," said Thrower. "As when Moses craved a vision of the Lord, and the Lord covered his eyes with His hand, only letting Moses see His back parts as he passed by."

"I mean, what if a man like me saw the Lord Jesus himself, only not looking like any painting of him, but instead looking like an overseer. I reckon that a man sees only what will make him understand the power of God, not the true majesty of the Lord."

Thrower nodded wisely. "It may well be," he said. "That's a plausible explanation. Or it might be that you only saw an angel."

There it was—that simple. From "what if a man like me" to Thrower saying "you saw an angel." That's how much alike these two men were. So Cavil told the whole story, for the first time ever, near seven years after it happened.

When he was done, Thrower took his hand and held it in a brotherly grip, looking him in the eye with a fierce-looking kind of expression. "To think of your sacrifice, mingling your flesh with that of these Black women, in order to serve the Lord. How many children?"

"Twenty-five that got born alive. You helped me bury the twenty-sixth inside Salamandy's belly this evening."

"Where are all these hopeful half-White youngsters?"

"Oh, that's half the labor I'm doing," said Cavil. "Till the Fugitive Slave Treaty, I used to sell them all south as soon as I could, so they'd grow up there and spread White blood throughout the Crown Colonies. Each one will be a missionary through his seed. Of course, the last few I've kept here. It ain't the safest thing, neither, Reverend Thrower. All my breeding-age stock is pure Black, and folks are bound to wonder where these mixup children come from. So far, though, my overseer, Lashman, he keeps his mouth shut if he notices, and nobody else ever sees them."

Thrower nodded, but it was plain his mind was on something else. "Only twenty-*five* of these children?"

"It's the best I could do," said Cavil. "Even a Black woman can't make a baby right off after a birthing."

"I meant—you see, I also had a—visitation. It's the reason why I came here, came touring through Appalachee. I was told that I would meet a farmer who also knew my Visitor, and who had produced twenty-six living gifts to God."

"Twenty-*six*."

"Living."

"Well, you see—well, ain't that just the way of it. You see, I wasn't including in my tally the very first one born, because his mother run off and stole him from me a few days before he was due to be sold. I had to refund the money in cash to the buyer, and it was no good tracking, the dogs couldn't pick up her scent. Word among the slaves was that she turned into a blackbird and *flew,* but you know the tales they tell."

"So—twenty-six then. And tell me this—is there some reason why the name 'Hagar' should mean anything to you?"

Cavil gasped. "No one knows I called the mother by that name!"

"My Visitor told me that Hagar had stolen away your first gift."

"It's Him. You've seen Him, too."

"To me he comes as—not an overseer. More like a scientist—a man of unguessable wisdom. Because *I* am a scientist, I imagine, besides my vocation as a minister. I have always supposed that He was a mere angel—listen to me, a *mere* angel—because I dared not hope that He was—was the Master himself. But now what you tell me—could it be that we have both entertained the presence of our Lord? Oh, Cavil, how can I doubt it? Why else would the Lord have brought us together like this? It means that I—that I'm forgiven."

"Forgiven?"

At Cavil's question, Thrower's face darkened.

Cavil hastened to reassure him. "No, you don't need to tell me if you don't want."

"I—it is almost unbearable to think of it. But now that I am clearly deemed acceptable—or at least, now that I've been given another chance—Brother Cavil, once I was given a mission to perform, one as dark and difficult and secret as your own. Except that where you have had the courage and strength to prevail, I failed. I tried, but I had not wit or vigor enough to overcome the power of the devil. I thought I was rejected, cast off. That's why I became a traveling preacher, for I felt myself unworthy to take a pulpit of my own. But now—"

Cavil nodded, holding the man's hands as tears flowed down his cheek.

At last Thrower looked up at him. "How do you suppose our—Friend—meant me to help you in your work?"

"I can't say," said Cavil. "But there's only one way I can think of, offhand."

"Brother Cavil, I'm not sure if I can take upon myself that loathsome duty."

"In my experience, the Lord strengthens a man, and makes it—bearable."

"But in my case, Brother Cavil—you see, I've never known a woman, as the Bible speaks of it. Only once have my lips touched a woman's, and that was against my will."

"Then I'll do my best to help you. How if we pray together good and long, and then I show you once?"

Well, that seemed like the best idea either of them could think of right offhand, and so they did it, and it turned out Reverend Thrower was a quick learner. Cavil felt a great sense of relief to have someone else join in, not to mention a kind of peculiar pleasure at having somebody watch him and then watching the other fellow in turn. It was a powerful sort of brotherhood, to have their seed mingled in the same vessel, so to speak. Like Reverend Thrower said, "When this field comes to harvest, Brother Cavil, we shall not guess whose seed came unto ripeness, for the Lord gave us this field together, for this time."

Oh, and then Reverend Thrower asked the girl's name. "Well, we baptized her as 'Hepzibah,' but she goes by the name 'Roach.'"

"Roach!"

"They all take animal names. I reckon she doesn't have too high an opinion of herself."

At that, Thrower just reached over and took Roach's hand

and patted it, as kindly a gesture as if Thrower and Roach was man and wife, an idea that made Cavil almost laugh right out. "Now, Hepzibah, you must use your Christian name," said Thrower, "and not such a debasing animal name."

Roach just looked at him wide-eyed, lying there curled up on the mattress.

"Why doesn't she answer me, Brother Cavil?"

"Oh, they never talk during this. I beat that out of them early—they always tried to talk me out of doing it. I figure better to have no words than have them say what the devil wants me to hear."

Thrower turned back to the woman. "But now I ask you to speak to me, Roach. You won't say devil words, will you?"

In answer, Roach's eyes wandered upward to where part of a bedsheet was still knotted around a rafter. It had been raggedly hacked off below the knot.

Thrower's face got kind of sick-looking. "You mean this is the room where—the girl we buried—"

"This room has the best bed," said Cavil. "I didn't want us doing this on a straw pallet if we didn't have to."

Thrower said nothing. He just left the room, pretty quick, plunging outside into the darkness. Cavil sighed, picked up the lantern, and followed him. He found Thrower leaning over the pump. He could hear Roach skittering out of the room where Salamandy died, heading for her own quarters, but he didn't give no never mind to her. It was Thrower—surely the man wasn't so beside himself that he'd throw up on the drinking water!

"I'm all right," whispered Thrower. "I just—the same room—I'm not at all superstitious, you understand. It just seemed disrespectful to the dead."

These northerners. Even when they understood somewhat

about slavery, they couldn't get rid of their notion of Blacks as if they was people. Would you stop using a room just because a mouse died there, or you once killed a spider on the wall? Do you burn down your stable just because your favorite horse died there?

Anyway, Thrower got himself together, hitched up his trousers and buttoned them up proper, and they went back into the house. Brother Cavil put Thrower in their guest room, which wasn't all that much used, so there was a cloud of dust when Cavil slapped the blanket. "Should have known the house slaves'd be slacking in this room," said Brother Cavil.

"No matter," said Thrower. "On a night this warm, I'll need no blanket."

On the way down the hall to his own bedroom, Cavil paused a moment to listen for his wife's breathing. As sometimes happened, he could hear her whimpering softly in her bedroom. The pain must be bad indeed. Oh Lord, thought Cavil, how many more times must I do Thy bidding before You'll have mercy and heal my Dolores? But he didn't go in to her—there was nothing he could do to help her, besides prayer, and he'd need his sleep. This had been a late night, and tomorrow had work enough.

Sure enough, Dolores had had a bad night—she was still asleep at breakfast time. So Cavil ended up eating with Thrower. The preacher put away an astonishingly large portion of sausage and grits. When his plate was clean for the third time, he looked at Cavil and smiled. "The Lord's service can give a man quite an appetite!" They both had a good laugh at that.

After breakfast, they walked outside. It happened they went near the woods where Salamandy had been buried. Thrower suggested looking at the grave, or else Cavil probably never would have known what the Blacks did in the night. There were footprints all over the grave itself, which was churned into mud. Now the drying mud was covered with ants.

"Ants!" said Thrower. "They can't possibly smell the body under the ground."

"No," said Cavil. "What they're finding is fresher and right on top. Look at that—cut-up entrails."

"They didn't—exhume her body and—"

"Not *her* guts, Reverend Thrower. Probably a squirrel or blackbird or something. They did a devil sacrifice last night."

Thrower immediately began murmuring a prayer.

"They know I forbid such things," said Cavil. "By evening, the proof of it would no doubt be gone. They're disobeying me behind my back. I won't have it."

"Now I understand the magnitude of the work you slaveowners have. The devil has an iron grip upon their souls."

"Well, never you mind. They'll pay for it today. They want blood dropped on her grave? It'll be their own. Mr. Lashman! Where are you! Mr. Lashman!"

The overseer had only just arrived for the day's work.

"A little half-holiday for the Blacks this morning, Mr. Lashman," said Cavil.

Lashman didn't ask why. "Which ones you want whipped?"

"All of them. Ten lashes each. Except the pregnant women, of course. But even they—one lash for each of them, across the thighs. And all to watch."

"They get a bit unruly, watching it, sir," said Lashman.

"Reverend Thrower and I will watch also," said Cavil.

While Lashman was off assembling the slaves, Thrower murmured something about not really wanting to watch.

"It's the Lord's work," said Cavil. "I have stomach enough to watch any act of righteousness. I thought after last night that you did too."

So they watched together as each slave in turn was

whipped, the blood dripping down onto Salamandy's grave. After a while Thrower didn't even flinch. Cavil was glad to see it—the man wasn't weak, after all, just a little soft from his upbringing in Scotland and his life in the North.

Afterward, as Reverend Thrower prepared to be on his way—he had promised to preach in a town a half-day's ride south—he happened to ask Cavil a question.

"I noticed that all your slaves seem—not old, you understand, but not young, either."

Cavil shrugged. "It's the Fugitive Slave Treaty. Even though my farm's prospering, I can't buy or sell any slaves— we're part of the United States now. Most folks keep up by breeding, but you know all my pickaninnies ended up south, till lately. And now I've lost me another breeder, so I'm down to five women now. Salamandy was the best. The others don't have so many years of babies left in them."

"It occurs to me," said Thrower. He paused in thought.

"What occurs to you?"

"I've traveled a lot in the North, Brother Cavil, and in most every town in Hio and Suskwahenny and Irrakwa and Wobbish, there's a family or two of Blacks. Now, you know and I know that they didn't grow on northern trees."

"All runaways."

"Some, no doubt, have their freedom legally. But many— certainly there are many runaways. Now, I understand that it's a custom for every slaveowner to keep a cachet of hair and nail clippings and—"

"Oh, yes, we take them from the minute they're born or the minute we buy them. For the Finders."

"Exactly."

"But we can't exactly send the Finders to walk every foot of ground in the whole North, hoping to run into one particular runaway buck. It'd cost more than the price of the slave."

"It seems to me that the price of slaves has gone up lately."

"If you mean that we can't buy one at any price—"

"That's what I mean, Brother Cavil. And what if the Finders don't have to go blindly through the North, relying on chance? What if you arranged to hire people in the North to scour the papers and take note of the name and age of every Black they see there? Then the Finders could go armed with information."

Well, that idea was so good that it stopped Cavil right short. "There's got to be something wrong with that idea, or somebody'd already be doing it."

"Oh, I'll tell you why nobody's done it so far. There's a good deal of ill-feeling toward slaveowners in the North. Even though northerners hate their Black neighbors, their misguided consciences won't let them cooperate in any kind of slave search. So any southerner who ever went north searching for a runaway soon learned that if he didn't have his Finder right with him, or if the trail was cold, then there was no use searching."

"That's the truth of it. Like a bunch of thieves up North, conspiring to keep a man from recovering his run-off stock."

"But what if you had northerners doing the searching for you? What if you had an agent in the North, a minister perhaps, who could enlist others in the cause, who could find people who could be trusted? Such an endeavor would be expensive, but given the impossibility of *buying* new slaves in Appalachee, don't you imagine people would be willing to pay enough to finance the work of recovering their runaways?"

"Pay? They'd pay double what you ask. They'd pay up front on the chance of you doing it."

"Suppose I charged twenty dollars to register their runaway—birthdate, name, description, time and circumstances of escape—and then charged a thousand dollars if I provide them with information leading to recovery?"

"Fifty dollars to register, or they won't believe you're serious. And another fifty whenever you send them information, even if it doesn't turn out to be the right one. And *three* thousand for runaways recovered healthy."

Thrower smiled slightly. "I don't wish to make an unfair profit from the work of righteousness."

"Profit! You got a lot of folks up there to pay if you're going to do a good job. I tell you, Thrower, you write up a contract, and then get the printer in town to run you off a thousand copies. Then you just go around and tell what you plan to one slaveowner in each town you come to in Appalachee. I reckon you'll have to get a new printing done within a week. We're not talking profit here, we're talking a valuable service. Why, I'll bet you get contributions from folks what *never* had a runaway. If you can make it so the Hio River stops being the last barrier before they get away clean, it'll not only return old runaways, it'll make the other slaves lose hope and stay home!"

Not half an hour later, Thrower was back outside and on his horse—but now he had notes written up for the contract and letters of introduction from Cavil to his lawyer and to the printer, along with letters of credit to the tune of five hundred dollars. When Thrower protested that it was too much, Cavil wouldn't even hear him out. "To get you started," said Cavil. "We both know whose work we're doing. It takes money. I have it and you don't, so take it and get busy."

"That's a Christian attitude," said Thrower. "Like the saints in the early Church, who had all things in common."

Cavil patted Thrower's thigh, where he sat stiff in the saddle—northerners just didn't know how to sit a horse. "We've had more in common than any other two men alive," said Cavil. "We've had the same visions and done the same works, and if that don't make us two peas in a pod, I don't know what will."

"When next I see the Visitor, if I should be so fortunate, I know that he'll be pleased."

"Amen," said Cavil.

Then he slapped Thrower's horse and watched him out of sight. My Hagar. He's going to find my Hagar and her little boy. Nigh on seven years since she stole my firstborn child from me. Now she'll come back, and this time she'll stay in chains and give me more children until she can't have no more. And as for the boy, he'll be my Ishmael. That's what I'll call him, too. Ishmael. I'll keep him right here, and raise him up to be strong and obedient and a true Christian. When he's old enough I'll hire him out to other plantations, and during the nights he'll go and carry on my work, spreading the chosen seed throughout Appalachee. Then my children will surely be as numberless as the sands of the sea, just like Abraham.

And who knows? Maybe then the miracle will happen, and my own dear wife will be healed, and she'll conceive and bear me a pure White child, my Isaac, to inherit all my land and all my work. Lord my Overseer, be merciful to me.

17

SPELLING BEE

Early January, with deep snow, and a wind sharp enough to slice your nose off—so of course that was a day for Makepeace Smith to decide *he* had to work in the forge all day, while Alvin went into town to buy supplies and deliver

PRENTICE ALVIN • 271

finished work. In the summer, the choice of jobs tended to go the other way.

Never mind, thought Alvin. He *is* the master here. But if I'm ever master of my own forge, and if I have me a prentice, you can bet he'll be treated fairer than I've been. A master and prentice ought to share the work alike, except for when the prentice plain don't know how, and then the master ought to teach him. That's the bargain, not to have a slave, not to always have the prentice take the wagon into town through the snow.

Truth to tell, though, Alvin knew he wouldn't have to take the wagon. Horace Guester's sleigh-and-two would do the job, and he knew Horace wouldn't mind him taking it, as long as Alvin did whatever errands the roadhouse needed doing in town.

Alvin bundled himself tight and pushed out into the wind—it was right in his face, from the west, the whole way up to the roadhouse. He took the path up by Miss Larner's house, it being the closest way with the most trees to break the wind. Course she wasn't in. It being school hours, she was with the children in the schoolhouse in town. But the old springhouse, it was Alvin's schoolhouse, and just passing by the door got him to thinking about his studies.

She had him learning things he never thought to learn. He was expecting more of ciphering and reading and writing, and in a way that's what she had him doing, right enough. But she didn't have him reading out of those primers like the children—like Arthur Stuart, who plugged away at his studies by lamplight every night in the springhouse. No, she talked to Alvin about ideas he never would've thought of, and all his writing and calculating was about such things.

Yesterday:

"The smallest particle is an atom," she said. "According

to the theory of Demosthenes, everything is made out of smaller things, until you come to the atom, which is smallest of all and cannot be divided."

"What's it look like?" Alvin asked her.

"I don't know. It's too small to see. Do *you* know?"

"I reckon not. Never saw anything so small but what you could cut it in half."

"But can't you *imagine* anything smaller?"

"Yeah, but I can split that too."

She sighed. "Well, now, Alvin, think again. If there *were* a thing so small it couldn't be divided, what would it be like?"

"*Real* small, I reckon."

But he was joking. It was a problem, and he set out to answer it the way he answered any practical problem. He sent his bug out into the floor. Being wood, the floor was a jumble of things, the broke-up once-alive hearts of living trees, so Alvin quickly sent his bug on into the iron of the stove, which was mostly all one thing inside. Being hot, the bits of it, the tiniest parts he ever saw clear, they were a blur of movement; while the fire inside, it made its own outward rush of light and heat, each bit of it so small and fine that he could barely hold the idea of it in his mind. He never really *saw* the bits of fire. He only knew that they had just passed by.

"Light," he said. "And heat. They can't be cut up."

"True. Fire isn't like earth—it can't be cut. But it can be changed, can't it? It can be extinguished. It can cease to be itself. And therefore the parts of it must become something else, and so they were not the unchangeable and indivisible atoms."

"Well, there's nothing smaller than those bits of fire, so I reckon there's no such thing as an atom."

"Alvin, you've got to stop being so empirical about things."

"If I knowed what that was, I'd stop being it."

"If I knew."

"Whatever."

"You can't always answer every question by sitting back and doodlebugging your way through the rocks outside or whatever."

Alvin sighed. "Sometimes I wish I never told you what I do."

"Do you want me to teach you what it means to be a Maker or not?"

"That's just *what* I want! And instead you talk about atoms and gravity and—I don't care what that old humbug Newton said, nor anybody else! I want to know how to make the—*place*." He remembered only just in time that there was Arthur Stuart in the corner, memorizing every word they said, complete with tone of voice. No sense filling Arthur's head with the Crystal City.

"Don't you understand, Alvin? It's been so long— thousands of years—that no one knows what a Maker really is, or what he does. Only that there were such men, and a few of the tasks that they could do. Changing lead or iron into gold, for instance. Water into wine. That sort of thing."

"I expect iron to gold'd be easier," said Alvin. "Those metals are pretty much all one thing inside. But wine— that's such a mess of different stuff inside that you'd have to be a—a—" He couldn't think of a word for the most power a man could have.

"Maker."

That was the word, right enough. "I reckon."

"I'm telling you, Alvin, if you want to learn how to do the things that Makers once did, you have to understand the nature of things. You can't change what you don't understand."

"And I can't understand what I don't see."

"Wrong! Absolutely false, Alvin Smith! It is what you *can* see that remains impossible to understand. The world you actually see is nothing more than an example, a special case. But the underlying principles, the order that holds it all together, *that* is forever invisible. It can only be discovered in the imagination, which is precisely the aspect of your mind that is most neglected."

Well, last night Alvin just got mad, which she said would only guarantee that he'd stay stupid, which he said was just fine with him as he'd stayed alive against long odds by being as pure stupid as he was without any help from *her.* Then he stormed on outside and walked around watching the first flakes of this storm start coming down.

He'd only been walking a little while when he realized that she was right, and he knowed it all along. Knew it. He always sent out his bug to see what was *there,* but then when he got set to make a change, he first had to think up what he *wanted* it to be. He had to think of something that wasn't there, and hold a picture of it in his mind, and then, in that way he was born with and still didn't understand, he'd say, See this? This is how you ought to be! And then, sometimes fast, sometimes slow, the bits of it would move around until they lined up right. That's how he always did it: separating a piece off of living rock; joining together two bits of wood; making the iron line up strong and true; spreading the heat of the fire smooth and even along the bottom of the crucible. So I do see what isn't there, in my mind, and that's what makes it *come* to be there.

For a terrible dizzying moment he wondered if maybe the whole world was maybe no more than what he imagined it to be, and if that was true then if he stopped imagining, it'd just go away. Of course, once he got his sense together he knew that if he'd been thinking it up, there wouldn't be so many strange things in the world that he never could've thought of himself.

So maybe the world was all dreamed up in the mind of God. But no, can't be that neither, because if God dreamed up men like White Murderer Harrison then God wasn't too good. No, the best Alvin could think of was that God worked pretty much the way Alvin did—told the rocks of the earth and the fire of the sun and stuff like that, told it all how it was supposed to be and then let it be that way. But when God told *people* how to be, why, they just thumbed their noses and laughed at him, mostly, or else they pretended to obey while they still went on and did what they pleased. The planets and the stars and the elements, they all might be thought up from the mind of God, but people were just too cantankerous to blame them on anybody but their own self.

Which was about the limit of Alvin's thinking last night, in the snow—wondering about what he could never know. Things like I wonder what God dreams about if he ever sleeps, and if all his dreams come true, so that every night he makes up a whole new world full of people. Questions that couldn't never get him a speck closer to being a Maker.

So today, slogging through the snow, pushing against the wind toward the roadhouse, he started thinking again about the original question—what an atom would be like. He tried to picture something so tiny that he couldn't cut it. But whenever he imagined something like that—a little box or a little ball or something—why, then he'd just up and imagine it splitting right in half.

The only way he couldn't split something in half was if it was so thin nothing could be thinner. He thought of it squished so flat it was thinner than paper, so thin that in that direction it didn't even *exist,* if you looked at it edge-on it would just plain not be there. But even then, he might not be able to split it along the edge, but he could still imagine turning it and slicing it across, just like paper.

So—what if it was squished up in another direction, too, so it was all edge, going on like the thinnest thread you ever dreamed of? Nobody could see it, but it would still be there, because it would stretch from here to there. He sure couldn't split that along the edge, and it didn't have any flat surface like paper had. Yet as long as it stretched like invisible thread from one spot to another, no matter how short the distance was, he could still imagine snipping it right in half, and each half in half again.

No, the only way something could be small enough to be an atom is if it had no size at all in any direction, not length nor breadth nor depth. That would be an atom all right— only it wouldn't even *exist*, it'd just be *nothing*. Just a place without anything in it.

He stood on the porch of the roadhouse, stamping snow off his feet, which did better than knocking for telling folks he was there. He could hear Arthur Stuart's feet running to open the door, but all he was thinking about was atoms. Because even though he'd just figured out that there couldn't be no atoms, he was beginning to realize it might be even crazier to imagine there *not* being atoms, so things could always get cut into smaller bits and *those* things into smaller bits, and those into even *smaller* bits, forever and ever. And when you think about it, it's got to be one or the other. Either you get to the bit that can't be split, and it's an atom, or you never do, and so it goes on *forever*, which is more than Alvin's head could hold.

Alvin found himself in the roadhouse kitchen, with Arthur Stuart piggyback, playing with Alvin's hat and scarf. Horace Guester was out in the barn stuffing straw into new bedticks, so Alvin asked Old Peg for use of the sleigh. It was hot in the kitchen, and Goody Guester didn't look to be in good temper. She allowed as how he could take the sled, but there was a price to pay.

"Save the life of a certain child, Alvin, and take Arthur Stuart with you," she said, "or I swear he'll do one more thing to rile me and end up in the pudding tonight."

It was true that Arthur Stuart seemed to be in a mood to make trouble—he was strangling Alvin with his own scarf and laughing like a fool.

"Let's do some lessons, Arthur," said Alvin. "Spell 'choking to death.'"

"C-H-O-K-I-N-G," said Arthur Stuart. "T-W-O. D-E-A-T-H."

Mad as she was, Goody Guester just had to break up laughing—not because he spelled "to" wrong, but because he'd spelled out the words in the most perfect imitation of Miss Larner's voice. "I swear, Arthur Stuart," she said, "you best never let Miss Larner hear you go on like that or your schooling days are over."

"Good! I hate school!" said Arthur.

"You don't hate school so much as you'd hate working with me in the kitchen every day," said Goody Guester. "All day every day, summer and winter, even swimming days."

"I might as well be a slave in Appalachee!" shouted Arthur Stuart.

Goody Guester stopped teasing and being mad, both, and turned solemn. "Don't even joke like that, Arthur. Somebody died once just to keep you from being such a thing."

"I know," said Arthur.

"No you don't, but you'd better just think before you—"

"It was my mama," said Arthur.

Now Old Peg started looking scared. She took a glance at Alvin and then said, "Never mind about that, anyway."

"My mama was a blackbird," said Arthur. "She flew so

high, but then the ground caught her and she got stuck and died."

Alvin saw how Goody Guester looked at him, even more nervous-like. So maybe there was something to Arthur's story of flying after all. Maybe somehow that girl buried up beside Vigor, maybe somehow she got a blackbird to carry her baby somehow. Or maybe it was just some vision. Anyway, Goody Guester had decided to act like it was nothing after all—too late to fool Alvin, of course, but she wouldn't know that. "Well, that's a pretty story, Arthur," said Old Peg.

"It's true," said Arthur. "I remember."

Goody Guester started looking even more upset. But Alvin knew better than to argue with Arthur about this blackbird idea he had, and about him flying once. The only way to stop Arthur talking about it was to get his mind on something else. "Better come with me, Arthur Stuart," said Alvin. "Maybe you got a blackbird mama sometime in your past, but I have a feeling your mama here in this kitchen is about to knead you like dough."

"Don't forget what I need you to buy for me," said Old Peg.

"Oh, don't worry. I got a list," said Alvin.

"I didn't see you write a thing!"

"Arthur Stuart's my list. Show her, Arthur."

Arthur leaned close to Alvin's ear and shouted so loud it like to split Alvin's eardrums right down to his ankles. "A keg of wheat flour and two cones of sugar and a pound of pepper and a dozen sheets of paper and a couple of yards of cloth that might do for a shirt for Arthur Stuart."

Even though he was shouting, it was his mama's own voice.

She purely hated it when he mimicked her, and so here she came with the stirring fork in one hand and a big old cleaver in the other. "Hold still, Alvin, so I can stick the fork in his mouth and shave off a couple of ears!"

"Save me!" cried Arthur Stuart.

Alvin saved him by running away, at least till he got to the back door. Then Old Peg set down her instruments of boy-butchery and helped Alvin bundle Arthur Stuart up in coats and leggings and boots and scarves till he was about as big around as he was tall. Then Alvin pitched him out the door into the snow and rolled him with his foot till he was covered with snow.

Old Peg barked at him from the kitchen door. "That's right. Alvin Junior, freeze him to death right before his own mother's eyes, you irresponsible prentice boy you!"

Alvin and Arthur Stuart just laughed. Old Peg told them to be careful and get home before dark and then she slammed the door tight.

They hitched up the sleigh, then swept out the new snow that had blown in while they were hitching it and got in and pulled up the lap robe. They first went on down to the forge again to pick up the work Alvin had to deliver—mostly hinges and fittings and tools for carpenters and leather-workers in town, who were all in the midst of their busiest season of the year. Then they headed out for town.

They didn't get far before they caught up to a man trudging townward—and none too well dressed, either, for weather like this. When they were beside him and could see his face, Alvin wasn't surprised to see it was Mock Berry.

"Get on this sleigh, Mock Berry, so I won't have your death on my conscience," said Alvin.

Mock looked at Alvin like his words was the first Mock even noticed somebody was there on the road, even though he'd just been passed by the horses, snorting and stamping through the snow. "Thank you, Alvin," said the man. Alvin slid over on the seat to make room. Mock climbed up beside him—clumsy, cause his hands were cold. Only when he was sitting down did he seem to notice Arthur Stuart sitting on the bench. And then it was like somebody slapped him—he started to get right back down off the sleigh.

"Now hold on!" said Alvin. "Don't tell me you're just as stupid as the White folks in town, refusing to sit next to a mixup boy! Shame on you!"

Mock looked at Alvin real steady for a long couple of seconds before he decided how to answer. "Look here, Alvin Smith, you know me better than that. I know how such mixup children come to be, and I don't hold against them what some White man done to their mama. But there's a story in town about who's the real mama of this child, and it does me no good to be seen coming into town with this child nearby."

Alvin knew the story well enough—how Arthur Stuart was supposedly the child of Mock's wife Anga, and how, since Arthur was plainly fathered by some White man, Mock refused even to have the boy in his own house, which led to Goody Guester taking Arthur in. Alvin also knew the story wasn't true. But in a town like this it was better to have such a story believed than to have the true story guessed at. Alvin wouldn't put it past some folks to try to get Arthur Stuart declared a slave and shipped on south just to be rid of him so there'd be no more trouble about schools and such.

"Never mind about that," said Alvin. "Nobody's going to see you on a day like this, and even if they do, Arthur looks like a wad of cloth, and not a boy at all. You can hop off soon as we get into town." Alvin leaned out and took Mock's arm and pulled him onto the seat. "Now pull up the lap robe and snuggle close so I don't have to take you to the undertaker on account of having froze to death."

"Thank you kindly, you persnickety uppity prentice boy." Mock pulled the lap robe up so high that it covered Arthur Stuart completely. Arthur yelled and pulled it down again so he could see over the top. Then he gave Mock Berry such a glare that it might have burnt him to a cinder, if he hadn't been so cold and wet.

When they got into town, there was sleighs a-plenty, but none of the merriment of the first heavy snowfall. Folks just went about their business, and the horses stood and waited, stamping their feet and snorting and steaming in the cold wind. The lazier sort of folks—the lawyers and clerks and such—they were all staying at home on a day like this. But the people with real work to do, they had their fires hot, their workshops busy, their stores open for business. Alvin made his rounds a-dropping off ironwork with the folks who'd called for it. They all put their signature on Makepeace's delivery book—one more slight, that he wouldn't trust Alvin to take cash, like he was a nine-year-old prentice boy and not more than twice that age.

On those quick errands, Arthur Stuart stayed bundled up on the sleigh—Alvin never stayed indoors long enough to warm up from the walk between sleigh and front door. It wasn't till they got to Pieter Vanderwoort's general store that it was worth going inside and warming up for a spell. Pieter had his stove going right hot, and Alvin and Arthur wasn't the first to think of warming up there. A couple of boys from town were there warming their feet and sipping tea with a nip or two from a flask in order to keep warm. They weren't any of the boys Alvin spent much time with. He'd throwed them once or twice, but that was true of every male creature in town who was willing to rassle. Alvin knew that these two—Martin, that was the one with pimples, and the other one was Daisy—I know that sounds like a crazy name for anyone but a cow, but that was his name all right—anyway, Alvin knew that these two boys were the kind who like to set cats afire and make nasty jokes about girls behind their back. Not the kind that Alvin spent much time with, but not any that he had any partickler dislike for, neither. So he nodded them good afternoon, and they nodded him back. One of them held up his flask to share, but Alvin said no thanks and that was that.

At the counter, Alvin pulled off some of his scarves, which felt good because he was so sweaty underneath; then he set to unwinding Arthur Stuart, who spun around like a top while Alvin pulled on the end of each scarf. Arthur's laughing brought Mr. Vanderwoort out from the back, and he set to laughing, too.

"They're so cute when they're little, aren't they," said Mr. Vanderwoort.

"He's just my shopping list today, aren't you, Arthur?"

Arthur Stuart spouted out his list right off, using his Mama's voice again. "A keg of wheat flour and two cones of sugar and a pound of pepper and a dozen sheets of paper and a couple of yards of cloth that might do for a shirt for Arthur Stuart."

Mr. Vanderwoort like to died laughing. "I get such a kick out of that boy, the way he talks like his mama."

One of the boys by the stove gave a whoop.

"I mean his adopted mama, of course," said Vanderwoort.

"Oh, she's probably his mama all right!" said Daisy. "I hear Mock Berry does a *lot* of work up to the roadhouse!"

Alvin just set his jaw against the answer that sprang to mind. Instead he hotted up the flask in Daisy's hand, so Daisy whooped again and dropped it.

"You come on back with me, Arthur Stuart," said Vanderwoort.

"Like to burned my hand off!" muttered Daisy.

"You just say the list over again, bit by bit, and I'll get what's wanted," said Vanderwoort. Alvin lifted Arthur over the counter and Vanderwoort set him down on the other side.

PRENTICE ALVIN • 283

"You must've set it on the stove like the blamed fool you are, Daisy," said Martin. "What is it, whiskey don't warm you up less it's boiled?"

Vanderwoort led Arthur into the back room. Alvin took a couple of soda crackers from the barrel and pulled up a stool near the fire.

"I didn't set it anywheres near the stove," said Daisy.

"Howdy, Alvin," said Martin.

"Howdy, Martin, Daisy," said Alvin. "Good day for stoves."

"Good day for nothing," muttered Daisy. "Smart-mouth pickaninnies and burnt fingers."

"What brings you to town, Alvin?" asked Martin. "And how come you got that baby buck with you? Or did you buy him off Old Peg Guester?"

Alvin just munched on his cracker. It was a mistake to punish Daisy for what he said before, and a worse mistake to do it again. Wasn't it trying to punish folks that brought the Unmaker down on him last summer? No, Alvin was working on curbing his temper, so he said nothing. Just broke off pieces of the cracker with his mouth.

"That boy ain't for sale," said Daisy. "Everybody knows it. Why, she's even trying to educate him, I hear."

"I'm educating my dog, too," said Martin. "You think that boy's learnt him how to beg or point game or anything useful?"

"But you got yourself the advantage there, Marty," said Daisy. "A dog's got him enough brains to know he's a dog, so he don't try to learn how to read. But you get one of these hairless monkeys, they get to thinking they're people, you know what I mean?"

Alvin got up and walked to the counter. Vanderwoort was coming back now, arms full of stuff. Arthur was tagging along behind.

"Come on behind the counter with me, Al," said Vanderwoort. "Best if you pick out the cloth for Arthur's shirt."

"I don't know a thing about cloth," said Alvin.

"Well, I know about cloth but I don't know about what Old Peg Guester likes, and if she ain't happy with what you come home with, I'd rather it be your fault than mine."

Alvin hitched his butt up onto the counter and swung his legs over. Vanderwoort led him back and they spent a few minutes picking out a plaid flannel that looked suitable enough and might also be tough enough to make patches on old trousers out of the leftover scraps. When they came back, Arthur Stuart was over by the fire with Daisy and Martin.

"Spell 'sassafras,' " said Daisy.

"Sassafras," said Arthur Stuart, doing Miss Larner's voice as perfect as ever. "S-A-S-S-A-F-R-A-S."

"Was he right?" asked Martin.

"Beats hell out of me."

"Now don't be using words like that around a child," said Vanderwoort.

"Oh, never you mind," said Martin. "He's our pet pickaninny. We won't do him no harm."

"I'm not a pickaninny," said Arthur Stuart. "I'm a mixup boy."

"Well, ain't that the truth!" Daisy's voice went so loud and high that his voice cracked.

Alvin was just about fed up with them. He spoke real soft, so only Vanderwoort could hear him. "One more whoop and I'll fill that boy's ears with snow."

"Now don't get riled," said Vanderwoort. "They're harmless enough."

"That's why I won't kill him." But Alvin was smiling, and so was Vanderwoort. Daisy and Martin were just playing, and since Arthur Stuart was enjoying it, why not?

Martin picked something off a shelf and brought it over to Vanderwoort. "What's this word?" he asked.

"Eucalyptus," said Vanderwoort.

"Spell 'eucalipidus,' mixup boy."

"Eucalyptus," said Arthur. "E-U-C-A-L-Y-P-T-U-S."

"Listen to that!" cried Daisy. "That teacher lady won't give time of day to us, but here we got her own voice spelling whatever we say."

"Spell 'bosoms,'" said Martin.

"Now that's going too far," said Vanderwoort. "He's just a boy."

"I just wanted to hear the teacher lady's voice saying it," said Martin.

"I know what you wanted, but that's behind-the-barn talk, not in my general store."

The door opened and, after a blast of cold wind, Mock Berry came in, looking tired and half-froze, which of course he was.

The boys took no notice. "Behind the barn don't got a stove," said Daisy.

"Then keep that in mind when you decide how to talk," said Vanderwoort.

Alvin watched how Mock Berry took sidelong glances at the stove, but made no move to go over there. No man in his right mind would choose not to go to the stove on a day like this—but Mock Berry knew there was worse things than being cold. So instead he just walked up to the counter.

Vanderwoort must've known he was there, but for a while he just kept on watching Martin and Daisy play spelling games with Arthur Stuart, paying no mind to Mock Berry.

"Suskwahenny," said Daisy.

"S-U-S-K-W-A-H-E-N-N-Y," said Arthur.

"I bet that boy could win any spelling bee he ever entered," said Vanderwoort.

"You got a customer," said Alvin.

Vanderwoort turned real slow and looked at Mock Berry without expression. Then, still moving slow, he walked over and stood in front of Mock without a word.

"Just need me two pounds of flour and twelve feet of that half-inch rope," said Mock.

"Hear that?" said Daisy. "He's a-fixing to powder his face white and then hang himself, I'll bet."

"Spell 'suicide,' boy," said Martin.

"S-U-I-C-I-D-E," said Arthur Stuart.

"No credit," said Vanderwoort.

Mock laid down some coins on the counter. Vanderwoort looked at it a minute. "Six feet of rope."

Mock just stood there.

Vanderwoort just stood there.

Alvin knew it was more than enough money for what Mock wanted to buy. He couldn't hardly believe Vanderwoort was raising his price for a man about as poor but hard-working as any in town. In fact, Alvin began to understand a little about why Mock stayed so poor. Now, Alvin knew there wasn't much he could do about it—but he could at least do what Horace Guester had once done for him with his master Makepeace—make Vanderwoort put things out in the open and stop pretending he wasn't being as unfair as he was being. So Alvin laid down the paper Vanderwoort had just written out for him. "I'm sorry to hear there's no credit," Alvin said. "I'll go fetch the money from Goody Guester."

Vanderwoort looked at Alvin. Now he could either make Alvin go fetch the money or say right out that there was credit for the *Guesters,* just not for Mock Berry.

Of course he chose another course. Without a word he went into the back and weighed out the flour. Then he measured out twelve feet of half-inch rope. Vanderwoort was known for giving honest measure. But then, he was also known for giving a fair price, which is why it took Alvin aback to see him do otherwise with Mock Berry.

Mock took his rope and his flour and started out.

"You got change," said Vanderwoort.

Mock turned around, looking surprised though he tried not to. He came back and watched as Vanderwoort counted out a dime and three pennies onto the counter. Then, hesitating a moment, Mock scooped them off the counter and dropped them into his pocket. "Thank you sir," he said. Then he went back out into the cold.

Vanderwoort turned to Alvin, looking angry or maybe just resentful. "I can't give credit to everybody."

Now, Alvin could've said something about at least he could give the same price to Blacks as Whites, but he didn't want to make an enemy out of Mr. Vanderwoort, who was after all a mostly good man. So Alvin grinned real friendly and said, "Oh, I know you can't. Them Berrys, they're almost as poor as me."

Vanderwoort relaxed, which meant it was Alvin's good opinion he wanted more than to get even for Alvin embarrassing him. "You got to understand, Alvin, it ain't good for trade if they come in here all the time. Nobody minds that mixup boy of yours—they're cute when they're little—but it makes folks stay away if they think they might run into one of them here."

"I always knowed Mock Berry to keep his word," said Alvin. "And nobody ever said he stole or slacked or any such thing."

"No, nobody ever told such a tale on him."

"I'm glad to know you count us both among your customers," said Alvin.

"Well, lookit here, Daisy," said Martin. "I think *Prentice* Alvin's gone and turned preacher on us. Spell 'reverend,' boy."

"R-E-V-E-R-E-N-D."

Vanderwoort saw things maybe turning ugly, so of course he tried to change the subject. "Like I said, Alvin, that mixup boy's bound to be the best speller in the county, don't you think? What I want to know is, why don't he go on and get into the county spelling bee next week? I think he'd bring Hatrack River the championship. He might even get the *state* championship, if you want my opinion."

"Spell 'championship,' " said Daisy.

"Miss Larner never said me that word," said Arthur Stuart.

"Well figure it out," said Alvin.

"C-H-A-M-P," said Arthur. "E-U-N-S-H-I-P."

"Sounds right to me," said Daisy.

"Shows what *you* know," said Martin.

"Can you do better?" asked Vanderwoort.

"*I'm* not going to be in the county spelling bee," said Martin.

"What's a spelling bee?" asked Arthur Stuart.

"Time to go," said Alvin, for he knew full well that Arthur Stuart wasn't a regular admitted student in the Hatrack River Grammar School, and so it was a sure thing he wouldn't be in no spelling bee. "Oh, Mr. Vanderwoort, I owe you for two crackers I ate."

"I don't charge my friends for a couple of crackers," said Vanderwoort.

"I'm proud to know you count me one of your friends," said Alvin. Alvin meant it, too—it took a good man to get caught out doing something wrong, and then turn around and treat the one that caught him as a friend.

Alvin wound Arthur Stuart back into his scarves, and

then wrapped himself up again, and plunged back into the snow, this time carrying all that he bought from Vanderwoort in a burlap sack. He tucked the sack under the seat of the sleigh so it wouldn't get snowed on. Then he lifted Arthur Stuart into place and climbed up after. The horses looked happy enough to get moving again—they only got colder and colder, standing in the snow.

On the way back to the roadhouse they found Mock Berry on the road and took him on home. Not a word did he say about what happened in the store, but Alvin knew it wasn't cause he didn't appreciate it. He figured Mock Berry was plain ashamed of the fact that it took an eighteen-year-old prentice boy to get him honest measure and fair price in Vanderwoort's general store—only cause the boy was White. Not the kind of thing a man loves to talk about.

"Give a howdy to Goody Berry," said Alvin, as Mock hopped off the sleigh up the lane from his house.

"I'll say you said so," said Mock. "And thanks for the ride." In six steps he was clean gone in the blowing snow. The storm was getting worse and worse.

Once everything was dropped off at the roadhouse, it was near time for Alvin's and Arthur's schooling at Miss Larner's house, so they headed on down there and threw snowballs at each other all the way. Alvin stopped in at the forge to give the delivery book to Makepeace. But Makepeace must've laid off early cause he wasn't there; Alvin tucked the book onto the shelf by the door, where Makepeace would know to look for it. Then he and Arthur went back to snowballs till Miss Larner came back.

Dr. Whitley Physicker drove her in his covered sleigh and walked her right up to her door. When he took note of Alvin and Arthur waiting around, he looked a bit annoyed. "Don't you boys think Miss Larner shouldn't have to do any more teaching on a day like this?"

Miss Larner laid a hand on Dr. Physicker's arm. "Thank you for bringing me home, Dr. Physicker," she said.

"I wish you'd call me Whitley."

"You're kind to me, Dr. Physicker, but I think your honored title suits me best. As for these pupils of mine, it's in bad weather that I do my best teaching, I've found, for they aren't wishing to be at the swimming hole."

"Not me!" shouted Arthur Stuart. "How do you spell 'championship'?"

"C-H-A-M-P-I-O-N-S-H-I-P," said Miss Larner. "Wherever did you hear that word?"

"C-H-A-M-P-I-O-N-S-H-I-P," said Arthur Stuart—in Miss Larner's voice.

"That boy is certainly remarkable," said Physicker. "A mockingbird, I'd say."

"A mockingbird copies the song," said Miss Larner, "but makes no sense of it. Arthur Stuart may speak back the spellings in *my* voice, but he truly knows the word and can read it or write it whenever he wishes."

"I'm not a mockingbird," said Arthur Stuart. "I'm a spelling bee championship."

Dr. Physicker and Miss Larner exchanged a look that plainly meant more than Alvin could understand just from watching.

"Very well," said Dr. Physicker. "Since I did in fact enroll him as a special student—at your insistence—he *can* compete in the county spelling bee. But don't expect to take him any farther, Miss Larner!"

"Your reasons were all excellent, Dr. Physicker, and so I agree. But *my* reasons—"

"Your reasons were overwhelming, Miss Larner. And I can't help but relish in advance the consternation of the people who fought to keep him out of school, when they watch him do as well as children twice his age."

"Consternation, Arthur Stuart," said Miss Larner.

"Consternation," said Arthur. "C-O-N-S-T-E-R-N-A-T-I-O-N."

"Good evening, Dr. Physicker. Come inside, boys. Time for school."

ARTHUR STUART WON the county spelling bee, with the word "celebratory." Then Miss Larner immediately withdrew him from further competition; another child would take his place at the state competition. As a result there was little note taken, except among the locals. Along with a brief notice in the Hatrack River newspaper.

Sheriff Pauley Wiseman folded up that page of the newspaper with a short note and put them in an envelope addressed to Reverend Philadelphia Thrower, The Property Rights Crusade, 44 Harrison Street, Carthage City, Wobbish. It took two weeks for that newspaper page to be spread open on Thrower's desk, along with the note, which said simply:

> Boy turned up here summer 1811, only a few weeks old best guess. Lives in Horace Guester's roadhouse, Hatrack River. Adoption don't hold water I reckon if the boy's a runaway.

No signature—but Thrower was used to that, though he didn't understand it. Why should people try to conceal their identity when they were taking part in works of righteousness? He wrote his own letter and sent it south.

A month later, Cavil Planter read Thrower's letter to a couple of Finders. Then he handed them the cachets he'd saved all these years, those belonging to Hagar and her stole-away Ishmael-child. "We'll be back before summer," said the black-haired Finder. "If he's yourn, we'll have him."

"Then you'll have earned your fee and a fine bonus as well," said Cavil Planter.

"Don't need no bonus," said the white-haired Finder. "Fee and costs is plenty."

"Well, then, as you wish," said Cavil. "I know God will bless your journey."

18

MANACLES

It was early spring, a couple of months before Alvin's nineteenth birthday, when Makepeace Smith come to him and said, "About time you start working on a journeyman piece, Al, don't you think?"

The words sang like redbird song in Alvin's ears, so he couldn't hardly speak back except to nod.

"Well, what do you think you'll make?" asked the master.

"I been thinking maybe a plow," said Alvin.

"That's a lot of iron. Takes a perfect mold, and no easy one, neither. You're asking me to put a good bit of iron at risk, boy."

"If I fail, you can always melt it back."

Since they both knew that Alvin had about as much chance of failing as he did of flying, this was pretty much empty talk—just the last rags of Makepeace's old pretense about how Alvin wasn't much good at smithing.

"Reckon so," said Makepeace. "You just do your best, boy. Hard but not too brittle. Heavy enough to bite deep, but light enough to pull. Sharp enough to cut the earth, and strong enough to cast all stones aside."

"Yes sir." Alvin had memorized the rules of the tools back when he was twelve years old.

There were some other rules that Alvin meant to follow. He had to prove to himself that he was a good smith, and not just a half-baked Maker, which meant that he'd use none of his knack, only the skills that any smith has—a good eye, knowledge of the black metal, the vigor of his arms and the skill of his hands.

Working on his journeyman piece meant he had no other duties till it was done. He started from scratch on this one, as a good journeyman always does. No common clay for the mold—he went upriver on the Hatrack to the best white clay, so the face of the mold would be pure and smooth and hold its shape. Making a mold meant seeing things all inside-out, but Alvin had a good mind for shapes. He patted and stroked the clay into place on the wooden frame, all the time seeing how the different pieces of the mold would give the cooling iron its plow shape. Then he baked the mold dry and hard, ready to receive the iron.

For the metal, he took from the pile of scrap iron and then carefully filed the iron clean, getting rid of all dirt and rust. He scoured the crucible, too. Only then was he ready to melt and cast. He hotted up the coal fire, running the bellows himself, raising and lowering the bellows handle just like he done when he was a new prentice. At last the iron was white in the crucible—and the fire so hot he could scarce bear to come near it. But he came near it anyway, tongs in hand, and hoisted the crucible from the fire, then carried it to the mold and poured. The iron sparked and dazzled, but the mold held true, no buckling or breaking in the heat.

Set the crucible back in the fire. Push the other parts of the mold into place. Gently, evenly, getting no splash. He had judged the amount of liquid iron just right—when the last part of the form slipped into place, just a bit of iron squeezed out evenly all around the edges, showing there was just enough, and scarce any waste.

And it was done. Nothing for it but to wait for the iron to cool and harden. Tomorrow he'd know what he'd wrought.

Tomorrow Makepeace Smith would see his plow and call him a man—a journey man, free to practice at any forge, though not yet ready to take on his own prentices. But to Alvin—well, he'd reached that point of readiness years ago. Makepeace would have only a few weeks short of the full seven years of Alvin's service—that's what he'd been waiting for, not for this plow.

No, Alvin's real journeyman work was yet to come. After Makepeace declared the plow good enough, then Alvin had yet another work to perform.

"I'M GOING TO turn it gold," said Alvin.

Miss Larner raised an eyebrow. "And what then? What will you tell people about a golden plow? That you found it somewhere? That you happened to have some gold lying about, and thought—this is just enough to make a plow?"

"You're the one what told me a Maker was the one who could turn iron to gold."

"Yes, but that doesn't mean it's wise to do it." Miss Larner walked out of the hot forge into the stagnant air of late afternoon. It was cooler, but not much—the first hot night of spring.

"More than gold," said Alvin. "Or at least not normal gold."

"Regular gold isn't good enough for you?"

"Gold is dead. Like iron."

"It isn't dead. It's simply—earth without fire. It never *was* alive, so it can't be dead."

"You're the one who told me that if I can imagine it, then maybe I can make it come to be."

"And you can imagine living gold?"

"A plow that cuts the earth with no ox to draw it."

She said nothing, but her eyes sparkled.

"If I could make such a thing, Miss Larner, would you consider as how I'd graduated from your school for Makers?"

"I'd say you were no longer a prentice Maker."

"Just what I thought, Miss Larner. A journeyman blacksmith and a journeyman Maker, both, if I can do it."

"And can you?"

Alvin nodded, then shrugged. "I think so. It's what you said about atoms, back in January."

"I thought you gave up on that."

"No ma'am. I just kept thinking—what is it you can't cut into smaller pieces? And then I thought—why, if it's got any size at all, it can be cut. So an atom, it's nothing more than just a place, one exact place, with no width at all."

"Euclid's geometric point."

"Well, yes ma'am, except that you said his geometry was all imaginary, and this is real."

"But if it has no size, Alvin—"

"That's what I thought—if it's got no size, then it's nothing. But it *isn't* nothing. It's a place. Only then I thought, it *isn't* a place—it just *has* a place. If you see the difference. An atom can be in one place, one pure geometric point like you said, but then it can *move*. It can be somewhere else. So, you see, it not only has place, it has a past and a future. Yesterday it was there, today it's here, and tomorrow over yonder."

"But it isn't *anything*, Alvin."

"No, I know that, it isn't any*thing*. But it ain't *nothing*, neither."

"Isn't. Either."

"I know all that grammar, Miss Larner, but I'm not thinking about that right now."

"You won't have good grammar unless you use it even when you're not thinking about it. But never mind."

"See, I start thinking, if this atom's got no size, how can anybody tell where it is? It's not giving off any light, because it's got no fire in it to give off. So here's what I come up with: Just suppose this atom's got no *size,* but it's still got some kind of mind. Some kind of tiny little wit, just enough to know where it is. And the only power it has is to move somewhere else, and know where it is *then.*"

"How could that be, a memory in something that doesn't exist?"

"Just suppose it! Say you got thousands of them just lying around, just going any which way. How can any of them tell where they are? Since all the others are moving any which way, nothing around it stays the same. But then suppose somebody comes along—and I'm thinking about God here—somebody who can show them a pattern. Show them some way to set still. Like he says—you, there, you're the center, and all the rest of you, you just stay the same distance away from him all the time. Then what have you got?"

Miss Larner thought for a moment. "A hollow sphere. A ball. But still composed of nothing, Alvin."

"But don't you see? That's why I knew that this was true. I mean, if there's one thing I know from doodlebugging, it's that everything's mostly empty. That anvil, it looks solid, don't it? But I tell you it's mostly empty. Just little bits of ironstuff, hanging a certain distance from each other, all patterned there. But most of the anvil is the empty space between. Don't you see? Those bits are acting just like the atoms I'm talking about. So let's say the anvil is like a mountain, only when you get real close you see it's made of gravel. And then when you pick up the gravel, it crumbles in your hand, and you see it's made of dust. And if you could pick up a single fleck of dust you'd see that it was just like the mountain, made of even tinier gravel all over again."

"You're saying that what we see as solid objects are really nothing but illusion. Little nothings making tiny spheres that are put together to make your bits, and pieces made from bits, and the anvil made from pieces—"

"Only there's a lot more steps between, I reckon. Don't you see, this explains everything? Why it is that all I have to do is imagine a new shape or a new pattern or a new order, and show it in my mind, and if I think it clear and strong enough, and command the bits to change, why—they do. Because they're *alive*. They may be small and none too bright, but if I show them clear enough, they can do it."

"This is too strange for me, Alvin. To think that everything is really nothing."

"No, Miss Larner, you're missing the point. The point is that everything is *alive*. That everything is made out of living atoms, all obeying the commands that God gave them. And just following those commands, why, some of them get turned into light and heat, and some of them become iron, and some water, and some air, and some of them our own skin and bones. All those things are real—and so those atoms are real."

"Alvin, I told you about atoms because they were an interesting theory. The best thinkers of our time believe there are no such things."

"Begging your pardon, Miss Larner, but the best thinkers never saw the things I saw, so they don't know diddly. I'm telling you that this is the only idea I can think of that explains it all—what I see and what I do."

"But where did these atoms come from?"

"They don't come from anywhere. Or rather, maybe they come from everywhere. Maybe these atoms, they're just there. Always been there, always will be there. You can't cut them up. They can't die. You can't make them and you can't break them. They're forever."

"Then God didn't create the world."

"Of course he did. The atoms were nothing, just places that didn't even know where they were. It's God who put them all into places so he'd know where they were, and so *they'd* know where they were—and everything in the whole universe is made out of them."

Miss Larner thought about it for the longest time. Alvin stood there watching her, waiting. He knew it was true, or at least truer than anything else he'd ever heard of or thought of. Unless she could think of something wrong with it. So many times this year she'd done that, point out something he forgot, some reason why his idea wouldn't work. So he waited for her to come up with something. Something wrong.

Maybe she would've. Only while she was standing there outside the forge, thinking, they heard the sound of horses cantering up the road from town. Of course they looked to see who was coming in such a rush.

It was Sheriff Pauley Wiseman and two men that Alvin never saw before. Behind them was Dr. Physicker's carriage, with old Po Doggly driving. And they didn't just pass by. They stopped right there at the curve by the forge.

"Miss Larner," said Pauley Wiseman. "Arthur Stuart around here?"

"Why do you ask?" said Miss Larner. "Who are these men?"

"He's here," said one of the men. The white-haired one. He held up a tiny box between his thumb and forefinger. Both the strangers looked at it, then looked up the hill toward the springhouse. "In there," said the white-haired man.

"You need any more proof than that?" asked Pauley Wiseman. He was talking to Dr. Physicker, who was now out of his carriage and standing there looking furious and helpless and altogether terrible.

"Finders," whispered Miss Larner.

"That's us," said the white-haired one. "You got a runaway slave up there, Ma'am."

"He is not," she said. "He is a pupil of mine, legally adopted by Horace and Margaret Guester—"

"We got a letter from his owner, giving his birthdate, and we got his cachet here, and he's the very one. We're sworn and certified, Ma'am. What we Find is found. That's the law, and if you interfere, you're obstructing." The man spoke real nice and quiet and polite.

"Don't worry, Miss Larner," said Dr. Physicker. "I already have a writ from the mayor, and that'll hold him till the judge gets back tomorrow."

"Hold him in *jail,* of course," said Pauley Wiseman. "Wouldn't want anybody to try to run off with him, now, would we?"

"Wouldn't do much good if they tried," said the white-haired Finder. "We'd just follow. And then we'll probably shoot them dead, seeing how they was thieves escaping with stolen property."

"You haven't even told the Guesters, have you!" said Miss Larner.

"How could I?" said Dr. Physicker. "I had to stay with *them,* to make sure they didn't just take him."

"We obey the law," said the white-haired Finder.

"There he is," said the black-haired Finder.

Arthur Stuart stood in the open door of the springhouse.

"Just stay where you are, boy!" shouted Pauley Wiseman. "If you move a muscle I'll whip you to jelly!"

"You don't have to threaten him," said Miss Larner, but there wasn't nobody to listen, since they were all running up the hill.

"Don't hurt him!" cried Dr. Physicker.

"If he don't run, he won't get hurt," said the white-haired Finder.

"Alvin," said Miss Larner. "Don't do it."

"They ain't taking Arthur Stuart."

"Don't use your power like that. Not to hurt someone."

"I tell you—"

"Think, Alvin. We have until tomorrow. Maybe the judge—"

"Putting him in jail!"

"If anything happens to these Finders, then the nationals will be in it, to enforce the Fugitive Slave Treaty. Do you understand me? It's not a local crime like murder. You'd be taken off to Appalachee to be tried."

"I can't do *nothing*."

"Run and tell the Guesters."

Alvin waited just a moment. If it was up to him, he'd burn their hands right off before he let them take Arthur. But already the boy was between them, their fingers digging into Arthur's arms. Miss Larner was right. What they needed was a way to win Arthur's freedom for sure, not some stupid blunder that would end up making things worse.

Alvin ran for the Guesters' house. It surprised him how they took it—like they'd been expecting it all the time for the last seven years. Old Peg and Horace just looked at each other, and without a word Old Peg started in packing—her clothes *and* Arthur Stuart's.

"What's she packing *her* things for?" asked Alvin.

Horace smiled, a real tight smile. "She ain't going to let Arthur spend a night in jail alone. So she'll have them lock her up right alongside him."

It made sense—but it was strange to think of people like Arthur Stuart and Old Peg Guester in jail.

"What are *you* going to do?" asked Alvin.

"Load my guns," said Horace. "And when they're gone, I'll follow."

Alvin told him what Miss Larner had said about the nationals coming if somebody laid hand on a Finder.

"What's the worst they can do to me? Hang me. I tell you, I'd rather be hanged than live in this house a single day if they take Arthur Stuart away and I done nothing to stop them. And I can do it, Alvin. Hell, boy, I must've saved fifty runaway slaves in my time. Po Doggly and me, we used to pick them up this side of the river and send them on to safety in Canada. Did it all the time."

Alvin wasn't a bit surprised to hear of Horace Guester being an Emancipationist—and not a talker, neither.

"I'm telling you this, Alvin, cause I need your help. I'm just one man and there's two of them. I got no one I can trust—Po Doggly ain't gone with me on something like this in a week of Christmases, and I don't know where he stands no more. But you—I know you can keep a secret, and I know you love Arthur Stuart near as much as my wife does."

The way he said it gave Alvin pause. "Don't *you* love him, sir?"

Horace looked at Alvin like he was crazy. "They ain't taking a mixup boy right out from under my roof, Al."

Goody Guester come downstairs then, with two bundles in homespun bags under her arms. "Take me into town, Horace Guester."

They heard the horses riding by on the road outside.

"That's probably them," said Alvin.

"Don't worry, Peg," said Horace.

"Don't *worry?*" Old Peg turned on him in fury. "Only two things are likely to happen out of this, Horace. Either I lose my son to slavery in the South, or my fool husband gets himself probably killed trying to rescue him. Of course I won't worry." Then she burst into tears and hugged Horace so tight it near broke Alvin's heart to see it.

It was Alvin drove Goody Guester into town on the roadhouse wagon. He was standing there when she finally wore down Pauley Wiseman so he'd let her spend the night in the cell—though he made her take a terrible oath about not trying to sneak Arthur Stuart out of jail before he'd do it.

As he led the way to the jail cell, Pauley Wiseman said, "You shouldn't fret none, Goody Guester. His master's no doubt a good man. Folks here got the wrong idea of slavery, I reckon."

She whirled on him. "Then you'll go in his place, Pauley? Seeing how it's so fine?"

"Me?" He was no more than amused at the idea. "I'm *White,* Goody Guester. Slavery ain't my natural state."

Alvin made the keys slide right out of Pauley's fingers.

"I'm sure getting clumsy," said Pauley Wiseman.

Goody Guester's foot just naturally ended up right on top of the key ring.

"Just lift up your foot, Goody Guester," said the sheriff, "or I'll charge you with aiding and abetting, not to mention resisting."

She moved her foot. The sheriff opened the door. Old Peg stepped through and gathered Arthur Stuart into her arms. Alvin watched as Pauley Wiseman closed and locked the door behind them. Then he went on home.

ALVIN BROKE OPEN the mold and rubbed away the clay that still clung to the face of the plow. The iron was smooth and hard, as good a plow as Alvin ever saw cast till then. He searched inside it and found no flaws, not big enough to mar the plow, anyway. He filed and rubbed, rubbed and filed till it was smooth, the blade sharp as if he meant to use it in a butcher shop instead of some field somewhere. He set it on top of the workbench. Then he sat there waiting while the sun rose and the rest of the world came awake.

In due time Makepeace came down from the house and looked at the plow. But Alvin didn't see him, being asleep. Makepeace woke him up enough to get him to walk back up to the house.

"Poor boy," said Gertie. "I bet he never even went to sleep last night. I bet he went on down and worked on that fool plow all night."

"Plow looks fair."

"Plow looks perfect, I'll bet, knowing Alvin."

Makepeace grimaced. "What do you know about iron-work?"

"I know Alvin and I know you."

"Strange boy. Ain't it the truth though? He does his best work when he stays up all night." Makepeace even had some affection in his voice, saying that. But Alvin was asleep in his bed by then and didn't hear.

"Sets such store by that mixup child," said Gertie. "No wonder he couldn't sleep."

"Sleeping now," said Makepeace.

"Imagine sending Arthur Stuart into slavery at his age."

"Law's the law," said Makepeace. "Can't say I like it, but a fellow has to live by the law or what then?"

"You and the law," said Gertie. "I'm glad we don't live on the other side of the Hio, Makepeace, or I swear you'd be wanting slaves instead of prentices—if you know the difference."

That was as pure a declaration of war as they ever gave each other, and they were all set for one of their rip-snorting knockabout break-dish fights, only Alvin was snoring up in the loft and Gertie and Makepeace just glared at each other and let this one go. Since all their quarrels came out the same, with all the same cruel things said and all the same hurts and harms done, it was like they just got tired and said, Pretend I just said all the things you hate worst in all the world to hear, and I'll pretend you said the things I hate worst back to me, and then let be.

Alvin didn't sleep all that long, nor all too well, neither. Fear and anger and eagerness all played through his body till he could hardly hold still, let alone keep his brain drifting with the currents of his dreams. He woke up dreaming of a black plow turned to gold. He woke up dreaming of Arthur Stuart being whipped. He woke up again thinking of aiming a gun at one of them Finders and pulling the trigger. He woke up again thinking of aiming at a Finder and *not* pulling the trigger, and then watching them go away dragging Arthur after them, him screaming all the time, Alvin, where are you! Alvin, don't let them take me.

"Wake up or hush up!" shouted Gertie. "You're scaring the children."

Alvin opened his eyes and leaned over the edge of the loft. "Your children ain't even here."

"Then you're scaring *me*. I don't know what you was dreaming, boy, but I hope that dream never comes even to my worst enemy—which happens to be my husband this morning, if you want to know the truth."

Her mentioning Makepeace made Alvin alert, yes sir. He pulled on his trousers, wondering when and how he got up to this loft and who pulled his pants and boots off. In just that little amount of time, Gertie somehow got food on the table—cornbread and cheese and a dollop of molasses. "I don't have time to eat, Ma'am," said Alvin. "I'm sorry, but I got to—"

"You got time."

"No Ma'am, I'm sorry—"

"Take the bread, then, you plain fool. You plan to work

all day with an empty belly? After only a morning's sleep? Why, it ain't even noon yet."

So he was chewing on bread when he come down the hill to the forge. There was Dr. Physicker's carriage again, and the Finders' horses. For a second Alvin thought—they come here cause Arthur Stuart got away somehow, and the Finders lost him, and—

No. They had Arthur Stuart with them.

"Good morning, Alvin," said Makepeace. He turned to the other men. "I must be about the softest master I ever heard of, letting my prentice boy sleep till near noon."

Alvin didn't even notice how Makepeace was criticizing him and calling him a prentice *boy* when his journeyman piece stood there finished on the workbench. He just squatted down in front of Arthur Stuart and looked him in the eyes.

"Stand back now," said the white-haired Finder.

Alvin didn't hardly notice him. He wasn't really seeing Arthur Stuart, not with his eyes, anyhow. He was searching his body for some sign of harm. None. Not yet anyway. Just the fear in the boy.

"You haven't told us yet," said Pauley Wiseman. "Will you make them or not?"

Makepeace coughed. "Gentlemen, I once made a pair of manacles, back in New England. For a man convicted of treason, being shipped back to England in irons. I hope I never make a manacle for a seven-year-old boy who done no harm to a living soul, a boy who played around my forge and—"

"Makepeace," said Pauley Wiseman. "I told them that if you made the manacles, they wouldn't have to use this."

Wiseman held up the heavy iron-and-wood collar that he'd left leaning against his leg.

"It's the law," said the white-haired Finder. "We bring runaway slaves back home in that collar, to show the others what happens. But him being just a boy, and seeing how it was his mama what run away and not him, we agreed to manacles. But it don't make no difference to me. We get paid either way."

"You and your damned Fugitive Slave Treaty!" cried Makepeace. "You use that law to make slavers out of us, too."

"I'll make them," said Alvin.

Makepeace looked at him in horror. "You!"

"Better than that collar," said Alvin. What he didn't say was, I don't intend for Arthur Stuart to wear those manacles a minute longer than tonight. He looked at Arthur Stuart. "I'll make you some manacles as don't hurt much, Arthur Stuart."

"Wisely done," said Pauley Wiseman.

"Good to see somebody with sense here," said the white-haired Finder.

Alvin looked at him and tried to hold all his hatred in. He couldn't quite do it. So his spittle ended up spattering the dust at the Finder's feet.

The black-haired Finder looked ready to throw a punch at him for that, and Alvin wouldn't've minded a bit to grapple with him and maybe rub his face in the dirt a minute or two. But Pauley Wiseman jumped right between them and he had sense enough to do his talking to the black-haired Finder, and not to Alvin. "You got to be a blame fool, setting to rassle with a blacksmith. Look at his arms."

"I could take him," said the Finder.

"You folks got to understand," said the white-haired Finder. "It's our knack. We can no more help being Finders than—"

"There's some knacks," said Makepeace, "where it'd be

better to die at birth than grow up and use it." He turned to Alvin. "I don't want you using my forge for this."

"Don't make a nuisance of yourself, Makepeace," said Pauley Wiseman.

"Please," said Dr. Physicker. "You're doing the boy more harm than good."

Makepeace backed off, but none too graciously.

"Give me your hands, Arthur Stuart," Alvin said.

Alvin made a show of measuring Arthur's wrists with a string. Truth was, he could see the measure of him in his mind, every inch of him, and he'd shape the iron to fit smooth and perfect, with rounded edges and no more weight than needed. Arthur wouldn't feel no pain from these manacles. Not with his body, anyhow.

They all stood and watched Alvin work. It was the smoothest, purest job they'd ever see. Alvin used his knack this time, but not so it'd show. He hammered and bent the strap iron, cutting it exactly right. The two halves of each manacle fit snug, so they wouldn't shift and pinch the skin. And all the time he was thinking how Arthur used to pump the bellows for him, or just stand there and talk to him while he worked. Never again. Even after they saved him tonight, they'd have to take him to Canada or hide him somehow—as if you could hide from a Finder.

"Good work," said the white-haired Finder. "I never saw me a better blacksmith."

Makepeace piped up from the dark corner of the forge. "You should be proud of yourself, Alvin. Why, let's make those manacles your journeyman piece, all right?"

Alvin turned and faced him. "My journeyman piece is that plow setting on the workbench, Makepeace."

It was the first time Alvin ever called his master by his first name. It was as clear as Alvin could let him know that the days of Makepeace talking to him like that were over now.

Makepeace didn't want to understand him. "Watch how you talk to me, boy! Your journeyman piece is what I say it is, and—"

"Come on, boy, let's get these on you." The white-haired Finder wasn't interested in Makepeace's talk, it seemed.

"Not yet," said Alvin.

"They're ready," said the Finder.

"Too hot," said Alvin.

"Well dip them in that bucket there and cool them off."

"If I do that, they'll change shape just a little, and then they'll cut the boy's arms so they bleed."

The black-haired Finder rolled his eyes. What did he care about a little blood from a mixup boy?

But the white-haired Finder knew that nobody'd stand for it if he didn't wait. "No hurry," he said. "Can't take too long."

They sat around waiting without a word. Then Pauley started in talking about nothing, and so did the Finders, and even Dr. Physicker, just jawing away like as if the Finders were any old visitors. Maybe they thought they were making the Finders feel more kindly so they wouldn't take it out on the boy once they had him across the river. Alvin had to figure that so he wouldn't hate them.

Besides, an idea was growing in his mind. It wasn't enough to get Arthur Stuart away tonight—what if Alvin could make it so even the Finders couldn't find him again?

"What's in that cachet you Finders use?" he asked.

"Don't you wish you knew," said the black-haired Finder.

"It's no secret," said the white-haired Finder. "Every slaveowner makes up a box like this for each slave, soon as he's bought or born. Scrapings from his skin, hair from his head, a drop of blood, things like that. Parts of his own flesh."

"You get his scent from that?"

"Oh, it ain't a scent. We ain't *bloodhounds,* Mr. Smith."

Alvin knew that calling him Mr. Smith was pure flattery. He smiled a little, pretending that it pleased him.

"Well then how does it help?"

"Well, it's our *knack,*" said the white-haired Finder. "Who knows how it works? We just look at it, and we—it's like we see the shape of the person we're looking for."

"It ain't like that," said the black-haired Finder.

"Well that's how it is for *me.*"

"I just know where he is. Like I can see his soul. If I'm close enough, anyway. Glowing like a fire, the soul of the slave I'm searching for." The black-haired Finder grinned. "I can see from a long way off."

"Can you show me?" asked Alvin.

"Nothing to see," said the white-haired Finder.

"I'll show you, boy," said the black-haired Finder. "I'll turn my back and y'all move that boy around in the forge. I'll point to him over my shoulder, perfect all the time."

"Come on now," said the white-haired Finder.

"We got nothing to do anyway till the iron cools. Give me the cachet."

The black-haired Finder did what he bragged—pointed at Arthur Stuart the whole time. But Alvin hardly saw that. He was busy watching from the inside of that Finder, trying to understand what he was doing, what he was *seeing,* and what it had to do with the cachet. He couldn't see how seven-year-old dried-up bits of Arthur Stuart's newborn body could show them where he was *now.*

Then he remembered that for a moment right at first the Finder hadn't pointed at all. His finger had wandered a little, and only after just that pause had he started pointing right at Arthur Stuart. Like as if he'd been trying to sort out which of the people behind him in the smithy was Arthur. The cachet wasn't for Finding—it was for recognizing. The

Finders saw everybody, but they couldn't tell who was who without a cachet.

So what they were seeing wasn't Arthur's mind, or Arthur's soul. They were just seeing a body, like every other body unless they could sort it out. And what they were sorting was plain enough to Alvin—hadn't he healed enough people in his life to know that people were pretty much the same, except for some bits at the center of each living piece of their flesh? Those bits were different for every single person, yet the same in every part of that person's flesh. Like it was God's way of naming them right in their flesh. Or maybe it was the mark of the beast, like in the book of Revelation. Didn't matter. Alvin knew that the only thing in that cachet that was the same as Arthur Stuart's body was that signature that lived in every part of his body, even the dead and cast-off parts in the cachet.

I can change those bits, thought Alvin. Surely I can change them, change them in every part of his body. Like turning iron into gold. Like turning water into wine. And then their cachet wouldn't work at all. Wouldn't help them at all. They could search for Arthur Stuart all they liked, but as long as they didn't actually see his face and recognize him the regular way, they'd never find him.

Best of all, they wouldn't even realize what happened. They'd still have the cachet, same as ever, and they'd know it hadn't been changed a bit because Alvin wouldn't change it. But they could search the whole world over and never find a body just like those specks in their cachet, and they'd never guess why.

I'll do it, thought Alvin. Somehow I'll figure a way to change him. Even though there must be millions of those signatures all through his body, I'll find a way to change every one. Tonight I'll do it, and tomorrow he'll be safe forever.

The iron was cool. Alvin knelt before Arthur Stuart and gently put the manacles in place. They fit his flesh so perfectly he might have cast them in a mold taken from Arthur's own body. When they were locked into place, with a length of light chain strung between them, Alvin looked Arthur Stuart in the eye. "Don't be afraid," he said.

Arthur Stuart didn't say a thing.

"I won't forget you," said Alvin.

"Sure," said the black-haired Finder. "But just in case you get ideas about remembering him while he's on his way home to his rightful master, I ought to tell you square—we never both of us sleep at the same time. And part of being a Finder is, we know if anybody's coming. You can't sneak up on us. Least of all you, smith boy. I could see *you* ten miles away."

Alvin just looked at him. Eventually the Finder sneered and turned away. They put Arthur Stuart onto the horse in front of the white-haired Finder. But Alvin figured that as soon as they got across the Hio, they'd have Arthur walking. Not out of meanness, maybe—but it wouldn't do no good for Finders to show themselves being kindly to a runaway. Besides, they had to set an example for the other slaves, didn't they? Let them see a boy seven years old walking along, feet bleeding, head bowed, and they'd think twice about trying to run off with their children. They'd know that Finders have no mercy.

Pauley and Dr. Physicker rode away with them. They were seeing the Finders to the Hio River and watching them cross the river, to make sure they did no hurt to Arthur Stuart while he was in free territory. It was the best they could do.

Makepeace didn't have much to say, but what he said, he said plain. "A real man would never put manacles on his own friend," said Makepeace. "I'll go up to the house and sign your journeyman papers. I don't want you in my smithy or my house another night." He left Alvin alone by the forge.

He'd been gone no more than five minutes when Horace Guester got to the smithy.

"Let's go," he said.

"No," said Alvin. "Not yet. They can see us coming. They'll tell the sheriff if they're being followed."

"We got no choice. Can't lose their trail."

"You know something about what I am and what I can do," said Alvin. "I've got them even now. They won't get more than a mile from the Hio shore before they fall asleep."

"You can do that?"

"I know what goes on inside people when they're sleepy. I can make that stuff start happening inside them the minute they're in Appalachee."

"While you're at it, why don't you kill them?"

"I can't."

"They aren't men! It wouldn't be murder, killing them!"

"They *are* men," said Alvin. "Besides, if I kill them, then it's a violation of the Fugitive Slave Treaty."

"Are you a lawyer now?"

"Miss Larner explained it to me. I mean she explained it to Arthur Stuart while I was there. He wanted to know. Back last fall. He said, 'Why don't my pa just kill them if some Finders come for me?' And Miss Larner, she told him how there'd just be more Finders coming, only this time they'd hang you and take Arthur Stuart anyway."

Horace's face had turned red. Alvin didn't understand why for a minute, not till Horace Guester explained. "He shouldn't call me his pa. I never wanted him in my house." He swallowed. "But he's right. I'd kill them Finders if I thought it'd do good."

"No killing," said Alvin. "I think I can fix it so they'll never find Arthur again."

"I know. I'm going to ride him to Canada. Get to the lake and sail across."

"No sir," said Alvin. "I think I can fix it so they'll never find him *anywhere*. We just got to hide him till they go away."

"Where?"

"Springhouse, if Miss Larner'll let us."

"Why there?"

"I got it hexed up every which way from Tuesday. I thought I was doing it for the teacher lady. But now I reckon I was really doing it for Arthur Stuart."

Horace grinned. "You're really something, Alvin. You know that?"

"Maybe. Sure wish I knew *what*."

"I'll go ask Miss Larner if we can make use of her house."

"If I know Miss Larner, she'll say yes before you finish asking."

"When do we start, then?"

It took Alvin by surprise, having a grown man ask *him* when they should start. "Soon as it's dark, I reckon. Soon as those two Finders are asleep."

"You can really *do* that?"

"I can if I keep watching them. I mean sort of watching. Keeping track of where they are. So I don't go putting the wrong people to sleep."

"Well, are you watching them now?"

"I know where they are."

"Keep watching, then." Horace looked a little scared, almost as bad as he did near seven years ago, when Alvin told him he knew about the girl buried there. Scared because he knew Alvin could do something strange, something beyond any hexings or knacks in Horace's ken.

Don't you know me, Horace? Don't you know that I'm still Alvin, the boy you liked and trusted and helped so many times? Finding out that I'm stronger than you thought, in ways you didn't think of, that don't mean I'm a whit more dangerous to you. No reason to be a-scared.

As if Horace could hear his words, the fear eased away from his face. "I just mean—Old Peg and I are counting on you. Thank God you ended up in this place, right at this time when we needed you so bad. The good Lord's looking out for us." Horace smiled, then turned and left the smithy.

What Horace said, it left Alvin feeling good, feeling sure of himself. But then, that was Horace's knack, wasn't it—to give folks the view of theirselves they most needed to see.

Alvin turned his thoughts at once to the Finders, and sent out his bug to stay with them, to keep track of the way their bodies moved like small black storms through the green-song around them, with Arthur Stuart's small song bright and clear between them. Black and White don't have nothing to do with bright and dark at heart, I reckon, thought Alvin. His hands stayed busy doing work at the forge, but for the life of him he couldn't pay real attention to it. He'd never watched somebody so far off before—except for that time he got helped by powers he didn't understand, inside Eight-Face Mound.

And the worst thing of all would be if he lost them, if they got away with Arthur Stuart, all because Alvin didn't pay attention close enough and lost that boy among all the beat-down souls of slaves in Appalachee and on beyond, in the deep South where all White men were servants to the other Arthur Stuart, King of England, and so all Blacks were slaves of slaves. Ain't going to lose Arthur in a place so bad. Going to hold on tight to him, like as if he got a thread to connect him to me.

Almost as soon as he thought of it, almost as soon as he imagined a thin invisible thread connecting him and that mixup boy, why, there it was. There was a thread in the air, a thread about as thin as what he imagined once trying to understand what an atom might be. A thread that only had size in one direction—the direction that led toward Arthur Stuart, connecting them heart to heart. Stay with him, Alvin told the thread, like as if it really was alive. And in answer it seemed to grow brighter, thicker, till Alvin was sure anybody who come along could see it.

But when he looked with his eyes, he couldn't see the thread at all; it only appeared to him again when he looked without eyes. It plain astonished him, that such a thing could come to be, created—not out of nothing—but created without pattern except the pattern found in Alvin's own mind. This is a Making. My first, thin, invisible Making—but it's real, and it's going to lead me to Arthur Stuart tonight, so I can set him free.

IN HER LITTLE house, Peggy watched Alvin and Arthur Stuart both, looking back and forth from one to the other, trying to find some pathway that led for Arthur's freedom without costing Alvin's death or capture. No matter how closely and carefully she looked, there was no such path. The Finders were too skilled with their terrible knack; on some paths, Alvin and Horace might carry Arthur off, but he'd only be found again and recaptured—at the cost of Alvin's blood or Alvin's freedom.

So she watched despairing as Alvin spun his almost nonexistent thread. Only then, for the first time, did she see some glimmer of a possibility of freedom in Arthur Stuart's heartfire. It came, not from the fact that the thread would lead Alvin to the boy—on many paths before he spun the thread, she had seen Alvin finding the Finders and putting them to sleep. No, the difference now was that Alvin could make the thread at all. The possibility of it had been so small that there had been no path that showed it. Or perhaps—something she hadn't thought of before—the very act of Making was such a violation of the natural order that her own knack couldn't see paths that relied on it, not until it was actually accomplished.

Yet even at the moment of Alvin's birth, hadn't she seen his glorious future? Hadn't she seen him building a city made of the purest glass or ice? Hadn't she seen his city filled with people who spoke with the tongues of angels and saw with the eyes of God? The fact that Alvin would Make, that was always probable, provided he stayed alive. But any one particular act of Making, that was never likely, never natural enough for a torch—even an extraordinary torch like Peggy—to see it.

She saw Alvin put the Finders to sleep almost as soon as it was dark and they could find a stopping place on the far side of the Hio. She saw Alvin and Horace meet in the smithy, preparing to set out through the woods to the Hio, avoiding the road so they wouldn't meet the sheriff and Dr. Physicker coming back from Hatrack Mouth. But she paid little heed to them. Now that there was new hope, she gave her full attention to Arthur's future, studying how and where his slender new paths of freedom were rooted to the present action. She could not find the clear moment of choice and change. To her that fact was proof that all depended on Alvin becoming a Maker, truly, on this night.

"O God," she whispered, "if thou didst cause this boy to be born with such a gift, I pray thee teach him Making now, tonight."

ALVIN STOOD BESIDE Horace, masked by shadows at the riverbank, waiting for a well-lighted riverboat to pass. Out on the boat, musicians were playing, and people danced a fancy quadrille on the decks. It made Alvin angry, to see them playing like children when a real child was being carried off to slavery tonight. Still, he knew they meant no harm, and knew it wasn't fair to blame others for being happy while somebody they don't even know might be grieving. By that measure there'd be no happiness in all the world, Alvin figured. Life being how it is, Alvin thought, there's not a moment in the day when there ain't at least a few hundred people grieving about something.

The ship had no sooner passed around a bend than they heard a crashing in the woods behind them. Or rather, Alvin heard the sound, and it only seemed like crashing to *him* because of his sense of the right order of things in the greenwood song. It took more than a few minutes before Horace heard it at all. Whoever it was sneaking up on them, he was right stealthy for a White man.

"Now I'm wishing for a gun," whispered Horace.

Alvin shook his head. "Wait and watch," he whispered—so faint his lips barely moved.

They waited. After a while, they saw a man step out of the woods and slither down the bank to the muddy edge of the water, where the boat rocked on the water. Seeing nobody there, he looked around, then sighed and stepped out into the boat, turned around and sat down in the stern, glumly resting his chin on his hands.

Suddenly Horace started chuckling. "Play fetch with my bones when I'm dead, but I do think that's old Po Doggly."

At once the man in the boat leaned back and Alvin could finally see him clear in the moonlight. It *was* Dr. Physicker's driver, sure enough. But this didn't seem to bother Horace none. He was already slipping down the riverbank, to splash out to the boat, climb aboard, and give Po Doggly such a violent hug the boat took on water. In only a second they both noticed that the boat was rocking out of kilter, and without a word they both shifted exactly right to balance the load, and then again without a word Po got the oars into the locks while Horace took a flat tin baling cup out from under his bench and commenced to dipping it and pouring it out overboard, again and again.

Alvin marveled for a moment at how smooth the two of them fit together. He didn't even have to ask—he knew from how they acted that they'd done this sort of thing a good many times before. Each knew what the other was going to do, so they didn't even have to think about it anymore. One man did his part, and the other his, and neither even had to check to make sure both parts were getting done.

Like the bits and pieces that made up everything in the world; like the dance of atoms Alvin had imagined in his mind. He'd never realized it before, but people could be like those atoms, too. Most of the time people were all disorganized, nobody knowing who anybody else was, nobody holding still long enough to trust or be trusted, just like Alvin imagined atoms might have been before God taught them who they were and gave them work to do. But here were two men, men that nobody'd ever figure even knew each other hardly, except as how everybody in a town like Hatrack River knows everybody else. Po Doggly, a onetime farmer reduced to driving for Dr. Physicker, and Horace Guester, the first settler in this place, and still prospering. Who'd've thought they could fit together so smooth? But it was because each one knew who the other was, knew it pure and true, knew it as sure as an atom might know the name God gave him; each one in his place, doing his work.

All these thoughts rushed through Alvin's mind so fast he hardly noticed himself thinking them, yet in later years he'd remember right enough that this was when he first understood: These two men, together, made something between them that was just as real and solid as the dirt under his feet, as the tree he was leaning on. Most folks couldn't

see it—they'd look at the two of them and see nothing but two
men who happened to be sitting in a boat together. But then,
maybe to other atoms it wouldn't seem like the atoms making up a bit of a iron was anything more than two atoms as
happened to be next to each other. Maybe you have to be
far off, like God, or anyhow bigger by far in order to see
what it is that two atoms make when they fit together in a
certain way. But just because another atom don't see the
connection don't mean it isn't real, or that the iron isn't as
solid as iron can be.

And if I can teach these atoms how to make a string
out of nothing, or maybe how to make iron out of gold, or
even—let it be so—change Arthur's secret invisible signature all through his body so the Finders wouldn't know him
no more—then why couldn't a Maker also do with people
as he does with atoms, and teach them a new order, and once
he finds enough that he can trust, build them together into
something new, something strong, something as real as iron.

"You coming, Al, or what?"

Like I said, Alvin hardly knew what thought it was he
had. But he didn't forget it, no, even sliding down the bank
into the mud he knew that he'd never forget what he thought
of just then, even though it'd take him years and miles and
tears and blood before he really understood it all the way.

"Good to see you, Po," said Alvin. "Only I kind of thought
we was doing something a mite secret."

Po rowed the boat closer in, slacking the rope and letting Alvin spider his way on board without getting his feet
wet. Alvin didn't mind that. He had an aversion to water,
which was natural enough seeing how often the Unmaker
tried to use water to kill him. But the water seemed to be
just water tonight; the Unmaker was invisible or far away.
Maybe it was the slender string that still hooked Alvin to

Arthur—maybe that was such a powerful Making that the Unmaker plain hadn't the strength to turn even this much water against Alvin.

"Oh, it's still secret, Alvin," said Horace. "You just don't know. Afore you ever got to Hatrack River—or anyway I mean afore you came back—me and Po, we used to go out and fetch in runaway slaves and help them on to Canada whenever we could."

"Didn't the Finders ever get you?" asked Alvin.

"Any slave got this far, that meant the Finders wasn't too close behind," said Po. "A good number that reached us stole their own cachet."

"Besides, that was afore the Fugitive Slave Treaty," said Horace. "Long as the Finders didn't kill us outright, they couldn't touch us."

"And in those days we had a torch," said Po.

Horace said nothing, just untied the rope from the boat and tossed it back onto shore. Po started in rowing the first second the rope was free—and Horace had already braced himself for the first lurch of the boat. It was a miracle, seeing how smooth they knew each other's next move before the move was even begun. Alvin almost laughed out loud in the joy of seeing such a thing, knowing it was possible, dreaming of what it might mean—thousands of people knowing each other that well, moving to fit each other just right, working together. Who could stand in the way of such people?

"When Horace's girl left, why, we had no way of knowing there was a runaway coming through here." Po shook his head. "It was over. But I knowed that with Arthur Stuart put in chains and dragged on south, why, there wasn't no way in hell old Horace wasn't going to cross the river and fetch him back. So once I dropped off them Finders and headed back away from the Hio a ways, I stopped the carriage and hopped on down."

"I bet Dr. Physicker noticed," said Alvin.

"Course he did, you fool!" said Po. "Oh, I see you're funning me. Well, he noticed. He just says to me, 'You be careful, them boys are dangerous.' And I said I'd be careful all right and then he says to me, 'It's that blame sheriff Pauley Wiseman. He didn't have to let them take him so fast. Might be we could've fought exerdiction if we could've held onto Arthur Stuart till the circuit judge come around. But Pauley, he did everything legal, but he moved so fast I just knew in my heart he wanted that boy gone, wanted him clean out of Hatrack River and never come back.' I believe him, Horace. Pauley Wiseman never did like that mixup boy, once Old Peg got the wind in her sails about him going to school."

Horace grunted; he turned the tiller just a little, exactly at the moment when Pauley slacked the oar on one side so the boat would turn slightly upstream to make the right landing on the far shore. "You know what I been thinking?" said Horace. "I been thinking your job just ain't enough to keep you busy, Po."

"I like my job good enough," said Po Doggly.

"I been thinking that there's a county election this fall, and the office of sheriff goes up for grabs. I think Pauley Wiseman ought to get turned out."

"And me get made sheriff? You think that's likely, me being a known drunk?"

"You ain't touched a drop the whole time you been with the doctor. And if we live through this and get Arthur back safe, why, you're going to be a hero."

"A hero hell! You crazy, Horace? We can't tell a soul about this or there'll be a reward out for our brains on rye bread from the Hio to Camelot."

"We ain't going to print up the story and sell copies, if that's what you mean. But you know how word spreads. Good folks'll know what you and me done."

"Then *you* be sheriff, Horace."

"Me?" Horace grinned. "Can you imagine me putting a man in jail?"

Po laughed softly. "Reckon not."

When they reached the shore, again their movements were swift and fit together just right. It was hard to believe it had been so many years since they worked together. It was like their bodies already knew what to do, so they didn't even have to think about it. Po jumped into the water— ankle deep is all, and he leaned on the boat so as not to splash much. The boat rocked a bit at *that,* of course, but without a bit of wasted motion Horace leaned against the rocking and calmed it down, hardly even noticing he was doing it. In a minute they had the bow dragged up onto the shore—sandy here, not muddy like the other side—and tied to a tree. To Alvin the rope looked old and rotten, but when he sent his bug inside to feel it out, he was sure it was still strong enough to hold the boat against the rocking of the river against the stern.

Only when all their familiar jobs was done did Horace present himself like militia on the town square, shoulders squared and eyes right on Alvin. "Well, now, Al, I reckon it's up to you to lead the way."

"Ain't we got to track them?" asked Po.

"Alvin knows where they are," said Horace.

"Well ain't that nice," said Po. "And does he know whether they got their guns aimed at our heads?"

"Yes," said Alvin. He said it in such a way as to make it plain that he didn't want no more questions.

It wasn't plain enough for Po. "You telling me this boy's a torch, or what? Most I heard was he got him a knack for shoeing horses."

Here was the bad part about having somebody else along. Alvin didn't have no wish to tell Po Doggly what all he could do, but he couldn't very well tell the man that he didn't trust him.

It was Horace came to the rescue. "Po, I got to tell you, Alvin ain't part of the story of this night."

"Looks to me like he's the biggest part."

"I tell you, Po, when this story gets told, it was you and me came along and happened to find the Finders asleep, you understand?"

Po wrinkled his brow, then nodded. "Just tell me this, boy. Whatever knack you got, you a Christian? I don't even ask that you be a Methodist."

"Yes sir," said Alvin. "I'm a Christian, I reckon. I hold to the Bible."

"Good then," said Po. "I just don't want to get myself all mixed up in devil stuff."

"Not with me," said Alvin.

"All right then. Best if I don't know what you do, Al. Just take a care not to get me killed because I don't know it."

Alvin stuck out his hand. Po shook it and grinned. "You blacksmiths got to be strong as a bear."

"Me?" said Alvin. "A bear gets in my way, I beat on his head till he's a wolverine."

"I like your brag, boy."

A moment's pause, and then Alvin led them off, following the thread that connected him to Arthur Stuart.

It wasn't all that far, but it took them an hour cutting through the woods in the dark—with all the leaves out, there wasn't much moonlight got to the ground. Without Alvin's sense of the forest around them, it would've taken three times as long and ten times the noise.

They found the Finders asleep in a clearing with a campfire dying down between them. The white-haired Finder was curled up on his bedroll. The black-haired Finder must've been left on watch; he was snoring away leaning against a tree. Their horses were asleep not far off. Alvin stopped them before they got close enough to disturb the animals.

Arthur Stuart was wide awake, sitting there staring into the fire.

Alvin sat there a minute, trying to figure how to do this. He wasn't sure how smart the Finders might be. Could they find scraps of dried skin, fallen-off hairs, something like that, and use it for a new cachet? Just in case, it wouldn't do no good to change Arthur right where he was; nor would it be too smart to head on out into the clearing where they might leave bits of their own selves, as proof of who stole Arthur away.

So from a distance, Alvin got inside the iron of the manacles and made cracks in all four parts, so they fell away to the ground at once, with a clank. The noise bothered the horses, who nickered a bit, but the Finders were still sleeping like the dead. Arthur, though, it didn't take him a second to figure out what was happening. He jumped to his feet all at once and started looking around for Alvin at the clearing's edge.

Alvin whistled, trying to match the song of a redbird. It was a pretty bad imitation, as birdcalls go, but Arthur heard it and knew that it was Alvin calling him. Without a moment's waiting or worrying, Arthur plunged right into the woods and not five minutes later, with a few more bad birdcalls to guide him, he was face to face with Alvin.

Of course Arthur Stuart made as if to give Alvin a big old hug, but Alvin held up a hand. "Don't touch anybody or anything," he whispered. "I've got to make a change in you, Arthur Stuart, so the Finders can't catch you again."

"I don't mind," said Arthur.

"I don't dare have a single scrap of the old way you used to be. You got hairs and skin and such all over in your clothes. So strip them off."

Arthur Stuart didn't hesitate. In a few moments his clothes were in a pile at his feet.

"Excuse me for not knowing a bit about this," said Po, "but if you leave those clothes a-lying there, them Finders'll know he come this way, and that points north to them sure as if we painted a big white arrow on the ground."

"Reckon you're right," said Alvin.

"So have Arthur Stuart bring them along and float them down the river," said Horace.

"Just make sure you don't touch Arthur or nothing," said Alvin. "Arthur, you just pick up your clothes and follow along slow and careful. If you get lost, give me a redbird whistle and I'll whistle back till you find us."

"I knew you was coming, Alvin," said Arthur Stuart. "You too, Pa."

"So did them Finders," said Horace, "and much as I wish we could arrange it, they ain't going to sleep forever."

"Wait a minute anyway," said Alvin. He sent his bug back into the manacles and drew them back together, fit them tight, joined the iron again as if it had been cast that way. Now they lay on the ground unbroken, fastened tight, giving no sign of how the boy got free.

"I don't suppose you're maybe breaking their legs or something, Alvin," said Horace.

"Can he *do* that from here?" asked Po.

"I'm doing no such thing," said Alvin. "What we want is for the Finders to give up searching for a boy who as far as they can tell doesn't exist no more."

"Well that makes sense, but I still like thinking of them Finders with their legs broke," said Horace.

Alvin grinned and plunged off into the forest, deliberately making enough noise and moving slow enough that the others could follow him in the near-darkness; if he wanted to, he could've moved like a Red man through the woods, making not a sound, leaving no whiff of a trail that anyone could follow.

They got to the river and stopped. Alvin didn't want Arthur getting into the boat in his present skin, leaving traces of himself all over. So if he was going to change him, he had to do it here.

"Toss them clothes, boy," said Horace. "Far as you can."

Arthur took a step or two into the water. It made Alvin scared, for with his inward eye he saw it as if Arthur, made of light and earth and air, suddenly got part of himself disappeared into the blackness of the water. Still, the water hadn't harmed them none on the trip here, and Alvin saw as how it might even be useful.

Arthur Stuart pitched his wad of clothes out into the river. The current wasn't all that strong; they watched the clothes turn lazily and float downstream, gradually drifting apart. Arthur stood there, up to his butt in water, watching the clothes. No, not watching them—he didn't turn a speck when they drifted far to the left. He was just looking at the north shore, the free side of the river.

"I been here afore," he said. "I seen this boat."

"Might be," said Horace. "Though you was a mite young to remember it. Po and I, we helped your mama into this very boat. My daughter Peggy held you when we got to shore."

"My sister Peggy," said Arthur. He turned around and looked at Horace, like as if it was really a question.

"I reckon so," said Horace, and that was the answer.

"Just stand there, Arthur Stuart," said Alvin. "When I change you, I got to change you all over, inside and out. Better to do that in the water, where all the dead skin with your old self marked in it can wash away."

"You going to make me White?" asked Arthur Stuart.

"Can you *do* that?" asked Po Doggly.

"I don't know what all is going to change," said Alvin. "I hope I don't make you White, though. That'd be like stealing away from you the part of you your mama gave you."

"They don't make White boys be slaves," said Arthur Stuart.

"They ain't going to make this partickler mixup boy a slave anyhow," said Alvin. "Not if I can help it. Now just stand there, stand right still, and let me figure this out."

They all stood there, the men and the boy, while Alvin studied inside Arthur Stuart, finding that tiny signature that marked every living bit of him.

Alvin knew he couldn't just go changing it willy-nilly, since he didn't rightly understand what all that signature was *for*. He just knew that it was somehow part of what made Arthur himself, and you don't just change that. Maybe changing the wrong thing might strike him blind, or make his blood turn to rainwater or something. How could Alvin know?

It was seeing the string still connecting them, heart to heart, that gave Alvin the idea—that and remembering what the Redbird said, using Arthur Stuart's own lips to say it. "The Maker is the one who is part of what he Makes." Alvin stripped off his own shirt and then stepped out into the water and knelt down in it, so he was near eye-to-eye with Arthur Stuart, cool water swirling gently around his waist. Then he put out his hands and pulled Arthur Stuart to him and held him there, breast to breast, hands on shoulders.

"I thought we wasn't supposed to touch the boy," said Po.

"Hush up you blame fool," said Horace Guester. "Alvin knows what he's doing."

I wish that was true, thought Alvin. But at least he had an idea what to do, and that was better than nothing. Now that their living skin was pressed together, Alvin could look and compare Arthur's secret signature with his own. Most of it was the same, exactly the same, and the way Alvin figured, that's the part that makes us both human instead of cows or frogs or pigs or chickens. That's the part I don't dare change, not a bit of it.

The rest—I can change that. But not any old how. What good to save him if I turn him bright yellow or make him stupid or something?

So Alvin did the only thing as made sense to him. He changed bits of Arthur's signature to be just like Alvin's own. Not *all* that was different—not all that much, in fact. Just a little. But even a little meant that Arthur Stuart had stopped being completely himself and started being partly Alvin. It seemed to Alvin that what he was doing was terrible and wonderful at the same time.

How much? How much did he have to change till the Finders wouldn't know the boy? Surely not all. Surely just *this* much, just *these* changes. There was no way to know. All that Alvin could do was guess, and so he took his guess and that was it.

That was only the beginning, of course. Now he started in changing all the other signatures to match the new one, each living bit of Arthur, one by one, as fast as he could. Dozens of them, hundreds of them; he found each new signature and changed it to fit the new pattern.

Hundreds of them, and hundreds more, and still he had changed no more than a tiny patch of skin on Arthur's chest. How could he hope to change the boy's whole body, going so slow?

"It hurts," whispered Arthur.

Alvin drew away from him. "I ain't doing nothing to hurt you, Arthur Stuart."

Arthur looked down at his chest. "Right here," he said, touching the spot where Alvin had been working.

Alvin looked in the moonlight and saw that indeed that spot seemed to be swollen, changed, darkened. He looked again, only not with his eyes, and saw that the rest of Arthur's body was attacking the part that Alvin changed, killing it bit by bit, fast as it could.

Of course. What did he expect? The signature was the way the body recognized itself—that's why every living bit of a body had to have that signature in it. If it wasn't there, the body knew it had to be a disease or something and killed it. Wasn't it bad enough that changing Arthur was taking so long? Now Alvin knew that it wouldn't do no good to change him at all—the more he changed him, the sicker he'd get and the more Arthur Stuart's own body would try to kill itself until the boy either died or shed the new changed part.

It was just like Taleswapper's old story, about trying to build a wall so big that by the time you got halfway through building it, the oldest parts of it had already crumbled to dust. How could you build such a wall if it was getting broke down faster than you could build it up?

"I can't," said Alvin. "I'm trying to do what can't be done."

"Well if you can't do it," said Po Doggly, "I hope you can fly, cause that's the only way you can get that boy to Canada before the Finders catch up with you."

"I can't," said Alvin.

"You're just tired," said Horace. "We'll all just hush up so you can think."

"Won't do any good," said Alvin.

"My mama could fly," said Arthur Stuart.

Alvin sighed in impatience at this same old story coming back again.

"It's true, you know," said Horace. "Little Peggy told me. That little black slave girl, she diddled with some ash and blackbird feathers and such, and flew straight up here. That's what killed her. I couldn't believe it the first time I realized the boy remembers, and we always kept our mouths shut about it hoping he'd forget. But I got to tell you, Alvin, it'd be a pure shame if that girl died just so you could give up on us at this same spot in the river seven years later."

Alvin closed his eyes. "Just shut your mouth and let me think," he said.

"I *said* that's what we'd do," said Horace.

"So *do* it," said Po Doggly.

Alvin hardly even heard them. He was looking back inside Arthur's body, inside that patch that Alvin changed. The new signature wasn't bad in itself—only where it bordered on the skin with the old signature, that was the only place the new skin was getting sick and dying. Arthur'd be just fine if Alvin could somehow change him all at once, instead of bit by bit.

The way that the string came all at once, when Alvin thought of it, pictured where it started and where it ended and what it *was*. All the atoms of it moving into place at the same time. Like the way Po Doggly and Horace Guester fit together all at once, each doing his own task yet taking into account all that the other man did.

But the string was clean and simple. This was hard—like he told Miss Larner, turning water into wine instead of iron into gold.

No, can't think of it that way. What I did to make the string was teach all the atoms what and where to be, because each one of them was alive and each one could obey me. But inside Arthur's body I ain't dealing with atoms, I'm dealing with these living bits, and each one of *them* is alive. Maybe it's even the signature itself that makes them alive, maybe I can teach them all what they ought to be—instead of moving each part of them, one at a time, I can just say—Be like this—and they'll do it.

He no sooner thought of it than he tried it. In his mind he

thought of speaking to all the signatures in Arthur's skin, all over his chest, all at once; he showed them the pattern he held in his mind, a pattern so complex he couldn't even understand it himself, except that he knew it was the same pattern as the signatures in this patch of skin he had changed bit by bit. And as soon as he showed them, as soon as he commanded them—Be like this! This is the way!—they changed. It all changed, all the skin on Arthur Stuart's chest, all at once.

Arthur gasped, then howled with pain. What had been a soreness in a patch of skin was now spread across his whole chest.

"Trust me," Alvin said. "I'm going to change you sure now, and the pain will stop. But I'm doing it under the water, where all the old skin gets carried off at once. Plug your nose! Hold your breath!"

Arthur Stuart was panting from the pain, but he did what Alvin said. He pinched his nose with his right hand, then took a breath and closed his mouth. At once Alvin gripped Arthur's wrist in his left hand and put his right hand behind the boy and plunged him under the water. In that instant Alvin held Arthur's body whole in his mind, seeing all the signatures, not one by one, but all of them; he showed them the pattern, the new signature, and this time thought the words so strong his lips spoke them. "This is the way! Be like this!"

He couldn't feel it with his hands—Arthur's body didn't change a whit that he could sense with his natural senses. But Alvin could still see the change, all at once, all in an instant, every signature in the boy's body, in the organs, in the muscles, in the blood, in the brain; even his hair changed, every part of him that was connected to himself. And what wasn't connected, what didn't change, that was washed away and gone.

Alvin plunged himself under the water, to wash off any part of Arthur's skin or hair that might have clung to him.

Then he rose up and lifted Arthur Stuart out of the water, all in one motion. The boy came up shedding waterdrops like a spray of cold pearls in the moonlight. He stood there gasping for breath and shaking from the cold.

"Tell me it don't hurt no more," said Alvin.

"Any more," said Arthur, correcting him just like Miss Larner always did. "I feel fine. Except cold."

Alvin scooped him up out of the water and carried him back to the bank. "Wrap him in my shirt and let's get out of here."

So they did. Not a one of them noticed that when Arthur imitated Miss Larner, he didn't use Miss Larner's voice.

PEGGY DIDN'T NOTICE either, not right away. She was too busy looking inside Arthur Stuart's heartfire. How it changed when Alvin transformed him! So subtle a change it was that Peggy couldn't even tell what it was Alvin was changing—yet in the moment that Arthur Stuart emerged from the water, not a single path from his past remained— not a single path leading southward into slavery. And all the new paths, the new futures that the transformation had brought to him—they led to such amazing possibilities.

During all the time it took for Horace, Po, and Alvin to bring Arthur Stuart back across the Hio and through the woods to the smithy, Peggy did nothing more than explore in Arthur Stuart's heartfire, studying possibilities that had never before existed in the world. There was a new Maker abroad in the land; Arthur was the first soul touched by him, and everything was different. Moreover, most of Arthur's futures were inextricably tied with Alvin. Peggy saw possibilities of incredible journeys—on one path a trip to Europe where Arthur Stuart would be at Alvin's side as the new Holy Roman Emperor Napoleon bowed to him; on another path a voyage into a strange island nation far to the south where Red men lived their whole lives on mats of floating seaweed; on another path a triumphant crossing into westward lands where the Reds hailed Alvin as the great unifier of all the races, and opened up their last refuge to him, so perfect was their trust. And always by his side was Arthur Stuart, the mixup boy—but now trusted, now himself gifted with some of the Maker's own power.

Most of the paths began with them bringing Arthur Stuart to her springhouse, so she was not surprised when they knocked at her door.

"Miss Larner," called Alvin softly.

She was distracted; reality was not half so interesting as the futures revealed now in Arthur Stuart's heartfire. She opened the door. There they stood, Arthur still wrapped in Alvin's shirt.

"We brought him back," said Horace.

"I can see that," said Peggy. She *was* glad of it, but that gladness didn't show up in her voice. Instead she sounded busy, interrupted, annoyed. As she was. Get on with it, she wanted to say. I've seen this conversation as Arthur overheard it, so get on with it, get it over with, and let me get back to exploring what this boy will be. But of course she could say none of this—not if she hoped to remain disguised as Miss Larner.

"They won't find him," said Alvin, "not as long as they don't actually see him with their eyes. Something—their cachet don't work no more."

"Doesn't work anymore," said Peggy.

"Right," said Alvin. "What we come for—came for—can we leave him with you? Your house, here, Ma'am, I've got it hexed up so tight they won't even think to come inside, long as you keep the door locked."

"Don't you have more clothes for him than this? He's been wet—do you want him to take a chill?"

"It's a warm night," said Horace, "and we don't want to be fetching clothes from the house. Not till the Finders come back and give up and go away again."

"Very well," said Peggy.

"We'd best be about our business," said Po Doggly. "I got to get back to Dr. Physicker's."

"And since I told Old Peg that I'd be in town, I'd better be there," said Horace.

Alvin spoke straight to Peggy. "I'll be in the smithy, Miss Larner. If something goes wrong, you give a shout, and I'll be up the hill in ten seconds."

"Thank you. Now—please go on about your business."

She closed the door. She didn't mean to be so abrupt. But she had a whole new set of futures. No one but herself had ever been so important in Alvin's work as Arthur was going to be. But perhaps that would happen with everyone that Alvin actually touched and changed—perhaps as a Maker he would transform everyone he loved until they all stood with him in those glorious moments, until they all looked out upon the world through the lensed walls of the Crystal City and saw all things as God must surely see them.

A knock on the door. She opened it.

"In the first place," said Alvin, "don't open the door without knowing who it is."

"I knew it was you," she said. Truth was, though, she didn't. She didn't even think.

"In the second place, I was waiting to hear you lock the door, and you never did."

"Sorry," she said. "I forgot."

"We went to a lot of work to save this boy tonight, Miss Larner. Now it's all up to you. Just till the Finders go."

"Yes, I know." She really was sorry, and let her voice reveal her regret.

"Good night then."

He stood there waiting. For what?

Oh, yes. For her to close the door.

She closed it, locked it, then returned to Arthur Stuart and hugged him until he struggled to get away. "You're safe," she said.

"Of course I am," said Arthur Stuart. "We went to a lot of work to save this boy tonight, Miss Larner."

She listened to him, and knew there was something wrong. What was it? Oh, yes, of course. Alvin had just said exactly those words. But what was wrong? Arthur Stuart was always imitating people.

Always imitating. But this time Arthur Stuart had repeated Alvin's words in his own voice, not Alvin's. She had never heard him do that. She thought it was his knack, that he was so natural a mimic he didn't even realize he was doing it.

"Spell 'cicada,'" she said.

"C-I-C-A-D-A," he answered. In his own voice, not hers.

"Arthur Stuart," she whispered. "What's wrong?"

"Ain't nothing wrong, Miss Larner," he said. "I'm home."

He didn't know. He didn't realize it. Never having understood how perfect a mimic he had been, now he didn't realize when the knack was gone. He still had the near-perfect memory of what others said—he still had all the words. But the voices were gone; only his own seven-year-old voice remained.

She hugged him again, for a moment, more briefly. She understood now. As long as Arthur Stuart remained himself, the Finders could have found him and taken him south into slavery. The only way to save him was to make him no longer completely himself. Alvin hadn't known, of course he hadn't, that in saving Arthur, he had taken away his knack, or at least part of it. The price of Arthur's freedom was making him cease to be fully Arthur. Did Alvin understand that?

"I'm tired, Miss Larner," said Arthur Stuart.

"Yes, of course," she said. "You can sleep here—in my bed. Take off that dirty shirt and climb in under the covers and you'll be warm and safe all night."

He hesitated. She looked into his heartfire and saw why; smiling, she turned her back. She heard a rustle of fabric and then a squeak of bedsprings and the swish of a small body sliding along her sheets into bed. Then she turned around, bent over him where he lay upon her pillow, and kissed him lightly on the cheek.

"Good night, Arthur," she said.

"Good night," he murmured.

In moments he was asleep. She sat at her writing table and pulled up the wick on her lamp. She would do some reading while she waited for the Finders to return. Something to keep her calm while she waited.

No, she wouldn't. The words were there on the page, but she made no sense of them. Was she reading Descartes or Deuteronomy? It didn't matter. She couldn't stay away from Arthur's new heartfire. Of course all the paths of his life changed. He wasn't the same person anymore. No, that wasn't quite true. He was still Arthur. Mostly Arthur.

Almost Arthur. Almost what he was. But not quite.

Was it worth it? To lose part of who he had been in order to live free? Perhaps this new self was better than the old; but that old Arthur Stuart was gone now, gone forever, even more surely than if he had gone south and lived the rest of his life in bitter slavery, with his time in Hatrack as a memory, and then a dream, and then a mythic tale he told the pickaninnies in the years just before he died.

Fool! she cried to herself in her heart. No one is the same person today that he was yesterday. No one had a body as young as it was, or a heart so naive, or a head so ignorant as it was. He would have been far more terribly transformed—malformed—by life in bondage than by Alvin's gentle changes. Arthur Stuart was more surely himself now than he would have been in Appalachee. Besides, she had seen all the dark paths that once dwelt in his heartfire, the taste of the lash, the stupefying sun beating down on him as he labored in the field, or the hanging rope that awaited him on the many paths that led to his leading or taking part in a slave revolt and slaughtering dozens of Whites as they lay in their beds. Arthur Stuart was too young to understand what had happened to him; but if he were old enough, if he could choose which future he'd prefer, Peggy had no doubt that he would choose the sort of future Alvin had just made possible.

In a way, he lost some of himself, some of his knack, and therefore some of the choices he might have had in life. But in losing those, he gained so much more freedom, so much more power, that he was clear winner in the bargain.

Yet as she remembered his bright face when he spelled words to her in her own voice, she could not keep herself from shedding a few tears of regret.

19

THE PLOW

The Finders woke up not long after Arthur Stuart's rescuers took him across the river.

"Look at this. Manacles still fastened tight. Good hard iron."

"Don't matter. They got them a good spell for sleeping and a good spell for slipping out of chains, but don't they know us Finders always find a runaway, once we got his scent?"

If you could've seen them, you'd think they was glad Arthur Stuart got loose. Truth was, these boys loved a good chase, loved showing folks that Finders just couldn't be shook loose. And if it so happened they put a fistful of lead shot through somebody's belly before the hunt was done, well, ain't that just the way of it? Like dogs on the trail of a bleeding deer.

They followed Arthur Stuart's path through the forest till they came to the water's edge. Only then did their cheerful looks give way to a kind of frown. They lifted up their eyes and looked across the water, searching for the heartfires of men abroad at this time of night, when all honest folk was bound to be asleep. The white-haired one, he just couldn't see far enough; but the black-haired one, he said, "I see a few, moving about. And a few not moving. We'll pick up the scent again in Hatrack River."

ALVIN HELD THE plow between his hands. He knew that he could turn it all to gold—he'd seen gold enough in his life to know the pattern, so he could show the bits of iron what they ought to be. But he also knew that it wasn't no ordinary gold that he wanted. That would be too soft, and as cold as any ordinary stone. No, he wanted something new, not just iron to gold like any alchemist could dream of, but a living gold, a gold that could hold its shape and strength better than iron, better than the finest steel. Gold that was awake, aware of the world around it—a plow that knew the earth that it would tear, to lay it open to the fires of the sun.

A golden plow that would know a man, that a man could trust, the way Po Doggly knew Horace Guester and each trusted the other. A plow that wouldn't need no ox to draw, nor added weight to force it downward into the soil. A plow that would know which soil was rich and which was poor. A sort of gold that never had been seen in all the world before, just like the world had never seen such a thin invisible string as Alvin spun between Arthur Stuart and himself today.

So there he knelt, holding the shape of the gold inside his mind. "Be like this," he whispered to the iron.

He could feel how atoms came from all around the plow and joined together with those already in the iron, forming bits much heavier than what the iron was, and lined up in different ways, until they fit the pattern that he showed them in his mind.

Between his hands he held a plow of gold. He rubbed his fingers over it. Gold, yes, bright yellow in the firelight from the forge, but still dead, still cold. How could he teach it to be alive? Not by showing it the pattern of his own flesh— that wasn't the kind of life it needed. It was the living atoms that he wanted to waken, to show them what they were compared to what they *could* be. To put the fire of life in them.

The fire of life. Alvin lifted the golden plow—much heavier now—and despite the heat of the slacking fire, he set it right amid the glowing charcoal of the forge.

THEY WERE BACK on their horses now, them Finders, walking them calmly up the road to Hatrack River, looking into every house and hut and cabin, holding up the cachet to match it with the heartfires that they found within. But nary a match did they find, nary a body did they recognize. They passed the smithy and saw that a heartfire burned inside, but it wasn't the runaway mixup boy. It was bound to be the smith what made the manacles, they knew it.

"I'd like to kill him," whispered the black-haired Finder. "I know he put that spell in the manacles, to make them so that boy could slip right out."

"Time enough for that after we find the pickaninny," said the white-haired Finder.

They saw two heartfires burning in the old springhouse, but neither one was like what they had in the cachet, so they went on, searching for a child that they might recognize.

THE FIRE WAS deep within the gold now, but all it was doing was melting it. That wouldn't do at all—it was life the plow needed, not the death of metal in the fire. He held the plowshape in his mind and showed it plain as can be to every bit of metal in the plow; cried out silently to every atom, It ain't enough to be lined up in the little shapes of gold—you need to hold this larger shape yourselves, no matter the fire, no matter what other force might press or tear or melt or try to maim you.

He could sense that he was heard—there was movement in the gold, movement against the downward slipping of the gold as it turned to fluid. But it wasn't strong enough, it wasn't *sure* enough. Without thinking, Alvin reached his hands into the fire and clung to the gold, showing it the plowshape, crying to it in his heart, Like this! Be like this! This is what you are! Oh, the pain of it burned something fierce, but he knew that it was right for his hands to be there, for the Maker is a part of what he makes. The atoms heard him, and formed themselves in ways that Alvin never even thought of, but the result of it all was that the gold now took the heat of the fire into itself without melting, without losing shape. It was done; the plow wasn't alive, exactly, not the way he wanted—but it could stand in the forgefire without melting. The gold was more than gold now. It was gold that knew it was a plow and meant to stay that way.

Alvin pulled his hands away from the plow and saw flames still dancing on his skin, which was charred in places, peeling back away from the bone. Silent as death, he plunged his hands into the water barrel and heard the sizzle of the fire on his flesh as it went out. Then, before the pain could come in full force, he set to healing himself, sloughing away the dead skin and making new skin grow.

He stood there, weakened from all his body had to do to heal his hands, looking into the fire at the gold plow. Just setting there, knowing its shape and holding to it—but that wasn't enough to make the plow alive. It had to know what a plow was for. It had to know why it lived, so it could act to fulfill that purpose. That was Making, Alvin knew it now; that was what Redbird come to say three years ago. Making wasn't like carpentry or smithy work or any such, cutting and bending and melting to force things into new shapes. Making was something subtler and stronger—making things *want* to be another way, a new shape, so they just naturally flowed that way. It was something Alvin had done for years without knowing what it was he was doing. When he thought he was doing no more than finding the natural cracks in stone, he was really making those cracks; by imagining where he wanted them to be, and showing it to the atoms within the bits within the pieces of the rock, he taught them to want to fulfill the shape he showed them.

Now, with this plow, he had done it, not by accident, but on purpose; and he'd taught the gold to be something stronger, to hold better to its shape than anything he'd ever Made before. But how could he teach it more, teach it to act, to move in ways that gold was never taught to move?

In the back of his mind, he knew that this golden plow wasn't the real problem. The real problem was the Crystal City, and the building blocks of *that* weren't going to be simple atoms in a metal plow. The atoms of a city are men and women, and they don't believe the shape they're shown with the simple faith that atoms have, they don't understand with such pure clarity, and when they act, their actions are never half so pure. But if I can teach this gold to be a plow and to be alive, then maybe I can make a Crystal City out of men and women; maybe I can find people as pure as the atoms of this gold, who come to understand the shape of the Crystal City and love it the way I did the moment I saw it when I climbed the inside of that twister with Tenskwa-Tawa. Then they'll not only hold that shape but also make it act, make the Crystal City a living thing much larger and greater than any one of us who are its atoms.

The Maker is the one who is part of what he makes.

Alvin ran to the bellows and pumped up the fire till the charcoal was glowing hot enough to drive any regular smith outside into the night air to wait till the fire slacked. But not Alvin. Instead he walked right up to the forge and climbed right into the heat and the flame. He felt the clothes burning right off his body, but he paid no mind. He curled himself around that plow and then commenced to healing himself, not piecemeal, not bit by bit, but healing himself by telling his whole body, all at once, Stay alive! Put the fire that burns you into this plow!

And at the same time, he told the plow, Do as my body does! Live! Learn from every living bit of me how each part has its purpose, and acts on it. I can't show you the shape you've got to be, or how it's done, cause I don't know. But I can show you what it's like to be alive, by the pain of my body, by the healing of it, by the struggle to stay alive. Be like this! Whatever it takes, however hard it is for you to learn, this is you, be like me!

It took forever, trembling in the fire as his body struggled with the heat, finding ways to channel it the way a river channels water, pouring it out into the plow like it was an ocean of golden fire. And within the plow, the atoms struggled to do what Alvin asked, wanting to obey him, not knowing how. But his call to them was strong, too strong not to hear; and it was more than a matter of hearing him, too. It was like they could tell that what he wanted for them was good. They trusted him, they wanted to be the living plow he dreamed of, and so in a million flecks of time so small that a second seemed like eternity to them, they tried this, they tried that, until somewhere within the golden plow a new pattern was made that knew itself to be alive exactly as Alvin wanted it to be; and in a single single moment the pattern passed throughout the plow and it was alive.

Alive. Alvin felt it moving within the curve of his body as the plow nestled down into the coals of the fire, cutting into it, plowing it as if it were soil. And because it was a barren soil, one that could bear no life, the plow rose quickly out of it and slipped outward, away from the fire toward the lip of the forge. It moved by deciding to be in a different place, and then being there; when it reached the brink of the forge it toppled off and tumbled to the smithy floor.

In agony Alvin rolled from the fire and also fell, also lay pressed against the cold dirt of the floor. Now that the fire no longer surrounded him, his body gained against the death of his skin, healing him as he had taught it to do, without him having to tell it what to do, without need of direction at all. Become yourself, that had been Alvin's command, and so the signature within each living bit of him obeyed the pattern it contained, until his body was whole and perfect, the skin new, uncallused, and unburned.

What he couldn't remove was the memory of pain, or the weakness from all the strength his body had given up. But he didn't care. Weak as he was, his heart was jubilant, because the plow that lay beside him on the ground was living gold, not because he made it, but because he taught it how to make itself.

THE FINDERS FOUND nothing, nowhere in town—yet the black-haired Finder couldn't see anyone running away, neither, not within the farthest distance that any natural man or horse could possibly have gone since the boy got taken back. Somehow the mixup boy was hiding from them, a thing they knew full well was pure impossible—but it must be so.

The place to look was where the boy had lived for all these years. The roadhouse, the springhouse, the smithy— places where folks were up unnatural late at night. They rode to near the roadhouse, then tied up their horses just off the road. They loaded their shotguns and pistols and set off on foot. Passing by the roadhouse they searched again, accounting for every heartfire; none of them was like the cachet.

"That cottage, with that teacher lady," said the white-haired Finder. "That's where the boy was when we found him before."

The black-haired Finder looked over that way. Couldn't see the springhouse through the trees, of course, but what he was looking for he could see, trees or not. "Two people in there," he said.

"Could be the mixup boy, then," said the white-haired Finder.

"Cachet says not." Then the black-haired Finder grinned nastily. "Single teacher lady, living alone, got a visitor this time of night? I know what kind of company she's keeping, and it ain't no mixup boy."

"Let's go see anyhow," said the white-haired Finder. "If'n you're right, she won't be putting out any complaint on how we broke in her door, or we'll just tell what we saw going on inside when we done it."

They had a good little laugh about that, and set off through the moonlight toward Miss Larner's house. They meant to kick in the door, of course, and have a good laugh when the teacher lady got all huffy about it and made her threats.

Funny thing was, when they actually got near the cottage, that plan just clean went out of their heads. They forgot all about it. Just looked again at the heartfires within and compared them to the cachet.

"What the hell are we doing up here?" asked the white-haired Finder. "Boy's bound to be at the roadhouse. We *know* he ain't here!"

"You know what I'm thinking?" said the black-haired one. "Maybe they killed him."

"That's plain crazy. Why save him, then?"

"How else do you figure they made it so we can't see him then?"

"He's in the roadhouse. They got some hex that hides him up, I'll bet. Once we open the right door there, we'll see him and that'll be that."

For a fleeting moment the black-haired Finder thought—well, why not look in this teacher lady's cottage, too, if they got a hex like that? Why not open *this* door?

But he no sooner had that thought than it just slipped away so he couldn't remember it, couldn't even remember *having* a thought. He just trotted away after the white-haired Finder. Mixup boy's bound to be in the roadhouse, that's for sure.

SHE SAW THEIR heartfires, of course, as the Finders came toward her cottage, but Peggy wasn't afraid. She had explored Arthur Stuart's heartfire all this time, and there was no path there which led to capture by these Finders. Arthur had dangers enough in the future—Peggy could see that—but no harm would come to the boy tonight. So she paid them little heed. She knew when they decided to leave; knew when the black-haired Finder thought of coming in; knew when the hexes blocked him and drove him away. But it was Arthur Stuart she was watching, searching out the years to come.

Then, suddenly, she couldn't hold it to herself any longer. She had to tell Alvin, both the joy and sorrow of what he had done. Yet how could she? How could she tell him that Miss Larner was really a torch who could see the million newborn futures in Arthur Stuart's heartfire? It was unbearable to keep all this to herself. She might have told Mistress Modesty, years ago, when she lived there and kept no secrets.

It was madness to go down to the smithy, knowing that her desire was to tell him things she couldn't tell without revealing who she was. Yet it would surely drive her mad to stay within these walls, alone with all this knowledge that she couldn't share.

So she got up, unlocked the door, and stepped outside. No one around. She closed the door and locked it; then again looked into Arthur's heartfire and again found no danger for the boy. He would be safe. She would see Alvin.

Only then did she look into Alvin's heartfire; only then did she see the terrible pain that he had suffered only minutes ago. Why hadn't she noticed? Why hadn't she seen? Alvin had just passed through the greatest threshold of his life; he had truly done a great Making, brought something new into the world, and she hadn't seen. When he faced the Unmaker while she was in far-off Dekane, she had seen his struggle—now, when she wasn't three rods off, why hadn't she turned to him? Why hadn't she known his pain when he writhed inside the fire?

Maybe it was the springhouse. Once before, near nineteen years ago, the day that Alvin was born, the springhouse had damped her gift and lulled her to sleep till she was al-most too late. But no, it couldn't be that—the water didn't run through the springhouse anymore, and the forgefire was stronger than that.

Maybe it was the Unmaker itself, come to block her. But as she cast about with her torchy sight, she couldn't see any unusual darkness amid the colors of the world around her, not close at hand, anyway. Nothing that could have blinded her.

No, it had to be the nature of what Alvin himself was do-ing that blinded her to it. Just as she hadn't seen how he would extricate himself from his confrontation with the Unmaker years ago, just as she hadn't seen how he would change young Arthur at the Hio shore tonight, it was just the same way she hadn't seen what he was doing in the forge. It was outside the futures that her knack could see, the particular Making he performed tonight.

Would it always be like that? Would she always be blinded when his most important work was being done? It made her angry, it frightened her—what good is my knack, if it des-erts me just when I need it most!

No. I didn't need it most just now. Alvin had no need of me or my sight when he climbed into the fire. My knack has never deserted me when it was *needed*. It's only my desire that's thwarted.

Well, he needs me now, she thought. She picked her way carefully down the slope; the moon was low, the shadows deep, so the path was treacherous. When she rounded the corner of the smithy, the light from the forgefire, spilling out onto the grass, was almost blinding; it was so red that it made the grass look shiny black, not green.

Inside the smithy Alvin lay curled on the ground, facing toward the forge, away from her. He was breathing heavily, raggedly. Asleep? No. He was naked; it took a moment to realize that his clothing must have burned off him in the forge. He hadn't noticed it in all his pain, and so had no memory of it; therefore she hadn't seen it happen when she searched for memories in his heartfire.

His skin was shockingly pale and smooth. Earlier today she had seen his skin a deep brown from the sun and the forgefire's heat. Earlier today he had been callused, with here and there a scar from some spark or searing burn, the normal accidents of life beside a fire. Now, though, his skin was as unmarked as a baby's, and she could not help herself; she stepped into the smithy, knelt beside him, and gently brushed her hand along his back, from his shoulder down to the narrow place above the hip. His skin was so soft it made her own hands feel coarse to her, as if she marred him just by touching him.

He let out a long breath, a sigh. She withdrew her hand.

"Alvin," she said. "Are you all right?"

He moved his arm; he was stroking something that lay within the curl of his body. Only now did she see it, a faint yellow in the double shadow of his body and of the forge. A golden plow.

"It's alive," he murmured.

As if in answer, she saw it move smoothly under his hand.

OF COURSE THEY didn't knock. At this time of night? They would know at once it couldn't be some chance traveler—it could only be the Finders. Knocking at the door would warn them, give them a chance to try to carry the boy farther off.

But the black-haired Finder didn't so much as try the latch. He just let fly with his foot and the door crashed inward, pulling away from the upper hinge as it did. Then, shotgun at the ready, he moved quickly inside and looked around the common room. The fire there was dying down, so the light was scant, but they could see that there was no one there.

"I'll keep watch on the stairs," said the white-haired Finder. 'You go out the back to see if anybody's trying to get out that way."

The black-haired Finder immediately made his way past the kitchen and the stairs to the back door, which he flung open. The white-haired Finder was halfway up the stairs before the back door closed again.

In the kitchen, Old Peg crawled out from under the table. Neither one had so much as paused at the kitchen door. She didn't know who they were, of course, but she hoped— hoped it was the Finders, sneaking back here because somehow, by some miracle, Arthur Stuart got away and they didn't know where he was. She slipped off her shoes and walked as quietly as she could from the kitchen to the common room, where Horace kept a loaded shotgun over the fireplace. She reached up and took it down, but in the process she knocked over a tin teakettle that someone had left warming by the fire earlier in the evening. The kettle clattered; hot water spilled over her bare feet; she gasped in spite of herself.

Immediately she could hear footsteps on the stairs. She ignored the pain and ran to the foot of the stairs, just in time to see the white-haired Finder coming down. He had a shotgun pointed straight at her. Even though she'd never fired a gun at a human being in her life, she didn't hesitate a moment. She pulled the trigger; the gun kicked back against her belly, driving the breath out of her and slamming her against the wall beside the kitchen door. She hardly noticed. All she saw was how the white-haired Finder stood there, his face suddenly relaxing till it looked as stupid as a cow's face. Then red blossoms appeared all over his shirt, and he toppled over backward.

You'll never steal another child away from his mama, thought Old Peg. You'll never drag another Black into a life of bowing under the whip. I killed you, Finder, and I think the good Lord rejoices. But even if I go to hell for it, I'm glad.

She was so intent on watching him that she didn't even notice that the door out back stood open, held in place by the barrel of the black-haired Finder's gun, pointed right at her.

ALVIN WAS SO intent on telling Peggy what he had done that he hardly noticed he was naked. She handed him the leather apron hanging from a peg on the wall, and he put it on by habit, without a thought. She hardly heard his words; all that he was telling her, she already knew from looking in his heartfire. Instead she was looking at him, thinking, Now he's a Maker, in part because of what I taught him. Maybe I'm finished now, maybe my life will be my own— but maybe not, maybe now I've just begun, maybe now I can treat him as a man, not as a pupil or a ward. He seemed to glow with an inner fire; and every step he took, the golden plow echoed, not by following him or tangling itself in his feet, but by slipping along on a line that could have been an orbit around him, well out of the way but close enough to be of use; as if it were a part of him, though unattached.

"I know," Peggy told him. "I understand. You *are* a Maker now."

"It's more than that!" he cried. "It's the Crystal City. I know how to build it now, Miss Larner. See, the city ain't the crystal towers that I saw, the city's the people inside it, and if I'm going to build the place I got to find the kind of folks who ought to be there, folks as true and loyal as this plow, folks who share the dream enough to want to build it, and keep on building it even if I'm not there. You see, Miss

Larner? The Crystal City isn't a thing that a single Maker can make. It's a city of Makers; I got to find all kinds of folks and somehow make Makers out of them."

She knew as he said it that this was indeed the task that he was born for—and the labor that would break his heart. "Yes," she said. "That's true, I know it is." And in spite of herself, she couldn't sound like Miss Larner, calm and cool and distant. She sounded like herself, like her true feelings. She was burning up inside with the fire that Alvin lit there.

"Come with me, Miss Larner," said Alvin. "You know so much, and you're such a good teacher—I need your help."

No, Alvin, not those words. I'll come with you for those words, yes, but say the other words, the ones I need so much to hear. "How can I teach what only you know how to do?" she asked him—trying to sound quiet, calm.

"But it ain't just for the teaching, either—I can't do this alone. What I done tonight, it's so hard—I need to have you with me." He took a step toward her. The golden plow slipped across the floor toward her, behind her; if it marked the outer border of Alvin's largest self, then she was now well within that generous circle.

"What do you need me for?" asked Peggy. She refused to look within his heartfire, refused to see whether or not there was any chance that he might actually—no, she refused even to name to herself what it was she wanted now, for fear that somehow she'd discover that it couldn't possibly be so, that it could never happen, that somehow tonight all such paths had been irrevocably closed. Indeed, she realized, that was part of why she had been so caught up in exploring Arthur Stuart's new futures; he would be so close to Alvin that she could see much of Alvin's great and terrible future through Arthur's eyes, without ever having to know what she would know if she looked into Alvin's own heartfire: Alvin's heartfire would show her whether, in his many futures, there were any in which he loved her, and married her, and put that dear and perfect body into her arms to give her and get from her that gift that only lovers share.

"Come with me," he said. "I can't even think of going on out there without you, Miss Larner. I—" He laughed at himself. "I don't even know your first name, Miss Larner."

"Margaret," she said.

"Can I call you that? Margaret—will you come with me? I know you ain't what you seem to be, but I don't care what you look like under all that hexery. I feel like you're the only living soul who knows me like I really am, and I—"

He just stood there, looking for the word. And she stood there, waiting to hear it.

"I love you," he said. "Even though you think I'm just a boy."

Maybe she would've answered him. Maybe she would've told him that she knew he was a man, and that she was the only woman who could love him without worshipping him, the only one who could actually be a helpmeet for him. But into the silence after his words and before she could speak, there came the sound of a gunshot.

At once she thought of Arthur Stuart, but it only took a moment to see that his heartfire was undisturbed; he lay asleep up in her little house. No, the sound came from farther off. She cast her torchy sight to the roadhouse, and there found the heartfire of a man in the last moment before death, and he was looking at a woman standing down at the foot of the stairs. It was Mother, holding a shotgun.

His heartfire dimmed, died. At once Peggy looked into her mother's heartfire and saw, behind her thoughts and feelings and memories, a million paths of the future, all jumbling together, all changing before her eyes, all becoming one single path, which led to one single place. A flash of searing agony, and then nothing.

"Mother!" she cried. "Mother!"

And then the future became the present; Old Peg's heart-fire was gone before the sound of the second gunshot reached the smithy.

ALVIN COULD HARDLY believe what he was saying to Miss Larner. He hadn't known until this moment, when he said it, how he felt about her. He was so afraid she'd laugh at him, so afraid she'd tell him he was far too young, that in time he'd get over how he felt.

But instead of answering him, she paused for just a moment, and in that moment a gunshot rang out. Alvin knew at once that it came from the roadhouse; he followed the sound with his bug and found where it came from, found a dead man already beyond all healing. And then a moment later, another gunshot, and then he found someone else dying, a woman. He knew that body from the inside out; it wasn't no stranger. It had to be Old Peg.

"Mother!" cried Miss Larner. "Mother!"

"It's Old Peg Guester!" cried Alvin.

He saw Miss Larner tear open the collar of her dress, reach inside and pull out the amulets that hung there. She tore them off her neck, cutting herself bad on the breaking strings. Alvin could hardly take in what he saw—a young woman, scarce older than himself, and beautiful, even though her face was torn with grief and terror.

"It's my mother!" she cried. "Alvin, save her!"

He didn't wait a second. He just tore on out of the smithy, running barefoot on the grass, in the road, not caring how the rough dirt and rocks tore into his soft, unaccustomed feet. The leather apron caught and tangled between his knees; he tugged it, twisted it to the side, out of his way. He could see with his bug how Old Peg was already past saving, but still he ran, because he had to *try,* even though he knew there was no reason in it. And then she died, and still he ran, because he couldn't bear not to be running to where that good woman, his good friend was lying dead.

His good friend and Miss Larner's mother. The only way that could be is if she was the torch girl what run off seven years ago. But then if she was such a torch as folks around her said, why didn't she see this coming? Why didn't she look into her own mother's heartfire and forsee her death? It made no sense.

There was a man in front of him on the road. A man running down from the roadhouse toward some horses tied to trees just over yonder. It was the man who killed Old Peg, Alvin knew that, and cared to know no more. He sped up, faster than he'd ever run before without getting strength from the forest around him. The man heard him coming maybe thirty yards off, and turned around.

"You, smith!" cried the black-haired Finder. "Glad to kill you too!"

He had a pistol in his hand; he fired.

Alvin took the bullet in his belly, but he didn't care about that. His body started work at once fixing what the bullet tore, but it wouldn't've mattered a speck if he'd been bleeding to death. Alvin didn't even slow down; he flew into the man, knocking him down, landing on him and skidding with him ten feet across the dirt of the road. The man cried out in fear and pain. That single cry was the last sound he made; in his rage, Alvin caught the man's head in such a grip that it took only one sharp jab of his other hand against the man's jaw to snap his neckbone clean in half. The man was already dead, but Alvin hit his head again and again with his fists, until his arms and chest and his leather apron was all covered with the black-haired Finder's blood and the man's skull was broke up inside his head like shards of dropped pottery.

Then Alvin knelt there, his head stupid with exhaustion and spent anger. After a minute or so he remembered that Old Peg was still lying there on the roadhouse floor. He knowed she was dead, but where else did he have to go? Slowly he got to his feet.

He heard horses coming down the road from town. That time of night in Hatrack River, gunshots meant only trouble. Folks'd come. They'd find the body in the road—they'd come on up to the roadhouse. No need for Alvin to stay to greet them.

Inside the roadhouse, Peggy was already kneeling over her mother's body, sobbing and panting from her run up to the house. Alvin only knew for sure it was her from her dress—he'd only seen her face but once before, for a second there in the smithy. She turned when she saw Alvin come inside. "Where were you! Why didn't you save her! You could have saved her!"

"I never could," said Alvin. It was wrong of her to say such a thing. "There wasn't time."

"You should have looked! You should have seen what was coming."

Alvin didn't understand her. "I can't see what's coming," he said. "That's *your* knack."

Then she burst out crying, not the dry sobs like when he first came in, but deep, gut-wrenching howls of grief. Alvin didn't know what to do.

The door opened behind him.

"Peggy," whispered Horace Guester. "Little Peggy."

Peggy looked up at her father, her face so streaked with

tears and twisted up and reddened with weeping that it was a marvel he could recognize her. "I killed her!" she cried. "I never should have left, Papa! I killed her!"

Only then did Horace understand that it was his wife's body lying there. Alvin watched as he started trembling, groaning, then keening loud and high like a hurt dog. Alvin never seen such grieving. Did my father cry like that when my brother Vigor died? Did he make such a sound as this when he thought that me and Measure was tortured to death by Red men?

Alvin reached out his arms to Horace, held him tight around the shoulders, then led him over to Peggy and helped him kneel there beside his daughter, both of them weeping, neither giving a sign that they saw each other. All they saw was Old Peg's body spread out on the floor; Alvin couldn't even guess how deeply, how agonizingly each one bore the whole blame for her dying.

After a while the sheriff came in. He'd already found the black-haired Finder's corpse outside, and it didn't take him long to understand exactly what happened. He took Alvin aside. "This is pure self-defense if I ever saw it," said Pauley Wiseman, "and I wouldn't make you spend three seconds in jail for it. But I can tell you that the law in Appalachee don't take the death of a Finder all that easy, and the treaty lets them come up here and get you to take back there for trial. What I'm saying, boy, is you better get the hell out of here in the next couple of days or I can't promise you'll be safe."

"I was going anyway," said Alvin.

"I don't know how you done it," said Pauley Wiseman, "but I reckon you got that half-Black pickaninny away from them Finders tonight and hid him somewhere around here. I'm telling you, Alvin, when you go, you best take that boy with you. Take him to Canada. But if I see his face again, I'll ship him south myself. It's that boy caused all this—

makes me sick, a good White woman dying cause of some half-Black mixup boy."

"You best never say such a thing in front of me again, Pauley Wiseman."

The sheriff only shook his head and walked away. "Ain't natural," he said. "All you people set on a monkey like it was folks." He turned around to face Alvin. "I don't much care what you think of me, Alvin Smith, but I'm giving you and that mixup boy a chance to stay alive. I hope you have brains to take it. And in the meantime, you might go wash off that blood and fetch some clothes to wear."

Alvin walked on back to the road. Other folks was coming by then—he paid them no heed. Only Mock Berry seemed to understand what was happening. He led Alvin on down to his house, and there Anga washed him down and Mock gave him some of his own clothes to wear. It was nigh onto dawn when Alvin got him back to the smithy.

Makepeace was setting there on a stool in the smithy door, looking at the golden plow. It was resting on the ground, still as you please, right in front of the forge.

"That's one hell of a journeyman piece," said Makepeace.

"I reckon," said Alvin. He walked over to the plow and reached down. It fairly leapt into Alvin's hands—not heavy at all now—but if Makepeace noticed how the plow moved by itself just before Alvin touched it, he didn't say.

"I got a lot of scrap iron," said Makepeace. "I don't even ask for you to go halves with me. Just let me keep a few pieces when you turn them into gold."

"I ain't turning no more iron into gold," said Alvin.

It made Makepeace angry. "That's *gold,* you fool! That there plow you made means never going hungry, never having to work again, living fine instead of in that rundown house up there! It means new dresses for Gertie and maybe a suit of clothes for me! It means folks in town saying Good morning to me and tipping their hats like I was a gentleman. It means riding in a carriage like Dr. Physicker, and going to Dekane or Carthage or wherever I please and not even caring what it costs. And you're telling me you ain't making no more *gold*?"

Alvin knew it wouldn't do no good explaining, but still he tried. "This ain't no common gold, sir. This is a living plow—I ain't going to let nobody melt it down to make coins out of it. Best I can figure, nobody could melt it even if they wanted to. So back off and let me go."

"What you going to do, plow with it? You blame fool, we could be kings of the world together!" But when Alvin pushed on by, headed out of the smithy, Makepeace stopped his pleading and started getting ugly. "That's my iron you used to make that golden plow! That gold belongs to *me*! A journeyman piece always belongs to the master, less'n he gives it to the journeyman and I sure as hell don't! Thief! You're stealing from me!"

"You stole five years of my life from me, long after I was good enough to be a journeyman," Alvin said. "And this plow—making it was none of your teaching. It's alive, Makepeace Smith. It doesn't belong to you and it doesn't belong to me. It belongs to itself. So let me just set it down here and we'll see who gets it."

Alvin set down the plow on the grass between them. Then he stepped back a few paces. Makepeace took one step toward the plow. It sank down into the soil under the grass, then cut its way through the dirt till it reached Alvin. When he picked it up, it was warm. He knew what that had to mean. "Good soil," said Alvin. The plow trembled in his hands.

Makepeace stood there, his eyes bugged out with fear. "Good Lord, boy, that plow *moved*."

"I know it," said Alvin.

"What are you, boy? The devil?"

"I don't think so," said Alvin. "Though I might've met him once or twice."

"Get on out of here! Take that thing and go away! I never want to see your face around here again!"

"You got my journeyman paper," said Alvin. "I want it."

Makepeace reached into his pocket, took out a folded paper, and threw it onto the grass in front of the smithy. Then he reached out and pulled the smithy doors shut, something he hardly ever did, even in winter. He shut them tight and barred them on the inside. Poor fool, as if Alvin couldn't break down them walls in a second if he really wanted to get inside. Alvin walked over and picked up the paper. He opened it and read it—signed all proper. It was legal. Alvin was a journeyman.

The sun was just about to show up when Alvin got to the springhouse door. Of course it was locked, but locks and hexes couldn't keep Alvin out, specially when he made them all himself. He opened the door and went inside. Arthur Stuart stirred in his sleep. Alvin touched his shoulder, brought the boy awake. Alvin knelt there by the bed and told the boy most all that happened in the night. He showed him the golden plow, showed him how it moved. Arthur laughed in delight. Then Alvin told him that the woman he called Mama all his life was dead, killed by the Finders, and Arthur cried.

But not for long. He was too young to cry for long. "You say she kilt one herself afore she died?"

"With your pa's own shotgun."

"Good for her!" said Arthur Stuart, his voice so fierce Alvin almost laughed, him being so small.

"I killed the other one myself. The one that shot her."

Arthur reached out and took Alvin's right hand and opened it. "Did you kill him with this hand?"

Alvin nodded.

Arthur kissed his open palm.

"I would've fixed her up if I could," said Alvin. "But she died too fast. Even if I'd been standing right there the second after the shot hit her, I couldn't've fixed her up."

Arthur Stuart reached out and hung onto Alvin around his neck and cried some more.

IT TOOK A day to put Old Peg into the ground, up on the hill with her own daughters and Alvin's brother Vigor and Arthur's mama who died so young. "A place for people of courage," said Dr. Physicker, and Alvin knew that he was right, even though Physicker didn't know about the runaway Black slave girl.

Alvin washed away the bloodstains from the floor and stairs of the roadhouse, using his knack to pull out what blood the lye and sand couldn't remove. It was the last gift he could give to Horace or to Peggy. Margaret. Miss Larner.

"I got to leave now," he told them. They were setting on chairs in the common room of the inn, where they'd been receiving mourners all day. "I'm taking Arthur to my folks' place in Vigor Church. He'll be safe there. And then I'm going on."

"Thank you for everything," said Horace. "You been a good friend to us. Old Peg loved you." Then he broke down crying again.

Alvin patted him on the shoulder a couple of times, and then moved over to stand in front of Peggy. "All that I am, Miss Larner, I owe to you."

She shook her head.

"I meant all I said to you. I still mean it."

Again she shook her head. He wasn't surprised. With her

mama dead, never even knowing that her own daughter'd come home, why, Alvin didn't expect she could just up and go. Somebody had to help Horace Guester run the road-house. It all made sense. But still it stabbed him to the heart, because now more than ever he knew that it was true—he loved her. But she wasn't for him. That much was plain. She never had been. A woman like this, so educated and fine and beautiful—she could be his teacher, but she could never love him like he loved her.

"Well then, I guess I'm saying good-bye," said Alvin. He stuck out his hand, even though he knew it was kind of silly to shake hands with somebody grieving the way she was. But he wanted so bad to put his arms around her and hold her tight the way he'd held Arthur Stuart when he was griev-ing, and a handshake was as close as he could come to that.

She saw his hand, and reached up and took it. Not for a handshake, but just holding his hand, holding it tight. It took him by surprise. He'd think about that many times in the months and years to come, how tight she held to him. Maybe it meant she loved him. Or maybe it meant she only cared for him as a pupil, or thanked him for avenging her mama's death—how could he know what a thing like that could mean? But still he held onto that memory, in case it meant she loved him.

And he made her a promise then, with her holding his hand like that; made her a promise even though he didn't know if she even wanted him to keep it. "I'll be back," he said. "And what I said last night, it'll always be true." It took all his courage then to call her by the name she gave him permission last night to use. "God be with you, Margaret."

"God be with you, Alvin," she whispered.

Then he gathered up Arthur Stuart, who'd been saying his own good-byes, and led the boy outside. They walked out back of the roadhouse to the barn, where Alvin had hidden the golden plow deep in a barrel of beans. He took off the lid and held out his hand, and the plow rose upward until it glinted in the light. Then Alvin took it up, wrapped it double in burlap and put it inside a burlap bag, then swung the bag over his shoulder.

Alvin knelt down and held out his hand the way he always did when he wanted Arthur Stuart to climb up onto his back. Arthur did, thinking it was all for play—a boy that age, he can't be grieving for more than an hour or two at a time. He swung up onto Alvin's back, laughing and bouncing.

"This time it's going to be a long ride, Arthur Stuart," said Alvin. "We're going all the way to my family's house in Vigor Church."

"Walking the whole way?"

"*I'll* be walking. *You're* going to ride."

"Gee-yap!" cried Arthur Stuart.

Alvin set off at a trot, but before long he was running full out. He never set foot on that road, though. Instead he took off cross country, over fields, over fences, and on into the woods, which still stood in great swatches here and there across the states of Hio and Wobbish between him and home. The greensong was much weaker than it had been in the days when the Red men had it all to themselves. But the song was still strong enough for Alvin Smith to hear. He let himself himself fall into the rhythm of the greensong, running as the Red men did. And Arthur Stuart—maybe he could hear some of the greensong too, enough that it could lull him to sleep, there on Alvin's back. The world was gone. Just him, Arthur Stuart, the golden plow—and the whole world singing around him. I'm a journeyman now. And this is my first journey.

20

CAVIL'S DEED

Cavil Planter had business in town. He mounted his horse early on that fine spring morning, leaving behind wife and slaves, house and land, knowing all were well under his control, fully his own.

Along about noon, after many a pleasant visit and much business well done, he stopped in at the postmaster's store. There were three letters there. Two were from old friends. One was from Reverend Philadelphia Thrower in Carthage, the capital of Wobbish.

Old friends could wait. This would be news about the Finders he hired, though why the letter should come from Thrower and not from the Finders themselves, Cavil couldn't guess. Maybe there was trouble. Maybe he'd have to go north to testify after all. Well, if that's what it takes, I'll do it, thought Cavil. Gladly I'll leave the ninety and nine sheep, as Jesus said, in order to reclaim the one that strayed.

It was bitter news. Both Finders dead, and so also the innkeeper's wife who claimed to have adopted Cavil's stolen firstborn son. Good riddance to her, thought Cavil, and he spared not a second's grief for the Finders—they were hirelings, and he valued them less than his slaves, since they weren't *his*. No, it was the last news, the worst news, that set Cavil's hands to trembling and his breath to stop. The man who killed one of the Finders, a prentice smith named Alvin, he ran off instead of standing trial—and took with him Cavil's son.

He took my son. And the worst words from Thrower were these: "I knew this fellow Alvin when he was a mere child, and already he was an agent of evil. He is our mutual

Friend's worst enemy in all the world, and now he has your most valued property in his possession. I wish I had better news. I pray for you, lest your son be turned into a dangerous and implacable foe of all our Friend's holy work."

With such news, how could Cavil go about the rest of the day's business? Without a word to the postmaster or to anybody, Cavil stuffed the letters into his pocket, went outside, mounted his horse, and headed home. All the way his heart was tossed between rage and fear. How could those northerner Emancipationist scum have let his slave, his son, get stole right out from under them, by the worst enemy of the Overseer? I'll go north, I'll make them pay, I'll find the boy, I'll—and then his thoughts would turn all of a sudden to what the Overseer would say, if ever He came again. What if He despises me now, and never comes again? Or worse, what if He comes and damns me for a slothful servant? Or what if He declares me unworthy and forbids me to take any more Black women to myself? How could I live if not in His service—what else is my life *for?*

And then rage again, terrible blasphemous rage, in which he cried out deep within his soul, O my Overseer! Why did You let this happen? You could have stopped it with a word, if You are truly Lord!

And then terror: Such a thing, to doubt the power of the Overseer! No, forgive me, I am truly Thy slave, O Master! Forgive me, I've lost everything, forgive me!

Poor Cavil. He'd find out soon enough what losing everything could mean.

He got himself home and turned the horse up that long drive leading to the house, only the sun being hot he stayed under the shade of the oaks along the south side of the road. Maybe if he'd rode out in the middle of the lane he would've been seen sooner. Maybe then he wouldn't have heard a woman cry out inside the house just as he was coming out from under the trees.

"Dolores!" he called. "Is something wrong?"

No answer.

Now, that scared him. It conjured up pictures in his mind of marauders or thieves or such, breaking into his house while he was gone. Maybe they already killed Lashman, and even now were killing his wife. He spurred his horse and raced around the house to the back.

Just in time to see a big old Black running from the back door of the house down toward the slave quarters. He couldn't see the Black man's face, on account of his trousers, which he didn't have on, nor any other clothing either—no, he was holding those trousers like a banner, flapping away in front of his face as he ran down toward the sheds.

A Black, no pants on, running out of my house, in which a woman was crying out. For a moment Cavil was torn between the desire to chase down the Black man and kill him with his bare hands and the need to go up and see to Dolores, make sure she was all right. Had he come in time? Was she undefiled?

Cavil bounded up the stairs and flung open the door to his wife's room. There lay Dolores in bed, her covers tight up under her chin, looking at him through wide-open, frightened eyes.

"What happened!" cried Cavil. "Are you all right?"

"Of course I am!" she answered sharply. "What are you doing home?"

That wasn't the answer you get from a woman who's just cried out in fear. "I heard you call out," said Cavil. "Didn't you hear me answer?"

"I hear everything up here," said Dolores. "I got nothing to do in my life but lie here and listen. I hear everything that's said in this house and everything that's done. Yes, I heard you call. But you weren't answering *me*."

Cavil was astonished. She sounded angry. He'd never heard her sound angry before. Lately he'd hardly heard a word from her at all—she was always asleep when he took breakfast, and their dinners together passed in silence. Now this anger—why? Why now?

"I saw a Black man running away from the house," said Cavil. "I thought maybe he—"

"Maybe he what?" She said the words like a taunt, a challenge.

"Maybe he hurt you."

"No, he didn't *hurt* me."

Now a thought began to creep into Cavil's mind, a thought so terrible he couldn't even admit he was thinking it. "What *did* he do, then?"

"Why, the same holy work that you've been doing, Cavil."

Cavil couldn't say a thing to that. She knew. She knew it all.

"Last summer, when your friend Reverend Thrower came, I lay here in my bed as you talked, the two of you."

"You were asleep. Your door was—"

"I heard everything. Every word, every whisper. I heard you go outside. I heard you talk at breakfast. Do you know I wanted to kill you? For years I thought you were the loving husband, a Christ-like man, and all this time you were rutting with these Black women. And then sold all your own babies as slaves. You're a monster, I thought. So evil that for you to live another minute was an abomination. But my hands couldn't hold a knife or pull the trigger on a gun. So I lay here and thought. And you know what I thought?"

Cavil said nothing. The way she told it, it made him sound so bad. "It wasn't like that, it was holy."

"It was adultery!"

"I had a vision!"

"Yes, your vision. Well, fine and dandy, Mr. Cavil Planter, you had a vision that making half-White babies was a good thing. Here's some news for you. I can make half-White babies, too!"

It was all making sense now. "He raped you!"

"He didn't rape me, Cavil. I invited him up here. I told him what to do. I made him call me his vixen and say prayers with me before and after so it would be as *holy* as what you did. We prayed to your damned Overseer, but for some reason he never showed up."

"It never happened."

"Again and again, every time you left the plantation, all winter, all spring."

"I don't believe it. You're lying to hurt me. You *can't* do that—the doctor said—it hurts you too bad."

"Cavil, before I found out what you done with those Black women, I thought I knew what pain was, but all that suffering was nothing, do you hear me? I could live through that pain every day forever and call it a holiday. I'm pregnant, Cavil."

"He raped you. That's what we'll tell everybody, and we'll hang him as an example, and—"

"Hang *him*? There's only one rapist on this plantation, Cavil, and don't think for a moment that I won't tell. If you lay a hand on my baby's father, I'll tell the whole county what you've been doing. I'll get up on Sunday and tell the church."

"I did it in the service of the—"

"Do you think they'll believe that? No more than I do. The word for what you done isn't holiness. It's concupiscence. Adultery. Lust. And when word gets out, when my baby is born Black, they'll turn against you, all of them. They'll run you out."

Cavil knew she was right. Nobody would believe him. He was ruined. Unless he did one simple thing.

He walked out of her room. She lay there laughing at him, taunting him. He went to his bedroom, took the shotgun down from the wall, poured in the powder, wadded it, then dumped in a double load of shot and rammed it tight with a second wad.

She wasn't laughing when he came back in. Instead she had her face toward the wall, and she was crying. Too late for tears, he thought. She didn't turn to face him as he strode to the bed and tore down the covers. She was naked as a plucked chicken.

"Cover me!" she whimpered. "He ran out so fast, he didn't dress me. It's cold! Cover me, Cavil—"

Then she saw the gun.

Her twisted hands flailed in the air. Her body writhed. She cried out in the pain of trying to move so quickly. Then he pulled the trigger and her body just flopped right down on the bed, a last sigh of air leaking out of the top of her neck.

Cavil went back to his room and reloaded the gun.

He found Fat Fox fully dressed, polishing the carriage. He was such a liar, he thought he could fool Cavil Planter. But Cavil didn't even bother listening to his lies. "Your vixen wants to see you upstairs," he said.

Fat Fox kept denying it all the way until he got into the room and saw Dolores on the bed. Then he changed his tune. "She made me! What could I do, Master! It was like you and the women, Master! What choice a Black slave got? I got to obey, don't I? Like the women and you!"

Cavil knew devil talk when he heard it, and he paid no mind. "Strip off your clothes and do it again," he said. Fat Fox howled and Fat Fox whined, but when Cavil jammed him in the ribs with the barrel, he did what he was told. He closed his eyes so he didn't have to see what Cavil's shotgun done to Dolores, and he did what he was told. Then Cavil fired the gun again.

In a little while Lashman came in from the far field, all a-lather with running and fearing when he heard the gunshots. Cavil met him downstairs. "Lock down the slaves, Lashman, and then go fetch me the sheriff."

When the sheriff came, Cavil led him upstairs and showed him. The sheriff went pale. "Good Lord," he whispered.

"Is it murder, Sheriff? I did it. Are you taking me to jail?"

"No sir," said the sheriff. "Ain't nobody going to call this murder." Then he looked at Cavil with this twisted kind of expression on his face. "What kind of man are you, Cavil?"

For a moment Cavil didn't understand the question.

"Letting me see your wife like that. I'd rather die before I let somebody see my wife like that."

The sheriff left. Lashman had the slaves clean up the room. There was no funeral for either one. They both got buried out where Salamandy lay. Cavil was pretty sure a few chickens died over the graves, but by then he didn't care. He was on his tenth bottle of bourbon and his ten-thousandth muttered prayer to the Overseer, who seemed powerful standoffish at a time like this.

Along about a week later, or maybe longer, here comes the sheriff again, with the priest and the Baptist preacher both. The three of them woke Cavil up from his drunken sleep and showed him a draught for twenty-five thousand dollars. "All your neighbors took up a collection," the priest explained.

"I don't need money," Cavil said.

"They're buying you out," said the preacher.

"Plantation ain't for sale."

The sheriff shook his head. "You got it wrong, Cavil. What happened here, that was bad. But you letting folks see your wife like that—"

"I only let *you* see."

"You ain't no gentleman, Cavil."

"Also, there's the matter of the slave children," said the Baptist preacher. "They seem remarkably light-skinned, considering you have no breeding stock but what's black as night."

"It's a miracle from God," said Cavil. "The Lord is lightening the Black race."

The sheriff slid a paper over to Cavil. "This is the transfer of title of all your property—slaves, buildings, and land—to a holding company consisting of your former neighbors."

Cavil read it. "This deed says all the slaves here on the land," he said. "I got rights in a runaway slave boy up north."

"We don't care about that. He's yours if you can find him. I hope you noticed this deed also includes a stipulation that you will never return to this county or any adjoining county for the rest of your natural life."

"I saw that part," said Cavil.

"I can assure you that if you break that agreement, it will be the end of your natural life. Even a conscientious, hardworking sheriff like me couldn't protect you from what would happen."

"You said no threats," murmured the priest.

"Cavil needs to know the consequences," said the sheriff.

"I won't be back," said Cavil.

"Pray to God for forgiveness," said the preacher.

"That I will." Cavil signed the paper.

That very night he rode out on his horse with a twenty-five-thousand-dollar draught in his pocket and a change of clothes and a week's provisions on a pack horse behind him. Nobody bid him farewell. The slaves were singing jubilation songs in the sheds behind him. His horse manured the end of the drive. And in Cavil's mind there was only one thought. The Overseer hates me, or this all wouldn't have happened. There's only one way to win back His love. That's to find that Alvin Smith, kill him, and get back my boy, my last slave who still belongs to me.

Then, O my Overseer, will You forgive me, and heal the terrible stripes Thy lash has torn upon my soul?

21

ALVIN JOURNEYMAN

Alvin stayed home in Vigor Church all summer, getting to know his family again. Folks had changed, more than a little—Cally was mansize now, and Measure had him a wife and children, and the twins Wastenot and Wantnot had married them a pair of French sisters from Detroit, and Ma and Pa was both grey-haired mostly, and moving slower than Alvin liked to see. But some things didn't change—there was playfulness in them all, the whole family, and the darkness that had fallen over Vigor Church after the massacre at Tippy-Canoe, it was—well, not *gone*— more like it had changed into a kind of shadow that was behind everything, so the bright spots in life seemed all the brighter by contrast.

They all took to Arthur Stuart right off. He was so young he could hear all the men of the town tell him the tale of Tippy-Canoe, and all that he thought of it was to tell them his own story—which was really a mish-mash of his real mama's story, and Alvin's story, and the story of the Finders and how his White mama killed one afore she died.

Alvin pretty much let Arthur Stuart's account of things stand uncorrected. Partly it was because why should he make Arthur Stuart out to be wrong, when he loved telling the tale so? Partly it was out of sorrow, realizing bit by bit that Arthur Stuart never spoke in nobody else's voice but his own. Folks here would never know what it was like to hear Arthur Stuart speak their own voice right back at them. Even so, they loved to hear the boy talk, because he still remembered all the words people said, never forgetting a scrap it seemed like. Why should Alvin mar what was left of Arthur Stuart's knack?

Alvin also figured that what he never told, nobody could ever repeat. For instance, there was a certain burlap parcel that nobody ever saw unwrapped. It wouldn't do no good for word to get around that a certain golden object had been seen in the town of Vigor Church—the town, which hadn't had many visitors since the dark day of the massacre at Tippy-Canoe, would soon have more company than they wanted, and all the wrong sort, looking for gold and not caring who got harmed along the way. So he never told a soul about the golden plow, and the only person who even knew he was keeping a secret was his close-mouthed sister Eleanor.

Alvin went to call on her at the store she and Armor-of-God kept right there on the town square, ever since before there *was* a town square. Once it had been a place where visitors, Red and White, came from far away to get maps and news, back when the land was still mostly forest from the Mizzipy to Dekane. Now it was still busy, but it was all local folks, come to buy or hear gossip and news of the outside world. Since Armor-of-God was the only grownup man in Vigor Church who wasn't cursed with Tenskwa-Tawa's curse, he was also the only one who could easily go outside to buy goods and hear news, bringing it all back in to the farmers and tradesmen of Vigor Church. It happened that today Armor-of-God was away, heading up to the town of Mishy-Waka to pick up some orders of glass goods and fine china. So Alvin found only Eleanor and her oldest boy, Hector, there, tending the store.

Things had changed a bit since the old days. Eleanor, who was near as good a hexmaker as Alvin, didn't have to conceal her hexes in the patterns of hanging flower baskets and arrangements of herbs in the kitchen. Now some of the hexes were right out in the open, which meant they could be much clearer and stronger. Armor-of-God must've let up a little on his hatred of knackery and hidden powers. That was a good thing—it was a painful thing, in the old days, to know how Eleanor had to pretend not to be what she was or know what she knew.

"I got something with me," said Alvin.

"So I see," said Eleanor. "All wrapped in a burlap bag, as still as stone, and yet it seems to me there's something living inside."

"Never you mind about that," said Alvin. "What's here is for no other soul but me to see."

Eleanor didn't ask any questions. She knew from those words exactly why he brought his mysterious parcel by. She told Hector to wait on any customers as came by, and then led Alvin out into the new ware-room, where they kept such things as a dozen kinds of beans in barrels, salt meat in kegs, sugar in paper cones, powder salt in waterproof pots, and spices all in different kinds of jars. She went straight to the fullest of the bean barrels, filled with a kind of green-speckle bean that Alvin hadn't seen before.

"Not much call for these beans," she said. "I reckon we'll never see the bottom of this barrel."

Alvin set the plow, all wrapped in burlap, on top of the beans. And then he made the beans slide out of the way, flowing around the plow smooth as molasses, until it sank right down to the bottom. He didn't so much as ask Eleanor to turn away, since she knew Alvin had power to do *that* much since he was just a little boy.

"Whatever's living in there," said Eleanor, "it ain't going to die, being dry down at the bottom of the barrel, is it?"

"It won't ever die," said Alvin, "at least not the way folks grow old and die."

Eleanor gave in to curiosity just enough to say, "I wish you could promise me that if anybody ever knows what's in there, so will I."

Alvin nodded to her. That was a promise he could keep. At the time, he didn't know how or when he'd ever show that plow to anybody, but if anybody could keep a secret, silent Eleanor could.

So anyway he lived in Vigor Church, sleeping in his old bedroom in his parents' house, lived there a good many weeks, well on toward July, and all the while he kept most of what happened in his seven-year prenticeship to himself. In fact he talked hardly more than he had to. He went here and there, a-calling on folks with his Pa or Ma, and without much fuss healing such toothaches and broken bones and festering wounds and sickness as he found. He helped at the mill; he hired out to work in other farmers' fields and barns; he built him a small forge and did simple repairs and solders, the kind a smith can do without a proper anvil. And all that time, he pretty much spoke when people spoke to him, and said little more than what was needed to do business or get the food he wanted at table.

He wasn't glum—he laughed at a joke, and even told a few. He wasn't solemn, neither, and spent more than a few afternoons down in the square, proving to the strongest farmers in Vigor Church that they weren't no match for a blacksmith's arms and shoulders in a rassling match. He just didn't have any gossip or small talk, and he never told a story on himself. And if you didn't keep a conversation going, Alvin was content to let it fall into silence, keeping at his work or staring off into the distance like as if he didn't even remember you were there.

Some folks noticed how little Alvin talked, but he'd been gone a long time, and you don't expect a nineteen-year-old to act the same as an eleven-year-old. They just figured he'd grown up to be a quiet man.

But a few knew better. Alvin's mother and father had some words between the two of them, more than once. "The boy's had some bad things happen to him," said his mother; but his father took a different view. "I reckon maybe he's had bad and good mixed in together, like most folks—he just doesn't know us well enough yet, after being gone seven years. Let him get used to being a man in this town, and not a boy anymore, and pretty soon he'll talk his leg off."

Eleanor, she also noticed Alvin wasn't talking, but since she also knew he had a marvelous secret living thing hidden in her bean barrel, she didn't fuss for a minute about something being *wrong* with Alvin. It was like she said to her husband, Armor-of-God, when he mentioned about how Alvin just didn't seem to have five words altogether for nobody. "He's thinking deep thoughts," said Eleanor. "He's working out problems none of us knows enough to help him with. You'll see—he'll talk plenty when he figures it all out."

And there was Measure, Alvin's brother who got captured by Reds when Alvin was; the brother who had come to know Ta-Kumsaw and Tenskwa-Tawa near as well as Alvin himself. Of course Measure noticed how little Alvin had told them about his prentice years, and in due time he'd surely be one Alvin could talk to—that was natural, seeing how long Alvin had trusted Measure and all they'd been through together. But at first Alvin felt shy even around

Measure, seeing how he had his wife, Delphi, and any fool could see how they hardly could stand to be more than three feet apart from each other; he was so gentle and careful with her, always looking out for her, turning to talk to her if she was near, looking for her to come back if she was gone. How could Alvin know whether there was room for him anymore in Measure's heart? No, not even to Measure could Alvin tell his tale, not at first.

One day in high summer, Alvin was out in a field building fences with his younger brother Cally, who was man-size now, as tall as Alvin though not as massive in the back and shoulders. The two of them had hired on for a week with Martin Hill. Alvin was doing the rail splitting—hardly using his knack at all, either, though truth to tell he could've split all the rails just by asking them to split themselves. No, he set the wedge and hammered it down, and his knack only got used to keep the logs from splitting at bad angles that wouldn't give full-length rails.

They must have fenced about a quarter mile before Alvin realized that it was peculiar how Cally never fell behind. Alvin split, and Cally got the posts and rails laid in place, never needing a speck of help to set a post into soil too hard or soft or rocky or muddy.

So Alvin kept his eye on the boy—or, more exactly, used his knack to keep watch on Cally's work—and sure enough, Alvin could see that Cally had something of Alvin's knack, the way it was long ago when he didn't half understand what he was doing with it. Cally would find just the right spot to set a post, then make the ground soft till he needed it to be firm. Alvin figured Cally wasn't exactly planning it. He probably thought he was finding spots that were naturally good for setting a post.

Here it is, thought Alvin. Here's what I know I've got to do: teach somebody else to be a Maker. If ever there was someone I should teach, it's Cally, seeing how he's got something of the same knack. After all, he's seventh son of a seventh son same as me, since Vigor was still alive when I was born, but long dead when Cally came along.

So Alvin just up and started talking as they worked, telling Cally all about atoms and how you could teach them how to be, and they'd be like that. It was the first time Alvin tried to explain it to anybody since the last time he talked to Miss Larner—Margaret—and the words tasted delicious in his mouth. This is the work I was born for, thought Alvin. Telling my brother how the world works, so he can understand it and get some control over it.

You can bet Alvin was surprised, then, when Cally all of a sudden lifted a post high above his head and threw it on the ground at his brother's feet. It had so much force—or Cally had so ravaged it with his knack—that it shivered into kindling right there where it hit. Alvin couldn't hardly even guess why, but Cally was plain filled with rage.

"What did I say?" asked Alvin.

"My name's Cal," said Cally. "I ain't been Cally since I was ten years old."

"I didn't know," said Alvin. "I'm sorry, and from now on you're Cal to me."

"I'm *nothing* to you," said Cal. "I just wish you'd go away!"

It was only right at this minute that Alvin realized that Cal hadn't exactly invited him to go along on this job—it was Martin Hill what asked for Alvin to come, and before that, the job had been Cal's alone.

"I didn't mean to butt into your work here," said Alvin. "It just never entered my head you wouldn't want my help. I know I wanted your company."

Seemed like everything Alvin said only made Cal seethe inside till now his face was red and his fists were clenched tight enough to strangle a snake. "I had a place here," said

Cal. "Then you come back. All fancy school taught like you are, using all them big words. And *healing* people without so much as touching them, just walking into their house and talking a spell, and when you leave everybody's all healed up from whatever ailed them—"

Alvin didn't even know folks had noticed he was doing it. Since nobody said a thing about it, he figured they all thought it was natural healing. "I can't think how that makes you mad, Cal. It's a good thing to make folks better."

All of a sudden there were tears running down Cal's cheeks. "Even laying hands on them, I can't always fix things up," said Cal. "Nobody even asks me no more."

It never occurred to Alvin that maybe Cal was doing his own healings. But it made good sense. Ever since Alvin left, Cal had pretty much been what Alvin used to be in Vigor Church, doing all his works. Seeing how their knacks were so much alike, he'd come close to taking Alvin's place. And then he'd done things Alvin never did when he was small, like going about healing people as best he could. Now Alvin was back, not only taking back his old place, but also besting Cal at things that only Cal had ever done. Now who was there for Cal to be?

"I'm sorry," said Al. "But I can teach you. That's what I was starting to do."

"I never seen them bits and what-not you're talking about," said Cal. "I didn't understand a thing you talked about. Maybe I just ain't got a knack as good as yours, or maybe I'm too dumb, don't you see? All I can be is the best I figure out for myself. And I don't need you proving to me that I can't never measure up. Martin Hill asking for you on this job, cause he knows you can make a better fence. And there you are, not even using your knack to split the rails, though I know you can, just to show me that *without* your knack you're a match for me."

"That's not what I meant," said Alvin. "I just don't use my knack around—"

"Around people as dumb as *me*," said Cal.

"I was doing a bad job explaining," said Alvin, "but if you'll let me, Cal, I can teach you how to change iron into—"

"Gold," said Cal, his voice thick with scorn. "What do you think I am? Trying to fool me with an alchemist's tales! If you knew how to do *that,* you wouldn't've come home poor. You know I once used to think you were the beginning and end of the world. I thought, when Al comes home, it'll be like old times, the two of us playing and working together, talking all the time, me tagging on, doing everything together. Only it turns out you still think I'm just a little boy, you don't say nothing to me except 'here's another rail' and 'pass the beans, please.' You took over all the jobs folks used to look to me to do, even one as simple as making a stout rail fence."

"Job's yours," said Alvin, shouldering his hammer. There was no point in trying to teach Cal anything—even if he *could* learn it, he could never learn it from Alvin. "I got other work to do, and I won't detain you any longer."

"*Detain* me," said Cal. "Is that a word you learned in a book, or from that ugly old teacher lady in Hatrack River that your ugly little mix-up boy talks about?"

Hearing Miss Larner and Arthur Stuart so scornfully spoken of, that made Alvin burn inside, especially since he had in fact learned to use phrases like "detain you any longer" from Miss Larner. But Alvin didn't say anything to show his anger. He just turned his back and walked off, back down the line of the finished fence. Cal could use his own knack and finish the fence himself; Alvin didn't even care about collecting the wages he'd earned in most of a day's work. He had other things on his mind—memories of Miss

Larner, partly, but mostly he was upset about how Cal hadn't wanted Alvin to teach him. Here he was the person in the whole world who had the best chance to learn it all as easy as a baby learning to suck, since it was his natural knack— only he didn't want to learn it, not from Alvin. It was something Alvin never would have thought possible, to turn down the chance to learn something, just because the teacher was somebody you didn't like.

Come to think of it, though, hadn't Alvin hated going to school with Reverend Thrower, cause of how Thrower always made him feel like he was somehow bad or evil or stupid or something? Could it be that Cal hated Alvin the way Alvin had hated Reverend Thrower? He just couldn't understand why Cal was so angry. Of all people in the world, Cal had no reason to be jealous of Alvin, because he could come closest to doing all that Alvin did; yet for that very reason, Cal was so jealous he'd never learn it, not without going through every step of figuring it out for himself.

At this rate, I'll never build the Crystal City, cause I'll never be able to teach Making to another soul.

It was a few weeks after that when Alvin finally tried again to talk to somebody, to see if he really could teach Making. It was on a Sunday, in Measure's house, where Alvin and Arthur Stuart had gone to take their dinner. It was a hot day, so Delphi laid a cold table—bread and cheese and salt ham and smoked turkey—and they all went outside to take the afternoon in the shade of Measure's north-facing kitchen porch.

"Alvin, I invited you and Arthur Stuart here today for a reason," said Measure. "Delphi and me, we already talked it over, and said a few things to Pa and Ma, too."

"Sounds like it must be pretty terrible, if it took that much talking."

"Reckon not," said Measure. "It's just—well, Arthur Stuart, here, he's a fine boy, and a good hard worker, and good company to boot."

Arthur Stuart grinned. "I sleep solid, too," he said.

"Fine sleeper," said Measure. "But Ma and Pa ain't exactly young no more. I think Ma's used to doing things in the kitchen all her own way."

"That she is," sighed Delphi, as if she had more than a little reason for knowing exactly how set in her ways Goody Miller was.

"And Pa, well, he's tiring out. When he gets home from the mill, he needs to lie down, have plenty of quiet around him."

Alvin thought he knew where the conversation was heading. Maybe his folks just weren't the quality of Old Peg Guester or Gertie Smith. Maybe they couldn't take a mix-up boy into their home or their heart. It made him sad to think of such a thing about his own folks, but he knew right off that he wouldn't even complain about it. He and Arthur Stuart would just pack up and set out on a road leading—nowhere in particular. Canada, maybe. Somewhere that a mix-up boy'd be full welcome.

"Mind you, they didn't say a thing like that to *me*," said Measure. "In fact, I sort of said it all to them. You see, me and Delphi, we got a house somewhat bigger than we need, and with three small ones Delphi'd be glad of a boy Arthur Stuart's age to help with kitchen chores like he does."

"I can make bread all myself," said Arthur Stuart. "I know Mama's recipe by heart. She's dead."

"You see?" said Delphi. "If he can make bread himself sometimes, or even just help me with the kneading, I wouldn't end up so worn out at the end of the week."

"And it won't be long before Arthur Stuart could help out in my work in the fields," said Measure.

"But we don't want you to think we're looking to hire him on like a servant," said Delphi.

"No, no!" said Measure. "No, we're thinking of him like another son, only growed up more than my oldest Jeremiah, who's only three and a half, which makes him still pretty much useless as a human being, though at least he isn't always trying to throw himself into the creek to drown like his sister Shiphrah—or like you when you were little, I might add."

Arthur Stuart laughed at that. "Alvin like to drowned *me* one time," said Arthur Stuart. "Stuck me right in the Hio."

Alvin felt pure ashamed. Ashamed of lots of things: The fact that he never told Measure the whole story of how he rescued Arthur Stuart from the Finders; the fact that he even thought for a minute that Measure and Ma and Pa might be trying to get rid of a mix-up boy, when the truth was they were squabbling over who got to have him in their home.

"It's Arthur Stuart's choice where to live, once he's invited," said Alvin. "He came home along with me, but I don't make such choices for him."

"Can I live here?" asked Arthur Stuart. "Cal doesn't much like me."

"Cal's got troubles of his own," said Measure, "but he likes you fine."

"Why didn't Alvin bring home something useful, like a horse?" said Arthur Stuart. "You eat like one, but I bet you can't even pull a two-wheel shay."

Measure and Delphi laughed. They knew Arthur Stuart was repeating something Cal had said, word for word. Arthur Stuart did it so often, folks came to expect it, and took delight in his perfect memory. But it made Alvin sad to hear it, because he knew that only a few months ago, Arthur Stuart would have said it in Cal's own voice, so even Ma couldn't've known without looking that it wasn't Cal himself.

"Is Alvin going to live down here too?" asked Arthur Stuart.

"Well, see, that's what we're thinking," said Measure. "Why don't you come on down here, too, Alvin? We can put you up in the main room here, for a while. And when the summer work's done, we can set to fixing up our old cabin—it's still pretty solid, since we ain't moved out of it but two years now. You can be pretty much on your own then. I reckon you're too old now to be living in your pa's house and eating at your ma's table."

Why, Alvin never would've reckoned it, but all of a sudden he found his eyes full of tears. Maybe it was the pure joy of having somebody notice he wasn't the same old Alvin Miller Junior anymore. Or maybe it was the fact that it was Measure, looking out for him like in the old days. Anyway, it was at that moment that Alvin first felt like he'd really come home.

"Sure I'll come down here, if you want me," Alvin said.

"Well there's no reason to cry about it," said Delphi. "I already got three babies crying every time they think of it. I don't want to have to come along and dab your eyes and wipe your nose like I do with Keturah."

"Well at least he don't wear diapers," said Measure, and he and Delphi both laughed like that was the funniest thing they ever heard. But actually they were laughing with pleasure at how Alvin had gotten so sentimental over the idea of living with them.

So Alvin and Arthur Stuart moved on down to Measure's house, and Alvin got to know his best-loved brother all over again. All the old things that Alvin once loved were still in Measure as a man, but there were new things, too. The tender way Measure had with his children, even after a spanking or a stiff talking to. The way Measure looked after his land and buildings, seeing all that needed doing, and then doing it, so there was never a door that squeaked for a second day, never an animal that was off its feed for a whole day without Measure trying to account for what was wrong.

Above all, though, Alvin saw how Measure was with Delphi. She wasn't a noticeably pretty girl, though not particularly ugly either; she was strong and stout and laughed loud as a donkey. But Alvin saw how Measure had a way of looking at her like the most beautiful sight he ever could see. She'd look up and there he'd be, watching her with a kind of dreamy smile on his face, and she'd laugh or blush or look away, but for a minute or two she'd move more graceful, walking partly on her toes maybe, like she was dancing, or getting set to fly. Alvin wondered then if he could ever give such a look to Miss Larner as would make *her* so full of joy that she couldn't hardly stay connected to the earth.

Then Alvin would lie there in the night, feeling all the subtle movements of the house, knowing without even using his doodlebug what the slow and gentle creaking came from; and at such times he remembered the face of the woman named Margaret who had been hiding inside Miss Larner all those months, and imagined her face close to his, her lips parted, and from her throat those soft cries of pleasure Delphi made in the silence of the night. Then he would see her face again, only this time twisted with grief and weeping. At such times his heart ached inside him, and he yearned to go back to her, to take her in his arms and find some place inside her where he could heal her, take her grief away, make her whole.

And because Alvin was in Measure's house, his wariness slipped away from him, so that his face again began to show his feelings. It happened, then, that once when Measure and Delphi exchanged such a look as they had between them, Measure happened to look at Alvin's face. Delphi was gone out of the room by then, and the children were long since in bed, so Measure was free to reach out a hand and touch Alvin's knee.

"Who is she?" Measure asked.

"Who?" asked Alvin, confused.

"The one you love till it takes your breath away just remembering."

For a moment Alvin hesitated, by long habit. But then the gateway opened, and all his story spilled out. He started with Miss Larner, and how she was really Margaret, who was the same girl who once was the torch in Taleswapper's stories, the one that looked out for Alvin from afar. But telling the story of his love for her led to the story of all she taught him, and by the time the tale was done, it was near dawn. Delphi was asleep on Measure's shoulder—she'd come back in sometime during the tale, but didn't last long awake, which was just as well, with her three children and Arthur Stuart sure to want breakfast on time no matter how late she stayed up in the night. But Measure was still awake, his eyes sparkling with the knowledge of what the Redbird said, of the living golden plow, of Alvin in the forgefire, of Arthur Stuart in the Hio. And also a deep sadness behind that light in Measure's eyes, for the murder Alvin had done with his own hands, however much it might have been deserved; and for the death of Old Peg Guester, and even for the death of a certain runaway Black slave girl Arthur Stuart's whole lifetime ago.

"Somehow I got to go out and find people I can teach to be Makers," said Alvin. "But I don't even know if somebody without a knack like mine can learn it, or how much they ought to know, or if they'd even want to know it."

"I think," said Measure, "that they ought to love the dream of your Crystal City before they ever know that they might learn to help in the making of it. If word gets out that there's a Maker who can teach Making, you'll get the sort of folks as wants to rule people with such power. But the Crystal City—ah, Alvin, think of it! Like living inside that twister that caught you and the Prophet all those years ago."

"Will you learn it, Measure?" asked Alvin.

"I'll do all I can to learn it," said Measure. "But first I make you a solemn promise, that I'll only use what you teach me to build up the Crystal City. And if it turns out I just can't learn enough to be a Maker, I'll help you any other way I can. Whatever you ask me to do, Alvin, that I'll do— I'll take my family to the ends of the Earth, I'll give up everything I own, I'll die if need be—anything to make the vision Tenskwa-Tawa showed you come true."

Alvin held him by both hands, held him for the longest time. Then Measure leaned forward and kissed him, brother to brother, friend to friend. The movement woke Delphi. She hadn't heard most of it, but she knew that something solemn was happening, and she smiled sleepily before she got up and let Measure take her off to bed for the last few hours till dawn.

That was the beginning of Alvin's true work. All the rest of that summer, Measure was his pupil and his teacher. While Alvin taught Making to Measure, Measure taught fatherhood, husbanding, manliness to Alvin. The difference was that Alvin didn't half realize what he was learning, while Measure won each new understanding, each tiny shred of the power of Makery, only after terrible struggle. Yet he *did* understand, bit by bit, and he did learn more than a little bit of Making; and Alvin began to understand, after many failed efforts, how to go about teaching someone else to "see" without eyes, to "touch" without hands.

And now, when he lay awake at night, he did not yearn so often for the past, but rather tried to imagine the future. Somewhere out there was the place where he should build the Crystal City; and out there, too, were the folks he had to find and teach them to love that dream and show them how to make it real. Somewhere there was the perfect soil that his living plow was meant to delve. Somewhere there was a woman he could love and live with till he died.

BACK IN HATRACK River, that fall there was an election, and it happened that because of certain stories floating around about who was a hero and who was a snake, Pauley Wiseman lost his job and Po Doggly got him a new one. Along about that time, too, Makepeace Smith come in to file a complaint about how back last spring his prentice run off with a certain item that belonged to his master.

"That's a long time waiting to file such a charge," said Sheriff Doggly.

"He threatened me," said Makepeace Smith. "I feared for my family."

"Well, now, you just tell me what it was he stole."

"It was a plow," said Makepeace Smith.

"A common plow? I'm supposed to find a common plow? And why in tarnation would he steal such a thing?"

Makepeace lowered his voice and said it all secret-like. "The plow was made of gold."

Oh, Po Doggly just laughed his head off, hearing that.

"Well, it's true, I tell you," said Makepeace.

"Is it, now? Why, I think that I believe you, my friend. But if there was a gold plow in your smithy, I'll lay ten to one that it was Al's, not yours."

"What a prentice makes belongs to the master!"

Well, that's about when Po started getting a little stern. "You start telling tales like that around Hatrack River, Makepeace Smith, and I reckon other folks'll tell how you kept that boy when he long since was a better smith than you. I reckon word'll get around about how you wasn't a fair

master, and if you start to charging Alvin Smith with stealing what only he in all this world could possibly make, I
think you'd find yourself laughed to scorn."

Maybe he would and maybe he wouldn't. It was sure that
Makepeace didn't try no legal tricks to try to get that plow
back from Alvin—wherever he was. But he told his tale,
making it bigger every time he told it—how Alvin was
always stealing from him, and how that golden plow was
Makepeace Smith's inheritance, made plowshape and
painted black, and how Alvin uncovered it by devil powers
and carried it off. As long as Gertie Smith was alive she
scoffed at all such tales, but she died not too long after Alvin
left, from a blood vein popping when she was a-screaming
at her husband for being such a fool. From then on, Makepeace had the story his own way, even allowing as how
Alvin killed Gertie herself with a curse that *made* her
veins pop open and bleed to death inside her head. It was a
terrible lie, but there's always folks as like to hear such tales,
and the story spread from one end of the state of Hio to the
other, and then beyond. Pauley Wiseman heard it. Reverend Thrower heard it. Cavil Planter heard it. So did a lot of
other folks.

Which is why when Alvin finally ventured forth from
Vigor Church, there was plenty of folks with an eye for
strangers carrying bundles about the size of a plowshare,
looking for a glint of gold under burlap, measuring strangers to see if they might be a certain run-off prentice smith
who stole his master's inheritance. Some of those folks even
meant to take it back to Makepeace Smith in Hatrack River,
if it happened they ever laid their hands upon the golden
plow. On the other hand, with some of those folks such a
thought never crossed their minds.

ALVIN
JOURNEYMAN

To Jason Lewis,
long-legged wanderer,
walker through woods,
dreamer of true dreams.

Acknowledgments

For the past few years, at every book signing or speech I gave, I was asked one question more than any other: Will there be another Alvin Maker book? The answer was always, Yes, but I don't know when. My original outline for *The Tales of Alvin Maker* had long since been abandoned, and while I knew certain incidents that would happen in this book, I still did not know enough about what would happen to Alvin, Peggy, Taleswapper, Arthur Stuart, Measure, Calvin, Verily Cooper, and others to be able to start writing.

At last the logjam broke and the story came right, or as near right as I could get it. As I composed, I was constantly aware of those hundreds of readers who were waiting for *Alvin Journeyman*. It was encouraging to know that this book was much looked for; it was also frightening, because I knew that for some, at least, the expectations would be so high that any story I wrote would be bound to disappoint. To the disappointed I can only express my regret that the reality is never as good as the anticipation (cf. Christmas); and to all who hoped for this book, I give my thanks for your encouragement.

I thank the many readers on America Online who came to the Hatrack River Town Meeting and downloaded each chapter of the manuscript as I wrote it, responding with many helpful comments. These sharp-eyed readers caught inconsistencies and dangling threads—questions raised in earlier books that needed to be resolved. Newel Wright, Jane Brady, and Len Olen, in particular, won my undying gratitude: Jane, by preparing a chronology of the events in the previous books, Newel, by saving me from two ghastly continuity errors, and Len, by a thorough proofreading that caught several errors that all the editors and I had missed. Thanks also go to David Fox for an insightful reading of the first nine chapters at a key point in the composition of the book.

Quite without my planning it, a peculiar and delightful community has grown up within the Hatrack River Town Meeting on AOL; people began to arrive, not as themselves, but as characters living within Alvin's world, and set up in trade or farming in that fictional town. Thus Hatrack River has taken on a life of its own. The temptation was irresistible to include mention of as many of these characters as I could within this storyline; I only regret that I couldn't work them all into the plot. If you want to know more about the wonderful characters these good people have created, come visit us online (keyword: Hatrack).

The only active online character I made extensive use of in this book was one I devised myself as a fictional foil, whom Kathryn Kidd (town identity: GoodyTradr) and I (town identity: HoracGuest) referred to from time to time in a comical way as a notorious gossip: Vilate Franker. A couple of years after we invented her, along came a good friend, Melissa Wunderly, who volunteered to portray her in the online community; so it was Melissa who brought her to life, false teeth, hexes, and all. Vilate's "best friend," however, was mine, and Melissa is not to be blamed for Vilate's unpleasant behavior in this book. And I appreciate Kathryn Kidd's allowing me to use her character, Goody Trader, at a couple of key moments.

I must tip my hat to Graham Robb, whose excellent, well-written *Balzac: A Biography* (Norton, 1994) gave me not only respite from writing but also the foundation of a character I personally enjoy.

As with many previous novels, each chapter was read as it emerged from the printer or the fax machine by my wife, Kristine; my son Geoffrey; and my friend and sometime collaborator, Kathryn H. Kidd. Their responses have been of incalculable value.

My thanks also go to those who keep our office and household functioning when I'm (too rarely) in writer mode: Kathleen Bellamy, who tends to the business, and Scott Allen, who keeps the computers and the house itself in running order. A tip of the hat also goes to Jason, Adam, and (on one occasion) Michael Lewis, for holes dug and holes filled; and to Emily, Kathryn, and Amanda Jensen for giving us those nights out.

If it weren't for Kristine, Geoffrey, Emily, Charlie Ben, and Zina Meg, I doubt that I would ever write at all: They make the work worth doing.

I

I THOUGHT I WAS DONE

I thought I was done writing about Alvin Smith. People kept telling me I wasn't, but I knew why. It's because they'd all heard Taleswapper and the way he tells stories. When he's done, it's all tied up neat in a package and you pretty much know what things meant and why they happened. Not that he spells it all out, mind you. But you just have this feeling that it all makes sense.

Well I ain't Taleswapper, which some of you might already have guessed, seeing how we don't look much alike, and I don't plan on becoming Taleswapper anytime soon, or anything much like him, not cause I don't reckon him to be a fine fellow, worthy of folks emulating him, but mainly because I don't see things the way he sees them. Things don't all make sense to me. They just happen, and sometimes you can extract a bit of sense from some calamity and sometimes the happiest day is just pure nonsense. There's no predicting it and there's *sure* no making it happen. Worst messes I ever saw folks get into was when they was trying to make things go in a sensible way.

So I set down what I knew of the earliest beginnings of Alvin's life right up till he made him the golden plow as his journeyman project, and I told how he went back to Vigor and set to teaching folks how to be Makers and how things already wasn't right with his brother Calvin and I thought I was done, because anybody who cares was there from then on to see for themselves or you know somebody who was. I told you the truth of how Alvin came to kill a man, so as to put to rest all the vicious rumors told about it. I told you how he came to break the runaway slave laws and I told you how Peggy Larner's mama came to die and believe me, that was pretty much the end of the story as far as I could see it.

But the ending didn't make sense of it, I reckon, and folks have been pestering me more and more about the early days and didn't I know more I could tell? Well sure I know. And I got nothing against telling it. But I hope you don't think that when I'm done telling all I know it'll finally be clear to everybody what everything that's happened was all about, because I don't know myself. Truth is, the story ain't over yet, and I hope it never will be, so the most I can hope to do is set down the way it looks to this one fellow at this exact moment, and I can't even promise you that tomorrow I won't come to understand it much better than anything I'm writing now.

My knack ain't storytelling. Truth is, Taleswapper's knack ain't storytelling either, and he'd be the first to tell you that. He collects stories, all right, and the ones he gathers are important so you listen because the tale itself matters. But you know he don't do nothing much with his voice, and he don't roll his eyes and use them big gestures like the real orators use. His voice ain't strong enough to fill a good-size cabin, let alone a tent. No, the telling ain't his knack. He's a painter if anything, or maybe a woodcarver or a printer or whatever he can use to tell or show the story but he's no genius at any of them.

Fact is if you ask Taleswapper what his knack is, he'll tell you he don't have none. He ain't lying—nobody can ever lay that charge at Taleswapper's door. No, he just set his heart on one knack when he was a boy, and all his life that seemed to him the only knack worth having and since he never got it (he thinks) why then he must not have no knack at all. And don't pretend you don't know what knack it was he wanted, because he practically slaps you in the face with it whenever he talks for long. He wanted the knack of prophecy. That's why he's always been so powerful jealous of Peggy Larner, because she's a torch and from childhood on she saw all the possible futures of people's lives, and while that's not the same thing as knowing *the* future— the way things will actually happen instead of how they might happen—it's pretty close. Close enough that I think Taleswapper would have been happy for five minutes of being a torch. Probably would have grinned himself to death within a week if such a thing happened.

When Taleswapper says he's got no knack, though, I'll tell you, he's wrong. Like a lot of folks, he has a knack and doesn't even know it because that's the way knacks work—it just feels as natural as can be to the person who's got it, as easy as breathing, so you don't think *that* could possibly be your unusual power because heck, that's *easy*. You don't know it's a knack till other people around you get all astonished about it or upset or excited or whatever feelings your knack seems to provoke in folks. Then you go, "Boy howdy, other folks can't *do* this! I got me a knack!" and from then on there's no putting up with you till you finally settle down and get back to normal life and stop bragging about how you can do this fool thing that you used to never be excited about back when you still had sense.

Some folks never know they got them a knack, though, because nobody else ever notices it either, and Taleswapper's that way. I didn't notice it till I started trying to collect all my memories and everything anybody ever told me about Alvin Maker's life. Pictures of him working that hammer in the forge every chance he got in case we ever forgot that he had an honest trade, hard come by with his own sweat, and didn't just dance through life like a quadrille with Dame Fortune as his loving partner—as if we ever thought Dame Fortune did anything more than flirt with him, and likely as not if he ever got close to her he'd find out she had the pox anyway; Fortune has a way of being on the side of the Unmaker, when folks start relying on her to save them. But I'm getting off the subject, which I had to read back to the beginning of this paragraph to see what in hell I was talking about (and I can hear you prickle-hearted prudes saying, What's he doing putting down curses on paper, hasn't he no sense of decent language? to which I say, When I curse it don't harm nobody and it makes my language more colorful and heaven knows I can use the color, and I can assure you I've studied cussing from the best and I know how to make my language a whole *lot* more colorful than it is right now, but I already tone myself down so you don't have apoplexy reading my words. I wouldn't want to spend half my life just going to the funerals of people who had a stroke from reading my book, so instead of criticizing me for the nasty words that creep into my writing why don't you praise me for the really ugly stuff that I virtuously chose to leave out? It's all how you choose to look at it, I think, and if you have time to rail on about my language, then you don't have enough to do and I'll be glad to put you in touch with folks who need more hands to help with *productive* labor), so anyway I looked back to the beginning of this paragraph *again* to see what the hell I was talking about and my point is that when I gathered all these stories together, I noticed that Taleswapper seems to keep showing up in the oddest places at *exactly* the moment when something important was about to happen, so that he ended up being a witness or even a participant in a remarkable number of events.

Now, let me ask you plain, my friends. If a man seems to know, down in his bones, when something important's about to happen, and where, and enough in advance that he can get his body over there to be a witness of it before it even starts, now ain't that prophecy? I mean why was it William Blake ever left England and came to America if it wasn't because he *knew* that the world was about to be torn open to give birth to a Maker again after all these generations? Just cause he didn't know it out in the open didn't mean that he wasn't a prophet. He thought he had to be a prophet with his mouth, but I say he's a prophet in his bones. Which is why he just happened to be wandering back to the town of Vigor Church, to Alvin's father's mill, for no reason he was aware of, at exactly the day and hour that Alvin's little brother Calvin Miller decided to run off and go study trouble in faraway places. Taleswapper had no idea what was going to happen, but folks, I tell you, he was *there,* and anybody who tells you Taleswapper's got no knack, including Taleswapper himself, is a blame fool. Of course I mean that in the nicest possible way, as Horace Guester would tell you.

So as I pick up my tale again that's the day I choose to start with, mostly because I can tell you from experience that *nothing* interesting happened during those long months when Alvin was still trying to teach a bunch of plain folks how to be a Maker like him instead of . . . well, all in time. Let's just say that while some of you are bound to criticize me for *not* telling all of Alvin's lessons about Makering and every single boring moment of every class he held trying to teach fish to hop, I can promise you that leaving out those days from my tale is an act of charity.

There's a lot of people and a lot of confusion in the story, too, and I can't help that, because if I made it all clear and simple that would be a lie. It was a mess and there was a lot of different people involved and also, to tell you the truth, there's a lot of things that happened that I didn't know about then and still don't know much about now. I'd like to say that I'm telling you all the important parts of the story, telling about all the important people, but I know perfectly well that there might be important parts that I just don't know about, and important people that I didn't realize were important. There's stuff that *nobody* knows, and stuff that them as knows ain't telling, or them as knows don't know they know. And even as I try to explain things as I understand them I'm still going to leave things out without meaning to, or tell you things twice that you already know, or contradict something that you know to be a fact, and all I can say is, I ain't no Taleswapper, and if you want to know the deepest truth, get him to unseal that back two-thirds of his little book and read you what he's got in *there* and I bet, for all he claims to be no prophet, I bet you'll hear things as will curl your hair, or uncurl it, depending.

There's one mystery, though, that I plain don't know the answer to, even though everything depends on it. Maybe if I tell you enough you'll figure it out for yourself. But what I don't understand is why Calvin went the way he did. He was a sweet boy, they all say it. He and Alvin were close as boys can be, I mean they fought but there was never malice in it and Cally grew up knowing Al would die for him. So what was it made jealousy start to gnaw at Calvin's heart and turn him away from his own brother and want to undo all his work? I heard a lot of the tale I'm about to tell you from Cally's own mouth, but you can be sure he never sat down and explained to me or anybody why he changed. Oh, he told plenty of folks why he hated Alvin, but there's no ring of truth in what he says about that, since he always accuses his brother of doing whatever his audience hates the most. To Puritans he says he came to hate Alvin because he saw him trucking with the devil. To Kingsmen he says he hated Alvin because he saw how his brother went so far as to murder a man just to keep him from recovering his own property, a runaway slave baby named Arthur Stuart (and don't *that* set them Royalists' teeth on edge, to think of a half-Black boy having the same name as the King!). Calvin always has a tale that justifies himself in the eyes of strangers, but never a word of explanation does he ever have to those of us who know the truth about Alvin Maker.

I just know this: When I first set eyes on Calvin, in Vigor Church during that year when Alvin tried to teach Makering, that year before he left, I'll tell you, folks, Calvin was already gone. In his heart every word that Alvin said was like poison. If Alvin paid no attention to him, Calvin felt neglected and said so. Then if Alvin *did* pay attention to him, Calvin got surly and sullen and claimed Alvin wouldn't leave him alone. There was no pleasing him.

But to say he was "contrary" don't explain a thing. It's just a name for the way he was acting, not an answer to the question of why he acted that way. I have my own guesses, but they're just guesses and no more, not even what they call "educated guesses" because there's no such thing as education so good it makes one man's guess any better than another's. Either you know or you don't, and I don't know.

I don't know why people who got what they need to be happy don't just go ahead and be happy. I don't know why lonely people keep shoving away everybody as tries to befriend them. I don't know why people blame weak and harmless folks for their troubles while they leave their real enemy alone to get away with all his harm. And I sure don't know why I bother to go to the trouble to write all this down when I know you still won't be satisfied.

Let me tell you one little thing about Calvin. I saw him one day taking class with Alvin, and for once he was paying attention, real close attention, heeding every word that came from his brother's lips. And I thought: He's finally come around. He finally realized that if he really wants to be a seventh son of a seventh son, if he really wants to be a Maker, he has to learn from Alvin how it's done.

And then the class ended, and I sat there watching Calvin as everybody else went on out to get back to their chores, until only me and Calvin was left in the room, and Calvin actually talks to me—mostly he ignored me like I wasn't there—he talks to me and in a few seconds I realize what he's doing. He's imitating Alvin. Not Alvin's regular voice, but Alvin's schoolteachery voice. You all remember when he got that way—I remember he learned that flowery fancy talk when he was studying with Miss Larner, before she came out of disguise and he realized she was the same Peggy Guester who kept his birth caul and protected him through his growing-up years. The big five-dollar words she learned in Dekane or from them books she read. Alvin wanted to sound refined like her, or sometimes he wanted to, anyway, and so he'd learn them words and use them and talk so fine you'd have thought he learned English from an expert instead of just growing up with it like the rest of us. But he couldn't keep it up. He'd hear himself talking so high-toned and he'd just suddenly laugh or make some joke and then he'd go back to talking like folks. And there was Calvin talking that same high-toned way, only he didn't laugh. He just did all his imitating and when he was done, he looked at me and said, "Was that right?"

As if I'd know!

And I says back to him, "Calvin, *sounding* like an educated man don't make you educated," and he says back to me, "I'd rather be ignorant and sound educated than be educated and sound ignorant," and I said, "Why?" and he says to me, "Because if you sound educated then nobody ever tests you to find out, but if you sound ignorant they never stop."

Here's my point. Well, maybe it's not the point I started out to make, but I long since lost track of *that*. So here's the point I want to make *now:* I know more about what happened during Alvin's year of wandering than anybody else on God's green Earth. But I also am aware of how many questions I still can't answer. So I reckon I'm the one as knows but seems ignorant. Which kind are you?

If you already figure you know this story, for heaven's sake stop reading now and save yourself some trouble. And if you're going to criticize me for not finishing the whole thing and tying it up in a bow for you, why, do us both a favor and write your own damn book, only have the decency to call it a romance instead of a history, because history's got no bows on it, only frayed ends of ribbons and knots that can't be untied. It ain't a pretty package but then it's not your birthday that I know of, so I'm under no obligation to give you a gift.

2

HYPOCRITES

Calvin was about fed up. Just this close to walking up to Alvin and . . . and something. Punching him in the nose, maybe, only he'd tried that afore and Alvin just caught him by the wrist and gripped him with those damn blacksmith muscles and he says, "Calvin, you know I could always throw you, do we have to do this now?" Alvin could always do everything better, or if he couldn't then it must not be worth doing. Folks all gathered around and listened to Alvin's babbling like it all made sense. Folks watched every move he made like he was a dancing bear. Only time they noticed Calvin was to ask him if he would kindly step aside so they could see Alvin a little better.

Step aside? Yep, I reckon I can step aside. I can step right out the door and out into the hot sun and right out onto the path going up the hill to the tree line. And what's to stop me from keeping right on? What's to stop me from walking on to the edge of the world and then jumping right off?

But Calvin didn't keep walking. He leaned against a big old maple and then hunkered down in the grass and looked out over Father's land. The house. The barn. The chicken coops. The pigpen. The millhouse.

Did the wheel ever turn in Father's mill anymore? The water passed useless through the chase, the wheel leaned forward but never moved, and so the stones inside were still, too. Might as well have left the huge millstone in the mountain, as to bring it down here to stand useless while big brother Alvin filled these poor people's minds with hopeless hopes. Alvin was grinding them up as surely as if he put their heads between the stones. Grinding them up, turning them to flour which Alvin himself would bake into bread and eat up for supper. He may have prenticed as a blacksmith all those years in Hatrack River, but here in Vigor Church he was a baker of brains.

Thinking of Alvin eating everybody's ground-up heads made Calvin feel nasty in a delicious kind of way. It made him laugh. He stretched his long thin legs out into the meadow grass and lay back against the trunk of the maple. A bug was scampering along the skin of his leg, up under his trousers, but he didn't bother to reach down and pull it out, or even to shake his leg to get it off. Instead, he got his doodlebug going, like a spare pair of eyes, like an extra set of fingers, looking for the tiny rapid flutter of the bug's useless stupid life and when he found it he gave it a little pinch, or really more like a squint, a tiny twitch of the muscles around his eyes, but that was all it took, just that little pinch and then the bug wasn't moving no more. Some days, little bug, it just don't pay to get up in the morning.

"That must be some funny story," said a voice.

Calvin fairly jumped out of his skin. How did somebody come on him unawares? Still, he didn't let himself show he'd been surprised. His heart might be beating fast inside his chest, but he still waited a minute before even turning around to look, and then he made sure to look about as uninterested as a fellow can look without being dead.

A bald fellow, old and in buckskins. Calvin knew him, of course. A far traveler and sometime visitor named Taleswapper. Another one who thought the world began with God and ended with Alvin. Calvin looked him up and down. The buckskins were about as old as the man. "Did you get them clothes off a ninety-year-old deer, or did your daddy and grandpa wear them all their lives to get them so worn out like that?"

"I've worn these clothes so long," said the old man, "that I sometimes send them on errands when I'm too busy to go, and nobody can tell the difference."

"I think I know you," said Calvin. "You're that old Taleswapper fellow."

"So I am," said the old man. "And you're Calvin, old Miller's youngest boy."

Calvin waited.

And here it came: "Alvin's little brother."

Calvin folded himself sitting down and then unfolded himself standing. He liked how tall he was. He liked looking down at the old man's bald head. "You know, old man, if we had another just like you, we could put your smooth pink heads together and you'd look like a baby's butt."

"Don't like being called Alvin's little brother, eh?" asked Taleswapper.

"You know where to go for your free meal," said Calvin. He started to walk away into the meadow. Having no destination in mind, of course, his walking pretty soon petered out, and he paused a moment, looking around, wishing there was something he wanted to do.

The old man was right behind him. Damn but the old boy was quiet! Calvin had to remember to keep a watch out for people. Alvin did it without thinking, dammit, and Calvin could do it too if he could just remember to remember.

"Heard you chuckling," said Taleswapper. "When I first walked up behind you."

"Well, then, I guess you ain't deaf yet."

"Saw you watching the millhouse and heard you chuckling and I thought, What does this boy see so funny in a mill whose wheel don't turn?"

Calvin turned to face him. "You were born in England, weren't you?"

"I was."

"And you lived in Philadelphia awhile, right? Met old Ben Franklin there, right?"

"What a memory you have."

"Then how come you talk like a frontiersman? You know and I know that it's supposed to be 'a mill whose wheel *doesn't* turn,' but here you are talking bad grammar as if you never went to school but I know you did. And how come you don't talk like other Englishmen?"

"Keen ear, keen eye," said Taleswapper. "A sharp one for details. Dull on the big picture, but sharp on details. I notice you talk worse than *you* know how, too."

Calvin ignored the insult. He wasn't going to let this old coot distract him with tricks. "I said how come you talk like a frontiersman?"

"Spend a lot of time on the frontier."

"I spend a lot of time in the chicken coop but that don't make me cluck."

Taleswapper grinned. "What do *you* think, boy?"

"I think you try to sound like the people you're telling your lies to, so they'll trust you, they'll think you're one of them. But you're not one of us, you're not one of anybody. You're a spy, stealing the hopes and dreams and wishes and memories and imaginings of everybody and leaving them nothing but lies in exchange."

Taleswapper seemed amused. "If I'm such a criminal, why ain't I rich?"

"Not a criminal," said Calvin.

"I'm relieved to be acquitted."

"Just a hypocrite."

Taleswapper's eyes narrowed.

"A hypocrite," Calvin said again. "Pretending to be what you're not. So other people will trust you, but they're trusting in a bunch of pretenses."

"That's an interesting idea, there, Calvin," said Taleswapper. "Where do you draw the line between a humble man who knows his own weaknesses but tries to act out virtues he hasn't quite mastered yet, and a proud man who pretends to have those virtues without the slightest intention of acquiring them?"

"Listen to the frontiersman now," said Calvin scornfully. "I knew you could shed that folksy talk the minute you wanted to."

"Yes, I can do that," said Taleswapper. "Just as I can speak French to a Frenchman and Spanish to a Spaniard and four kinds of Red talk depending on which tribe I'm with. But you, Calvin, do you speak Scorn and Mockery to everyone? Or just to your betters?"

It took Calvin a moment to realize that he had been put

down, hard and low. "I could kill you without using my hands," he said.

"Harder than you think," said Taleswapper. "Killing a man, that is. Why not ask your brother Alvin about it? He's done it the once, for just cause, whereas you think of killing a man because he tweaks your nose. And then you wonder why I call myself your better."

"You just want to put me down because I named you for what you are. Hypocrite. Like all the others."

"*All* the others?"

Calvin nodded grimly.

"*Everyone* is a hypocrite except Calvin Miller?"

"Calvin *Maker*," said Calvin. Even as he said it, he knew it was a mistake; he had never told anyone the name by which he thought of himself, and now he had blurted it out, a boast, a brag, a *demand*, to this most unsympathetic of listeners. This man who was most likely, of all men, to repeat Calvin's secret dream to others.

"Well, now it seems to be unanimous," said Taleswapper. "We're all pretending to be something that we're not."

"I *am* a Maker!" Calvin insisted, raising his voice, even though he knew he was making himself seem even weaker and more vulnerable. He just couldn't stop himself from talking to this slimy old man. "I've got all the knack for it that Alvin ever had, if anyone would bother to notice!"

"Made any millstones lately, without tools?" asked Taleswapper.

"I can make stones in a fence fit together like as if they growed that way out of the ground!"

"Healed any wounds?"

"I killed a bug crawling on my leg just a moment ago without so much as laying a hand on it."

"Interesting. I ask of healing and you answer with killing. Doesn't sound like a Maker to me."

"You said yourself that Alvin killed a man!"

"With his hands, not with his knack. A man who had just murdered an innocent woman who died to protect her son from captivity. The bug—was it going to harm you or anyone?"

"Yes, there you are, Alvin is always righteous and wonderful, while Calvin can't do nothing right! But Alvin hisself told me the story of how he caused a bunch of roaches to get theirselfs kilt when he was a boy and—"

"And you learned nothing from his story, except that you have the power to torment insects."

"*He* gets to do what he wants and then talks about how he's learned better now, but if *I* do the same things then I'm not worthy! I can't be taught any of his secrets because I'm not *ready* for them only I *am* ready for them, I'm just not ready to let Alvin decide *how* I'll use the knack I was born with. Who tells *him* what to do?"

"The inner light of virtue," said Taleswapper, "for lack of a clearer name."

"Well what about *my* inner light?"

"I imagine that your parents ask themselves this very question, and often."

"Why can't *I* be allowed to figure things out on my own like Alvin did?"

"But of course you *are* being allowed to do *exactly* that," said Taleswapper.

"No I'm not! He sits there trying to explain to those bone-headed no-knack followers of his how to get inside other things and learn what they are and how they're shaped inside and then ask them to take on new forms, as if that's a thing that folks can learn—"

"But they *do* learn it, don't they?"

"If you call an inch a year moving, then I guess you can call that learning," said Calvin. "But me, the one who actually understands everything he says, the one who could actually put it all to use, he won't even let me in the room. If I stay there he just tells stories and makes jokes and won't teach a *thing* until I leave, and why? I'm his best pupil, ain't I? I learn it all, I soak it in fast and I can use it on the instant, but he won't teach me! He calls them others 'apprentice Makers' but me he won't even take on for a single lesson, all because I don't bow down and worship whenever he starts talking about how a Maker can never use his power to destroy, but only to build, or he loses it, which is nonsense, since a man's knack is his knack and—"

"It seems to me," said Taleswapper, his voice sharp enough to cut through Calvin's raging, "that you are a singularly unteachable young man. You ask Alvin to teach you, and he tries to do it, but then you refuse to listen because *you* know what's nonsense and what matters, *you* know that a man doesn't have to make in order to be a Maker, *you* already know so much I'm surprised you still wait around here, wishing for Alvin to teach you things that you plainly have no desire to know."

"I want him to teach me how to get into the small of things!" cried Calvin. "I want him to teach me how to change people the way he changed Arthur Stuart so the Finders couldn't Find him anymore! I want him to teach me how to get inside bones and blood vessels, how to turn iron to gold! I want me a golden plow like his and he won't teach me *how!*"

"And it has never occurred to you," said Taleswapper, "that when he speaks of using the power of Making only to build things up, never to tear them down, he might be teaching you precisely the thing you are asking? Oh, Calvin, I'm so sorry to see that your mama did have one stupid child after all."

Calvin felt the rage explode inside himself, and before he knew what he was doing he knocked the old man down and straddled his hips, pounding on his frail old ribs and belly. It took many blows before he realized that the old man wasn't fighting back. Have I killed him? Calvin wondered. What will I do if he's dead? They'll have me for murder, then. They won't understand how he provoked me, begging for a beating. It's not like I planned to kill him.

Calvin put his fingers to Taleswapper's throat, feeling for a pulse. It was there, feeble, but it probably was always feeble, given how old the fellow was.

"Didn't quite kill me, eh?" whispered Taleswapper.

"Didn't feel like it," said Calvin.

"How many men will you have to beat up before everyone agrees that you're a Maker?"

Calvin wanted to hit him again. Didn't this old man learn anything?

"You know, if you hurt people enough, eventually they'll all call you whatever you want. Maker. King. Captain. Boss. Master. Holy One. Pick your title, you can beat people into calling you that. But you don't change yourself a bit. All you do is change the meanings of those words, so they all mean the same thing: Bully."

Calvin, hot with shame, got up and stood over him. He restrained himself from kicking the old man until his head was jelly. "You've got a knack for words," he said.

"True words in particular," said Taleswapper.

"Lies, from all I can see," said Calvin.

"A liar sees lies," said Taleswapper. "Even when they aren't there. Just as a hypocrite sees hypocrites whenever he runs across good people. Can't stand to think that anyone might *really* be what you only pretend to be."

"You did say one true thing," said Calvin. "About its making no sense me waiting around here for Alvin to teach me what he plainly means to keep secret. I should've realized that Alvin wasn't never going to teach me anything, because he's afraid if people see me doing all the things he can do, he won't be king of the hill anymore. I have to find it out on my own, just like he did."

"You have to find it out by learning the same things he did," said Taleswapper. "Alone or as his pupil, though, I don't think you're capable of learning those things."

"You're wrong," said Calvin. "I'll prove it to you."

"By learning to master your own will and use your power only to build things, only to help others?"

"By going out into the world and learning everything and coming back and showing Alvin who's got the real Maker's knack and who's just pretending."

Taleswapper propped himself up on one elbow. "But Calvin, your actions here today have made the answer to that question as plain as day."

Calvin wanted to kick him in his face. Silence that mouth. Break that shiny pate and watch the brains spill out into the meadow grass.

Instead he turned away and took a few steps toward the woods. He had a destination this time. East. Civilization. The cities, the lands where people lived together cheek by jowl. Among them there would be those who could teach him. Or, failing that, those he could experiment with until he learned all that Alvin knew, and more. Calvin was wrong to have stayed here so long. Foolish to have kept hoping that he'd ever get any love or help from Alvin. I worshipped him, that was my mistake, thought Calvin. It took this bone-headed old fool to show me the kind of contempt that people have for me. Always comparing me to Alvin, perfect Alvin, Alvin the Maker, Alvin the virtuous son.

Alvin the hypocrite. He does with his power just what I want to do—only he's so subtle about it that people don't even realize he's controlling them. Tell us what to do, Alvin!

Teach us how to Make, Alvin! Does Alvin ever say, It's not your knack, you poor fool, I can't teach you how to do this any more than I can teach a fish to walk? No. He pretends to teach them, helps them get a few pathetic illusory successes so they stay with him, his obedient servants, his disciples.

Well, I'm not one of them. I'm my own man, smarter than he is, and more powerful, too, if I can just learn what I need to learn. After all, Alvin was only a seventh son for a couple of moments after he was born, until our oldest brother Vigor died. But I have been a seventh son my whole life, and still am one today. Before long I'm bound to surpass Alvin. I'm the real Maker. The real thing. Not a hypocrite. Not a pretender.

"When you see Alvin, tell him not to follow me. He won't see me again until I'm ready for him to square off against me, Maker against Maker."

"There can never be a battle of Maker against Maker," said Taleswapper.

"Oh?"

"Because if there's a battle," said Taleswapper, "it's because one of them, at least, is not a Maker at all, but rather its opposite."

Calvin laughed. "That old wives' tale? About some supposed Unmaker? Alvin tells the stories, but it's all a bunch of hogwash to make him look like more of a hero."

"I'm not surprised that you don't believe in the Unmaker," said Taleswapper. "The first lie the Unmaker always tells is that he doesn't exist. And his true servants always believe him, even as they carry out his work in the world."

"So I'm the Unmaker's servant?" asked Calvin.

"Of course," said Taleswapper. "I have the bruises on my body now to prove it."

"Those bruises prove you're a weak man with a big mouth."

"Alvin would have healed me and strengthened me," said Taleswapper. "That's what *Makers* do."

Calvin couldn't take any more of this. He kicked the man right in the face. He could feel Taleswapper's nose break under the ball of his foot; then the old man flopped back into the grass and lay there still. Calvin didn't even bother to check his pulse. If he was dead, so be it. The world would be a better place without his lies and rudeness.

Not until he was well into the woods, about five minutes later, did the enormity of what he had done flow over him. Killed a man! I might have killed a man, and left him to die!

I should have healed him before I left. The way Alvin healed people. Then he would have *known* that I'm truly a Maker, because I healed him. How could I have missed such an opportunity to show what I can do?

At once he turned and raced back through the forest, dodging the roots, skittering down a bank he had so eagerly climbed only moments before. But when, panting, he emerged into the meadow, the old man wasn't there, though bits of blood still clung to the grass and pooled where his head had lain. Not dead, then. He got up and walked, so he can't be dead.

What a fool I was, thought Calvin. Of course I didn't kill him. I'm a Maker. Makers don't destroy things, they build them. Isn't that what Alvin always tells me? So if I'm a Maker, nothing I do can possibly be destructive.

For a moment he almost headed down the hill toward the millhouse. Let Taleswapper accuse him in front of everybody. Calvin would simply deny it, and let them work out how to deal with the problem. Of course they'd all believe Taleswapper. But Calvin only needed to say, "That's his knack, to make people believe his lies. Why else would you trust in this stranger instead of Alvin Miller's youngest boy, when you all know I don't go around beating people up?" It was a delicious scene to contemplate, with Father and Mother and Alvin all frozen into inaction.

But a better scene was this: Calvin free in the city. Calvin out of his brother's shadow.

Best of all, they couldn't even get up a group of men to follow him. For here in the town of Vigor Church, the adults were all bound by Tenskwa-Tawa's curse, so that any stranger they met, they had to tell him the story of how they slaughtered the innocent Reds at Tippy-Canoe. If they didn't tell the story, their hands and arms would become covered with dripping blood, mute testimony of their crime. Because of that they didn't venture out into the world where they might run into strangers. Alvin himself might come looking for him, but no one else except those who had been too young to take part in the massacre would be able to join with him. Oh, yes, their brother-in-law Armor, he wasn't under the curse. And maybe Measure wasn't really under the curse, because he took it on himself, even though he wasn't part of the battle. So maybe he could leave. But that still wouldn't be much of a search party.

And why would they bother to search for him anyway? Alvin thought Calvin was a nothing. Not worth teaching. So how could he be worth following?

My freedom was always just a few steps away, thought Calvin. All it took was my realizing that Alvin was *never* going to accept me as his true friend and brother. Taleswapper showed me that. I should thank him.

Hey, I already gave him all the thanks he deserved.

Calvin chuckled. Then he turned and headed back into the forest. He tried to move as silently as Alvin always did, moving through the forest—a trick Al had learned from the wild Reds back before they either gave up and got civilized or moved across the Mizzipy into the empty country of the west. But despite all his efforts, Calvin always ended up making noise and breaking branches.

For all I know, Calvin told himself, Alvin makes just as much noise, and simply uses his knack to make us *think* he's quiet. Because if everybody *thinks* you're silent, you *are* silent, right? Makes no difference at all.

Wouldn't it be just like that hypocrite Alvin to have us all thinking he's in such harmony with the greenwood when he's really just as clumsy as everyone else! At least I'm not ashamed to make an honest noise.

With that reassuring thought, Calvin plunged on into the underbrush, breaking off branches and disturbing fallen leaves with every step.

3

WATCHERS

While Calvin was a-setting out on his journey to wherever, trying not to think about Alvin with every step, there was someone else already on a journey, also wishing she could stop thinking about Alvin. That's about where the semblance ends, though. Because this was Peggy Larner, who knew Alvin better and loved Alvin more than any living soul. She was riding in a coach along a country road in Appalachee, and she was at least as unhappy as Calvin ever was. Difference was, she blamed her woes on nary a soul but her own self.

In the days after her mother was murdered, Peggy Larner figured that she would stay in Hatrack River for the rest of her life, helping her father tend his roadhouse. She was done with the great matters of the world. She had set her hand to meddling in them, and the result had been that she didn't tend to her own backyard and so she failed to see her mother's death looming. Preventable, easily, it was so dependent upon merest chance; a simple word of warning and her mother and father would have known the Slave Finders were coming back that night, and how many of them there were, and how armed, and through what door coming. But Peggy had been watching the great matters of the world, had been minding her foolish love for the young journeyman smith named Alvin who had learned to make a plow of living gold and then asked her to marry him and go with him through the world to do battle with the Unmaker, and all the while the Unmaker was destroying her own life through the back door, with a shotgun blast that shredded her mother's flesh and gave Peggy the most terrible of burdens to carry all her life. What kind of child does not watch out to save her own mother's life?

She could not marry Alvin. That would be like rewarding herself for her own selfishness. She would stay and help her father in his work.

And yet she couldn't do even that, not for long. When her father looked at her—or rather, when he wouldn't look at her—she felt his grief stab to her heart. He knew she could have prevented it. And though it was his great effort not to reproach her with it, she didn't need to hear his words to know what was in his heart. No, nor did she need to use her knack to see his heart's desire, his bitter memories. She knew without looking, because she knew him deep, as children know parents.

There came a day, then, when she could bear it no longer. She had left home once before, as a girl, with a note left behind. This time she left with more courage, facing her father and telling him that she couldn't stay.

"Have I lost my daughter then, as well as my wife?"

"Your daughter you have as well as ever," said Peggy. "But the woman who could have prevented your wife's death, and failed to do it—that woman can't live here anymore."

"Have I said anything? Have I by word or deed—"

"It's your knack to make folks feel welcome under your roof, Father, and you've done your best with me. But there's no knack can take away the terrible burden charged to my soul. There's no love or kindness you can show toward me that will hide—from *me*—what you suffer at the very sight of me."

Father knew he couldn't deceive his daughter any longer, her being a torch and all. "I'll miss you with all my heart," he said.

"And I'll miss you, Father," she answered. With a kiss, with a brief embrace, she took her leave. Once again she rode in Whitley Physicker's carriage to Dekane. There she visited with a family that had done her much kindness, once upon a time.

She didn't stay long, though, and soon she took the coach down to Franklin, the capital of Appalachee. She knew no one there, but she soon would—no heart could remain closed to her, and she quickly found those people who hated the institution of slavery as much as she did. Her mother had died for taking a half-Black boy into her home, into her family as her own son, even though by law he belonged to some White man down in Appalachee.

The boy, Arthur Stuart, was still free, living with Alvin in the town of Vigor Church. But the institution of slavery, which had killed both the boy's birth mother and his adoptive mother, that lived on, too. There was no hope of changing it in the King's lands to the south and east, but Appalachee was the nation that had won its freedom by the

sacrifice of George Washington and under the leadership of
Thomas Jefferson. It was a land of high ideals. Surely she
could have some influence here, to root out the evil of slavery from this land. It was in Appalachee that Arthur Stuart
had been conceived by a cruel master's rape of his helpless
slave. It was in Appalachee, then, that Peggy would quietly
but deftly maneuver to help those who hated slavery and
hinder those who would perpetuate it.

She traveled in disguise, of course. Not that anyone here
would know her, but she didn't like being called by the name
of Peggy Guester, for that was also her mother's name. Instead she passed as Miss Larner, gifted teacher of French,
Latin, and music, and in that guise she went about tutoring,
here a few weeks, there a few weeks. It was master classes
that she taught, teaching the schoolmasters in various towns
and villages.

Though her public lessons were conscientiously taught,
what concerned her most was seeking out the heartfires of
those who loathed slavery, or those who, not daring to admit their loathing, were at least uncomfortable and apolo-
getic about the slaves they owned. The ones who were
careful to be gentle, the ones who secretly allowed their
slaves to learn to read and write and cipher. These good-
hearted ones she dared to encourage. She called upon them
and said words that might turn them toward the paths of life,
however few and faint they were, in which they gained courage and spoke out against the evil of slavery.

In this way, she was still helping her father in his work.
For hadn't old Horace Guester risked his life for many years,
helping runaway slaves make it across the Hio and on north
into French territory, where they would be no longer slaves,
where Finders could not go? She could not live with her
father, she could not remove any part of his burden of grief,

but she could carry on his work, and might in the end make his work unnecessary, for it would have been accomplished, not a slave at a time, but all the slaves of Appalachee at once.

Would I then be worthy to return and face him? Would I be redeemed? Would Mother's death mean something then, instead of being the worthless result of my carelessness?

Here was the hardest part of her discipline: She refused to let any thought of Alvin Smith distract her. Once he had been the whole focus of her life, for she was present at his birth, peeled the birth caul from his face, and for years thereafter used the power of the dried-up caul to protect him against all the attacks of the Unmaker. Then, when he became a man and grew into his own powers enough that he could mostly protect himself, he was still the center of her heart, for she came to love the man he was becoming. She had come home to Hatrack River then, in disguise for the first time as Miss Larner, and there she gave him and Arthur Stuart the kind of book learning that they both hungered for. And all the time she was teaching him, she was hiding behind the hexes that hid her true face and name, hiding and watching him like a spy, like a hunter, like a lover who dared not be seen.

It was in that disguise that he fell in love with her, too. It was all a lie, a lie I told him, a lie I told myself.

So now she would not search for his bright heartfire, though she knew she could find it in an instant, no matter how far away he was. She had other work in her life. She had other things to achieve or to undo.

Here was the best part of her new life: Everyone who knew anything about slavery knew that it was wrong. The ignorant—children growing up in slave country, or people who had never kept slaves or seen them kept or even known a Black man or woman—they might fancy that there was nothing wrong with it. But those who knew, they all understood that it was evil.

Many of them, of course, simply told themselves lies or made excuses or flat-out embraced the evil with both arms—anything to keep their way of life, to keep their wealth and leisure, their prestige, their honor. But more were made miserable by the wealth that came from the labor and suffering of the Blacks that had been stolen from their native land and brought against their will to this dark continent of America. It was these whose hearts Peggy reached for, especially the strong ones, the ones who might have the courage to make a difference.

And her labors were not in vain. When she left a place, people were talking—no, to be honest they were quarreling—over things that before had never been openly questioned. To be sure, there was suffering. Some of those whose courage she had helped awaken were tarred and feathered, or beaten, or their houses and barns burnt. But the excesses of the slavemasters served only to expose to others the necessity of taking action, of winning their freedom from a system that was destroying them all.

She was on this errand today. A hired carriage had come to fetch her to a town called Baker's Fork, and she was well on the way, already hot and tired and dusty, as summer travelers always were, when all of a sudden she felt curious to see what was up a certain road.

Now, Peggy wasn't one to be curious in any ordinary way. Having had, since childhood, the knack of knowing people's inmost secrets, she had learned young to shy away from simple curiosity. Well she knew that there were some things folks were better off not knowing. As a child she would have given much not to know what the children her age thought of her, the fear they had of her, the loathing because of her strangeness, because of the hushed way their parents talked of her. Oh, she would have been glad not to know the secrets of the men and women around her. Curiosity was its own punishment, when you were sure of finding the answer to your question.

So the very fact that she felt curious about, of all things, a rutted track in the low hills of northern Appalachee—that was the most curious thing of all. And so, instead of trying to follow the track, she looked inside her own heartfire to see what lay down that road. But every path she saw in which she called to the carriage driver and bade him turn around and follow the track, every one of those paths led to a blank, a place where what might happen there could not be known.

It was a strange thing for her, not to know at all what the outcome might be. Uncertainty she was used to, for there were many paths that the flow of time could follow. But not to have a glimmer, that was new indeed. New and—she had to admit—attractive.

She tried to warn herself off, to tell herself that if she couldn't see, it must be the Unmaker blocking her, there must be some terrible fate down that road.

But it didn't *feel* like the Unmaker. It felt right to follow the track. It felt *necessary*, though she tingled a bit with the danger of it. Is this how other people feel all the time? she wondered. Knowing nothing, the future all a blank, able to rely only on feelings like this? Is this tingling what George Washington felt just before he surrendered his army to the rebels of Appalachee and then turned himself over to the king he had betrayed? Surely not, for old George was certain enough of the outcome. Maybe it's what Patrick Henry felt when he cried out, Give me liberty or give me death, having no notion which of the two, if either, he might win. To act without knowing . . .

"Turn around!" she called.

The driver didn't hear her over the clattering of the horses' hooves, the rattling and creaking of the carriage.

She thumped on the roof of the carriage with her umbrella. "Turn around!"

The driver pulled the horses to a stop. He slid open the tiny door that allowed words to pass between driver and passengers. "What, ma'am?"

"Turn around."

"I ain't took no wrong turn, ma'am."

"I know that. I want to follow that track we just passed."

"That just leads on up to Chapman Valley."

"Excellent. Then take me to Chapman Valley."

"But it's the school board in Baker's Fork what hired me to bring you."

"We're going to stop the night anyway. Why not Chapman Valley?"

"They got no inn."

"Nevertheless, either turn the carriage around or wait here while I *walk* up that track."

The door slid shut—perhaps more abruptly than necessary—and the carriage took a wide turn out into the meadow. It had been dry these past few days, so the turn went smoothly, and soon they were going up the track that had made her so curious.

The valley, when she saw it, was pretty, though there was nothing remarkable about its prettiness. Except for the rough woods at the crests of the surrounding hills, the whole valley was tamed, the trees all in the place where they were planted, the houses all built up to fit the ever-larger families that lived there. Perhaps the walls were more crisply painted, and perhaps a whiter white than other places—or perhaps that was just what happened to Peggy's perceptions, because she was looking especially sharp to see what had piqued her curiosity. Perhaps the orchard trees were older than usual, more gnarled, as if this place had been settled long ago, the earliest of the Appalachee settlements. But what of that? Everything in America was newish; there was bound to be someone in this town who still remembered its founding. Nothing west of the first range of mountains was any older than the lifespan of the oldest citizen.

As always, she was aware of the heartfires of the people dwelling here, like sparks of light that she could see even in the brightest part of noon, through all walls, behind all hills, in all attics or basements where they might be. They were the ordinary folk of any town, perhaps a bit more content than others, but not immune to the suffering of life, the petty resentments, the griefs and envies. Why had she come here?

They came to a house with no one home. She rapped on the roof of the carriage again. The horses were whoaed to a stop, and the little door opened. "Wait here," she said.

She had no idea why this house, the empty one, drew her curiosity. Perhaps it was the way it had obviously grown up around a tiny log cabin, growing first prosperous, then grand, and finally nothing more than large, as aesthetics gave way to the need for more room, more room. How, in such a large and well-tended place, could there be no one home?

Then she realized that she heard singing coming from the house. And laughter from the yard. Singing and laughter, and yet not a heartfire to be seen. There had never been such a strange thing in all her life. Was this a haint house? Did the restless dead dwell here, unable to let go of life? But who ever heard of a haint that laughed? Or sang such a cheery song?

And there, running around the house, was a boy not more than six, being chased by three older girls. Not one with a heartfire. But from the dirt on the boy's face and the rage in the eyes of the red-faced girls, these could not be the spirits of the dead.

"Hallo, there!" cried Peggy, waving.

The boy, startled, looked at her. That pause was his undoing, for the girls caught up to him and fell to pummeling him with much enthusiasm; his answer was to holler with equal vigor, cursing them roundly. Peggy didn't know them, but had little doubt that the boy, in the fashion of all boys, had done some miserable mischief which outraged the girls— his sisters? She also had little doubt that the girls, despite the inevitable protests of innocence, had no doubt provoked *him* before, but in subtle, verbal ways so that he could never point to a bruise and get his mother on his side. Such was the endless war between male and female children. Stranger or not, however, Peggy could not allow the violence of the girls to get out of hand, and it seemed they were not disposed to go lightly in their determined battering of the bellowing lad. They were pursuing the beating, not as a holiday, but as if it were their bread-and-butter labor, with an overseer who would examine their handiwork later and say, "I'd say the boy was well beaten. You get your day's pay, all right!"

"Let up now," she said, striding across the goat-cropped yard.

They ignored her until she was on them and had two of the girls by the collars. Even then, they kept swinging with their fists, not a few of the blows landing on Peggy herself, while the third girl took no pause. Peggy had no choice but to give the two girls she had hold of a stern push, sending them sprawling in the grass, while she dragged the third girl off the boy.

As she had feared, the boy hadn't done well under the girls' blows. His nose was bleeding, and he got up only slowly; when the girl Peggy was holding lunged at him, he scurried on all fours to evade her.

"Shame on you," said Peggy. "Whatever he did, it wasn't worth this!"

"He killed my squirrel!" cried the girl she held.

"But how can you have had a squirrel?" asked Peggy. "It would be cruel of *you* to pen one up."

"She was never penned," said the girl. "She was my friend. I fed her and these others saw it—she came to me and I kept her alive through the hard winter. He knew it! He was jealous that the squirrel came to me, and so he killed it."

"It was a squirrel!" the boy shouted—hoarsely and rather weakly, but it was clear he *meant* it to be a shout. "How should I know it was yours?"

"Then you shouldn't have killed any," said another of the girls. "Not till you were sure."

"Whatever he did to the squirrels," said Peggy, "even if he was malicious, it was wrong of you and unchristian to knock him down and hurt him so."

The boy looked at her now. "Are you the judge?" he asked.

"Judge? I think not!" said Peggy with a laugh.

"But you can't be the Maker, that one's a boy. I think you're a judge." The boy looked even more certain. "Aunt Becca said the judge was coming, and then the Maker, so you can't be the Maker because the judge ain't come yet, but you could be the judge because the judge comes first."

Peggy knew that other folks often took the words of children to be nonsense, if they didn't understand them immediately. But Peggy knew that the words of children were always related to their view of the world, and made their own sense if you only knew how to hear them. Someone had told them—Aunt Becca, it was—that a judge and a Maker were coming. There was only one Maker that Peggy knew of. Was Alvin coming here? What was this place, that the children knew of Makers, and had no heartfires?

"I thought your house was standing empty," said Peggy, "but I see that it is not."

For indeed there now stood a woman in the doorway, leaning against the jamb, watching them placidly as she slowly stirred a bowl with a wooden spoon.

"Mama!" cried the girl that Peggy still held. "She has me and won't let go!"

"It's true!" cried Peggy at once. "And I still won't let go, till I'm sure she won't murder the boy here!"

"He killed my squirrel, Mama!" cried the girl.

The woman said nothing, just stirred.

"Perhaps, children," said Peggy, "we should go talk to this lady in the doorway, instead of shouting like river rats."

"Mother doesn't like you," said one of the girls. "I can tell."

"That's a shame," said Peggy. "Because I like *her*."

"Do not," said the girl. "You don't know her, and if you did you *still* wouldn't like her because nobody does."

"What a terrible thing to say about your mother," said Peggy.

"I don't have to like her," said the girl. "I *love* her."

"Then take me to this woman that you love but don't like," said Peggy, "and let me reach my own conclusions about her."

As they approached the door, Peggy began to think that the girls might be right. The woman certainly didn't look welcoming. But for that matter, she didn't look hostile, either. Her face was empty of emotion. She just stirred the bowl.

"My name is Peggy Larner." The woman ignored her outstretched hand. "I'm sorry if I shouldn't have intervened, but as you can see the boy was taking some serious injury."

"Just my nose is bloody, is all," said the boy. But his limp suggested other less visible pains.

"Come inside," said the woman.

Peggy had no idea whether the woman was speaking just to the children, or was including her in the invitation. If it could be called an invitation, so blandly she spoke it, not looking up from the bowl she stirred. The woman turned away, disappearing inside the house. The children followed. So, finally, did Peggy.

No one stopped her or seemed to think her action strange. It was this that first made her wonder if perhaps she had fallen asleep in the carriage and this was some strange dream, in which unaccountable unnatural things happen which nevertheless excite no comment in the land of dreams, where there is no custom to be violated. Where I am now is not real. Outside waits the carriage and the team of four horses, not to mention the driver, as real and mundane a fellow as ever belched in the coachman's seat. But in here, I have stepped into a place beyond nature. There are no heart-fires here.

The children disappeared, stomping somewhere through the wood-floored house, and at least one of them went up or down a flight of stairs; it had to be a child, there was so much vigor in the step. But there were no sounds that told Peggy where to go, or what purpose was being served by her coming here. Was there no order here? Nothing that her presence disrupted? Would no one but the children ever notice her at all?

She wanted to go back outside, return to the carriage, but now, as she turned around, she couldn't remember what door she had come through, or even which way was north. The windows were curtained, and whatever door she had come through, she couldn't see it now.

It was an odd place, for there was cloth everywhere, folded neatly and stacked on all the furniture, on the floors, on the stairs, as if someone had just bought enough to make

432 • *Orson Scott Card*

Becca snorted. "My husband's name is Isaac."

That was Ta-Kumsaw's White name. "Don't quibble with me," said Peggy. "Something called me here. If it wasn't you, who was it?"

"My untalented sister. The one who breaks threads whenever she touches the loom."

Aunt Becca, the children had called the weaver. "Is your sister the mother of the children I met?"

"The murderous little boy who kills squirrels for sport? His brutal sisters? I think of them as the four horses of the apocalypse. The boy is war. The sisters are still sorting themselves out among the other forces of destruction."

"You speak metaphorically, I hope," said Peggy.

"I hope not," said Becca. "Metaphors have a way of holding the most truth in the least space."

"Why would your sister have brought me here? She didn't seem to know me at the door."

"You're the judge," said Becca. "I found a purple thread of justice in the loom, and it was you. I didn't want you here, but I knew that you'd come, because I knew my sister would have you here."

"Why? I'm no judge. I'm guilty myself."

"You see? Your judgment includes everyone. Even those who are invisible to you."

"Invisible?" But she knew before asking what it was that Becca meant.

"Your vision, your torching, as you quaintly call it—you see where people are in the many paths of their lives. But I am not on the path of time. Nor is my sister. We don't belong anywhere in your prophecies or in the memories of those who know us. Only in the present moment are we here."

"Yet I remember your first word long enough to make sense of the whole sentence," said Peggy.

a thousand dresses with and the tailors and seamstresses were yet to arrive. Then she realized that the piles were of one continuous cloth, flowing off the top of one stack into the bottom of the next. How could there be a cloth so long? Why would anyone make it, instead of cutting it and sending it out to get something made from it?

Why indeed. How foolish of her not to realize it at once. She knew this place. She hadn't visited it herself, but she had seen it through Alvin's heartfire, years ago.

He was still in Ta-Kumsaw's thrall in those days. The Red warrior took Alvin with him and brought him into his legend, so that those who now spoke of Alvin Smith the Finderkiller, or Alvin Smith and the golden plow, had once spoken of the same boy, little knowing it, when they spoke of the evil "Boy Renegado," the White boy who went with Ta-Kumsaw in all his travels in the last year before his defeat at Fort Detroit. It was in that guise that Alvin came here, and walked down this hall, yes, turning right here, yes, tracking the folded cloth into the oldest part of the house, the original cabin, into the slanting light that seems to have no source, as if it merely seeped in through the chinks between the logs. And here, if I open this door, I will find the woman with the loom. This is the place of weaving.

Aunt Becca. Of course she knew the name. Becca, the weaver who held the threads of all the lives in the White man's lands in North America.

The woman at the loom looked up. "I didn't want you here," she said softly.

"Nor did I plan to come," said Peggy. "The truth is, I had forgotten you. You slipped my mind."

"I'm supposed to slip your mind. I slip all minds."

"Except one or two?"

"My husband remembers me."

"Ta-Kumsaw? He isn't dead, then?"

"Ah," said Becca. "The judge insists on correctness of speech. Boundaries are not so clear, Margaret Larner. You remember perfectly now; but what will you remember in a week from now? What you forget of me, you'll forget so completely that you won't remember that you once knew it. Then my statement will be true, but you'll forget that I said it."

"I think not."

Becca smiled.

"Show me the thread," said Peggy.

"We don't do that."

"What harm can it do? I've already seen all the possible paths of my life."

"But you haven't seen which one you'll choose," said Becca.

"And you have?"

"At this moment, no," said Becca. "But in the moment that contains all moments, yes. I've seen the course of your life. That isn't why you came, though. Not to find out something as stupid as whether you'll marry the boy you've nurtured all these years. You will or you won't. What is that to me?"

"I don't know," said Peggy. "I wonder why you exist at all. You change nothing. You merely see. You weave, but the threads are out of your control. You are meaningless."

"So you say," said Becca.

"And yet you have a life, or had one. You loved Ta-Kumsaw—or Isaac, whatever name you use. So loving some boy, marrying him, that didn't always seem stupid to you."

"So you say," said Becca.

"Or do you include yourself in that? Do you call yourself stupid in having loved and married? You can't pretend to be inhuman when you loved and lost a man."

"Lost?" she asked. "I see him every day."

"He comes here? To Appalachee?"

Becca hooted. "I think not!"

"How many threads broke under your hand with that pass of the shuttlecock?" asked Peggy.

"Too many," said Becca. "And not enough."

"Did you break them? Or did they simply happen to break?"

"The thread grew thin. The life wore out. Or it was cut. It isn't the thread that cuts the life, it's the death that cuts the thread."

"So you keep a record, is that it? The weaving causes nothing, but simply records it all."

Becca smiled thinly. "Passive, useless creatures that we are, but we must weave."

Peggy didn't believe her, but there was no use in arguing. "Why did you bring me here?"

"I told you. I didn't."

"Why did *she* bring me here?"

"To judge."

"What is it that I'm supposed to judge?"

Becca passed the shuttlecock from her right hand to her left. The loom slammed forward, then dropped back. She passed the shuttlecock from her left hand to her right. Again, the frame slammed forward, weaving the threads tight.

This *is* a dream, thought Peggy. And not a very pleasant one. Why can't I ever wake up to escape from some foolish useless dream?

"Personally," said Becca, "I think you've already made your judgment. It's only my sister thinks that you deserve a second chance. She's very romantic. She thinks that you deserve some happiness. My own feeling is that human happiness is a very random thing, and bestows itself willy-nilly, and there's not much deserving about the matter."

"So it's myself that I'm supposed to judge?"

Becca laughed.

One of the girls stuck her head into the room. "Mother says it's nasty and uncompassionate when you laugh during the weaving," she said.

"Nanner nanner," said Becca.

The girl laughed lightly, and Becca did too.

"Mother mixed up something really vile for your supper. *With* dumplings."

"Vileness with dumplings," said Becca. "Do sup with me."

"Let the *judge* do that," said the girl. "She really *is* a bossy one. Telling *us* about right and wrong." With that the girl disappeared.

Becca clucked for a moment. "The children are so full of themselves. Still very impressed with the idea that they aren't part of the normal world. You must forgive them for being arrogant and cruel. They couldn't have hurt their brother much, because they haven't the strength to strike a blow that will really harm him."

"He bled," said Peggy. "He limped."

"But the squirrel died," said Becca.

"You keep no threads for squirrels."

"*I* keep no threads for them. But that doesn't mean their threads aren't woven."

"Oh, tell me flat out. Don't waste my time with mysteries."

"I haven't been," said Becca. "No mysteries. I've told you everything that's useful. Anything else I told you might affect your judgment, and so I won't do it. I let my sister have her way, bringing you here, but I'm certainly *not* going to bend your life any more than that. You can leave whenever you want—that's a choice, and a judgment, and I'll be content with it."

"Will *I?*"

"Come back in thirty years and tell me."

"Will I be—"

"If you're still alive then." Becca grinned. "Do you think

I'm so clumsy as to let slip your real span of years? I don't even know it. I haven't cared enough to look."

Two girls came in with a plate and a bowl and a cup on a tray. They set it on a small table near the loom. The plate was covered with a strange-smelling food. Peggy recognized nothing about it. Nor was there anything that she might have called a dumpling.

"I don't like it when people watch me eat," said Becca.

But Peggy was feeling very angry now, with all the elusiveness of Becca's conversation, and so she did not leave as courtesy demanded.

"Stay, then," said Becca.

The girls began to feed her. Becca did nothing to seek out the food. She kept up the perfect rhythm of her weaving, just as she had done throughout their conversation. The girls deftly maneuvered spoon or fork or cup to find their Aunt Becca's mouth, and then with a quick slurp or bite or sip she had the food. Not a drop or crumb was spilled on the cloth.

It could not always be like this, thought Peggy. She married Ta-Kumsaw. She bore a daughter to him, the daughter that went west to weave a loom among the Reds beyond the Mizzipy. Surely those things were not done with the shuttlecock flying back and forth, the loom slamming down to tamp the threads. It was deception. Or else it involved things Peggy was not going to understand however she tried.

She turned and left the room. The hall ended in a narrow stair. Sitting on the top step was, she assumed, the boy—she could see only his bare feet and trouser legs. "How's the nose?" she asked.

"Still hurts," said the boy. He scooched forward and dropped down a couple of steps by bouncing on his bottom.

"But not too bad," she said. "Healing fast."

"They was only *girls*," he said scornfully.

"You didn't think such scorn of them when they were pounding on you," she said.

"But you didn't hear me callin' uncle, did you? You didn't hear no uncle from me."

"No," said Peggy. "No uncle from you."

"I got me an uncle, though. Big Red man. Ike."

"I know of him."

"He comes most every day."

Peggy wanted to demand information from him. How does Ta-Kumsaw get here? Doesn't he live west of the Mizzipy? Or is he dead, and comes only in the spirit?

"Comes through the west door," said the boy. "We don't use that one. Just him. It's the door to my cousin Wieza's cabin."

"Her father calls her Mana-Tawa, I think."

The boy hooted. "Just giving her a Red name don't mean he can hold on to her. She don't belong to him."

"Whom does she belong to?"

"To the loom," he said.

"And you?" asked Peggy. "Do you belong to the loom?"

He shook his head. But he looked sad.

Peggy said it as she realized it: "You want to, don't you."

"She ain't going to have no more daughters. She don't stop weaving for him anymore. So she can't go. She'll just be there forever."

"And nephews can't take her place?"

"Nieces can, but my sisters ain't worth pigslime, in my opinion, which happens to be correck."

"Correct," said Peggy. "There's a *t* on the end."

"Correckut," the boy said. "But what I think is they ought to spell the words the way folks say 'em, stead of making us say 'em the way they're spelt."

Peggy had to laugh. "You have a point. But you can't just start spelling words any which way. Because you don't say them the same as someone from, say, Boston, and so pretty soon you and he would be spelling things so differently that you couldn't read each other's letters or books."

"Don't want to read his damn old books," said the boy. "I don't even know no boys in Boston."

"Do you have a name?"

"Not for *you* to know," said the boy. "You think I'm stupid? You're so thick with hexes you think I'm going to give you power over my name?"

"The hexes are to hide me from others."

"What do you have to hide for? Ain't nobody looking for you."

The words struck her hard. Nobody looking for her. Well, there it was. Once she had hidden so she could return to her own house without her family knowing her. Whom was she hiding from now?

"Perhaps I'm hiding from myself. Perhaps I don't want to be what I'm supposed to be. Or perhaps I don't want to keep living the life I already started to live."

"Perhaps you don't know squat about it," he said.

"Perhaps."

"Oh, don't be so mysterious, you silly old lady."

Silly she might accept, but *old?* "I'm not that many years older than you."

"When people say *perhaps* it's cause they're lying. Either they don't believe the thing they're saying, or they *do* believe it only they don't want to admit they do."

"You're a very wise young man."

"And the *real* liars change the subject the minute the truth comes up."

Peggy regarded him steadily. "You were waiting for me, weren't you?"

"I knew what Aunt Becca would do. She don't tell nobody nothin'."

"And you're going to tell me?"

"Not me! That's trouble too deep for me to get into." He smiled. "But you did stop the three witches from making soup of me. So I got you thinking in the right direction, if you've got the brains to see it." With that he jumped up and she listened as his feet slapped up the stairs and he was gone.

The choice was for Peggy to be happy. Becca said that, or said that her sister said it—though it was hard to imagine that blank-faced woman caring a whit whether anybody was happy or not. And now the boy got her talking about why she was hiding behind hexes, and said that he had guided her. The choice she was being offered was obvious enough now. She had buried herself in her father's work of breaking the back of slavery, and had stopped looking out for Alvin. They wanted her to look back again. They wanted her to reach out for him.

She stormed back into the cabin. "I won't do it," she said. "Caring for that boy is what killed my mother."

"Excuse me but I think a shotgun is what did for her," said Becca.

"A shotgun I could have prevented."

"So you say," said Becca.

"Yes, I say so."

"Your mother's thread broke when she decided to pick up a shotgun and do some killing of her own rather than trust to Alvin. Her boy Arthur was safe. She didn't need to kill, but when she chose to do that, she chose to die. Do you think you could have changed her mind about that?"

"Don't expect me to accept easy answers."

"No, I expect you to make all the answers as hard as possible. But sometimes it's the easy answers that are true."

"So it's back to the old days? Watching Alvin? Am I supposed to fall in love with him? Marry him? Watch him die?"

"I don't much care either way. My sister thinks you'll be

happier with him than without him, and he's dead either way, in the long run, but then aren't we all? Most women that aren't killed by having babies live to be widows. What of that?"

What *of* that? Just because she could foresee so many ways for Alvin to die didn't mean that she should avoid loving him. She knew that, rationally. But fear wasn't rational.

"You spend your whole life grieving for those that haven't died yet," said Becca. "What a waste of an interesting knack."

"Interesting?"

"You *could* have had the knack of making shoe leather supple. Just see how happy that would've made you."

Peggy tried to imagine herself as a cobbler and had to laugh. "I suppose that I'd rather know than not know, mostly."

"Exactly. Knowing hurts sometimes, especially when you can't do anything to change it."

But there was something furtive in her, the way she said that. "Can't do anything to change it my left eye!" said Peggy.

"Don't use curses you don't understand," said Becca.

"You *do* make changes. *You* don't think the loom is immutable, not one bit."

"It's dangerous to change. The consequences are unpredictable."

"You saw Ta-Kumsaw dead at Detroit. So you picked up Alvin's thread and you—"

"What do you know about the loom!" cried Becca. "What do you know about watching the threads flow under your hands and seeing all the grief and pain and suffering and thinking! It doesn't matter, they're God's cattle and he can herd them how he likes, only then you find the one you love more than life and God has him slaughtered by the treachery of the French and the hatred of the English and for *nothing,* his whole life meaningless and lost and nothing changed by it except a few legends and songs, and here I am, still loving him, a widow forever because he's gone! So yes, I found the one who could save him. I knew if they met, they'd love each other and save each other."

"But what you did caused the massacre at Tippy-Canoe," said Peggy. "The people of Vigor Church thought Alvin had been kidnapped and tortured to death, so they slaughtered Tenskwa-Tawa's people in vengeance. Now they have a curse on them, all because you—"

"Because Harrison took advantage of their rage. Do you think there wouldn't have been a massacre anyway?"

"But the blood wouldn't have been on the same hands, would it?"

Becca wept, and her tears fell onto the cloth.

"Shouldn't you dry those tears?" asked Peggy.

"If tears could mar this cloth, there'd be no cloth left."

"So you of all people know the cost of meddling with the course of others' lives."

"And you of all people know the cost of failing to meddle when the time was right." Becca raised her head and continued her work. "I saved him, and that was my goal. Those who died would have died anyway."

"Yet here I am because your sister wants me to look after Alvin."

"Here you are because we only see the threads and then half-guess as to what they mean and who they are. We know the young Maker's thread—there's no way to miss it in this cloth. Besides, I moved it once, I twined it with my Isaac's thread. Do you think I could lose track of it after that? I'll show you, if you promise not to look beyond the inch of cloth I show."

"I promise not to look. But I can't help what I chance to see."

"Chance to see this, then."

Peggy looked at the cloth, knowing that the sight of it was rarely given to those not of the loom. Alvin's thread was obvious, shimmering light, with all colors in it; but it was no thicker than any other, and it looked frail, easily snapped by careless handling. "You dared to move this one?"

"It returned of itself to its own place," said Becca. "I only borrowed it for a while. And he saved his brother Measure. Eight-face mound opened up for him. I tell you there are forces at work in his life far stronger than my power to move the threads."

"More powerful than me, too."

"You are one of the forces. Not all of them, not the greatest of them, but you are one. Look. See how the threads cross him. His brothers and sisters, I think. He is closely entwined with his family. And see how these threads are brightening, taking on more hues. He's teaching them to be Makers."

Peggy hadn't known that. "Isn't that dangerous?"

"He can't do his work alone," said Becca. "So he teaches others to help him in it. He's more successful at it than he knows."

"This one," said Peggy, pointing to the brightest of the other threads. It veered off widely, wandering through the cloth far from the rest of the family.

"His brother. Also a seventh son of a seventh son," said Becca. "Though the eighth, if you count the one who died."

"But the seventh of those alive when he was born," said Peggy. "Yes, there's power in him."

"Look," said Becca. "See how he was at the beginning. Every bit as bright as Alvin's. There was near as much in him then as in Alvin. And no more forces working against him than Alvin overcame. Fewer, really, because by the time he came into his own you and Alvin between you had the Unmaker at bay. At least, all the killing tricks. But the Unmaker found another way to undo the boy. Hate and envy.

If you love Alvin, Peggy, find his younger brother's heart-fire. Somehow he must be brought back before it's too late."

"Why? I don't know anything about Calvin, except his name and Alvin's hopes for him."

"Because the way the threads are going now, when his rejoins Alvin's, Alvin's comes to an end."

"He kills him?"

"How should I know? We learn what we can learn, but the threads say little except by their movement through the cloth. You will know. That's why she called you. Not just for your own happiness, but because . . . as she said, because I owe it to the Maker. I used him once to save my love. Didn't I owe you the same chance? That's what she said. But we knew that if I showed you this at first, before you chose, you would help him out of duty. For the grand cause, not for love of him."

"But I hadn't decided to watch him again."

"So you say," said Becca.

"You're very smug," said Peggy, "for a woman who has made such a botch of things herself."

"I inherited a botch," said Becca. "One day my mother, who crossed the ocean and brought us here, one day she took her hands from the loom and walked away. My sister and I came in with her supper and found her gone. We were both married, but I had borne a child for my husband, and in those days my sister had none. So I took the loom, and she went to her husband. And all the time, I was furious at my mother for going away like that. Fleeing her duty." Becca stroked the threads, gently, even gingerly. "Now I think I understand. The price of holding all these lives in our hands is that we scarcely have a life ourselves. My mother wasn't good at this, because her heart wasn't in it. Mine is, and if I made a mistake to save my husband's life, perhaps you can judge me more kindly knowing that I had already given up my life with my husband in order to fill my mother's place."

"I didn't mean to condemn you," said Peggy, abashed.

"Nor did I mean to justify myself to you," said Becca. "And yet you did condemn me, and I did justify myself. I hold my mother's thread here. I know where she is. But I'll never know, really, why she did what she did. Or what might have happened if she stayed." Becca looked up at Peggy. "I don't know much, but what I know, I know. Alvin must go out into the world. He must leave his family—let them learn Making on their own now, as he did. He must rejoin Calvin before the boy has been completely turned by the Unmaker. Otherwise, Calvin may be not only his death, but also the undoing of all the Maker's works."

"I have an easy answer," said Peggy. "I'll find Calvin and make sure he never comes home."

"You think you have the power to control a Maker's life?"

"Calvin is no Maker. How could he be? Think what Alvin had to do, to come into his own."

"Nevertheless, you never had the power to stand against Alvin, even when he was a child. And he was kind at heart. I think Calvin isn't governed by the same sense of decency."

"So I can't stand against him," said Peggy. "Nor can I send Alvin out on errands. He's not mine to command."

"Isn't he?" asked Becca.

Peggy buried her face in her hands. "I don't want him to love me. I don't want to love him. I want to continue my struggle against slavery here in Appalachee."

"Oh, yes. Using your knack to meddle with the cloth, aren't you?" said Becca. "Do you know where it leads?"

"To liberty for the slaves, I hope."

"Perhaps," she said. "But the sure thing is this: It leads to war."

Peggy looked up grimly. "I see warsigns down all the

paths. Before I started doing this, I saw those signs." Grieving mothers. The terror of battle in young men's lives.

"It begins as a civil war in Appalachee, but it ends as a war between the King on the one side and the United States on the other. Brutal, bloody, cruel . . ."

"Are you saying I should stop? That I should let these monsters continue to rule over the Blacks they kidnapped and all their children forever?"

"Not at all," said Becca. "The war comes because of a million different choices. Your actions push things that way, but you aren't the only cause. Do you understand? If war is the only way to free the slaves, then isn't the war worth all the suffering? Are lives wasted, when they end for such a cause?"

"I can't judge this sort of thing," said Peggy.

"But that's not true," said Becca. "Only you are fit to judge, because only you see the outcomes that might result. By the time I see things they've become inevitable."

"If they're inevitable, then why are you bothering to tell me to try to change them?"

"Almost inevitable. Again, I spoke imprecisely. I can't meddle with the threads on a grand scale. I can't foresee the consequences of change. But a single thread—sometimes I can move it without undoing the whole fabric. I didn't know a way to move Calvin that would make a difference. But I could move you. I could bring the judge here, the one who sees with the blindfold over her eyes. So I've done that."

"I thought you said your sister did it."

"Well, she's the one who decided it must be done. But only I could touch the thread."

"I think you spend a lot of your time lying and concealing things."

"Quite possibly."

"Like the fact that the western door leads into Ta-Kumsaw's land west of the Mizzipy."

"I never lied about that, or concealed it either."

"And the eastern door, where does that lead?"

"It opens in my auntie's house in Winchester, back in England. See? I conceal nothing."

"You have but one daughter," said Peggy, "and she's already got a loom of her own. Who will take your place here?"

"None of your business," said Becca.

"Nothing is none of my business now," said Peggy. "Not after you picked up my thread and moved it here."

"I don't know who will take my place. Maybe I'll be here forever. I'm not my mother. I won't quit and force this on an unwilling soul."

"When it comes time to choose, look at the boy," said Peggy. "He's wiser than you think."

"A boy's hands on the loom?" Becca's face bore an expression that suggested she had just tasted something awful.

"Before any talent for weaving," said Peggy, "doesn't the weaver have to care about the threads coming into the cloth? He may have killed a squirrel, but I don't think he loves death."

Becca regarded her steadily. "You take too much upon yourself."

"As you said. I'm a judge."

"You'll do it, then?"

"What, watch Alvin? Yes. Though I know I'll have a broken heart six times over before I bury him, yes, I'll turn my eyes back to that boy."

"That man."

"That Maker," said Peggy.

"And the other?"

"I'll meddle if I can find a way."

Becca nodded. "Good." She nodded again. "We're done, now. The doors will lead you out of the house."

That was all the good-bye that Peggy got. But what Becca

said was true. Where once Peggy couldn't see a way out, now every corridor led to a door standing open, with the daylight outside. She didn't want to go through the doors back into her own world, though. She wanted to pass through the doors in the old cabin. The east door, into England. The west door, into Red country. Or the south door—where did it lead?

Nevertheless, it was this time and place where she belonged. There was a carriage waiting for her, and work to do, stirring up war by encouraging compassion for the slaves. She could live with that, yes, as Becca had said. Didn't Jesus himself say that he came to bring, not peace, but war? Turning brother against brother? If that's what it takes to remove the stain of slavery from this land, then so be it. I speak only of peaceful change—if others choose to kill or die rather than let the slaves go free, that is their choice, and I didn't cause it.

Just as I didn't cause my mother to take up the gun and kill the Finder who was, after all, only obeying the law, unjust as the law might be. He wouldn't have found Arthur Stuart, hidden as he was in my house, his very smell changed by Alvin's Making, and his presence hidden behind all the hexes Alvin had put there. I didn't kill her. And even if I could have prevented what she did, it wouldn't have changed who she was. She was the woman who would make such a choice as that. That was the woman I loved, her fierce angry courage along with everything else. I am not guilty of her death. The man who shot her was. And she was the one, not I, who placed her in harm's way.

Peggy strode out into the sunlight feeling invigorated, light of step. The air tasted sweet to her. The place with no heartfires had rekindled her own.

She got back into the carriage and it took her without further distractions to an inn well north of Chapman Valley. She spent the night there, and then the next day rode on to

Baker's Fork. Once there, she held her master classes, teaching schoolmasters and gifted students, and in between conversing with this man or that woman about slavery, making comments, scorning those who mistreated slaves, declaring that as long as anyone had such power over other men and women, there would be mistreatment, and the only cure for it was for all men and women to be free. They nodded. They agreed. She spoke of the courage it would take, how the slaves themselves bore the lash and had lost all; how much would White men and women suffer in order to free them? What did Christ suffer, for the sake of others? It was a strong and measured performance that she gave. She did not retreat from it one bit, even though she knew now that it would lead to war. Wars have been fought for foolish causes. Let there be one, at last, in a good cause, if the enemies of decency refuse to soften their hearts.

Amid all the teaching and all the persuasion, she did find time, a scrap of an hour to herself, sitting at the writing desk in one old plantation widow's home. It was the very desk where, moments before, the woman had manumitted all her slaves and hired them on as free workingmen and workingwomen. Peggy saw in her heartfire when the choice was made that she would end up with her barns burnt and her fields spoiled. But she would lead these newfreed Blacks northward, despite all harassment and danger. Her courage would become legendary, a spark that would inspire other brave hearts. Peggy knew that in the end, the woman would not miss her fine house and lovely lands. And someday twenty thousand Black daughters would be given the woman's name. Why am I named Jane? they would ask their mothers. And the answer would come: Because once there was a woman by that name who freed her slaves and protected them all the way north, and then hired and looked after them until they learned the ways of free men and women and could stand on their own. It is a name of great honor. No one would know of the schoolteacher who came one day and gave open words to the secret longings of Jane's heart.

At that writing desk, Peggy took the time to write a letter and address it. Vigor Church, in the state of Wobbish. It would get to him, of course. As she sealed it, as she handed it over to the postal rider, she looked at long last toward the heartfire that she knew best, knew even better than her own. In it she saw the familiar possibilities, the dire consequences. But they were different now, because of the letter. Different . . . but better? She couldn't guess. She wasn't judge enough to know. Right and wrong were easy for her. But good and bad, better and worse, those were still too tricky. They kept sliding past each other strangely and changing before her eyes. Perhaps there was no judge who could know that; or if there was, he wasn't talking much about it.

The messenger took the letter and carried it north, where in another town he handed it to a rider who paid him what he thought the letter might be worth on delivery, minus half. The second rider took it on north, in his meandering route, and finally he stood in a store in the town of Vigor Church, where he asked about a man named Alvin Smith.

"I'm his brother-in-law," said the storekeeper. "Armor-of-God Weaver. I'll pay you for the letter. You don't want to go any farther into the town, or up there, either. You don't want to listen to the tale those people have to tell."

The tone of his voice convinced the rider. "Five dollars, then," he said.

"I'll wager you only paid the rider who gave it to you a single dollar, thinking the most you could get from me was two. But I'll pay you the five, if you still ask for it, because I'm willing to be cheated by a man who can live with himself after doing it. It's you that'll pay most, in the end."

"Two dollars, then," said the rider. "You didn't have to get personal about it."

Armor-of-God took out three silver dollars and laid them in the man's hand. "Thank you for honest riding, friend," he said. "You're always welcome here. Stay for dinner with us."

"No," the man said. "I'll be on my way."

As soon as he was gone, Armor-of-God laughed and told his wife, "He only paid fifty cents for that letter, I'll wager. So he still thinks he cheated me."

"You need to be more careful with our money, Armor," she answered.

"Two dollars to cause a man a little spiritual torment that perhaps could change his life for the better? Cheap enough bargain, I'd say. What is a soul worth to God? Two dollars, do you think?"

"I shudder to think what some men's souls will be marked down to when God decides to close the shop," said his wife. "I'll take the letter up to Mother's house. I'm going there today anyway."

"Measure's boy Simon comes down for the mail," said Armor-of-God.

She glared at him. "I wasn't going to read it."

"I didn't say you were." But still he didn't hand her the letter. Instead he laid it on the counter, waiting for Measure's oldest boy to come and fetch it up the hill to the house where Alvin was teaching people to be Makers. Armor-of-God still wasn't happy about it. It seemed unreligious to him, improper, against the Bible. And yet he knew Alvin was a good boy, grown to be a good man, and whatever powers of witchery he had, he didn't use them to do harm. Could it be truly against God and religion for him to have such powers, if he used them in a Christian way? After all, God created the world and all things in it. If God didn't want there to be Makers, he didn't have to create any of them.

So what Alvin was doing must be in line with the will of God.

Sometimes Armor-of-God felt perfectly at peace with Alvin's doings. And sometimes he thought that only a devil-blinded fool would think even for a moment that God was happy with any sort of witchery. But those were all just thoughts. When it came to action, Armor-of-God had made his decision. He was with Alvin, and against whoever opposed him. If he was damned for it, so be it. Sometimes you just had to follow your heart. And sometimes you just had to make up your mind and stick with it, come hell or high water.

And nobody was going to mess with Alvin's letter from Peggy Larner. Especially not Armor-of-God's wife, who was a good deal too clever with hexery herself.

Far away in another place, Peggy saw the changes in the heartfires and knew the letter was now in Alvin's family. It would do its work. The world would change. The threads in Becca's loom would move. It is unbearable to watch without meddling, thought Peggy. And then it is unbearable to watch what my meddling causes.

4

QUEST

Even before Miss Larner's letter came, Alvin was feeling antsy. Things just wasn't going the way he planned. After months of trying to turn his family and neighbors into Makers, it was looking like a job for six lifetimes, and try as he might, Alvin couldn't figure out how he was going to have more than one lifetime to work with.

Not that the teaching was a failure—he couldn't call it an

outright bust, not yet, considering that some of them really were learning how to do some small Makings. It's just that Making wasn't their knack. Alvin had figured out that there wasn't no knack that another person couldn't learn, given time and training and wit enough and plain old stick-to-it-iveness. But what he hadn't taken into account was that Making was like a whole bunch of knacks, and while some of them could grasp this or that little bit of it, there was hardly any who seemed to show a sign of grasping the whole of it. Measure sometimes showed a glimmer. More than a glimmer, really. He could probably be a Maker himself if only he didn't keep getting distracted. But the others—there was no way they were going to be anything like what Alvin was. So if there was no hope of success, what was the point of trying?

Whenever he got to feeling discouraged like that, though, he'd just tell himself to shut his mouth and stick to his work. You don't get to be a Maker by changing your plan every few minutes. Who can follow you then? You stick to it. Even when Calvin, the only natural born Maker among them, even when he refused to learn anything and finally took himself off to do who knows what sort of mischief in the wide world, even then you don't give up and go off in search of him because, as Measure pointed out to the men who wanted to get up a search party, "You can't force a man to be a Maker, because forcing folks to do things is to Unmake them."

Even when Alvin's own father said, "Al, I marvel at what you can do, but it's enough for me that you can do it. My part was done when you were born, it seems to me. Ain't no man alive but what he isn't proud to have his son pass him up, which you done handily, and I don't aim to get back into the race." Even then, Alvin determined grimly to go on teaching while his father went back to the mill and began to clean it up and get it ready to grind again.

"I can't figure out," said Father, "if my milling is Making or Unmaking. The stones grind the grain and break it apart into dust, so that's Unmaking. But the dust is flour, and you can use it to make bread and cake that the maize or wheat can't be made into, so milling might be just a step along the road to Making. Can you answer me that, Alvin? Is grinding flour Making or Unmaking?"

Well, Alvin could answer it glib enough, that it was Making for sure, but it kept nagging at him, that question. I set out to make Makers out of these people, my family, my neighbors. But am I really just grinding them up and Unmaking them? Before I started trying to teach them, they were all content with their own knacks or even their own lack of a knack, when you come down to it. Now they're frustrated and they feel like failures and why? Is it Making to turn people into something that they weren't born to be? To be a Maker is good—I know it, because I am one. But does that mean it's the only good thing to be?

He asked Taleswapper about it, of course. After all, Taleswapper didn't show up for no reason, even if the old coot had no notion what the reason was himself. Maybe he was there to give Alvin some answers. So one day when the two of them were chopping wood out back, he asked, and Taleswapper answered like he always did, with a story.

"I heard a tale once about how a man who was building a wall as fast as he could, but somebody else was tearing it down faster than he could build it up. And he wondered how he could keep the wall from being torn down completely, let alone ever finish it. And the answer was easy: You can't build it alone."

"I remember that tale," said Alvin. "That tale is why I'm here, trying to teach these folks Making."

"I just wonder," said Taleswapper, "if you might be able to stretch that story, or maybe twist it a little and wring a bit more useful truth out of it."

"Wring away," said Alvin. "We'll find out whether the story is a wet cloth or a chicken's neck when you're done wringing."

"Well maybe what you need isn't a bunch of other stone-masons, cutting the stone and mixing the mortar and plumbing the wall and all those jobs. Maybe what you need is just a lot of cutters, and a lot of mortar mixers, and a lot of surveyors, and so on. Not everybody has to be a Maker. In fact, maybe all you need is just the one Maker."

The truth of what Taleswapper was saying was obvious; it had already occurred to Alvin many times, in other guises. What took him by surprise was how tears suddenly came to his own eyes, and he said softly, "Why does that make me so desperate sad, my friend?"

"Because you're a good man," said Taleswapper. "An evil man would delight to find out that he was the only one who could rule over a great many people working in a common cause."

"More than anything I don't want to be alone anymore," said Alvin. "I've been alone. Almost my whole time as a prentice in Hatrack River, I felt like there was nobody to take my part."

"But you were never alone the whole time," said Taleswapper.

"If you mean Miss Larner looking out for me—"

"Peggy is who I meant. I can't see why you still call her by that false name."

"That's the name of the woman I fell in love with," said Alvin. "But she knows my heart. She knows I killed that man and I didn't have to."

"The man who murdered her mother? I don't think she holds it against you."

"She knows what kind of man I am and she doesn't love

me, that's what," said Alvin. "So I *am* alone, the minute I leave this place. And besides, leaving here is like lining up all these people and slapping their faces and saying, You failed so I'm gone."

At that Taleswapper just laughed. "That is plain foolishness and you know it. Truth is you've already taught them everything, and now it's just a matter of practice. They don't need you here anymore."

"But nobody needs me anywhere else," said Alvin.

Taleswapper laughed again.

"Stop laughing and tell me what's funny."

"A joke you have to explain isn't going to be funny anyway," said Taleswapper, "so there ain't no point in explaining it."

"You're no help," said Alvin, burying the head of his axe in the chopping stump.

"I'm a great help," said Taleswapper. "You just don't want to be helped yet."

"Yes I do! I just don't need riddles, I need answers!"

"You need somebody to tell you what to do? That's a surprise. Still an apprentice then, after all? Want to turn your life over to somebody else? For how long, another seven years?"

"I may not be a prentice anymore," said Alvin, "but that don't mean I'm a master. I'm just a journeyman."

"Then hire on somewhere," said Taleswapper. "You've still got things to learn."

"I know," said Alvin. "But I don't know where to go to learn it. There's that crystal city I saw in the twister with Tenskwa-Tawa. I don't know how to build it. I don't know *where* to build it. I don't even know *why* to build it, except that it ought to exist and I ought to make it exist."

"There you are," said Taleswapper. "Like I said, you've already taught everybody here everything you know, twice over. All you're doing now is helping them practice—and cheating now and then by helping them, don't think I haven't noticed."

"When I use my knack to help them, I tell them I helped," said Alvin, blushing.

"And then they feel like failures anyway, figuring that your help was all that made anything happen, and nothing of their own doing. Alvin, I think I *am* giving you your answer. You've done what you can here. Leave Measure to help them, and the others who've learned a bit of it here and there. Let them work things out on their own, the way you did. Then you go out into the world and learn more of the things you need to know."

Alvin nodded, but in his heart he still refused to believe it. "I just can't see what good it is to go out to try to learn when you know as well as I do there's not another Maker in the world right now, unless you count Calvin which I don't. Who am I going to learn from? Where am I going to go?"

"So you're saying that there's no use in just wandering around, seeing what happens and learning as you can?"

Taleswapper's face was so wry as he said this that Alvin knew at once there was a double meaning. "Just because *you* learn that way doesn't mean *I* can. You're just collecting stories, and there's stories everywhere."

"There's Making almost everywhere, too," said Taleswapper. "And where there isn't Making, there's still old made things being torn down, and you can learn from them, too."

"I can't go," said Alvin. "I can't go."

"Which is to say, you're afraid."

Alvin nodded.

"You're afraid you'll kill again."

"I don't think so. I know I won't. Probably."

"You're afraid you'll fall in love again."

Alvin hooted derisively.

"You're afraid you'll be alone out there."

"How could I be alone?" he asked. "I'd have my golden plow with me."

"That's another thing," said Taleswapper. "That living plow. What did you make it for, if you keep it in darkness all the time and never use it?"

"It's gold," said Alvin. "People want to steal it. Many a man would kill for that much gold."

"Many a man would kill for that much tin, for that matter," said Taleswapper. "But you remember what happened to the man who was given a talent of gold, and buried it in the earth."

"Taleswapper, you're plumb full of wisdom today."

"Brimming over," said Taleswapper. "It's my worst fault, splashing wisdom all over other people. But most of the time it dries up real fast and doesn't leave a stain."

Alvin grimaced at him. "Taleswapper, I'm not ready to leave home yet."

"Maybe folks have to leave home *before* they're ready, or they never get ready at all."

"Was that a paradox, Taleswapper? Miss Larner taught me about paradox."

"She's a fine teacher and she knows all about it."

"All I know about paradox is that if you don't shovel it out of the stable, the barn gets to stinking real bad and fills up with flies."

Taleswapper laughed at that, and Alvin joined in laughing, and that was the end of the serious part of the conversation. Only it clung to Alvin, the whole thing, knowing that Taleswapper thought he should leave home, and him not having a clue where he would go if he did leave, and not being willing to admit failure, either. All kinds of reasons for staying. Most important reason of all was simply being home. He'd spent half his childhood away from his family, and it was good to sit down at his mother's table every day. Good to see his father standing at the mill. Hear his father's voice, his brothers' voices, his sisters' voices laughing and quarreling and telling and asking, his mother's voice, his mother's sharp sweet voice, all of them covering his days and nights like a blanket, keeping him warm, all of them saying to him, You're safe here, you're known here, we're your people, we won't turn on you. Alvin had never heard him a symphony in his life, or even more than two fiddles and a banjo at the same time, but he knew that no orchestra could ever make a music more beautiful than the voices of his family moving in and out of their houses and barns and the millhouse and the shops in town, threads of music binding him to this place so that even though he knew Taleswapper was right and he ought to leave, he couldn't bring himself to go.

How did Calvin ever do it? How did Calvin leave this music behind him?

Then Miss Larner's letter came.

Measure's boy Simon brought it, him being five now and old enough to run down to Armor-of-God's store to pick up the post. He could do his letters now, too, so he didn't just give the letter over to his grandma or grandpa, he took it right to Alvin himself and announced at the top of his lungs, "It's from a woman! She's called Miss Larner and she makes real purty letters!"

"*Pretty* letters," Alvin corrected him.

Simon wasn't to be fooled. "Oh, Uncle Al, you're the only person around here as says it like that! I'd be plumb silly to fall for a joke like that!"

Alvin pried up the sealing wax and unfolded the letter. He knew her handwriting from the many hours he had tried to imitate it, studying with her back in Hatrack River. His hand was never as smooth, could never flow the way hers did. Nor was he as eloquent. Words weren't his gift, or at

least not the formal, elegant words Miss Larner—Peggy—
used in writing.

> *Dear Alvin,*
>
> *You've overstayed in Vigor Church. Calvin's a great
> danger to you, and you must go find him and reconcile
> with him; if you wait for him to come back to you, he
> will bring the end of your life with him.*
>
> *I can almost hear you answer me: I ain't afraid to see
> my life end. (I know you still say ain't, just to spite me.)
> Go or stay, that's up to you. But I can tell you this. Ei-
> ther you will go now, of your own free will, or you will
> go soon anyway, but not freely. You're a journeyman
> smith—you will have your journey.*
>
> *Perhaps in your travels we shall encounter each other.
> It would please me to see you again.*
>
> > *Sincerely,*
> > *Peggy*

Alvin had no idea what to make of this letter. First she
bosses him around like a schoolboy. Then she talks teas-
ingly about how he still says *ain't.* Then she as much as asks
him to come to her, but in such a cold way as to chill him
to the bone—"It would please me to see you again" indeed!
Who did she think she was, the Queen? And she signed the
letter "sincerely" as if she was a stranger, and not the woman
that he loved, and that once said she loved him. What was she
playing at, this woman who could see so many futures?
What was she trying to get him to do? It was plain there was
more going on than she was saying in her letter. She thought
she was so wise, since she knew more about the future than
other folks, but the fact was that she could make mistakes
like anybody else and he didn't want her telling him what

to *do,* he wanted her to tell him what she *knew* and let him make up his own mind.

One thing was certain. He wasn't going to drop everything and take off in search of Calvin. No doubt she knew exactly where he was and she hadn't bothered to tell him. What was *that* supposed to accomplish? Why should he go off searching for Calvin when she could send him a letter and tell him, not where Calvin was right now, but where Calvin would *be* by the time Alvin caught up with him? Only a fool takes off on foot trying to follow the flight of a wild goose.

I know I've got to leave here sometime. But I'm not going to leave in order to chase down Calvin. And I'm not going to leave because the woman I almost married sends me a bossy letter that doesn't even hint that she still loves me, if she ever really did. If Peggy was so sure that he'd go soon anyway, because he had to, well, then he might as well just wait around and see what it was that would make him go.

5

TWIST

America was too small a country for Calvin. He knew that now. It was all too new. The powers of a land took time to ripen. The Reds, they knew the land, but they were gone. And the Whites and Blacks who lived here now, they had only shallow powers, knacks and hexes, spells and dreams. Nothing like the ancient music that Alvin had talked about. The greensong of the living forest. Besides, the Reds were gone, so whatever it was they knew, it must have been weak. Failure was proof enough of that.

Even before Calvin knew in his mind where he was headed, his feet knew. East. Sometimes a bit north, sometimes a bit south, but always east. At first he thought he was just going to Dekane, but when he got there he just worked for a day or two to get a bit of coin and some bread in his belly, and then he was off over the mountains, following the new railroad into Irrakwa, where he could sneer a little at men and women who were Red in body but White in dress and speech and soul. More work, more coin, more practice at using his Making here and there. Pranks, mostly, because he didn't dare use his knack out in the open where folks would take notice and spread word of him. Just little favors for houses where they treated him good, like driving all the mice and roaches off their property. And a little bit of getting even with those who turned him away. Sending a rat to die in a well. Causing a leak in the roof over a flour barrel. That one was hard, making the wood swell and then shrink. But he could work with the water. The water lent itself to his use better than any other element.

Turned out that Irrakwa wasn't where his feet were taking him, either. He worked his way across Irrakwa to New Holland, where the farmers all spoke Dutch, and then down the Hudson to New Amsterdam.

He thought when he came to the great city on the tip of Manhattan Island that this might be the place he was looking for. Biggest city in the U.S.A. And it wasn't hardly Dutch anymore. Everybody spoke English for business, and on top of that Calvin counted a dozen languages before he stopped caring how many. Not to mention strange accents of English from places like York and Glasgow and Monmouth. Surely all the lores of the world were gathered here. Surely he could find teachers.

So he stayed for days, for a week. He tried the college farther up the island, but they wanted him to study intellectual things instead of the lore of power, and soon enough Calvin figured out that none of them high-toned professors knew anything useful anyhow. They treated him like he was crazy. One old coot with a white goat-beard spent half an hour trying to convince Calvin to let the man study *him,* like as if he was some strange specimen of bug. Calvin only stayed for the whole half hour so he'd have time to loosen all the bindings of all the books on the man's shelves. Let him wonder about Calvin's kind of madness as the pages of every book he picked up fell out and scattered on the floor.

If the professors weren't worth nothing, the street wasn't much better. Oh, he heard about loremasters and wizards and such. Gypsies bragged on some cursemonger. Irishmen knew of a priest who had special ways. Frenchmen and Spaniards heard of witches or child-saints or whatever. One Portugee told of a free Black woman who could make your enemy's crotch turn as smooth and blank as an armpit— which, according to the story, was how she got her freedom, after doing that to her master's firstborn son and threatening to do it next to him. But every one of them kept retreating out of sight. He'd find out who knew the loremaster, and then go to that person and find out that he only knew somebody else who knew the powerful one, and so on and so on, like constables searching through the night for a fugitive who kept slipping away into alleys.

In the meantime, though, Calvin learned to live in a city and he liked it. He liked the way that you could disappear right out in the open. Nobody knew you. Nobody expected anything from you. You were what you wore. When he arrived he dressed like a rube from the country, and so people expected him to be stupid and awkward and, what the hell, he was. But in a few days he realized how his clothes gave him away and he bought some city garb from a used-garment house. That was when people started being willing to talk to him. And he learned to change his speech a little, too. Talk faster, get rid of some of the drawl. Shake off the country twang. He knew he gave himself away with every word he said, but he was getting better. People didn't ask him to repeat himself as much. And by the end of the week, he was no more out of place than any of the other immigrants. That was as good as it got—it wasn't as if anybody was actually *from* New Amsterdam. Except maybe for some old Dutch landlords hiding in their mansions up-island.

Rumors of wisdom, but no wisdom to be had in this town. Well, what did he expect? Anybody who really knew the powers of the old world would hardly have to board some miserable boat and sail west at risk of life and limb in order to come live in some sinkhole of a slum in New Amsterdam. No, the people of Europe who understood power were still in Europe—because they were running things there, and didn't have no reason to leave.

And who was the most powerful one of all? Why, the man whose victories had caused all these people of the dozen languages to flock to American shores. The man who drove the aristocrats out of France, and then conquered Spain and the Holy Roman Empire and Italy and Austria and then for some reason stopped at the Russian border and the English Channel, declared peace and held on, iron-fisted but, as they said, tenderhearted, so that pretty soon nobody in Italy or Austria or the low countries or anywhere, really, was wishing for their old rulers to come back. That was the man who understood power. That was the man who was fit to teach Calvin what he needed to know.

Only trouble was, why would a man so powerful ever agree to speak to a poor farmboy from Wobbish? And how was that poor farmboy ever going to find passage across the ocean? If only Alvin had bothered to teach him how to turn iron into gold. Now *that* would be useful. Imagine a whole steam locomotive turned to solid gold. Fire up the engine and the whole damn thing would melt down—but it would melt down into pools of gold. Just put in a dipper and draw it out and there was passage to France, and not in no steerage, neither. First-class passage, and a fine hotel in Paris. Fine clothes, too, so that when he walked into the American embassy the flunkies would bow and scrape and take him straight to the ambassador and the ambassador would take him straight to the imperial palace where he would be presented to Napoleon himself and Napoleon would say, Why should I meet with you, an ordinary citizen of a second-rate country in the wild lands of the west? And Calvin would take three dipperfuls of gold out of his pockets and set them heavily in Napoleon's hands and say, How much of this do you want? I know how to make more. And Napoleon would say, I have all the taxes of Europe to buy me gold. What do I need with your pathetic handfuls? And Calvin would say, Now you have a bit more gold than you had before. Look at your buttons, sir. And Napoleon would look at the brass buttons on his coat and they would be gold, too, and he would say, What do you want from me, sir? That's right, he'd call Calvin "sir" and Calvin would say, All I want is for you to teach me the ways of power.

Only if Calvin knew how to turn iron or brass into gold, he sure as hell wouldn't need no help from Napoleon Bonaparte, Emperor of Earth or whatever fool title the man had given himself in his latest promotion. It was one of those circular dilemmas that he always kept running into. If he had enough power to attract Napoleon's attention, he wouldn't need Napoleon. And, because he needed Napoleon, there was no chance that any of his underlings would let Calvin come anywhere near him.

Calvin wasn't stupid. He wasn't no rube, whatever the city

people thought. He knew that powerful men didn't let just anybody come in and chat.

But I do have some powers, thought Calvin. I do have some powers, and I can wangle a way, once I get across the pond. That's what the sophisticated people called the Atlantic Ocean—the pond. Once I get across the pond. Might have to learn French, but they say Napoleon speaks English, too, from his days as a general in Canada. One way or another, I'll get to see him and he'll take me on as his apprentice. Not apprenticed like to take over his empire after him, but instead to do the same thing in America. Bring the Crown Colonies and New England and the United States all under one flag. And Canada, too. And Florida. And then maybe he'd turn his eyes across the Mizzipy and see how good a job old Tenskwa-Tawa would do at holding back a *Maker* who wanted to cross and conquer Red country.

All dreams. All stupid foolish dreams of a boy sleeping in a cheap boardinghouse and doing lousy odd jobs to earn a few cents a day. Calvin knew that, but he also knew that if he couldn't turn a knack like his into money and power he didn't deserve nothing better than those lousy beds and wormy meals and backbreaking jobs.

One thing, though. Folks on the street were getting used to the idea that Calvin was searching for something, and finally the old woman he bought apples from—the one who'd given him an apple his first day there when he was out of money, since she was a country girl herself, she said; the one who from that day to this found no more worms or flies in her fruit—she said to him, "Well I hope you've talked to the Bloody Man, he knows stuff."

"Bloody Man?"

"You know, the one as tells horrible stories or when he can't find nobody new to tell it to, his hands are dripping with blood. Everybody knows the Bloody Man. He come here because the curse on him is, he has to find new people every day to tell his story to, and where you going to find a good supply of new people all the time?"

Of course Calvin knew by now exactly who she was talking about. "Harrison is *here?*"

"You know him?"

"Know *of* him. He called hisself—himself—governor of Wobbish for a while. Slaughtered Tenskwa-Tawa's people at Tippy-Canoe."

"That's the one. Dreadful story. Thank heaven I only had to hear it the once. But there's some kind of power in the fact that his hands get all bloody. I mean, that's strange, ain't it? All them other folks you hear about, you never actually see them do nothing, if you know what I mean. But you can see the blood. That's power, I reckon."

"Reckon so." Again he corrected himself. "I think so."

"Might as well say, 'I imagine so,' if you're trying to get all highfalutin."

"Just don't want to sound country, that's all."

"Then you'd better learn French. All the high-tone folks do. Here we are in a Dutch city where everybody speaks English, and they go into their toney restaurants and order their food in French! What did the *French* ever have to do with New Amsterdam? You want to eat in French, you go to Canada, that's what I say!"

He listened to her diatribe until he could finally get free—which meant when she finally got a customer—and then he set out to find Harrison. White Murderer Harrison. Calvin knew all about the curse on him, from the stories told by his own father and neighbors, and he'd sometimes imagined Harrison walking country roads from town to town, folks throwing him out before he could come in and start telling his awful tale. It never occurred to him that Harrison would come to the city, but it made sense, once you thought about it. Bloody Man.

He found him in an alleyway behind a restaurant where he got fed every night by a manager who didn't want him accosting his customers. "It's a stiff punishment," said the manager. "I had a landlord in Kilkenny who believed in that kind of justice. Punishments that went on forever. Permanent shame. I think it's wrong. I don't care much what the man did. Let him without sin among you, and all that. So he eats back of my restaurant. Long as he doesn't hurt trade."

"Aren't you the generous one," said Calvin.

"You got a mouth on you, boy. In fact I *am* generous, and open-minded, too, and just because I know it and take credit for it doesn't make it any less true. So you can take your little winking sort of wit and leave my establishment if you're going to eat my food and then sit in judgment on me."

"I haven't eaten your food."

"But you will," said the man, "because, as I said, I *am* generous, and you look hungry. Now get back to the kitchen and you can tell the cook to give you something for yourself and something for Bloody Man out in the alley. If you come with his food, he'll talk to you, right enough. He'll probably tell you his story, for that matter."

"I know his story."

"Everybody might know a story, but it's never the same story they know. Now get away from my door, you look like a street rat."

Calvin looked down at his clothes and realized, yes, he had bought clothing to blend in, but what he blended in with was the street, not the city. He'd have to do something about that before he went to Paris. Have to become, if not a gentleman, then at least a tradesman. Not a street rat.

He didn't like people who called themselves generous,

but the fact was the food in the kitchen was good. The cook didn't give him no scraps or scrapings. He got food that was decent and there was plenty. How did this manager stay in business, being so generous to the poor? No doubt he was cheating his boss. He could afford to be generous, since he didn't have to pay for it himself. Most virtues were like that. People could take pride in how virtuous they were, but the fact was that as soon as virtue got expensive or inconvenient, it was amazing how fast it gave way to practical concerns.

The man's generosity got him this much: No roaches or mice in his kitchen.

Out in the alleyway, Bloody Man was sipping from a wine bottle. He saw Calvin and his eyes went hungry. Calvin laughed. "I hear you've got a story to tell."

"They still sending boys like you to find me, as a prank?"

"No prank. I know your story, mostly. Just wanted to meet you my own self, I guess."

Harrison offered him the wine bottle. "Best thing about this place," he said. "Besides that they don't run me off in the first place. When somebody opens a bottle of wine and doesn't finish it at the table, the manager refuses to pour from that bottle to anyone else. So it comes out into the alley."

"The big surprise," said Calvin, "is that there ain't ten dozen other hungry drunks here."

Harrison laughed. "They used to. But they got sick of hearing me tell my story and now I have the alley to myself. That's how I like it."

But Calvin could hear it in his voice that it was a lie. He didn't like it that way. He was hungry for company.

"Might as well start telling me the story. Between bites, if you want," said Calvin.

Harrison started eating. Calvin could see a remnant of table manners. Once he had been a civilized man.

Between bites, Harrison told the tale. All of it: How he had some Reds from south of the Hio come and kidnap two White boys in order to blame it on Tenskwa-Tawa, the so-called Red Prophet. Only the boys were rescued somehow and fell in with the Prophet's brother, Ta-Kumsaw. But that didn't matter because Harrison still used the kidnapping to rile up the White folks in the northern part of Wobbish, the ones as lived nearest to the Prophet's village at Tippy-Canoe. So Harrison was able to raise an army to go wipe out Prophetstown. And then at the last minute, who shows up but one of the kidnapped boys. Well, Harrison sees nothing for it but to have the boy killed, and everything seems to be working. The Reds just stand there, letting the musketfire and the grapeshot mow them down until nine out of ten of them was dead, the whole meadow a sheet of blood flowing down into the Tippy-Canoe, only it was too much for those White men—they *called* themselves men—because they all stopped shooting before the job was done, and then up comes that boy who was supposed to be dead and he wasn't even injured, and he tells the truth to everybody and then the Red Prophet puts a curse on all of them there and the worst curse on Harrison, including that he has to tell a new person every day and . . .

"You're telling it all wrong," said Calvin.

Harrison looked at him angrily. "You think after all these years I don't know how to tell the tale? If I tell it any other way, I get blood on my hands and believe me, it looks bad. People throw up when they see me. Looks like I stuck my hands in a corpse up to my elbows."

"Telling it *your* way has you living in an alley, eating from charity and drinking leftover wine," said Calvin.

Harrison squinted at him. "Who *are* you?"

"The boy you tried to kill is my brother Measure. The other boy you had them kidnap is my brother Alvin."

"And you came to gloat?"

"Do I look like I'm gloating? No, I left home because I got sick of their righteousness, knowing everything and not having respect for nobody else."

Harrison winked. "I never liked people like that."

"You want to hear how you *ought* to tell your tale?"

"I'm listening."

"The Reds were at war with the Whites. They weren't using the land but they didn't want White farmers to use it, either. They just couldn't share even though there was plenty of room. Tenskwa-Tawa claimed to be peaceful, but you knew that he was gathering all those thousands of Reds together in order to be Ta-Kumsaw's army. You had to do *something* to rile up the Whites there to put a stop to this menace. So yes, you had two boys kidnapped, but you never gave orders for anybody to be killed—"

"If I say *that* the blood just leaps onto my hands on the spot—"

"I'm sure you've thought of all the possible lies, but hear me out," said Calvin.

"Go on."

"You didn't order anybody killed. That was just lies your enemies told about you. Lies originating with Alvin Miller Junior, now called Alvin Smith. After all, Alvin was the Boy Renegado, the White boy who went everywhere with Ta-Kumsaw for a year. He was Ta-Kumsaw's friend—we'll use the word *friend* because we're in decent company—so of course he lied about you. It was your battle at Tippy-Canoe that broke the back of Ta-Kumsaw's plans. If you hadn't struck then and there, Ta-Kumsaw would have been victorious later at Fort Detroit, and Ta-Kumsaw would have driven all the civilized folks out of the land west of the Appalachees and Red armies would be descending on the cities of the east, raiding out of the mountains and—why, thanks to you and your courage at Tippy-Canoe, the Reds have been driven west of the Mizzipy. You opened up all the western lands to safe colonization."

"My hands would be dripping before I said all that."

"So what? Hold them up and say, 'Look what the Red Witch Tenskwa-Tawa did to punish me. He covered my hands with blood. But I'm glad to pay that price. The blood on my hands is the reason why White men are building civilization right to the shores of the Mizzipy. The blood on my hands is the reason why people in the east can sleep easy at night, without so much as a thought about Reds coming and raping and killing the way those savages always did.'"

Harrison chuckled. "Every word you've said is the profoundest bull hockey, my boy, I hope you know that."

"You just need to decide whether you're going to let Tenskwa-Tawa have the final victory over you."

"Why are you telling me this? What's in it for you?"

"I don't know. I came looking for you thinking you might know something of power, but when I heard you tell that weasely weakling tale I knew that you didn't know nothing that a *man* could use. In fact, I knew more than *you.* So, seeing how I was going to ask you to share, it seemed only fair to share right back."

"How kind of you." His sarcasm was inescapable.

"I don't think so. I just picture the look on my brother Alvin's face when you tell everbody he was the Boy Renegado. You say *that,* and nobody'll believe him if he testifies against you. In fact, he'll have to hide himself, when you think of all the terrible things folks believe about the Boy Renegado. How he was the cruelest Red of them all, killing and torturing so even the Shaw-Nee puked."

"I remember those tales."

"You hold up those bloody hands, my friend, and then make them mean what *you* want them to mean."

Harrison shook his head. "I can't live with the blood."

"So you *have* a conscience, eh?"

Harrison laughed. "The blood gets in my *food*. It stains my clothes. It makes people sick."

"If I were you, I'd eat with gloves on and I'd wear dark clothes."

Harrison was through eating. So was Calvin.

"So you want me to do this to hurt your brother."

"Not hurt him. Just keep him silent and out of sight. You've spent, what, eight years living like a dog. Now it's his turn."

"There's no going back," said Harrison. "Once I tell lies, I'll have bloody hands till the day I die."

Calvin shrugged. "Harrison, you're a liar and a murderer, but you love power more than life. Unfortunately you're piss-poor at getting it and keeping it. Ta-Kumsaw and Alvin and Tenskwa-Tawa played you for a sucker. I'm telling you how to undo what they done to you. How to set yourself free. I don't give a rat's front teeth whether you do what I said or not." He got up to go.

Harrison half-rose and clutched at Calvin's pantlegs. "Someone told me that Alvin, he's a Maker. That he has real power."

"No he doesn't," said Calvin. "Not for you to worry about. Because, you see, my friend, he can only use his power for *good,* never to harm nobody."

"Not even me?"

"Maybe he'll make an exception for you." Calvin grinned wickedly. "I know *I* would."

Harrison withdrew his hands from Calvin's clothing. "Don't look at me like that, you little weasel."

"Like what?" asked Calvin.

"Like I'm scum. Don't *you* judge *me*."

"Can you tell me a single good reason why not?"

"Because whatever else I did, boy, I never betrayed my own brother."

Now it was Calvin's turn to look into the face of contempt. He spat on the ground near Harrison's knees. "Eat pus and die," he said.

"Was that a curse?" asked Harrison jeeringly as Calvin walked away. "Or merely a friendly warning?"

Calvin didn't answer him. He was already thinking of other things. How to raise the money to get passage east, for one thing. First class. He was going to go first class. Maybe what he needed to do was see if his knack extended to causing money to fall out of some shopkeeper's money-bag as he carried his earnings to the bank. If he did it right, no one would see. He wouldn't get caught. And even if someone saw the money fall out and him pick it up, they could only accuse him of finding dropped money, since he never laid a hand on the bag. That would work. It would be easy enough. So easy that it was stupid that Alvin had never done it before. The family could have used the money. There were some hard years. But Alvin was too selfish ever to think of anybody but himself, or anything but his stupid plan of trying to teach Making to people with no knack for it.

First-class passage to England, and from there across the channel to France. New clothes. It wouldn't take much to get that kind of money. A lot of money changed hands in New Amsterdam, and there was nothing to stop some of it from falling onto the street at Calvin's feet. God had given him the power, and that meant that it must be the will of God for him to do it.

Wouldn't it be a hoot if Harrison actually took Calvin's advice?

6

TRUE LOVE

Amy Sump didn't care what her friends or anybody said. What she felt for Alvin Maker was love. Real love. True, deep, abiding love that would withstand the test of time.

If only he would pay any attention to her openly, so others could see it. Instead all he ever did was give her those glances that made her heart flutter so within her. She worried sometimes that maybe it was just his Makerness, his knack or whatever it was. Worried that he was somehow reaching inside her chest and making her heart turn over and her whole body quiver. But no, that wasn't the sort of thing that Makers did. In fact maybe he didn't even *know* about her love for him. Maybe his glances were really searching looks, hoping to see in her face some sign of her love. That was why she no longer tried to hide her maidenly blushes when her heart beat so fast and her face felt all hot and tingly. Let him see how his gaze transforms me into a quivering mass of devoted worshipfulness.

How Amy longed to go to the teaching sessions where Alvin worked with a dozen or so grownups at once, telling them how a Maker had to see the world. How she would love to hear his voice for hours on end. Then she would discover the true knack within her, and both she and her beloved Alvin would rejoice to discover that she was secretly a Maker herself, so that the two of them together would be able to remake the world and fight off the evil nasty Unmaker together. Then they would have a dozen babies, all of them Makers twice over, and the love of Alvin and Amy Maker would be sung for a thousand generations throughout the whole world, or at least America, which was pretty much the same thing as far as Amy cared.

But Amy's parents wouldn't let her go. "How could Alvin possibly concentrate on teaching anybody anything with you making cow-eyes at him the whole time?" her mother said, the heartless old hag. Not as cruel as her father, though, telling her, "Get some control over yourself, girl! Or I'm going to have to get you some love diapers to keep you from embarrassing yourself in public. Love diapers, do you understand me?" Oh, she understood him, the nasty man. Him of the cranks and pulleys, pipes and cables. Him of pumps and engines and machinery, who had no understanding of the human heart. "The heart's just a pump itself, my girl," he said, which showed him to be a deeply totally impossibly eternally abysmally ignorant machine of a man his own self but said nothing about the truth of the universe. It was her beloved Alvin who understood that all things were alive and had feelings—all things *except* her father's hideous dead machines, chugging away like walking corpses. A steam-powered lumbermill! Using fire and water to cut wood! What an abomination before the Lord! When she and Alvin were married, she'd get Alvin to stop her father from making any more machines that roared and hissed and chugged and gave off the heat of hell. Alvin would keep her in a sylvan wonderland where the birds were friends and the bugs didn't bite and they could swim naked together in clear pools of water and he would swim to her in real life instead of just in her dreams and he would reach out and embrace her and their naked bodies would touch under the water and their flesh would meet and join and . . .

"No such thing," said her friend Ramona.

Amy felt herself grow hot with anger. Who was Ramona to decide what was real and what wasn't? Couldn't Amy tell her dreams to *somebody* without having to keep saying it was just a dream instead of pretending that it was real, that his arms had been around her? Didn't she remember it as clearly—no, far *more* clearly—than anything that had ever happened to her in real life?

"Did so happen. In the moonlight."

"When!" said Ramona, her voice dripping with contempt.

"Three nights ago. When Alvin *said* he was going out into the woods to be alone. He was really going to be with me."

"Well where is there a pool of clear water like that? Nothing like that around here, just rivers and streams, and you *know* Alvin never goes into the Hatrack to swim or nothing."

"Don't you know *anything?*" said Amy, trying to match her best friend's disdain. "Haven't you heard of the green-song? How Alvin learned from them old Reds how to run through the forest like the wind, silent and not even so much as bending a branch? He can run a hundred miles in an hour, faster than any railroad train. It wasn't any kind of pool around *here,* it was so far away that it would take anybody from Vigor Church three days to get there on a good horse!"

"Now I know you're just lying," said Ramona.

"He can do that *any day,*" insisted Amy hotly.

"*He* can, but *you* can't. You screech when you brush up into a spiderweb, you dunce."

"I'm not a dunce I'm the best student in the school *you're* the dunce," said Amy all in a breath—it was an epigram she had often used before. "I held Alvin's *hand* is what, and he carried me along, and then when I got tired he picked me up in those blacksmith's arms of his and carried me."

"And then I'm *sure* he really took off all his clothes and you took off all of yours, like you was a couple of weasels or something."

"Muskrats. Otters. Creatures of water. It wasn't nakedness, it was naturalness, the freeness of two kindred souls who have no secrets from each other."

"Well, what a bunch of beautifulness," said Ramona. "Only I think if it really happened it would be *disgustingness* and *revoltingness,* him coming up and hugging you in your complete and utter *starkersness.*"

Amy knew that Ramona was making fun of her but she wasn't sure why making up words like *disgustingness* made the idiotic girl laugh and almost fall off the tree branch where they were sitting.

"You have no appreciation of beauty."

"You have no appreciation of *truth,*" said Ramona. "Or should I say, of 'truthfulness.'"

"You calling me a liar?" said Amy, giving her a little push.

"Hey!" cried Ramona. "No fair! I'm farther out on the branch so there's nothing for me to grab onto."

Amy pushed her again, harder, and Ramona wobbled, her eyes growing wide as she clutched at the branch.

"Stop it you little liar!" cried Ramona. "I'll tell what lies you've been saying."

"They *aren't* lies," said Amy. "I remember it as clearly as . . . as clearly as the sunlight over the fields of green corn."

"As clearly as the grunting of the hogs in my father's sty," said Ramona, in a voice that matched Amy's for dreaminess.

"Of course true love would be beyond your ability to imagine."

"Yes, my imaginingness is the epitaph of feebleness."

"Epitome, not epitaph," Amy said.

"Oh, if only I could have your sublimeness of correctness, your wiseness."

"Stop *ness*ing all the time."

"*You* stop."

"I don't do that."

"Do so."

"Do not."

"Eat worms," said Ramona.

"On brain salad," said Amy. And now that they were back to familiar playful argument, they both broke into laughter and talked about other things for a while.

And if things had stayed that way, maybe nothing would have happened. But on the way back home in the gathering dusk, Ramona asked one last time, "Amy, telling truth, cross your heart, friend to friend, swear to heaven, remember forever, tell me that you didn't really actually with your own flesh and blood go swimming naked with Alvin Smith—"

"Alvin *Maker.*"

"Tell me it was a dream."

Almost Amy laughed and said, Of course it was a dream, you silly girl.

But in Ramona's eyes she saw something: wide-eyed wonder at the idea that such things were possible, and that someone Ramona actually knew might have done something so wicked and wonderful. Amy didn't want to see that look of awe change to a look of knowing triumph. And so she said what she knew she shouldn't say. "I wish it was a dream, I honestly do, Ramona. Because when I think back on it I long for him all the more and I wonder when he'll dare to speak to my father and tell him that he wants me for his wife. A man who's done a thing like that with a girl— he's got to marry her, doesn't he?"

There. She had said it. The most secret wonderful dream of her heart. Said it right out.

"You've got to tell your papa," said Ramona. "He'll see to it Alvin marries you."

"I don't want him to be forced," said Amy. "That's silly. A man like Alvin can only be enticed into marriage, not pushed into it."

"Everybody thinks you're all goo-goo over Alvin and he doesn't even see you," said Ramona. "But if he's going off with you a swimming starkers in some faraway pond that only he can get to, well, I don't think that's right. I honestly don't."

"Well, I don't care what you think," said Amy. "It *is* right and if you tell I'll cut off all your hair and tat it into a doily and *burn* it."

Ramona burst out laughing. "Tat it into a *doily?* What kind of power does *that* have?"

"A six-sided doily," said Amy portentously.

"Oh, I'm trembling. Made out of my own hair, too. Silly, you can't do things like that, that's what Black witches do, make things out of hair and burn them or whatever."

As if that was an argument. Alvin did Red magic; why couldn't Amy learn to do Black magic, when her Makering knack was finally unlocked? But there was no use arguing about that sort of thing with Ramona. Ramona thought she knew better than anybody. It was a marvel that Amy even bothered to keep her as a best friend.

"I'm going to tell," said Ramona. "Unless you tell me right now that it's all a lie."

"If you tell I'll kill you," said Amy.

"Tell me it's a lie, then."

Tears sprang unbidden to Amy's eyes. It was *not* a lie. It was a dream. A true dream, of true love, a dream that came from the paths of secretness within her own and Alvin's hearts. He dreamed the same dream at the same time, she knew it, and he felt her flesh against his as surely as she felt his against hers. That made it true, didn't it? If a man and a woman both remembered the realness of each other's bodies pressing against each other, then how was that anything but a true experience? "I love Alvin too much to lie about such a thing. Cut my tongue out if any part of it is false!"

Ramona gasped. "I never believed you till now."

"But you tell *no* one," said Amy. Her heart swelled with satisfaction over her victory. Ramona finally believed her. "Swear."

"I swear," said Ramona.

"Show me your fingers!" cried Amy.

Ramona brought her hands out from behind her. The fingers weren't crossed, but that didn't prove they weren't crossed a few moments ago.

"Swear again now," said Amy. "When I can see your hands."

"I *swear,*" said Ramona, rolling her eyes.

"It's our beautiful secret," said Amy, turning and walking away.

"Ours and Alvin's," said Ramona, uncrossing her ankles and following her.

7
───

BOOKING PASSAGE

It didn't take Calvin too long to figure out that it was going to take a powerful long time to earn enough money to buy passage to Europe as a gentleman. A long time and a lot of work. Neither idea sounded attractive.

He couldn't turn iron into gold, but there was plenty of things he *could* do, and he thought about them long and hard. He wasn't sure, but he didn't reckon them banks could keep him out of their vaults for long if he got to working on what all was holding them together. Still, there was a chance of being caught, and that would be the ruination of all his dreams. He thought of putting out his shingle as a Maker, but that would bring a kind of fame and attention that wouldn't stand in his favor later, not to mention all the accusations of charlatanry that would be bound to come. He was already hearing rumors of Alvin—or rather, of some prentice smith out west who turned an iron plow into gold. Half those who told the tale did it with rolled eyes, as if to say, I'm sure some western farmboy has a Maker's knack, that's likely, yes!

Sometimes Calvin wished it was a different knack he had. For instance, he could do with a torch's knack about now. Seeing the future—why, he could see which property to buy, or which ship to invest in! But even then he'd have to have a partner to put up the money, since he had nothing now. And hanging around New Amsterdam getting rich wasn't what he wanted. He wanted to learn Makering, or whatever it was that Napoleon could teach him. Having set his sights so high, the petty businessmen of Manhattan were hardly the partners he wanted.

There's more than one way to skin a cat, as the saying went. If he couldn't easily get the money for his first-class voyage, why not go direct to the source of all voyages? So it was that he found himself walking the wharfs of Manhattan, along the Hudson and the East River. It was entertaining in its own right, the long, sleek sailing ships, the clunky, smoky steamers, the stevedores shouting and grunting and sweating, the cranes swinging, the ropes and pulleys and nets, the stink of fish and the bawling of the gulls. Who would have guessed, when he was a boy rowdying in a millhouse in Vigor Church, that one day he would be here on the edge of the land, drinking in the liquorous scents and sounds and sights of the life of the sea.

Calvin wasn't one to get lost in reverie and contemplation, though. He had his eye out for the right ship, and from time to time stopped to ask a stevedore of a loading ship what the destination might be. Those as were bound for Africa or Haiti or the Orient were no use to him, but them with European destinations got a thorough looking-over. Until at last he found the right one, a bright and tall-masted English ship with a captain of some breeding who didn't seem to raise his voice at all, though all the men did his will, working hard and working smart under his eye. Everything was clean, and the cargo included trunks and parcels carefully loaded up the ramp instead of being tossed around carelesslike.

Naturally, the captain wouldn't think of talking to a boy Calvin's age, wearing Calvin's clothes. But it wasn't hard for Calvin to think of a plan to get the captain's attention.

He walked up to one of the stevedores and said, "Scuse me, sir, but there's a sharp leak a-going near the back of the boat, on the further side."

The stevedore looked at him oddly. "I'm not a sailor."

"Neither am I, but I think the captain'll thank them as warns him of the problem."

"How can you see it, if it's under the water?"

"Got a knack for leaks," said Calvin. "I'd hurry and tell him, if I were you."

Saying it was a knack was enough for the stevedore, him being an American, even if he *was* a Dutchman by his accent. The captain, of course, wouldn't care diddly about knacks, being an Englishman, which under the Protectorate had a law against knacks. Not against having them, just against believing they existed or attempting to use them. But the captain was no fool, and he'd send somebody to check, knack or no knack.

Which is how it happened. The stevedore talking to his

foreman; the foreman to some ship's officer; each time there was a lot of pointing at Calvin and staring at him as he non-chalantly whistled and looked down at the waterline of the ship. To Calvin's disappointment, the officer didn't go to the captain, but instead sent a sailor downstairs into the dark cellar of the ship. Calvin had to provide something for him to see, so now he sent out his doodlebug and got into the wood, right where he'd said the leak was. It was a simple thing to let the planks get just a little loose and out of posi-tion under the waterline, which sent a goodly stream of water spurting into the cellar of the ship. Just for the fun of it, when he figured the sailor must be down there looking at it, Calvin opened and closed the gap, so the leak was some-times a fine spray, sometimes a gush of water, and some-times just a trickle. Like blood seeping from a wound with an intermittent tourniquet. Bet he never saw no leak like that before, thought Calvin.

Sure enough, in a few minutes the sailor was back, acting all agitated, and now the officer barked orders to several seamen, then went straight to the captain. This time, though, there wasn't no finger-pointing. The officer wasn't going to give Calvin none of the credit for finding the leak. That re-ally got Calvin's goat, and for a minute he thought of sink-ing the boat then and there. But that wouldn't do him no good. Time enough to put that greedy ambitious officer in his place.

When the captain went below, Calvin put on a fine show for him. Instead of causing one leak to spurt and pulse, Calvin shifted the leak from one place to another—a gush here, a gush there. By now it had to be obvious that there wasn't nothing natural about that leak. There was a good deal of stirring on the deck, and a lot of sailors started rush-ing below. Then, to Calvin's delight, a fair number started rushing back onto the deck and onto the gangplank, heading for dry land where there wasn't no strange powers causing leaks in the boat.

Finally the captain came on deck, and this time the officer wasn't taking all the credit for himself. He pointed to the foreman, who pointed to the stevedore, and pretty soon they were all pointing at Calvin.

Now, of course, Calvin could stop fiddling with the leak. He stopped it cold. But he wasn't done. As the captain headed for the gangplank, Calvin sent his bug to seek out all the nearby rats that he could sense lurking under the wharf and among the crates and barrels and on the other ships. By the time the captain got halfway down the gangplank, a couple of dozen rats were racing up the very same bridge, heading for the ship. The captain tried in vain to shoo them back, but Calvin had filled them with courage and grim determination to reach the deck—food, food, Calvin was promising them—and they merely dodged and went on. Dozens more were streaming across the planking of the pier, and the captain was fairly dancing to avoid tripping on rats and falling on his face. On deck, sailors with mops and bowling pins were striking at the rats, trying to knock or sweep them off into the sea.

Then, as suddenly as he had launched the rats, Calvin sent them a new message: Get off this ship. Fire, fire. Leaks. Drowning. Fear.

Squealing and scurrying, all the rats that he had sent aboard came rushing back down the gangplank and all the lines and cables connecting the ship to the shore. And all the rats that had already been aboard, lurking in the cargo hold and in the dark wet cellar and in the hidden caves in the joints and beams of the ship, they also gushed up out of the hatches and portholes like water bubbling out of a new spring. The captain stopped cold to watch them leave. Finally, when all the rat traffic had disappeared into their hiding places on the wharf and the other ships, the captain turned toward Calvin and strode to him. Through it all the man had never lost his dignity—even while dancing to avoid the rats. My kind of man, thought Calvin. I must watch him to learn how gentlemen behave.

"How did you know there was a leak on my ship?" asked the captain.

"You're an Englishman," said Calvin. "You don't believe in what I can see and do."

"Nevertheless, I believe in what *I* can see, and there was nothing natural about that leak."

"I'd say them rats might have been doing it. Good thing for you they all left your ship."

"Rats and leaks," said the captain. "What do you want, boy?"

"I want to be called a man, sir," said Calvin. "Not a boy."

"Why do you wish harm to me and my ship? Has someone of my crew done you an offense?"

"I don't know what you're talking about," said Calvin. "I reckon you're not such a fool as to blame the one as told you you had a leak."

"I'm also not such a fool as to think you knew of anything you didn't have the power to cause or cure at will. Were the rats your doing as well?"

"I was as surprised as you were by their behavior," said Calvin. "Didn't seem natural, all them rats rushing *onto* a sinking ship. But then they seemed to come to their senses and leave again. Every single rat, I daresay. Now, that would be an interesting voyage, wouldn't it—to cross the ocean without any loss of your food supply to the nibbling of rats."

"What do you want from me?" asked the captain.

"I stopped to do you a favor, with no thought of benefit to my own self," said Calvin, trying to sound like an educated Englishman and knowing from the expression on the captain's face that he was failing pathetically. "But it happens that I am in need of first-class passage to Europe."

The captain smiled thinly. "Why in the world would you want to book passage on a leaking ship?"

"But sir," said Calvin, "I've got a sort of knack for spotting leaks. And I can promise you that if I were aboard your ship, during the whole voyage there'd be not a single leak, even in the stoutest storm." Calvin had no idea whether he could keep a ship tight during all the stresses of a storm at sea, but odds were that he'd never have to find out, either.

"Correct me if I'm wrong," said the captain, "but am I to guess that if I take you on my ship, first class, without your paying a farthing, I'll find no problem with leaks and not a rat on my ship? While if I refuse, I'll find my ship at the bottom of the harbor?"

"That would be a rare disaster," said Calvin. "How could such a well-made ship possibly sink faster than your boys could pump?"

"I saw how the leak moved from place to place. I saw how strangely the rats behaved. I may not believe in your American knacks, but I know when I'm in the presence of unaccountable power."

Calvin felt pride flush through his body like ale.

Suddenly he felt the barrel of a pistol just under his breastbone. He looked down to see that the captain had somehow come up with a weapon.

"What's to stop me from blowing a hole in your belly?" asked the captain.

"The likelihood of your dancing on the end of an American rope," said Calvin. "There ain't no law against knacks here, sir, and saying that somebody was doing witchery ain't cause enough to kill him the way it is in England."

"But it's to England you're going," said the captain.

"What's to stop me from taking you on my ship, then having you arrested the moment you step ashore?"

"Nothing," said Calvin. "You could do that. You could even kill me in my sleep during the voyage and cast my body overboard into the sea, telling all the others that you had to dispose of the body of a plague victim as quickly as possible. You think I'm a fool, not to think of that stuff?"

"So go away and leave me and my ship alone."

"If you killed me, what would keep the planks from pulling free of the beams of your boat? What would stop your boat from turning into scraps of lumber bobbing on the water?"

The captain eyed him curiously.

"First-class passage is ludicrous for you. The other first-class passengers would snub you at once, and no doubt they'd assume I'd brought you aboard as my catamite. It would ruin my career anyway, to permit an uncouth, unlettered ruffian like you to sail among my gentle passengers. To put it plainly, young master, you may have power over rats and planks, but you have none over rich men and women."

"Teach me," said Calvin.

"There aren't enough hours in the day or days in the week."

"Teach me," said Calvin again.

"You come here threatening me with destruction of my ship by the evil powers of Satan, and then dare to ask me to teach you to be a gentleman?"

"If you believed my powers were from the devil," said Calvin, "then why didn't you once say a prayer to ward me off?"

The captain glared at him for a moment, then smiled, grimly but not without genuine mirth. "Touché," he said.

"Whatever the devil *that* means," said Calvin.

"It's a fencing term," said the captain.

"I must've put up ten miles of fences in my life," said Calvin. "Post and rail, stone, wire, and picket, every kind, and I never heard of no tooshay."

The captain's smile broadened. "There is something attractive in your challenge. You may have some interesting . . . what do you call them . . . knacks? But you're still a poor boy from the farm. I've taken many a peasant lad and turned him into a first-rate seaman. But I've never taken a boy who wasn't a gentleman born and turned him into something that could pass for civilized."

"Consider me the challenge of your life."

"Oh, believe me, I already do. I haven't altogether decided not to kill you, of course. But it seems to me that since you mean to cause me trouble anyway, why not accept the challenge and see if I can work a miracle just as inexplicable and impossible as any of the nasty pranks you've played on me this morning?"

"First class, not steerage," Calvin insisted.

The captain shook his head. "Neither one. You'll travel as my cabin boy. Or rather, my cabin boy's boy. Rafe is a good three years younger than you, I imagine, but he knows from birth all that you are so desperate to learn. With you to help him, perhaps he'll have enough free time to teach you. And I'll oversee you both. On several conditions, though."

Calvin didn't see as how the captain was in much of a position to set conditions, but he listened civil-like all the same.

"No matter what powers you have, survival at sea depends on instant and perfect obedience from everyone on board the ship. Obedience to *me*. You know nothing of the sea and I gather you don't care about learning seamanship, either. So you will do nothing that interferes with my authority. And you will obey me yourself. That means that when I say piss, you don't even look for a pot, you just whip it out and pee."

"In front of others, I'll do a fine show of obedience, unless you command me to kill myself or some such foolishness."

"I'm not a fool," said the captain.

"All right, I'll do like you say."

"And you'll keep your mouth shut until you learn—in *private*—to talk in some way approximating gentlemanly speech. Right now if you open your mouth you confess your low origins and you will embarrass yourself and me in front of my crew and the other officers and passengers."

"I know how to keep my mouth shut when I need to."

"And when you reach England, our deal is done and you leave no curse on my ship."

"Now you've asked too much," said Calvin. "What I need is your introduction to other high-class people. And passage to France."

"To France! Aren't you aware that England is at war with France?"

"You *have* been ever since Napoleon conquered Austria and Spain. What's that to me?"

"In other words, reaching England doesn't mean I'll be rid of you."

"That's right," said Calvin.

"So why don't I just kill myself now and spare myself all this adventure before you send me to an early grave?"

"Because them as is my friends will prosper in this world and there ain't nothing much bad that can happen to them."

"And all I have to do is maintain my status as your friend, is that it?"

Calvin nodded.

"But someday, isn't it going to occur to you that if the only reason I'm kind to you is out of terror that you'll destroy my ship, I'm not really your friend at all?"

Calvin smiled. "That just means you'll have to try extra hard to convince me that you really mean it."

The officer who had first heard Calvin's message now approached the captain diffidently. "Captain Fitzroy," he said. "The leaking seems to have stopped, sir."

"I know," said the captain.

"Thank you sir," said the officer.

"Get everyone back to work, Benson," said the captain.

"Some of the American stevedores and sailors won't get back on that ship no matter what we say, sir."

"Pay them off and hire others," said the captain. "That will be all, Benson."

"Yes sir." Benson turned around and headed back toward the gangplank.

Calvin, in the meantime, had heard the air of crisp command in Captain Fitzroy's voice and wondered how a man could learn to use his voice like a sharp hot knife, slicing through other men's will like warm butter.

"I would say you've already caused me more trouble than you're worth," said Captain Fitzroy. "And I personally doubt that you have it in you to learn to be a gentleman, though heaven knows there are plenty that have the title who are every bit as ignorant and boorish as you. But I will accept your coercive agreement, in part because I find you fascinating as well as despicable."

"I don't know what all them words mean, Captain Fitzroy, but I know this—Taleswapper once told us how when kings have bastards, the babies get the last name 'Fitzroy.' So no matter what I am, your name says you're a son of a bitch."

"In my case, the great-great-grandson of a bitch. The second Charles sowed his wild oats. My great-great-grandmother, a noted actress of semi-noble origins, entered into a liaison with him and managed to get her child recognized as royal before the parliament deprived him of his head. My family has had its ups and downs since the end of the monarchy, and there have been Lords Protector who thought that our association with the royal family made us dangerous. But we managed to survive and even, in recent years, prosper. Unfortunately, I'm the younger son of a younger son, so I had the choice of the church or the army or the sea. Until meeting you, I did not regret my choice. Do you have a name, my young extortionist?"

"Calvin," he said.

"And are you of such a benighted family that you have but the one name to spend as your patrimony?"

"Maker," said Calvin. "Calvin Maker."

"How deliciously vague. Maker. A general term that can be construed in many ways while promising no particular skill. A Calvin of all trades. And master of none?"

"Master of rats," said Calvin, smiling. "And leaks."

"As we have seen," said Captain Fitzroy. "I will have your name enrolled as part of the ship's company. Have your gear aboard by nightfall."

"If you have someone follow me to kill me, your ship—"

"Will dissolve into sawdust, yes, the threat has already been made," said Fitzroy. "Now you only have to worry about how much I actually care for my ship."

With that, Fitzroy turned his back on Calvin and headed up the gangplank. Calvin almost made him slip and take a pratfall, just to pierce that dignity. But there was a limit, he knew, to how far he could push this man. Especially since Calvin hadn't the slightest idea how to carry out his threat to make the ship fall apart if they killed him. Either he could make the ship leak or stop leaking, but either way he had to be there and alive to do it. If Fitzroy ever realized that his worst threats were pure bluff, how long would he let Calvin live?

Get used to it, Calvin, he told himself. Plenty of people

have wanted Alvin dead, too, but he got through it all. We Makers must have some kind of protection, it's as simple as that. All of nature is looking out for us, to keep us safe. Fitzroy won't kill me because I can't be killed.

I hope.

8

LEAVETAKING

For some reason Alvin's classroom of grownup women just wasn't going well today. They were distracted, it seemed like, and Goody Sump was downright hostile. It finally came to a head when Alvin started working with their herb boxes. He was trying to help them find their way into the greensong, the first faintest melody, by getting their sage or sorrel or thyme, whatever herb they chose, to grow one specially long branch. This was something Alvin reckoned to be fairly easy, but once you mastered it, you could pretty much get into harmony with any plant. However, only a couple of the women had had much success, and Goody Sump was not one of them. Maybe that was how come she was so testy—her laurel wasn't even thriving, let alone showing lopsided growth on one branch.

"The plants don't make the same music they did back when the Reds were tending the woods," Alvin said. He was going to go on and explain how they could do, in a small way, what the Reds did large, but he didn't get a chance, because that was the moment Goody Sump chose to erupt.

She leapt from her chair, strode over to the herb table, and brought her fist right down on top of her own laurel, capsizing the pot and spattering potting soil and laurel leaves all over the table and her own dress. "If you think them Reds was so much better why don't you just go live with *them* and carry off *their* daughters to secret randy views!"

Alvin was so stunned by her unprovoked rage, so perplexed by her inscrutable words, that he just looked at her gape-mouthed as she pulled what was left of her laurel out of what was left of the soil, pulled off a handful of leaves, and threw them in his face, then turned and stalked out of the room.

As soon as she was gone, Alvin tried to make a joke out of it. "I reckon there's some folks as don't take natural to agriculture." But hardly anybody laughed.

"You got to overlook her behavior, Al," said Sylvy Godshadow. "A mother's got to believe her own daughter, even if everybody else knows she's spinning moonbeams."

Since Goody Sump had five daughters, and Alvin had heard nothing significant about any of them lately, this information wasn't much help. "Is Goody Sump having some trouble at home?" he asked.

The women all looked around at each other, but not a one would meet his eyes.

"Well, it looks to me like everybody here knows somewhat as hasn't yet found its way to my ears," said Alvin. "Anybody mind explaining?"

"We're not gossips," said Sylvy Godshadow. "I'm surprised you'd think to accuse us." With that, she stood up and started for the door.

"But I didn't call nobody a gossip," said Alvin.

"Alvin, I think before you criticize others, you'd comb the lice out of your own hair," said Nana Pease. And she was up and off, too.

"Well, what are the rest of you waiting for?" said Alvin. "If you all wanted a day off of class, you only had to ask. It's a sure thing *I'm* done for the day."

Before he could even get started sweeping up the spilt soil, the other ladies had all flounced out.

Alvin tried to console himself by muttering things he'd heard his own father mutter now and then over the years, things like "Women" and "Can't do nothing to please 'em" and "Might as well shoot yourself first thing in the morning." But none of that helped, because this *wasn't* just some normal display of temper. These were levelheaded ladies, every one of them, and here they were up in arms over plain nothing, which wasn't natural.

It wasn't till afternoon that Alvin realized something serious was wrong. A couple of months ago, Alvin had asked Clevy Sump, Goody Sump's husband, to teach them all how to make a simple one-valve suction pump. It was part of Alvin's idea to teach folks that making is making, and everybody ought to know everything they can possibly learn. Alvin was teaching them hidden powers of Making, but they ought to be learning how to make with their hands as well. Secretly Alvin also hoped that when they saw how tricky and careful it was to make fine machinery like Clevy Sump did, they'd realize that what Alvin was teaching wasn't much harder if it was harder at all. And it was working well enough.

Except that today, after the noon bread and cheese, he went on out to the mill to find the men gathered around the wreckage of the pumps they'd been making. Every one of them was broke in pieces. And since the fittings were all metal, it must have took some serious work to break it all up. "Who'd do a thing like this?" Alvin asked. "There's a lot of hate goes into something like *this*." And thinking of hate, it made Alvin wonder if maybe Calvin hadn't come back secretly after all.

"There's no mystery who done it," said Winter Godshadow. "I reckon we ain't got us a pump-making teacher no more."

"Yep," said Taleswapper. "This looks like a specially thorough way of telling us, 'Class dismissed.'"

Some of the men chuckled. But Alvin could see that he wasn't the only one angry at the destruction. After all, these pumps were nearly completed, and all these men had put serious work into making them. They counted on them at their own houses. For many of them, it meant the end of drawing water, and Winter Godshadow in particular had got him a plan to pipe the water right into the kitchen, so his wife wouldn't even have to go outdoors to fetch it. Now their work was undone, and some of them weren't taking kindly to it.

"Let me talk to Clevy Sump about this," said Alvin. "I can't hardly believe it was him, but if it was, whatever's the problem I bet it can be set to rights. I don't want none of you getting angry at him before he's had his say."

"We ain't angry at *Clevy,*" said Nils Torson, a burly Swede. His heavy-lidded gaze made it clear who he *was* angry at.

"Me?" said Alvin. "You think *I* done this?" Then, as if he could hear Miss Larner's voice in his ear, he corrected himself: "*Did* this?"

Murmurs from several of the men assented to the proposition.

"Are you crazy? Why would I go to all this trouble? I'm not an Unmaker, boys, you know that, but if I was, don't you think I could tear up these pumps a lot more thoroughly without taking half so much trouble?"

Taleswapper cleared his throat. "Perhaps you and I ought to talk alone about this, Alvin."

"They're accusing me of wrecking all their hard work and it ain't so!" said Alvin.

"Ain't nobody accusin' nobody of nothin'," said Winter Godshadow. "God follows all. God sees all deeds."

Usually when Winter got into his God-talking moods, the others would sort of back off and pretend to be busy paring their nails or something. But not this time—this time they were nodding and murmuring their agreement.

"Like I said, Alvin, let's you and me have a word. In fact, I think we ought to go on up to the house and talk to your father and mother."

"Talk to me right here," said Alvin. "I'm not some little boy to be taken out behind the woodshed and given a licking in private. If I stand accused of something that everybody knows about except me . . ."

"We ain't accusing," said Nils. "We're pondering."

"Pondering," echoed a couple of the others.

"Tell me here and now what you're pondering," said Alvin. "Because whatever I'm accused of, if it's true I want to make it right, and if it's false I want to set it straight."

They looked at each other back and forth, until finally Alvin turned to Taleswapper. "*You* tell me."

"I only repeat tales that I believe to be true," said Taleswapper. "And this one I believe to be a flat-out lie told by a dreamy-hearted girl."

"Girl? What girl?" and then, putting together Goody Sump's behavior and what Clevy Sump had done to the pumps, and remembering the dreamy expression in one girl's eyes when she sat there in the children's class paying no intelligent attention to a thing that Alvin said, he jumped to a certain conclusion and whispered her name. "Amy."

To Alvin's consternation, some of the men took the fact that he came up with her name as proof that Amy was telling the truth about whatever it was she had said. "See?" they murmured. "See?"

"I'm done with this," said Nils. "I'm done. I'm a farmer.

Corn and hogs, that's my knack if I have me any." When he left, several other men went with him.

Alvin turned to the others. "I *don't* know what I'm accused of, but I can promise you this, I've done nothing wrong. In the meantime, it's plain there's no use in holding class today, so let's all go home. I reckon there's a way to salvage every one of these pumps, so your work isn't lost. We'll get back to it tomorrow."

As they left, some of the men touched Alvin's shoulder or punched his arm to show their support. But some of the support was of a kind he didn't much like. "Can't hardly blame you, pretty little calf-eyed thing like that." "Women is always reading more into things than a man means."

Finally Alvin was alone with Taleswapper.

"Don't look at me," said Taleswapper. "Let's go on up to the house and see if your father's heard the stories yet."

When they got there, it was like a family council was already in session. Measure, Armor-of-God, and Father and Mother were all gathered around the kitchen table. Arthur Stuart was kneading dough—small as he was, he was good with bread and liked doing it, so Mother had finally given in and admitted that a woman could still be mistress of her own house even if somebody else made the bread.

"Glad you're here, Al," said Measure. "You'd think a piece of silliness like this would just get laughed out of town. I mean, these folks should *know* you."

"Why should they?" asked Mother. "He's been gone most of the past seven years. When he left he was a scrub-size boy who'd just spent a year running around the countryside with a Red warrior. When he come back he was full of power and majesty and scared the pellets out of all the bunny-hearts around here. What do they know of his character?"

"Would somebody please tell me what this is *about?*" Alvin said.

"You mean they haven't?" asked Father. "They were powerful quick to tell your mother and Measure and Armor-of-God."

Taleswapper chuckled. "Of course they didn't tell Alvin. Those who believe the tale assume he already knows. And those who don't believe it are plain ashamed that anyone could say such silly slander."

Measure sighed. "Amy Sump told her friend Ramona, and Ramona told her mama, and her mama went straight to Goody Sump, and she went straight to her husband, and he like to went crazy because he can't conceive that every male creature larger than a mouse isn't hottin' up after his nubian daughter."

"Nubile," Alvin corrected him.

"Yeah yeah," said Measure. "I know, you're the one who reads the books, and now's *sure* the time to correct my grammar."

"Nubians are Black Africans," said Alvin. "And Amy ain't no Black near as I can figure."

"This might be a good time to shut up and listen," said Measure.

"Yes *sir,*" said Alvin.

"If only you had left when that torch girl sent you that warning," said Mother. "It's a plain fool who stays inside a burning house because he wants to see the color of the flames."

"What's Amy saying about me?" asked Alvin.

"Pure nonsense," said Father. "About you running off in the Red way, a hundred miles in a night through the woods, taking her to a secret lake where you swum nekkid and other such indecencies."

"With *Amy?*" asked Alvin, incredulous.

"Meaning that you'd do it with someone else?" asked Measure.

"I'd do such a thing with nobody," said Alvin. "Ain't decent, and besides, there ain't enough unbroken living forest these days to *get* a hundred miles in a night. I can't make half so good a speed through fields and farms. The greensong gets noisy and busted up and I get too tired trying to hear it and *why* is anybody believing such silliness?"

"Because they think you can do anything," said Measure.

"And because a good number of these men have noticed Amy filling out of late," said Armor-of-God, "and they know that if *they* had the power, and if Amy was as moony toward them as she plainly is toward you, they'd have her naked in a lake in two seconds flat."

"You're too cynical about human nature," said Taleswapper. "Most of these fellows are the wishing kind. But they know Alvin is a doer, not just a wisher."

"I hardly noticed her except to think she was sure slow to learn, considering how tight she seemed to pay attention," said Alvin.

"To *you* she was paying attention. Not to what you said or taught," said Measure.

"Well it ain't so. I didn't do anything to her or with her, and . . ."

"And even if you did it would be plain disaster if you married her," said Mother.

"*Married* her!" cried Alvin.

"Well of course if it was true, you'd have to marry her," said Father.

"But it *ain't* true."

"You got any witnesses of that?" asked Measure.

"Witnesses of what? How can I have witnesses that it didn't happen? Everybody's my witness—everybody didn't see any such thing."

"But she says it happened," said Measure. "And you're the only other one who knows whether she's lying or not. So either she's a plain liar and you're innocently accused, or she's a brokenhearted lied-to seduced girl and you're the cad who got the use of her and now won't do the decent thing, and nobody can prove either way."

"So *you* don't even believe me?"

"Of course we believe you," said Father. "Do you think we're insane? But our believing you ain't any kind of evidence. Measure's been reading law, and he explained it to us."

"Law?" asked Alvin.

"Well, afore you come home from Hatrack River, anyway. And now and then since. I reckon somebody in the family ought to know something about the law."

"But you mean you think this might come to court?"

"Might," said Measure. "That's what the Sumps were saying. Get them a lawyer from Carthage City instead of one of the frontier lawyers as has a shingle out here in Vigor Church. Lots of publicity."

"But they can't convict me of anything!"

"Breach of promise. Indecent liberties with a child. All depends on how many jurors think that where there's smoke, there's fire."

"Indecent liberties with a . . ."

"That one's a hanging offense, all right," said Measure. "But I hear that's the charge that Clevy wants to bring."

"Doesn't matter if they convict you or not," said Taleswapper.

"Matters to *me*," said Mother.

"Either way, the tale will spread. Alvin the so-called Maker, taking advantage of young girls. You can't let this go to trial," said Taleswapper.

Alvin saw at once how such rumors, such publicity as a trial would bring, it would bring down his work, make it impossible to attract others to come and learn Making at Vigor Church.

Not that he was doing much good teaching Making anyway.

"Miss Larner," murmured Alvin.

"Yep," said Taleswapper. "She warned you. Leave now freely, or leave later because you have to."

"Why should he be driven from his own home just because a horny lying little . . ." Mother's voice trailed off.

Alvin sat in the ensuing silence, recognizing his foolishness. "I spose I'm a plain fool for not heeding Miss Larner." And then, stiffening his back, he closed his eyes and said, "There's another way. So I don't have to leave at all."

"What's that?" asked Measure.

"I could marry her."

"No!" cried Mother and Father at once.

"Why not just sign a confession?" asked Armor-of-God.

"You can't marry her," said Measure.

"It's what she wants," said Alvin. "You can bet she'd say yes, and her father and mother would have to agree to it."

"Agree to it—and then despise you ever after," said Father.

"Doesn't matter about his reputation or what people think of him or anything, compared to this," said Measure. "Waking up every morning and seeing Amy Sump in bed next to you, and knowing the only reason she's there is because she slandered you—tell me what kind of home you'll make, the two of you, for your babies?"

Alvin thought about that for a moment and nodded. "I guess marriage ain't much of a solution. More like starting a whole new set of problems."

"Ah, good," said Father. "I was afraid we'd raised us a fool."

"So I sneak off like a thief, and everybody reckons Amy was telling the truth and I ran off."

"Not likely," said Measure. "We'll let it be known that you left because your work is too important to be distracted by this nonsense. You'll be back when Amy starts telling the truth, and in the meantime, you'll be studying up on . . . whatever. Learning something."

"Learning how to build the Crystal City," murmured Taleswapper.

They all looked at him.

"You don't know how, do you, Alvin?" asked Taleswapper. "While you're busy trying to make Makers out of these people, you don't even know yourself what the Crystal City really is, or how to make it."

Alvin nodded. "That's right."

"So . . . it isn't even a lie," said Taleswapper. "You *do* have much to learn, and you're overdue to learn it. Why, you're even grateful to Amy for showing you that you've been hanging around here far too long. Measure's been learning right good. He's far enough ahead of the others that he can go on teaching in your absence. And him being a married man, no schoolgirl's going to get some foolish notion about *him*."

"I don't know," said Measure. "I'm pretty cute."

"You have my bags packed yet, Taleswapper?" asked Alvin.

"Ain't as if you need much luggage," said Taleswapper. "You're going to be traveling small and fast. I reckon there's only one burden that will weigh you down much. A certain farm implement."

"I couldn't leave it here?" asked Alvin.

"Not safe," said Taleswapper. "Not safe for your family, to have the rumor get about that the Maker is gone but he left the golden plow behind."

"Not safe for *him* to have the rumor say he took it with him," said Mother.

"Nobody on this planet is safer than Alvin, if he wants to be," said Measure.

"So I just pick up the plow, put it in a gunnysack, and head on out?" asked Alvin.

"That's about the best plan," said Armor-of-God. "Though I bet your ma will insist on you taking some salt pork with you, and a change of clothes."

"And me."

They all turned to the source of the small piping voice.

"He's taking me with him," said Arthur Stuart.

"You'd only slow him down, boy," said Father. "You got a good heart, but short legs."

"He ain't in no hurry," said Arthur, "specially figuring as he don't know where he's going."

"The point is you'd be in the way," said Armor-of-God. "He'd always have to be thinking of you, trying to keep you out of harm's way. There's plenty of places in this land where a free half-Black boy is going to get folks' dander up, and that won't be much help to Alvin either."

"You're talking like you think you got a choice," said Arthur. "But if Alvin goes, I go, and that's it. You can lock me in a closet, but someday I'll get out and then I'll follow him and find him or die trying."

They all looked at him in consternation. Arthur Stuart had been near silent since coming to Vigor after his adopted mother was murdered back in Hatrack River. Silent but hardworking, cooperative, obedient. This was a complete surprise, this attitude from him.

"And besides," said Arthur Stuart, "while Alvin's busy looking after the whole world, I'll be there to look after *him*."

"I think the boy should go," said Measure. "The Unmaker plainly ain't done with Alvin yet. He needs somebody to watch his back. I think Arthur's got it in him."

And that was pretty much it. Nobody could size up a fellow like Measure could.

Alvin walked to the hearth and pried up four stones. Nobody would have guessed that anything was hid under them, because until he raised the stones there wasn't so much as a crack in the mortar. He didn't dig in the earth under the stones; the plow was buried eight feet deep, and shoveling would have taken all day, not to mention the dismantling of the entire hearth. No, he just held out his hands and called to the plow, and willed the earth to float it up to him. A moment later, the plow bobbed to the surface of the soil like a cork on a still pond. Alvin could hear a couple of sharp breaths behind him—it still got to folks, even his own family, when he showed his knack so openly. Also, the gold had such a luster to it. As if, even in the pitch black of the darkest moonless stormy night, that plow would still be visible, the gold burning its way even through your closed eyelids to imprint its shining life straight onto your eyes, straight into your brain. The plow trembled under Alvin's hand.

"We got us a journey to take," Alvin murmured to the warm gold. "And maybe along the way we'll figure out what I made you for."

An hour later, Alvin stood at the back door of the house. Not that it took him an hour to pack—he'd spent most of the time down at the mill, fixing the pumps. Nor had he spent any of the time on farewells. They hadn't even sent word to any of the family that he was going, because word would get out and the last thing Alvin needed was for folks to be lying in wait for him when he headed into the forest. Mother and Father and Measure and Armor would have to carry his words of love and Godblessyou to his brothers and sisters and nieces and nephews.

Alvin hitched the bag with the plow and his change of clothes in it over his shoulder. Arthur Stuart took his other hand. Alvin scanned the hexes he'd laid in place around the house and made sure they were still perfect in their sixness, undisturbed by wind or meddling. All was in order. It was the only thing he could do for his family in his absence, was to keep wardings about to fend off danger.

"Don't you worry about Amy, neither," said Measure. "Soon as you're gone, she'll notice some other strapping boy and pretty soon the dreams and stories will be about *him* and folks'll realize that you never done nothing wrong."

"Hope you're right," said Alvin. "Because I don't intend to stay away for long."

Those words hung in the silence for a moment, because they all knew it was quite possible that this time Alvin might be gone for good. Might never come home. It was a dangerous world, and the Unmaker had plainly gone to some trouble to get Alvin out of here and onto the road.

He kissed and hugged all around, taking care not to let the heavy plow smack into anybody. And then he was off for the woods behind the house, sauntering so as to give anyone watching him the impression that this was just a casual errand he was on, and not some life-changing escape. Arthur Stuart had ahold of his left hand again. And to Alvin's surprise, Taleswapper fell into step right beside him.

"You coming with me, then?" asked Alvin.

"Not far," said Taleswapper. "Just to talk a minute."

"Glad to have you," said Alvin.

"I just wondered if you've given any thought to finding Peggy Larner," said Taleswapper.

"Not even for a second," said Alvin.

"What, are you mad at her? Hell, boy, if you'd just listened to her . . ."

"You think I don't know that? You think I haven't been thinking of that this whole time?"

"I'm just saying that you two was on the verge of marrying

back there in Hatrack River, and you could do with a good wife, and she's the best you'll ever find."

"Since when do you meddle?" asked Alvin. "I thought you just collected stories. I didn't think you made them happen."

"I was afraid you'd be angry at her like this."

"I'm not angry at her. I'm angry at myself."

"Alvin, you think I don't know a lie when I hear it?"

"All right, I *am* angry. She knew, right? Well, why didn't she just *tell* me? Amy Sump is going to tell lies about you and force you to leave, so get out now before her childish imaginings ruin everything."

"Because if she said that, you wouldn't have left, would you, Alvin? You would have stayed, figuring you could make everything work out fine with Amy. Why, you would have taken her aside and told her not to love you, right? And *then* when she started talking about you, there'd be witnesses who remembered how she stayed after class one day and was alone with you, and then you *would* be in trouble because even *more* people would believe her story and—"

"Taleswapper, I wish you sometime would learn the knack of shutting up!"

"Sorry," said Taleswapper. "I just don't have any gift for that. I just blather on, annoying people. The fact is that Peggy told you as much as she could without making things worse."

"That's right. In her judgment, she decided how much I was entitled to know, and that's all she told me. And then you have the gall to tell me I should go *marry* her?"

"I'm not following your logic here, Al," said Taleswapper.

"What kind of marriage is it, when my wife knows *everything* but she never tells me enough to make up my own mind! Instead she always makes up my mind for me. Or tells me exactly what she needs to tell me in order to get me to do what *she* thinks I ought to do."

"But you didn't do what she said you ought to do. You stuck around."

"So that's the life you want for me? Either to obey my wife in everything, or wish I had!"

Taleswapper shrugged. "I'm still not getting your objection."

"It's this simple: A grownup man doesn't want to be married to his mother. He wants to make his own decisions."

"I'm sure you're right," said Taleswapper. "And who's this grownup man you're talking about?"

Alvin refused to be baited. "I hope someday it's me. But it'll never be me if I tie myself to a torch. I owe much to Miss Larner. And I owe even more to the girl she was before she became a teacher, the girl who watched over me and saved my life again and again. No wonder I loved her. But marrying her would have been the worst mistake of my life. It would have made me weak. Dependent. My knack might have remained in my hands, but it would be entirely at her service, and that's no way for a man to live."

"A *grownup* man, you mean."

"Mock me all you want, Taleswapper. I notice *you* got no wife."

"I must be a grownup, then," said Taleswapper. But now there was an edge to his voice, and after gazing at Alvin for just another moment, he turned and walked back the way they'd come together.

"I never seen Taleswapper mad like that before," said Arthur Stuart.

"He doesn't like it when folks throw his own advice back in his face," said Alvin.

Arthur Stuart said nothing. Just waited.

"All right, let's go."

At once Arthur turned and started walking.

"Well, wait for me," said Alvin.

"Why?" said Arthur Stuart. "You don't know where we're going, either."

"Reckon not, but I'm bigger, so I get to choose which nowhere we head for."

Arthur laughed a little. "I bet there's not a single direction you can choose where there isn't *somebody* standing in your road, somewhere. Even if it's halfway around the world."

"I don't know about that," said Alvin. "But I know for sure that no matter which way we go, eventually we'll run into the ocean. Can you swim?"

"Not an ocean's worth I can't."

"So what good are *you,* then?" said Alvin. "I was counting on you to tow me across."

Hand in hand they plunged deeper into the woods. And even though Alvin didn't know where he was going, he did know this: The greensong might be weak and jumbled these days, but it was still there, and he couldn't help but fall into it and start moving in perfect harmony with the greenwood. The twigs leaned out of his way; the leaves were soft under his feet, and soon he was soundless, leaving no trail behind him and making no disturbance as he went.

That night they camped on the shore of Lake Mizogan. If you could call it camping, since they made no fire and built no shelter. They broke out of the woods late in the afternoon and stood there on the shore. Alvin remembered being at this lake—not quite this spot, but not far off either—when Tenskwa-Tawa had called a whirlwind and cut his feet and walked out on the bloody water, taking Alvin with him, drawing him up into the whirlwind and showing him visions. It was then that Alvin first saw the Crystal City and knew that he would build it someday, or rather rebuild it, since it had existed once before, or maybe more than once. But the storm was gone, a distant memory; Tenskwa-Tawa and his people were gone, too, most of them dead and the rest of them in the west. Now it was just a lake.

Once Alvin would have been afraid of the water, for it was water that the Unmaker had used to try to kill him, over and over, when he was a child. But that was before Alvin grew into his knack and became a true Maker that night in the forge, turning iron into gold. The Unmaker couldn't touch him through water anymore. No, the Unmaker's tool would be more subtle now. It would be people. People like Amy Sump, weak-willed or greedy or dreamy or lazy, but all of them easily used. It was people who held danger for him now. Water was safe enough, for them as could swim, and that was Alvin.

"How about a dip in the water?" Alvin asked.

Arthur shrugged. It was when they dipped together in the water of the Hio that the last traces of Arthur's old self got washed away. But there'd be none of that now. They just stripped down and swam in the lake as the sun set, then lay down in the grass to dry off, the moonlight making the water shine, a breeze making the humid air cool enough for sleeping. In the whole journey they hadn't said a word till they got to the shore of the lake, just moved in perfect harmony through the wood; even now as they swam, they still said nothing, and hardly splashed they were so much in harmony with everything, with each other. So it startled Alvin when Arthur spoke to him, lying there in the dark.

"This is what Amy dreamed of, ain't it?"

Alvin thought of that for a moment. Then he got up and put on his clothes. "I reckon we're dry now," he said.

"You think maybe she had a true dream? Only it wasn't her, it was me?"

"I didn't do no hugging or unnatural things when we was naked in the water," said Alvin.

Arthur laughed. "Ain't nothin' unnatural about what *she* dreamed of."

"It wasn't no true dream."

Arthur got up and put his clothes on, too. "I heard the greensong this time, Alvin. Three times I let go of your hand, and I still heard it for the longest time before it started fading and I had to catch your hand or get left behind."

Alvin nodded as if that was what he expected. But it wasn't. In all his teaching of the folks of Vigor Church, he hadn't even *tried* to teach Arthur Stuart much, sending him instead to the schoolhouse to learn reading and ciphering. But it was Arthur who might well be his best student after all.

"You going to become a Maker?" asked Alvin.

Arthur shook his head. "Not me," he said. "Just going to be your friend."

Alvin didn't say aloud the thought of his heart: To be my friend, you might just have to be a Maker. He didn't have to say it. Arthur already understood.

The wind rose a little in the night, and far away, out over the lake, lightning brightened the underside of distant clouds. Arthur breathed softly in his sleep; Alvin could hear him in the stillness, louder than the whisper of distant thunder. It should have made him feel lonely, but it didn't. The breaths in the darkness beside him could have been Ta-Kumsaw on their long journey so many years ago, when Alvin had been called the Boy Renegado and the fate of the world seemed to hang in the balance. Or it might have been his brother Calvin when as boys they shared a room; Alvin remembered him as a baby in a cradle, then in a crib, the child's eyes looking up to him as if he were God, as if he knew something no other human knew. Well, I did know it, but I lost Calvin anyway. And I saved Ta-Kumsaw's life, but couldn't do a thing to save his cause, and he is lost to me also, across the river in the fog of the Red west.

And the breathing could have been a wife, instead of just a dream of a wife. Alvin tried to imagine Amy Sump there in the darkness, and even though Measure was right that it would have been a miserable marriage, the fact was that her face was pretty, and in this moment of solitary wakefulness Alvin could imagine that her young body was sweet and warm to the touch, her kiss eager and full of life and hope.

Quickly he shrugged off that image. Amy was not for him, and even to imagine her like that felt akin to some kind of awful crime. He could never marry someone who worshipped him. Because his wife would not be married to the Maker named Alvin; his wife would be married to the man.

It was Peggy Larner he thought of then. He imagined leaning up on one elbow and looking at her when the low distant lightning cast a brush of light across her face. Her hair loose and tousled in the grass. Her ladylike hands no longer controlled and graceful with studied gestures, but now casually flung out in sleep.

To his surprise tears came to his eyes. In a moment he realized why: She was as impossible for him as Amy, not because she would worship him, but because she was more committed to his cause than he was. She loved, not the Maker, and certainly not the man, but rather the Making and the thing made. To marry her would be a kind of surrender to fate, for she was the one who saw futures that might arise out of all possible present choices, and if he married her he would be no man at all, not because she would mean to unman him, but because he himself would not be so stupid as not to follow her advice. Freely he would follow her, and thus freely lose his freedom.

No, it was Arthur lying there beside him, this strange boy

who loved Alvin beyond all reason and yet demanded nothing from him; this boy who had lost a part of himself in order to be free, and had replaced it with a part of Alvin.

The parallel was suddenly obvious to Alvin, and for a moment he was ashamed. I did to Arthur just what I fear that Peggy Larner might do to me. I took away a part of him and replaced it with myself. Only he was so young and his danger so great that I didn't ask him or explain, nor could he have understood me if I tried. He had no choice. I still have one.

Would I be as content as Arthur, if once I gave myself to Peggy?

Perhaps someday, Alvin thought. But not now. I'm not ready yet to give myself to someone, to surrender my will. The way Arthur has to me. The way parents do to their children, giving their lives over to the needs of helpless selfish little ones. The road is open before me, all roads, all possibilities. From this grassy bed beside Lake Mizogan I can go anywhere, find all that is findable, do all that is doable, make all that can be made. Why should I build a fence around myself? Leash myself to one tree? Not even a horse, not even a dog was loyal enough to do such a mad thing to itself.

From infancy on his knack had captured him. Whether as a child in his family, as Ta-Kumsaw's traveling companion, as a prentice smith, or as a teacher of would-be Makers, he had been hobbled by his knack. But not now.

The lightning flashed again, farther off this time. There would be no rain here tonight. And tomorrow he would get up and go south, or north, or west, or east, as the idea struck him, seeking whatever goal seemed desirable. He had left home to get away, not to go toward anything. There was no greater freedom than that.

9

COOPER

Peggy Larner kept watch on both of those bright heart-fires: Alvin as he wandered through America, Calvin as he made his way to England and prepared for his audience with Napoleon. There was little change in the possible futures that she saw, for neither man's plan was one whit altered.

Alvin's plan, of course, was no plan at all. He and Arthur Stuart, traveling afoot, made their way westward from Mizogan, past the growing town of Chicago and on until the dense fogs of the Mizzipy turned them back. Alvin had entertained a vague hope that he, at least, would be permitted to pass to the Mizzipy and beyond, but if such a thing would ever be possible, it certainly was not possible now. So he went north all the way to High Water Lake, where he boarded one of the new steamboats that was carrying iron ore to Irrakwa, where it would be loaded on trains and carried the rest of the way to the coal country of Suskwahenny and Pennsylvania, to feed into the new steel mills. "Is that Making?" asked Arthur Stuart, when Alvin explained the process to him. "Turning iron into steel?"

"It's a sort of Making," said Alvin, "where earth is forced by fire. But the cost is high, and the iron aches when it's been transformed like that. I've seen some of the steel they've made. It's in the rails. It's in the locomotives. The metal screams all the time, a soft sound, very high, but I can hear it."

"Does that mean it's evil to use steel?" asked Arthur Stuart.

"No," said Alvin. "But we should only use it when it's worth the cost of such suffering. Maybe someday we'll find a better way to bring the iron up to strength. I *am* a smith. I won't deny the forgefire or refuse the hammer and the anvil. Nor will I say that the foundries of Dekane are somehow worse than my small forge. I've been inside the flame. I know that the iron can live in it too, and come out unhurt."

"Maybe that's what we're wandering for," said Arthur Stuart. "For you to go to the foundries and help them make steel more kindly."

"Maybe," said Alvin, and they rode the train to Dekane and Alvin applied for work in a foundry and learned by watching and doing all the things there was to know about the making of steel, and in the end he said, "I found a way, but it takes a Maker to do it, or pretty close." And there it was: If Alvin was to change the world, it required him to do what he had already half-failed at doing back in Vigor Church, which was to make more Makers. They left the steeltowns and went on east and as Peggy watched Alvin's heartfire she saw no change, no change, no change. . . .

And then one day, of a sudden, for no reason she could see in Alvin's life, a thousand new roads opened up and down every one of them was a man that she had never seen before. A man who called himself Verily Cooper and spoke like a book-learned Englishman and walked beside Alvin every step of his life for years. Down that path the golden plow was fixed with a perfect handle and leapt to life under human hands. Down that path the Crystal City rose skyward and the fog at the Mizzipy shore cleared for a few miles and Red folk stood on the western shore and gladly greeted White folk come on coracles and rafts to trade with them and speak to them and learn from them.

But where did this Verily Cooper come from, and why had he now so suddenly appeared in Alvin's life?

Only later in the day did it occur to Peggy that it was none of Alvin's doing that brought this man to him, but rather someone else. She looked to Calvin's heartfire—so far away she had to look deep through the ground to see him in England, around the curve of the Earth—and there she saw that it was he who had made the change, and by the simplest of choices. He took the time to charm a Member of Parliament who invited him to tea, and even though Calvin knew that this man had nothing for him, on a whim, the merest chance, he decided he would go. That decision transformed Calvin's own futures only slightly. Nothing much was changed, except this: Down almost every road, Calvin spent an hour at the tea sitting beside a young barrister named Verily Cooper, who listened avidly to all that Calvin had to say.

Was it possible, then, that Calvin was part of Alvin's making after all? He went to England with the undoing of all of Alvin's works in his heart; and yet, by whim, by chance—if there was such a thing as chance—he would have an encounter that would almost surely bring Verily Cooper to America. To Alvin Smith. To the golden plow, the Crystal City, the opening of the Mizzipy fog.

ARISE COOPER WAS an honest hardworking Christian. He lived his life as close to purity as he could, given the finite limits of the human mind. Every commandment he learned of, he obeyed; every imperfection he could imagine, he purged from his soul. He kept a detailed journal every day, tracking the doings of the Lord in his life.

For instance, on the day his second son was born, he wrote: "Today Satan made me angry at a man who insisted on measuring the three kegs I made him, sure that I had given him short measure. But the Spirit of God kindled forgiveness within my heart, for I realized that a man might become suspicious because he had been so often cheated by devilish men. Thus I saw that the Lord had trusted me to teach this man that not all men will cheat him, and I bore his insult with patience. Sure enough, as Jesus taught, when I answered vileness with kindness the stranger did part from my coopery as my friend instead of my enemy, and with a wiser eye about the workings of the Lord among men. Oh how great thou art, my beloved God, to turn my sinful heart into a tool to serve thy purposes in this world! At nightfall entered into the world my second son, whom I name Verily, Verily, I Say Unto You, Except Ye Become As A Little Child Ye Shall In No Wise Enter Into The Kingdom Of Heaven."

If anyone thought the name a bit excessive, they said nothing to Arise Cooper, whose own name was also a bit of scripture: Arise And Come Forth. Nor did the child's mother, whose own name was the shortest verse in scripture: He Wept. They all knew that the baby's whole name would almost never be used. Instead he was known as Verily, and as he grew up the name would often be shortened to Very.

It was not the name that was Verily Cooper's heaviest burden. No, there was something much darker that cast its shadow upon the boy very early in his life.

Arise's wife, Wept, came to him one day when Verily was only two years old. She was agitated. "Arise, I saw the boy playing with scraps today, building a tower of them."

Arise cast his mind through all the evil that one might do with wood scraps from the cooper's trade and could think of only one. "Was it a representation of the tower of Babel?"

Wept looked puzzled. "It might be, or might not. What would I know of that, since the boy speaks not a word yet?"

"What, then?" asked Arise, impatient now because she had not got straight to the point. No, no, he was impatient because he had guessed wrong and now was a bit ashamed of himself. It was a sin to try to put the blame on her for ill feelings of his own causing. In his heart he prayed for forgiveness even as she went on.

"Arise, he built high with the scraps, but they fell over, again and again. I saw him and thought, The Lord of heaven teaches our little one that the works of man are all futility, and only the works of God can last. But then he gets on his face this look of grim determination, and now he studies each scrap of wood as he builds with it, laying it in place all careful-like. He builds and he builds and he builds, until the last scrap is higher than his own head, and still it stands."

Arise was uncertain what she meant by this, or why it troubled her.

"Come, husband, and see the working of our baby's hand."

Arise followed her into the kitchen. No one else was there, though this was the busiest cooking time of the day. Arise could see why they had all fled. For the pile of scrap wood rose higher than reason or balance should have allowed. The blocks lay every which way, balanced perfectly no matter how odd or precarious the fit with the blocks above and below.

"Knock it down at once," said Arise.

"Do you think that didn't occur to me?" asked Wept. She flung out her arm and dashed the tower to the ground. It fell, but all in one motion, and even lying on the ground the blocks remained attached to each other as surely as if they were glued.

"He must have been playing with the mucilage," said Arise, but he knew even as he said it that it wasn't so.

He knelt beside the supine tower and tried to separate a block from the end. He couldn't pry it away. He picked up the whole tower and dashed it across his knee. It bruised him but did not break. Finally, by standing on the middle of it and lifting one end with all his strength, he broke the tower, but it took as much force as if he were breaking a sturdy plank. And when he examined the torn ends, he saw that the tower had broken in the middle of a block, and not at the joint between them.

He looked at his wife, and knew what he should say to her. He should tell her that it was obvious her son had been possessed by Satan, to such a point that the lad was now fully empowered with extraordinary witchery. When such a word was said, there would be no choice but to take the boy to the magistrate, who would administer the witch tests. The boy, being too young and speechless to confess or recant, would burn as the court's sentence, if he did not drown during the trial.

Arise had never questioned the rightness of the laws that kept England pure of witchery and the other dark doings of Satan. No more would they exile witches to America—the only result of that old policy had been a nation possessed by the Devil. The scripture was clear, and there was no room for mercy: Thou shalt not suffer a witch to live.

And yet Arise did not say to his wife the words that would force them to give their baby to the magistrate for discipline. For the first time in his life, Arise Cooper, knowing the truth, did not act upon it.

"I say we burn this odd-shaped board," said Arise. "And forbid the child to play with blocks. Watch him close, and teach him to live each moment in close obedience to the laws of God. Until he has learned, let no other woman look after him out of your presence."

He looked his wife in the eye, and Wept looked back at him. At first her eyes were wide with surprise at his words; then surprise gave way to relief, and then to determination. "I will watch him so close that Satan will have no opportunity to whisper in his ear," she said.

"We can afford to have a cook to supervise the work of the serving girls from now on," said Arise. "The raising of this most difficult son is in our hands. We *will* save him from the Devil. No other work is more important than this."

Thus it was that Verily Cooper's upbringing became difficult and interesting. He was beaten more than any other child in the family, for his own good, for Arise well knew that Satan had made an inroad in the child's heart at an early age. Thus all signs of rebellion, disrespect, and sin must be driven out vigorously.

If little Verily was resentful of the special discipline he received compared to his older brother and his younger sisters, he said nothing of it—perhaps because complaint always resulted in swift blows from a birch rod. He learned to live with such punishment and even, after a little while, to take some pride in it, for the other children looked at him in awe, seeing how much beating he took without so much as crying—and for offenses which, in them, would have brought no more than a sharp look from their parents.

Verily was quick to learn. The birch rod taught him which of his actions were merely the normal mischief of a growing boy, and which were regarded as signs that Satan was laboring mightily for possession of his soul. When the neighborhood boys were building a snow fort, for instance, if he built sloppily and carelessly like they did, there was no punishment. But when he took special care to make the blocks fit smoothly and seamlessly together, he got such a caning that his buttocks bled. Likewise, when he helped his father in the shop, he learned that if he joined the staves of a barrel loosely, as other men did it, barely holding them together inside the hoops, relying on the liquid the barrel would eventually hold to swell the wood and make the joints truly airtight, then it was all right. But if he chose the wood carefully and concentrated to fit them so the wood joined perfectly, and the barrel held air as tight as a pig's bladder, his father beat him with the sizing tool and drove him from the shop.

By the time he was ten, Verily no longer went openly into his father's shop, and it seemed that his father didn't mind having him stay away. Yet still it galled him to see the work that the shop turned out without his help, for Verily could sense the roughness, the looseness of the fit between the staves of the kegs and the barrels and the butts. It grated on him. It made him tingle between the shoulder blades just to think of it, until he could hardly stand it. He took to rising in the middle of the night and going into the shop and re-building the worst of the barrels. No one guessed what he had done, for he left no scraps behind. All he did was un-hoop the barrel, refit the staves, and draw the hoops back on, more tightly than before.

The result was, first, that Arise Cooper got a name for making the best barrels in the midlands; second, that Ver-ily was often sleepy and lazy-seeming during the day, which led to more beatings, though nothing like as severe as the ones he got when he really concentrated on making things fit together; and third, that Verily learned to live with con-stant deception, hiding what he was and what he saw and what he felt and what he did from everyone around him. It was only natural that he should be drawn to the study of law.

Lazy as Verily sometimes seemed, he had a sharp mind with his studies—Arise and Wept both saw it, and instead of contenting themselves with the local taxpaid teacher, they sent him to an academy that was normally only for the sons of squires and rich men. The taunting and mockery that Verily endured from the other boys because of his rough accent and homely clothing was hardly noticeable to Very—such poundings as the boys inflicted on him were nothing com-pared to the beatings he was inured to, and any abuse that didn't cause physical pain didn't even enter Very's consciousness. All he cared about was that at school he didn't have to live in fear all the time, and the teachers loved it when he studied carefully and saw how ideas fit together. What he could only do in secret with his hands, he could do openly with his mind.

And it wasn't just ideas. He began to learn that if he concentrated on the boys around him, really listening to them, watching how they acted, he could see them as clearly as he saw bits of wood, seeing exactly where and how each boy might fit well with each other boy. Just a word here and there, just an idea tossed into the right mind at the right time, and he made the boys of his dormitory into a cohesive band of loving friends. As much as they were willing, that is. Some were filled with deep rage that made it so that the better they fit, the more surly and suspicious they became. Verily couldn't help that. He couldn't change a boy's heart—he could only help him find where his natural inclinations would make him fit most comfortably with the others.

No one saw it, though—no one saw that it was Verily who made these boys into the tightest group of friends that had ever passed through this school. The masters saw that they were friends, but they also saw that Verily was the one misfit who never quite belonged. They could not have imagined that he was the cause of the others' extraordinary closeness. And that was fine with Very. He suspected that if they knew what he was doing, it would be like being home with Father again, only now it wouldn't be birch rods.

For in his studies, particularly in religion class, Verily finally came to understand what the beatings were all about. Witchery. Verily Cooper had been born a witch. No wonder his father looked haunted all the time. Arise Cooper had suffered a witch to live, and those canings, far from being an act of rage or hatred, were really designed to help Verily learn to disguise the evil born in him so that no one would ever know that Arise and Wept Cooper had concealed a witchchild in their own home.

But I'm not a witch, Verily finally told himself. Satan never came to me. And what I do causes no harm. How can it be against God to make barrels tight, or help boys find the best chance of friendship between them? How have I ever used my powers except to help others? Was that not what Christ taught? To be the servant of all?

By the time Verily was sixteen, a sturdy and rather good-looking young man of some education and impeccable manners, he had become a thoroughgoing skeptic. If the dogmas about witchery could be so hopelessly wrong, how could any of the teachings of the ministers be relied upon? It left Verily Cooper at loose ends, intellectually speaking, for all his teachers spoke as if religion were the cornerstone of all other learning, and yet all of Very's actual studies led him to the conclusion that sciences founded upon religion were uncertain at best, utterly bogus at worst.

Yet he breathed no word of these conclusions. You could be burned as an atheist just as fast as you could be burned as a witch. And besides, he wasn't sure he didn't believe in *anything*. He just didn't believe in what the ministers said.

If the preachers had no idea of what was good or evil, where could he turn to learn about right and wrong? He tried reading philosophy at Manchester, but found that except for Newton, the best the philosophers had to offer was a vast sea of opinion with a few blocks of truth floating here and there like wreckage from a sunken ship. And Newton and the scientists who followed him had no soul. By deciding that they would study only that which could be verified under controlled conditions, they had merely limited their field of endeavor. Most truth lay outside the neat confines of science; and even within those boundaries, Verily Cooper, with his keen eye for things which did not fit, soon found that while the pretense of impartiality was universal, the fact of it was very rare. Most scientists, like most philosophers and most theologians, were captives of received opinion. To swim against the tide was beyond their powers, and so truth remained scattered, unassembled, waterlogged.

At least lawyers knew they were dealing with tradition, not truth; with consensus, not objective reality. And a man who understood how things fit together might make a real contribution. Might save a few people from injustice. Might even, in some far distant year, strike a blow or two against the witchery laws and spare those few dozen souls a year so incautious as to be caught manipulating reality in unapproved ways.

As for Arise and Wept, they were deeply gratified when their son Verily left home expressing no interest in the family business. Their oldest child, Mocky (full name: He Will Not Be Mocked Cooper), was a skilled barrelmaker and popular both inside and outside the family. He would inherit everything. Verily would go to London and Arise and Wept would no longer be responsible for him. Verily even gave them a quit-claim against the family estate, though they hadn't asked for it. When Arise accepted the document, twenty-one-year-old Verily took the birch rod from where it hung on the wall, broke it over his knee, and fed it into the kitchen fire. There was no further discussion of the matter. All understood: What Verily chose to do with his powers was his own business now.

Verily's talents were immediately noticed. He was invited to join several law firms, and finally chose the one that gave him the greatest independence to choose his own clients. His reputation soared as he won case after case; but what impressed the lawyers who truly understood these things was not the number of victories, but rather the even larger

number of cases that were settled—justly—without even going to trial. By the time Verily turned twenty-five, it was
becoming a custom several times a month for both parties
in hotly contested lawsuits to come to Verily and beg him
to be their arbiter, completely sidestepping the courts: such
was his reputation as a wise and just man. Some whispered
that in due course he would become a great force in politics. Some dared to wish that such a man might someday
be Lord Protector, if that office were only filled by election,
like the presidency of the United States.

The United States of America—that motley, multilingual,
mongrel, mossbacked republic that had somehow, kingless
and causeless, arisen by accident between the Crown Lands
and New England. America, where men wearing buckskin
were said to walk the halls of Congress along with Reds,
Dutchmen, Swedes, and other semi-civilized specimens
who would have been ejected from Parliament before they
could speak a word aloud. More and more Verily Cooper
turned his eyes to that country; more and more he yearned
to live in a place where his gift for making things fit together could be used to the fullest. Where he could join
things together with his hands, not just with his mind and
with his words. Where, in short, he could live without deception.

Maybe in such a land, where men did not have to lie about
who they were in order to be granted the right to live, maybe
in such a land he could find his way to some kind of truth,
some kind of understanding about what the universe was
for. And, failing that, at least Verily could be free there.

The trouble was, it was English law that Verily had studied, and it was English clients who were on the way to making him a rich man. What if he married? What if he had
children? What kind of life would he make for them in

America, amid the forest primeval? How could he ask a wife to leave civilization and go to Philadelphia?

And he wanted a wife. He wanted to raise children. He wanted to prove that goodness wasn't beaten into children, that fear was not the fount from which virtue flowed. He wanted to be able to gather his family in his arms and know that not one of them dreaded the sight of him, or felt the need to lie to him in order to have his love.

So he dreamed of America but stayed in London, searching in high society to find the right woman to make a family with. By now his homely manners had been replaced by university fashion and finally with courtliness that made him welcome in the finest houses. His wit, never biting, always deep, made him a popular guest in the great salons of London, and if he was never invited to the same dinners or parties as the leading theologians of the day, it was not because he was thought to be an atheist, but rather because there were no theologians regarded as his equal in conversation. One had to place Verily Cooper with at least one who could hold his own with him—everyone knew that Very was far too kindhearted to destroy fools for public entertainment. He simply fell silent when surrounded by those of dimmer wit; it was a shameful thing for a host when word spread that Verily Cooper had been silent all night long.

Verily Cooper was twenty-six years old when he found himself at a party with a remarkable young American named Calvin Miller.

Verily noticed him at once, because he didn't fit, but it wasn't because of his Americanness. In fact, Verily could see at once that Calvin had done a good job of acquiring a veneer of manners that kept him from the most egregious faux pas that bedevilled most Americans who attempted to make their way in London. The boy was going on about his effort to learn French, joking about how abominably untalented he was at languages; but Verily saw (as did many others) that this was all pretense. When Calvin spoke French each phrase came out with splendid accents, and if his vocabulary was lacking, his grammar was not.

A lady near Verily murmured to him, "If he's bad at languages, I shudder to imagine what he's *good* at."

Lying, that's what he's good at, thought Verily. But he kept his mouth shut, because how could he possibly know that Calvin's every word was false, except because he knew that nothing fit when Calvin was speaking? The boy was fascinating if only because he seemed to lie when there was no possible benefit from lying; he lied for the sheer joy of it.

Was this what America produced? The land that in Verily's fantasies was a place of truth, and this was what was spawned there? Maybe the ministers were not wholly wrong about those with hidden powers—or "knacks," as the Americans quaintly called them.

"Mr. Miller," said Verily. "I wonder, since you're an American, if you have any personal knowledge of knacks."

The room fell silent. To speak of such things—it was only slightly less crude than to speak of personal hygiene. And when it was rising young barrister Verily Cooper doing the asking . . .

"I beg your pardon?" asked Calvin.

"Knacks," said Verily. "Hidden powers. I know that they're legal in America, and yet Americans profess to be Christian. Therefore I'm curious about how such things are rationalized, when here they are considered to be proof of one's enslavement to Satan and worthy of a sentence of death."

"I'm no philosopher, sir," said Calvin.

Verily knew better. He could tell that Calvin was suddenly more guarded than ever. Verily's guess had been right.

This Calvin Miller was lying because he had much to hide. "All the better," said Verily. "Then there's a chance that your answer will make sense to a man as ignorant of such matters as I am."

"I wish you'd let me speak of other things," said Calvin. "I think we might offend this company."

"Surely you don't imagine you were invited here for any reason other than your Americanness," said Verily. "So why do you resist talking about the most obvious oddity of the American people?"

There was a buzz of comment. Who had ever seen Verily be openly rude like this?

Verily knew what he was doing, however. He hadn't interviewed a thousand witnesses without learning how to elicit truth even from the most flagrant habitual liar. Calvin Miller was a man who felt shame sharply. That was why he lied—to hide himself from anything that would shame him. If provoked, however, he would respond with heat, and the lies and calculation would give way to bits of honesty now and then. In short, Calvin Miller had a dander, and it was up.

"Oddity?" asked Calvin. "Perhaps the odd thing is not having knacks, but rather denying that they exist or blaming them on Satan."

Now the buzz was louder. Calvin, by speaking honestly, had shocked and offended his pious listeners more than Verily's rudeness had. Yet this *was* a cosmopolitan crowd, and there *were* no ministers present. No one left the room; all watched, all listened with fascination.

"Take that as your premise, then," said Verily. "Explain to me and this company how these occult knacks came into the world, if not caused by the influence of the Devil. Surely you won't have us believe that we Englishmen burn people to death for having powers given to them by God?"

Calvin shook his head. "I see that you want merely to provoke me, sir, into speaking in ways that are against the law here."

"Not so," said Verily. "There are three dozen witnesses in this salon right now who would testify that far from initiating this conversation, you were dragged into it. Furthermore, I am not asking you to preach to us. I'm merely asking you to tell us, as scientists, what Americans believe. It is no more a crime to tell about American beliefs concerning knacks than it is to report on Muslim harems and Hindu widow-burning. And this is a company of people who are eager to learn. If I'm wrong, please, let me be corrected."

No one spoke up to correct him. They were, in fact, dying to hear what the young American would say.

"I'd say there's no consensus about it," said Calvin. "I'd say that no one knows what to think. They just use the knacks that they have. Some say it's against God. Some say God made the world, knacks included, and it all depends on whether the knacks are used for righteousness or not. I've heard a lot of different opinions."

"But what is the wisest opinion that you've heard?" insisted Verily.

He could feel it the moment Calvin decided on his answer: It was a kind of surrender. Calvin had been flailing around, but now he had given in to the inevitable. He was going to tell, if not the truth, then at least a true reporting of somebody else's truth.

"One fellow says that knacks come because of a natural affinity between a person and some aspect of the world around him. It's not from God *or* Satan, he says. It's just part of the random variation in the world. This fellow says that a knack is really a matter of winning the trust of some part of reality. He reckons that the Reds, who don't believe in knacks, have found the truth behind it all. A White man gets it in his head he has a knack, and from then on all he works on is honing that particular talent. But if, like the Reds, he saw knacks as just an aspect of the way all things are connected together, then he wouldn't concentrate on just one talent. He'd keep working on all of them. So in this fellow's view, knacks are just the result of too much work on one thing, and not enough work on all the rest. Like a hodsman who carries bricks only on his right shoulder. His body's going to get twisted. You have to study it all, learn it all. Every knack is within our power to acquire it, I reckon, if only we . . ."

His voice trailed off.

When Calvin spoke again, it was in the crisp, clear, educated-sounding way he must have learned since reaching England. Only then did Verily and the others realize that his accent had changed during that long speech. He had shed the thin coating of Englishness and shown the American.

"Who is this man who taught you all this lore?" asked Verily.

"Does it matter? What does such a rough man know of nature?" Calvin spoke mockingly; but he was lying again, Verily knew it.

"This 'rough man,' as you call him. I suspect he says a great deal more than the mere snippet you've given us today."

"Oh, you can't stop him from talking, he's so full of his own voice." The bitterness in Calvin's tone was a powerful message to Verily: This is sincere. Calvin resents whoever this frontier philosopher is, resents him deeply. "But I'm not about to bore this company with the ravings of a frontier lunatic."

"But you don't think he's a lunatic, do you, Mr. Miller?" said Verily.

A momentary pause. Think of your answer quickly, Calvin Miller. Find a way to deceive me, if you can.

"I can't say, sir," said Calvin. "I don't think he knows half as much as he lets on, but I wouldn't dare call my own brother a liar."

There was a sudden loud eruption of buzzing. Calvin Miller had a brother who philosophized about knacks and said they weren't from the Devil.

More important to Verily was the fact that Calvin's words obviously didn't fit in with the world he actually believed in. Lies, lies. Calvin obviously believed that his brother was very wise indeed; that he probably knew *more* than Calvin was willing to admit.

At this moment, without realizing it himself, Verily Cooper made the decision to go to America. Whoever Calvin's brother was, he knew something that Verily wanted desperately to learn. For there was a ring of truth in this man's ideas. Maybe if Verily could only meet him and talk to him, he could make Verily's own knack clear to him. Could tell him why he had such a talent and why it persisted even though his father tried to beat it out of him.

"What's your brother's name?" asked Verily.

"Does that matter?" asked Calvin, a faint sneer in his voice. "Planning a visit to the backwoods soon?"

"Is that where you're from? The backwoods?" asked Verily.

Calvin immediately backtracked. "Actually, no, I was exaggerating. My father was a miller."

"How did the poor man die?" asked Verily.

"He's not dead," said Calvin.

"But you spoke of him in the past tense. As if he were no longer a miller."

"He still runs a mill," said Calvin.

"You still haven't told me your brother's name."

"Same as my father's. Alvin."

"Alvin Miller?" asked Verily.

"Used to be. But in America we still change our names

with our professions. He's a journeyman smith now. Alvin Smith."

"And you remain Calvin Miller because . . ."

"Because I haven't chosen my life's work yet."

"You hope to discover it in France?"

Calvin leapt to his feet as if his most terrible secret had just been exposed. "I have to get home."

Verily also rose to his feet. "My friend, I fear my curiosity has made you feel uncomfortable. I will stop my questioning at once, and apologize to this whole company for having broached such difficult subjects tonight. I hope you will all excuse my insatiable curiosity."

Verily was at once reassured by many voices that it had been most interesting and no one was angry with or offended by anyone. The conversation broke into many smaller chats.

In a few moments, Verily managed to maneuver himself close to the young American. "Your brother, Alvin Smith," he said. "Tell me where I can find him."

"In America," said Calvin; and because the conversation was private, he did not conceal his contempt.

"Only slightly better than telling me to search for him on Earth," said Verily. "Obviously you resent him. I have no desire to trouble you by asking you to tell me any more of his ideas. It will cost you nothing to tell me where he lives so I can search him out myself."

"You'd make a voyage across the ocean to meet with a boy who talks like a country bumpkin in order to learn what he thinks about knacks?"

"Whether I make such a voyage or merely write him a letter is no concern of yours," said Verily. "In the future I'm bound to be asked to defend people accused of witchery. Your brother may have the arguments that will allow me to save a client's life. Such ideas can't be found here in England because it would be the ruin of a man's career to explore too assiduously into the works of Satan."

"So why aren't you afraid of ruining your own career?" said Calvin.

"Because whatever he knows, it's true enough to make a liar like you run halfway around the world to get away from the truth."

Calvin's expression grew ugly with hate. "How dare you speak to me like that! I could . . ."

So Verily had guessed right about the way Calvin fit into his own family back home. "The name of the town, and you and I will never have to speak again."

Calvin paused for a moment, weighing the decision. "I take you at your word, Mr. Rising Young Barrister Esquire. The town is Vigor Church, in Wobbish Territory. Near the mouth of Tippy-Canoe Creek. Go find my brother if you can. Learn from him—if you can. Then you can spend the rest of your life wondering if maybe you wouldn't have been better off trying to learn from *me*."

Verily laughed softly. "I don't think so, Calvin Miller. I already know how to lie, and alas, that's the only knack you have that you've practiced enough to be truly accomplished at it."

"In another time I would have shot you dead for that remark."

"But this is an age that loves liars," said Verily. "That's why there are so many of us, acting out lives of pretense. I don't know what you're hoping to find in France, but I can promise you, it will be worthless to you in the long run, if your whole life up to that moment is a lie."

"Now you're a prophet? Now you can see into a man's heart?" Calvin sneered and backed away. "We had a deal. I told you where my brother lives. Now stay away from me." Calvin Miller left the party, and, moments later, so did

Verily Cooper. It was quite a scandal, Verily's acting so rudely in front of the whole company like that. Was it quite safe to invite him to dinners and parties anymore?

Within a week that question ceased to matter. Verily Cooper was gone: resigned from his law firm, his bank accounts closed, his apartment rented. He sent a brief letter to his parents, telling them only that he was going to America to interview a fellow about a case he was working on. He didn't add that it was the most important case of his life: his trial of himself as a witch. Nor did he tell them when, if ever, he meant to return to England. He was sailing west, and would then take whatever conveyance there was, even if it was his own feet on a rough path, to meet this fellow Alvin Smith, who said the first sensible thing about knacks that Verily had ever heard.

On the very day that Verily Cooper set sail from Liverpool, Calvin Miller stepped onto the Calais ferry. From that moment on, Calvin spoke nothing but French, determined to be fluent before he met Napoleon. He wouldn't think of Verily Cooper again for several years. He had bigger fish to fry. What did he care about what some London lawyer thought of him?

10

WELCOME HOME

Left to himself, Alvin likely wouldn't have come back to Hatrack River. Sure, it was his birthplace, but since his folks moved on before he was even sitting up by himself he didn't have no memories of the way it was then. He knew that the oldest settlers in that place were Horace

Guester and Makepeace Smith and old Vanderwoort, the Dutch trader, so when he was born the roadhouse and the smithy and the general store must have been there already. But he couldn't conjure up no pictures in his memory of such a little place.

The Hatrack River he knew was the village of his prenticeship, with a town square and a church with a preacher and Whitley Physicker to tend the sick and even a post office and enough folks with enough children that they got them up a subscription and hired them a schoolteacher. Which meant it was a real town by then, only what difference did that make to Alvin? He was stuck there from the age of eleven, bound over to a greedy master who squeezed the last ounce of work out of "his" boy while teaching him as little as possible, as late as possible. There was scarce any money, and neither time to get any pleasure from it nor pleasures to be bought if you had the time.

Even so, miserable as his prenticeship was, he might have looked back on Hatrack River with some fondness. There was Makepeace's shrewish wife Gertie, who nevertheless was a fine cook and had a spot of kindness for the boy now and then. There was Horace and Old Peg Guester, who remembered his birth and made him feel welcome whenever he had a moment to visit with them or do some odd job to help them out. And as Alvin got him a name for making perfect hexes and doing better ironwork than his master, there was plenty of visits from all the other folks in town, asking for this, asking for that, and all sort of pretending they didn't know Alvin was the true master in that smithy. Wouldn't want to rile up old Makepeace, cause then he'd take it out on the boy, wouldn't he? But he was a good one with his hands, that boy Alvin.

So Alvin might have made him some happy memories of the place, the way folks always finds a way to dip into their own past and draw out wistful moments, even if those very moments was lonely or painful or downright hellish to live through at the time.

For Alvin, though, all those childish and youthish memories was swallowed up in the way it ended. Right at the happiest time, when he was falling in love with Miss Larner while trying to pick up some decent book learning, them Slave Finders came for little Arthur Stuart and everything went ugly. They even forced Alvin to make the manacles that Arthur would wear back into slavery. Then Alvin and Horace Guester took their life in their hands and went to fetch back the boy, and Alvin changed Arthur Stuart deep inside and washed away his old self in the Hio, so the Finders could never match him up with the bits of hair and flesh in their cachet. So even then, it might have still been hopeful, a good memory of a bad time that turned out fine.

Then that last night, standing in the smithy with Miss Larner, Alvin told her he loved her and asked her to marry him and she might have said yes, she had a look in her eyes that said yes, he thought. But at that very moment Old Peg Guester killed one Finder and got herself killed by the other. Only then did Alvin find out that Miss Larner was really Little Peggy, Peg's and Horace's long-lost daughter, the torch girl who saved Alvin's life when he was a little baby. What a thing to find out about the woman you love, in the exact moment that you're losing her forever.

But he wasn't really thinking of losing Miss Larner then. All he could think of was Old Peg, gruff and sharp-tongued and loving old Peg, shot dead by a Slave Finder, and never mind that she shot one of them first, they was in her house without leave, trespassing, and even if the law gave them the right to be there, it was an evil law and they was evil to make their living by it and it didn't none of it matter then, anyway, because Alvin was so angry he wasn't thinking straight. Alvin found the one as killed Old Peg and snapped his neck with one hand, and then he beat his head against the ground until the skull inside the skin was all broke up like a pot in a meal sack.

When Alvin's fury died, when the white-hot rage was gone, when deep justice stopped demanding the death of the killer of Old Peg, all that was left was the broken body in his arms, the blood on his apron, the memory of murder. Never mind that nobody in Hatrack River would ever call him a killer for what he done that night. In his own heart he knew that he had Unmade his own Making. For that moment he had been the Unmaker's tool.

That dark memory was why none of the other memories could ever turn light in Alvin's heart. And that's why Alvin probably wouldn't never have come back to Hatrack River, left to himself.

But he wasn't left to himself, was he? He had Arthur Stuart with him, and to that little boy the town of Hatrack River was nothing but pure golden childhood. It was setting and watching Alvin work in the smithy, or even pumping the bellows sometimes. It was listening to the redbird song and knowing the words. It was hearing all the gossip in the town and saying it back all clever so the grownups clapped their hands and laughed. It was being the champion speller of the whole town even though for some reason they wouldn't let him into the school proper. And yes, sure, the woman he called Mother got herself killed, but Arthur didn't see that with his own eyes, and anyway, he *had* to go back, didn't he? Old Peg his adopted mother who killed a man to save him and died her own self, she lay buried on a hill behind the roadhouse. And in a grave on the same hill lay Arthur's true mother, a little Black slavegirl who used her secret African powers to make wings for herself so she could fly with the baby in her arms, she could fly all the way north to where her baby would be safe, even though she herself died from the journey. How could Arthur Stuart not return to that place?

Don't go thinking that Arthur Stuart ever asked Alvin to go there. That wasn't the way Arthur thought about things. He was going along with Alvin, not telling Alvin where to go. It was just that when they talked, Arthur kept going on about this or that memory from Hatrack River until Alvin reached his own conclusion. Alvin reckoned that it would make Arthur Stuart happy to go back to Hatrack River, and then it never crossed Alvin's mind that his own sadness might outweigh Arthur's happiness. He just up and left Irrakwa, where they happened to be that week in late August of 1820. Up and left that land of railroads and factories, coal and steel, barges and carriages and men on horseback going back and forth on urgent errands. Left that busy place and came through quiet woods and across whispering streams, down deer paths and along rutted roads until the land started looking familiar and Arthur Stuart said, "I've been here. I know this place." And then, in wonder: "You brung me home, Alvin."

They came from the northeast, passing the place where the railroad spur was fixing to pass near Hatrack River and cross the Hio into Appalachee. They came across the covered bridge over the Hatrack that Alvin's own father and brothers built, like a monument to their dead oldest brother Vigor, who got mashed by a tree carried on a storm flood while he was crossing the river. They came into town on the same road his family used. And, just like Alvin's family, they passed the smithy and heard the ringing of hammer on iron on anvil.

"Ain't that the smithy?" asked Arthur Stuart. "Let's go see Makepeace and Gertie!"

"I don't think so," said Alvin. "In the first place, Gertie's dead."

"Oh, that's right," said the boy. "Blew out a blood vein screaming at Makepeace, didn't she?"

"How'd you hear that?" asked Alvin. "You don't miss much gossip, do you, boy?"

"I can't help what people talk about when I'm right there," said Arthur Stuart. And then, back to his original idea: "I reckon it wouldn't be proper anyway, to visit Makepeace before seeing Papa."

Alvin didn't tell him that Horace Guester hated it when Arthur called him Papa. Folks got the wrong impression, like maybe Horace himself was the White half of that mixup boy, which wasn't so at all but folks will talk. When Arthur got older, Alvin would explain to him that he ought to not call Horace Papa anymore. For now, though, Horace was a man and a man would have to bear the innocent offense of a well-meaning boy.

The roadhouse was twice as big as before. Horace had built on a new wing that doubled the front, with the porch continuing all along it. But that wasn't hardly the only difference—the whole thing was faced with clapboards now, whitewashed and pretty as you could imagine against the deep green of the forest that still snuck as close to the house as it dared.

"Well, Horace done prettied up the place," said Alvin.

"It don't look like itself no more," said Arthur Stuart.

"Anymore," Alvin corrected him.

"If you can say 'done prettied up' then I can say 'no more,'" said Arthur Stuart. "Miss Larner ain't here to correct us no more anyhow."

"That should be 'no more nohow,'" said Alvin, and they both laughed as they walked up onto the porch.

The door opened and a somewhat stout middle-aged woman stepped through it, almost running into them. She carried a basket under one arm and an umbrella under the other, though there wasn't a sign of rain.

"Excuse me," said Alvin. He saw that she was hedged about with hexes and charms. Not many years ago, he would have been fooled by them like any other man (though he would always have seen where the charms were and how the hexes worked). But he had learned to see past hexes of illusion, and that's what these were. These days, seeing the truth came so natural to him that it took real effort to see the illusion. He made the effort, and was vaguely saddened to see that she was almost a caricature of feminine beauty. Couldn't she have been more creative, more *interesting* than this? He judged at once that the real middle-aged woman, somewhat thick-waisted and hair salted with grey, was the more attractive of the two images. And it was a sure thing she was the more interesting.

She saw him staring at her, but no doubt she assumed it was her beauty that had him awed. She must have been used to men staring at her—it seemed to amuse her. She stared right back at him, but *not* looking for beauty in him, that was for sure.

"You were born here," she said, "but I've never seen you before." Then she looked at Arthur Stuart. "But you were born away south."

Arthur nodded, made mute by shyness and by the over-whelming force of her declaration. She spoke as if her words were not only true, but superseded all other truth that had ever been thought of.

"He was born in Appalachee, Missus. . . ." In vain Alvin waited for her reply. Then he realized that he was supposed to assume, seeing her young beautiful false image, that she was a Miss rather than a Missus.

"You're bound for Carthage City," said the woman, speaking to Alvin again, and rather coldly.

"I don't think so," said Alvin. "Nothing for me there."

"Not yet, not yet," she said. "But I know you now. You must be Alvin, that prentice boy old Makepeace is always going on about."

"I'm a journeyman, ma'am. If Makepeace isn't saying that part, I wonder how much of what he says *is* true."

She smiled, but her eyes weren't smiling. They were calculating. "Aha. I think there's the makings of a good story in that. Just needs a bit of stirring."

At once Alvin regretted having said so much to her. Why *had* he spoken up so boldly, anyway? He wasn't a one to babble on to strangers, especially when he was more or less calling another fellow a liar. He didn't want trouble with Makepeace, but now it looked pretty sure he was going to get it anyway. "I wish you'd tell me who you are, ma'am."

It wasn't *her* voice that answered. Horace Guester was in the doorway now. "She's the postmistress of Hatrack River, on account of her uncle's brother-in-law being the congressman from some district in Suskwahenny and he had some pull with the president. We're all hoping to find a candidate in the election this fall who'll promise to throw her out so we can vote for him for president. Failing that, we're going to have to up and hang her one of these days."

The postmistress got a sort of half-smile on her face. "And to think Horace Guester's knack is to make folks feel welcome!"

"What would the charge be, in the hanging?" asked Alvin.

"Criminal gossip," said Horace Guester. "Rumor aforethought. Sniping with malice. Backbiting with intent to kill. Of course I mean all that in the nicest possible way."

"I do no such thing," said the postmistress. "And my name, since Horace hasn't deigned to utter it yet, is Vilate

Franker. My grandmother wasn't much of a speller, so she named my mother Violet but spelled it Vilate, and when my mother grew up she was so ashamed of grandmama's illiteracy that she changed the pronunciation to rhyme with 'plate.' However, I am *not* ashamed of my grandmother, so I pronounce it 'Violet,' as in the delicate flower."

"To rhyme," said Horace, "with Pilate, as in Pontius the handwasher."

"You sure talk a lot, ma'am," said Arthur Stuart. He spoke in all innocence, simply observing the facts as he saw them, but Horace hooted and Vilate blushed and then, to Alvin's shock, clicked with her tongue and opened her mouth wide, letting her upper row of teeth drop down onto the lower ones. False teeth! And such a horrible image—but neither Arthur nor Horace seemed to see what she had done. Behind her wall of illusion, she apparently thought she could get away with all kinds of ugly contemptuous gestures. Well, Alvin wasn't going to disabuse her. Yet.

"Forgive the boy," said Alvin. "He hasn't learned when's the right time to speak his mind."

"He's right," she said. "Why shouldn't he say so?" But she dropped her teeth at the boy again. "I find it irresistible to tell stories," she went on. "Even when I know my listeners don't care to hear them. It's my worst vice. But there are worse ones—and I thank the good Lord I don't have *those*."

"Oh, I like stories, too," said Arthur Stuart. "Can I come listen to you talk some more?"

"Any time you like, my boy. Do you have a name?"

"Arthur Stuart."

It was Vilate's turn to hoot with laughter. "Any relation to the esteemed king down in Camelot?"

"I was named after him," he said, "but far as I know we ain't no kin."

Horace spoke up again. "Vilate, you won yourself a convert cause the poor boy's got no guile and less sense, but kindly stand aside of this door and let me welcome in this man who was born in my house and this boy who grew up in it."

"There's obviously parts of this story that I haven't heard yet," said Vilate, "but don't trouble yourself on my account— I'm sure I'll get a much fuller version from others than I would ever get from you. Good day, Horace! Good day, Alvin! Good day, my young kingling. Do come see me, but don't bring me any of Horace's cider, it's sure to be poisoned if he knows it's for me!" With that she bustled off the porch and out onto the hard-packed dirt of the road. Alvin saw the illusions dazzle and shimmer as she went. The hexes weren't quite so perfect from the rear. He wondered if others ever saw through her when she was going away.

Horace watched her grimly as she walked up the road. "We pretend that we're only pretending to hate each other, but in fact we really do. The woman's evil, and I mean that serious. She has this knack of knowing where something or somebody's from and where they're bound to end up, but she uses that to piece together the nastiest sort of gossip and I swear she reads other people's mail."

"Oh, I don't know," said Alvin.

"That's right, my boy, you ain't been here for the past year and you *don't* know. A lot of changes since you left."

"Well, let me in, Mr. Guester, so I can set down and maybe eat some of today's stew and have a drink of something— even poisoned cider sounds good about now."

Horace laughed and embraced Alvin. "Have you been gone so long you forgot my name is Horace? Come in, come in. And you too, young Arthur Stuart. You're always welcome here."

To Alvin's relief, Arthur Stuart said nothing at all, and so naturally among the things he didn't say was "papa."

They followed him inside and from then on till they laid down for naps in the best bedroom, they were in Horace's hospitable care. He fed them, gave them hot water for washing their hands and feet and faces, took their dirty clothes for laundering, stuffed more food in them, and then personally tucked them into bed after making them watch him put clean sheets on the bed "just so you *know* I still keep my dear Peg's high standards of cleanliness even if I am just an old widower living alone."

The mention of his late wife was all it took, though, to bring memory flooding back. Tears came into Arthur Stuart's eyes. Horace at once began to apologize, but Alvin stilled him with a smile and a gesture. "He'll be all right," he said. "It's coming home, and her not here. Those are good tears and right to shed them."

Arthur reached out and patted Horace's hand. "I'll be all right, Papa," he said.

Alvin looked at Horace's face and was relieved to see that instead of annoyance, his eyes showed a kind of rueful gladness at hearing the name of Papa. Maybe he was thinking of the one person who had the true right to call him that, his daughter Peggy, who had come home in disguise and was too soon gone, and who knew if he'd ever see her again. Or maybe he was thinking of the one who taught Arthur Stuart to call him Papa, the dear wife whose body lay in the hilltop plot behind the roadhouse, the woman who was always faithful to him even though he never deserved her goodness, being (as only he in all the world believed) a man of evil.

Soon Horace backed on out of the room and closed the door, and Arthur Stuart quietly cried himself to sleep in Alvin's arms. Alvin lay there, wanting to doze, too, for a little while. It was good to be home, or as near to home as Alvin could figure in these days when he wondered what home even was. Carthage City was where he was bound to end up, eh? Why would he go there to live? Or would he only go there to die? What did this Vilate Franker actually know, anyway? He lay there, sleepless, wondering about her, wondering if she could really be as evil as Horace Guester said. Alvin had met true evil in his life, but he still persisted in thinking it was awful rare, and the word was bandied about too much by those who didn't understand what real badness was.

What he could not let himself think of was the only other woman he had known who fenced herself around with hexes. Rather than remember Miss Larner, who was really Little Peggy, he finally drifted into sleep.

WHAT AN INTERESTING boy, thought Vilate as she walked away from the roadhouse. Not at all like the shifty little weasel I expected after the things Makepeace Smith has said. But then, nobody trusts shifty little weasels well enough to be betrayed by them—it's strong, fine-looking men as tricks folks into thinking they're as open-hearted as they are open-faced. So maybe every word Makepeace said was true. Maybe Alvin did steal some precious hoard of gold that he found while digging a well. Maybe Alvin did fill up the well where the gold was found and dig another a few yards off, hoping nobody'd notice. Maybe he did shape it like a plow and pretend that he had turned iron into gold so he could run off with Makepeace's treasure trove. What's that to me? thought Vilate. It wasn't my gold, and never could be, as long as Makepeace had it. But if it happens to be a golden plow that Alvin has in that bag he carries over his shoulder, why, then it might end up being anybody's gold.

Anybody strong enough might take it away by brute force, for instance. Anybody cruel enough might kill Alvin and take it from the corpse. Anybody sneaky enough could take it out of Alvin's room as he slept. Anybody rich enough could hire lawyers to prove something against Alvin in court and take it away by force of law. All kinds of ways to get that plow, if you want it bad enough.

But Vilate would never stoop to coercion. She wouldn't even *want* that golden plow, if it existed, unless Alvin gave it to her of his own free will. As a gift. A love-gift, perhaps. Or . . . well, she'd settle for a guilt gift, if it came to that. He looked like a man of honor, but the way he was staring at her . . . well, she knew that look. The man was smitten. The man was hers, if she wanted him.

Play this right, Vilate, she told herself. Set the stage. Make *him* come after you. Let no one say you set your cap for him.

Her best friend was waiting for her in the kitchen shed back of the post office when she got there. "So what do you think of that Alvin?" she asked, before Vilate even had time to greet her.

"Trust you to get the news before I can tell you myself." Vilate set to work stoking up the fine cast-iron stove with a bread oven in it that made her the envy of the women in Hatrack River.

"Five people saw you on the roadhouse porch greeting him, Vilate, and the word reached me before your foot touched the street, I'm sure."

"Then those are idle people, I'd say, and the devil has them."

"No doubt you'd know—I'm sure the devil gives you a new list every time he makes another recruit."

"Of course he does. Why, everyone knows the devil lives right here in my fancy oven." Vilate cackled with glee.

"So . . ." said her best friend impatiently. "What do you think of him?"

"I don't think he's that much," said Vilate. "Working-man's arms, of course, and tanned like any low-class boy.

His talk is rather coarse and country-like. I wonder if he can even read."

"Oh, he can read all right. Teacher lady taught him when he lived here."

"Oh, yes, the fabled Miss Larner who was so clever she got her prize student to win a spelling bee, which caused the slave finders to get wind of a half-Black boy and ended up killing Horace Guester's wife, Miss Larner's own mother. A most unnatural woman."

"You do find a way to make the story sound right ugly," said her friend.

"Is there a pretty version of it?"

"A sweet love story. Teacher tries to transform the life of a half-Black boy and his rough-hewn friend, a prentice smith. She falls in love with the smith boy, and turns the half-Black lad into a champion speller. Then the forces of evil take notice—"

"Or God decides to strike down her pride!"

"I do think you're jealous of her, Vilate. I do think that."

"Jealous?"

"Because she won the heart of Alvin Smith, and maybe she still owns it."

"Far as I can tell, his heart's still beating in his own chest."

"And is the gold still shining in his croker sack?"

"You talk sweet about Miss Larner, but you always assume *I* have the worst motives." Vilate had the stove going nicely now, and put on a teapot to boil as she began cutting string beans and dropping them in a pan of water.

"Because I know you so well, Vilate."

"You *think* you know me, but I'm full of surprises."

"Don't you drop your teeth at *me,* you despicable creature."

"They dropped by themselves," said Vilate. "I never do it on purpose."

"You're such a liar."

"But I'm a beautiful liar, don't you think?" She flashed her best smile at her friend.

"I don't understand what men see in women anyway," her friend answered. "Hexes or no hexes, as long as a woman has her clothes on a man can't see what he's interested in anyhow."

"I don't know about *all* men," said Vilate. "I think some men love me for my character."

"A character of sterling silver, no doubt—never mind a little tarnish, you can wipe *that* off with a little polish."

"And some men love me for my wit and charm."

"Yes, I'm sure they do—if they've been living in a cave for forty years and haven't seen a civilized woman in all that time."

"You can tease me all you want, but I know you're jealous of me, because Alvin Smith is already falling in love with me, the poor hopeless boy, while he'll never give a look at you, not a single look. Eat your heart out, dear."

Her best friend just sat there with a grumpy face. Vilate had really hit home with that last one. The teapot sang. As always, Vilate set out two teacups. But, as always, her best friend sniffed the tea but never drank it. Well, so what? Vilate never failed in her courtesy, and that's what mattered.

"Makepeace is going to take him to court."

"Ha," said Vilate. "You heard *that* already, too?"

"Oh, no. I don't know if Makepeace Smith even knows his old prentice is back in town—though you can bet that if the word reached *me* that fast, it got to him in half the time! I just know that Makepeace has been bragging so much on how Alvin robbed him that if he don't serve papers on the boy, everybody's going to know it was just empty talk. So he's *got* to bring the boy to trial, don't you see?"

Vilate smiled a little smile to herself.

"Already planning what you're going to bring to him in jail?" asked her friend.

"Or something," said Vilate.

ALVIN WOKE FROM his nap to find Arthur Stuart gone and the room half-dark. The traveling must have taken more out of him than he thought, to make him sleep the afternoon away.

A knock on the door. "Open up, now, Alvin," said Horace. "The sheriff's just doing his job, he tells me, but there's no way out of it."

So it must have been a knock on the door that woke him in the first place. Alvin swung his legs off the bed and took the single step that got him to the door. "It wasn't barred," he said as he opened it. "You only had to give it a push."

Sheriff Po Doggly looked downright sheepish. "Oh, it's just Makepeace Smith, Alvin. Everybody knows he's talking through his hat, but he's gone and got a warrant on you, to charge you with stealing his treasure trove."

"Treasure?" asked Alvin. "I never heard of no treasure."

"Claims you dug up the gold digging a well for him, and moved the well so nobody'd know—"

"I moved the well cause I struck solid stone," said Alvin. "If I found gold, why would that make me move the well? That don't even make sense."

"And that's what you'll say in court, and the jury will believe you just fine," said Sheriff Doggly. "Everybody knows Makepeace is just talking through his hat."

Alvin sighed. He'd heard the rumors flying hither and yon about the golden plow and how it was stolen from a blacksmith that Alvin prenticed with, but he never thought Makepeace would have the face to take it to court, where he'd be proved a liar for sure. "I give you my word I won't leave town till this is settled," said Alvin. "But I've got Arthur Stuart to look after, and it'd be right inconvenient if you locked me up."

"Well, now, that's fine," said Doggly. "The warrant says you have a choice. Either you surrender the plow to me for safekeeping till the trial, or you sit in jail *with* the plow."

"So the plow is the only bail I can pay, is that it?" asked Alvin.

"Reckon that's the long and short of it."

"Horace, I reckon you'll have to look after the boy," said Alvin to the innkeeper. "I didn't bring him here to put him back in your charge, but you can see I got small choice."

"Well, you could put the plow in Po's keeping," said Horace. "Not that I mind keeping the boy."

"No offense, Sheriff, but you wouldn't keep the plow safe a single night," said Alvin, smiling wanly.

"Reckon I could do just fine," said Po, looking a mite offended. "I mean, even if I lock you up, you don't think I'd let you keep the plow in the cell with you, do you?"

"Reckon you *will*," said Alvin mildly.

"Reckon not," said Po.

"Reckon you think you could keep it safe," said Alvin. "But what you don't know is how to keep folks safe from the plow."

"So you admit you have it."

"It was my journeypiece," said Alvin. "There are witnesses of that. This whole charge is nonsense, and you and everybody else knows it. But what'll the charge be if I give you this plow and somebody opens the sack and gets struck blind? What's the charge then?"

"Blind?" asked Po Doggly, glancing at Horace, as if his old friend the innkeeper could tell him whether he was having his leg pulled.

"You think you can tell your boys not to look in the sack, and that's going to be enough?" said Alvin. "You think they won't just try to take a peek?"

"Blind, eh?" said Po.

Alvin picked up the sack from where it had lain beside him on the bed. "And who's going to carry the plow, Po?"

Sheriff Doggly reached out to take it, but no sooner had his hands closed around the sack than he felt the hard metal inside shift and dance under his hands, sliding away from him. "Stop doing that, Alvin!" he demanded.

"I'm just holding the top of the sack," said Alvin. "What shelf you going to keep this on?"

"Oh, shut up, boy," said Doggly. "I'll let you keep it in the cell. But if you plonk somebody over the head with that thing and make an escape, I'll find you and the charge won't be no silly tale from Makepeace Smith, I promise you."

Alvin shook his head and smiled.

Horace laughed out loud. "Po, if Al wanted to escape from your jail, he wouldn't have to do no head plonking."

"I'm just telling you, Al," said the sheriff. "Don't push your luck with me. There's a outstanding extradition order from Appalachee about standing trial for the death of a certain dead Slave Finder."

Suddenly Horace's genial manner changed, and in a quick movement he had the sheriff pressed into the doorjamb so tight it looked like it might make a permanent difference in his posture. "Po," said Horace, "you been my dearest friend for many a year. We done in the dark of night what would get us kilt for doing in daylight, and trusted each other's life through it all. If you ever bring a charge or even *try* to extradite this boy for killing the *Slave Finder* who killed my Margaret in my own house, I will do a little justice on you with my own two hands."

Po Doggly squinted and looked the innkeeper in the eye. "Is that a threat, Horace? You want me to break my oath of office for you?"

"How can it be a threat?" said Horace. "You know I meant it in the nicest possible way."

"Just come along to jail, Alvin," said Doggly. "I reckon if the town ladies don't have meals for you, Horace here will bring you roadhouse stew every night."

"I keep the plow?" asked Alvin.

"I ain't coming near that thing," said the sheriff. "*If* it's a plow. *If* it's gold." Doggly gestured him to pass through the door and come into the hall. Alvin complied. The sheriff followed him down the narrow hall to the common room, where about two dozen people were standing around waiting to see what the sheriff had been after. "Alvin, nice to see you," several of them greeted him. They looked kind of embarrassed, seeing how Alvin was in custody. "Not much of a welcome, is it?" said Ruthie Baker, her face grim. "I swan, that Makepeace Smith has bit himself a tough piece of gristle with this mischief."

"Just bring me some of them snickerdoodles in jail," said Alvin. "I been hankering for them the whole way here."

"You can bet the ladies'll be quarreling all day about who's to feed you," said Ruth. "I just wish dear old Peg had been here to greet you." And she burst into quick, sentimental tears. "Oh, I wish I didn't cry so easy!"

Alvin gave her a quick hug, then looked at the sheriff. "She ain't passing me no file to saw the bars with," he said. "So is it all right if I . . ."

"Oh, shut up, Alvin," said Sheriff Doggly. "Why the hell did you even come back here?"

At that moment the door swung open and Makepeace

Smith himself strode in. "There he is! The thief has been apprehended at last! Sheriff, make him give me my plow!"

Po Doggly looked him in the eye. Makepeace was a big man, with massive arms and legs like tree trunks, but when the sheriff faced him Makepeace wilted like a flower. "Makepeace, you get out of my way right now."

"I want my plow!" Makepeace insisted—but he backed out the door.

"It ain't your plow till the court says it's your plow, if it ever does," said the sheriff.

Horace Guester chimed in. "It ain't your plow till you show you know how to make one just like it."

But Alvin himself said nothing to Makepeace. He just walked on out of the roadhouse, pausing in the doorway only to tell Horace, "You let Arthur Stuart visit me all he wants, you hear?"

"He'll want to sleep right in the cell with you, Alvin, you know that!"

Alvin laughed. "I bet he can fit right through the bars, he's so skinny."

"I made those bars!" Makepeace Smith shouted. "And they're too close together for anyone to fit through!"

Ruth Baker shouted back, just as loudly. "Well, if you made those bars, little Arthur can no doubt *bend* them out of the way!"

"Come on now, folks," Sheriff Doggly said. "I'm just making a little arrest here, so stand clear and let me bring the prisoner on through. While you, Makepeace, are exactly three words away from being arrested your own self for obstructing justice and disturbing the peace."

"Arrest *me!*" cried Makepeace.

"Now you're just *one* word away," said Sheriff Doggly. "Come on, any word will do. Say it. Let me lock you up, Makepeace. You know I'm dying to."

Makepeace knew he was. He clamped his mouth shut and took a few steps away from the roadhouse porch. But then he turned to watch, and let himself smile as he saw Alvin getting led away down the street toward the courthouse, and the jail out back.

11

JAIL

Calvin's French was awful—but that was hardly his worry. Talking he had done in England, and plenty of it, until he learned to imitate the cultured accents of a refined gentleman. But here in Paris, talking was useless—harmful, even. One did not become a figure of myth and rumor by chatting. That's one thing Calvin had learned from Alvin, all right, even though Alvin never meant to teach it. Alvin never tooted his own horn. So every Tom, Dick, and Sally tooted it for him. And the quieter he got, the more they bragged on him. That was what Calvin did from the moment he arrived in Paris, kept his silence as he went about healing people.

He had been working on healing—like Taleswapper said, that was a knack people would appreciate a lot more than a knack for killing bugs. No way could Calvin do the subtle things that Alvin talked about, seeing the tiny creatures that spread disease, understanding the workings of the little bits of life out of which human bodies were built. But there *were* things within Calvin's grasp. Gross things, like bringing the edges of open wounds together and getting the skin to scar over—Calvin didn't rightly understand how he did it, but he could sort of squinch it together in his mind and the scar-stuff would grow.

Getting skin to split, too, letting the nasty fluids spew out—that was impressive indeed, especially when Calvin did it with beggars on the city streets. Of course, a lot of the beggars had phony wounds. Calvin could hardly heal *those,* and he wouldn't make himself many friends by making the painted scars slide off beggars' faces. But the real ones—he could help some of them, and when he did, he was careful to make sure plenty of people could see exactly what happened. Could see the healing, but could not hear him brag or boast, or even promise in advance what would happen. He would make a great show of it, standing in front of the beggar, ignoring the open hand or the proffered cup, looking down instead at the wound, the sore, the swelling. Finally the beggar would fall silent, and so would the onlookers, their attention at last riveted on the spot that Calvin so intently watched. By then, of course, Calvin had the wound clearly in mind, had explored it with his doodling bug, had thought through what he was going to do. So in that exact moment of silence he reached out with his bug and gave the new shape to the skin. The flesh opened or the wound closed, whatever was needed.

The onlookers gasped, then murmured, then chattered. And just when someone was about to engage him in conversation, Calvin turned and walked away, shaking his head and refusing to speak.

The silence was far more powerful than any explanation. Rumors of him spread quickly, he knew, for in the cafe where he supped (but did no healing) he heard people speaking of the mysterious silent healer, who went about doing good as Jesus did.

What Calvin hoped would not get spread about was the fact that he wasn't exactly healing people, except by chance. Alvin could get into the deep hidden secrets of the body and do real healing, but Calvin couldn't see that small. So the wound might drain and close, but if there was a deep infection it would come right back. Still, some of them might be healed, for all he knew. Not that it would really help them—how would they beg, without a wound? If they were smart, they'd get away from him before he could take away the coin they used to buy compassion. But no, the ones with real injury wanted to be healed more than they wanted to eat. Pain and suffering did that to people. They could be wise and careful when they felt fine. Add a little pain to the mix, though, and all they wanted was whatever would make the pain go away.

It took a surprisingly long time before one of the Emperor's secret police came to see him. Oh, a gendarme or two had witnessed what he did, but since he touched no one and said nothing, they also did nothing, said nothing to him. And soldiers—they were beginning to seek him out, since so many veterans had injuries from their days in service, and half the cripples Calvin helped had old companions from the battle lines they went to see, to show the healing miracle that Calvin had brought them. But no one with the furtive wariness of the secret police was ever in the crowd, not for three long weeks—weeks in which Calvin had to keep moving his operation from one part of the city to another, lest someone he had already healed come back to him for a second treatment. What good would all this effort do if the rumor began to get about that the ones he healed didn't stay healed?

Then at last a man came, a middle-sized man of bourgeois clothing and modest demeanor, but Calvin saw the tension, the watchfulness—and, most important, the brace of pistols hidden in the pockets of his coat. This one would report to the Emperor. So Calvin made quite sure that the secret policeman was in a good position to see all that transpired when he healed a beggar. Nor did it hurt that even before the silence fell and he did the healing, everyone was murmuring things like, "Is he the one? I heard he healed that one-legged beggar near Montmartre," though of course Calvin had never even attempted to heal someone with a missing limb. Even Alvin might not be able to do something as spectacular as *that*. But it didn't hurt that such a rumor was about. Anything to get him into the presence of the Emperor, for everyone knew that he suffered agonies from the gout. Pain in the legs—he will bring me to him to end the pain in his legs. For the pain, he'll teach me all he knows. Anything to remove the pain.

The healing ended. Calvin walked away, as usual. To his surprise, however, the secret policeman left by quite another route. Shouldn't he follow me? Whisper to me that the Emperor needs me? Would I come and serve the Emperor? Oh, but I'm not sure I can be of help. I do what I can, but many wounds are stubborn and refuse to be fully healed. Oh, that's right, Calvin meant to promise *nothing*. Let his deeds speak for themselves. He would make the Emperor's leg feel better for a while—he was sure he could do that—but no one would ever be able to say that Calvin Miller had promised that the healing would be permanent, or even that there would be any kind of healing at all.

But he had no chance to say these things, for the secret policeman went another way.

That evening, as he waited for his supper at the cafe, four gendarmes came into the cafe, laughing as if they had just come off duty. Two went toward the kitchen—apparently they knew someone there—while the other two jostled, clumsy and laughing, among the tables. Calvin smiled a moment and then looked out the window.

The laughing stopped. Harsh hands seized his arms and lifted him out of his chair. All four gendarmes were around him now, not laughing at all. They bound his wrists together and hobbled his legs. Then they half-dragged him from the cafe.

It was astonishing. It was impossible. This had to be a response to the report of the secret policeman. But why would they arrest him? What law had he broken? Was it simply that he spoke English? Surely they understood the difference between an Englishman and an American. The English were still at war with France, or something like war, anyway, but the Americans were neutral, more or less. How dare they?

For a moment, painfully hobbling along with the gendarmes at the too-brisk pace they set for him, Calvin toyed with the idea of using his Makering power to loose the bonds and stand free of them. But they were all armed, and Calvin had no desire to tempt them to use their weapons against an escaping prisoner.

Nor did he waste effort, after the first few minutes, trying to persuade them that some terrible mistake was underway. What was the point? They knew who he was; someone had told them to arrest him; what did they care whether it was a mistake or not? It wasn't *their* mistake.

Half an hour later, he found himself stripped and thrown into a miserable stinking cell in the Bastille.

"Welcome to the Land of the Guillotine!" croaked someone farther up the corridor. "Welcome, O pilgrim, to the Shrine of the Holy Blade!"

"Shut up!" cried another man.

"They sliced through another man's neck today, the one who was in the cell you're in now, new boy! That's what happens to Englishmen here in Paris, once somebody decides that you're a spy."

"But I'm not English!" Calvin cried out.

This was greeted with gales of laughter.

PEGGY SET DOWN her pen in weariness, closed her eyes in disgust. Wasn't there some kind of plan here? The One who sent Alvin into the world, who protected him and prepared him for the great work of building the Crystal City, didn't that One have some kind of plan? Or was there no plan? No, there had to be some meaning in the fact that this very day, in Paris, Calvin was locked up in prison, just as Alvin was in prison in Hatrack River. The Bastille, of course, was a far cry from a second-story room in the back of the courthouse, but jail was jail—they were both locked in, for no good reason, and with no idea of how it would all come out.

But Peggy knew. She saw all the paths. And, finally, she closed up her pen, put away the papers she had been writing on, and got up to tell her hosts that she would have to leave earlier than she expected. "I'm needed elsewhere, I think."

BONAPARTE'S NEPHEW WAS a weasel who thought he was an ermine. Well, let him have his delusion. If men didn't have delusions, Bonaparte wouldn't be Emperor of Europe and Lawgiver of Mankind. Their delusions were his truth; their hungers were his heart's desire. Whatever they wanted to believe about themselves, Bonaparte helped them believe it, in exchange for control over their lives.

Little Napoleon, the lad called himself. Half of Bonaparte's nephews had been named Napoleon, in an effort to curry favor, but only this one had the effrontery to use the name at court. Bonaparte wasn't quite sure if this meant that Little Napoleon was bolder than the others, or simply too stupid to realize how dangerous it was to dare to use the Emperor's own name, as if to assert one's claim to succeed him. Seeing him now, marching in here like a mechanical soldier—as if he had some secret military accomplishment that no one knew about but which entitled him to strut about playing the general—Bonaparte wanted to laugh in his face and expose in front of all the world Little Napoleon's dreams of sitting on the throne, ruling the world, surpassing his uncle's accomplishments. Bonaparte wanted to look him in the eye and say, "You couldn't even fill my pisspot, you vainglorious mountebank."

Instead he said, "What good wind blows you here, my little Napoleon?"

"Your gout," said the lad.

Oh, no. Another cure. Cures found by fools usually did more harm than good. But the gout was a curse, and . . . let's see what he has.

"An Englishman," said Little Napoleon. "Or, to speak more accurately, an American. My spies have watched him—"

"*Your* spies? These are different spies from the spies I pay?"

"The spies you assigned to me for supervision, Uncle."

"Ah, those spies. They do still remember they work for me, don't they?"

"Remember it so well that instead of simply following orders and watching for enemies, they have also watched for someone who might help you."

"Englishmen in Europe are all spies. Someday after some notable achievement when I'm very very popular I will round them all up and guillotine them. Monsieur Guillotin—now *that* was a useful fellow. Has he invented anything else lately?"

"He's working on a steam-powered wagon, Uncle."

"They already exist. We call them locomotives, and we're laying track all over Europe."

560 • *Orson Scott Card*

"Ah, but *he* is working on one that doesn't have to run on rails."

"Why not a steam-powered balloon? I can't understand why that has never worked. The engine would propel the craft, and the steam, instead of being wastefully discharged into the atmosphere, would fill the balloon and keep the craft aloft."

"I believe the problem, Uncle, is that if you carry enough fuel to travel more than twenty or thirty feet, the whole thing weighs too much to get off the ground."

"That's why inventors exist, isn't it? To solve problems like that. Any fool could come up with the basic idea—*I* came up with it, didn't I? And when it comes to such matters I'm plainly a fool, as most men are." Bonaparte had long since learned that such modest remarks always got repeated by onlookers in the court and did much to endear him to the people. "It's Monsieur Guillotin's job to . . . well, never mind, the machine that bears his name is enough of a contribution to mankind. Swift, sure, and painless executions—a boon to the unworthiest of humans. A very Christian invention, showing kindness to the least of Jesus' brethren." The priests would repeat that one, and from the pulpit, too.

"About this Calvin Miller," said Little Napoleon.

"And my gout."

"I've seen him drain a swollen limb just by standing on the street staring at a beggar's pussing wound."

"A pussing wound isn't the gout."

"The beggar had his trousers ripped open to show the wound, and this American stood there looking for all the world as if he were dozing off, and then suddenly the skin erupted with pus and all of it drained out, and then the wound closed without a single stitch. Neither he nor any man touched the leg. It was quite a demonstration of remarkable healing powers."

"You saw this yourself?"

"With my own eyes. But only the once. I can hardly go about secretly, Uncle. I look too much like your esteemed self."

No doubt Little Napoleon imagined that this was flattery. Instead it sent a faint wave of nausea through Bonaparte. But he let nothing show in his face.

"You now have this healer under arrest?"

"Of course. Waiting for your pleasure."

"Let him sweat."

Little Napoleon cocked his head a moment, studying Bonaparte, probably trying to figure out what plan his uncle had for the healer, and why he didn't want to see him right away. The one thing he would never think of, Bonaparte was quite sure, was the truth: that Bonaparte hadn't the faintest idea what to do about a healer who actually had power. It made him uneasy thinking about it. And he remembered the young White boy who had come with the Red general, Ta-Kumsaw, to visit him in Fort Detroit. Could this American be the same one?

Why should he even make such a connection? And why would that boy in Detroit matter, after all these years? Bonaparte was uncertain about what it all meant, but it felt to him as if forces were at work, as if this American in the Bastille were someone of great importance to him. Or perhaps not to him. To someone, anyway.

Bonaparte's leg throbbed. Another episode of gout was starting. "Go away now," he said to Little Napoleon.

"Do you want information from the American?" asked Little Napoleon.

"No," said Bonaparte. "Leave him alone. And while you're at it, leave *me* alone, too."

ALVIN HAD A steady stream of visitors in the courthouse jail. It seemed like they all had the same idea. They'd sidle right up to the bars, beckon him close, and whisper (as if the deputy didn't know right well what they was talking about), "Don't you have some way to slip on out of here, Alvin?"

What, they believed he hadn't thought of it? Such a simple matter, to soften the stone and pull one of the bars out. Or, for that matter, he could make the metal of a bar flow away from the stone it was embedded in. Or dissolve the bar entirely. Or push against the stone and press on through, walking through the wall into freedom. Such things would be easy enough for Alvin. As a child he had played with stone and found softness and weakness in it; as a prentice blacksmith, he had come to understand iron from the heart out. Hadn't he crawled into the forgefire and turned an iron plowshare to living gold?

Now, locked in this prison, he thought of leaving, thought of it all the time. Thought of hightailing it off into the woods, with or without Arthur Stuart—the boy was happy here, so why take him away? Thought of the sun on his back, the wind in his face, the greensong of the forest now so faint to him through stone and iron that he could hardly hear it.

But he told himself what he told those friendly folk who meant so well. "I need to be shut of this whole affair before I go off. So I mean to stand trial here, get myself acquitted, and then go on without fear of somebody tracking me down and telling the same lies on me again."

And then they always did the same thing. Having failed to persuade him to escape, they'd eye his knapsack and whisper, "Is it in there?"

And the boldest of them would say what they were all wishing. "Can I see it?"

His answer was always the same. He'd ask about the weather. "Think it's a hard winter coming on?" Some picked up slower than others, but after a while they all realized he wasn't going to answer a blame thing about the golden plow or the contents of his knapsack, not a word one way or the other. Then they'd make some chat or take up his used dishes, them as brought food, but it never took long and soon they was on their way out of the courthouse to tell their friends and family that Alvin was looking sad kind of but he still wasn't saying a thing about that gold plow that Makepeace claimed was his own gold treasure stolen by the boy back in his prentice days.

One day Sheriff Doggly brought in a fellow that Alvin recognized, sort of, but couldn't remember why or who. "That's the one," said the stranger. "Got no respect for any man's knack except his own." Then Alvin recollected well enough—it was the dowser who picked the spot for Alvin to dig a well for Makepeace Smith. The spot where Alvin dug right down to a sheet of thick hard rock, without finding a drop of water first. No doubt Makepeace meant to use him as a witness that Alvin's well wasn't in the spot the dowser chose. Well, that was true enough, no disputing it. The dowser fellow wasn't going to testify to anything that Alvin wouldn't have admitted freely his own self. So let them plot their plots. Alvin had the truth with him, and that was bound to be enough, with twelve jurors of Hatrack River folk.

The visits that really cheered him were Arthur's. Two or three times a day, the boy would blow in from the square like a leaf getting tucked into an open door by a gust of wind. "You just got to meet that feller John Binder," he'd say. "Ropemaker. Some folks is joking how if they decide to hang you, he'll be the one as makes the rope, but he just shuts 'em right up, you should hear him, Alvin. 'No rope of mine is going to hang no Maker,' he says. So even though you never met him I count him as a friend. But I tell you, they say his ropes *never* unravel, never even *fray,* no matter where you cut em. Ain't that some knack?"

And later in the same day, he'd be on about someone else. "I was out looking for Alfreda Matthews, Sophie's cousin, she's the one lives in that shack down by the river, only the river's a long windy thing and I couldn't find her and in fact it was getting on toward dark and I couldn't rightly find myself, and then here I am face to face with this Captain Alexander, he's a ship's captain only who knows what he's doing so far from the sea? But he lives around here doing tinkering and odd fixing, and Vilate Franker says he must have done some terrible crime to have to hide from the sea, or maybe there was some great sea beast that swallowed up his ship and left only him alive and now he daresn't go back to sea for fear the beast—she calls it La Vaya Than, which Goody Trader says is Spanish for 'Ain't this a damn lie,' do you know Goody Trader?"

"Met her," says Alvin. "She brung me some horehound drops. Nastiest candy I ever ate, but I reckon for them as loves horehound they were good enough. Strange lady. Squatted right outside the door here pondering for the longest time until she finally gets up and says 'Humf, you're the first man I ever met what didn't need *nothing* and here you are in jail.'"

"They say that's her knack, knowing what a body needs even when he don't know himself," said Arthur. "Though I *will* say that Vilate Franker says that Goody Trader is a humbug just like the alligator boy in the freak show in Dekane, which you wouldn't take me to see cause *you* said if he was real, it was cruel to gawk at him, and—"

"I remember what I said, Arthur Stuart. You don't have to gossip to me about *me.*"

"Anyway, what was I talking about?"

"Lost in the woods looking for old drunken Freda."

"And I bumped into that sea captain, anyway, and he looks me in the eye and he says, 'Follow me,' and I go after him about ten paces and he sets me right in the middle of a deer track and he says, 'You just go along this way and when you reach the river again, you go upstream about three rods.' And you know what? I did what he said and you know what?"

"You found Freda."

"Alfreda Matthews, and she was stone drunk of course but I splashed her face with some water and I done what you said folks ought to do, I emptied her jug out and boy howdy, she was spitting mad, I like to had to out-dance the devil just to keep from getting hit by them rocks she threw!"

"Poor lady," said Alvin. "But it won't do no good as long as there's folks to give her another jug."

"Can't you do like you did with that Red Prophet?"

Alvin looked at him sharp. "What do you think you know about *that?*"

"Just what your own mama told me back in Vigor Church, about how you took a drunken one-eyed Red and made a prophet out of him."

Alvin shook his head. "No sir, she got it wrong. He was a prophet all along. And he wasn't a drunk the way Freda's a drunk. He took the likker into him to drown out the terrible black noise of death. That's what I fixed, and then he didn't need that likker no more. But Freda—there's something else in her that hungers for it, and I don't understand it yet."

"I told her to come to you though, so I reckon you oughta know and that's why I told you she's a-coming to get healed."

Alvin shook his head.

"Did I do wrong?"

"No, you done right," said Alvin. "But there's nothing I

can do for her beyond what she oughta do for herself. She knows the likker's eating her up, stealing her life away from her. But I'll talk to her and help her if I can."

"They say she can tell you when rain's coming. If she's sober."

"Then how would anybody know she has such a knack?" asked Alvin.

Arthur just laughed and laughed. "I reckon she must have been sober *once,* anyway. And it was raining!"

When Arthur Stuart left, Alvin pondered the tales he told. Some of Arthur's chat was just gossip. There was some powerful gossips in Hatrack River these days, and the way Alvin figured it, the two biggest gossips was Vilate Franker, who Alvin had met and knew she was living inside a bunch of lying hexes, and Goody Trader, who he didn't really know yet except for what he gleaned from her visit. Her real name was either Chastity or Charity—Vilate said it was Chastity, but other folks said the other. She went by Goody, short for Goodwife, seeing how she'd been married three times and kept all them husbands happy till they croaked, accidental every time, though again Vilate managed to give Arthur the impression that they wasn't truly accidental. Them two women was at war all the time, that much was plain—hardly a word one said as wasn't contradicted flat out by the other. Now, neither one of these ladies invented gossip, nor was it so that Hatrack River didn't have rumors and tales before the two of them moved here. But it was plain that Arthur was visiting both of them every day, and both of them was filling him full of tales until Alvin could hardly make sense of it and it was a sure thing that Arthur didn't really understand the half of what he'd been told.

Alvin knew for himself that Vilate was deceptive and spiteful. But Goody might be just the same or worse, only she was better at it so Alvin couldn't see it so plain. Hard to tell. And that business with Goody Trader saying Alvin didn't need nothing—well, what was *that?*

But behind all the gossip and quarreling, there was something else that struck Alvin as pretty strange. Mighty knacks was thick underfoot in Hatrack River. Most towns might have somebody with something of a knack that you might notice. Most knacks, though, was pretty plain. A knack for soup. A knack for noticing animal tracks. Useful, but nothing to write a letter to your daddy about. A lot of folks had no idea what their own knack was, because it was so easy for them and not all that remarkable in the eyes of other folks. But here in Hatrack River, the knacks was downright astonishing. This sea captain who could help you find your way even when you didn't know you was lost. And Freda—Alvin pooh-poohed it to Arthur Stuart, but there was folks in town as swore she didn't just *predict* rain, if you sobered her up in a dry season she could *bring* it. And Melyn, a Welsh girl who can harp and sing so you forget everything while she's doing it, forget it all and just sit there with a stupid smile on your face because you're so happy—she came and played for Alvin and he could feel how the sound that flowed from her could reach inside him like a doodle-bug scooting through the earth, reach inside and find all the knots and loosen them up and just make him feel good.

It was power like he'd been trying to teach the folks back in Vigor, only they could hardly understand it, could hardly get but a glimmer of it now and then, and here it was so thick on the ground you could rake it up like leaves. Maggie who helped out in Goody Trader's store, she could ride any horse no matter how wild, plenty of witnesses of that. And one who scared Alvin a little, a girl named Dorcas Bee who could draw portraits of folks that not only looked like their outward face, but also showed everything that was inside them—Alvin didn't know what to make of her, and even with his eyes he couldn't rightly understand how she did it.

Any one of these folks would be remarkable in whatever town they lived in, no matter if it was as big as New Amsterdam or Philadelphia. Yet here they were living in the middle of nowhere, Hatrack River of all places, swelling the numbers of the town but yet nobody seemed to find it remarkable at all that so many knacks was gathered here.

There's a reason for it, Alvin thought. Got to be a reason for it. And I have to know it, because there's going to be a jury of these knacky folks, and they're going to decide whether Makepeace Smith is a plain liar—or I am. Only this town is full of lies, since the things Vilate Franker says and the things Goody Trader says can't all be true at the same time. Full of lies and, yes, miseries. Alvin could feel that there was something of the Unmaker going on, but couldn't lay hands on it or find who it was. Hard to find the Unmaker when the Unmaker didn't want to be found. Especially hard from a jail cell, where all you got was rumor and brief visits.

Well, they wasn't *all* brief. Vilate Franker herself came and stayed sometimes half an hour at a time, even though there wasn't no place to sit down. Alvin couldn't figure what she wanted. She didn't gossip with him, rightly speaking—all of *her* gossip Alvin got secondhand from Arthur Stuart. No, Vilate came to him to talk about philosophy and poetry and such, things that no man or woman had talked to him about since Miss Larner. Alvin wondered if maybe Vilate was trying to charm him, but since he couldn't see the beauty-image from her hexes, he didn't rightly know. She sure wasn't pretty to *him*. But the more she talked, the more he liked her company, till he found himself looking forward to her coming every day. More than anybody except Arthur Stuart, truth be known, and as they talked, Alvin would lie down on the cot in the ceil and he'd close his eyes and then he didn't have to see either her unprettiness *or* her hexery, he could just hear the words and think the ideas and see the visions that she conjured in him. She'd say poetry and the words had music inside him. She'd talk of Plato and Alvin understood and it made him feel wise in a way that the adulation of folks back in Vigor Church never did.

Was this some knack of hers? Alvin didn't know, just plain couldn't tell. He only knew that it was only during her visits that he could completely forget that he was in jail. And it dawned on him, after a week or so, that he might just be falling in love. That the feelings that he had only ever had toward Miss Larner were getting waked up, just a little, by Vilate Franker. Now wouldn't that beat all? Miss Larner had been pretty and young, using knacks to make herself look plain and middle-aged. Now here was a woman plain and middle-aged using knacks that made other folks think she was pretty and young. How opposite could you be? But in both cases, it was the mature woman without obvious beauties that he delighted in.

And yet, even as he wondered if he was falling in love with Vilate, every now and then, in his lonely hours especially after dark, he would think of another face entirely. A young girl back in Vigor, the girl whose lies had driven him from home in the first place, the girl who claimed he had done forbidden things with her. He found himself thinking of those forbidden things, and there was a place in his heart where he wished he *had* done them. If he had, of course he would have married her. In fact, he would have married her before doing them, because that was right and the law and Alvin wasn't no kind of man to do wrong by a woman or break no law if he could help it. But in his imaginings in the dark there wasn't no law nor right and wrong neither, he just woke up sweating from a dream in which the girl wasn't no liar after all, and then he was plain ashamed of himself, and couldn't figure out what was wrong with him, to be falling in love with a woman of words and ideas and experience during the day, but then to be hot with passion for a stupid lying girl who just happened to be pretty and flat-out in love with him once upon a time back home.

I am an evil man, thought Alvin at times like that. Evil and unconstant. No better than them faithless fellows who can't leave women alone no matter what. I am the kind of man that I have long despised.

Only even that wasn't true, and Alvin knew it. Because he hadn't done a blamed thing wrong. Hadn't *done* anything. Had only imagined it. Imagined . . . and enjoyed. Was that enough to make him evil? "As a man thinketh in his heart, so is he," said the scripture. Alvin remembered it because his mother quoted it all the time till his father barked back at her, "That's just your way of saying that all men are devils!" and Alvin wondered if it was true—if all men had evil in their hearts, and those men as were good, maybe they were simply the ones who controlled theirselves so well they could act contrary to their heart's desire. But if that were so, then no man was good, not one.

And didn't the Holy Book say that, too?

No man good, not one. Not me, neither. Maybe me least of all.

And that was his life in that jail in Hatrack River. Darker and darker thoughts about his own worthiness, falling in love with two women at once, caught up in the gossip of a town where the Unmaker was surely at work, and where knacks abounded.

CALVIN WAS PRETTY good with stone—he always did all right with that. Well, not always. He wasn't *born* finding the natural weaknesses of stone. But after Alvin went off to be a prentice to a smith, Calvin started trying to do what he saw or heard of his big brother doing. In those days he was still hoping to show Alvin how good he was at Makering when he got back, to hear his brother say to him, "Calvin, why, you're most as good as I am!" Which Alvin never said, nor even close to it. But it was true, at least about stone. Stone was easy, really, not like flesh and bone. Calvin could find his way into the stone, part it, shift it.

Which is what he started doing right away with the Bastille, of course. He didn't know why the secret police had put him inside those walls, clammy and cold. It wasn't a dungeon, not like in those stories, where the prisoner never sees any light except when a guard comes down with a torch, so he can go blind without knowing it. There was light enough, and a chair to sit on and a bed to lie on and a chamber pot that got emptied every day, once he figured out he was supposed to leave it by the door.

It was still a prison, though.

It took Calvin about five minutes to figure out that he could pretty much dissolve the whole locking mechanism, but he remembered just in time that getting out of his cell wasn't exactly the same thing as getting out of the Bastille. He couldn't make himself invisible, and Maker or not, a musket ball would knock him down or maim him or kill him like any other man.

He'd have to find another way out. And that meant going right through the wall, right through stone. Trouble was, he didn't have any idea whether he was forty feet up or twenty feet under the street level. Or if the wall at the back of his cell opened on the outside or into an inner courtyard. Who might see if a gap appeared in the wall? He couldn't just remove a stone—he had to remove it in one piece, so he could put it back after if he had to.

He waited till night, then began working on a stone block right near floor level. It was heavy, and he didn't know of any way to make it lighter. Nor was there some subtle way to make stone move across stone. Finally he just softened the stone, plunged his fingers into it, then let it harden around his fingers, so he had a grip right in the middle of the stone block. Now, as he pulled on it, he made a thin layer of the stone turn liquid on the bottom and sides, so it was easier to pull it out, once he got it moving. It also made it silent as rock slid across rock. Except for the loud thud as the back of the stone dropped out of the hole and fell the few inches to the floor.

A breeze came through the cell, making it all the cooler. He slid the stone out of the way and then lay down and thrust his head and shoulders into the gap.

He was maybe twelve feet above the ground and directly over the head of a group of a dozen soldiers marching from somewhere to somewhere. Fortunately, they didn't look up. But that didn't keep Calvin's heart from beating halfway out of his chest. Once they were past, though, he figured he could go feetfirst through the hole and drop safely down to the ground and just walk away into the streets of Paris. Let them wonder how he got a stone out of the wall. That'd teach them to lock up folks who heal beggars.

He was all set to go, his feet already going into the hole, when it suddenly dawned on him that escaping was about as dumb a thing as he could do. Wasn't he here to see the Emperor? If he became a fugitive, that wasn't going to be too helpful. Bonaparte had powers that even Alvin didn't know about. Calvin *had* to learn them, if he could. The smart thing to do was sit tight here and see if somehow, someone in the chain of command might realize that a fellow who could heal beggars might be able to help with Bonaparte's famous gout.

So he got his back into it and hefted the stone back up into the gap and shoved it into place. He left the finger holes in it—it was dark at the back of the cell and besides, maybe if they noticed those holes in the stone they'd have more respect for his powers.

Or maybe not. How could he know? Everything was out of his control now. He hated that. But if you want to get something, you got to put yourself in the way of getting it.

Now that he wasn't trying to escape—but knew that he could if he wanted to—Calvin spent the days and nights lying on his cot or pacing his cell. Calvin wasn't good at being alone. He'd learned that on his trek through the woods after leaving Vigor. Alvin might be happy running along like a Red, but Calvin soon abandoned the forest tracks and got him on a road and hitched a ride on a farmer's wagon and then another and another, making friends and talking for company the whole way.

Now here he was stuck again, and even if the guards had been willing to talk to him, he didn't know the language. It hadn't bothered him that much when he was free to walk the streets of Paris and feel himself surrounded by the bustle of busy city life. Here, though, his inability to so much as ask a guard what day it was . . . it made him feel crippled.

Finally he began to amuse himself with mischief. It was no trouble at all to get his doodle bug inside the lock mechanism and ruin the guard's key by softening it when he inserted it. When the guard took the key back out, it had no teeth and the door was still locked. Angry, the guard stalked off to get another key. This time Calvin let him open the door without a problem—but what was it that made the first key lose its teeth?

And it wasn't just his own lock. He began to search far and wide with his doodle bug until he located the other occupied cells. He played games with their locks, too, including fusing a couple of them shut so no key could open them, and ruining a couple of others so they couldn't be locked at all. The shouting, the stomping, the running, it kept Calvin greatly entertained, especially as he imagined what the guards must be thinking. Ghosts? Spies? Who could be doing these strange things with the locks in the Bastille?

He also learned a few things. Back in Vigor, whenever he sat down for long he'd either get impatient and get up and move again, or he'd start thinking about Alvin and get all angry. Either way, he didn't spend all that much time testing the limits of his powers, not since Alvin came home. Now, though, he found that he could send his doodle bug right far, and into places that he'd never seen with his own eyes. He began to get used to moving his bug through the stone, feeling the different textures of it, sensing the wooden frames to the heavy doors, the metal hinges and locks. Damn, but he was good at this!

And he explored his own body with that doodle bug, and the bodies of the other prisoners, trying to find what it was that Alvin saw, trying to see deep. He experimented a little on the other prisoners' bodies, too, making changes in their legs the way he'd have to change Bonaparte's leg. Not that any of them had gout, of course—that was a rich man's disease, and nobody in prison was rich, even if they had money on the outside. Still, he could get a mental chart of what a more-or-less healthy leg looked like, on the inside. Get some idea of what he needed to do to get the Emperor's leg back in good shape.

Truth to tell, though, he didn't understand much more about legs after a week of this than he did at the beginning.

A week. A week and a half. Every day, more and more often, he'd walk to the wall, squat down, and put his fingers into those finger holes. He'd pull the stone a little bit, or maybe sometimes more, and once or twice all the way out of the wall, wanting to slide through the hole and walk away to freedom. Always, after a little thought, he put it back. But it took more thought every day. And the longing to be gone got stronger and stronger.

It was a blame fool plan anyway, like all his plans, when you came right down to it. Calvin was a fool to think they'd let some unknown American boy have access to the Emperor.

He had the stone out of the wall for what he thought might well be the last time, when he heard the steps in the corridor. Nobody ever came along here this late at night! No time to get the stone back in place, either. So . . . was it go, or stay? They'd see the stone out of the wall no matter what he did. So did he want to face the consequences, which might include seeing the Emperor, but might just as easy mean facing the guillotine; or did he duck through the hole and get out into the street before they got the door open?

LITTLE NAPOLEON GRUMBLED to himself. All these days, the Emperor could have asked about the American healer any time. But no, it had to be in the middle of the night, it had to be *tonight,* when Little Napoleon had reserved the best box for the opening of a new opera by some Italian, what's-his-name. He wanted to tell the Emperor that tonight was *not* convenient, he should find another toady to do his bidding. But then the Emperor smiled at him and suggested that he had others who could do such a menial job, and he shouldn't waste his nephew's time on such unimportant matters . . . and what could Little Napoleon do? He couldn't let the Emperor realize that he could be replaced by some flunky. No, he insisted, No, Uncle, I'll go myself, it'll be my pleasure.

"I just hope he can do what you promised," Bonaparte said.

The bastard was playing with him, that was the truth. He knew as well as Little Napoleon did that there was no promise of anything, just a report. But if it pleased the Emperor to make his nephew sweat with fear that maybe he'd be made a fool of, well, emperors were allowed to toy with other people's feelings.

The guard made a great noise about marching down the stone corridor and fumbling a long time with the keys.

"What, fool, are you giving the prisoner time to stop digging his tunnel and hide the evidence?"

"There be no tunnels from this floor, my lord," the turnkey said.

"I know that, fool. But what's all the fumble with the keys?"

"Most of them are new, my lord, and I don't recognize which one opens which door, not as easy as I used to."

"Then get the old keys and don't waste my time!"

"The old keys been stripped, or the locks was broken, my lord. It's been crazy, you wouldn't believe it."

"I *don't* believe it," said Little Napoleon grumpily. But he did, really—he had heard something about some sabotage or some kind of rare lock rust or something in the Bastille.

The key finally slid into the lock, and the door creaked open. The turnkey stepped in and shone his lantern about, to make sure the prisoner was in his place and not poised to jump him and take the keys. No, this one, the American boy, he was sitting far from the door, leaning against the opposite wall.

Sitting on what? The turnkey took a step or two closer, held the lantern higher.

"Mon dieu," murmured Little Napoleon.

The American was sitting on a large stone block from the wall, with a gap that led right out to the street. No man could have lifted such a block out of the wall with his bare hands—how could he even get hold of it? But having moved it somehow, what did this American fool do but sit down and wait! Why didn't he escape?

The American grinned at him, then stood up, still smiling, still looking at Little Napoleon—and then plunged his hands into the stone right up to his elbows, as easy as if the stone had been a water basin.

The turnkey screeched and ran for the door.

The American pulled his hands back out of the stone—except that one of them was in a fist now. He held out the stone to Little Napoleon, who took it, hefted it. It was stone, as hard as ever—but it was shaped with the print of the inside of a man's palms and fingers. Somehow this fellow could reach into solid rock and grab a lump of stone as if it were clay.

Little Napoleon reached into his memory and pulled out some English from his days in school. "What are your name?" he asked.

"Calvin Maker," said the American.

"Speak you the French?"

"Not a word," said Calvin Maker.

"Go *avec* me," said Little Napoleon. *"Avec . . ."*

"With," said the boy helpfully. "Go with you."

"Oui. Yes."

The Emperor had finally asked for the boy. But now Little Napoleon had serious misgivings. There was nothing about the healing of beggars to suggest the boy might have power over solid stone. What if this Calvin Maker did something to embarrass him? What if—it was beyond imagining, but he had to imagine it—what if he killed Uncle Napoleon?

But the Emperor had asked for him. There was no undoing *that*. What was he going to do, go tell Uncle that the boy he'd brought to heal his gout just *might* decide to plunge his hands into the floor and pull up a lump of marble and brain him with it? That would be political suicide. He'd be living on Corsica tending sheep in no time. If he didn't get to watch the world tumble head over heels as his head rolled down into the basket from the guillotine.

"Go go go," said Little Napoleon. "Wiss me."

The turnkey was huddled in a far corner of the corridor. Little Napoleon aimed a kick in his direction. The man was so far gone that he didn't even dodge. The kick landed squarely, and with a whimper the turnkey rolled over like a cabbage.

The American boy laughed out loud. Little Napoleon didn't like his laugh. He toyed with the idea of drawing his knife and killing the boy on the spot. But the explanation to the Emperor would be dangerous. "So you tried for weeks to get me to see him, and he was an assassin all along?" No, whatever happened, the American would see the Emperor.

Calvin Maker would see Napoleon Bonaparte . . . while Little Napoleon would see if God would answer a most fervent prayer.

12

LAWYERS

"You know the miller's boy, Alvin, is in jail up in Hatrack River." The stranger leaned on the counter and smiled.

"I reckon we heard about it," said Armor-of-God Weaver.

"I'm here to help get the truth about Alvin, so the jury can make the right judgment up in Hatrack. They don't know Alvin as well as folks around here are bound to. I just need to get some affidavits about his character." The stranger smiled again.

Armor-of-God nodded. "I reckon this is the place for affidavits, if the truth about Alvin is what you're after."

"That I am. I take it you know the young man yourself?"

"Well enough." Armor-of-God figured if he was going to find out what this fellow was doing, it was best not to say he was married to Alvin's sister. "But I reckon you don't know what you're getting into up here, friend. You'll get more than the affidavits you're after."

"Oh, I've heard tell about the massacre at Tippy-Canoe, and the curse that folks here are under. I'm a lawyer. I'm used to hearing grim stories from people I'm defending."

"Defending, eh?" asked Armor. "You a lawyer as defends people, is that it?"

"That's what I'm best known for, in my home in Carthage City."

Armor nodded again. He might live in Carthage City now, but his accent said New England. And he might try some folksy talk, but it was a lawyer's version of it, to put folks off guard. This man could talk like the Bible if he wanted to. He could talk like Milton. But Armor didn't let on that he didn't trust the man. Not yet. "So when folks here tell you how they slaughtered Reds what never done nobody no harm, you can hear that without batting an eye, is that it?"

"I can't guarantee I won't do any eye-batting, Mr. Weaver. But I'll listen, and when it's done, I'll get on with the business that brought me here."

Now it's time. "And what business is that?" asked Armor.

The man blinked. Already batting an eye, thought Armor. That was right quick.

"I told you, Mr. Weaver. Getting affidavits about Alvin the miller's son."

"In order to tell people in Hatrack River about his true character, I remember. The thing is, out of the last eight years, Alvin spent seven in Hatrack, and only one here in Vigor Church. We knowed him as a child, you bet, but lately I'd say it's the people of Hatrack River as knows him best. So the way I see it, you're here to get a picture of Alvin that folks in Hatrack *don't* know. And the only reason for that is because you need to change their point of view about the boy. And since I know for a fact that Alvin is respected in Hatrack, you can only be here to try to dig up some dirt on the boy in order to do him harm. Have I just about got it? Friend?"

The lawyer's sudden lack of a cheerful smile was all the confirmation Armor needed. "Dirt is the farthest thing from my mind, Mr. Weaver. I come here with an open mind."

"An open mind, and free talk about how you defend people and all so as to make folks think you're on Alvin's side, instead of being hired to do your best to destroy folks' good opinion of him. So I reckon the fact that you're here means that Alvin's friends better get somebody else to go around collecting affidavits in his favor, since you won't be satisfied until you dig up some lies."

The man stiffened and stepped back. "I see that you're rather a partisan about the matter. I hope you can tell me what I said to give offense."

"Why, the only offense you gave was thinking that because I'm not a lawyer I must be dumb as a dog's butt."

"Well, no matter what conclusion you have reached, I assure you that as an officer of the court I seek nothing more than the simple truth."

"Officer of the court, is it? Well, I happen to know that *all* lawyers is called officers of the court. Even when they're hired by a private party to do mischief, because you sure as God lives wasn't hired by the county attorney down in Hatrack, because *he* would've give you a letter of introduction and you wouldn't have tried none of these pussyfooting pre-varicating misrepresenting shenanigans."

The stranger put his hat back on his head and pushed it down right firm. Armor suppressed the impulse to reach out and push it down still firmer. As the stranger reached the door, Armor called out one last question. "Do you have a name, so we can inquire with the state bar association about any outstanding actions against you?"

The lawyer turned and smiled, even broader than when he was trying to fool Armor. "My name is Daniel Webster, Mr. Weaver, and my client is truth and justice."

"Truth and justice must pay a damn sight better in New England than it does out here," said Armor. "You *are* from New England, aren't you?"

"I was born there, and raised there, but saw no future for myself in that benighted backward place. So I came to the United States, where the laws are founded on the rights of man instead of the dynastic claims of monarchs or the worn-out theology of Puritans."

"Ah. So nobody's paying you?"

"I didn't say that, Mr. Weaver."

"Who's paying you, then? Ain't the county, and it ain't the state. And it sure can't be Makepeace Smith, since he's got him hardly four bits to rub together."

"I'm representing a consortium of concerned citizens of Carthage City, who are determined to see that justice prevails even in the benighted backwaters of the state of Hio."

"A consortium. That anything like a public house? Or a brothel?"

"How amusing."

"Name me a name, Mr. Webster. I happen to be mayor of this town, such as it is, and you're here practicing law, after a fashion, and I think I have a right to know who's sending lawyers up here to collect lies about our respected citizens."

"Do you own a gun of any kind, Mr. Weaver?"

"I do, friend."

"Then why should I reveal the names of my clients to an armed and angry man of a town that is so proud of being a nest of murderers that they brag out the whole story to any unfortunate visitor who happens by? Also, mayors have no right to inquire about anything from an attorney about his relations with his clients. Good day, Mr. Weaver."

Armor watched the Webster fellow out the door, then put on his hat, called out to his oldest boy to leave off soapmaking and watch the store, and took off at a jog up and over the hill to his in-laws' house. His wife would be there, since she was the best of the women at doing Alvin's Makery stuff and so was in much demand as a teacher and a fashioner of—much as Armor hated it—hexes. The family needed to know what was going on, that Alvin had enemies from the capital who were spending money on a lawyer to come dig up dirt about the boy. There was no way around it now— they had to get them a lawyer for Alvin, somehow. And not no country cousin, either. It had to be a city lawyer who knew all the same tricks as this Webster fellow. Armor vaguely remembered having heard of this man somewhere. He was spoke of with awe in some circles, and having talked to him and heard his golden voice and his quick answers and the way he made a lie sound like the natural truth even to someone who knew it was deception—well, Armor knew it would take some finding to get them a lawyer who could best him. And finding was going to be complicated by another problem—paying.

CALVIN HAD NO idea what he was supposed to do upon meeting the Emperor. The man's title was a throwback to ancient Rome, to Persia, to Babylon. But there he sat in a straight-back chair instead of a throne, his leg up on a cushioned bench; and instead of courtiers there were only secretaries, each scribbling away on a writing desk until an order or letter or edict was finished, then leaping to his feet and rushing from the room as the next secretary began to scribble furiously as Bonaparte dictated in a continuous stream of biting, lilting, almost Italian-sounding French.

As the dictation proceeded, Calvin, with guards on either side of him (as if that could stop him from making the floor collapse under the Emperor if he felt like it), watched silently. Of course they did not invite him to sit down; even Little Napoleon, the Emperor's nephew, remained standing. Only the secretaries could sit, it seemed, for it was hard to imagine how they could write without a lap.

At first Calvin simply took in the surroundings; then he studied the face of the Emperor, as if that slightly pained expression contained some secret which, if only examined long enough, would yield the secrets of the sphinx. But soon Calvin's attention drifted to the leg. It was the gout that he had to cure, if he was to make any headway. And Calvin had no idea what caused the gout or even how to figure it out. That was Alvin's province.

For a moment it occurred to Calvin that maybe he ought to beg permission to write to his brother so he could get Alvin over here to cure the Emperor and win Calvin's freedom. But he immediately despised himself for the cowardly thought. Am I a Maker or not? And if a Maker, then Alvin's equal. And if Alvin's equal, why should I summon him to bail me out of a situation which, for all I know right now, might need no bailing?

He sent his doodling bug into Napoleon's leg.

It wasn't the sort of swelling that Calvin was used to in the festering sores of beggars. He didn't understand what the fluids were—not pus, that was certain—and he dared not simply make them flow back into the blood, for fear that they might be poisons that would kill the very man he came to learn from.

Besides, was it really in Calvin's best interests to cure this man? Not that he knew how to do it—but he wasn't sure he really ought to try. What he needed was not the momentary gratitude of a cured man, but the continuing dependence of a sufferer who needed Calvin's ministration for relief. Temporary relief.

And this was something Calvin *did* understand, to a point. He had learned long ago how to find the nerves in a dog or squirrel and give them a sort of tweak, an invisible pinch. Sometimes it set the animal to squealing and screeching till Calvin almost died from laughing. Other times the creature didn't show pain, but limped along as if that pinched limb didn't even exist. One time a perfectly healthy dog dragged around its hindquarters till its belly and legs were rubbed raw in the dirt and Father was all set to shoot the poor thing to put it out of its misery. Calvin took mercy on the beast then and unpinched the nerve so it could walk again, but after that it never did walk right, it sort of sidled, though whether that was from the pinch Calvin gave it or from the damage caused by dragging its butt through the dirt for most of a week Calvin had no way to guess.

What mattered was that pinching of the nerve, to remove all feeling—Bonaparte might limp, but it would take away the pain. Relief, not a cure.

Which nerve? It wasn't like Calvin had them all charted out. That sort of methodical thinking was Alvin's game. In England, Calvin had realized that this was one of the crucial differences between him and his brother. There was a new word a fellow just coined at Cambridge for people who were ploddingly methodical like Alvin: *scientist*. While Calvin, with dash and flair and verve and, above all, the spirit of improvisation, *he* was an artist. Trouble was, when it came to getting at the nerves in Bonaparte's leg, Calvin couldn't very well experiment. He didn't think a strong friendship would develop between the Emperor and him if it began with the Emperor squealing and screeching like a tortured squirrel.

He pondered that for a while until, watching a secretary rise up and rush from the room, it occurred to him that Bonaparte's weren't the only legs around. Now that it mattered that Calvin find out exactly which nerve did what, and that his pinch deadened pain instead of provoking it, he had to play the scientist and test many legs until he got it right.

He started with the secretary who was next in line, a shortish fellow (smaller even than the Emperor, who was a man of scant stature) who fidgeted a little in his chair. Uncomfortable? Calvin asked him silently. Then let's see if we can find you some relief. He sent his bug into the man's right leg, found the most obvious nerve, and pinched.

Not a wince, not a grimace. Calvin was annoyed. He pinched harder. Nothing.

Then the current secretary jumped to his feet and rushed from the room. It was now the turn of the short fellow Calvin had pinched. The man tried to shift his body in his chair, to adjust the position of the lapdesk, but to Calvin's delight a look of astonishment came over the man's face, followed by a blush as he had to reach down and move his right leg with his hands. So. That large nerve—or was it a bundle of very fine nerves?—had nothing to do with feeling. Instead they seemed to control movement. Interesting.

The fellow wrote in silence, but Calvin knew that all he was really thinking about was what would happen when he had to jump up and run from the room. Sure enough, when the edict ended—it was about the granting of a special tax exemption to certain vintners in southern France because of a bad harvest—the man leapt up, spun around, and

586 • *Orson Scott Card*

sprawled on the floor, his right leg tangled with his left like the fishing lines of children.

Every eye turned to the poor fellow, but not a word was spoken. Calvin watched with amusement as he got up on his hands and his left knee, while the right leg hung useless. The knee bent well enough, of course, and the man got it under his body so it *looked* like it might work, but twice he tried to put weight on it and twice he fell again.

Bonaparte, looking annoyed, finally spoke to him. "Are you a secretary, sir, or a clown?"

"My leg, sir," said the miserable clerk. "My right leg seems not to work just now."

Bonaparte turned sharply to the guards detaining Calvin. "Help him out of here. And fetch someone to clean up the spilled ink."

The guards hauled the man to his feet and started to move him toward the door. Now it was time for Little Napoleon to assert himself. "Take his desk, fools," said the Emperor's nephew. "And the inkwell, and the quill, and the edict, if it isn't spoiled."

"And how will they do all that?" asked Bonaparte testily. "Seeing they have to hold up this one-legged beggar?" Then he looked expectantly at Little Napoleon's face.

It took a moment for Little Napoleon to realize what the Emperor wanted of him, and an even longer moment for him to swallow his pride enough to do it. "Why, of course, Uncle," he said, with careful mildness. "I shall gladly pick it up myself, sir."

Calvin suppressed a smile as the proud man who had arrested him now knelt down and gathered up papers, lapdesk, quill, and inkwell, carefully avoiding getting a single drop of ink on himself. By now the secretary Calvin had pinched was out of the room. He thought of sending out his bug to find the man and unpinch the nerve, but he wasn't sure where he had gone and anyway, what did it matter? It was just a secretary.

When Little Napoleon was gone, Bonaparte resumed dictating, but now his delivery was not rapid and biting. Rather he halted, corrected himself now and then, and sometimes lapsed into silence for a time, as the secretary sat with pen poised. At such moments Calvin would cause the ink on the quill to flow to the tip and drop off suddenly onto the paper—ah, the flurry of blotting! And of course this only served to distract the Emperor all the more.

There remained, however, the matter of legs. Calvin explored each secretary in turn, finding other nerves to pinch, ever so slightly. He left the nerves of movement alone now; it was the nerves of pain that he was finding now, charting his progress by the widened eyes, flushed faces, and occasional gasps of the unfortunate secretaries. Bonaparte was not unaware of their discomfort—it distracted him all the more. Finally, when a man gasped at a particularly sharp pinch—Calvin's touch was not always precise with such slender things as nerves—Bonaparte turned himself in his chair, wincing at the pain in his own leg, and said, as best Calvin could understand his French, "Do you mock me with these pains and moans? I sit here in agony, making no sound, while you, with no more pain than that of sitting too long to take letters, moan and gasp and wince and sigh until I can only imagine I am trapped with a choir of hyenas!"

At that moment Calvin finally got it right, giving just the right amount of pressure to a secretary's pain nerve that all feeling vanished, and instead of the man wincing, his face relaxed in relief. That's it, thought Calvin. That's how it's done.

He almost sent his bug right into Bonaparte's leg to do that same little twist and make the Emperor's pain go away. Fortunately he was distracted by the opening of the door. It was a scullery maid with a bucket and rags to clean up the ink from the marble floor. Bonaparte glared at her, and she almost dropped her things and fled, except that he at once softened his expression. "My rage is at my pain, girl," he said to her. "Come in and do your work, no one minds."

With that she gathered her courage, scurried to the drying ink, set down the bucket with a clank and a slosh, and set to work scrubbing.

By now Calvin had come to his senses. What good would it do to take away Bonaparte's pain if the Emperor didn't *know* that it was Calvin doing it? Instead he practiced the soothing twist of the nerves on all the secretaries, to their undoubted relief, and as he did he began to sense a sort of current, a humming, a vibration on the nerves that were actually carrying pain at the instant he twisted them, so that he could get even more precise, taking away not all the feeling in a leg, but just the pain itself. Finally he got to the scullery maid, to the pain she always felt in her knees as she knelt on hard cold floors to do her work. So sudden was the relief, and so sharp and constant had been the pain, that she cried aloud, and again Bonaparte glared at the interruption.

"Oh sir," she said, "forgive me, but I suddenly felt no pain in my knees."

"Lucky you," said Bonaparte. "Along with this miracle, do you also find that you see no ink on the floor?"

She looked down. "Sir, with all my scrubbing, I can't get up the whole stain. I'm afraid it's gone down into the stone, sir."

Calvin at once sent his doodling bug into the surface of the marble and discovered that the ink had, indeed, penetrated beyond the reach of her scrubbing. Now was the chance to have Bonaparte notice him, not as a prisoner—even his guards were gone—but as a man of power. "Perhaps I can help," he said.

Bonaparte looked at him as if seeing him for the first

time, though Calvin was quite aware that the Emperor had sized him up several times over the past half-hour. Bonaparte spoke to him in accented English. "Was it for scullery work you came to Paris, my dear American friend?"

"I came to serve you, sir," said Calvin. "Whether with a stained floor or a pained leg, I care not."

"Let's see you with floors first," said Bonaparte. "Give him the rags and bucket, girl."

"I don't need them," said Calvin. "I've already done it. Have her scrub again, and this time the stain will come right up."

Bonaparte glowered at the idea of serving as interpreter for an American prisoner and a scullery maid, but his curiosity got the better of his dignity and he gave the girl the order to scrub again. This time the ink came right up, and the stone was clean again. It had been child's play for Calvin, but the awe in the girl's face was the best possible advertisement for his wondrous power. "Sir," she said, "I had only to pass the rag over the stain and it was gone!"

The secretaries were eyeing Calvin carefully now—they weren't fools, and they clearly suspected him of causing both their discomfort and their relief, though some of them were pinching the legs to try to restore feeling after Calvin's first, clumsier attempts at numbing pain. Now Calvin went back into their legs, restored feeling, and then gave the more delicate twist that removed pain. They watched him warily, as Bonaparte looked back and forth between his clerks and his prisoner.

"I see you have been busy playing little jokes on my secretaries."

Without an answer, Calvin reached into the Emperor's leg and, for just a moment, removed all pain. But only for a moment; he soon let it come back.

Bonaparte's face darkened. "What kind of man are you,

to take away my pain for a moment and then send it back to me?"

"Forgive me, sir," said Calvin. "It's easy to cure the pain I caused myself, in your men. Or even the pain from hours of kneeling, scrubbing floors. But the gout—that's hard, sir, and I know of no cure, nor of any relief that lasts more than a little while."

"Longer than five seconds, though—I'll wager you know how to do *that*."

"I can try."

"You're the clever one," said Bonaparte. "But I know a lie. You can take away the pain and yet you choose not to. How dare you hold me hostage to my pain?"

Calvin answered in mild tones, though he knew he took his life in his hands to say such a bold thing in *any* tone: "Sir, you have held my whole body prisoner this whole time, when I was free before. I come here and find you already a prisoner of pain, and you complain to *me* that I do not set *you* free?"

The secretaries gasped again, but not in pain this time. Even the scullery maid was shocked—so much so that she knocked her bucket over, spilling soapy, inky water over half the floor.

Calvin quickly made the water evaporate from the floor, then made the residue of ink turn to fine, invisible dust.

The scullery maid went screaming from the room.

The secretaries, too, were on their feet. Bonaparte turned to them. "If I hear any rumor of this, you will all go to the Bastille. Find the girl and silence her—by persuasion or imprisonment, she deserves no torture. Now leave me alone with this extortionist, while I find out what he wants to get from me."

They left the room. As they were going, Little Napoleon

and the guards returned, but Bonaparte sent them away as well, to his nephew's ill-concealed fury.

"All right, we're alone," said Bonaparte. "What do you want?"

"I want to heal your pain."

"Then heal it and have done."

Calvin took the challenge, twisted the nerves just right, and saw Bonaparte's face soften, losing the perpetual wince. "Such a gift as that," murmured the Emperor, "and you spend it cleaning floors and taking stones from prison walls."

"It won't last," said Calvin.

"You mean you choose not to make it last," said Bonaparte.

Calvin took the unusual step of telling the plain truth, sensing that Bonaparte would know if anything he said was a lie. "It's not a cure. The gout is still there. I don't understand the gout and I can't cure it. I can take away the pain."

"But not for long."

Truthfully, Calvin answered, "I don't know how long."

"And for what payment?" asked Bonaparte. "Come on, boy, I know you want something. Everyone does."

"But you're Napoleon Bonaparte," said Calvin. "I thought you knew what every man wanted."

"God doesn't whisper it in my ear, if that's what you think. And yes, I know what you want but I have no idea why you've come to me for it. You're hungry to be the greatest man on Earth. I've met men with ambition like yours before—and women, too. Unfortunately I can't easily bend such ambition into subservience to my interests. Generally I have to kill them, because they're a danger to me."

Those words went like a knife through Calvin's heart.

"But you're different," said Bonaparte. "You mean me no harm. In fact, I'm just a tool to you. A means of gaining advantage. You don't want my kingdom. I rule all of Europe, northern Africa, and much of the ancient East, and yet you want me only to tutor you in preparation for a much greater game. What game, on God's green Earth, might that be?"

Calvin never meant to tell him, but the words came blurting out. "I have a brother, an older brother, who has a thousand times my power." The words galled him, burned his throat as he said them.

"And a thousand times your virtue, too, I think," said Bonaparte. But those words had no sting for Calvin. Virtue, as Alvin defined it, was waste and weakness. Calvin was proud to have little of it.

"Why hasn't your brother challenged me?" asked Bonaparte. "Why hasn't he shown his face to me in all these years?"

"He's not ambitious," said Calvin.

"That is a lie," said Bonaparte, "even though in your ignorance you believe it. There is no such thing as a living human being without ambition. St. Paul said it best: Faith, ambition, and love, the three driving forces of human life."

"I believe it was hope," said Calvin. "Hope and charity."

"Hope is the sweet weak sister of ambition. Hope is ambition wishing to be liked."

Calvin smiled. "That's what I've come for," he said.

"Not to heal my gout."

"To ease your pain, as you ease my ignorance."

"With powers like yours, what do you need with my small world-conquering gifts?" Bonaparte's irony was plain and painful.

"My powers are nothing compared to my brother's, and he is the only teacher I can learn them from. So I need other powers that he doesn't have."

"Mine."

"Yes."

"Then how do I know that you won't turn on me and try to take my empire?"

"If I wanted it I could have it now," said Calvin.

"It's one thing to terrify people with displays of power," said Bonaparte. "But terror only gets you obedience when you're there. I have the power to hold men obedient to me even when my back is turned, even when there's no chance I'd ever catch them in wrongdoing. They love me, they serve me with their whole hearts. Even if you sent every building in Paris crashing to the street, it wouldn't win the people's loyalty."

"That's why I'm here, because I know that."

"Because you want to win the loyalty of your brother's friends," said Bonaparte. "You want them to spurn your brother and put you in his place."

"Call me Cain if you want, but yes," said Calvin. "Yes."

"I can teach you that," said Bonaparte. "But no pain. And no little games with the pain, either. If the pain comes back, I'll have you killed."

"You can't even hold me in a prison if I don't want to stay there."

"When I decide to kill you, boy, you won't even see it coming."

Calvin believed him.

"Tell me, boy—"

"Calvin."

"Boy, don't interrupt me, don't correct me." Bonaparte smiled sweetly. "Tell me, Calvin, weren't you afraid that I would win *your* loyalty and put your gifts to use in my service?"

"As you said," Calvin answered, "your powers have scant effect on people with ambition as great as your own. It's only really the goodness in people that you turn against them to control them. Their generosity. Isn't that right?"

"In a sense, though it's much more complicated than that. But yes."

Calvin smiled broadly. "Well, then, you see? I knew I was immune."

Bonaparte frowned. "Are you so sure of that? So proud to be a man utterly devoid of generosity?"

Calvin's smile faded just a little. "Old Boney, the terror of Europe, the toppler of empires—Old Boney is shocked at *my* lack of compassion?"

"Yes," said Bonaparte. "I never thought I'd see the like. A man I'll never have power over . . . and yet I will let you stay with me, for the sake of my leg, and I'll teach you all that can be taught. For the sake of my leg."

Calvin laughed and nodded. "Then you've got a deal."

Only later, as he was being shown to a luxurious apartment in the palace, did it occur to Calvin to wonder if, perhaps, Bonaparte's admission that Calvin could not be controlled might not be just a ploy; if, perhaps, Bonaparte already had control over Calvin but, like all the Emperor's other tools, Calvin continued to think that he was free.

No, he told himself. Even if it's true, what good will it do me to think about it? The deed's done or it's not done, and either way I'm still myself and still have Alvin to deal with. A thousand times more powerful than me! A thousand times more virtuous! We'll see about that when the time comes, when I take your friends away from you, Alvin, the way you stole my birthright from *me,* you thieving Esau, you pit-digging Reuben, you jealous taunting Ishmael. God will give me my birthright, and has given me Bonaparte to teach me how to accomplish something with it.

ALVIN DIDN'T REALIZE he was doing it. Daytimes he thought he was bearing his imprisonment right well, putting on a cheerful face for his visitors, singing now and then—harmonizing with the jailors when they knew the song and joined in. It was a jaunty sort of imprisonment, and everyone was saying that it was a shame for Alvin to be all cooped up, but wasn't he taking it like a soldier?

In his sleep, though, his hatred for the jail walls, for the sameness and lifelessness of the place, it came out in another kind of song, an inward music that harmonized with the greensong that once had filled this part of the world. It was the music of the trees and the lesser plants, of the insects and spiders, of the furred and finny creatures that dwelt in the leaves, on the ground, in the earth, or in the cold streams and unstoppable rivers. And Alvin's inner voice was tuned to it, knew all the melodies, and instead of harmonizing with jailors his heart sang with free creatures.

And they heard his song that went unheard by human ears. In the tattered remnants of the ancient woods, in the new growth where a few abandoned fields were four or ten years fallow, they heard him, the last few bison, the still deer, the hunting cats and the sociable coyotes and the timber wolves. The birds above all heard him, and they came first, in twos, in tens, in flocks of hundreds, visiting the town and singing with his music for a while, daybirds coming in the nighttime, until the town was wakened by the din of so many songs all at once. They came and sang an hour and left again, but the memory of their song lingered.

First the birds, and then the song of coyotes, the howl of wolves, not so near as to be terrifying, but near enough to fill the untuned hearts of most folks with a kind of dread, and they woke with nightsweats. Raccoon prints were all over, and yet there was no tearing or thievery, and no more than the usual number of chickens were taken, though foxfeet had trodden on every henhouse roof. Squirrels a-gathering their nuts ran fearlessly through the town to leave small offerings outside the courthouse. Fish leapt in the Hatrack and in other nearby streams, a silver dance in the sparkling moonlit water, the drops like stars falling back into the stream.

Through it Alvin slept, and most folks also slept, so only gradually did the word spread that the natural world was all aflutter, and then only a few began to link it with Alvin being in jail. Logical folks said there couldn't be no connection. Dr. Whitley Physicker boldly said, when asked (and sometimes when no one asked at all), "I'm the first to say it's wrong to have that boy locked up. But that doesn't imply that the swarming of harmless unstinging bees through the town last night meant anything at all except that perhaps this will be a hardish winter. Or perhaps a mild one. I'm not a great reader of bees. But it's *nothing* to do with Alvin in jail because nature hardly concerns itself with the legal disputes of human beings!"

True enough, but, as a lawyer might say, irrelevant. It wasn't Alvin in jail that disturbed nature, it was Alvin singing in his dreams that drew them. And those few in town who could hear some faint echo of his song—ones like John Binder, for instance, and Captain Harriman, who had heard such silent stirrings all their lives—why, they didn't wake up to the birdsong and the coyotes yipping and the wolves howling and the patter of squirrel feet on shingles. Those things just fit into their own dreams, for to them it all belonged, it all fit, and Alvin's song and the natural greensong of the world spoke peace to them deep in their hearts. They heard the rumors but didn't understand the fuss. And if Drunken Freda drank a little less and slept a little better, who would notice it besides herself?

VERILY COOPER CAME to Vigor Church the hard way, but then everybody did. What with the town's reputation for making travelers listen to a hard dark story, it's no wonder nobody put a stagecoach route there. The railroad wasn't out that far west yet, but even if it was, it wasn't likely there'd be a Vigor Station or even a spur. The town that Armor-of-God Weaver once expected to be the gateway to the west was now a permanent backwater.

So it was railroad—shaky and stinky, but fast and cheap—to Dekane, and stagecoach from there. By sheerest chance, Verily's route took him right through the town of Hatrack River, where the man he was coming to meet, Calvin's brother Alvin, was locked up. But this was the express coach and it didn't stop in Hatrack for a leisurely meal at Horace Guester's roadhouse, where no doubt Verily would have heard talk that stopped his journey right there. Instead he rode on to Carthage City, changed to a slow coach heading northwest into Wobbish, and then got out at a sleepy little ferry town and bought him a horse and a saddle and a pack mule for his luggage, which wasn't all that much but more than he wanted to have on the horse he was riding. From there it was a simple matter of riding north all day, stopping at a farmhouse at night, and riding another day until, late in the afternoon, just as the sun was setting, he came to Armor's general store, where lamps were lit and Verily hoped he might find a night's lodging.

"I'm sorry," said the man at the door. "We don't take in lodgers—not much call for them in this town. The miller's family up the road takes in such lodgers as we get, but . . . well, friend, you might as well come in. Because most of the miller's family is right here in my store, and besides, there's a tale they have to tell you before you or they can go to bed tonight."

"I've been told of it," said Verily Cooper, "and I'm not afraid to hear it."

"So you came here on purpose?"

"With those signs on the road, warning travelers away?"

Verily stepped through the doorway. "I have a horse and a mule to attend to—"

His words were heard by the people gathered on stools and chairs and leaning on the store counter. Immediately two young men with identical faces swung themselves over the counter. "I've got the horse," said one.

"Which gives me the mule—and his baggage, no doubt."

"And I've got the saddle," said the first. "I think it comes out even."

Verily Cooper stuck out his hand in the forthright American manner he had already learned. "I'm Verily Cooper," he said.

"Wastenot Miller," said one of the boys.

"And I'm Wantnot," said the other.

"Puritans, from the naming of you," said Verily.

"Not on a bet," said a thick-bodied middle-aged man who was sitting on a stool in the corner. "Naming babies for virtues ain't no monopoly of religious fanatics from New England."

For the first time Verily felt suspicion in the air, and he realized that they had to be wondering who he was and what his business was here. "There's not more than one miller in town, is there?" he asked.

"Only me," said the thickset man.

"Then you must be Alvin Miller, Senior," said Verily, striding up to him and thrusting out his hand.

The miller took it warily. "You've got me pegged, young feller, but all I know about you is that you come here late in the day, nobody knew you was coming, and you talk like a highfalutin Englishman with a lot of education. Had us a preacher here for a while who talked like you. Not anymore though." And from the tone of his voice, Verily gathered that the parting hadn't been a pleasant one.

"My name is Verily Cooper," he said. "My father's trade is barrelmaking, and I learned the trade as a boy. But you're right, I did get an education and I'm now a barrister."

The miller looked puzzled. "Barrelmaker to barrister," he said. "I got to say I don't rightly know the difference."

The man who greeted him at the door helped out. "A barrister is an English lawyer."

The dry tone of his voice and the way everyone stiffened up told Verily that they had something against lawyers here. "Please, I assure you, I left that profession behind when I left England. I doubt that I'd be allowed to practice law here in the United States, at least not without some kind of examination. I didn't come here for that, anyway."

The miller's wife—or so Verily guessed from her age, for she wasn't sitting by the man—spoke up, and with a good deal less hostility in her voice than her husband had had. "A man comes from England especially to come to the town in America that lives every day in shame. I admit I'm curious, lawyer or no lawyer. What *is* your business here?"

"Well, I met a son of yours, I think. And what he told me—"

It was almost comic, the way they all suddenly leaned forward. "You saw Calvin?"

"The very one," said Verily. "An interesting young man."

They reserved comment.

Well, if there was one thing Verily had learned as a lawyer, it was that he didn't have to fill every silence with his own speech. He couldn't be sure of this family's attitude toward Calvin—after all, Calvin was such an accomplished liar he must have practiced the art here at home before trying to use it to make his way in the world. So he might be hated. Or he might be loved and yearned for. Verily didn't want to make a mistake.

Finally, predictably, it was Calvin's mother who spoke up. "You saw my boy? Where was he? How was he?"

"I met him in London. He has the language and bearing of quite a clever young man. Seems to be in good health, too."

They nodded, and Verily saw that they seemed to be relieved. So they did love him, and had feared for him.

A tall, lanky man of about Verily's age stretched out his long legs and leaned back on his stool. "I'm pretty near certain that you didn't come all this way just to tell us Calvin was a-doing fine, Mr. Cooper."

"No, indeed not. It was something Calvin said." Verily looked around at them again, this large family that was at once welcoming and suspicious of a stranger, at once concerned and wary about a missing son. "He spoke of a brother of his." At this Verily looked at the lanky one who had just spoken. "A son with talents that exceeded Calvin's own."

The lanky one hooted and several others chuckled. "Don't go telling us no stories!" he said. "Calvin wouldn't never speak of Alvin that way!"

So the lanky one wasn't Alvin Junior after all. "Well, let's just say that I read between the lines, so to speak. You know that in England, the use of hidden powers and arcane arts is severely punished. So we Englishmen remain quite ignorant of such matters. I gathered, however, that if there was one person in the world who could teach me how to understand such things, it might well be Calvin's brother Alvin."

They all agreed with that, nodding, some even smiling.

But the father remained suspicious. "And why would an English lawyer be looking to learn more about such things?"

Verily, to his own surprise, was at a loss for words. All his thought had been about finding Alvin the miller's son—but of course they would have to know why he cared so much about hidden powers. What could he say? All his life he had been forced to hide his gift, his curse; now he found he couldn't just blurt it out, or even hint.

Instead, he strode to the counter and picked up a couple of large wooden spools of thread that were standing there, presumably so that customers could reel off the length of thread they wanted and wind it onto a smaller spool. He put the ends of the spools together, and then found the perfect fit for them, so that no man could pull them apart.

He handed the joined spools to the miller. At once the man tried to pull them apart, but he didn't seem surprised when he failed. He looked at his wife and smiled. "Lookit that," he said. "A lawyer who knows how to do something useful. That's a miracle."

The spools got passed around, mostly in silence, until they got to the lanky young man leaning back on his stool. Without a moment's reflection, he pulled the spools apart and set them on the counter. "Spools ain't no damn good stuck together like that," he said.

Verily was stunned. "You *are* the one," he said. "You *are* Alvin."

"No, sir," said the young man. "My name is Measure, but I've been learning somewhat of my brother's skill. That's his main work these days, is teaching folks how to do the same Makering stuff that he does, and I reckon I'm learning it about as good as anybody. But you—I *know* he'd want to meet you."

"Yes," said Verily, making no effort to hide his enthusiasm. "Yes, that's what I've come for. To learn from him—so I'm glad to hear that he wants to teach."

Measure grinned. "Well, he wants to teach, and you want to learn. But I got a feeling you two are going to have to do each other a different kind of service before that can happen."

Verily was not surprised. Of course there would be some kind of price, or perhaps a test of loyalty or trustworthiness. "I'll do whatever it takes to have a Maker teach me what my gift is for and how to use it well."

Mrs. Miller nodded. "I think you just might do," she said. "I think perhaps God brought you here."

Her husband snorted.

"It would be enough if he brought you to teach my husband manners, but I fear that may be beyond even the powers of a benevolent God," she said.

"I hate it when you talk like old Reverend Thrower," said the miller grumpily.

"I know you do, dear," said his wife. "Mr. Cooper, suppose you *did* need to practice law, not in Wobbish, but in the state of Hio. How long would it take you to prepare to take the test?"

"I don't know," he said. "It depends on how far American legal practice has diverged from English common law and equity. Perhaps only a few days. Perhaps much longer. But I assure you, I didn't come here to practice law, but rather to study higher laws."

"You want to know why you found us all down here at Armor's store?" asked the miller. "We were having a meeting, to try to figure out how to raise the money to hire us a lawyer. We knew we needed a good one, a first-rate one, but we also knew that some rich and secret group in Carthage had already hired them the best lawyers in Hio to work against us. So the question was, who could we hire, and how in the world could we pay him? My wife thinks God brung you, but my own opinion is that you brung your own self, or in another way of looking at it, my boy Alvin brung you. But who knows, I always say. You're here. You're a lawyer. And you want something from Alvin."

"Are you proposing an exchange of services?" asked Verily.

"Not really," Measure interrupted, rising from his stool. Verily had always thought of himself as rather a tall man, but this young farmer fairly towered over him. "Alvin would teach you for free, if you want to learn. The thing is, you pretty much *got* to do us that legal service before Alvin can take you on as a pupil. That's just the way it is."

Verily was baffled. Either it was barter or it wasn't.

The storekeeper spoke up from behind him, laughing. "We're all talking at each other every whichaway. Mr. Cooper, the legal service we need from you is to defend Alvin Junior at his trial. He's in jail over in Hatrack River, charged with stealing a man's gold and my guess is they're going to pile on a whole bunch of other charges, too. They're out to put that boy in prison for a long time, if not hang him, and you coming along here just now—well, you got to see that it looks mighty fortunate to us."

"In jail," Verily said.

"In Hatrack River," said Armor.

"I just rode through there not a week ago."

"Well, you passed by the courthouse where they got him locked up."

"Yes, I'll do it. When is the trial?"

"Oh, pretty much whenever you want. The judge there is a friend of Alvin's, as are most of the townfolk, or most of them as amount to much, anyway. They can't just let him go, much as they'd like to. But they'll delay the trial as long as you need to get admitted to the bar."

Verily nodded. "Yes, I'll do it. But . . . I'm puzzled. You have no idea whether I'm a *good* lawyer or not."

Measure hooted with laughter. "Come on, friend, you think we're blind? Look at your clothes! You're rich, and you didn't get that way from barrelmaking."

"Besides," said Armor, "you have that English accent, those gentlemanly airs. The jury in Hatrack River will mostly be on Alvin's side. Everything you say is going to sound powerful clever to them."

"You're saying that I don't actually have to be very good. I just have to be English, an attorney-at-law, alive, and present in the courtroom."

"Pretty much, yep," said Armor.

"Then you have an attorney. Or rather, your son does. If he wants me, that is."

"He wants to get out of jail and have his name cleared," said Measure solemnly. "And he wants to teach folks how to be Makers. I think you'll fit right in with what he wants."

"Come here!" The command came from Mrs. Miller, and Verily obediently walked to her. She reached out and took his right hand and held it in both of hers. "Mr. Verily Cooper," she said, "will you be a true friend to my son?"

He realized that it was an oath she was asking for, an oath with his whole heart in it. "Yes, ma'am. I will be his true friend."

It wasn't quite silence that followed his promise. There was the sound of breaths long pent being released. Verily had never been the answer to anyone's heartfelt wish before. It was rather exhilarating. And a bit terrifying, too.

Wastenot and Wantnot came back in. "Horse and mule are unloaded, fed, watered, and stabled."

"Thank you," said Verily.

The twins looked around. "What's everybody grinning for?"

"We got us a lawyer for Alvin," said Measure.

Wastenot and Wantnot grinned, too. "Well, heck, then let's go home to bed!"

"No," said the miller. "One more item of business we got to do."

At once the cheerful mood faded.

"Have a seat, Mr. Cooper," said the miller. "We have a

tale to tell you. A sad one, and it ends with all the men of this town, except Armor here, and Measure—it ends with all of us in shame."

Verily sat down to listen.

13

MANEUVERS

Vilate brought him another pie. "I couldn't finish the last one," Alvin said. "You think my stomach is a bottomless pit?"

"A man of your size and strength needs something to keep the meat on his bones," said Vilate. "And I haven't figured out yet how to make half a pie."

Alvin chuckled. But as she slid the pie under the iron-barred door of the cell, Alvin noticed that she had some new hexes on her, not to mention a come-hither and a beseeching. Most hexes he recognized right off—he'd made a few of them in his own time, for protection or warding, and even for concealment and mildness of heart, which made for a deeper kind of safety but were much harder to make. What Vilate had today, though, was beyond Alvin's ken. And since they probably wouldn't work on him, or not too well, he couldn't rightly tell what they'd be for. Nor could he ask her.

Some kind of concealment, maybe. It seemed related to an overlook-me hex, which was always very subtle and usually worked only in one direction.

Alvin bent down, picked up the pie, and set it on the small table they'd allowed him.

"Alvin," she said softly.

"Yes?" he answered.

"Sh."

He looked up, wondering what the secrecy was about.

"I don't want to be heard," she said. She glanced toward the half-open door leading to the sheriff's office, where the guard was no doubt eavesdropping. She beckoned to Alvin.

What went through his mind then made him a little shy. Was she perhaps thinking some of the same romantic thoughts about him that he had thought about her on some of these lonely nights? Maybe she knew somehow that he alone could see past her false charms of beauty and liked her for who she really was. Maybe she thought of him as someone she could come to love, as he had wondered sometimes about her, seeing as how his first love was lost to him.

He came closer. "Alvin, do you want to escape from here?" she whispered. She leaned her forehead on the bars. Her face was so close. Was she, in some shy way, offering a kiss?

He reached down and touched her chin, lifted her face. Did she want him to kiss her? He smiled ruefully. "Vilate, if I wanted to escape, I—"

He didn't get to finish his sentence, didn't get to say, I reckon I could walk on out of here any old day. Because at that moment the deputy swung the door open and looked into the jail. He immediately got a frantic look on his face, and scanned right past them as if he didn't see them at all. "How in the hell!" he cried, then rushed from the jail. Alvin heard his feet pounding down the hall as he called out, "Sheriff! Sheriff Doggly!"

Alvin looked down at Vilate. "What was *that* all about?" he asked.

Vilate dropped her teeth at him, then smiled. "How should I know, Alvin? But I reckon this is a dangerous time to be talking about what I come to talk about." She picked up her skirts and rushed from the jail.

Alvin had no idea what her visit had been about, but he knew this much: Whatever her new hexes did, they were involved with the deputy and what he saw when he came in. And since there was a come-hither and a beseeching, Vilate might well have been the reason the deputy came into the room in the first place, and the reason he panicked so fast and rushed out without investigating any further.

She dropped the upper plate of her teeth to show contempt for me, thought Alvin. Just like she did to Horace, her enemy. Somehow I've become her enemy.

He looked at the pie sitting on the cot. He picked it up and slid it back under the door.

Five minutes later, the deputy came back with the sheriff and the county attorney. "What the hell was this all about!" Sheriff Doggly demanded. "There he is, just like always! Billy Hunter, you been drinking?"

"I swear there wasn't a soul here," said the deputy. "I saw Vilate Franker go in with a pie—"

"Sheriff, what's he talking about?" said Alvin. "I saw him come in here not five minutes ago and start yelling and running down the hall. It scared poor Vilate so she took on out of here like she had a bear after her."

"He was *not* here, I'd swear to that before God and all the angels!" said Billy Hunter.

"I was right here by the door," said Alvin.

"Maybe he was bending over to get the pie and you didn't see him," said the sheriff.

"No sir," said Alvin, unwilling to lie. "I was standing right up. There's the pie—you can have it if you want, I told Miz Vilate that I didn't finish the last one."

"I don't want none of your pie," said Billy. "Whatever you did, you made me look like a plain fool."

"It don't take no help from Alvin to make you look that way," said Sheriff Doggly. Marty Laws, the county attorney, hooted at the joke. Marty had a way of laughing at just the right time to make everything worse.

Billy glared at Alvin.

"Now, Alvin, we got to put you on your parole," said Marty. "You can't just go taking jaunts out of the jail whenever you feel like it."

"So you *do* believe me," said the deputy.

Marty Laws rolled his eyes.

"*I* don't believe nobody," said Sheriff Doggly. "And Alvin ain't taking no jaunts, are you, Alvin?"

"No sir," said Alvin. "I have not stirred from this cell."

None of them bothered to pretend that Alvin *couldn't* have escaped whenever he wanted.

"You calling me a liar?" asked Billy.

"I'm calling you mistaken," said Alvin. "I'm thinking maybe somebody fooled you into thinking what you thought and seeing what you saw."

"Somebody's fooling somebody," said Billy Hunter.

They left. Alvin sat on the cot and watched as an ant canvassed the floor of the jail, looking for something to eat. There's a pie right there, just a little that way . . . and sure enough, the ant turned, heeding Alvin's advice though of course the words themselves were just too hard a thing to fit into an ant's tiny mind. No, the ant just got the message of food and a direction, and in a minute or two it was up the pie dish and walking around on the crust. Then it headed out to find its friends and bring them for lunch. Might as well somebody get some good out of that pie.

Vilate's hexes were for concealment, all right, and they were aimed at the door. She had got him to stand close so that he'd be included in her strong overlook-me, so Billy Hunter had looked and couldn't see that anybody was there.

But why? What possible good could she accomplish from such a bit of tomfoolery as that?

Underneath all his puzzlement, though, Alvin was mad. Not so much at Vilate as he was mad at himself for being such a plain fool. Getting all moony-eyed about a woman with false teeth and vanity hexes, for pete's sake! Liking her even when he knew she was a plain gossip and suspected that half the tales she told him weren't true.

And the worst thing was, when he saw Peggy again—*if* he saw Peggy again—she'd know just how stupid he was, falling for a woman that he knew was all tricks and lies.

Well, Peggy, when I fell in love with *you* you were all tricks and lies, too, you know. Remember *that* when you're thinking I'm the biggest fool as ever lived.

The door opened and Billy Hunter came back in, stalked over to the cell door, and picked up the pie. "No sense this going to waste even if you are a liar," said Billy.

"As I said, Billy, you're welcome to it. Though I sort of half-promised it to an ant a minute ago."

Billy glared at him, no doubt thinking that Alvin was making fun of him instead of telling the plain truth. Well, Alvin was, kind of. Making fun out of the situation, anyway. He'd have to talk this over with Arthur Stuart when the boy came back, see if he had any idea what Vilate might have meant by this charade.

The ant came back, leading a line of her sisters. All they found was a couple of crumbs of crust. But those were something, weren't they? Alvin watched as they struggled to maneuver the big chunks of pastry. To help them out, he sent his doodlebug to break the pieces into smaller loads. The ants made short work of them then, carrying out the crumbs in a line. A feast in the anthill tonight, no doubt.

His stomach growled. Truth to tell, he could have used that pie, and might not have left much behind, neither. But he wasn't eating nothing that came from Vilate Franker, never again. That woman wasn't to be trusted.

Dropped her teeth at me, he thought. Hates me. Why?

THERE WAS NO way around it. Even with the best possible luck in choosing a jury, even with this new English fellow as Alvin's lawyer, Little Peggy saw no better than a three-in-four chance of him being acquitted, and that wasn't good enough odds. She would have to go to him. She would have to be available to testify. Even with all the newcomers in Hatrack, one thing was certain: If Peggy the torch said a thing was true, she would be believed. The people of Hatrack knew that she saw the truth, and they also knew— sometimes to their discomfiture—that she never said what wasn't true, though they were grateful enough that she didn't tell every truth she knew.

Only Peggy herself could count how many terrible or shameful or mournful secrets she had left unmentioned. But that was neither here nor there. She was used to carrying other people's secrets around inside her, used to it from the earliest time of her life, when she had to face her father's dark secret of adultery. Since then she had learned not to judge. She had even come to love Mistress Modesty, the woman with whom her father, old Horace Guester, had been unfaithful. Mistress Modesty was like another mother to her, giving her, not the life of the body, but the life of the mind, the life of mannered society, the life of grace and beauty that Peggy valued perhaps too highly.

Perhaps too highly, because there wasn't going to be too much of grace and beauty in Alvin's future, and like it or not, Peggy was tied to that future.

What a lie I tell myself, she thought. "Like it or not" indeed. If I chose to, I could walk away from Alvin and not care whether he stayed in jail or got himself drowned in the

Hio or whatnot. I'm tied to Alvin Smith because I love him, and I love what he can be, and I want to be part of all that he will do. Even the hard parts. Even the ungraceful, unmannered, stupid parts of it.

So she headed for Hatrack River, one stage at a time.

On a certain day she passed through the town of Wheelwright in northern Appalachee. It was on the Hio, not far upriver from where the Hatrack flowed into it. Close enough to home that she might have hired a wagon and taken the last ferry, trusting that the moonlight and her ability as a torch would get her home safely. Might have, except that she stopped for dinner at a restaurant she had visited before, where the food was fresh, the flavors good, and the company reputable—a welcome change in all three categories, after long days on the road.

While she was eating, she heard some kind of tumult outside—a band playing, rather badly but with considerable enthusiasm; people shouting and cheering. "A parade?" she asked her waiter.

"You know the presidential election's only a few weeks off," said the waiter.

She knew, but had scarcely paid attention. Somebody was running against somebody else for some office or other in every town she passed through, but it hardly mattered, compared to the matter of stopping slavery, not to mention her concerns about Alvin. It made no difference to her, up to now, who won these elections. In Appalachee, as in the other slave states, there wasn't a soul dared to run openly as an anti-slavery candidate—that would be a ticket for a free suit of tar and feathers and a rail ride out of town, if not worse, for those as loved slavery were violent at heart, and those as hated it were mostly timid, and wouldn't stand together. Yet.

"Some sort of stump speech?" she asked.

"I reckon it's old Tippy-Canoe," said the waiter.

She blanched, knowing at once whom the man referred to. "Harrison?"

"Reckon he'll carry Wheelwright. But not farther south, where the Cherriky tribe is right numerous. They figure him to be the man to try to take away their rights. Won't amount to much in Irrakwa, neither, that being Red country. But, see, White folks isn't too happy about how the Irrakwa control the railroads and the Cherriky got them toll roads through the mountains."

"They'd vote for a murderer, out of nothing more than envy?"

The waiter smiled thinly. "There's them as says just because a Red witch feller put a spell on Tippy-Canoe don't mean he did nothing wrong. Reds get mad over any old thing."

"Slaughtering thousands of innocent women and children—silly of them to take offense."

The waiter shrugged. "I can't afford to have strong opinions on politics, ma'am."

But she saw that he *did* have strong opinions, and they were not the same as hers.

Paying for the meal—and leaving two bits on the table for the waiter, for she saw no reason to punish a man in his livelihood because of his political views—she made haste outside to see the fuss. A few rods up the street, a wagon had been made over into a sort of temporary rostrum, decked out with the red, white, and blue bunting of the flag of the United States. Not a trace of the red and green colors of the old flag of independent Appalachee, before it joined the Union. Of course not. Those had been the Cherriky colors—red for the Red people, green for the forest. Patrick Henry and Thomas Jefferson had adopted them as the colors of a free Appalachee; it was for that flag that George Washington died. But now, though other politicians still invoked the old loyalties, Harrison could hardly want to bring to mind the alliance between Red and White that won freedom for Appalachee from the King at Camelot. Not with those bloody hands.

Hands that even now dripped blood as they gripped the podium. Peggy, standing on the wooden sidewalk across the street, looked over the heads of the cheering crowd to watch William Henry Harrison's face. She looked in his eyes first, as any woman might study any man, to see his character. Quickly enough, though, she looked deeper, into the heartfire, seeing the futures that stretched out before him. He had no secrets from her.

She saw that every path led to victory in the election. And not just a slight victory. His leading opponent, a hapless lawyer named Andrew Jackson from Tennizy, would be crushed and humiliated—and then suffer in the ignominious position of vice-president into which the leading loser in each election was always forced. A cruel system, Peggy had always thought, the political equivalent of putting a man in the stocks for four years. It was significant that both candidates were from the new states in the west; even more significant that both were from territories that permitted slavery. Things were taking a dark turn indeed. And darker yet were the things she saw in Harrison's mind, the plans he and his political cronies meant to carry out.

Their most extravagant ideas had little hope of success— only a few paths in Harrison's heartfire led to the union with the Crown Lands that he hoped for; he would never be a duke; what a pathetic dream, she thought. But he would certainly succeed in the political destruction of the Reds in Irrakwa and Cherriky, because the Whites, especially in the west, were ready for it, ready to break the power of a people that Harrison dared to speak of as savages. "God didn't bring the Christian race to this land in order to share it with heathens and barbarians!" cried Tippy-Canoe, and the people cheered.

Harrison would also succeed in spreading slavery beyond its present locale, permitting slave owners to bring slaves to property in the free states and continue to own them and force them to serve on such property—as long as the slave owner continued to own any amount of land in a slave state and cast his vote there. It was precisely to achieve this end that most of Harrison's backers were behind him. It was the matter of Reds that would sweep Tippy-Canoe into office, but once there, it was the matter of slavery that would give him his power base in Congress.

This was unbearable. Yet she bore it, watching on into the afternoon as he ranted and exhorted, periodically lifting his bloody hands skyward to remind the crowd. "*I* have tasted the treacherous wrath of the secret powers of the Red man, and I'll tell you, if this is all they can do, well, that's good, because it ain't much! Sure, I can't keep a shirt clean"—and they laughed at that, over and over, each variation on the tedious details of life with bloody hands—"and ain't a soul willing to lend me a hankie"—laughter again—"but they can't stop me from telling you the plain truth, and they can't stop a Christian people from electing the one man proven to be willing to stand up against the Red traitors, the barbarians who dress like White men but secretly plan to own everything the way they own the railroads and the mountain toll roads and . . ."

And on and on. Confounded nonsense, all of it, but the crowd only grew as the afternoon passed, and by dark, when Harrison finally climbed down from his pulpit, he was carried away on the shoulders of his supporters to be watered with beer and stuffed with some sort of rough food, whatever would make the crowd think of him as one of them, while Peggy Larner stood gripping the rail on the sidewalk, seeing down every path that this man was the undoing of all her work, that this man would be the cause of the death and suffering of countless more Reds than had already died or suffered at his hands.

If she had had a musket in her hands at that moment, she might have gone after him and put a ball through his heart.

But the murderous rage passed quickly and shamefully. I am not a one who kills, she thought. I am one who frees the slave if I can, not one who murders the master.

There had to be a way to stop him.

Alvin would know. She had to get to Hatrack River all the more urgently, not just to help with Alvin's trial, but to get his help in stopping Harrison. Perhaps if he went to Becca's house and used the doorways in her ancient cabin to let him visit with Tenskwa-Tawa—surely the Red Prophet would do something to make his curse against White Murderer Harrison more effective. Though she didn't see such an outcome down any of the paths in Alvin's heartfire, she never knew when some act of hers or of someone else's might open up new paths that led to better hopes.

It was too late that day, though. She would have to spend the night in Wheelwright and finish her journey to Hatrack River the next day.

"I COME TO you, sir, with the good wishes of your family," said the stranger.

"I confess I didn't catch your name," said Alvin, unfolding himself from his cot. "It's pretty late in the evening."

"Verily Cooper," said the stranger. "Forgive my late arrival. I thought it better that we speak tonight, since the first matter of your defense before the court is in the morning."

"I know the judge is finally going to start choosing him a jury."

"Yes, that's important, of course. But under the advice of

616 • *Orson Scott Card*

an outside lawyer, a Mr. Daniel Webster, the county attorney has introduced some unpleasant motions. As, for instance, a motion requiring that the contested property be placed under the control of the court."

"The judge won't go for that," said Alvin. "He knows that the second this plow is out of my hands, some rough boys from the river, not to mention a few greedier souls from town, will move heaven and earth to get their hands on it. The thing's made of gold—that's all they know and care about it. But who are you, Mr. Cooper, and what does all this have to do with you?"

"I'm your attorney, Mr. Smith, if you'll have me." He handed Alvin a letter.

Alvin recognized Armor-of-God's handwriting at once, and the signatures of his parents and his brothers and sisters. They all signed, affirming that they found Mr. Cooper to be a man of good character and assuring him that someone was paying a high-powered lawyer from New England named Daniel Webster to sneak around and collect lies from anyone as had a grievance against him in Vigor Church. "But I've done no harm to anyone there," said Alvin, "and why would they lie?"

"Mr. Smith, I have to—"

"Call me Alvin, would you? 'Mr. Smith' always sounds to me like my old master Makepeace, the fellow whose lies got me into this fix."

"Alvin," said Cooper again. "And you must call me Verily."

"Whatever."

"Alvin, it has been my experience that the better a man you are, the more folks there are who resent you for it, and find occasion to get angry at you no matter how kindly meant your deeds may be."

"Well then, I'm safe enough, not being such a remarkable good man."

Cooper smiled. "I know your brother Calvin," he said.

Alvin raised an eyebrow. "I'd like to say that any friend of Calvin's is a friend of mine, but I can't."

"Calvin's hatred of you is, I believe, one of the best recommendations of your character that I could think of. It's because of his account of you that I came to meet you. I met him in London, you see, and determined then and there to close my legal practice and come to America and see the man who can teach me who and what I am, and what it's for."

With that, Cooper bent down and took up Alvin's Testament, the book that lay open on the floor beside his cot. He closed it, then handed it back to Alvin.

Alvin tried to thumb it open, but the pages were fused shut as tight as if the book were one solid block of wood with a leather cover.

Verily took it back from him for only a moment, then returned it yet again. This time the book fell open to the exact page that Alvin had been reading. "I could have died for that in England," said Verily. "It was the wisdom of my parents and my own ability to learn to hide these powers that kept me alive all these years. But I have to know what it is. I have to know why God lets some folks have such powers. And what to do with them. And who you are."

Alvin lay back on his cot. "Don't this beat all," he said. "You crossed an ocean to meet me?"

"I had no idea at the time that I might be of service to you. In fact, I must say that it occurs to me that perhaps some providential hand led me to the study of law instead of following my father's trade as a cooper. Perhaps it was known that one day you would face the silver tongue of Daniel Webster."

"You got you a tongue of gold, then, Verily?" asked Alvin.

"I hold things together," said Verily. "It's my . . . knack, as you Americans call it. That is what the law does. I use the law to hold things together. I see how things fit."

"This Webster fellow—he's going to use the law to try to tear things apart."

"Like you and the plow."

"And me and my neighbors," said Alvin.

"Then you understand the dilemma," said Verily. "Up till now you've been known as a man of generosity and kindness to all. But you have a plow made of gold that you won't let anyone see. You have fantastic wealth which you share with no one. This is a wedge that Webster will attempt to use to split you from your community like a rail from a log."

"When gold comes into it," said Alvin, "folks start to finding out just how much love and loyalty is worth to them, in cash money."

"And it's rather shameful, don't you think, how cheap the price can be sometimes." Verily smiled ruefully.

"What's *your* price?"

"When you get free of this place, you let me go with you, to learn from you, to watch you, to be part of all you do."

"You don't even know me, and you're proposing marriage?"

Verily laughed. "I suppose it sounds like that, doesn't it."

"Without none of the benefits, neither," said Alvin. "I'm right comfortable taking Arthur Stuart along with me because he knows when to keep silent, but I don't know if I can take having a fellow who wants to pick my brains tagging along with me every waking minute."

"I'm a lawyer, so my trade is talk, but I promise you that if I didn't know when and how to keep silence, I'd never have lived to adulthood in England."

"I can't give you no promises," said Alvin. "So I reckon you ain't my attorney after all, since I can't make your fee."

"There's one promise you can make me," said Verily. "To give me an honest chance."

Alvin studied the man's face and decided he liked the look of him, though he wished as more than once before that he had Peggy's knack of seeing inside a fellow's mind instead of just being able to check out the health of his organs.

"Yes, I reckon I can make that promise, Verily Cooper," said Alvin. "An honest chance you'll have, and if that's fee enough for you, then you're my attorney."

"Then the deed is done. And now I'll let you go back to sleep, excepting only for one question."

"Ask it."

"This plow—how vital is it to you that the plow remain in your hands, and no one else's?"

"If the court demands that I give it up, I'll buck this jail and live in hiding the rest of my days before I'll let any other hand touch the plow."

"Let's be precise. Is it the possession of it that matters, or the very seeing and touching of it?"

"I don't get your question."

"What if someone else could see and touch it in your presence?"

"What good would that do?"

"Webster will argue that the court has the right and duty to determine that the plow exists and that it's truly made of gold, in order to make just compensation possible, if the court should determine that you need to pay Mr. Make-peace Smith the cash value of the plow."

Alvin hooted. "It never crossed my mind, in all this time in jail, that maybe I could buy old Makepeace off."

"I don't think you can," said Verily. "I think it's the plow he wants, and the victory, not the money."

"True enough, though I reckon if the money's all he can get . . ."

"So tell me, as long as the plow is in your possession . . ."

"I guess it depends on who's doing the looking and the touching."

"If you're there, nobody can steal it, am I right?" asked Verily.

"Reckon that's true," said Alvin.

"So how free a hand do I have?"

"Makepeace can't be the one to touch it," said Alvin. "Not out of any meanness on my part, but here's the thing: The plow's alive."

Verily raised an eyebrow.

"It don't breathe and it don't eat or nothing like that," said Alvin. "But the plow is alive under a man's hand. Depending on the man. But for Makepeace to touch the plow while he's living in the midst of a black lie—I don't know what would happen to him. I don't know if it'd be safe for him ever to touch metal again. I don't know what the hammer and anvil would do to him, if his hands touched the plow with his heart so black."

Verily leaned his face against the bars, closed his eyes.

"Are you unwell?" asked Alvin.

"Sick with the thrill of at last staring knowledge in the face," said Verily. "Sick with it. Faint with it."

"Well, don't puke on the floor, I'll have to smell it all night." Then Alvin grinned.

"I was thinking more of fainting," said Verily. "Not Makepeace, or anyone else who's living in a . . . black lie. Makes me wonder about my opponent, Mr. Daniel Webster."

"Don't know him," said Alvin. "Might be an honest man, for all I know. A lying man might have an honest attorney, don't you think?"

"He might," said Verily. "But such a combination would only work to destroy the lying man in the end."

"Well hell, Verily, a lying man destroys himself in the end every time anyway."

"Do you know that? I mean, the way you know the plow is alive?" asked Verily.

"I reckon not," said Alvin. "But I have to believe it's true, or how could I trust anybody?"

"I think you're right, in the long run," said Verily. "In the long run, a lie ties itself in knots and eventually people come to see that it's a lie. But the long run is very, very long. Longer than life. You could be long dead before the lie dies, Alvin."

"You warning me of something in particular?" asked Alvin.

"I don't think so," said Verily. "The words just sounded like something I had to say and you had to hear."

"You said them. I heard them." Alvin grinned. "Good night, Verily Cooper."

"Good night, Alvin Smith."

PEGGY LARNER GOT to the ferry bright and early in the morning, wearing her urgency like a tight corset so she could hardly breathe. White Murderer Harrison was going to be president of the United States. She had to talk to Alvin, and this river, this Hio, was standing in her way.

But the ferry was on the other side of the river, which made perfect sense, since the farmers on the other side would need to have it earliest, to bring their goods to market. So she had to wait, urgency or not. She could see the ferry already being poled along, tied to a metal ring that slid along the cable that crossed the river some forty feet overhead. Only that frail connection kept the whole thing from being washed downriver; and she imagined that when the river was in flood they didn't run the ferry at all some days, since even if the cable were strong enough, and the ring, and the rope, there'd be no trees strong enough to tie the ends to without fear of one or the other of them pulling out of the ground. Water was not to be tamed by cables, rings, or ropes, any more than dams or bridges, hulls or rafts, pipes or gutters, roofs or windows or walls or doors. If she had learned anything in her early years of looking out for Alvin, it was the untrustworthiness of water, the sneakiness of it.

There was the river to be crossed, though, and she would cross it.

As so many others had crossed. She thought of how many times her father had snuck down to the river and taken a boat across to rescue some runaway slave and bring him north to safety. She thought of how many slaves had come without help to this water, and, not knowing how to swim, had either despaired and waited for the Finders or the dogs to get them, or struck out anyway, breasting the water until their feet found no purchase on the bottom mud and they were swept away. The bodies of such were always found on some downriver bank or bar or snag, made white by the water, bloated and horrible in death; but the spirit, ah, the spirit was free, for the owner who thought he owned the woman or the man, that owner had lost his property, for his property would not be owned whatever it might cost. So the water killed, yes, but just reaching this river meant freedom of one kind or another to those who had the courage or the rage to take it.

Harrison, though, would take away all meaning from this river. If his laws came to be, the slave who crossed would still be a slave no matter what; only the slave who died would be free.

One of the ferrymen, the one poling on this side, he looked familiar to her. She had met him before, though he'd not been missing an ear then, nor had he any kind of scar on his face. Now a gash marked him with a faint white line, a little puckering and twisting at the eyebrow and the lip. It had been a wicked fight. Once no one had been able to lay a hand of harm on this rough man, and in the sure knowledge of that he had been a bully. But someone took that lifelong hex away from him. Alvin had fought this man, fought him in defense of Peggy herself, and when the fight was done, this river rat had been undone. But not completely; and he was alive still, wasn't he?

"Mike Fink," she said softly when he stepped ashore.

He looked sharp at her. "Do I know you, ma'am?"

Of course he didn't. When they met before, not two years ago, she was covered in hexes that made her look many years older. "I don't expect you to remember me," she said. "You must take many thousands of people a year across the river."

He helped her hoist her traveling bags onto the ferry. "You'll want to sit in the middle of the raft, ma'am." She sat down on the bench that ran the middle of the raft. He stood near her, waiting, while another couple of people sauntered over to the ferry—locals, obviously, since they had no luggage.

"A ferryman now," she said.

He looked at her.

"When I knew you, Mike Fink, you were a full-fledged river rat."

He smiled wanly. "You was that lady," he said. "Hexed up six ways to Tuesday."

She looked at him sharply. "You saw through them?"

"No ma'am. But I could feel them. You watched me fight that Hatrack River boy."

"I did."

"He took away my mother's hex," said Mike.

"I know."

"I reckon you know damn near everything."

She looked at him again. "You seem to be abundant in knowledge yourself, sir."

"You're Peggy the torch, of Hatrack River town. And the boy as whupped me and stole my hex, he's in jail in Hatrack now, for stealing gold off'n his master when he was a prentice smith."

"And I suppose that pleases you?" asked Peggy.

Mike Fink shook his head. "No ma'am."

And in truth, as she looked into his heartfire, she saw no future in which he harmed Alvin.

"Why are you still here? Not ten miles from Hatrack Mouth, where he shamed you?"

"Where he made a man of me," said Mike.

She was startled then, for sure. "That's how you think of it?"

"My mother wanted to keep me safe. Tattooed a hex right into my butt. But what she never thought of was, what kind of man does it make a fellow, to never get hurt no matter what harm he causes to others? I've killed folks, some bad, but some not so bad. I've bit off ears and noses and broken limbs, too, and all the time I was doing it, I never cared a damn, begging your pardon, ma'am. Because nothing ever hurt me. Never touched me."

"And since Alvin took away your hex, you've stopped hurting people?"

"Hell no!" Mike Fink said, then roared with laughter. "Why, you sure don't know a thing about the river, do you! No, every last man I ever beat in a fight had to come find me, soon as word spread that a smith boy whupped me and made me howl! I had to fight every rattlesnake and weasel, every rat and pile of pigshit on the river all over again. You see this scar on my face? You see where my hair hangs straight one side of my head? That's two fights I damn near lost. But I won the rest! Didn't I, Holly!"

The other ferryman looked over. "I wasn't listening to your brag, you pitiful scab-eating squirrel-fart," he said mildly.

"I told this lady I won every fight, every last one of them."

"That's right enough," said Holly. "Course, mostly you just shot them dead when they made as if to fight you."

"Lies like that will get you sent to hell."

"Already got me a room picked out there," said Holly, "and you to empty my chamberpot twice't a day."

"Only so's you can lick it out after!" hooted Mike Fink.

Peggy felt repulsed by their crudity, of course; but she also felt the spirit of camaraderie behind their banter.

"What I don't understand, Mr. Fink, is why you never sought vengeance against the boy who beat you."

"He wasn't no boy," said Fink. "He was a man. I reckon he was probably born a man. *I* was the boy. A bully boy. He knew pain, and I didn't. He was fighting for right, and I wasn't. I think about him all the time, ma'am. Him and you. The way you looked at me, like I was a crusty toad on a clean bedsheet. I hear tell he's a Maker."

She nodded.

"So why's he letting them hold him in jail?"

She looked at him quizzically.

"Oh, come now, ma'am. A fellow as can wipe the tattoo off my butt without touching it, he can't be kept in no natural jail."

True enough. "I imagine he believes himself to be innocent, and therefore he wants to stand trial to prove it and clear his name."

"Well he's a damn fool, then, and I hope you'll tell him when you see him."

"And why will I give him this remarkable message?"

Fink grinned. "Because I know something he don't know. I know that there's a feller lives in Carthage City who wants Alvin dead. He plans to get Alvin exerdited to Kenituck—"

"Extradited?"

"That means one state tells another to give them up a prisoner."

"I know what it means," said Peggy.

"Then what was you asking, ma'am?"

"Go on with your story."

"Only when they take Alvin in chains, with guards awake and watching him day and night, they'll never take him to Kenituck for no trial. I know some of the boys they hired to take him. They know that on some signal, they're to walk away and leave him alone in chains."

"Why haven't you told the authorities?"

"I'm telling *you,* ma'am," said Mike Fink, grinning. "And I already told myself and Holly."

"Chains won't hold him," said Peggy.

"You reckon not?" said Mike. "There was some reason that boy took the tattoo off my butt. If hexes had no power over him, I reckon he never would've had to clean mine off, do you think? So if he needed to get rid of my hex, then I reckon them as understands hexes right good might be able to make chains that'd hold him long enough for somebody to come with a shotgun and blow his head off."

But she had seen nothing of the kind in his future.

"Course it'll never happen," said Mike Fink.

"Why not?" she asked.

"Cause I owe that boy my life. My life as a man, anyway, a man worth looking at in the mirror, though I ain't half so pretty as I was before he dealt with me. I had a grip on that boy in my arms, ma'am. I meant to kill him, and he knowed it. But he didn't kill me. More to the point, ma'am, he broke both my legs in that fight. But then he took pity on me. He had mercy. He must've knowed I wouldn't live out the night with broke legs. I had too many enemies, right there among my friends. So he laid hands on my legs and he fixed them. Fixed my legs, so the bones was stronger than before. What kind of man does that to a man as tried to kill him not a minute before?"

"A good man."

"Well, many a good man might wish to, but only one good man had the power," said Mike. "And if he had the power to do that, he had the power to kill me without touching me. He had the power to do whatever he damn well pleased, begging your pardon. But he had mercy on me, ma'am."

That was true—the only surprise to Peggy was that Mike Fink understood it.

"I aim to pay the debt. As long as I'm alive, ma'am, ain't no harm coming to Alvin Smith."

"And that's why you're here," she said.

"Came here with Holly as soon as I found out what was getting plotted up."

"But why here?"

Mike Fink laughed. "The portmaster at Hatrack Mouth knows me real good, and he don't trust me, I wonder why. How long you reckon it'd be afore the Hatrack County sheriff was on my back like a sweaty shirt?"

"I suppose that also explains why you haven't made yourself known to Alvin directly."

"What's he going to think when he sees me, but that I've come to get even? No, I'm watching, I'm biding my time, I ain't showing my hand to the law nor to Alvin neither."

"But you're telling me."

"Because you'd know it anyway, soon enough."

She shook her head. "I know this: There's no path in your future that has you rescuing Alvin from thugs."

His face grew serious. "But I got to, ma'am."

"Why?"

"Because a good man pays his debts."

"Alvin won't think you're in his debt, sir."

"Don't matter to me what he thinks about it, I feel the debt so the debt's going to be paid."

"It's not just debt, is it?"

Mike Fink laughed. "Time to push this raft away and get it over to the north shore, don't you think?" He hooted twice, high, as if he were some kind of steam whistle, and Holly hooted back and laughed. They set their poles against the floating dock and pushed away. Then, smooth as if they were dancers, he and Holly poled them across the river, so smoothly and deftly that the line that tied them to the cable never even went taut.

Peggy said nothing to him as he worked. She watched instead, watched the muscles of his arms and back rippling under the skin, watched the slow and graceful up-and-down of his legs as he danced with the river. There was beauty in it, in him. It also made her think of Alvin at the forge, Alvin at the anvil, his arms shining with sweat in the firelight, the sparks glinting from the metal as he pounded, the muscles of his forearms rippling as he bent and shaped the iron. Alvin could have done all his work without raising a hand, by the use of his knack. But there was a joy in the labor, a joy from making with his own hands. She had never experienced that—her life, her labors, all were done with her mind and whatever words she could think of to say. Her life was all about knowing and teaching. Alvin's life was all about feeling and making. He had more in common with this one-eared scar-faced river rat than he had with her.

This dance of the human body in contest with the river, it was a kind of wrestling, and Alvin loved to wrestle. Crude as Fink was, he was Alvin's natural friend, surely.

They reached the other shore, bumping squarely against the floating dock, and the shoreman lashed the upstream corner of the raft to the wharf. The men with no luggage jumped ashore at once. Mike Fink laid down his pole and, sweat still dripping down his arms and from his nose and grizzled beard, he made as if to pick up her bags.

She laid a hand on his arm to stop him. "Mr. Fink," she said. "You mean to be Alvin's friend."

"I had in mind more along the lines of being his champion, ma'am," he said softly.

"But I think what you really want is to be his friend."

Mike Fink said nothing.

"You're afraid that he'll turn you away, if you try to be his friend in the open. I tell you, sir, that he'll *not* turn you away. He'll take you for what you are."

Mike shook his head. "Don't want him to take me for that."

"Yes you do, because what you are is a man who means to be good, and undo the bad he's done, and that's as good as any man ever gets."

Mike shook his head more emphatically, making drops of sweat fly a little; she didn't mind the ones that struck on her skin. They had been made by honest work, and by Alvin's friend.

"Meet him face to face, Mr. Fink. Be his friend instead of his rescuer. He needs friends more. I tell you, and you know that I know it: Alvin will have few true friends in his life. If you mean to be true to him, and never betray him, so he can trust you always, then I can promise you he may have a few friends he loves as much, but none he loves more than you."

Mike Fink knelt down and turned his face away toward

the river. She could see from the glinting that his eyes were awash with tears. "Ma'am," he said, "that's not what I was daring to hope for."

"Then you need more courage, my friend," she said. "You need to dare to hope for what is good, instead of settling for what is merely good enough." She stood up. "Alvin has no need of your violence. But your honor—that he can use." She lifted both her bags herself.

At once he leapt to his feet. "Please ma'am, let me . . ."

She smiled at him. "I saw you take such joy from wrestling with the river just now. It made me want to do a little physical work myself. Will you let me?"

He rolled his eyes. "Ma'am, in all the tales of you I've heard around here, I never heard you was *crazy*."

"You have something to add to the legend, then," she said, winking. She stepped onto the floating dock, bags in hand. They were heavy, and she almost regretted turning down his help.

"I heard all you said," Mike told her, coming up behind her. "But please don't shame me by letting me be seen empty-handed while a fine lady carried her own luggage."

Gratefully she turned and handed the bags to him. "Thank you," she said. "I think some things must be built up to."

He grinned. "Maybe I'll build up to going to see Alvin face to face."

She looked into his heartfire. "I'm sure of it, Mr. Fink."

As Fink put her bags into the carriage in which the men who had crossed with them impatiently waited for her, she wondered: I just changed the course of events. I brought Mike Fink closer than he would ever have come on his own. Have I done something that will save Alvin in the end? Have I given him the friend that will confound his enemies?

She found Alvin's heartfire almost without trying. And no, there was no change, no change, except for a day when

Mike Fink would go away from a prison cell in tears, knowing that Alvin would surely die if he wasn't there, but knowing also that Alvin refused to have him, refused to let him stand guard.

But it was not the jail in Hatrack River. And it was not anytime soon. Even if she hadn't changed the future much, she'd changed it a little. There'd be other changes, too. Eventually one of them would make the difference. One of them would turn Alvin away from the darkness that would engulf the end of his life.

"God be with you, ma'am," said Mike Fink.

"Call me Miss Larner, please," said Peggy. "I'm not married."

"So far, anyway," he said.

Even though he hardly slept the night before, Verily was too keyed up to be sleepy as he entered the courtroom. He had met Alvin Smith, after all these weeks of anticipation, and it was worth it. Not because Alvin had overawed him with wisdom—time enough to learn from him later. No, the great and pleasant surprise was that he liked the man. He might be a bit roughhewn, more American and more countrified than Calvin. What of that? He had a glint of humor in his eyes, and he seemed so direct, so open . . .

And I am his attorney.

The American courtroom was almost casual, compared to the English ones in which Verily had always litigated up to now. The judge had no wig, for one thing, and his robe was a little threadbare. There could hardly be any majesty of law here; and yet law was law, and justice was not utterly unconnected to it, not if the judge was honest, and there was no reason to think he wouldn't be.

He called the court into session and asked for motions. Marty Laws rose quickly. "Motion to have the golden plow removed from the prisoner and placed into the custody of the court. It doesn't make any sense for the very item in question to remain in the possession of the prisoner when . . ."

"Didn't ask for arguments," said the judge. "I asked for motions. Any others?"

"If it please the court, I move for dismissal of all charges against my client," said Verily.

"Speak up, young man, I couldn't hear a word you said."

Verily repeated himself, more loudly.

"Well, wouldn't that be nice," said the judge.

"When the court is ready for argument, I'll be glad to explain why."

"Explain now, please," said the judge, looking just a little annoyed.

Verily didn't understand what he had done wrong, but he complied. "The point at issue is a plow that all agree is made of solid gold. Makepeace Smith has not a scintilla of evidence that he was ever in possession of such a quantity of gold, and therefore he has no standing to bring a complaint."

Marty Laws pounced at once. "Your Honor, that's what this whole trial is designed to prove, and as for evidence, I don't know what a scintilla is, unless it has something to do with *The Odyssey*—"

"Amusing reference," said the judge, "and quite flattering to me, I'm sure, but please sit back down on your chairybdis until I ask for rebuttal, which I won't have to ask for because the motion to dismiss is denied. Any other motions?"

"I've got one, Your Honor," said Marty. "A motion to postpone the matter of extradition until after—"

"Extradition!" cried the judge. "Now what sort of nonsense is this!"

"It was discovered that there was an outstanding warrant of extradition naming the prisoner, demanding that he be

sent to Kenituck to stand trial for the murder of a Slave
Finder in the act of performing his lawful duty."

This was all news to Verily. Or was it? The family had
told him some of the tale—how Alvin had changed a half-
Black boy so the Finders could no longer identify him, but
in their search for the boy they got into the roadhouse where
his adopted parents lived, and there the boy's mother had
killed one of the Finders, and the other had killed her, and
then Alvin had come up and killed the one that killed her,
but not until after the Finder had shot him, so it was obviously self-defense.

"How can he be tried for this?" asked Verily. "The determination of Pauley Wiseman, who was sheriff at the
time, was that it was self-defense."

Marty turned to the man sitting, up to now silently, beside him. The man arose slowly. "My learned friend from
England is unaware of local law, Your Honor. Do you mind
if I help him out?"

"Go ahead, Mr. Webster," said the judge.

So . . . the judge had already had dealings with Mr. Webster, thought Verily. Maybe that meant he was already
biased; but which way?

"Mr.—Cooper, am I right?—Mr. Cooper, when Kenituck, Tennizy, and Appalachee were admitted to the union
of American states, the Fugitive Slave Treaty became the
Fugitive Slave Law. Under that law, when a Slave Finder engaged in his lawful duty in one of the free states is interfered with, the defendant is tried in the state where the
owner of the slave being pursued has his legal residence. At
the time of the crime, that state was Appalachee, but the
owner of the slave in question, Mr. Cavil Planter, has relo-
cated in Kenituck, and so that is where by law Mr. Smith
will have to be extradited to stand trial. If it is found there
that he acted in self-defense, he will of course be set free.

Our petition to the court is to set aside the matter of extradition until after the conclusion of this trial. I'm sure you'll agree that this is in the best interests of your client."

So it seemed, on the surface. But Verily was no fool—if it *was* in the best interest of Alvin Smith, Daniel Webster would not be so keen on it. The most obvious motive was to influence the jury. If people in Hatrack, who mostly liked Alvin, came to believe that by convicting him of stealing Makepeace's plow they might keep him from being extradited to a state where he would surely be hanged, they might convict him for his own good.

"Your Honor, my client would like to oppose this motion and demand an immediate hearing on the matter of extradition, so it may be cleared up before he stands trial on the charges here."

"I don't like that idea," said the judge. "If we have the hearing and approve the extradition, then this trial takes second place and off he goes to Kenituck."

Marty Laws whispered to Verily, "Don't be daft, boy! I'm the one as pushed Webster into agreeing to this, it's crazy to send him to Kenituck."

For a moment Verily wavered. But by now he had some understanding of how Webster and Laws fit together. Laws might believe that he had persuaded Webster to put off the extradition, but Verily was pretty sure the reality went the other way. Webster wanted extradition postponed. Therefore Verily didn't.

"I'm quite aware of that," said Verily, a statement that had become true not five seconds before. "Nevertheless, we wish an immediate hearing on the matter of extradition. I believe that is my client's right. We don't wish the jury to be aware of a matter of extradition hanging over him."

"But *we* don't want the defendant leaving the state while

still in possession of Makepeace Smith's gold!" cried Webster.

"We don't know whose gold it is yet," said the judge. "This is all pretty darn confusing, I must say. Sounds to me like the prosecution is pleading the defense's cause, and vice-versa. But on general principles I'm inclined to give the capital charge precedence over a matter of larceny. So the extradition hearing will be—how long do you boys need?"

"We could be ready in this afternoon," said Marty.

"No you can't," said Verily. "Because you have to obtain evidence that at present is almost certainly in Kentuck."

"Evidence!" Marty looked genuinely puzzled. "Of what? All the witnesses of Alvin's killing that Finder fellow live right here in town."

"The crime for which extradition is mandatory is not killing a Finder, plain and simple. It's interfering with a Finder who is in pursuit of his lawful duty. So you must not only prove that my client killed the Finder—you must prove the Finder was in lawful pursuit of a particular slave." The thread that Verily was holding to was what the Miller family back in Vigor had told him about Alvin changing the half-Black boy so the Finders couldn't Find him anymore.

Marty Laws leaned close to Daniel Webster and they conferred for a moment. "I believe we'll have to bring us a Slave Finder over the river from Wheelwright," said Laws, "and fetch the cachet. Only that's in Carthage City, so . . . by horse and then by train . . . day after tomorrow?"

"That works for me," said the judge.

"If it please the court," said Webster.

"Nothing has pleased me much so far today," said the judge. "But go ahead, Mr. Webster."

"Since there is some considerable history of people hiding the slave in question, we'd like him taken into custody immediately. I believe the boy is in this courtroom right now." He turned and looked straight at Arthur Stuart.

"On the contrary," said Verily Cooper. "I believe the boy Mr. Webster is indicating is the adopted son of Mr. Horace Guester, the owner of the roadhouse in which I have taken lodging, and therefore he has presumptive rights as a citizen of the state of Hio, which decrees that he is presumed to be a free man until and unless it is proven otherwise."

"Hell's bells, Mr. Cooper," said Marty Laws, "we all know the Finders picked the boy out and took him back across the river in chains."

"It is my client's position that they did so in error, and a panel of impartial Finders will be unable, using only the cachet, to pick the boy out from a group of other boys if his race is concealed from them. We propose this as the first matter for the court to demonstrate. If the panel of Finders cannot pick out the boy, then the Finders who died in this town were *not* pursuing their lawful business, and therefore Kentuck has no jurisdiction because the Fugitive Slave Law does not apply."

"You're from England and you don't know diddly about what these Finders can do," said Marty, quite upset now. "Are you trying to get Arthur Stuart sent off in chains? And Alvin hanged?"

"Mr. Laws," said the judge, "you are the state's attorney in this matter, not Mr. Smith's or Mr. Stuart's."

"For crying out loud," said Marty.

"And if the Fugitive Slave Law does not apply, then I submit to the court that Alvin Smith has already been determined by the sheriff and attorney of Hatrack County to have acted in self-defense, and therefore to bring charges now would put him in double jeopardy, which is forbidden by—"

"I know exactly who and what forbids double jeopardy," said the judge, now getting a little edgy with Verily.

What am I doing wrong? Verily wondered.

"All right, since it's Mr. Smith's neck that's on the line, I'll deny the prosecution's motion and grant the defense motion to set up a blind test of a panel of Finders. Let's add another day—we'll meet on Friday to see if they can identify Arthur Stuart. As for putting Arthur in custody, I'll ask the boy's adopted father—is old Horace in the court today?"

Horace stood up. "Here I am, sir," he said.

"You going to make my life difficult by hiding this boy, so I have to lock you up for the rest of your natural life for contempt of court? Or are you going to keep him in plain sight and bring him to court for that test?"

"I'll bring him," said Horace. "He ain't going nowheres as long as Alvin's in jail, anyhow."

"Don't get cute with me, Horace, I'm just warning you," said the judge.

"Got no intention of being cute, dammit," murmured Horace as he sat back down.

"Don't curse in my courtroom, either, Mr. Guester, and don't insult me by assuming that my grey hair means I'm deaf." The judge rapped with his gavel. "Well, that does it for motions and—"

"Your Honor," said Verily.

"That's me," said the judge. "What, you got another motion?"

"I do," said Verily.

"And there's the matter of arguments on the motion to produce the plow," offered Marty Laws helpfully.

"Dammit," muttered the judge.

"I heard that, judge!" cried Horace Guester.

"Bailiff, put Mr. Guester outside," said the judge.

They all waited while Horace Guester got up and hurried out of the courtroom.

"What's your new motion, Mr. Cooper?"

"I respectfully request to know the position of Mr. Webster in this courtroom. He seems not to be an official of the county of Hatrack or the state of Hio."

"Ain't you co-counsel or some other fool thing?" asked the judge of Daniel Webster.

"I am," said Webster.

"Well, there you have it."

"Begging your pardon, Your Honor, but it seems plain to me that Mr. Webster's fees are not being paid by the county. I respectfully request to know who *is* paying him, or if he is acting out of the goodness of his heart."

The judge leaned on his desk and cocked his head to look at Daniel Webster. "Now that you mention it, I do recall never seeing you represent anybody as wasn't either very rich or very famous, Mr. Webster. I'd like to know myself who's paying you."

"I'm here volunteering my services," said Webster.

"So if I put you under oath and ask you to tell me if your time and expenses here are or are not being paid by someone other than your own self, you would say that you are receiving no payment? Under oath?"

Webster smiled faintly. "I'm on retainer, and so my expenses are paid, but not for this case specifically."

"Let me ask it another way. If you don't want the bailiff to put you out with Mr. Guester, tell me who's paying you."

"I am on retainer with the Property Rights Crusade, located at 44 Harrison Street in the city of Carthage in the state of Wobbish." Webster smiled thinly.

"Does that answer your respectful request, Mr. Cooper?" the judge asked.

"It does, Your Honor."

"Then I'll declare this—"

"Your Honor!" cried Marty Laws. "The matter of possession of the plow."

"All right, Mr. Laws," said the judge. "Time for brief arguments."

"It's absurd for the defendant to remain in possession of the property in question, that's all," said Marty.

"Since the defendant himself is in the custody of the county jail," said Verily Cooper, "and the plow is in his possession, then, like his clothing and his pen and ink and paper and everything else in his possession, the plow is obviously in the custody of the county jail as well. The state's motion is moot."

"How do we know that the defendant even *has* the plow?" asked Marty Laws. "Nobody's seen it."

"That's a point," said the judge, looking at Verily.

"Because of special properties of the plow," said Verily, "the defendant feels it unwise to let it out of his sight. Nevertheless, if the state wishes to designate three officers of the court to see it . . ."

"Let's keep it simple," said the judge. "Mr. Laws, Mr. Cooper, and I will go see this plow today, as soon as we finish here."

Verily noticed with pleasure that Daniel Webster flushed with anger as he realized he was not going to be treated as an equal and invited along. Webster tugged at Laws's coat and then whispered in his ear.

"Um, Your Honor," said Laws.

"What message are you delivering for Mr. Webster?" asked the judge.

"We can't exactly call me, you, and Mr. Cooper as witnesses, us being, um, what we are," said Laws.

"I thought the point of this was to make sure the plow existed," said the judge. "If you and me and Mr. Cooper see it, then I think we can fairly well assure everybody it exists."

"But in the trial, we'll want people other than the defendant and Mr. Makepeace Smith to be able to testify about the plow."

"Plenty of time for worrying about that later. I'm sure we can get a few witnesses to see it by then, too. How many do you want?"

Another whispered conference. "Eight will do fine," said Laws.

"You and Mr. Cooper get together in the next while and decide which eight people you'll settle on as witnesses. In the meantime, the three of us will go visit Mr. Alvin Smith in prison and get an eyeful of this marvelous legendary mythical golden plow that has—how did you put it, Mr. Cooper?"

"Special properties," said Verily.

"You Englishmen have such a fine way with words."

Once again, Verily could sense some kind of nastiness directed toward him from the judge. As before, he had no idea what he had done to provoke it.

Still, the judge's inexplicable annoyance aside, things had gone rather well.

Unless, of course, the Millers had been all wrong and the Slave Finders *could* identify Arthur Stuart as the wanted runaway. Then there'd be problems. But . . . the nicest thing about this case was that if Verily performed quite badly, making it certain that Alvin would be hanged or Arthur Stuart returned to slavery, Alvin, being a Maker, could always just take the boy and go away; and not a soul could stop them if Alvin didn't want to be stopped, or find them if Alvin didn't want to be found.

Still, Verily had no intention of doing badly. He intended to win spectacularly. He intended to clear Alvin's name of all charges so the Maker would be free to teach him all that he wanted to know. And another, deeper motive, one which he did not try to hide from himself though he would never have admitted it to another: He wanted the Maker to respect him. He wanted Alvin Smith to look him in the eye and say, "Well done, friend."

That would be good. Verily Cooper wanted that good thing.

14

WITNESSES

All the time of waiting hadn't been so bad, really. Nothing was happening in the jail, but Alvin didn't mind being alone and doing nothing. It gave him thinking time. And thinking time was making time, he reckoned. Not like he used to do as a boy, making bug baskets out of pulled-up grass to keep the Unmaker back. But making things in his head. Trying to remember the Crystal City as he saw it in the waterspout with Tenskwa-Tawa. Trying to figure how such a place was made. Can't teach folks how to make it if I don't know what it is myself.

Outside the jail he knew that the Unmaker was moving in the world, tearing down a little here, knocking over a little there, setting a wedge in every tiny crack it found. And there were always people searching for the Unmaker, for some awful destructive power outside themselves. Poor fools, they always thought that Destruction was merely destruction, they were using it and when they were done with it, they'd set to building. But you don't build on a foundation of destruction. That's the dark secret of the Unmaker, Alvin thought. Once he sets you to tearing down, it's hard to get back to building, hard to get your own self back. The digger wears out the ground *and* the spade. And once you let yourself be a tool in the Unmaker's hand, he'll wear you out, he'll tear you down, he'll dull you and hole you and all the time you'll be thinking you're so sharp and fine and bright and whole, and you never know till he lets go of you, lets you drop and fall. What's that clatter? Why, that was me. That was me, sounding like a wore-out tool. What you leaving me for? I still got use left in me!

But you don't, not when the Unmaker's got you.

What Alvin figured out was that when you're Making, you don't use people like tools. You don't wear them out to achieve *your* purpose. You wear yourself out helping them achieve *theirs.* You wear yourself out teaching and guiding, persuading and listening to advice and letting folks persuade *you,* when it happens they're right. So instead of one ruler and a bunch of wore-out tools, you got a whole city of Makers, all of them free fellow-citizens, hard workers every one . . .

Except for one little problem. Alvin couldn't teach Making. Oh, he could get people to sort of set their minds right and their work would be enhanced a little. And a few people, like Measure, mostly, and his sister Eleanor, they learned a thing or two, they caught a glimmer. But most was in the dark.

And then there comes a one like this lawyer from England, this Verily Cooper, and he was just born knowing how to do in a second what Measure could only do after a whole day's struggle. Sealing a book shut like it was a single block of wood and cloth, and then opening it again with no harm to any of the pages and the letters still stuck on the surfaces. That was some Making.

What did he have to teach Verily? He was born knowing. And how could he hope to teach those as wasn't born knowing? And anyway how could he teach anything when he didn't know how to make the crystal out of which the city would be made?

You can't build a city of glass; it'll break, it can't hold weight. You can't build out of ice, either, because it ain't clear enough and what about summer? Diamonds, they're strong enough, but a city made of diamond, even if he could find or make so much of it—no way would they be allowed to use such rich stuff for building, there'd be folks to tear it down in no time, each one stealing a bit of wall to make hisself rich, and pretty soon the whole thing would be like a Swiss cheese, more hole than wall.

Oh, Alvin could spin himself through these thoughts and wonderings, through memories and words of books he read when Miss Larner—when Peggy—was teaching him. He could keep his mind occupied in solitude and not mind it a bit, though he also sure didn't mind when Arthur Stuart came to talk to him about goings on.

Today, though, things were happening. Verily Cooper would be fending off motions for this and that, and even if he was a good lawyer, he was from England and he didn't know the ways here, he could make mistakes, but there wasn't a blame thing Alvin could do about it even if he did. He just had to put his trust in other folks and Alvin hated that.

"Everyone hates it," said a voice, a so-familiar voice, a dreamed-of, longed-for voice with which he had had many a debate in his memory, many a quarrel in his imagination; a voice that he dreamed of whispering gently to him in the night and in the morning.

"Peggy," he whispered. He opened his eyes.

There she was, looking just as she would if he had conjured her up, only she was real, he hadn't done no conjuring.

He remembered his manners and stood up. "Miss Larner," he said. "It was kind of you to come and visit me."

"Not so much kind as necessary," she said, her tone businesslike.

Businesslike. He sighed inwardly.

She looked around for a chair.

He picked up the stool that stood inside the cell and impulsively, thoughtlessly handed it right through the bars to her. He hardly even noticed how he made the bits of iron bar and the strands of woodstuff move apart to let each other through; only when he saw Peggy's wide, wide eyes did he realize that of course she'd never seen anybody pass wood and iron right through each other like that.

"Sorry," he said. "I've never done that before, I mean without warning or nothing."

She took the stool. "It was very thoughtful of you," she said. "To provide me with a stool."

He sat down on his cot. It creaked under him. If he hadn't toughened up the material, it would have given way under his weight days ago. He was a big man and he used furniture kind of rough; he didn't mind if it complained out loud now and then.

"They're doing pretrial motions in court today, I understand."

"I watched part of it. Your lawyer is excellent. Verily Cooper?"

"I think he and I ought to be friends," Alvin said. He watched for her reaction.

She nodded. "Do you really want me to tell you what I know about the possible courses your friendship might take?"

Alvin sighed. "I do, and I don't, and you know it."

"I'll tell you that I'm glad he's here. Without him you'd have no chance of getting through this trial."

"So now I'll win?"

"Winning isn't everything, Alvin."

"But losing is nothing."

"If you lost the case but kept your life and your life's

work, then losing would be better than winning, and dying for it, don't you think?"

"I'm not on trial for my life!"

"Yes you are," said Peggy. "Whenever the law gets its hands on you, those who use the law to their own advantage will also turn it against you. Don't put your trust in the laws of men, Alvin. They were designed by strong men to improve their power over weaker ones."

"That's not fair, Miss Larner," said Alvin. "Ben Franklin and them others as made the first laws—"

"They meant well. But the reality for you is that whenever you put yourself in jail, Alvin, your life is in grave danger every moment."

"You came to tell me that? You know I can walk out of here whenever I want."

"I came so I could tell you when to walk away, if the need comes."

"I want my name cleared of Makepeace's lies."

"I also came to help with that," she said. "I'm going to testify."

Alvin thought of that night when Goody Guester died, Peggy's mother, though he hadn't known that Miss Larner was really Peggy Guester until she knelt weeping over her mother's ruined body. Right till the moment they heard the first gunshot, he and Peggy had been on the verge of declaring their love for each other and deciding to marry. And then her mother killed the Finder, and the other Finder killed her, and Alvin got there way too late to heal her from the shotgun blast, and all he could do was kill the man that shot her, kill him with his bare hands, and what did that do? What good did that do? What kind of Making was that?

"I don't want you to testify," he said.

"I wasn't looking forward to it myself," she said. "I won't do it if it's not needed. But you have to tell Verily Cooper what and who I am, and tell him that when he's all done with his other witnesses, he's to look to me, and if I nod, he's to call me as a witness, no arguments. Do you understand me? I'll know better than either of you whether my testimony is necessary or not."

Alvin heard what she said and knew he'd go along, but there was a part of him that was seething with anger even though he didn't know why—he'd been longing to see her for more than a year now, and suddenly she was here and all he wanted to do was yell at her.

Well, he didn't yell. But he did speak up in a voice that sounded less than kind. "Is that what you come back for? To tell poor stupid Alvin and his poor stupid lawyer what to do?"

She looked sharp at him. "I met an old friend of yours at the ferry."

For a moment his heart leapt within him. "Ta-Kumsaw?" he whispered.

"Goodness no," she said. "He's out west past the Mizzipy for all I know. I was referring to a fellow who once had a tattoo on an unmentionable part of his body, a Mr. Mike Fink."

Alvin rolled his eyes. "I guess the Unmaker's assembling all my enemies in one place."

"On the contrary," said Peggy. "I think he's no enemy. I think he's a friend. He swears he means only to protect you, and I believe him."

He knew she meant him to take that as proof that the man could be trusted, but he was feeling stubborn and said nothing.

"He came to the Wheelwright ferry in order to be close enough to keep an eye on you. There's a conspiracy to get you extradited to Kentuck under the Fugitive Slave Law."

"Po Doggly told me he wasn't going to pay no mind to that."

"Well, Daniel Webster is here precisely to see to it that whether you win or lose here, you get taken to Kenituck to stand trial."

"I won't go," said Alvin. "They'd never let me get to trial."

"No, they never would. That's what Mike Fink came to watch out for."

"Why is he on my side? I took away his hex of protection. It was a strong one. Near perfect."

"And he's suffered a few scars and lost an ear since then. But he's also learned compassion. He values the exchange. And you healed his legs. You left him with a fighting chance."

Alvin thought about that. "Well, you never know, do you. I thought of him as a stone killer."

"I think that a good person can sometimes do wrong out of ignorance or weakness or wrong thinking, but when hard times come, the goodness wins out after all. And a bad person can often seem good and trustworthy for a long time, but when hard times come, the evil in him gets revealed."

"So maybe we're just waiting for hard enough times to come in order to find out just how bad I am."

She smiled wryly. "Modesty is a virtue, but I know you too well to think for a minute you believe you're a bad man."

"I don't think much about whether I'm good or bad. I think a lot about whether I'm going to be worth a damn or not. Right now I reckon myself to be worth about six bits."

"Alvin," she said, "you never used to swear in front of me."

He felt the rebuke but he rather liked the feeling of annoying her. "It's just the bad in me coming out."

"You're very angry with me."

"Yes, well, you know all, you see all."

"I've been busy, Alvin. You've been doing your life's work, and I've been doing mine."

"Once upon a time I hoped it might be the same work," said Alvin.

"It will never be the same work. Though our labors may complement each other. I will never be a Maker. I only see what is there to be seen. While you imagine what might be made, and then make it. Mine is by far the lesser gift, and mostly useless to you."

"That's the purest nonsense I ever heard."

"I don't speak nonsense," she said sharply. "If you don't think my words sound true, then think again until you understand them."

He imagined her as he used to see her, the severe-looking teacher lady at least ten years older than Peggy really was; she still knew how to use her voice like a rap across the knuckles. "It ain't useless to me to know what's coming in the future."

"But I don't *know* what's coming. I only know what *might* come. What seems likely to come. There are so many paths the future might take. Most people stumble blindly along, plunging into this or that path that I see in their heart-fire, heading for disaster or delight. Few have your power, Alvin, to open up a new path that did not exist. There was no future in which I saw you push that stool through the bars of the cell. And yet it was an almost inevitable act on your part. A simple expression of the impulsiveness of a young man. I see in people's heartfires the futures that are possible for them in the natural course of events. But you can set aside the laws of nature, and so you can't be properly accounted for. Sometimes I can see clearly; but there are deep gaps, dark and wide."

He got up from the cot and came to the bars, held them,

knelt down in front of her. "Tell me how I find out how to make the Crystal City."

"I don't know how you do it. But I've seen a thousand futures in which you do."

"Tell me where I look then, in order to learn!"

"I don't know. Whatever it is, it doesn't follow the laws of nature. Or at least I think that's why I can't see it."

"Vilate Franker says my life ends in Carthage City," said Alvin.

She stiffened. "How does she know such a thing?"

"She knows where things come from and where they'll end up."

"Don't go to Carthage City. Never go there."

"So she's right."

"Never go there," she whispered. "Please."

"I got no plans for it," he said. But inside his heart he thought: She cares for me after all. She still cares for me.

He might have said something about it, or she might have talked a bit more tenderly and less businesslike. *Might* have, but then the door opened and in trooped the sheriff and the judge and Marty Laws and Verily Cooper.

"Scuse us," said Sheriff Doggly. "But we got us a courtroom thing to do here."

"I'm at your service, gentlemen," said Alvin, rising at once to his feet. Peggy also rose, then stooped to move the stool out of the way of the door.

The sheriff looked at the stool.

"It was so kind of you to allow Alvin's stool to be placed outside the bars for me," said Peggy.

Po Doggly looked at her. He hadn't given any such order, but he decided not to argue the point. Alvin was Alvin.

"Explain things to your client," said the judge to Verily Cooper.

"As we discussed last night," said Verily, "we'll need to have various witnesses view the plow. The three of us will be enough to ascertain that the plow exists, that it appears to be made of gold, and . . ."

"That's all right," said Alvin.

"And we've agreed that after the jury is empaneled, we'll select eight more witnesses who can testify to the existence and nature of the plow in open court."

"As long as the plow stays in here with me," said Alvin. He glanced toward Sheriff Doggly.

"The sheriff already knows," said the judge, "that he is *not* one of the designated witnesses."

"Blame it all, Your Honor!" said Doggly. "It sets in here for weeks in my jail and I can't even *see* it?"

"I don't mind if he stays," said Alvin.

"I do," said the judge. "It's better if he doesn't regale his deputies with tales of how big and how gold the thing is. I know we can trust Mr. Doggly. But why exacerbate the temptation that must already afflict at least some of his deputies?"

Alvin laughed.

"What's so funny, Mr. Smith?" asked the judge.

"How everybody's all pretending they know what in hell the word *exacerbate* means." They all joined him in laughter.

When it died down, Sheriff Doggly was still in the room. "I'm waiting to escort the lady out," he said.

Alvin rolled his eyes. "She saw the plow on the night that it was made."

"Nevertheless," said the judge, "three witnesses on this official occasion. You can show it to every visitor in the jail if you want to, but on this occasion, we have agreed to three, and three it is."

Peggy smiled at the judge. "You are a man of extraordinary integrity, sir," she said. "I'm glad to know you're presiding at this trial."

When she was gone and the sheriff had closed the door to the jail, the judge looked at Alvin. "That was Peggy Guester? The torch girl?"

Alvin nodded.

"She grew up prettier than I ever expected," said the judge. "I just wish I knew whether she was being sarcastic."

"I don't think so," said Alvin. "But you're right, she has a way of saying even nice things as if she's only barely holding back from telling a bunch of stuff that ain't so nice."

"Whoever marries that one," said the judge, "he better have a thick skin."

"Or a stout stick," said Marty Laws, and then he laughed. But he laughed alone, and soon fell silent, vaguely embarrassed, uncertain why his joke had fallen so flat.

Alvin reached under the cot and slid out the burlap bag that held the plow. He pulled back the mouth of the sack, so the plow sat exposed, surrounded by burlap, shining golden in the light from the high windows.

"I'll be damned," said Marty Laws. "It really is a plow, and it really is gold."

"*Looks* gold," said the judge. "I think if we're to be honest witnesses, we have to touch it."

Alvin smiled. "I ain't stopping you."

The judge sighed and turned to the county attorney. "We forgot to get the sheriff to open the cell door."

"I'll fetch him," said Marty.

"Please cover the plow, Mr. Smith," said the judge.

"Don't bother," said Alvin. He reached over and opened the cell door. The latch didn't even so much as make a sound; nor did the hinges squeak. The door just opened, silent and smooth.

The judge looked down at the latch and lock. "Is this broken?" he asked.

"Don't worry," said Alvin. "It's working fine. Come on in and touch the plow, if you want."

Now that the door was open, they hung back. Finally Verily Cooper stepped in, the judge after him. But Marty held back. "There's something about that plow," he said.

"Nothing to be worried about," said Alvin.

"You're just bothered because the door opened so easy," said the judge. "Come on in, Mr. Laws."

"Look," said Marty. "It's trembling."

"Like I told you," said Alvin, "it's alive."

Verily knelt down and reached out a hand toward the plow. With no one touching it yet, the plow slid toward him, dragging the burlap with it.

Marty yelped and turned his back, pressing his face into the wall opposite the cell door.

"You can't be much of a witness with your back turned," said the judge.

The plow slid to Verily. He laid his hand on the top of it. It slowly turned under his hand, turned and turned, around and around, smooth as an ice skater.

"It *is* alive," he said.

"After a fashion," said Alvin. "But it's got a mind of its own, so to speak. I mean, it's not like I've tamed it or nothing."

"Can I pick it up?" asked Verily.

"I don't know," said Alvin. "Nobody but me has ever tried."

"It would be useful," said the judge, "if we could heft it to see if it weighs like gold, or if it's some other, lighter alloy."

"It's the purest gold you'll ever see in your life," said Alvin, "but heft it if you can."

Verily squatted, got his hands under the plow, and lifted. He grunted at the weight of it, but it stayed in his hands as he lifted it. Still, there was some struggle with it. "It wants to turn," said Verily.

"It's a plow," said Alvin. "It reckon it wants to find good soil."

"You wouldn't actually plow with this, would you?" said the judge.

"I can't think why else I made it, if it ain't for plowing. I mean, if I was making a bowl I got the shape wrong, don't you think?"

"Can you hand it to me?" asked the judge.

"Of course," said Verily. He stepped close to the judge and held the plow as the older man wrapped his hands around it. Then Verily let go.

At once the plow began to buck in the judge's hands. Before the judge could drop it, Alvin reached out and rested his right hand on the plow's face. Immediately it went still.

"Why didn't it do that with Mr. Cooper?" asked the judge, his voice trembling a little.

"I reckon it knows Verily Cooper is my attorney," said Alvin, grinning.

"While I am impartial," said the judge. "Perhaps Mr. Laws is correct not to handle it."

"But he has to," said Verily. "He's the most important one to see it. He has to assure Mr. Webster and Makepeace Smith that it's the real plow, the gold plow, and that it's safe here in the jailhouse."

The judge handed the plow to Alvin, then left the cell and put his hand on Marty Laws's shoulder. "Come now, Mr. Laws, I've handled it, and even if it bucks a bit, it won't harm you."

Laws shook his head.

"Marty," said Alvin. "I don't know what you're afraid of, but I promise you that the plow won't hurt you, and you won't hurt it."

Marty turned sideways. "It was so bright," he said. "It hurt my eyes."

"Just a glint of sunlight," said the judge.

"No sir," said Marty. "No, Your Honor. It was bright. It was bright from way down deep inside itself. It shone right into me. I could feel it."

The judge looked at Alvin.

"*I* don't know," said Alvin. "It's not like I've been showing it to folks."

"I know what he means," said Verily. "I didn't see it as light. But I felt it as warmth. When the bag fell open, the whole place felt warmer. But there's no harm in it, Mr. Laws. Please—I'll hold it with you."

"As will I," said the judge.

Alvin held the plow out to them.

Marty slowly turned so he could watch, his head partly averted, as the other two witnesses got their hands on and under the plow. Only then did he sidle forward and gingerly lay his fingertips on and under the golden plowshare. He was sweating something awful, and Alvin felt plain sorry for him, but couldn't begin to understand what the man was going through. The plow had always felt comfortable and friendly-like to him. What did it mean to Marty?

When the thing didn't hurt him, Marty gained confidence, and shifted his hands to get some of the weight of the plow. Still his eyes were squinted and he looked sidelong, as if to protect one eye in case the other one was suddenly blinded. "I can hold it alone, I guess," he said.

"Let Mr. Smith keep his hand on it, so it doesn't buck," said the judge.

Alvin left his hand, but the others took their hands away, and Marty held the plow alone.

"I reckon it weighs like gold," said Marty.

Alvin reached under the plow and got hold of it. "I got it now, Marty," he said.

Marty let go—reluctantly, it seemed to Alvin.

"Anyway, I reckon you can see why I don't just let anyone have a grab at it," said Alvin.

"I'd hate to think what shape I'd be in if I dropped it on my toe," said the judge.

"Oh, it lands easy," said Alvin.

"It really is alive," said Verily softly.

"You're a bold fellow," said the judge to Alvin. "Your attorney was quite adamant about having a hearing on the extradition matter before we even empanel a jury about the larceny business."

Alvin looked at Verily. "I reckon my attorney knows what he's doing."

"I told them," said Verily, "that my defense would be that the finder was not engaged in lawful business, since by the cachet they carried, Arthur Stuart could not possibly be identified."

Alvin knew that this was more a question than a statement. "They walked right by Arthur Stuart that night," said Alvin.

"We are going to bring a group of Slave Finders from Wheelwright to see if they can pick Arthur Stuart from a group of boys about his age," said Verily. "Their faces and hands will be hidden, of course."

"Make sure," said Alvin, "to get a couple of Mock Berry's boys in the group, along with whatever White boys you settle on. I reckon those as spends their whole lives looking for Black folks might have some ways of spotting which is which, even if they got gloves on and bags over their heads."

"Mock Berry?" asked the judge.

"He's a Black fellow," explained Marty. "Free Black, mind you. Him and Anga his wife, they've got a passle of young folks in a cabin in the woods not far from the roadhouse."

"Well, that's a good idea, to have some Black boys in the

mix," said the judge. "And maybe I'll see to a few other things to make things stay fair." He reached out to the plow, which Alvin still held in his hands. "Mind if I touch it one more time?"

He did; the plow trembled under his hand.

"If the jury should decide that this is truly Makepeace Smith's gold," said the judge, "I wonder how he's going to get it home?"

"Your Honor," Marty protested.

The judge glared at him. "Don't you even for a *moment* imagine that I'm going to be anything but completely fair and impartial in the conduct of this trial."

Marty shook his head and held out his hands as if to ward off the very *thought* of partiality.

"Besides," said the judge. "You saw what you saw, too. You going to turn the trial over to Mr. Webster, now that you seen it move and shine and whatnot?"

Marty shook his head. "The point at issue is whether Alvin Smith made the plow with gold that belonged to Makepeace. What the plow is like, its other properties—I don't see but what that's completely irrelevant."

"Exactly," said the judge. "All we needed to verify right now is that it exists, it's gold, and it should remain in Alvin's custody while Alvin remains in the custody of the sheriff. I think we've determined all three points to everyone's satisfaction. Right, gentlemen?"

"Right," said Marty.

Verily smiled.

Alvin put the plow back in the burlap bag.

As they left the cell, the judge carefully closed the door until the latch clicked. Then he tried to open it and couldn't. "Well, I'm glad to see the jail is secure." He didn't grin when he said it. He didn't have to.

Po Doggly looked beside himself with curiosity as they

emerged from the jail into the outer office. In moments he was inside the jail, looking through bars at Alvin, hoping to catch a glint of gold.

"Sorry, Sheriff," said Alvin. "All put away."

"You got no sense of sport, Alvin," said Doggly. "You couldn't even leave the top open a little bit?"

"I won't mind a bit if you're one of the eight," said Alvin. "Let's see what happens."

"Not a bad idea," said Doggly. "And thank you for not minding. I won't do that, though. Better to use eight ordinary citizens, instead of a public official. I'm just curious, you know. Never saw that much gold in all my life, and I'd like to be able to tell my grandchildren."

"So would I," said Alvin. And then: "Sheriff Doggly, Peggy Larner wouldn't still be out there, would she?"

"No. Sorry, Al. She's gone. Reckon she went on home to say howdy to her pa."

"Reckon so," said Alvin. "No matter."

ARTHUR STUART WOULD never have called himself a spy. He couldn't help it that he was short. He couldn't help it that his skin was dark and that, being shy, he tended to stand in shadows and hold very, very still so people overlooked him quite easily. He wasn't aware that some of the greensong from his long journeys with Alvin still lingered with him, a melody in the back of his mind, so that his step was unusually quiet, twigs tended to bend out of his way, and boards didn't often squeak under his step.

But when it came to his visit to Vilate's house, well, it wasn't no accident she didn't see him. In fact, he made it a point not to step on the porch of the post office, so he couldn't very well walk through the front door and make the bell ring. Nor, when he got around to the back of Vilate Franker's house, did he knock on her back door or ask her permission before climbing up on her rain barrel and leaning over to look through her window into her kitchen, where the teapot simmered on the stove and Vilate sat drinking tea and carrying on quite a lively conversation with . . .

With a salamander.

Not a lizard—even from the window, Arthur Stuart could see there were no scales. Besides, you didn't have to be some kind of genius to know a salamander from a lizard at five paces. Arthur Stuart was a boy, and boys tended to know such things. Moreover, Arthur Stuart had been an unusually solitary and inquisitive boy, and he had a way with animals, so even if some other boy might make a mistake, Arthur Stuart never would. It was a salamander.

Vilate would say something, and then sip her tea, glancing up from the cup now and then to nod or murmur something—"Mm-hm"; "I know"; "Isn't it just awful?"—as if the salamander was saying something.

But the salamander didn't say nothing. Didn't even look at her, most of the time, though truth to tell you never quite knew for sure what a salamander was looking at, because if one eye was looking there, the other might be looking here and how would you know? Still and all, Arthur was pretty sure it looked right at him. Knew he was there. But didn't seem to get alarmed or nothing, so Arthur just kept on looking and listening.

"A man shouldn't trifle with a lady's affections," she was saying. "Once a man goes down that road, the lady has a right to protect herself as best she can."

Another sip. Another nod.

"Oh, I know. And the worst of it is, people are going to think so badly of me. But everyone knows that Alvin Smith has hidden powers. Of course I couldn't help myself."

Another sip. And then, abruptly, tears streamed out of her eyes.

"Oh, my dear, dear soul, my friend, my beloved trusted friend, how can I do this? I really do care for the boy. I really do care for him. Why oh why couldn't he have loved me? Why did he have to spurn me and make me do this?"

And so it went. Arthur wasn't no dummy. He knew right off that Vilate Franker was planning some kind of devilment against Alvin, and he sort of hoped she might mention what it was, though that wasn't too likely, since all she talked about was how bad she felt and how she hated to do it but it was a lady's right to defend her honor even though it might involve giving the appearance of having *no* honor but that's why it was so good having such a good, true, wonderful *friend*.

Ah, the tears that flowed. Ah, the sighs. Ah, the quart of tea she consumed while Arthur leaned on the sill, watching, listening.

Oddly, though, as soon as the tears were done, her face just went clean. Not a streak. Not a trace of redness around the eyes. Not a sign that she had even shed a tear.

The tea eventually took its toll. Vilate slid her chair back and rose to her feet. Arthur knew where the privy was; he immediately jumped from the rain barrel and ran around the front of the house before the door even opened leading out to the back. Then, knowing she couldn't possibly hear the bell, he opened the post office door, went inside, clambered over the counter, and made his way into the kitchen from the front of the house. There was the salamander, licking a bit of tea that had spilled from the saucer. As Arthur entered, the salamander lifted its head. Then it scurried back and forth, making a shape on the table. One triangle. Another triangle crossing it.

A hex.

Arthur moved to the chair where Vilate had been sitting. Standing, his head was just about at the height her head was at when she was seated. And as he leaned over her chair, the salamander changed.

No, not really. No, the salamander disappeared. Instead, a woman was sitting in the chair across from him.

"You're an evil little boy," the woman said with a sad smile.

Arthur hardly even noticed what she said. Because he knew her. It was Old Peg Guester. The woman he called Mother. The woman who was buried under a certain stone marker on the hill behind the roadhouse, near his real mother, the runaway slave girl he never met. Old Peg was there.

But it wasn't Old Peg. It was the salamander.

"And you imagine things, you nasty boy. You make up stories."

Old Peg used to call him her "nasty boy," but it was a tease. It was when he repeated something someone else had said. She would laugh and call him nasty boy and give him a hug and tell him not to repeat *that* remark to anyone.

But this woman, this pretend Old Peg, she meant it. She thought he was a nasty boy.

He moved away from the chair. The salamander was back on the table and Old Peg was gone. Arthur knelt by the table to look at the salamander at eye level. It stared into his eyes. Arthur stared back.

He used to do this for hours with animals in the forest. When he was very little, he understood them. He came away with their story in his mind. Gradually that ability faded. Now he caught only glimmers. But then, he didn't spend as much time with animals anymore. Maybe if he tried hard enough . . .

"Don't forget me, salamander," he whispered. "I want to know your story. I want to know who taught you how to make them hexes on the table."

He reached out a hand, then slowly let a single finger

come to rest on the salamander's head. It didn't recoil from him; it didn't move even when his finger made contact. It just looked at him.

"What are you doing indoors?" he whispered. "You don't like it indoors. You want to be outside. Near the water. In the mud. In the leaves. With bugs."

It was the kind of thing Alvin did, murmuring to animals, suggesting things to them.

"I can take you back to the mud if you want. Come with me, if you want. Come with me, if you can."

The salamander raised a foreleg, then slowly set it down. One step closer to Arthur.

And from the salamander he thought he felt a hunger, a desire for food, but more than that, a desire for . . . for freedom. The salamander didn't like being a prisoner.

The door opened.

"Why, Arthur Stuart," said Vilate. "Imagine you coming to visit."

Arthur had sense enough not to jump to his feet as if he was doing something wrong. "Any letters for Alvin?" he asked.

"Not a one."

Arthur didn't even mention the salamander, which was just as well, because Vilate never even looked at it. You'd think that if a lady was caught with a live salamander—or even a dead one, for that matter—on her kitchen table, she'd at least offer some explanation.

"Want some tea?" she asked.

"Can't stay," said Arthur.

"Oh, next time then. Give Alvin my love." Her smile was sweet and beautiful.

Arthur reached out his hand, right in front of her, and touched the salamander's back.

She didn't notice. Or at least she gave no sign of noticing.

He moved away, backed out of the room, hopped the counter, and ran out the front door, hearing the bell ring behind him as he went.

If the salamander was a prisoner, who had captured it? Not Vilate—the salamander was making hexes to fool her into seeing somebody there. Though Arthur was willing to bet that it wasn't Old Peg Guester that Vilate saw. But the salamander wasn't fooling her out of its own free will, because all it wanted was to be free to go back to being an ordinary salamander again.

He'd have to tell Alvin about this, that was sure. Vilate was planning to do something rotten to him, and the salamander that walked out hexes on the kitchen table, it had something to do with the plot.

How could Vilate be so stupid that she didn't even see me touching her salamander? Why didn't she get upset when she saw me in the kitchen when she got back from the privy?

Maybe she wanted me to see the salamander. Or maybe someone else wanted me to see it.

Wanted me to see Mother.

For a moment, walking along the dusty main street of Hatrack River, he lost control of himself, almost let himself cry thinking about Mother, thinking about seeing her sitting across from him.

It wasn't real, he told himself. It was all fakery. Humbug. Hoaxification. Whoever was behind all this was a liar, and a mean liar at that. Nasty boy indeed. Evil boy. He wasn't no evil boy. He was a good boy and the real Peg Guester would know that, she wouldn't say nothing like that to him. The real Peg Guester would hug him up tight and say, "My good boy, Arthur Stuart, you are my own good boy."

He walked it off. He walked the tears right out of his eyes, and when the sad feelings went away, another feeling came in its place. He was plain mad. Got no right making him see Mama. Got no right. I hate you, whoever you are, making me see my Mama calling me names like that.

He trotted up the stairs into the courthouse. The only good thing about Alvin being in jail was that Arthur Stuart always knew where he was.

IT WAS HARD for Napoleon to believe that he had once come *this* close to killing the American boy Calvin. Hard to remember how frightened he had been to see the boy's power. How for the first few days, Napoleon had watched him closely, had hardly slept for fear that the boy would do something to him in the night. Remove his legs, for instance. That would be a cure for the gout! It only occurred to him because of the number of times he had wished, in the throes of agony, that in one of his battles a cannonball had severed his leg. Stumping around on sticks couldn't be worse than this. And the boy brought such relief. Not a cure . . . but a cessation of the pain.

In exchange for that, Napoleon was content to let Calvin manipulate him. He knew who was really in control, and it wasn't an upstart, ignorant American boy. Who cared if Calvin thought he was clever, doling out a day's relief from pain in exchange for another lesson on how to govern men? Did he really imagine Napoleon would teach him anything that would give him the upper hand? On the contrary, with every hour, every day they spent together, Napoleon's control over a boy who *could* have been uncontrollable grew stronger, deeper. And Calvin had no idea.

They never understood, none of them. They all thought they served Napoleon out of love and admiration, or out of greed and self-interest, or out of fear and discretion. Whatever motive drove them, Napoleon fed it, got control of it. Some were impelled by shame, and some by guilt; some by ambition, some by lust, some even by their excess of piety—for when the occasion demanded, Napoleon could convince some spiritually starved soul that he was God's chosen servant on Earth. It wasn't hard. None of it was hard, when you understood other people the way Napoleon did. They gave off their desires like sweat, like the smell of an athlete after the contest or a soldier after a battle, like the smell of a woman—Napoleon didn't even have to think, he simply said the word, the exact words they needed to hear to win them to him.

And on those rare occasions when someone was immune to his words, when they had some sort of protective amulet or hex, each one more clever than the last—well, that's what guards were for. That's why there was a guillotine. The people knew that Napoleon was not a cruel man, that few indeed were ever punished under his rule. They knew that if a man was sent to the guillotine, it was because the world would be better off with that particular mouth detached from those lungs, with those hands unconnected to that head.

Calvin? Ah, the boy could have been dangerous. The boy had the power to save himself from the guillotine, to stop the blade from striking his neck. The boy might have been able to prevent anything that didn't come as a complete surprise. How would the Emperor have defeated him? Perhaps a little opium to dull him; he had to sleep sometime. But it didn't matter. No need to kill after all. Only a little study, a little patience, and Napoleon had him.

Not as his servant—no, this American boy was clever, he was watching for that, he was careful not to allow himself to succumb to any attempt by Napoleon to turn him into a slave, into one of those servants who looked at their Emperor with adoring eyes. Now and then Napoleon made a remark, a sort of feint, so Calvin would *think* he was fending off the Emperor's best strokes. But in fact, Napoleon had no need for this boy's loyalty. Just his healing touch.

This boy was driven by envy. Who would have guessed it? All that innate power, such gifts from God or Nature or whatever, and the boy was wasting it all because of envy for his older brother Alvin. Well, he wasn't about to tell Calvin he had to stop letting those feelings control him! On the contrary, Napoleon fed them, subtly, with little queries now and then about how Alvin might have done this or that, or comments about how awful it was having to put up with younger brothers who simply haven't the ability to measure up to one's own ability. He knew how this would rankle, how it would fester in Calvin's soul. A worm, twisting its way through the boy's judgment, eating tunnels in it. I have you, I have you. Look across the ocean, your gaze fixed upon your brother; you might have challenged me for the empire here, for half the world, but instead all you can think about is some useless fellow in homespun or deerskin or whatever who can make polished stone with his bare hands and heal the sick.

Heal the sick. That's the one that Napoleon was working on now. He knew perfectly well that Calvin was deliberately not healing him; he also knew that if Calvin ever got the idea that Napoleon was really in command, he'd probably flee and leave him with the gout again. So he had to keep a delicate balance: Taunt him because his brother could heal and he couldn't; at the same time, convince him that he'd already learned all the Emperor had to teach, that it was just a matter of practice now before he was as good at controlling other men.

If it worked out well, the boy, filled with confidence that he had squeezed the last drop of knowledge from Napoleon's mind, would finally show off that he was a match for

666 • *Orson Scott Card*

his brother after all. He would heal the Emperor, then leave
the court at once and sail back to America to challenge his
brother—to attempt, using Napoleon's teachings, to get control over him.

Of course, if he got there and nothing he learned from
the Emperor worked, well, he'd be back for vengeance!
But Napoleon really was teaching him. Enough to play on
the weaknesses of weak men, the fears of fearful men, the
ambitions of proud men, the ignorance of stupid men. What
Calvin didn't notice was that Napoleon wasn't teaching
him any of the truly difficult arts: how to turn the virtues of
good men against them.

The most hilarious thing was that Calvin was surrounded
by the very best men, the most difficult ones that Napoleon
had won over. The Marquis de La Fayette, for instance—he
was the servant who bathed the Emperor. It would never
occur to Calvin that Napoleon would keep his most dangerous enemies near him, oblivious to how he humiliated
them. If Calvin only understood, he would realize that this
was *real* power. Evil men, weak men, fearful men—they
were so easy to control. It was only when men of virtue fell
under Napoleon's control that he felt at last the confidence
to reach for power, to unseat the king and take his place,
to conquer Europe and impose his peace upon the warring
nations.

Calvin never sees that, because he is himself a fearful and
ambitious man, and does not realize that others might be
fearless and generous. No wonder he resents his older
brother so much! From what Calvin said of him, it seemed
to Napoleon that Alvin would be a very difficult case indeed, a very hard one to break. In fact, knowing that Calvin's brother existed was enough to cause Napoleon to hold
off on his plan of building up his armies in Canada with an
eye to conquering the three English-speaking nations of

America. No reason to do anything to make Alvin Smith turn his eyes eastward. That was a contest Napoleon did not want to embark on.

Instead he would send Calvin home, armed with great skill at subversion, deception, corruption, and manipulation. He'd have no control over Alvin, of course, but he would surely be able to deceive him, for Napoleon well knew that just as evil, weak, and fearful people saw their own base motives in other people's actions, so also the virtuous tended to assume the noblest of motives for other people's acts; why else were so many awful liars so successful at bilking others? If good people weren't so trusting of bad ones, the human race would have died out long ago—most women never would have let most men near them.

Let the brothers battle it out. If anyone can get rid of the threat of this Alvin Smith, it's his own brother, who can get close to him—not me, with all my armies, with all my skill. Let them fight.

But not until my leg is healed.

"My dear Leon, you mustn't drift off with the covers down like that."

It was La Fayette, checking on him before sleep. Napoleon let the fellow pull his blanket up. It was a coolish night; it was good to have such tender concern from a loving man of great responsibility, dependability, creativity. I have in my hands the best of men, and under my thumb the worst of them. My record is much better than God's. Clearly the old fellow chose the wrong son to make his only begotten. If I'd been in Jerusalem in the place of that dullard Jesus, I'd never have been crucified. I would have had Rome under my control in no time, and the whole world converted to my doctrine.

Maybe that's what this Alvin was—God's second try! Well, Napoleon would help with the script. Napoleon would send Alvin Smith his Judas.

"You need your sleep, Leon," said La Fayette.

"My mind is so full," said Napoleon.

"Of happy things, I pray."

"Happy indeed."

"No pain in your leg? It's good to have that American boy here, if he keeps you from that dreadful suffering."

"I know that when I'm in pain I'm so difficult to live with," said Napoleon.

"Not at all, never. Don't even think it. It's a joy to be with you."

"Do you ever miss it, my Marquis? The armies, the power? Government, politics, intrigues?"

"Oh, Leon! How could I miss it? I have it all through you. I watch what you do and I marvel. I never could have done so well. I'm at school with you every day; you are the superb master."

"Am I?"

"The master. The master of all is my dear Leon. How truly they named your house in Corsica, my dear. Buona Parte. Good parts. You are truly the lion of good parts."

"How sweet of you to say so, my Marquis. Good night."

"God bless you."

The candle retreated from the room, and moonlight returned its dim light through the curtains.

I know you're studying me, Calvin. Sending your doodling bug, as you so quaintly call it, into my legs, to find the cause of the gout. Figure it out. Be as smart as your brother about this one thing, so I can finally get rid of you and the pain both.

VERILY HAD KNOWN debased men in his life; he had been offered large sums of money to defend one now and then, but his conscience was not for sale. He remembered one of them who, thinking that his minions had not been clear about just how *much* money he was offering, came to see Verily in person. When he finally realized that Verily was not simply holding out for a higher price, he looked quite hurt. "Really, Mr. Cooper, why isn't my money as good as anyone else's?"

"It isn't your money, sir," said Verily.

"What, then? What is your objection?"

"I keep imagining: What if, through some gross miscarriage of justice, I won?"

Livid, the man hurled vile threats at him and left. Verily never knew whether it was this man or another who sent an assassin after him—a pathetic attempt, knifework in the dark. Verily saw the blade and the assassin's vicious smile—obviously the fellow had chosen a profession that allowed him to satisfy his own predilections—and caused the blade to drop off the knife and shatter at the man's feet. The man couldn't have looked more crestfallen if Verily had made a eunuch of him.

Debased men, but they all had something in common: They showed a keen regard for virtue, and tried to dress themselves in that costume. Hypocrisy, for all its bad reputation, at least showed a decent respect for goodness.

These Slave Finders, however, were not noble enough to be hypocrites. Not having risen above the level of reptiles and sharks, they showed no awareness of their own despicableness, and thus made no attempt to hide what they were. One was almost tempted to admire their brazenness, until one remembered what callous disregard for decency they must have in order to spend their lives, in exchange for mere money, chasing down the most helpless of their fellow-beings and returning them to lives of bondage, punishment, and despair.

Verily was pleased that Daniel Webster seemed to be almost as repulsed by these men as he was. Fastidiously the New England lawyer disdained to shake their hands, managing to be busy with his papers as each one arrived. Nor did he even bother to learn their names; having once ascertained that the entire group contracted for was properly assembled, he then addressed them only as a group, and without quite looking any of them in the eye. If they noticed his aloofness, they made no remark and showed no resentment. Perhaps this is how they were always treated. Perhaps those who hired them always did so with distaste, washing their hands after passing them the cachet of the slave they were to hunt down, washing again after giving them their Finder's fee. Didn't they understand that it is the murderer who is filthy, and not the knife?

It was ten-thirty in the morning before the Finders, seated at a single long table before the judge's bench, were satisfied that they had got the information they needed from the cachet belonging to a certain Cavil Planter of Oily Spring, Kenituck. The judge had the deposition, carefully taken by Mr. Webster at Mr. Planter's home in Carthage City, Wobbish. Planter had attempted to assert that the cachet was a collection of nail and hair clippings and a bit of dried skin taken from one Arthur Stuart of Hatrack River; but Webster insisted that he state the exact legal situation, which was that the items in the cachet were taken from an unnamed baby born on his farm in Appalachee to a slave woman belonging to Mr. Planter at the time, who had shortly afterward escaped—with, as Planter insisted on adding, the help of the devil, who gave her the power to fly, or so it was rumored among the ignorant and superstitious slaves.

The Finders were ready; the boys were led in, one at a time, and lined up in a row in front of them. All the boys were dressed in ordinary clothing, and all were more or less of a size. Their hands were covered, not with gloves, but with burlap bags tied above their elbows; a finer sacking material also covered their heads with loose-fitting hoods. No scrap of skin was visible; care had even been taken to make sure there was no gap between the buttons of their shirts. And just in case, a large placard with a number on it hung from each boy's neck, completely covering his shirtfront.

Verily watched carefully. Was there some difference between the Black sons of Mock Berry and the White boys? Something about their walk, their stance? Indeed, there were differences among the boys—this one's pose of insouciance, that one's nervous fidgeting—but Verily could not tell which were White and which were Black. Certainly he could not tell which one was Arthur Stuart, the boy who was not fully of either race. This did not mean, however, that the Finders did not know or could not guess.

Alvin assured him, though, that their knack would be useless to them, since Arthur Stuart was no longer a fair match for the cachet.

And Alvin was right. The Finders looked puzzled when the last boy was brought in and the judge said, "Well, which of them matches the cachet?" Clearly they had expected to know instantly which of them was their prey. Instead, they began to murmur.

"No conference," said the judge. "Each of you must reach his conclusion independently, write down the number of the boy you think matches the cachet, and have done with it."

"Are you sure someone hasn't held out the boy in question?" asked one Slave Finder.

"What you are asking me," said the judge, "is if I am either corrupt or a fool. Would you care to specify which accusation you are inquiring about?"

After that the Finders puzzled in silence.

"Gentlemen," said the judge—and was his tone somewhat dry when he called them that? "You have had three minutes. I was told your identification would be instant. Please write and have done."

They wrote. They signed their papers. They handed them to the judge.

"Please, return to your seats while I tabulate the results," said the judge.

Verily had to admire the way the judge showed no expression as he sorted through the papers. But it also frustrated him. Would there be *no* hint of the outcome?

"I'm disappointed," said the judge. "I had expected that the much-vaunted powers and the famous integrity of the Slave Finders would give me unanimous results. I had expected that you would either unanimously point the finger at one boy, or unanimously declare that the boy could not be one of this group. Instead, I find quite a range of answers. Three of you did declare under penalty of perjury that none of these boys matched the cachet. But four of you have named various boys—again, under penalty of perjury. Specifically, the four of you named three different boys. The only two who seemed to be in agreement both happened to be seated together, at my far right. Since you are the only two who agree in accusing one of the boys, I think we'll check your assertion first. Bailiff, please remove the hood from the head of boy number five."

The bailiff did as he was asked. The boy was Black, but he was not Arthur Stuart.

"You two—are you certain, do you swear before God, that this is the boy who matches the cachet? Remember please that it is your license to practice your profession in the state of Wobbish that hangs in the balance, for if you are found to be unreliable or dishonest, you will never be permitted to bring a slave back across the river again."

What they also knew, however, was that if they now backed down, they would be liable for charges of perjury. And the boy *was* Black.

"No sir, I am certain this is the boy," said one. The other nodded emphatically.

"Now, let's look at the other two boys that were named. Take the hoods from numbers one and two."

One of them was Black, the other White.

The Finder who named a White boy covered his face with his hands. "Again, knowing that your license is at stake, are you both prepared to swear that the boy you named is an exact match?"

The Finder who named the White boy began to stammer, "I don't know, I just don't, I was sure, I thought it was . . ."

"The answer is simple—do you continue to swear that this boy is an exact match, or did you lie under oath when you named him?"

The Finders who had sworn that the cachet matched no one were smiling now—they knew, obviously, that the others had lied, and were enjoying their torment.

"I did not lie," said the Finder who named the White boy.

"Neither did I," said the other defiantly. "And I *still* think I'm right. I don't know how these other boys could get it so wrong."

"But you—*you* don't think you're right, do you? You don't think some miracle turned that slave baby White, do you?"

"No, sir. I must be . . . mistaken."

"Give me your license. Right now."

The miserable Finder stood up and handed the judge a leather case. The judge took from the case a piece of paper with an official seal on it. He wrote in the margin and then on the back; then he signed it and crimped it with his own seal. "There you go," he said to the Finder. "You understand that if you're ever caught attempting to practice the profession of Slave Finding in the state of Hio, you will be arrested and tried and, when convicted, you will face at least ten years in prison?"

"I understand," said the humiliated man.

"And you are also aware that Hio maintains a reciprocity arrangement with the states of Huron, Suskwahenny, Irrakwa, Pennsylvania, and New Sweden? So that the same or similar penalties will apply to you there if you attempt to practice this profession?"

"I understand," he said again.

"Thank you for your help," said the judge. "You should only be grateful that you were incompetent, for if I had cause to suspect you of perjury, it would have been prison *and* the lash, I assure you, for if I thought that you had willfully named this boy falsely, I would have no mercy on you. You may go."

The others obviously got the message. As the unfortunate man fled the courtroom, the other three who had named one boy or another steeled themselves for what was to come.

"Sheriff Doggly," said the judge, "would you kindly inform us of the identity of these two boys who stand identified by three of our panel of Finders?"

"Sure, Your Honor," said Doggly. "These two is Mock Berry's boys, James and John. Peter's near growed and Andrew and Zebedee was too small."

"You're sure of their identity?"

"They've lived here in Hatrack all their lives."

"Any chance that either of them is, in fact, the child of a runaway slave?"

"No chance. For one thing, the dates are all wrong. They're both way too old—the Berry boys is always short for their age, kind of late-blooming roses if you know what I mean, then they just shoot up like spring grass, cause Peter's about the tallest fellow around here. But these boys, they was already clever little tykes well known around town before ever the slave that cachet belongs to was born."

The judge turned to the Finders. "Well, now. I wonder how it happens that you appointed for slavery these two freeborn Black children."

One of them spoke up immediately. "Your Honor, I will protest this whole procedure. We were not brought here to be placed on trial ourselves, we were brought here to practice our profession and—"

The gavel slammed down on the desk. "You were brought here to practice your profession, that is true. Your profession requires that when you make an identification, it must be assumed by all courts of law to be both honest and accurate. Whenever you practice your profession, here or in the field, your license is on the line, and you know it. Now, tell me at once, did you lie when you identified these boys, or were you merely mistaken?"

"What if we was just guessing?" one of them asked. Verily almost laughed out loud.

"Guessing, in this context, would be lying, since you were swearing that the boy you named was a match for the cachet, and if you had to guess, then he was not a match. Did you guess?"

The man thought about it for a moment. "No sir, I didn't lie. I was just plain wrong I reckon."

Another man tried a different tack. "How do we know this sheriff isn't lying?"

"Because," said the judge, "I already met all these boys, and their parents, and saw their birth records in the county archive. Any more questions before you decide whether you'll lose your license or be bound over for trial as perjurers?"

The two remaining Finders quickly agreed that they had been mistaken. Everyone waited while the judge signed and sealed the limitation on their licenses. "You gentlemen may also go."

They went.

Verily rose to his feet. "Your Honor, may I request that these young men who were not identified be allowed to remove their hoods? I fear that they may be growing quite uncomfortable."

"By all means. Bailiff, it's certainly time."

The hoods came off. The boys all looked relieved. Arthur Stuart was grinning.

To the three remaining Finders, the judge said, "You are under oath. Do you swear that none of these boys matches the cachet belonging to Mr. Cavil Planter?"

They all swore to it.

"I commend you for having the honesty to admit to not finding a match, when others were clearly tempted to find a match no matter what. I find your profession loathsome, but at least the three of you practice it honestly and with reasonable competence."

"Thank you, Your Honor," said one of them; the others, however, seemed to know they had just been insulted.

"Since this proceeding is a legal hearing under the Fugitive Slave Law, I don't have to have your signatures on anything, but I'd prefer it if you'd stay long enough to sign your names to an affirmation that specifically states that this young man, the mixup boy named Arthur Stuart, is definitely not a match with the cachet. Can you sign such a statement under oath before God?"

They could. They did. They were dismissed.

"Mr. Webster, I can't think what in the world you'd have to say, but since you represent Mr. Cavil Planter in this matter, I must ask you for any statement you'd like to make on this matter before I issue my finding."

Webster rose slowly to his feet. Verily wondered what the

man could have the audacity to say, in the face of such evidence—what whining, sniveling complaint or protest he might utter.

"Your Honor," said Webster, "it is obvious to me that my client is the victim of fraud. Not today, Your Honor, for these proceedings have clearly been honest. No, the fraud was more than a year ago, when two Finders, hoping to collect a fee they had not earned, named this boy as Mr. Planter's property and proceeded to commit murder and get themselves killed in the effort to enslave a free boy. My client, believing them to be honest, naturally proceeded to secure the redress to which he would have been entitled by law; but now, I can assure you that as soon as my client learns that he was put upon most sorely by those Finders, he will be as horrified as I am by how close he came to enslaving a free child and, what is worse, extraditing for prosecution the young man named Alvin Smith, who it now seems was acting in proper self-defense when he killed the second of those malicious, lying, fraudulent men pretending to be Finders." Webster sat back down.

It was a pretty speech. Webster's voice was lovely to hear. The man should go into politics, Verily thought. His voice would be a noble addition to the halls of Congress in Philadelphia.

"You pretty much summed up my summing up," said the judge. "It is the finding of this court that Arthur Stuart is not the property of Mr. Cavil Planter, and therefore the Finders who were trying to take him back to Appalachee were not acting lawfully, and therefore the interference Margaret Guester and Alvin Smith offered them was legal and appropriate under the circumstances. I declare Alvin Smith to be absolved of all responsibility, criminal or civil, in the deaths of these Finders, and I declare Margaret Guester to be posthumously absolved in like manner. Under the terms of the Fugitive Slave Law, there may be no further attempt by anyone under any circumstances to bring Arthur Stuart into slavery regardless of any additional evidence—this action is final. Likewise there may be no further attempt to try Alvin Smith on any charges arising out of the illegal expedition undertaken by those fraudulent Finders, including their death. This action, likewise, is final."

Verily loved hearing those words, for all that language insisting that such actions were final had been placed in the law for the purpose of blocking any effort on the part of antislavery forces to interfere with the recapture of a slave or the punishment of those who helped a runaway. This time, at least, that finality would work against the proponents of slavery. Hoist on their own petard.

The bailiff took the burlap bags off the boys' hands. The judge, the sheriff, Verily, and Marty Laws all shook the boys' hands and gave them—except Arthur, of course—the two bits they were entitled to for their service to the court. Arthur got something more precious. Arthur got a copy of the judge's decision making it illegal for him to be accosted by anyone searching for runaway slaves.

Webster shook Verily's hand, quite warmly. "I'm glad things worked out this way," he said. "As you know, in our profession we are sometimes called upon to represent clients in actions that we wish they would not pursue."

Verily held his silence—he supposed that for most lawyers this was probably true.

"I'm glad that my presence here will not result in anyone entering a life of slavery, or of your client being extradited under false charges."

Verily couldn't leave that statement alone. "And you would have been sad to see him extradited, if this hearing had turned out otherwise?"

"Oh, not at all," said Webster. "If the Finders had identified young Mr. Stuart, then justice would have demanded that your client be tried in Kenituck for murder."

"Justice?" Verily didn't try to keep the contempt from his voice.

"The law *is* justice, my friend," said Webster. "I know of no other measure available to us as mortal men. God has a better justice than ours, but until angels sit upon the bench, the justice of law is the best justice we can have, and I, for one, am glad we have it."

If Verily had been tempted to feel even a glimmer of guilt over the fact that Arthur Stuart really was Cavil Planter's slave, by law, and that, again by law, Alvin Smith really should have been extradited, there was no chance of it now. Webster's narrow view of justice was just as truly satisfied by this outcome as Verily's much broader perspective. By God's justice, Arthur should be free and Alvin held to no penalty, and so the outcome had been just. But Webster's justice was as well served, for the letter of the law required the matching of the cachet to the slave, and if it so happened that Arthur Stuart had been changed somehow by a certain Maker so the cachet no longer matched—well, the law made no provision for exceptions, and so, as Webster had said, the law being satisfied, justice must also have been done.

"I'm grateful to know your mind upon the matter," said Verily. "I look forward to discovering, in my client's trial for larceny, precisely what your commitment to justice is."

"And so you shall," said Webster. "The gold belongs to Makepeace Smith, not his former apprentice. So when justice is done, Makepeace Smith will have his gold."

Verily smiled at him. "It shall be a contest, then, Mr. Webster."

"When two giants meet in battle," said Webster, "one giant will fall."

"And loud shall be the noise thereof," said Verily.

Webster took only a moment to realize that Verily was teasing him about his golden-voiced oratory; and when he did, instead of being insulted, he threw back his head and laughed, warmly, loudly, cheerfully. "I like you, Mr. Cooper! I shall enjoy all that lies ahead of us!"

Verily let him have the last word. But in his own mind, he answered, Not all, Mr. Webster. You shall not enjoy it all.

NO ONE PLANNED a meeting, but they arrived at Alvin's cell that evening almost at the same time, as if someone had summoned them. Verily Cooper had come to discuss what would happen during the selection of the jury and perhaps gloat a little over the easy victory in the hearing that morning; he was joined by Armor-of-God Weaver, who brought letters from family and wellwishers in Vigor Church; Arthur Stuart of course was there, as he was most evenings; Horace Guester had brought a bowl of roadhouse stew and a jug of the fresh cider—Alvin wouldn't take the cider that had turned, it dulled his mind; and no sooner were they all assembled in and around the open cell than the outer door opened and the deputy showed in Peggy Larner and a man that none but Alvin recognized.

"Mike Fink, as I live and breathe," said Alvin.

"And you're that smithy boy who bent my legs and broke my nose." Mike Fink smiled, but there was pain in the smile, and no one was sure but what there might not be a quarrel here.

"I see some scars and marks on you, Mr. Fink," said Alvin, "but I reckon from the fact you're standing here before us that those are marks of fights you won."

"Won fair and square, and hard fought," said Fink. "But I killed no man as didn't require me to, on account of trying to stick a knife in me and there being no other way to stop them."

"What brings you here, Mr. Fink?" asked Alvin.

"I owe you," said Fink.

"Not that I know of," said Alvin.

"I owe you and I mean to repay."

Still his words were ambiguous, and Arthur Stuart noticed how Papa Horace and Armor-of-God braced themselves to take on the powerful body of the riverman, if need arose.

It was Peggy Larner who made it clear. "Mr. Fink has come to give us information about a plot against Alvin's life. And to offer himself as a bodyguard, to make sure no harm comes to you."

"I'm glad to know you wanted to give me warning," said Alvin. "Come on in and sit down. You can share the floor with me, or sit on my cot—it's stronger than it looks."

"Don't have much to tell. I think Miss Larner already told you what I learned before, about a plot to kill you as they took you back for trial in Kenituck. Well, the men I know—if you can rightly call them men—haven't been fired from the plan. In fact what I heard this very afternoon was to pay no nevermind to how the extradition was squished—"

"Quashed," offered Verily Cooper helpfully.

"Mashed," said Fink. "Whatever. They got to pay no heed to it, because they'll still be needed. The plan is for you not to leave the town of Hatrack River alive."

"And what about Arthur Stuart?" asked Alvin.

"Not a word about no mixup boy," said Fink. "The way I see it, they don't give a damn about the boy, he's just an excuse for them to get you kilt."

"Please watch . . ." Alvin began, mildly enough, but Mike Fink didn't need to hear him finish saying "your language with the lady."

"Beg your pardon, Miss Larner," he said.

"Don't that beat all," said Alvin admiringly. "He's already beginning to sound like one of your students." But was there a bite in his tone?

There was certainly a bite in Peggy's answer. "I'd rather hear him swear than hear you say 'don't' for 'doesn't.' "

Alvin leaned close to Mike Fink to explain, though he never took his eyes from Peggy's face. "You see, Miss Larner knows all the words, and she knows just where they ought to be."

Arthur Stuart could see the fury in her face, but she held her tongue. It was some kind of fight going on between the two of them; but what was it about? Miss Larner had *always* corrected their grammar, ever since she tutored Alvin and Arthur together when she was the schoolteacher in Hatrack River.

What puzzled Arthur Stuart all the more was the way the older men—not Verily, but Horace and Armor-of-God and even Mike Fink—sort of glanced around at each other and half-smiled like they all understood *exactly* what was going on between Alvin and Peggy, understood it better than those two did their own selves.

Mike Fink spoke up again. "Getting back to matters of life and death instead of grammar . . ."

At which point Horace murmured under his breath, "And lovers' spats."

"I'm sorry to say I can't learn no more of their plans than that," said Fink. "It's not like we're dear friends or nothing— more like they'd be as happy to stab me in the back as pee on my boots, depending on whether their knife or their . . . whatever . . . was in their hands." He glanced again at Peggy

Larner and blushed. Blushed! That grizzled face, scarred and bent by battle, that missing ear, but still the blood rushed into his face like a schoolboy rebuked by his schoolmarm.

But before the blush could even fade, Alvin had his hand on Fink's arm and pulled him down to sit beside him on the floor, and Alvin threw an easy arm over his shoulder. "You and me, Mike, we just can't remember how to talk fine in front of some folks and plain in front of others. But I'll help you if you'll help me."

And there, in one easy moment, Alvin had put Mike Fink back to rights. There was just a kind of plain sincerity in Alvin's way of speaking that even when you knew he was trying to make you feel better, you didn't mind. You knew he cared about you, cared enough to try to make you feel better, and so you *did* feel better.

Thinking of Alvin making folks feel better made Arthur Stuart remember something that Alvin did to make *him* feel better. "Why don't you sing that song, Alvin?"

Now it was Alvin's turn to blush in embarrassment. "You know I ain't no singer, Arthur. Just because I sung it to you . . ."

"He made up a song," said Arthur Stuart. "About being locked up in here. We sung it together yesterday."

Mike Fink nodded. "Seems like a Maker got to keep making something."

"I got nothing to *do* but think and sing," said Alvin. "*You* sing it, Arthur Stuart, not me. You've got a good singing voice."

"I'll sing it if you want," said Arthur. "But it's your song. You made it up, words and tune."

"You sing it," said Alvin. "I don't even know if I'd remember all the words."

Arthur Stuart dutifully stood up and started to sing, in his piping voice:

I meant to be a journeyman,
To wander on the earth.
As quick as any fellow can
I left the country of my birth—
It's fair to say I ran.

Arthur Stuart looked over at Alvin. "You got to sing the chorus with me, anyway."

So together they sang the rollicking refrain:

At daybreak I'll be risin',
For never will my feet be still,
I'm bound for the horizon—oh!
I'm bound for the horizon.

Then Arthur went back to the verse, but now Alvin joined him in a kind of tenor harmony, their voices blending sweetly to each other.

Till I was dragged from bed
And locked inside a little cell.
My journeys then were in my head
On all the roads of hell.

With the next verse, though, when Arthur began it, Alvin didn't join in, he just looked confused.

Alone with my imagining
I dreamt the darkest dream—

"Wait a minute, Arthur Stuart," said Alvin. "That verse isn't really part of this song."

"Well it fits, and you sung it to this tune your own self."

"But it's a nonsense dream, it don't mean a thing."

"I like it," said Arthur. "Can't I sing it?"

Alvin waved him to go ahead, but he still looked embarrassed.

> *Alone with my imagining*
> *I dreamt the darkest dream,*
> *Of tiny men, a spider's sting,*
> *And in a land of smoke and steam*
> *An evil golden ring.*

"What does that *mean?*" asked Armor-of-God.

"I don't know," said Alvin. "I wonder if sometimes I don't accidentally end up with somebody else's dream. Maybe that was a dream that belonged to somebody of ancient days, or maybe somebody who ain't even been born yet. Just a spare dream and I chanced to snag on it during my sleep."

Verily Cooper said, "When I was a boy, I wondered if the strange people in my dreams might not be just as real as me, and I was in *their* dreams sometimes too."

"Then let's just hope they don't wake up at a inconvenient moment," said Mike Fink dryly.

Arthur Stuart went on with the last verse.

> *The accusations all were lies*
> *And few believed the tale,*
> *So I was patient, calm and wise.*
> *But legs grow weak inside a jail*
> *And something in you dies.*

"This song may be the saddest one I ever heard," said Horace Guester. "Don't you *ever* have a cheerful thought in here?"

"The chorus is pretty sprightly," said Arthur Stuart.

"I had cheerful thoughts today," said Alvin, "thinking of

four Slave Finders losing their license to carry off free men and put them into bondage in the south. And now I'm cheerful again, knowing that the strongest man I ever fought is now going to be my bodyguard. Though the sheriff may not take kindly to it, Mr. Fink, since he thinks I'm safe enough as long as I'm in the care of him and his boys."

"And you are safe," said Peggy. "Even those deputies that don't like you would never raise a hand against you or allow you to be less than safe."

"There's no danger, then?" asked Horace Guester.

"Grave danger," said Peggy. "But not from the deputies, and most particularly not till the trial is over, and Alvin prepares to leave. That's when we'll need more than a bodyguard to die along with Alvin. We'll need subterfuge to get him out of town in one piece."

"Who says I'll die?" asked Fink.

Peggy smiled thinly. "Against any five men I think you two would do well."

"So there'll be more than five?" asked Alvin.

"There may be," said Peggy. "Nothing is clear right now. Things are in flux. The danger is real, though. The plot's in place and men have been paid. You know when money's involved, even assassins feel obliged to fulfill their contracts."

"But for the nonce," said Verily Cooper, "we're not to worry about our safety, or Alvin's?"

"Prudence is all that's needed," said Peggy.

"I don't know why we're putting our trust in knackery," said Armor-of-God. "Our Savior is guard enough for us all."

"Our Savior will resurrect us," said Peggy, "but I haven't noticed that Christians end up any less dead at the end of life than heathens."

"Well, one thing's sure," said Horace Guester. "If it wasn't for knackery Alvin wouldn't be in this blamed fix."

"Did you like the song?" asked Alvin. "I mean, I thought

Arthur sung it real good. Real well. Very well." Each correction won a bit more of a smile from Miss Larner.

"*Sang* it very well," said Peggy. "But each version of the sentence was better than the one before!"

"I got another verse," said Alvin. "It's not really part of the song, on account of it isn't true yet, but do you want to hear it?"

"You got to sing it alone, I don't know another verse," said Arthur Stuart.

Alvin sang:

> *I trusted justice not to fail.*
> *The jury did me proud.*
> *Tomorrow I will hit the trail*
> *And sing my hiking song so loud*
> *It's like to start a gale!*

They all laughed, and allowed as how they hoped he could soon sing it for real. By the time the meeting ended, they'd decided that Armor-of-God, with Mike Fink to watch his back and keep him safe, would head for Carthage City and learn all he could about the men who were paying Daniel Webster's salary and see for sure if they were the same ones paying the river rats and other scoundrels to lie in wait to take Alvin's life. Other than that, everything was in Verily Cooper's hands. And to hear him tell it, it was up to the witnesses and the jury. Twelve good men and true.

THERE WAS A long line at the county clerk's office as Peggy came in for the first day of Alvin's trial. "Early voters," Marty Laws explained. "Folks that worry maybe the weather will keep them from casting their ballot election day. This Tippy-Canoe campaign has folks pretty riled up."

"Do you think they're voting for or against?"

"I'm not sure," said Marty. "You're the one who'd know, aren't you?"

Peggy didn't answer. Yes, she *would* know, if she cared to look. But she feared what she'd see.

"It's Po Doggly who knows about politics around here best. He says that if it was all up or down on the whole Red business, Tippy-Canoe wouldn't get him a vote. But he's also been playing on the western pride thing. How Tippy-Canoe is from our side of the Appalachee Mountains. Which don't make much sense to me, seeing as how Old Hickory—Andy Jackson—he's every bit as western as Harrison. I think folks worry about how Andy Jackson, being from Tennizy, he's probably too much for slavery. Folks around here don't want to vote in somebody who'll make the slavery thing any worse than it is."

Peggy smiled grimly. "I wish they knew Mr. Harrison's real position on slavery."

Marty cocked an eyebrow. "You know something I don't know?"

"I know that Harrison is the candidate that those who wish to expand slavery into the northern states will want to support."

"Ain't a soul here who wants to see that happen."

"Then they shouldn't vote for Harrison—if he becomes president, it *will* happen."

Marty stared long and hard at her. "Do you know this the way most folks know their political opinions, or do you know it as . . . as . . ."

"I know it," said Peggy. "I don't say that of mere opinions."

Marty nodded and looked off into space. "Well damn. Wouldn't you know it."

"You have a habit of betting on the wrong horse lately," said Peggy.

"You can say that again," said Marty. "I kept telling Makepeace for years that there wasn't a case against Alvin and I wasn't going to get him extradited from Wobbish. But then he showed up here, and what could I do? I had Makepeace, and he had him a witness besides himself. And you never know what juries are going to do. I think it's a bad business."

"Then why don't you move to dismiss the charges?" asked Peggy.

Marty glowered. "I can't do that, Miss Peggy, for the plain good reason that there *is* a case to be made. I hope this English lawyer Alvin's folks found for him can win him free. But I'm not going to roll over and play dead. What you got to understand, Miss Peggy, is I like most of the people in this county, and most of the time the folks I got to prosecute, they're people that I like. I don't prosecute them because I don't like them. I prosecute them because they done wrong, and the people of Hatrack County elected me to set things right. So I hope Alvin gets off, but if he does, it won't be because I failed to fulfill my responsibilities."

"I was there on the night the plow was made. Why don't you call *me* as a witness?"

"Did you see it made?" asked Marty.

"No. It was already finished when I saw it."

"Then what exactly are you a witness *of?*"

Peggy didn't answer.

"You want to get on that stand because you're a torch, and the people of Hatrack know you're a torch, and if you say Makepeace is lying, they'll believe you. But here's the thing I worry about, Miss Peggy. I know you and Alvin was once sweet for each other, and maybe still are. So how do I know that if you get on the stand, you won't commit some grievous sin against the God of truth in order to win the freedom of this boy?"

Peggy flushed with anger. "You know because you know my oath is as good as anyone's and better than most."

"If you get on the stand, Miss Peggy, I will rebut you by bringing up witnesses to say you lived in Hatrack for many months in complete disguise, lying to everyone that whole time about who you were. Covered with hexes, pretending to be a middle-aged spinster schoolteacher when the whole time you were seeing the smith's prentice boy under the guise of tutoring him. I know you had your reasons for doing all those things. I know there was a reason why on the night the plow was supposedly made, the same night your mother was killed, you and Alvin were seen running from the smithy together, only Alvin was stark naked. Do you get my drift, Miss Peggy?"

"You're advising me not to testify."

"I'm telling you that while some folks will believe you, others will be sure you're just helping Alvin as his co-conspirator. My job is to make sure every possible doubt of your testimony is introduced."

"So you *are* Alvin's enemy, and the enemy of truth." Peggy hurled the words, meaning them to bite.

"Accuse me all you like," said Marty, "but my job is to make the case that Alvin stole that gold. I don't think your testimony, based entirely on your unverifiable claim as a torch that Makepeace is a liar, should be allowed to stand unchallenged. If it did stand that way, then every half-baked dreamspeaker and soothsayer in the country would be able to say whatever he pleased and juries would believe them, and then what would happen to justice in America?"

"Let me understand you," said Peggy. "You plan to discredit me, destroy my reputation, and convict Alvin, all for the sake of justice in America?"

"As I said," Marty repeated, "I hope your lawyer can do as good a job defending Alvin as I'm going to do prosecuting him. I hope he can find as much damning evidence against my witnesses as Mr. Webster and I have found concerning Alvin. Because, frankly, I don't *like* my witnesses much, and I think Makepeace is a greedy lying bastard who should go to jail himself for perjury but I can't prove it."

"How can you live with yourself, then, working in the service of evil when you know so clearly what is good?"

"It's also good for the public prosecutor to prosecute, instead of setting himself up as judge."

Peggy nodded gravely. "As so often is the case, there is no clear choice that has all the good on its side, opposed to one that is nothing but bad."

"That's the truth, Peggy. That's God's honest truth."

"You advise me not to testify."

"Nothing of the kind. I just warned you of the price you'd pay for testifying."

"It's unethical for us to have had this conversation, isn't it?"

"A little bit," said Marty. "But your pa and I go back a long way."

"He'd never forgive you if you discredited me."

"I know, Miss Peggy. And that would break my heart." He nodded his good-bye, touching his forehead as if to tip the hat he wasn't wearing indoors. "Good day to you."

Peggy followed him into the courtroom.

That first morning was spent questioning the eight witnesses who had been shown the golden plow. First was Merlin Wheeler, who rolled in on his wheelchair. Peggy knew that Alvin had offered once, years ago, to heal him so he could walk again. But Merlin just looked him in the eye and said, "I lost the use of my legs to the same men who killed my wife and child. If you can bring them back, then we'll see about my legs." Alvin didn't understand then, and truth to tell, Peggy didn't really understand now. How did it help his wife and children for Merlin to go around in a wheelchair all the time? But then, maybe it helped Merlin himself. Maybe it was like wearing widow's weeds. A public symbol of how he was crippled by the loss of those he loved best. Anyway, he made a sturdy witness, mostly because people knew he had a knack for seeing what was fair and right, making him a sort of informal judge, though it wasn't all that common for both parties in a dispute to agree to get him to arbitrate for him. One or the other of them, it seemed, always felt it somehow inconvenient to have the case decided by a man who was truly evenhanded and fair. Anyway, the jury was bound to listen when Wheeler said, "I ain't saying the plow's bewitched cause I don't know how it got to be the way it is. I'm just saying that it appears to be gold, it hefts like gold, and it moves without no hand touching it."

Wheeler set the tone for all the others. Albert Wimsey was a clockmaker with a knack for fine metalwork, who fled to America when his business rivals accused him of using witchery in making his clocks—when *he* said the plow was gold, he spoke with authority, and the jury would entertain no further doubt about the metal it was made of. Jan Knickerbacker was a glassmaker who was said to have an eye to see things more clearly than most folks. Ma Bartlett was a frail old lady who once was a schoolteacher but now lived in the old cabin in the woods that Po Doggly built when he first settled in the area; she got a small pension from somewhere and mostly spent her days under an oak tree by Hatrack River, catching catfish and letting them go. People went to her to find out if they could trust other folks, and she was always right, which made it so many a budding romance got nipped in the bud, until folks sort of shied away from asking certain questions of her.

Billy Sweet made candy, a young and gullible young fellow that nobody took all that seriously, but you couldn't help but like him no matter how foolish the things he said and did. Naomi Lerner made a little money tutoring, but her knack was ignorance, not teaching—she could spot ignorance a mile away, but wasn't much good at alleviating it. Joreboam Hemelett was a gunsmith, and he must have had a touch of fire knackery because it was well known that no matter how damp a day it might be, the powder in a Hemelett gun always ignited. And Goody Trader—whose first name was rumored to be either Chastity or Charity, both names used ironically by those who didn't like her—kept a general store on the new end of Main Street, where she was well known to stock her shelves, not just with the things folks wanted, but also with the things they needed without knowing it.

All through their testimony, about hefting the plow, about how it moved, or hummed, or trembled, or warmed their hands, the jurors' eyes were drawn again and again to the burlap sack under Alvin's chair. He never touched it or did anything to call attention to it, but his body moved as if the plow inside the sack were the fulcrum of his balance. They wanted to see for themselves. But they knew, from Alvin's posture, that they would not see it. That these eight had seen for them. It would have to be enough.

The eight witnesses were well known to the people in town, all of them trusted (though Billy Sweet was only trusted *this* far, seeing as how he was so trusting himself that any liar could get him to believe any fool thing) and all of them well enough liked, apart from the normal quarrels of small-town life. Peggy knew them all, better than they knew each other, of course, but perhaps it was that very knowledge of them that blinded her to a thing that only Arthur Stuart seemed to notice.

Arthur was sitting beside her in the courtroom, watching the testimony, wide-eyed. It was only when all eight of the witnesses were done testifying that he leaned up to Peggy and whispered, "Sure are a lot of folks with sharp knacks here in Hatrack, aren't there?"

Peggy grew up around here, and for all that a lot of folks had moved in after she left, she always felt that she pretty much knew everybody. But was that so? She had run off the first time just before Alvin got to Hatrack to start his prenticeship with Makepeace Smith, and in the more than eight years since then, she had only spent that single year in Hatrack—less than a year, really—when she was in disguise. During those eight years a lot of people had moved in. More, in fact, by twice, than had lived here at the time she left. She had scanned their heartfires, routinely, because she wanted to get a sense of who lived in this place.

But she hadn't realized until Arthur's whispered remark that of the newcomers, an unusual number had quite remarkable knacks. It wasn't that the eight witnesses were different from the rest of the town. Knacks were thick on the ground here, much more so than any other place that Peggy had visited.

Why? What brought them here?

The answer was easy and obvious—so obvious that Peggy doubted it at once. Could they really have been drawn here because Alvin was here? It was in Hatrack that the prentice learned to hone his knack until it became an all-encompassing power of powers. It was here that Alvin made the living plow. Was there something about his Making that drew them? Something that kindled a fire inside them and set their feet to wandering until they came to rest in this place, where Making was in the air?

Or was it more than that? Was there Someone perhaps guiding them, so it wasn't just the makery in Hatrack that drew them, but rather the same One who had brought Alvin to this town? Did it mean there was purpose behind it all, some master plan? Oh, Peggy longed to believe *that,* for it would mean she was not responsible for making things turn out all right. If God is tending to things here, then I can put away my broom and set aside my needle and thread, I have neither cleaning nor stitchery to do. I can simply be about my business.

One way or the other, though, it was plain that Hatrack River was more than just the town where Alvin happened to be in jail right now. It was a place where people of hidden powers congregated in goodly numbers. Just as Verily Cooper had crossed the sea to meet Alvin, perhaps unwittingly all these others had also crossed sea or mountains or vast reaches of prairie and forest to find the place where the Maker Made his golden plow. And now these eight had handled the plow, had seen it move, knew it was alive. What did it mean to them?

For Peggy, to wonder was to find out: She looked at their heartfires and found something startling. On past examination, none of them had shown paths in their future that were closely tied to Alvin's. But now she found that their lives were bound up in his. All of them showed many paths into the future that led to a crystal city by the banks of a river.

For the first time, the Crystal City of Alvin's vision in the tornado was showing up in someone else's future.

She almost fainted from the relief of it. It wasn't just a formless dream in Alvin's heart, with no path guiding her as to how he would get there. It could be a reality, and if it was, all of these eight souls would be a part of it.

Why? Just because they had touched the living plow? Was that what the thing was? A tool to turn people into citizens of the Crystal City?

No, not that. No, it would hardly be the free place Alvin dreamed of, if folks were forced to be citizens because of touching some powerful object. Rather the plow opened up a door in their lives so they could enter into the future they most longed for. A place, a time where their knacks could be brought to full fruition, where they could be part of something larger than any of them were capable of creating on their own.

She had to tell Alvin. Had to let him know that after all that trying in Vigor Church to teach those of feeble knack how to do what they could not really do, or not easily, here in his true birthplace his citizens were already assembling, those who had the natural gifts and inclinations that would make them co-Makers with him.

Another thought struck her, and she began to look into the heartfires of the jurors. Another group of citizens, randomly chosen—and again, while not all had spectacular knacks, they were all people whose knacks defined them, people who might well have been searching for what their gifts might mean, what they were *for*. People who, consciously or not, might well have found themselves gravitating toward the place where a Maker had been born. A place where iron was turned to gold, where a mixup boy had been changed so a cachet no longer named him as a slave. A place where people with knacks and talents and dreams might find purpose, might build something together, might become Makers.

Did they know how much they needed Alvin? How much their hopes and dreams depended on him? Of course not. They were jurors, trying to stay impartial. Trying to judge according to the law. And that was good. That was a kind of Making, too—keeping to the law even when it hurt your heart to do it. Maintaining good order in the community. If they showed favoritism to one person just because they admired him or needed him or liked him or even loved him, that would be the undoing of justice, and if justice were ever undone, were ever openly disdained, then that would be the end of good order. To corrupt justice was the Unmaker's trick. Verily Cooper would have to prove his case, or at least disprove Makepeace Smith's assertions; he would have to make it *possible* for the jury to acquit.

But if they did acquit, then the paths that opened in their heartfire were like the paths of the witnesses: They would be with Alvin one day, building great towers of shimmering crystal rising into the sky, catching light and turning it into truth the way it had happened when Tenskwa-Tawa took Alvin up into the waterspout.

Should I tell Alvin that his fellow-Makers are here around him in this courtroom? Would it help his work or make him overconfident to know?

To tell or not to tell, the endless question that Peggy wrestled with. Next to that one, Hamlet's little quandary was downright silly. Contemplations of suicide were always the Unmaker's work. But truth-telling and truth-hiding—it could go either way. The consequences were unpredictable.

Of course, for ordinary people consequences were *always* unpredictable. Only torches like Peggy were burdened by having such a clear idea of the possibilities. And there weren't many torches like Peggy.

MAKEPEACE WASN'T A very good witness in his own cause. Surly and nervous—not a winning combination, Verily knew. But that was why Laws and Webster had put him on first, so that his negative impression would be forgotten after the testimony of more likable—and believable—witnesses.

The best thing Verily could do, in this case, was to let Makepeace have his say—as memorably as possible, as negatively as possible. So he made no objection when Makepeace peppered his account with slurs on Alvin's character. "He was always the laziest prentice I ever had." "I never could get the boy to do nothing without standing over him and yelling in his ear." "He was a slow learner, everybody knowed that." "He ate like a pig even on days when he didn't lift a finger." The onslaught of slander was so relentless that everyone was getting uncomfortable with it—even Marty Laws, who was starting to glance at Verily to see why he wasn't raising any objections. But why should Verily object, when the jurors were shifting in their seats and looking away from Makepeace with every new attack on Alvin? They all knew these were lies. There probably wasn't a one of them that hadn't come to the smithy hoping that Alvin rather than his master would do the work. Alvin's skill was famous—Verily had learned that from overhearing casual conversation in the roadhouse at evening meals—so all Makepeace was doing was damaging his own credibility.

Poor Marty was trapped, however. He couldn't very well cut short Makepeace Smith's testimony, since it was the foundation of his whole case. So the questioning went on, and the answering, and the slander.

"He made a plow out of plain iron. I saw it, and so did Pauley Wiseman who was sheriff then, and Arthur Stuart, and the two dead Finders. It was setting on the workbench when they come by to get me to make manacles for the boy. But I wouldn't make no manacles, no sir! That's not decent work for a smith, to make the chains to take a free boy into slavery! So what do you know but Alvin himself, who *said* he was such a friend to Arthur Stuart, *he* up and says he'll make the manacles. That's the kind of boy he was and is today—no loyalty, no decency at all!"

Alvin leaned over to Verily and whispered in his ear. "I know it's wicked of me, Verily, but I want so bad to give old Makepeace a bad case of rectal itch."

Verily almost laughed out loud.

The judge shot him a glare, but it wasn't about his near laughter. "Mr. Cooper, aren't you going to object to any of these extraneous comments upon your client's character?"

Verily rose slowly to his feet. "Your Honor, I am sure the jury will know *exactly* how seriously to take all of Mr. Makepeace Smith's testimony. I'm perfectly content for them to remember both his malice and his inaccuracy."

"Well, maybe that's how it's done in England, but I will instruct the jury to *ignore* Mr. Smith's malice, since there's no way to know whether his malice came as a result of the events he has recounted, or predated them. Furthermore, I will instruct Mr. Smith to make no more aspersions on the defendant's character, since those are matters of opinion and not of fact. Did you understand me, Makepeace?"

Makepeace looked confused. "I reckon so."

"Continue, Mr. Laws."

Marty sighed and went on. "So you saw the iron plow, and Alvin made the manacles. What then?"

"I told him to use the manacles as his journeyman piece. I thought it would be fitting for a traitorous scoundrel to go through his whole life knowing that the manacles he made for his friend were the—"

The judge interrupted, again glaring at Verily. "Makepeace, it's words like 'traitorous scoundrel' that's going to get you declared in contempt of court. Do you understand me now?"

"I been calling a spade a spade all my life, Your Honor!" Makepeace declared.

"At this moment you're digging a very deep hole with it," said the judge, "and I'm the man to bury you if you don't watch your tongue!"

Cowed, Makepeace put on a very solemn look and faced forward. "I apologize, Your Honor, for daring to live up to my oath to speak the truth, the whole truth, and nothing but the—"

The gavel came down.

"Nor will I allow sarcasm directed at this bench, Mr. Smith. Continue, Mr. Laws."

And so it went, till Makepeace had finished with his tale. It truly was a weak and whining little complaint. First there was an iron plow, made of the very iron Makepeace had provided for the journeyman piece. Then there was a plow made of solid gold. Makepeace could only think of two possibilities. First, that Alvin had somehow used some sort of hexery to change the iron into gold, in which case it was made from the iron Makepeace had given him and, according to time-honored tradition and the terms of Alvin's prentice papers, the plow belonged to Makepeace. Or it was a different plow, not made from Makepeace's iron, in which case where did Alvin get such gold? The only time Alvin had ever done enough digging to bring up buried treasure like that was when he was digging a well for Makepeace, which he dug in the wrong place. Makepeace was betting Alvin had dug in the right place first, found the gold, and then hid it by digging in another spot for the actual well. And if the gold was found on Makepeace's land, well, it was Makepeace's gold that way, too.

Verily's cross-examination was brief. It consisted of two questions.

"Did you see Alvin take gold or anything like gold out of the ground?"

Angry, Makepeace started to make excuses, but Verily waited until the judge had directed him to answer the question yes or no.

"No."

"Did you see the iron plow transformed into a golden plow?"

"Well so what if I didn't, the fact is there *ain't* no iron plow so where *is* it then?"

Again, the judge told him to answer the question yes or no. "No," said Makepeace.

"No more questions for this witness," said Verily.

As Makepeace got up and left the witness box, Verily turned to the judge. "Your Honor, the defense moves for immediate dismissal of all charges, inasmuch as the testimony of this witness is not sufficient to establish probable cause."

The judge rolled his eyes. "I hope I'm not going to have to listen to motions like that after *every* witness."

"Just the pathetic ones. Your Honor," said Verily.

"Your point is made. Your motion is denied. Mr. Laws, your next witness?"

"I would like to have called Makepeace's wife, Gertie, but she passed away more than a year ago. Instead, with the court's permission, I will call the woman who was doing kitchen help for her the day the golden plow was first . . . evidenced. Anga Berry."

The judge looked at Verily. "This will make her testimony hearsay, after a fashion. Do you have any objection, Mr. Cooper?"

Alvin had already assured Verily that nothing Anga could say would do him any possible harm. "No objection, Your Honor."

ALVIN LISTENED AS Anga Berry testified. She didn't really witness to anything except that Gertie told her about Makepeace's accusations the very next morning, so the charge wasn't one he dreamed up later. On cross-examination, Verily was kind to her, only asking her whether Gertie Smith had said anything to lead Anga to believe she thought Alvin was as bad a boy as Makepeace said.

Marty rose to his feet. "Hearsay, Your Honor."

Impatiently the judge replied, "Well, Marty, we *know* it's

hearsay. It was for hearsay that *you* called her in the first place!"

Abashed, Marty Laws sat back down.

"She never said nothing about his smithery or nothing," said Anga. "But I know Gertie set quite a store by the boy. Always helped her out, toted water for her whenever she asked—that's the *worst* job—and he was good with the children and just . . . always helping. She never said a bad word about him, and I reckon she had a high opinion of his goodness."

"Did Gertie ever tell you he was a liar or deceiver?" asked Verily.

"Oh, no, unless you count hiding some job he was doing till it was done, so as to surprise her. If *that's* deception, then he done that a couple of times."

And that was it. Alvin was relieved to know that Gertie hadn't been unkind to him behind his back, that even after her death she was a friend to him. What surprised Alvin was how glum Verily was when he sat down at the table next to him. Marty was busy calling his next witness, a fellow named Hank Dowser whose tale Alvin could easily guess— this was a man who *did* have malice and it wouldn't be pleasant to hear him. Still, he hadn't seen anything either, and in fact the well-digging had nothing to do with the plow so what did it matter? Why did Verily look so unhappy?

Alvin asked him.

"Because there was no reason for Laws to call that woman. She worked against his case and he had to know that in advance."

"So why did he call her?"

"Because he wanted to lay the groundwork for something. And since she didn't say anything new during his examination of her, it must have been during the cross-examination that the new groundwork was laid."

"All you asked Anga was whether Gertie had the same low opinion of me that her husband had."

Verily thought for a moment. "No. I also asked her if you had ever deceived Gertie. Oh, I'm such a fool. If only I could recall those words from my lips!"

"What's wrong with that?" asked Alvin.

"He must have some witness that calls you a deceiver, a witness who is otherwise irrelevant to this case."

In the meantime, the dowser, in a state of high dudgeon, was speaking of how uppity Makepeace's prentice was, how he dared to tell a dowser how to dowse. "He's got no respect for any man's knack but his own!"

Verily spoke up. "Your Honor, I object. The witness is not competent to testify concerning my client's respect or lack of it toward other people's knacks in general."

The objection was sustained. Hank Dowser was a quicker learner than Makepeace; there was no more problem with him. He quickly established that the prentice had obviously dug the well in a different place from the place where Hank had declared water could be found.

Verily had only one question for him. "Was there water in the place where he dug the well?"

"That's not the question!" declared Hank Dowser.

"I'm sorry to have to tell you, Mr. Dowser, that I am the one authorized by this court to ask questions at this time, and I tell you that it *is* the question that I would like you to answer. At this time."

"What was the question?"

"Did my client's well reach water?"

"It reached a *kind* of water. But compared to the pure water *I* found, I'm sure that what he got was a sludgy, scummy, foul-tasting brew."

"Do I take it that your answer is yes?"

"Yes."

And that was that.

For his next witness, Marty called a name that sent a shiver down Alvin's spine. "Amy Sump."

A very attractive girl arose from the back of the courtroom and walked down the aisle.

"Who is *she?*" asked Verily.

"A girl from Vigor with a *very* active imagination."

"About what?"

"About how she and I did what a man has no business doing with a girl so young."

"Did you?"

Alvin was annoyed by the question. "Never. She just started telling stories and it grew from there."

"Grew?"

"That's why I took off from Vigor Church, to give her lies a chance to settle down and die out."

"So she started telling stories about you and you *fled?*"

"What does it have to do with the plow and Makepeace Smith?"

Verily grimaced. "A certain matter of whether you deceive people or not. Marty Laws roped me in."

Marty was explaining to the judge that, because he had had no chance to talk with this witness himself beforehand, his illustrious co-counsel would conduct the examination. "The girl is young and fragile, and they have established a rapport."

Verily thought that the idea of Webster and Amy having rapport wasn't very promising when it came to getting honest testimony from her, but he had to tread carefully. She was a child, and a girlchild at that. He couldn't seem to be hostile or fearful of her before she spoke, and in cross-examination he'd have to proceed delicately lest he seem to be a bully.

Unlike Makepeace Smith and Hank Dowser, who were

obviously angry and malicious, Amy Sump was absolutely believable. She spoke shyly and reluctantly. "I don't want to get Alvin in no trouble, sir," she said.

"And why not?" asked Daniel Webster.

Her answer came in a whisper. "Because I still love him."

"You . . . you still love him?" Oh, Webster was a fine actor, worthy of the boards in Drury Lane. "But how can you—why do you still love him?"

"Because I am with child," she whispered.

A buzzing arose through the courtroom.

Again, Webster feigned grieved surprise. "You are with . . . Are you married, Miss Sump?"

She shook her head. Glistening tears flew from her eyes onto her lap.

"Yet you are with child. The child of some man who didn't even have the decency to make an honest woman of you. *Whose* child, Miss Sump?"

This was already out of control. Verily leapt to his feet. "Your Honor, I object on the grounds that this can have *no* conceivable connection with—"

"It goes to the issue of deception, Your Honor!" cried Daniel Webster. "It goes to the issue of a man who will say whatever it takes to get his way, and then absconds without so much as a farewell, having taken away that which is most precious from the very one who trusted him!"

The judge smacked down his gavel. "Mr. Webster, that was such a fine summing up that I'm inclined to charge the jury and end the trial. Unfortunately this is *not* the end of the trial and I'd appreciate it if you'd refrain from jumping up on a stump and making a speech when it ain't speechifying time."

"I was responding to my worthy opponent's objection."

"Well, you see, Daniel, that's where you made your mistake. Because his objection was addressed to me, me being the judge here, and I didn't really need your help at that moment. But I'm grateful to know that your help is right there, ready for me, if ever I *do* need it."

Webster answered the sarcasm with a cheerful smile. What did he care? His point was already made.

"The objection is overruled, Mr. Cooper," said the judge. "Who is the father of your child, Miss Sump?"

She burst into tears—still on cue, despite the interruption. "Alvin," she said, sobbing. Then she looked up and gazed soulfully across the court into Alvin's eyes. "Oh, Al, it ain't too late! Come back and make a wife of me! I love you so!"

15

LOVE

Verily Cooper, doing his best to hide his astonishment, turned languidly to look at Alvin. Then he raised an eyebrow.

Alvin looked vaguely sad. "It's true she's pregnant," he whispered. "But it ain't true I'm the father."

"Why didn't you tell me if you knew?" Verily whispered.

"I didn't know till she said it. Then I looked and yes, there's a baby growing in her womb. About the size of a nib. No more than three weeks along."

Verily nodded. Alvin had been in jail for the past month, and traveling far from Vigor Church for several months before that. The question was whether he could get the girl to admit under cross-examination that she was barely a month along in her pregnancy.

In the meantime, Daniel Webster had gone on, eliciting

from Amy a lurid account of Alvin's seduction of her. No doubt about it, the girl told a convincing story, complete with all kinds of details that made it sound true. It seemed to Verily that the girl wasn't lying, or if she was, she believed her own lies. For a few moments he had doubts about Alvin. Could he have done this? The girl was pretty and desirable and from the way she talked, she was certainly willing. Just because Alvin was a Maker didn't mean he wasn't a man all the same.

He quickly shook off such thoughts. Alvin Smith was a man with self-control, that was the truth. And he had honor. If he really did such things with this child, he'd certainly marry her and not leave her to face the consequences alone.

It was a measure of how dangerous the girl's testimony was, if she could get Alvin's own attorney to doubt him.

"And then he left you," said Daniel Webster.

Verily thought of objecting, but figured there was no point.

"It was my own fault, I know," said Amy, breaking down—again—into pathetic tears. "I shouldn't have told my best friend Ramona about Alvin and me, because she mouthed it around to everybody and they didn't understand about our true love and so of course my Alvin had to leave because he has great works to do in the world, he can't be tied down to Vigor Church just now. I didn't want to come here and testify! I want him to be free to do whatever he needs to do! And if my baby grows up without a pa, at least I can tell my child that she comes of noble blood, with Makery as her heritage!"

Oh, that was a nice touch, making her the suffering saint who is content that "her" Alvin is a lying seducing deceiving abandoning bastard-making cradle-robber, because she loves him so.

It was time for cross-examination. This had to proceed delicately indeed. Verily couldn't give a single hint that he believed her; at the same time, he didn't dare to be seen to attack her, because the jury's sympathy was all with the girl right now. The seeds of doubt had to be planted gently.

"I'm sorry you had to come all the way down here. It must be a hard journey for a young lady in your delicate condition."

"Oh, I'm doing all right. I just puke once in the morning and then I'm fine for the rest of the day."

The jury laughed. A friendly, sympathetic, believing laugh. Heaven help me, thought Verily.

"How long have you known you were going to have a baby?"

"A long time," she said.

Verily raised an eyebrow. "Now, that's a pretty vague answer. But before you hear my next question, I just want you to remember that we can bring your mother and father down here if need be, to establish the exact time this pregnancy began."

"Well I didn't tell them till just a few days ago," said Amy. "But I've been pregnant for—"

Verily raised his hand to silence her, and shook his head. "Be careful, Miss Sump. If you think for just a minute, you'll realize that your mother certainly knows and your father probably knows that you couldn't possibly have been pregnant for more than a few weeks."

Amy looked at him in a puzzled way for a long moment. Then dawning realization came across her face. She finally realized: Her mother would know, from washing rags, when she last menstruated. And it wasn't months and months ago.

"Like I was going to say all along, I got pregnant in the last month. Sometime in the last month."

"And you're sure that Alvin is the father?"

She nodded. But she was no fool. Verily knew she was doing the math in her head. She obviously had counted on being able to lie and say she'd been pregnant for months, since before Alvin left Vigor; when the baby was born she could say it had taken so long because it was a Maker's child, or some such nonsense. But now she had to have a better lie.

Or else she'd been planning this lie all along. That, too, was possible.

"Of course he is," she said. "He comes to me in the night even now. He's really excited about the baby."

"What do you mean by 'even now'?" asked Verily. "You know that he's in jail."

"Oh, posh," said Amy. "What's a jail to a man like him?"

Once again, Verily realized that he'd been playing into Webster's hands. Everybody knew Alvin had hidden powers. They knew he worked in stone and iron. They knew he could get out of that jail whenever he wanted.

"Your Honor," said Verily, "I reserve the right to recall this witness for further cross-examination."

"I object," said Daniel Webster. "If he recalls Miss Sump then she's *his* witness, it won't be cross-examination, and she's not a hostile witness."

"I need to lay the groundwork for further questioning," said Verily.

"Lay all you want," said the judge. "You'll have some leeway, but it won't be cross. The witness may step down, but don't leave Hatrack River, please."

Webster stood again. "Your Honor, I have a few questions on redirect."

"Oh, of course. Miss Sump, I beg your pardon. Please remain seated and remember you're still under oath."

Webster leaned back in his chair. "Miss Sump, you say that Alvin comes to you in the night. How does he do that?"

"He slips out of his cell and right through the walls of the jail and then he runs like a Red man, all caught up in . . . in . . . Redsong, so he reaches Vigor Church in a single hour and he ain't even tired. No, he is *not* tired!" She giggled.

Redsong. Verily had had enough conversation with Alvin by now to know that it was greensong, and if he'd really had any intimacy with this girl she'd know that. She was remembering things she'd heard from his lessons months and months ago in Vigor Church, when she went to class with people trying to learn to be Makers. That's all this was—the imaginings of a young girl combined with scraps of things she learned about Alvin. But it might take the golden plow away from him, and perhaps more important, it might send him to jail and destroy his reputation forever. This was not an innocent fib, and for all her pretense at loving Alvin, she knew exactly what she was doing to him.

"Does he come to you every night?"

"Oh, he can't do that. Just a couple of times a week."

Webster was done with her, but now Verily had a couple more questions. "Miss Sump, *where* does Alvin visit you?"

"In Vigor Church."

"You're only a girl, Miss Sump, and you live with your parents. Presumably you are supervised by them. So my question is quite specific—where are you when Alvin visits you?"

She was momentarily flustered. "Different places."

"Your parents let you go about unchaperoned?"

"No, I mean—we always start out at home. Late at night. Everybody's asleep."

"Do you have a room of your own?"

"Well, no. My sisters sleep in the same room with me."

"So where do you meet Alvin?"

"In the woods."

"So you deceive your parents and sneak into the woods at night?"

The word *deceive* was a red flag to her. "I don't deceive nobody!" she said, with some heat.

"So they know you're going to the woods alone to meet Alvin."

"No. I mean—I know they'd stop me, and it's true love between us, so—I don't sneak out, because Papa bars the door and he'd hear me so I—at the county fair I was able to slip away and—"

"The county fair was in broad daylight, not at night," said Verily, hoping he was right.

"Argumentative!" shouted Webster. But his interruption served not to help the girl but fluster her more.

"If this happens a couple of times a week, Miss Sump, you surely don't depend on the county fair to provide you with opportunities, do you?" asked Verily.

"No, that was just the once, just the one time. The other times . . ."

Verily waited, refusing to ease her path by filling her long silence with words. Let the jury see her making things up as she went along.

"He comes into my room, all silent. Right through the walls. And then he takes me out the same way, silent, through the walls. And then we run with the Redsong to the place where he gives me his love by moonlight."

"It must be an amazing experience," said Verily. "To have your lover appear at your bedside and raise you up and carry you through the walls and take you silently across miles and miles in an instant to an idyllic spot where you have passionate embraces by moonlight. You're in your nightclothes. Doesn't it get cold?"

"Sometimes, but he can make the air warm around me."

"And what about moonless nights? How do you see?"

"He . . . makes it light. We can always see."

"A lover who can do the most miraculous things. It sounds quite romantic, wouldn't you say?"

"Yes, it is, very very romantic," said Amy.

"Like a dream," said Verily.

"Yes, like a dream."

"I object!" cried Webster. "The witness is a child and doesn't realize the way the defense attorney can misconstrue her innocent simile!"

Amy was quite confused now.

"What did I say?" she asked.

"Let me ask it very clearly," said Verily Cooper. "Miss Sump, isn't it possible that your memories of Alvin come from a dream? That you dreamed all this, being in love with a strong and fascinating young man who was too old even to notice you?"

Now she understood why Webster had objected, and she got a cold look in her eye. She knows, thought Verily. She knows she's lying, she's not deceived, she knows exactly what she's doing and hates me for tripping her up, a little. "My baby ain't no dream, sir," she said. "I never heard of no dream as gives a girl a baby."

"No, I've never heard of such a dream, either," said Verily. "Oh, by the way, how long ago was the county fair?"

"Three weeks ago," she said.

"You went with your family?"

Webster interrupted, demanding to know the relevance.

"She gave the county fair as a specific instance of meeting Alvin," explained Verily, when the judge asked. The judge told him to proceed. "Miss Sump," said Verily, "tell me how you got off by yourself to meet Alvin at the fair. Had you already arranged to meet him there?"

"No, it was—he just showed up there."

"In broad daylight. And no one recognized him?"

"Nobody saw him but me. That's a fact. That's—it's a thing he can do."

"Yes, we're beginning to realize that when it comes to spending time with you, Alvin Smith can and will do the most amazing, miraculous things," said Verily.

Webster objected, Verily apologized, and they went on. But Verily suspected that he was on a good track here. The way Amy made her story so believable was by adding detail. When it came to the events that didn't happen, the details were all dreamy and beautiful—but she wasn't just making them up, it was clear she had really had such dreams, or at least daydreams. She was speaking from memory.

But there must be another memory in her mind—the memory of her time with the man who was the true father of the child she carried. And Verily's hunch was that her mention of the county fair, which didn't fit in at all with the pattern she had established for her nighttime assignations with Alvin, was tied in with that real encounter. If he could get her drawing on memory with this one . . .

"So only you could see him. I imagine that you went off with him? May I ask you where?"

"Under the flap of the freak show tent. Behind the fat lady."

"Behind the fat lady," said Verily. "A private place. But . . . why there? Why didn't Alvin whisk you away into the forest? To some secluded meadow by a crystal stream? I can't imagine it was very comfortable for you—in the straw, perhaps, or on the hard ground, in the dark . . ."

"That's just the way Alvin wanted it," she said. "I don't know why."

"And how long did you spend there behind the fat lady?"

"About five minutes."

Verily raised an eyebrow. "Why so hasty?" Then, before Webster could object, he plunged into his next question. "So Alvin escaped from the Hatrack County jail in broad daylight, journeyed all the way to Pisgah Church on the far side of the state of Wobbish from here, in order to spend five minutes with you behind the fat lady?"

Webster spoke up again. "How can this young girl be expected to know the defendant's motivations for whatever bizarre acts he performs?"

"Was that an objection?" asked the judge.

"It doesn't matter," said Verily. "I'm through with her for now." And this time he let a little contempt into his voice. Let the jury see that he no longer had any regard for this girl. He hadn't destroyed her testimony, but he had laid the groundwork for doubt.

It was three in the afternoon. The judge adjourned them for the day.

ALVIN AND VERILY had supper in his cell that night, conferring over what was likely to happen the next day, and what had to happen in order to acquit him. "They actually haven't proved anything about Makepeace," said Verily. "All they're doing is proving you're a liar in general, and then hoping the jury will think this removes all reasonable doubt about you and the plow. The worst thing is that every step of the way, Webster and Laws have played me like a harp. They set me up, I introduced an idea they were hoping I'd bring up in my cross-examination, and presto! There's the groundwork for the next irrelevant, character-damaging witness."

"So they know the legal tricks in American courts better than you do," said Alvin. "You know the law. You know how things fit together."

"Don't you see, Alvin? Webster doesn't care whether you're convicted or not—what he loves is the stories the newspapers are writing about this trial. Besmirching your reputation. You'll never recover from that."

"I don't know about never," said Alvin.

"Stories like this don't disappear. Even if we manage to find the man who impregnated her—"

"Oh, I know who it was," said Alvin.

"What? How could you—"

"Matt Thatcher. He's a couple of years younger than me, but all us boys knew him in Vigor. He was always a rapscallion of the first stripe, and when I was back there this past year he was always full of brag about how no girl could resist him. Every now and then some fellow'd have to beat him up cause of something he said about the fellow's sister. But after last year's county fair, he was talking about how he drove his tent spike into five different girls in the freak show tent behind the fat lady."

"But that was more than a year ago."

"A boy like Matt Thatcher don't got much imagination, Verily. If he found himself a spot that worked once, he'll be back there. For what it's worth, though, he never did name any of the girls he supposedly got last year, so we all figured he just found the spot and *wished* he could get himself some girl to go with him there. I just figure that this year he finally succeeded."

Verily leaned back on his stool, sipping his mug of warm cider. "The thing that puzzles me is, Webster must have found Amy Sump when he visited in Vigor Church long before I got there. *Before* the county fair, too. She must not have been pregnant when he found her."

Alvin smiled and nodded. "I can just imagine him telling Amy's parents, 'Well it's a good thing she's not with child. Though if she were, I dare say Alvin's wandering days would be over.' And she listens and goes and gets herself pregnant with the most willing but stupid boy in the county."

Verily laughed. "You imitate his voice quite well, sir!"

"Oh, I'm nothing at imitations. I wish you could have heard Arthur Stuart back in the old days. Before . . ."

"Before?"

"Before I changed him so the Finders couldn't identify him."

"So you didn't just subvert their cachet. You changed the boy himself."

"I made him just a little bit less Arthur and a little bit more Alvin. I'm not glad of it. I miss the way he could make hisself sound like anybody. Even a redbird. He used to sing right back to the redbird."

"Can't you change him back? Now that he has the official court decision, he can never be hauled into court again."

"Change him back? I don't know. It was hard enough changing him the first time. And I don't think I remember well enough how he used to be."

"The cachet has the way he used to be, doesn't it?"

"But I don't have the cachet."

"Interesting problem. Arthur doesn't seem to mind the change, though, does he?"

"Arthur's a sweet boy, but what he doesn't mind now he might well come to mind later, when he's old enough to know what I done to him." Alvin was drumming on his empty dish now. Clearly his mind kept going back to the trial. "I got to tell you, it's only going to get worse tomorrow, Verily."

"How so?"

"I didn't understand it till now, till what Amy said about me sneaking out of jail and all. But now I know what the plan is. Vilate Franker came in here covered with hexes, maneuvered me close enough to her that the same hex worked on me, too—an overlook-me, and a right good one. Then in comes Billy Hunter, one of the deputies, and when he looks in the cell, he doesn't see anybody at all. He runs off and gets the sheriff, and when he comes back, Vilate's gone but here *I* am, and I tell them I been nowhere, but Billy Hunter knows what he saw—or didn't see—and they're going to bring him into court, and Vilate too. Vilate too."

"So they'll have a witness to corroborate that you have indeed left your cell during your incarceration here."

"And Vilate's likely to say anything. She's a notorious gossip. Goody Trader plain hates her, and so does Horace Guester. She also thinks of herself as quite a beauty, though those particular hexes don't work on me no more. Anyway Arthur Stuart saw her . . ."

"I was here when Arthur told you about her. About the salamander."

"That ain't no regular salamander, Verily. That's the Unmaker. I've met it before. Used to come on me more direct-like. A shimmering in the air, and there it was. Trying to take me over, rule me. But I wouldn't have it, I'd make something—a bug basket—and he'd go away. Nowadays I'd be more likely to make up some silly rhyme or song and commit it to memory to drive him back. But here's the thing—the Unmaker has a way of being different things to different people. There was a minister in Vigor Church, Reverend Philadelphia Thrower; he saw the Unmaker as an angel, only it was a kind of terrible angel, and one time— well, it doesn't matter. Armor-of-God saw it, not me. With Vilate the Unmaker's got that salamander doing some kind of hexery that makes Vilate see . . . somebody. Somebody who talks to her and tells her things. Only that somebody is really speaking the words of the Unmaker. You know what Arthur Stuart saw. Old Peg Guester, the woman who was the only mother he knew. The Unmaker appears as somebody you can trust, somebody who fulfills your most heartfelt dream, but in the process he perverts every-thing so that without quite realizing it, you start destroying everything and everybody around you. This whole thing, you don't have to look toward Webster to find the conspiracy. The Unmaker is all the connection they need. Putting together Amy Sump and Vilate Franker and Makepeace Smith and Daniel Webster and . . . not one of them thinks he's doing something all that awful. Amy probably thinks she really loves me. Maybe so does Vilate. Makepeace has probably talked himself into believing the plow really belongs to him. Daniel Webster probably believes I really am a scoundrel. But . . ."

"But the Unmaker makes everything work together to undo you."

Alvin nodded.

"Alvin, that makes no sense," said Verily. "If the Unmaker's really out to Unmake everything, then how can he put together such an elaborate plan? That's a kind of Making, too, isn't it?"

Alvin lay back on the cot and whistled for a moment. "That's right," he said.

"The Unmaker sometimes Makes things, then?"

"No," said Alvin. "No, the Unmaker can't Make nothing. Can't. He just takes what's already there in twists and bends and breaks it. So I was wrong. The Unmaker's working on all these people, but if it's all fitting together into a plan, then somebody's planning it. Some person."

Verily chuckled. "I think we already have the answer," he said. "Your speculation about Daniel Webster. He discovers Amy Sump as he searches in Vigor Church for any kind of dirt about you. She wasn't part of any plan, just a girl who started pretending that her daydreams were true. But then he puts into her head the idea of getting pregnant and the idea of testifying against you to clip your wings and force you to come home. She works out the rest herself, her own plan— the Unmaker doesn't have to teach her anything. Then Daniel Webster comes here to Hatrack and of course he meets the town gossip as he searches for dirt about you here. Vilate Franker barely knows you, but she *does* know everybody else's story, and they converse many times. He happens to let slip how Amy Sump's story will just sound like the imaginings of a dreamy but randy young girl unless they can get some kind of evidence that you actually do leave your cell. And then Vilate comes up with her *own* plan and the Unmaker just sits back and encourages her."

"So the plan is all coming from Daniel Webster, only he doesn't even know it," said Alvin. "He wishes for something, and then it just happens to come true."

"Don't give him too much credit for integrity," said Verily. "I suspect this is a method he's been using for a long time, wishing for some key piece of evidence, and then trusting in his client or one of his client's friends to come up with the testimony that he needs. He never quite soils his hands, but the effect is the same. Yet nothing can ever be proven—"

The outer door opened, and Po Doggly came in with Peggy Larner. "Sorry to interrupt your supper and confabulation, gentlemen," said the sheriff, "but something's come up. You got you a visitor with special circumstances, he's come a long way but he can only come in and see you after dark and I'm the only guard as can let him in, on account of he already sat me down and told me a tale."

Alvin turned to Verily. "That means it's someone from home. Someone besides Armor-of-God. Someone who's under the curse."

"He shouldn't be under it," said Peggy. "If it weren't for his grand gesture of including himself in a curse he didn't personally deserve."

"Measure," said Alvin. To Verily he explained, "My older brother."

"He's coming," said the sheriff. "Arthur Stuart's leading him in with his hat low and his eyes down so he won't see anybody who doesn't already know the story. Doesn't want to spend all night telling folks about the massacre at Tippy-Canoe. So the doors will be open here, but I'll still be outside, watching. Not that I think you'd try to escape, Alvin."

"You mean you don't think I've been making twice-a-week trips to Vigor Church?"

"For *that* girl? I don't think so." With that, Doggly walked out, leaving the outer door open.

Peggy came on in and joined Alvin and Verily inside Alvin's cell. Verily stood up to offer her his stool, but with a gesture she declined to sit.

"Howdy, Peggy," said Alvin.

"I'm fine, Alvin. And you?"

"You know I never did any of those things she said," he told her.

"Alvin," she said, "I know that you *did* find her attractive. She saw that you paid her a little special attention. She began to dream and wish."

"So you're saying it's my fault after all?"

"It's her fault that dreams turned into lies. It's your fault that she had hopeless dreams like that in the first place."

"Well why don't I just shoot myself before I ever look at a woman with desire? It always seems to turn out pretty lousy when I do."

She looked as if he slapped her. As usual, Verily felt a keen sense of being left out of half of what went on in Alvin's life. Why should it bother him so much? He wasn't there, and they were under no obligation to explain. Still, it was embarrassing. He got up. "Please, I'll step outside so you can have this conversation alone."

"No need," said Peggy. "I'm sure Arthur is almost here with Measure by now."

"She doesn't want to talk to me," said Alvin to Verily. "She'll try to get me acquitted because she wants to see the Crystal City get built, only she can't offer me a lick of help in trying to figure out how to build it, seeing as how I don't know and she seems to know everything. But just cause she wants me acquitted doesn't mean she actually likes me or thinks I'm worth spending time with."

"I don't like being in the middle of this," said Verily.

"You're not," said Peggy. "There's no 'this' to be in the middle of."

"There never *was* no 'this,' either, was there?" asked Alvin.

Verily was quite sure he had never heard a man sound so miserable.

Peggy took a moment to answer. "I'm not—there was and is a—it hasn't a thing to do with you, Alvin."

"What doesn't have a thing to do with me? My still being crazy in love with you after a whole year with only one letter from you, and that one as cold as you please, like I was some kind of scoundrel you still had to do business with or something? Is that the thing that doesn't have anything to do with me? I asked you to marry me once. I understand that things have been pretty bleak since then, your mother getting killed and all, that was terrible, and I didn't press you, but I did write to you, I did think about you all the time, and—"

"And I thought of you, Alvin."

"Yes, well, *you're* a torch, so you *know* I'm thinking about you, or you do if you care to look, but what do *I* know when there's no sign from you? What do I know except what you tell me? Except what I see in your face? I know I looked in your face that night in the smithy, I looked in your eyes and I thought I saw love there, I thought I saw you saying yes to me. Did I make that up? Is that the 'this' that there isn't one of?"

Verily was thoroughly miserable, being forced to be a witness of this scene. He had tried to make his escape before; now it was clear they didn't want him to go. If only he knew how to disappear. How to sink through the floor.

It was Arthur who saved him. Arthur, with Measure in tow; and, just as the sheriff had said, Measure had his hat so low and his head bent so far down that he really did need Arthur Stuart to lead him by the hand. "We're here," said Arthur. "You can look up now."

Measure looked up. "Al," he said.

"Measure!" Alvin cried. It took about one stride each, with those two long-legged men, for them to be in each other's embrace. "I've missed you like my own soul," said Alvin.

"I've missed you too, you ugly scrawny jailbird," said Measure. And in that moment, Verily felt such a pang of jealousy that he thought his heart would break. He was ashamed of the feeling as soon as he was aware of it, but there it was: He was jealous of that closeness between brothers. Jealous because he knew that he would never be that close to Alvin Smith. He would always be shut out, and it hurt so deeply that for a moment he thought he couldn't breathe.

And then he did breathe, and blocked that feeling away in another part of himself where he didn't have to stare it in the face.

In a few minutes the greetings were over, and they were down to business. "We found out Amy was gone and it didn't take no genius to figure out where she went. Oh, at first the rumor was she got pregnant at the county fair and was sent off to have the baby somewhere, but we all remembered the tales she told about Alvin and Father and I went

to her pa and got it out of him right quick, that she was off
to testify in Hatrack. He didn't like it much, but they're paying them and he needs the money and his daughter swears
it's true but you could tell looking at him that he don't believe her lies either. And in fact as we were leaving he says,
When I find out who it was got my daughter pregnant I'm
going to kill him. And Pa says, No you ain't. And Mr. Sump
he says, I am so because I'm a merciful man, and killing
him's kinder than making him marry Amy."

They all laughed at that, but in the end they knew it wasn't
exactly funny.

"Anyhow, Eleanor says, Amy's best friend is that mouse
of a girl Ramona and I'm going to get the truth out of her."

Alvin turned to Verily. "Eleanor's our sister, Armor-of-
God's wife."

Another reminder that he wasn't inside this circle. But
also a reminder that Alvin thought of him and wanted to
include him.

"So Eleanor gets Ramona and sets her down inside that
hex you made for her in the shop, Alvin, the one that makes
liars get so nervous, only I don't know as how it was really
needed. Eleanor says to her, Who's the father of Amy's baby,
and Ramona says, How should I know? only it's a plain lie,
and finally when Eleanor won't let up, Ramona says, Last
time I told the truth it only caused Alvin Maker to have to
run away cause of Amy's lies, but she *swore* it was true,
she *swore* it and so I believed her but now she's saying it
was Alvin got her pregnant and I know that's not true
cause she got into the freak show tent with—"

Alvin held up his hand. "Matt Thatcher?"

"Of course," said Measure. "Why we didn't just castrate
him along with the pigs I don't know."

"She *saw* them or is it hearsay?" asked Verily.

"Saw them and stood guard where they went under the

tent and heard Amy cry out once and heard Matt panting
and then it was done and she asked Amy what it was like
and Amy looked positively stricken and says to her, It's awful and it hurts. Ramona's got no doubt Amy was a virgin
up till then, so all the other stories is lies."

"She's not competent to testify about Amy's virginity,"
said Verily, "but she'd still be a help. It would take care of
the pregnancy and make it plain that Amy is something of
a liar. Reasonable doubt. How long will it take to get her
down here?"

"She's here," said Peggy. "I got her to the roadhouse and
Horace Guester's feeding her."

"I'll want to talk to her tonight," said Verily. "This is
good. This is something. And until now, we had nothing."

"*They* have nothing," said Peggy. "And yet . . ."

"And yet they'd convict me if they voted right now,
wouldn't they?" Alvin asked.

Peggy nodded. "I thought they knew you better."

"This is all so extraneous to Makepeace's assertions,"
said Verily. "None of this would have been permitted in an
English court."

"Next time somebody tries to get me arrested for larceny
and a crazy girl claims to be pregnant by me, I'll arrange to
have it tried in London," said Alvin, grinning.

"Good idea," said Verily. "Besides, we have a much
higher grade of crazy girls in England."

"I'm going to testify," said Peggy.

"I don't think so," said Alvin.

"You aren't a witness of anything," said Verily.

"You saw how the rules go in this court," said Peggy.
"You can work me in."

"It won't help," said Verily. "They'll chalk it up to your
being in love with Alvin."

Alvin sighed and lay back on his cot.

"No they won't," said Peggy. "They know me."

"They know Alvin, too," said Verily.

"Don't mean to contradict you, sir," said Arthur Stuart, "but everybody knows Miss Larner here is a torch, and everybody knows that before she tells a lie, you can boil an egg in a pan of snow."

"If I testify, he won't be convicted," said Peggy.

"No," said Alvin. "They'll drag you through the mud. Webster doesn't care about convicting me, you know that. He only wants to destroy me and everybody near me, because that's what the people who hired him want."

"We don't even know who they are," said Verily.

"I don't know their names, but I know who they are and what they want. To you it looks as though Amy's testimony is a sidetrack, but it's Amy's testimony they wanted. And if they could get testimony about me and Peggy in the smithy on the night the plow was made—"

"I'm not afraid of their calumnies," said Peggy.

"It ain't calumnies I'm talking about, it's the plain truth," said Alvin. "I was naked, we was alone in the smithy. Can't help what conclusions folks draw from that, and so I won't have you getting on the stand and all that story coming out in the papers in Carthage and Dekane and heaven knows where else. We'll do it another way."

"Ramona will be a help," said Verily.

"Not Ramona either," said Alvin. "It does no good to have one friend betray another for my sake."

The others were flabbergasted.

"You got to be joking!" cried Measure. "After I brought her all the way here? And she wants to testify."

"I'm sure she does," said Alvin. "But after the papers are through hacking at Amy, how will Ramona feel *then?* She'll always remember that she betrayed a friend. That's a hard one. It'll hurt her. Won't it, Peggy?"

"Oh, you actually want my advice about something?"

"I want the truth. I've been telling the truth, and so have you, so just say it."

"Yes," said Peggy. "It would hurt Ramona greatly to testify against Amy."

"So we won't do it," said Alvin. "Nor do I want to see Vilate humiliated by having her hexes removed. She sets a store by being taken for beautiful."

"Alvin," said Verily, "I know you're a good man and wiser than me, but surely you can see that you can't let courtesy to a few individuals destroy all that you were put here on this earth to do!"

The others agreed.

Alvin looked as miserable as Verily had ever seen a man look, and Verily had seen men condemned to hang or burn. "Then you *don't* understand," he said. "It's true that sometimes people have to suffer to make something good come to be. But when I have it in my power to save them from suffering it, and bear it myself, well then that's part of what I do. That's part of Making. If I have it in my power, then I bear it. Don't you see?"

"No," said Peggy. "You *don't* have it in your power."

"Is that the honest torch talking? Or my friend?"

She hesitated only a moment. "Your friend. This passage in your heartfire is dark to me."

"I figured it was. And I think the reason is because I got to do some Making. I got to do something that's never been done before, to Make something new. If I do it, then I can go on. If I don't, then I go to jail and my path through life takes another course."

"*Would* you go to jail?" asked Arthur Stuart. "Would you really stay in prison for years and years?"

Alvin shrugged. "There are hexes I can't undo. I think if I was convicted, they'd see to it that I was bound about like that. But even if I could get away, what would it matter? I couldn't do my work here in America. And I don't know that my work could be done anywhere else. If there's any reason to my life at all, then there's a reason I was born here and not in England or Russia or China or something. Here's where my work's to be done."

"So you're saying that I can't use the two best witnesses to defend you?" asked Verily.

"My best witness is the truth. Somebody's going to speak it, that's for sure. But it won't be Miss Larner, and it won't be Ramona."

Peggy leaned down and looked Alvin in the eye, their faces not six inches apart. "Alvin Smith, you wretched boy, I gave my childhood to you, to keep you safe from the Unmaker, and now you tell me I have to stand by and watch you throw all that sacrifice away?"

"I already asked you for the whole rest of your life," said Alvin. "What do I want with your ruin? You lost your childhood for me. You lost your mother for me. Don't lose any more. I would have taken everything, yes, and given you everything too, but I won't take less because I can't give less. You'll take nothing from me, so I'll take nothing from you. If that don't make sense to you then you ain't as smart as you let on, Miss Larner."

"Why don't those two just get married and make babies?" said Arthur Stuart. "Pa said that."

Her face stony, Peggy turned away from them. "It has to be on *your* terms, doesn't it, Alvin. Everything on your terms."

"*My* terms?" said Alvin. "It wasn't my terms to say these things to you in front of others, though at least it's my friends and not strangers who have to hear them. I love you, Miss Larner. I love you, Margaret. I don't want you in that courtroom, I want you in my arms, in my life, in all my dreams and works for all time to come."

Peggy clung to the bars of the jail, her face averted from the others.

Arthur Stuart walked around to the outside of the cell and looked guilelessly up into her face. "Why don't you just marry him instead of crying like that? Don't you love him? You're real pretty and he's a good-looking man. You'd have damn cute babies. Pa said that."

"Hush, Arthur Stuart," said Measure.

Peggy slid down until she was kneeling, and then she reached through the bars and took Arthur Stuart's hands. "I can't, Arthur Stuart," she said. "My mother died because I loved Alvin, don't you see? Whenever I think of being with him, it just makes me feel sick and . . . guilty . . . and angry and . . ."

"My mama's dead too, you know," said Arthur Stuart. "My Black mama and my White mama both. They both died to save me from slavery. I think about that all the time, how if I'd never been born they'd both still be alive."

Peggy shook her head. "I know you think of that, Arthur, but you mustn't. They want you to be happy."

"I know," said Arthur Stuart. "I ain't as smart as you, but I know *that.* So I do my best to be happy. I'm happy most of the time, too. Why can't you do that?"

Alvin whispered an echo to his words. "Why can't you do that, Margaret?"

Peggy raised her chin, looked around her. "What am I doing here on the floor like this?" She got to her feet. "Since you won't take my help, Alvin Smith, then I've got work to do. There's a war in the future, a war over slavery, and a million boys will die, in America and the Crown Colonies and even New England before it's done. My work is to make sure those boys don't die in vain, to make sure that when it's over the slaves are free. That's what my mother died for, to free one slave. I'm not going to pick just one, I'm going to save them all if I can." She looked fiercely at the men who watched her, wide-eyed. "I've made my last sacrifice for Alvin Smith—he doesn't need my help anymore."

With those words she strode to the outer door.

"I do so," murmured Alvin, but she didn't hear him, and then she was gone.

"If that don't beat all," said Measure. "I ask you, Alvin, why didn't you just fall in love with a thunderstorm? Why don't you just go propose to a blizzard?"

"I already did," said Alvin.

Verily walked to the door of the cell. "I'm going to interview Ramona tonight in case you change your mind, Alvin," he said.

"I won't," said Alvin.

"I'm quite sure, but other than that there's nothing else I *can* do." He debated saying the next words, but decided that he might as well. What did he have to lose? Alvin was going to go to prison and Verily's journey to America was going to turn out to have been in vain. "I must say that I think you and Miss Larner are a perfect match. The two of you together must have more than seventy percent of the world's entire store of stupid bullheadedness."

It was Verily's turn to head for the outer door. Behind him as he left, he heard Alvin say to Measure and Arthur: "That's my lawyer." He wasn't sure if Alvin spoke in pride or mockery. Either way, it only added to his despair.

BILLY HUNTER'S TESTIMONY was pretty damaging. It was plain that he liked Alvin well enough and had no desire to make him look bad. But he couldn't change what he saw and had to tell the truth—he'd looked into the jail and there was nowhere Alvin and Vilate could have hidden.

Verily's cross-examination consisted merely of ascertaining that when Vilate entered the cell, Alvin was definitely there, and that the pie she left behind tasted right good. "Alvin didn't want it?" asked Verily.

"No sir. He said . . . he said he sort of promised it to an ant."

Some laughter.

"But he let you have it anyway," said Verily.

"I guess so, yes."

"Well, I think that shows that Alvin is unreliable indeed, if he can't keep his word to an ant!"

There were some chuckles at Verily's attempt at humor, but that did nothing to ameliorate the fact that the prosecution had cut into Alvin's credibility, and rather deeply at that.

It was Vilate's turn then. Marty Laws laid the groundwork, and then came to the key point. "When Mr. Hunter looked into the jail and failed to see you and Alvin, where were you?"

Vilate made a great show of being reluctant to tell. He was relieved to see, however, that she wasn't quite the actress Amy Sump had been, perhaps because Amy half-believed her own fantasies, while Vilate . . . well, this was no schoolgirl, and these were no fantasies of love. "I should never have let him talk me into it, but . . . I've been alone too long."

"Just answer the question, please," asked Laws.

"He took me through the wall of the jail. We passed through the wall. I held his hand."

"And where did you go?"

"Fast as the wind we went—I felt as though we were flying. For a time I ran beside him, taking strength from his hand as he held mine and led me along; but then it became too much for me, and I, fainting, could not go on. He sensed this in that way of his and gathered me into his arms. I was quite swept away."

"Where did you go?"

"To a place where I've never been."

There were some titters at that, which seemed to fluster

her a little. Apparently she was not aware of her own double entendre—or perhaps she was a better actress than Verily thought.

"By a lake. Not a large one, I suppose—I could see the far shore. Waterbirds were skimming the lake, but on the grassy bank where we . . . reclined . . . we were the only living things. This beautiful young man and I. He was so full of promises and talk of love and . . ."

"Can we say he took advantage of you?" asked Marty.

"Your Honor, he's leading the witness."

"He did *not* take advantage of me," Vilate said. "I was a willing participant in all that happened. The fact that I regret it now does not change the fact that he did *not* force me in any way. Of course, if I had known then how he had said the same things, done the same things with that girl from Vigor Church . . ."

"Your Honor, she has no personal knowledge of—"

"Sustained," said the judge. "Please limit your responses to the questions asked."

Verily had to admire her skill. She managed to sound as if she were defending Alvin rather than trying to destroy him. As if she loved him.

16

TRUTH

When it came Verily's turn to question Vilate, he sat for a moment contemplating her. She was the picture of complacent confidence, with her head just slightly cocked to the left, as if she were somewhat—but not very—curious to hear what he would ask of her.

"Miss Franker, I wonder if you can tell me—when you passed through the wall from the jail, how did you get up to ground level?"

She looked momentarily confused. "Oh, is the jail below ground? Well, I suppose when we went through the wall, we—no, of course we didn't. The jail is on the second floor of the courthouse, and it's about a ten-foot drop to the ground. That was mean of you, to try to trick me."

"My question still stands," said Verily. "That must have been quite a drop, coming through the wall into nothing."

"We handled it gently. We . . . floated to the ground. It was part of the remarkable experience. If I had known you wanted so much detail, I'd have said so from the start."

"So Alvin . . . floats."

"He *is* a remarkable young man."

"I imagine so," said Verily. "In fact, one of his extraordinary talents is the ability to see through hexes of illusion. Did you know that?"

"No, I . . . no." She looked puzzled.

"For instance, he sees through the hex you use to keep people from seeing that little trick you play with your false teeth. Did you know that?"

"Trick!" She was mortified. "False teeth! What a terrible thing to say!"

"Do you or do you not have false teeth?"

Marty Laws was on his feet. "Your Honor, I can't see what relevancy false teeth have to the case at hand."

"Mr. Cooper, it does seem a little extraneous," said the judge.

"Your Honor has allowed the prosecution to cast far afield in trying to impugn the veracity of my client. I think the defense is entitled to the same latitude in impugning the veracity of those who claim my client is a deceiver."

"False teeth is a bit personal, don't you think?" asked the judge.

"And accusing my client of seducing her *isn't?*" asked Verily.

The judge smiled. "Objection overruled. I think the prosecution opened the door wide enough for such questions."

Verily turned back to Vilate. "Do you have false teeth, Miss Franker?"

"I do not!" she said.

"You're under oath," said Verily. "For instance, didn't you waggle your upper plate at Alvin when you said that he was a beautiful young man?"

"How can I waggle an upper plate that I do not have?" she said.

"Since that is your testimony, Miss Franker, would you be willing to appear in court without those four amulets you're wearing, and without the shawl with the hexes sewn in?"

"I don't have to sit here and . . ."

Alvin leaned over and tugged at Verily's coattail. Verily wanted to ignore him, because he knew that Alvin was going to forbid him to pursue this line any further. But there was no way he could pretend that he didn't notice a movement so broad that the whole court saw it. He turned back to Alvin, ignoring Vilate's remonstrances, and let Alvin whisper in his ear.

"Verily, you know I didn't want—"

"My duty is to defend you as best I—"

"Verily, ask her about the salamander in her handbag. Get it out in the open if you can."

Verily was surprised. "A salamander? But what good will that do?"

"Just get it out in the open," said Alvin. "On a table in

734 • *Orson Scott Card*

the open. It won't run away. Even with the Unmaker possessing it, salamanders are still stupid. You'll see."

Verily turned back to face the witness. "Miss Franker, will you kindly show us the lizard in your handbag?"

Alvin tugged on his coat again. Mouth to ear, he whispered, "Salamanders ain't lizards. They're amphibians, not reptiles."

"Your pardon, Miss Franker. Not a lizard. An amphibian. A salamander."

"I have no such—"

"Your Honor, please warn the witness about the consequences of lying under—"

"If there's such a creature in my handbag, I don't have any idea who put it there or how it got there," said Vilate.

"Then you won't object if the bailiff looks in your bag and removes any amphibious creatures he might find?"

Overcoming her uncertainty, Vilate replied, "No, not at all."

"Your Honor, who is on trial here?" asked Marty Laws.

"I believe the issue is truthfulness," said the judge, "and I find this exercise fascinating. We've watched you come up with scandal. Now I'll be interested to see an amphibian."

The bailiff rummaged through the handbag, then suddenly hooted and jumped back. "Excuse me, Your Honor, it's up my sleeve!" he said, trying to maintain his composure as he wriggled and danced around.

With a flamboyant gesture, Verily swept his papers off the defense table and pulled it out into the middle of the courtroom. "When you retrieve the little fellow," he said, "set him here, please."

Alvin leaned back on his chair, his legs extended, his ankles crossed, looking for all the world like a politician who just won an election. Under his chair, the plow lay still inside its sack.

Alone of all the people in the court, Vilate paid no attention whatever to the salamander. She simply sat as if in a trance; but no, that wasn't it. No, she sat as if she were at a soiree where something slightly rude was being said, and she was pretending to take no notice of it.

Verily had no idea what would come of this business with the salamander, but since Alvin wouldn't let him try any other avenue to discredit Vilate or Amy, he'd have to make it do.

ALVIN HAD BEEN watching Vilate during her testimony—watching close, not just with his eyes, but with his inner sight, seeing the way the material world worked together. One of the first things he marked was the way Vilate cocked her head just a little before answering. As if she were listening. So he sent out his doodlebug and let it rest in the air, feeling for any tremors of sound. Sure enough, there *were* some, but in a pattern Alvin had never seen before. Usually, sound spread out from its source like waves from a rock cast into a pond, in every direction, bouncing and reverberating, but also fading and growing weaker with distance. This sound, however, was channeled. How was it done?

For a while he was in danger of becoming so engrossed in the scientific question that he might well forget that he was on trial here and this was the most dangerous but possibly the weakest witness against him. Fortunately, he caught on to what was happening very quickly. The sound was coming from two sources, very close together, moving in parallel. As the sound waves crossed each other, they interfered with each other, turning the sound into mere turbulence in the air. When Alvin listened closely, he could hear the faint hiss of the chaotic noise. But in the direction where the sound waves were perfectly parallel, they not only didn't interfere with each other, but rather seemed to increase the power of the sound. The result was that for someone sitting exactly in Vilate's position, even the faintest whisper would be audible; but for anyone anywhere else in the courtroom, there would be no sound at all.

Alvin found this curious indeed. He hadn't known that the Unmaker actually used sound to talk to his minions. He had supposed that somehow the Unmaker spoke directly into their minds. Instead, the Unmaker spoke from two sound sources, close together. Then Alvin had to smile. The old saying was true: The liar spoke out of both sides of his mouth.

Looking with his doodlebug into Vilate's handbag, Alvin soon found the source of the sound. The salamander was perched on the top of her belongings, and the sound was coming from its mouth—though salamanders had no mechanism for producing a human voice. If only he could hear what the salamander was saying.

Well, if he wasn't mistaken, that could be arranged. But first he needed to get the salamander out into the open, where the whole court could see where its speech was coming from. That was when he began to pay attention to the proceedings again—only to discover, to his alarm, that Verily was about to defy him and try to take away Vilate's beautiful disguise. He reached out and tugged on Verily's coat, and whispered a rebuke that was as mild as he could make it. Then he told him to get the salamander out of the bag.

Now, with the salamander in a panic, trapped in the bailiff's dark sleeve, it took Alvin a few moments to get his doodlebug inside the creature and start to help it calm down—to slow the heartbeat, to speak peace to it. Of course he could feel no resistance from the Unmaker. That was no surprise to Alvin. The Unmaker was always driven back by his Making. But he could sense the Unmaker, lurking, shimmering in the background, in the corners of the court, waiting to come back into the salamander so it could speak to Vilate again.

It was a good sign, the fact that the Unmaker needed the help of a creature in order to speak to Vilate. It suggested that she was not wholly consumed by the lust for power or Unmaking, so that the Unmaker could not speak to her directly.

Alvin didn't really know that much about the Unmaker, but with years in which to speculate and reason about it, he had come to a few conclusions. He didn't really think of the Unmaker as a person anymore, though sometimes he still called it "him" in his own thoughts. Alvin had always seen the Unmaker as a shimmering of air, as something that retreated toward his peripheral vision; he believed now that this was the true nature of the Unmaker. As long as a person was engaged in Making, the Unmaker was held at bay; and, in fact, most people weren't particularly attractive to it. It was drawn only to the most extraordinary of Makers—and the most prideful destroyers (or destructively proud; Alvin wasn't sure if it made a difference). It was drawn to Alvin in the effort to undo him and all his works. It was drawn to others, though, like Philadelphia Thrower and, apparently, Vilate Franker, because they provided the hands, the lips, the eyes that would allow the Unmaker to do its work.

What Alvin guessed, but could not know, was that the people to whom the Unmaker appeared most clearly had a kind of power over it. That the Unmaker, having been drawn into relations with them, could not suddenly free itself. Instead, it acted out the role that its human ally had prepared for it. Reverend Thrower needed an angelic visitor that was ripe with wrath—so that was what the Unmaker became for him. Vilate needed something else. But the Unmaker could not withhold itself from her. It could not sense that there was danger in being exposed, unless Vilate sensed that danger herself. And since Vilate was unable to be rational enough to know there even *was* a salamander—something Alvin had learned from Arthur Stuart's report—there was a good chance that the Unmaker could be led to expose itself to the whole courtroom, as long as Alvin worked carefully and took Vilate by surprise.

So he watched as the bailiff finally took the calm—well, calmer, anyway—salamander from the collar of his shirt, whither it had fled, and set it gently on the table. Gradually Alvin withdrew his doodlebug from the creature, so that the Unmaker could come back into possession of it. Would it come? Would it speak again to Vilate, as Alvin hoped?

It did. It would.

The column of sound arose again.

Everyone could see the salamander's mouth opening and closing, but of course they heard nothing and so it looked like the random movements of an animal.

"Do you see the salamander?" asked Verily.

Vilate looked quizzical. "I don't understand the question."

"On this table in front of you. Do you see the salamander?"

Vilate smiled wanly. "I think you're trying to play with me now, Mr. Cooper."

A whisper arose in the courtroom.

"What I'm trying to do," said Verily, "is determine just how reliable an observer you are."

Daniel Webster spoke up. "Your Honor, how do we know there isn't some trick going on that the defense is playing? We already know that the defendant has remarkable hidden powers."

"Have patience, Mr. Webster," said the judge. "Time enough for rebuttal on redirect."

In the meantime, Alvin had been playing with the double column of sound coming from the salamander and leading straight to Vilate. He tried to find some way to bend it, but of course could not, since sound must travel in a straight line—or at least to bend it was beyond Alvin's power and knowledge.

What he could do, though, was set up a counterturbulence right at the source of one of the columns of sound, leaving the other to be perfectly audible, since there would be no interference from the column Alvin had blocked. The sound would still be faint, however; Alvin had no way of knowing whether it could be heard well enough for people to understand it. Only one way to find out.

Besides, this might be the new thing he had to Make in order to get past the dark place in his heartfire where Peggy couldn't see.

He blocked one of the columns of sound.

VERILY WAS SAYING, "Miss Franker, since everyone in the court but you is able to see this salamander—"

Suddenly, a voice from an unexpected source became audible, apparently in midsentence. Verily fell silent and listened.

It was a woman's voice, cheery and encouraging. "You just sit tight, Vilate, this English buffoon is no match for you. You don't have to tell him a single thing unless you want to. That Alvin Smith had his chance to be your friend, and he turned you down, so now you'll show him a thing or two about a woman scorned. He had no idea of your cleverness, you sly thing."

"Who is that!" demanded the judge.

Vilate looked at him, registering nothing more than faint puzzlement. "Are you asking me?" she said.

"I am!" the judge replied.

"But I don't understand. Who is what?"

The woman's voice said, "Something's wrong but you just stay calm, don't admit a thing. Blame it on Alvin, whatever it is."

Vilate took a deep breath. "Is Alvin casting some kind of spell that affects everyone but me?" she asked.

The judge answered sharply. "Someone just said, 'Blame it on Alvin, whatever it is.' Who was it that said that?"

"Ah! Ah! Ah!" cried the woman's voice—which was obviously coming from the salamander's mouth. "Ah! How could he hear me? I talk only to you! I'm *your* best friend, Vilate, nobody else's! They're trying to trick you! Don't admit a thing!"

"I . . . don't know what you mean," said Vilate. "I don't know what you're hearing."

"The woman who just said, 'Don't admit a thing,'" said Verily. "Who is that? Who is this woman who says she's your best friend and no one else's?"

"Ah! Ah! Ah! Ah!" cried the salamander.

"My best friend?" asked Vilate. Suddenly her face was a mask of terror—except for her mouth, which still wore a pretty grin. Sweat beaded on her forehead.

On impulse, Verily strode to her and took hold of her shawl. "Please, Miss Franker, you seem overwarm. Let me hold your shawl for you."

Vilate was so confused she didn't realize what he was doing until it was done. The moment the shawl came from her shoulders, the smile on her mouth disappeared. In fact, the face that everyone knew so well was gone, replaced by the face of a middle-aged woman, somewhat wrinkled and sunburnt; and most remarkable of all, her mouth was wide open and inside it, the upper plate of her false teeth were clicking up and down, as if she were raising and lowering it with her tongue.

The buzz in the courtroom became a roar.

"Verily, dammit," said Alvin. "I told you not to—"

"Sorry," said Verily. "I see you need that shawl, Miss Franker." Quickly he replaced it.

Aware now of what he had done to her, she snatched the shawl close to her. The clicking false teeth were immediately replaced by the same lovely smile she had worn before, and her face was again thin and young.

"I believe we have some idea of the reliability of this witness," said Verily.

The salamander cried out, "They're winning, you foolish ninny! They trapped you! They tricked you, you silly twit!"

Vilate's face lost its composure. She looked frightened. "How can you talk like that to me," she whispered.

Vilate wasn't the only one who looked frightened. The judge himself had shrunk back into the far corner of his space behind the bench. Marty Laws was sitting on the back of his chair, his shoes on the seat.

"To whom are you speaking?" asked the judge.

Vilate turned her face away from judge and salamander both. "My friend," she said. "My best friend, I thought." Then she turned to the judge. "All these years, no one else has ever heard her voice. But you hear her now, don't you?"

"I do," said the judge.

"You're telling them too much!" cried the salamander. Was its voice changing?

"Can you see her?" asked Vilate, her voice thin and quavering. "Do you see how beautiful she is? She taught me how to be beautiful, too."

"Shut up!" cried the salamander. "Tell them nothing, you bitch!"

Yes, the voice was definitely lower in pitch now, thick in the throat, rasping.

"I can't see her, no," said the judge.

"She's not my friend, though, is she," said Vilate. "Not really."

"I'll rip your throat out, you . . ." The salamander let fly with a string of expletives that made them all gasp.

Vilate pointed at the salamander. "She made me do it! She told me to tell those lies about Alvin! But now I see she's really hateful! And not beautiful at all! She's not beautiful, she's ugly as a . . . as a newt!"

"Salamander," said the judge helpfully.

"I hate you!" Vilate cried at the salamander. "Get away from me! I don't want to see you ever again!"

The salamander seemed poised to move—but not away from her. It looked more as if it meant to spring from the table, leap the distance between it and Vilate, and attack her as its hideous voice had threatened.

ALVIN WAS SEARCHING carefully through the salamander's body, trying to find where and how the Unmaker had control of it. But however it was done, it left no physical evidence that Alvin could see.

He realized, though, that it didn't matter. There were ways to get a person free of another person's control—an off-my-back hex. Couldn't it work for the salamander, if it was perfectly done? Alvin marked out in his mind the exact spots on the table where the hex would need to be marked, the order of the markings, the number of loops that would have to be run linking point to point.

Then he sent his doodlebug into that part of the salamander's brain where such sense as it had resided. Freedom, he whispered there, in the way he had that animals could understand. Not words, but feelings. Images. The salamander seeking after food, mating, scampering over mud, through leaves and grass, into cool mossy stone crevices. Free to do that instead of living in a dry handbag. The salamander longed for it.

Just do this, said Alvin silently into the salamander's mind. And he showed it the loops to make to get to the first mark.

The salamander had been poised to leap from the table. But instead it ran the looping pattern, touched one toe on the exact point; Alvin made it so the toe penetrated the wood just enough to make a mark, though no human eye could have seen it, the mark was so subtle. Scamper, loop, mark, and mark again. Six tiny prickings of the table's surface, and then a bound into the middle of the hex.

And the Unmaker was gone.

THE SALAMANDER RACED in a mad pattern, too fast to follow clearly; ran, then stopped stockstill in the middle of the table.

And then, suddenly, the intelligence seemed to go out of its movements. It no longer looked at Vilate. No longer looked at anyone in particular. It nosed across the table. Not certain yet whether the spell that bound the creature was done or not, no one moved toward it. It ran down the table leg, then scurried straight toward Alvin. It nosed the sack under his chair that contained the plow. It ran inside the sack.

Consternation broke out in the courtroom. "What's happening!" cried Marty Laws. "Why did it go in that sack!"

"Because it was spawned in that sack!" cried Webster. "You can see now that Alvin Smith was the source of all this mischief! I have seen the face of the devil and he sits cocky as you please in yonder chair!"

The judge banged with his gavel.

"He's not the devil," said Vilate. "The devil wears a much more lovely face than that." Then she burst into tears.

"Your Honor," said Webster, "the defendant and his lawyer have turned this court into a circus!"

"Not until after you turned it into a cesspool of scandalous lies and filthy innuendoes!" Verily roared back at him.

And as he roared, the spectators burst into applause.

The judge banged the gavel again. "Silence! Come to order, or I'll have the bailiff clear the court! Do you hear me?"

And, after a time, silence again reigned.

Alvin bent over and reached into the sack. He took out the limp body of the salamander.

"Is it dead?" asked the judge.

"No, sir," said Alvin. "She's just asleep. She's very, very tired. She's been rode hard, so to speak. Rode hard and given nothing to eat. It ain't evidence of nothing now, Your Honor. Can I give her to my friend Arthur Stuart to take care of till she has her strength back?"

"Does the prosecution have any objection?"

"No, Your Honor," said Marty Laws.

At the same time, Daniel Webster rose to his feet. "This salamander never *was* evidence of anything. It's obvious that it was introduced by the defendant and his lawyer and was always under their command. Now they've taken possession of an honest woman and broken her! Look at her!"

And there sat beautiful Vilate Franker, tears streaming down her smooth and beautiful cheeks.

"An honest woman?" she said softly. "You know as well as I do how you hinted to me about how you needed corroboration for that Amy Sump girl, how if you just had some way of proving that Alvin did *indeed* leave the jail, then she would be believed and no one would believe Alvin. Oh, you sighed and pretended that you weren't suggesting anything to me, but I knew and you knew, and so I learned the hexes from my friend and we did it, and now there you sit, lying again."

"Your Honor," said Webster, "the witness is clearly distraught. I can assure you she has misconstrued the brief conversation we had at supper in the roadhouse."

"I'm sure she has, Mr. Webster," said the judge.

"I have not misconstrued it," said Vilate, furious, whirling on the judge.

"And I'm sure you have not," said the judge. "I'm sure you're both completely correct."

"Your Honor," said Daniel Webster, "with all due respect, I don't see—"

"No, you don't see!" cried Vilate, standing up in the witness box. "You claim to see an honest woman here? I'll show you an honest woman!"

She peeled her shawl off her shoulders. At once the illusion of beauty about her face disappeared. Then she reached down and pulled the amulets out of her bodice and lifted their chains from around her neck. Her body changed before their eyes: Now she was not svelte and tall, but of middle height and a somewhat thickened middle-aged body. There was a stoop to her shoulders, and her hair was more white than gold. "*This* is an honest woman," she said. Then she sank down into her seat and wept into her hands.

"Your Honor," said Verily, "I believe I have no more questions for this witness."

"Neither does the prosecution," said Marty Laws.

"That's not so!" cried Webster.

"Mr. Webster," said Marty Laws quietly, "you are discharged from your position as co-counsel. The testimony of the witnesses you brought me now seems inappropriate to use in court, and I think it would be prudent of you to retire from this courtroom without delay."

A few people clapped, but a glare from the judge quieted them.

Webster began stuffing papers into his briefcase. "If you are alleging that I behaved unethically to any degree—"

"Nobody's alleging anything, Mr. Webster," said the judge, "except that you have no further relationship with the county attorney of Hatrack County, and therefore it's appropriate for you to step to the other side of the railing and, in my humble opinion, to the other side of the court-room door."

Webster rose to his full height, tucked his bag under his arm, and without another word strode down the aisle and out of the courtroom.

On his way out, he passed a middle-aged woman with brown-and-grey hair who was moving with some serious intent toward the judge's bench. No, toward the witness stand, where she stepped into the box, put her arm around Vilate Franker's shoulders, and helped the weeping woman rise to her feet. "Come now, Vilate, you did very bravely, you did fine, we're right proud of you."

"Goody Trader," Vilate murmured, "I'm so ashamed."

"Nonsense," said Goody Trader. "We all want to be beautiful, and truth to tell, I think you still are. Just—mature, that's all."

The spectators watched in silence as Goody Trader led her erstwhile rival from the courtroom.

"Your Honor," said Verily Cooper, "I think it should be clear to everyone that it is time to return to the real issue before the court. We have been distracted by extraneous witnesses, but the fact of the matter is that it all comes down to Makepeace Smith and Hank Dowser on one side, and Alvin Smith on the other. Their word against his. Unless the prosecution has more witnesses to call, I'd like to begin my defense by letting Alvin give his word, so the jury can judge between them at last."

"Well said, Mr. Cooper," said Marty Laws. "That's the real issue, and I'm sorry I ever moved away from it. The prosecution rests, and I think we'd all like to hear from the defendant. I'm glad he's going to speak for himself, even though the constitution of the United States allows him to decline to testify without prejudice."

"A fine sentiment," said the judge. "Mr. Smith, please rise and take the oath."

Alvin bent over, scooped up the sack with the plow in it, and hoisted it over his shoulder as easy as if it was a loaf of bread or a bag of feathers. He walked to the bailiff, put one hand on the Bible and raised the other, sack and all. "I do solemnly swear to tell the truth, the whole truth, and nothing but the truth so help me God," he said.

"Alvin," said Verily, "just tell us all how this plow came to be."

Alvin nodded. "I took the iron my master gave me—that's Makepeace, he was my master in those days—and I melted it to the right hotness. I'd already made my plow mold, so I poured it in and let it cool enough to strike off the mold, and then I shaped and hammered and scraped all the imperfections out of it, till near as I could tell it had the shape of a plow as perfect as I could do it."

"Did you use any of your knack for Making as you did it?" asked Verily.

"No sir," said Alvin. "That wouldn't be fair. I wanted to earn the right to be a journeyman smith. I did use my doodlebug to inspect the plow, but I made no changes except with my tools and my two hands."

Many of the spectators nodded. They knew something of this matter, of wanting to do something with their hands, without the use of the extraordinary knacks that were so common in this town these days.

"And when it was done, what did you have?"

"A plow," said Alvin. "Pure iron, well shaped and well tempered. A good journeyman piece."

"Whose property was that plow?" asked Verily. "I ask you not as an expert on law, but rather as the apprentice you were at the time you finished it. Was it your plow?"

"It was mine because I made it, and his because it was his iron. It's custom to let the journeyman keep his piece, but I knew it was Makepeace's right to keep it if he wanted."

"And then you apparently decided to change the iron."

Alvin nodded.

"Can you explain to the court your reasoning on the matter?"

"I don't know that it could be called reasoning, rightly. It wasn't rational, as Miss Larner would have defined it. I just knew what I wanted it to be, really. This had nothing to do with going from prentice to journeyman smith. More like going from prentice to journeyman Maker, and I had no master to judge my work, or if I do, he's not yet made hisself known to me."

"So you determined to turn the plow into gold."

Alvin waved off the idea with one hand. "Oh, now, that wouldn't be hard. I've known how to change one metal to another for a long time—it's easier with metals, the way the bits line up and all. Hard to change air, but easy to change metal."

"You're saying you could have turned iron to gold at any time?" asked Verily. "Why didn't you?"

"I reckon there's about the right amount of gold in the world, and the right amount of iron. A man doesn't need to make hammers and saws, axes and plowshares out of gold—he needs iron for that. Gold is for things that need a soft metal."

"But gold would have made you rich," said Verily.

Alvin shook his head. "Gold would have made me famous. Gold would have surrounded me with thieves. And it wouldn't have got me one step closer to learning how to be a proper Maker."

"You expect us to believe that you have no interest in gold?"

"No sir. I need money as much as the next fellow. At that time I was hoping to get married, and I hardly had a penny to my name, which isn't much in the way of prospects. But for most folks gold stands for their hard labor, and I don't see how I should have gold that didn't come from *my* hard labor, too. It wouldn't be fair, and if it's out of balance like that, then it ain't good Making, if you see my point."

"And yet you *did* transform the plow into gold, didn't you?"

"Only as a step along the way," said Alvin.

"Along the way to what?"

"Well, you know. To what the witnesses all said they seen. This plow ain't common gold. It moves. It acts. It's alive."

"And that's what you intended?"

"The fire of life. Not just the fire of the forge."

"How did you do it?"

"It's hard to explain to them as don't have the sight of a doodlebug to get inside things. I didn't create life inside it—that was already there. The bits of gold *wanted* to hold the shape I'd given them, that plow shape, so they fought against the melting of the fire, but they didn't have the strength. They didn't know their *own* strength. And I couldn't teach them, either. And then all of a sudden I thought to put my own hands into the fire and *show* the gold how to be alive, the way I was alive."

"Put your hands into the fire?" asked Verily.

Alvin nodded. "It hurt something fierce, I'll tell you—"

"But you're unscarred," said Verily.

"It was hot, but don't you see, it was a Maker's fire, and finally I understood what I must have known all along, that a Maker is part of what he Makes. I had to be in the fire along with the gold, to show it how to live, to help it find its own heartfire. If I knew exactly how it works I could do a better job of teaching folks. Heaven knows I've tried but ain't nobody learned it aright yet, though a couple or so is getting there, step by step. Anyway, the plow came to life in the fire."

"So now the plow was as we have seen it—or rather, as we have heard it described here."

"Yes," said Alvin. "Living gold."

"And in your opinion, whom does that gold belong to?"

Alvin looked around at Makepeace, then at Marty Laws, then at the judge. "It belongs to itself. It ain't no slave."

Marty Laws rose to his feet. "Surely the witness isn't asserting the equal citizenship of golden plows."

"No sir," said Alvin. "I am not. It has its own purpose in being, but I don't think jury duty or voting for president has much to do with it."

"But you're saying it doesn't belong to Makepeace Smith and it doesn't belong to you either," said Verily.

"Neither one of us."

"Then why are you so reluctant to yield possession of it to your former master?" asked Verily.

"Because he means to melt it down. He said as much that very next morning. Of course, when I told him he couldn't do that, he called me thief and insisted that the plow belonged to him. He said a journeyman piece belongs to the master unless he gives it to the journeyman and, I think he said, 'I sure as hell don't!' Then he called me thief."

"And wasn't he right? Weren't you a thief?"

"No sir," said Alvin. "I admit that the iron he gave me

was gone, and I'd be glad to give that iron back to him, five-fold or tenfold, if that's what the law requires of me. Not that I stole it from him, mind you, but because it no longer existed. At the time, of course, I was angry at him because I was ready to be a journeyman years before, but he held me to all the years of the contract anyway, pretending all the time that he didn't know I was already the better smith—"

Among the spectators, Makepeace leapt to his feet and shouted, "A contract is a contract!"

The judge banged the gavel.

"I kept the contract, too," said Alvin. "I worked the full term, even though I was kept as a servant, there wasn't a thing he could teach me after the first year or so. So I figured at the time that I had more than earned the price of the iron that was lost. Now, though, I reckon that was just an angry boy talking. I can see that Makepeace was within his rights, and I'll be glad to give him the price of the iron, or even make him another iron plow in place of the one that's gone."

"But you won't give him the actual plow you made."

"If he gave me gold to make a plow, I'd give him back as much gold as he gave me. But he gave me iron. And even if he had a right to that amount of gold, he doesn't have the right to *this* gold, because if it fell into his hands, he'd destroy it, and such a thing as this shouldn't be destroyed, specially not by them as has no power to make it again. Besides, all his talk of thief was before he saw the plow move."

"He saw it move?" asked Verily.

"Yes sir. And then he said to me, 'Get on out of here. Take that thing and go away. I never want to see your face around here again.' As near as I can recall them, those were his exact words, and if he says otherwise then God will witness against him at the last day, and he knows it."

Verily nodded. "So we have your view on it," he said.

"Now, as to Hank Dowser, what about the matter of digging somewhere other than the place he said?"

"I knew it wasn't a good place," said Alvin. "But I dug where he said, right down till I reached solid stone."

"Without hitting water?" asked Verily.

"That's right. So then I went to where I knew I should have dug in the first place, and I put the well there, and it's drawing pure water even today, I hear tell."

"So Mr. Dowser was simply wrong."

"He wasn't wrong that there was water there," said Alvin. "He just didn't know that there was a shelf of rock and the water flowed under it. Bone dry above. That's why it was a natural meadow—no trees grew there, then or now, except some scrubby ones with shallow roots."

"Thank you very much," said Verily. Then, to Marty Laws: "Your witness."

Marty Laws leaned forward on his table and rested his chin on his hands. "Well, I can't say as how I have much to ask. We've got Makepeace's version of things, and we've got your version. I might as well ask you, is there any chance that you didn't actually turn iron into gold? Any chance that you *found* the gold in that first hole you dug, and then shaped it into a plow?"

"No chance of that, sir," said Alvin.

"So you didn't hide that old iron plow away in order to enhance your reputation as a Maker?"

"I never looked for no reputation as a Maker, sir," said Alvin. "And as for the iron, it ain't iron anymore."

Makepeace nodded. "That's all the questions I've got."

The judge looked back at Verily. "Anything more from you?"

"Just one question," said Verily. "Alvin, you heard the things Amy Sump said about you and her and the baby she's carrying. Any truth to that?"

Alvin shook his head. "I never left the jail cell. It's true that I left Vigor Church at least partly because of the stories she was putting out about me. They were false stories, but I needed to leave anyway, and I hoped that with me gone, she'd forget about dreaming me into her life and fall in love with some fellow her own age. I never laid a hand on her. I'm under oath and I swear it before God. I'm sorry she's having trouble, and I hope the baby she's carrying turns out fine and strong and makes a good son for her."

"It's a boy?" asked Verily.

"Oh yes," said Alvin. "A boy. But not my son."

"Now we're finished," said Verily.

It was time for final statements, but the judge didn't give the word to begin. He leaned back in his chair and closed his eyes for a long moment. "Folks, this has been a strange trial, and it's taken some sorry turns along the way. But right now there's only a few points at issue. If Makepeace Smith and Hank Dowser are right, and the gold was found not made, then I think it's fair to say the plow is flat out Makepeace's property."

"Damn straight!" cried Makepeace.

"Bailiff, take Makepeace Smith into custody please," said the judge. "He's spending the night in jail for contempt of court, and before he can say another word I'll inform him that every word he says will add another night to his sentence."

Makepeace nearly burst, but he didn't say another word as the bailiff led him from the courtroom.

"The other possibility is that Alvin made the gold out of iron, as he says, and that the gold is something called 'living gold,' and therefore the plow belongs to itself. Well, I can't say the law allows any room for farm implements to be self-owning entities, but I will say that since Makepeace

754 • *Orson Scott Card*

gave Alvin a certain weight of iron, then if Alvin made that iron disappear, he owes Makepeace the same weight of iron back again, or the monetary equivalent in legal tender. This is how it seems to me at this moment, though I know the jury may see other possibilities that escape me. The trouble is that right now I don't know how the jury can possibly make a fair decision. How can they forget all the business about Alvin maybe or maybe not having scandalous liaisons? A part of me says I ought to declare a mistrial, but then another part of me says, that wouldn't be right, to make this town go through yet another round of this trial. So here's what I propose to do. There's one fact in all of this that we can actually test. We can go out to the smithy and have Hank Dowser show us the spot where he called for the well to be dug. Then we can dig down and see if we find either the remnants of some treasure chest—and water—or a shelf of stone, the way Alvin said, and not a drop of water. It seems to me then we'll at least know something, whereas at the present moment we don't know much at all, except that Vilate Franker, God bless her, has false teeth."

Neither the defense nor the prosecution had any objections.

"Then let's convene this court at Makepeace's smithy at ten in the morning. No, not tomorrow—that's Friday, election day. I see no way around it, we'll have to do it Monday morning. Another weekend in jail, I'm afraid, Alvin."

"Your Honor," said Verily Cooper. "There's only the one jail in this town, and with Makepeace Smith forced to share a cell in the same room with my client—"

"All right," said the judge. "Sheriff, you can release Makepeace when you get Alvin back over there."

"Thank you, Your Honor," said Verily.

"We're adjourned till ten on Monday." The gavel struck and the spectacle ended for the day.

DECISIONS

Because Calvin used to keep to himself so much in Vigor Church, he always thought of himself as a solitary sort of fellow. Everybody in Vigor who wasn't besotted with Alvin turned out to be pretty much of an idiot, when it came down to it. What did Calvin want with pranks like luring skunks under porches or pushing over outhouses? Alvin had him cut out of anything that mattered, and any other friends he might have had didn't amount to much.

In New Amsterdam and London, Calvin was even more alone, being concentrated as he was on the single-minded goal of getting to Napoleon. It was the same on the streets of Paris, when he was going around trying to get a reputation as a healer. And once he got the Emperor's attention, it was all study and work.

For a while. Because after a few weeks it became pretty clear that Napoleon was going to stretch out his teaching as long and slow as possible. Why should he do otherwise? As soon as Calvin was satisfied that he had learned enough, he'd leave and then Napoleon would be the victim of gout. Calvin toyed with the idea of putting on some pressure by increasing Napoleon's pain, and with that in mind he went and found the place in the Emperor's brain where pain was registered. He had some idea of using his doodling bug to poke directly into that place of pure agony, and then see if Napoleon didn't suddenly remember to teach Calvin a few things that he'd overlooked till now.

That was fine for daydreaming, but Calvin wasn't no fool. He could do that agony trick once, and get one day's worth of teaching, but then before he next fell asleep, he'd better be long gone from Paris, from France, and from anywhere on God's green Earth where Napoleon's agents might find him. No, he couldn't force Napoleon. He had to stay and put up with the excruciatingly slow pace of the lessons, the sheer repetitiveness. In the meantime, he observed carefully, trying to see what it was Napoleon was doing that Calvin didn't understand. He never saw a thing that made sense.

What was left for him, then, but to try out the things Napoleon *had* taught him about manipulating other people, and see if he could figure out more by pure experimentation? That was what finally brought him into contact with other people—the desire to learn how to control them.

Trouble was, the only people around were the staff, and they were all busy. What's worse, they were also under Napoleon's direct control, and it wouldn't do to let the Emperor see that somebody else was trying to win control of his toadies. He might get the wrong idea. He might think Calvin was trying to undermine his power, which wasn't true— Calvin didn't care a hoot about taking Napoleon's place. What was a mere Emperor when there was a Maker in the world?

Two Makers, that is. Two.

Who could Calvin try out his new-learned powers on? After a little wandering around the palace and the government buildings, he began to realize that there was another class of person altogether. Idle and frustrated, they were Calvin's natural subjects: the sons of Napoleon's clerks and courtiers.

They all had roughly the same biography: As their fathers rose to positions of influence, they got sent away to steadily better boarding schools, then emerged at sixteen or seventeen with education, ambition, and no social prestige whatsoever, which meant that most doors were closed to them except to follow in their fathers' footsteps and become completely dependent upon the Emperor. For some of them, this was perfectly all right; Calvin left those hardworking, contented souls alone.

The ones he found interesting were the desultory law students, the enthusiastically untalented poets and dramatists, the gossiping seducers looking around for women rich enough to be desirable and stupid enough to be taken in by such pretenders. Calvin's French improved greatly the more he conversed with them, and even as he followed Napoleon's lessons and learned to find what vices drove these young men, so he could flatter and exploit and control them, he also discovered that he enjoyed their company. Even the fools among them were entertaining, with their lassitude and cynicism, and now and then he found some truly clever and fascinating companions.

Those were the most difficult to win control of, and Calvin told himself that it was the challenge rather than the pleasure of their company that kept him coming back to them again and again. One of them most of all: Honoré. A skinny, short man with prematurely rotten teeth, he was a year older than Calvin's brother Alvin. Honoré was without manners; Calvin soon learned that it wasn't because he didn't know how to behave, but rather because he wished to shock people, to show his contempt for their stale forms, and most of all because he wished to command their attention, and being faintly repulsive all the time had the desired effect. He might start with their contempt or disgust, but within fifteen minutes he always had them laughing at his wit, nodding at his insights, their eyes shining with the dazzlement of his conversation.

Calvin even allowed himself to think that Honoré had some of the same gift Napoleon had been born with, that by studying him Calvin might learn a few of the secrets the Emperor still withheld.

At first Honoré ignored Calvin, not in particular but in the general way that he ignored everyone who had nothing to offer him. Then he must have heard from someone that Calvin saw the Emperor every day, that in fact the Emperor used him as his personal healer. At once Calvin became acceptable, so much so that Honoré began inviting him along on his nighttime jaunts.

"I am studying Paris," said Honoré. "No, let me correct myself—I am studying humankind, and Paris has a large enough sampling of that species to keep me occupied for many years. I study all people who depart from the norm, for their very abnormalities teach me about human nature: If the actions of this man surprise me, it is because I must have learned, over the years, to expect men to behave in a different way. Thus I learn not only the oddity of the one, but also the normality of the many."

"And how am I odd?" asked Calvin.

"You are odd because you actually listen to my ideas instead of my wit. You are an eager student of genius, and I half suspect that you may have genius yourself."

"Genius?" asked Calvin.

"The extraordinary spirit that makes great men great. It is perfect piety that turns men into saints or angels, but what about men who are indifferently pious but perfectly intelligent or wise or perceptive? What do they become? Geniuses. Patron saints of the mind, of the eye, of the mind's eye! I intend, when I die, to have my name invoked by those who pray for wisdom. Let the saints have the prayers of those who need miracles." He cocked his head and looked up at Calvin. "You're too tall to be honest. Tall men always tell lies, since they assume short men like me will never see clearly enough to contradict them."

"Can't help being tall," said Calvin.

"Such a lie," said Honoré. "You wanted to be tall when

you were young, just as I wanted to be closer to the earth, where my eye could see the details large men miss. Though I do hope to be fat someday, since fatness would mean I had more than enough to eat, and that, my dear Yankee, would be a delicious change. It's a commonplace idea that geniuses are never understood and therefore never become popular or make money from their brilliance. I think this is pure foolishness. A true genius will not only be smarter than everyone else, but will be *so* clever that he'll know how to appeal to the masses without compromising his brilliance. Hence: I write novels."

Calvin almost laughed. "Those silly stories women read?"

"The very ones. Fainting heiresses. Dullard husbands. Dangerous lovers. Earthquakes, revolutions, fires, and interfering aunts. I write under several *noms de plume,* but my secret is that even as I master the art of being popular and therefore rich, I am also using the novel to explore the true state of humankind in this vast experimental tank known as Paris, this hive with an imperial queen who surrounds himself with drones like my poor stingless unflying father, the seventh secretary of the morning rotation—you gave him a hotfoot once, you miserable prankster, he wept that night at the humiliation of it and I vowed to kill you someday, though I think I probably won't—I have never kept a promise yet."

"When do you write? You're here all the time." Calvin gestured to include the environs of the government buildings.

"How would you know, when you *aren't* here all the time? By night I pass back and forth between the grand salons of the cream of society and the finest brothels ever created by the scum of the earth. And in the mornings, when you're taking emperor lessons from M. Bonaparte, I hole up in my miserable poet's garret—where my mother's housekeeper brings me fresh bread every day, so don't weep for me yet, not until I get syphilis or tuberculosis—and I write furiously, filling page after page with scintillating prose. I tried my hand at poetry once, a long play, but I discovered that by imitating Racine, one learns primarily to become as tedious as Racine, and by studying Molière, one learns that Molière was a lofty genius not to be trifled with by pathetic young imitators."

"I haven't read either of them," said Calvin. In truth he had never heard of either one and only deduced that they were dramatists from the context.

"Nor have you read my work, because in fact it is not yet genius, it is merely journeyman work. In fact I fear sometimes that I have the ambition of a genius, the eye and ear of a genius, and the talent of a chimneysweep. I go down into the filthy world, I come up black, I scatter the ashes and cinders of my research onto white papers, but what have I got? Paper with black marks all over it." Suddenly he gripped Calvin's shirtfront and pulled him down until they were eye to eye. "I would cut off my leg to have a talent like yours. To be able to see *inside* the body and heal or harm, give pain or relieve it. I would cut off both legs." Then he let go of Calvin's shirt. "Of course, I wouldn't give up my more fragile parts, for that would be too great a disappointment to my dear Lady de Berny. You will be discreet, of course, and when you gossip about my affair with her you will never admit you heard about it from me."

"Are you really jealous of me?" asked Calvin.

"Only when I am in my right mind," said Honoré, "which is rare enough that you don't yet interfere with my happiness. You are not yet one of the major irritations of my life. My mother, now—I spent my early childhood pining for some show of love from her, some gentle touch of affection, and instead was always greeted with coldness and reproof.

Nothing I did pleased her. I thought, for many years, that it was because I was a bad son. Then, suddenly, I realized that it was because she was a bad mother! It wasn't me she hated, it was my father. So one year when I was away at school, she took a lover—and she chose well, he is a very fine man whom I respect greatly—and got herself impregnated and gave birth to a monster."

"Deformed?" asked Calvin, curious.

"Only morally. Otherwise he is quite attractive, and my mother dotes on him. Every time I see her fawning on him, praising him, laughing at his clever little antics, I long to do as Joseph's brothers did and put him in a pit, only *I* would never be softhearted enough to pull him out and sell him into mere slavery. He will also probably be tall and she will see to it he has full access to her fortune, unlike myself, who am forced to live on the pittance my father can give me, the advances I can extort from my publishers, and the generous impulses of the women for whom I am the god of love. After careful contemplation, I have come to the conclusion that Cain, like Prometheus, was one of the great benefactors of humankind, for which of course he must be endlessly tortured by God, or at least given a very ugly pimple in his forehead. For it was Cain who taught us that some brothers simply cannot be endured, and the only solution is to kill them or have them killed. Being a man of lazy disposition, I lean toward the latter course. Also one cannot wear fine clothes in prison, and after one is guillotined for murder, one's collars never stay on properly; they're always sliding off to one side or the other. So I'll either hire it done or see to it he gets employed in some miserable clerical post in a faroff colony. I have in mind Reunion in the Indian Ocean; my only objection is that its dot on the globe is large enough that Henry may not be able to see the entire circumference of his island home at once. I want him to feel himself in prison every waking moment. I suppose that is uncharitable of me."

Uncharitable? Calvin laughed in delight, and regaled Honoré in turn with tales of his own horrible brother. "Well, then," said Honoré, "you must destroy him, of course. What are you doing here in Paris, with a great project like that in hand!"

"I'm learning from Napoleon how to rule over men. So that when my brother builds his Crystal City, I can take it away from him."

"Take it away! Such shallow aims," said Honoré. "What good is taking it away?"

"Because he built it," said Calvin, "or he *will* build it, and then he'll have to see me rule over all that he built."

"You think this because you are a nasty person by nature, Calvin, and you don't understand nice people. To you, the end of existence is to control things, and so you will never build anything, but rather will try to take control of what is already in existence. Your brother, though, is by nature a Maker, as you explain it; therefore he cares nothing about who rules, but only about what exists. So if you take away the rule of the Crystal City—when he builds it—you have accomplished nothing, for he will still rejoice that the thing exists at all, regardless of who rules it. No, there is nothing else for you to do but let the city rise to its peak—and then tear it down into such a useless heap of rubble that it can never rise again."

Calvin was troubled. He had never thought this way, and it didn't feel good to him. "Honoré, you're joking, I'm sure. *You* make things—your novels, at least."

"And if you hated me, you wouldn't just take away my royalties—my creditors do that already, thank you very much. No, you would take my very books, steal the copyright, and then revise them and revise them until nothing of truth or beauty or, more to the point, my genius remained in them, and then you would continue to publish them under my name, causing me to be shamed with every copy sold. People would read and say, 'Honoré de Balzac, such a fool!' That is how you would destroy me."

"I'm not a character in one of your novels."

"More's the pity. You would speak more interesting dialogue if you were."

"So you think I'm wasting my time here?"

"I think you're *about* to waste your time. Napoleon is no fool. He's never going to give you tools powerful enough to challenge his own. So leave!"

"How can I leave, when he depends on me to keep his gout from hurting? I'd never make it to the border."

"Then heal the gout the way you used to heal those poor beggars—that was a cruel thing for you to do, by the way, a miserable selfish thing, for how did you think they were going to feed their children without some suppurating wound to excite pity in passersby and eke out a few sous from them? Those of us who were aware of your one-man messianic mission had to go about after you, cutting off the legs of your victims so they'd be able to continue to earn their livelihood."

Calvin was appalled. "How could you do such a thing!"

Honoré roared with laughter. "I'm joking, you poor literal-minded American simpleton!"

"I can't heal the gout," said Calvin, coming back to the subject that interested him: his own future.

"Why not?"

"I've been trying to figure out how diseases are caused. Injuries are easy. Infections are, too. If you concentrate, anyway. Diseases have taken me weeks. They seem to be caused by tiny creatures, so small I can't see them individually, only *en masse*. Those I can destroy easily enough, and cure the disease, or at least knock it back a little and give the body a chance to defeat it on its own. But not all diseases are caused by those tiny beasts. Gout baffles me completely. I have no idea what causes it, and therefore I can't cure it."

Honoré shook his oversized head. "Calvin, you have such native talents, but they have been bestowed unworthily upon you. When I say you must heal Napoleon, of course I don't care whether you actually cure the gout. It isn't the gout that bothers him. It's the *pain* of the gout. And you already cure that every day! So cure it once and for all, thank Napoleon kindly for his lessons, and get out of France as quickly as possible! Have done with it! Get back about your life's work! I'll tell you what—I'll even pay your passage to America. No, I'll do more. I'll come with you to America, and add the study of that astonishingly crude and vigorous people to my vast store of knowledge about humankind. With your talent and my genius, what is there we couldn't accomplish?"

"Nothing," said Calvin happily.

He was especially happy because not five minutes before, Calvin had decided that he wanted Honoré to accompany him to America, and so by the tiniest of gestures, by certain looks and signs that Honoré was never aware of, he caused the young novelist to like him, to be excited by the work that Calvin had to do, and to want so much to be a part of it that he would come home to America with him. Best of all, Calvin had brought it off so skillfully that Honoré obviously had no idea that he had been manipulated into it.

In the meantime, Honoré's idea of curing Napoleon's pain once and for all appealed to him. That place in the brain where pain resided still waited for him. Only instead of stimulating it, all he had to do was cauterize it. It would not only cure Napoleon's gout, but would also cure all other pains he might feel in the future.

So, having thought of it, having decided to do it, that night Calvin acted. And in the morning, when he presented himself to the Emperor, he saw at once that the Emperor knew what he had done.

"I cut myself this morning, sharpening a pen," said Napoleon. "I only knew it when I saw the blood. I felt no pain at all."

"Excellent," said Calvin. "I finally found the way to end your pain from gout once and for all. It involved cutting off *all* pain for the rest of your life, but it's hard to imagine you'd mind."

Napoleon looked away. "It was hard for Midas to imagine that he would not want *everything* he touched to turn to gold. I might have bled to death because I felt no pain."

"Are you rebuking me?" said Calvin. "I give you a gift that millions of people pray for—to live a life without pain—and you're rebuking me? You're the Emperor—assign a servant to watch you day and night in order to make sure you don't unwittingly bleed to death."

"This is permanent?" asked Napoleon.

"I can't cure the gout—the disease is too subtle for me. I never pretended to be perfect. But the pain I could cure, and so I did. I cured it now and forever. If I did wrong, I'll restore the pain to you as best I can. It won't be a pleasant operation, but I think I can get the balance back to about what it was before. Intermittent, wasn't it? A month of gout, and then a week without it, and then another month?"

"You've grown saucy."

"No sir, I merely speak French better, so my native sauciness can emerge more clearly."

"What's to stop me from throwing you out, then? Or having you killed, now that I don't need you anymore?"

"Nothing has ever stopped you from doing those things," said Calvin. "But you don't needlessly kill people, and as for throwing me out—well, why go to the trouble? I'm ready to leave. I'm homesick for America. My family is there."

Napoleon nodded. "I see. You decided to leave, and then finally cured my pain."

"My beloved Emperor, you wrong me," said Calvin. "I found I could cure you, and then decided to leave."

"I still have much to teach you."

"And I have much to learn. But I fear I'm not clever enough to learn from you—the last several weeks you have taught me and taught me, and yet I keep feeling as if I have learned nothing new. I'm simply not a clever enough pupil to master your lessons. Why should I stay?"

Napoleon smiled. "Well done. Very well done. If I weren't Napoleon, you would have won me over completely. In fact, I would probably be paying your passage to America."

"I was hoping you would, anyway, in gratitude for a pain-free life."

"Emperors can't afford to have petty emotions like gratitude. If I pay your passage it's not because I'm grateful to you, it's because I think my purpose will be better served with you gone and alive than with you, say, here and alive or, perhaps, here and dead, or the most difficult possibility, gone and dead." Napoleon smiled.

Calvin smiled back. They understood each other, the Emperor and the young Maker. They had used each other and now were done with each other and would cast each other aside—but with style.

"I'll take the train to the coast this very day, begging your consent, sir."

"My consent! You have more than my consent! My servants have already packed your bags and they are doubtless at the station as we speak." Napoleon grinned, touched his forelock in an imaginary salute, and then watched as Calvin rushed from the room.

Calvin the American Maker and Honoré Balzac the annoyingly ambitious young writer, both gone from the country in the same day. And the pain of the gout now gone from him.

I'll have to be careful getting into the bath. I might scald myself to death without knowing it. I'll have to get someone else to climb into the water before me. I think I know just the young servant girl who should do it. I'll have to have her scrubbed first, so she doesn't foul the water for me. It will be interesting to see how much of the pleasure of the bath came from the slight pain of hot water. And was pain a part of sexual pleasure? It would be infuriating if the boy had interfered with *that*. Napoleon would have to have him hunted down and killed, if the boy had ruined that sport for him.

It didn't take long for the ballots to be counted in Hatrack River—by nine P.M. Friday, the elections clerk announced a decisive victory countywide for Tippy-Canoe, old Red Hand Harrison. Some had been drinking all through the election day; now the likker began to flow in earnest. Being a county seat, Hatrack drew plenty of farmers from the hinterland and smaller villages, for whom Hatrack was the nearest metropolis, having near a thousand people now; it was swollen to twice that number by ten in the evening. As word came in from each of the neighboring counties and from some across river that Tippy-Canoe was winning there, too, guns were shot off and so were mouths, which led to fisticuffs and a lot of traffic into and out of the jail.

Po Doggly came in about ten-thirty and asked Alvin if he'd mind too much being put on his own parole to go spend the night in the roadhouse—Horace Guester was standing bail for him, and did he give his solemn oath etcetera etcetera because the jail was needed to hold drunken brawlers ten to a cell. Alvin took the oath and Horace and Verily escorted him through back lots to the roadhouse. There was plenty of drinking and dancing downstairs in the common room of the roadhouse, but not the kind of rowdiness that prevailed at rougher places and out in the open, where wagons filled with likker were doing quite a business. Horace's party, as always, was for locals of the more civilized variety. Still, it wouldn't do no good for Alvin to show his face there and get rumors going, especially since there was bound to be some in the crowds infesting Hatrack River as wasn't particular friends of Alvin's—and a few that *was* particular friends of Makepeace's. Not to mention them as was always a particular friend of any amount of gold that might be obtained by stealth or violence. It was up the back stairs for Alvin, and even then he stooped and had his face covered and said nary a word the whole jaunt.

Up in Horace's own bedroom, where Arthur Stuart and Measure already had cots, Alvin paced the room, touching the walls, the soft bed, the window as if he had never seen such things before. "Even cooped up in here," said Alvin, "it's better than a cell. I hope never to be back in such a place again."

"Don't know how you've stood it this far," said Horace. "I'd go plain bonkers in a week."

"Who's to say he didn't?" said Measure.

Alvin laughed and agreed with him. "I was crazy not to let Verily go with his plans, I know that," said Alvin.

"No, no," said Verily. "You were right, you came through in your own defense."

"But what if I hadn't figured out how to let the salamander's voice be heard? I've been thinking about that ever since yesterday. What if I hadn't done it? They was all talking like I could do anything, like I could fly or do miracles on the moon just by thinking about it. I wish I could. Sometimes I wish I could. It's still nip and tuck with the jury, ain't it, Verily?"

Verily agreed that it was. But they all knew that he wasn't likely to get convicted of anything now—assuming, of course, that the shelf of rock was still there in the spot Hank Dowser marked for a well. The real damage was to his good name. The real damage was to the Crystal City, which now would be harder to build because of all them stories going around about how Alvin Smith seduced young girls and old women and walked through walls to get to them. Never mind that the story had turned out to be lies and foolishness— there was always folks stupid enough to say, "Where there's smoke there's fire," when the saying should have been, "Where there's scandalous lies there's always malicious believers and spreaders-around, regardless of evidence."

The whooping and hollering in the street, with youngsters or drunken oldsters riding their horses at a breakneck speed up and down until Sheriff Doggly or some deputy could either stop the horse or shoot it, that guaranteed no sleep for anyone, not early, anyway. So they were all still awake, even Arthur Stuart, when two more men came into the common room of the roadhouse, looking wore out and dirty from hard travel. They waited at the counter, nursing a mug of cider each, till Horace came downstairs to check on things and recognized them at once. "Come on up, he's here, he's upstairs," whispered Horace, and the three of them was up the stairs in a trice.

"Armor," said Alvin, greeting him with a brotherly hug. "Mike." And Mike Fink got him a hug as well. "You picked a good night to return."

"We picked a *damn* good night," said Fink. "We was afraid we might be too late. The plan was to take you out of the jail and hang you as part of the election night festivities. Glad the sheriff thought ahead."

"He just needed the space for drunk and disorderly," said Alvin. "I don't think he had any inkling about no plot."

"There's twenty boys here," said Fink. "Twenty at least, all of them well paid and likkered up. I hope well enough paid that they're *really* likkered up so they'll just fall down, puke, and go to sleep, and then slink off home to Carthage in the morning."

"I doubt it," said Measure. "I been caught up in plots against Alvin before. Somebody once pretty much took me apart."

Fink looked at him again. "You wasn't so tall then," he said. "I was plain ashamed of what I done to you," he said. "It was the worst thing I ever done."

"I didn't die," said Measure.

"Not for lack of trying on my part," said Fink.

Verily was baffled. "You mean this man tried to kill you, Measure?"

"Governor Harrison ordered it," said Measure. "And it was years ago. Before I was married. Before Alvin came here to Hatrack River as a prentice boy. And if I recall aright, Mike Fink was a little prettier in those days."

"Not in my heart," said Frank. "But I bore you no malice, Measure. And after Harrison had me do that to you, I left him, I wanted no truck with him. It don't make up for nothing, but it's the truth, that I'm not a man who'd let such as him boss me around, not anymore. If I thought you was the type of man to get even, I wouldn't run, I'd let you do it. But you ain't that kind of man."

"Like I said," Measure answered, "no harm done. I learned some things that day, and so did you. Let's have done with that now. You're Alvin's friend now, and that makes you my friend as long as you're loyal and true."

There were tears in Mike Fink's eyes. "Jesus himself couldn't be more kind to me, and me less deserving."

Measure held out his hand. Mike took and held it. Just for a second. Then it was done, and they set it behind them and went on.

"Found out a few things," said Armor-of-God. "But I'm glad Mike was with me. Not that he had to do any violence, but there was a couple of times that some fellows didn't take kindly to the questions I was asking."

"I did throw a fellow into a horsetrough," said Fink, "but I didn't hold him under or nothing so I don't think that counts."

Alvin laughed. "No, I reckon that was just playing around."

"It's some old friends of yours behind all this, Alvin," said Armor-of-God. "The Property Rights Crusade is mostly Reverend Philadelphia Thrower and a couple of clerks opening letters and mailing out letters. But there's some money people behind him, and he's behind other people who need money."

"Like?" asked Horace.

"Like one of his first and longest and loyalest contributors is a fellow name of Cavil Planter, who once owned him a farm in Appalachee and still clings to a certain cachet like it was gold bullion," said Armor-of-God, with a glance at Arthur Stuart.

Arthur nodded. "You're saying that's the white man as raped my mama to make me."

"Most likely," said Armor-of-God.

Alvin stared at Arthur Stuart. "How do you know about such things?"

"I hear everything," said Arthur Stuart. "I don't forget none of it. People said things about that stuff when I was too young to understand it, but I remembered the words and said them to myself when I was older and *could* understand them."

"Damn," said Horace. "How was Old Peg and me supposed to know he'd be able to figure it out later?"

"You did nothing wrong," said Verily. "You can't help the knacks your children have. My parents couldn't predict what I'd do, either, though heaven knows they tried. If Arthur Stuart's knack let him learn things that were painful to know, then I'd also have to say his inward character was strong enough to deal with it and let him grow up untroubled by it."

"I ain't troubled by it, that's true," said Arthur Stuart. "But I'll never call him my pa. He hurt my mama and he wanted to make a slave of me, and that's no pa." He looked at Horace Guester. "My own Black mama died trying to get me here, to a real pa and to a ma who'd take her place when she died."

Horace reached out and patted the boy's hand. Alvin knew how Horace had never liked having the boy call him his father, but it was plain Horace had reconciled himself to it. Maybe it was because of what Arthur just said, or maybe it was because Alvin had taken the boy away for a year and Horace was realizing now that his life was emptier without this half-Black mixup boy as his son.

"So this Cavil Planter is one of the money men behind Thrower's little group," said Verily. "Who else?"

"A lot of names, we didn't get but a few of them but it's prominent people in Carthage, and all of them from the proslavery faction, either openly or clandestine," said Armor. "And I'm pretty sure about where most of the money's going *to*."

"We know some of it went to pay Daniel Webster," said Alvin.

"But a lot more of it went to help with White Murderer Harrison's campaign for president," said Armor.

They fell silent, and in the silence more gunshots went off, more cheering, more galloping of horses and whooping and hollering. "Tippy-Canoe just carried him another county," said Horace.

"Maybe he won't do so well back east," said Alvin.

"Who knows?" said Measure. "I can guarantee you he didn't get a single vote in Vigor Church. But that ain't enough to turn the tide."

"It's out of our hands for now," said Alvin. "Presidents ain't forever."

"I think what's important here," said Verily, "is that the same people whose candidate for president just won the election are also out to get you killed, Alvin."

"I'd think about lying low for a while," said Measure.

"I *been* lying low," said Alvin. "I had about all the low-lying I can stand."

"Being in jail so's they know right where you be ain't lying low," said Mike Fink. "You got to be where they don't think to look for you, or where if they do find you they can't do nothing to hurt you."

"The first place I can think of that fills those requirements is the grave," said Alvin, "but I reckon I don't want to go there yet."

There was a soft rap on the door. Horace went to it, whispered, "Who's there?"

"Peggy," came the answer.

He opened the door and she came in. She looked around at the assembled men and chuckled. "Planning the fate of the world here?"

Too many of them remembered what happened the last time they met together for her casual tone to be easily accepted. Only Armor and Fink, who weren't there in Alvin's cell that night, greeted her with good cheer. They filled her in on all that had happened, including the fact that Harrison's election was taken for a sure thing all along the route from Carthage City to Hatrack.

"You know what I don't think is fair?" said Arthur Stuart. "That old Red Hand Harrison is walking around with blood dripping off'n him and they made him president, while Measure here has to stay half-hid and all them other good folks daresn't leave Vigor Church cause of that curse. It seems to me like the good folks is still punished and the worsest one got off scot-free."

"Seems the same to me," said Alvin. "But it ain't my call."

"Maybe it ain't and maybe it is," said Arthur Stuart.

They all looked at him like he was a mess on the floor. "How is it Alvin's call?" asked Verily.

"That Red chief ain't dead, is he?" said Arthur Stuart. "That Red prophet what put the curse on, right? Well, him as puts on a curse can take it off, can't he?"

"Nobody can talk to them wild Reds no more," said Mike Fink. "They fogged up the river and nobody can get across. There ain't even no trade with New Orleans no more, damn near broke my heart."

"Maybe nobody can get across the river," said Arthur Stuart. "But Alvin can."

Alvin shook his head. "I don't know," he said. "I don't think so. Besides, I don't know if Tenskwa-Tawa's going to see things the same way as us, Arthur. He might say, The White people of America are bringing destruction on themselves by choosing White Murderer Harrison to be their leader. But the people of Vigor Church will be saved from that destruction because they respected the curse I gave them. So he'll say the curse is really a blessing."

"If he says that," said Measure, "then he ain't as good a man as I thought."

"He sees things a different way, that's all," said Alvin. "I'm just saying you can't be sure what he'll say."

"Then *you* can't be sure either," said Armor-of-God.

"I'm thinking something, Alvin," said Measure. "Miss Larner here told me somewhat about how she and Arthur figured out there's a lot of people with sharp knacks in this place. Maybe drawn here cause you was born here, or cause you made the plow here. And there's all them people you've been teaching up in Vigor, folks who maybe don't got so sharp a knack but they know the things you taught them, they know the way to live. And I also have my own idea that maybe the curse forced us all to live together there, so we had to get along no matter what, we had to learn to make peace among ourselves. If the curse was lifted from the folks of Vigor Church, them as wanted to could come here and teach them as has the knacks. And teach them meantime how to live together in harmony."

"Or folks from here could go there," said Alvin. "Even if the curse ain't lifted."

Measure shook his head. "There's like a hundred people or more in Vigor Church who's already trying to follow the Maker way. Nobody here even knows about it, really. So if you said to the folks in Vigor, please come to Hatrack, they'd come; but if you said to the folks in Hatrack, please come to Vigor, they'd laugh."

"But the river's still fogged up," said Mike Fink, "and the curse is still on."

"If it comes to that," said Miss Larner, "there might be another way to talk to Tenskwa-Tawa without crossing the river."

"You got a pigeon knows the way to the Red Prophet's wigwam?" asked Horace, scoffing.

"I know a weaver," said Miss Larner, "who has a door that opens into the west, and I know of a man named Isaac who uses that door." She looked at Alvin, and he nodded.

"I don't know what you're talking about," said Measure, "but if you think you can talk to Tenskwa-Tawa, then I hope you'll do it. I hope you will."

"I will for you," said Alvin. "For your sake and the sake of my family and friends in Vigor Church, I'll ask even though I fear the answer will be worse than no."

"What could be worse than no?" asked Arthur Stuart.

"I could lose a friend," said Alvin. "But when I weigh that friend against the people of Vigor and the hope that they might help teach other folks to be Makers and help build the Crystal City—then I don't see as how I've got no choice. I was a child when I went there, though, to that weaver's house." He was silent for a moment. "Miss Larner knows the way, if she'll guide me there." It was his turn to look at her, waiting. After a moment's hesitation, she nodded.

"One way or another, though," said Verily Cooper, "you *will* leave this place as soon as the trial's over."

"Win or lose," said Alvin. "Win or lose."

"And if anybody tries to stop him or harm him, they'll have to deal with me first," said Mike Fink. "I'm going with you, Alvin, wherever you go. If these people have the president in their pocket, they're going to be all the more dangerous and you ain't going nowhere without me to watch your back."

"I wish I was younger," said Armor-of-God. "I wish I was younger."

"I don't want to travel alone," said Alvin. "But there's work to be done here, especially if the curse is lifted. And you have responsibilities, too, you married men. It's only the single ones, really, who are free to wander as I'll have to wander. Whatever I find out at the weaver's house, whatever happens when and if I talk to Tenskwa-Tawa, I still have to learn how to build the Crystal City."

"Maybe Tenskwa-Tawa can tell you," said Measure.

"If he knows, then he could have told me back when you and I was boys and in his company," said Alvin.

"I'm unmarried," said Arthur Stuart. "I'm coming with you."

"I reckon so," said Alvin. "And Mike Fink, I'll be glad of your company, too."

"I'm not married either," said Verily Cooper.

Alvin looked at him oddly. "Verily, you're already a dear friend, but you're a lawyer, not a woodsman or a wandering tradesman or a river rat or whatever the rest of us are."

"All the more reason you need me," said Verily. "There'll be laws and courts, sheriffs and jails and writs wherever you go. Sometimes you'll need what Mike Fink has to offer. And sometimes you'll need me. You can't deny me, Alvin Smith. I came all this way to learn from you."

"Measure knows all I know by now. He can teach you as well as I can, and you can help him."

Verily looked at his feet for a moment. "Measure's learned from you, and you from him, since you're brothers and have been for a long time. May it not be taken as an offense, I beg you, if I say that I'd be glad of a chance to learn from you directly for a while, Alvin. I mean to belittle no one else by saying that."

"No offense taken," said Measure. "If you hadn't said it, I would have."

"These three then to go with me on the long road," said Alvin. "And Miss Larner to go with me as far as Becca Weaver's house."

"I'll go too," said Armor-of-God. "Not the whole road, but as far as the weavers. So I can bring back word about what Tenskwa-Tawa says. I hope you'll forgive my presumption, but I crave the chance to be the one as brings the good news to Vigor Church, if they're set free."

"And if they're not?"

"Then they need to learn that too, and from me."

"Then our plans are laid, such as they are," said Alvin.

"All except how to get out of Hatrack River alive, with all these thugs and ruffians about," said Verily Cooper.

"Oh, me and Armor already got that figured out," said Mike Fink with a grin. "And we pretty much won't have to beat nobody to a pulp to do it, neither, if we're lucky."

There was such glee in Mike Fink's face when he said it, though, that more than one of the others wondered whether Mike really thought it would be *good* luck not to have to pulverize somebody. Nor were a few of them altogether sure that they didn't wish to do a little pulp-beating themselves, if push came to shove.

Fink and Armor-of-God were about to head downstairs with Horace then, to freshen up from their journey before he put them to bed in his attic, a good clean space but one he never rented out, just in case of late-night sudden visitors like these, when Measure called out, "Mike Fink."

Fink turned around.

"There's a story I got to tell you before I go to sleep tonight," he said.

Fink looked puzzled for a moment.

"Measure's under the curse," said Armor-of-God. "He's got to tell you or he'll go to bed with bloody hands."

"I came this close to being under the curse myself," said Fink. "But you? How did you get under it?"

"He took it on himself," said Miss Larner. "But that doesn't mean the same rules don't apply."

"But I already know the story."

"That'll make the telling of it easier," said Measure. "But I got to do it."

"I'll come back up when I've peed and et," said Fink. "Begging your pardon, ma'am."

There they were, then, looking at each other, Alvin and

ALVIN JOURNEYMAN • 779

Peggy—but once again with Verily Cooper, Arthur Stuart, and Measure looking on.

"Don't the two of you get tired of playing out your scenes in front of an audience?"

"There's no scene to play," said Miss Larner.

"Too bad," said Alvin. "I thought this was the part of the play where I says to you, 'I'm sorry,' and you says to me—"

"I say to you, There is nothing to be sorry for."

"And I say to you, Is so. And you say, Is not. Is so, Is not, Is so, back and forth till we bust out laughing."

At which she burst out laughing.

"I was right, you didn't need to testify," Alvin said.

Her face went stern at once.

"Hear me out, for pete's sake, cause you were right too, if it came right down to it, it wasn't my place to tell you whether or not you could testify. It's not my decision whether you get to make this sacrifice or that one, or whether it's worth it. You decide your own sacrifices, and I decide mine. Instead of me bossing you about it, I should have just asked you to hold off and see if I could manage without. And you would have said yes. Wouldn't you."

She looked him in the eye. "Probably not," she said. "But I *should* have."

"So maybe we ain't so bullheaded after all."

"The day after—no, two days later—that's when we're not so bullheaded."

"That'll do, if we just stay friends till we soften up a little."

"You're not ready for married life, Alvin," said Miss Larner. "You still have many leagues to travel, and until you're ready to build the Crystal City, you have no need of me. I'm not going to sit home and pine for you, and I'm not going to try to tag along with you when the companions you need are men like these. Speak to me when your journey's done. See if we still need each other then."

"So you admit we need each other now."

"I'm not debating with you now, Alvin. I concede no points to you, and petty contradictions will not be explained or reconciled."

"These men are my witnesses, Margaret. I will love you forever. The family we make together, that will be our best Making, better than the plow, better than the Crystal City."

She shook her head. "Be honest with yourself, Alvin. The Crystal City will stand forever, if you build it right. But our family will be gone in a few lifetimes."

"So you admit we'll have a family."

She grinned. "You should run for office, Alvin. You'd lose, but the debates would be entertaining." She was turning toward the door when it opened without a knock. It was Po Doggly, his eyes wide. He scanned the room till he saw Alvin. "What are you doing sitting there like that, and not a gun in the room!"

"I wasn't robbing any of them, and they wasn't robbing me," said Alvin. "We didn't think to bring guns along."

"There was a break-in at the jail. A man claiming to be Amy Sump's father riled up the crowd and about thirty men broke into the courthouse and overpowered Billy Hunter and took away his keys. They hauled every damn prisoner out of there and started beating on them till they told which one of them was you. I got there before they killed anybody and I run them off all right, but they can't get far from town in one night and I don't know but what somebody's going to tell them where you are so I want you to sleep with guns tonight."

"Don't worry about it," said Miss Larner. "They won't come here tonight."

Po looked at her, then at Alvin. "You sure?"

"Don't even post a guard, Po," said Miss Larner. "It will only draw attention to the roadhouse. The men hired to kill

Alvin are all cowards, really, so they had to get drunk in order to make the attempt. They'll sleep it off tonight."

"And go away after that?"

"Make sure the trial is well guarded, and after that if Alvin is acquitted he'll leave Hatrack and your nightmares will be over."

"They broke into my jail," said Doggly. "I don't know who your enemies are, boy, but if I was you I'd get rid of that golden plow."

"It ain't the plow," said Alvin. "Though some of them probably thinks it is. But plow or no plow, the ones as want me dead would be sending boys like those after me."

"And you really don't want my protection?" asked Doggly.

Both Alvin and Miss Larner agreed that they did not.

When Po made his good-byes and was ready to leave, Miss Larner slipped her arm through his. "Take me downstairs, please, and on to the room I'm sharing with my new friend Ramona." She gave not so much as a backward glance at Alvin.

Measure hooted once—after the door was closed. "Alvin, is she testing you? Just to make sure that you'll *never* turn wife-beater, no matter what the provocation?"

"I got a feeling I ain't seen provocation yet." But Alvin was smiling when he said it, and the others got the idea he didn't mind the idea of sparring with Miss Larner now and then—sparring with words, that is, words and looks and winks and nasty grins.

After the candles were doused and the room was dark and still, with all of them in bed and wishing to sleep, Alvin murmured: "I wonder what they meant to do to me."

Nobody asked who he meant; Measure didn't have to. "They meant to kill you, Alvin. Does it matter what method they used? Hanging. Burning alive. A dozen musket balls. Do you really care which way you die?"

"I'd like to have a corpse decent-looking enough that the coffin can be open and my children can bear to look at me and say good-bye to me."

"You're dreaming then," said Measure. "Cause even right now I don't know how no wife and children could bear to look at you, though I daresay they'll say good-bye readily enough."

"I expect they were going to hang me," said Alvin. "If you ever see folks about to hang me, don't waste your time or risk your life trying to save me. Just come along after they've given up on me so you can get me on home."

"So you got no fear of the rope," said Measure.

"Nor fear of drowning or suffocation," said Alvin. "Nor falling—I can fix up breaks and make the rocks soft under me. But fire, now. Fire and beheading and too many bullets, those can take me right off. I could use some help if you see them going at me like that."

"I'll try to remember that," said Measure.

MONDAY MORNING BEHIND the smithy, everyone was gathered by ten o'clock; but from dawn onward, heavily armed deputies were on guard all around the site. The judge arranged things so the whole jury could see, as well as Marty Laws, Verily Cooper, Alvin Smith, Makepeace Smith, and Hank Dowser. "This court is now in session," said the judge loudly. "Now, Hank Dowser, you show us the exact place you marked."

Verily Cooper spoke up. "How do we know he'll mark the same place?"

"Cause I'll dowse it again," said Hank Dowser, "and the same spot will still be best."

Alvin spoke up then. "There's water everywhere here. There's not a place you can pick where there won't be water if you just go far enough down."

Hank Dowser whirled on him and glared. "There it is! He's got no respect for any man's knack except his own! You think I don't know there's water most everywhere? The question is, is the water pure? Is it close to the surface? That's what I find—the easy dig, the clean water. And I'll tell you, by the use of hickory and willow wands, that the water is purest here, and closest to the surface here, and so I mark this spot, as I would have more'n a year ago! Tell me, Alvin Journeyman, if you're so clever, is this or is it not the same spot I marked, exactly?"

"It is," said Alvin, sounding a little abashed. "And I didn't mean to imply that you weren't a real dowser, sir."

"You didn't exactly mean *not* to imply it either, though, did you!"

"I'm sorry," said Alvin. "The water is purest here, and closest to the surface, and you truly found it twice the same, the exact spot."

The judge intervened. "So after this unconventional courtroom exchange, which seems appropriate to this unconventional courtroom, you both agree that this is the spot where Alvin says he dug the first well and found nothing but solid impenetrable stone, and where it is Makepeace's contention that there was no such stone, but rather a buried treasure which Alvin stole and converted to his own use while telling a tale of turning iron into gold."

"For all we know he hid my iron underground here!" cried Makepeace.

The judge sighed. "Makepeace, please, don't make me send you to jail again."

"Sorry," muttered Makepeace.

The judge beckoned to the team of workingmen he'd arranged to come do the digging. Paying them would come out of the county budget, but with four diggers it couldn't take long to prove one or the other right.

They dug and dug, the dirt flying. But it was a dryish dirt, a little moist from the last rain which was only a week ago, but no hint of a watery layer. And then: *chink*.

"The treasure box!" cried Makepeace.

A few moments later, after scraping and prying, the foreman of the diggers called out, "Solid stone, Your Honor! Far as we can reach. Not no boulder, neither—feels like bedrock if'n I ever saw it."

Hank Dowser's face went scarlet. He muscled his way to the hole and slid down the steep side. With his own handkerchief he brushed away the soil from the stone. After a few minutes of examination, he stood up. "Your Honor, I apologize to Mr. Smith, as graciously, I hope, as he just apologized to me a moment ago. Not only is this bedrock—which I did not see, for I have never found such a sheet of water *under* solid stone like this—but also I can see old scrape marks against the stone, proving to me that the prentice boy *did* dig in this spot, just as he said he did, and reached stone, just as he said he did."

"That don't prove he didn't find gold along the way!" cried Makepeace.

"Summations to the jury!" the judge called out.

"In every particular that we could test," said Verily Cooper, "Alvin Smith has proven himself to be truthful and reliable. And all the county has to assail him is the unproven and unprovable speculations of a man whose primary motive seems to be to get his hands upon gold. There are no witnesses but Alvin himself of how the gold came to be shaped like a plow, or the plow came to be made of gold. But we have eight witnesses, not to mention His Honor, myself, and my respected colleague, not to mention Alvin himself, all swearing to you that this plow is not just gold, but also alive. What possible property interest can Makepeace Smith have in an object which clearly belongs to itself and only keeps company with Alvin Smith for its own protection? You have more than a reasonable doubt—you have a certainty that my client is an honest man who has committed no crime, and that the plow should stay with him."

It was Marty Laws's turn then. He looked like he'd had sour milk for breakfast. "You've heard the witnesses, you've seen the evidence, you're all wise men and you can figure this out just fine without my help," said Laws. "May God bless your deliberations."

"Is that your summing up?" demanded Makepeace. "Is that how you administer justice in this county? I'll support your opponent in the next local election, Marty Laws! I swear you haven't heard the end of this!"

"Sheriff, kindly arrest Mr. Makepeace Smith again, three days this time, contempt of court and I'll consider a charge of attempted interference with the course of justice by offering a threat to a sitting judge in order to influence the outcome of a case."

"You're all ganging up against me! All of you are in this together! What did he do, Your *Honor,* bribe you? Offer to share some of that gold with you?"

"Quickly, Sheriff Doggly," said the judge, "before I get angry with the man."

When Makepeace's shouting had died down enough to proceed, the judge asked the jury, "Do we need to traipse on back to the courtroom for hours of deliberation? Or should we just stand back and let you work things out right here?"

The foreman whispered to his fellow jurors; they whispered back. "We have a unanimous verdict, Your Honor."

"What say you, etcetera etcetera?"

"Not guilty of all charges," said the foreman.

"We're done. I commend both attorneys for fine work in a difficult case. And to the jury, my commendation for cutting through the horse pucky and seeing the truth. Good citizens all. This court stands adjourned until the next time somebody brings a blame fool charge against an innocent man, at least that's what I'm betting on." The judge looked around at the people, who were still standing there. "Alvin, you're free to go," he said. "Let's all go home."

OF COURSE THEY didn't all go; nor, strictly speaking, was Alvin free. Right now, surrounded by a crowd and with a dozen deputies on guard, he was safe enough. But as he gripped the sack with the plow inside, he could almost feel the covetings of other men directed toward that plow, that warm and trembling gold.

He wasn't thinking of that, however. He was looking over at Margaret Larner, whose arm was around young Ramona's waist. Someone was speaking to Alvin—it was Verily Cooper, he realized, congratulating him or something, but Verily would understand. Alvin put a hand on Verily's shoulder, to let him know that he was a good friend even though Alvin was about to walk away from him. And Alvin headed on over to Miss Larner and Ramona.

At the last moment he got shy, and though he had his eyes on Margaret all the way through the crowd, it was Ramona he spoke to when he got there. "Miss Ramona, it was brave of you to come forward, and honest too." He shook her hand.

Ramona beamed, but she was also a little upset and nervous. "That whole thing with Amy was my fault I think. She was telling *me* those tales about you, and I was doubting her, which only made her insist more and more. And she stuck to it so much that for a while I believed maybe it *was* true and that's when I told my folks and that's what started all the rumors going, but then when she went with Thatch under the freak show tent and she comes out pregnant but babbling about how it was you got her that way, well, I had my chance then to set things straight, didn't I? And then I didn't get to testify!"

"But you told my friends," said Alvin, "so the people who matter most to me know the truth, and in the meantime you didn't have to hurt your friend Amy." In the back of his mind, though, Alvin couldn't shake the bitter certainty that there would always be some who believed her charges, just as he was sure that she would never recant. She would go on telling those lies about him, and some folks at least would go on believing them, and so he would be known for a cad or worse no matter how clean he lived his life. But that was spilled milk.

Ramona was shaking her head. "I don't reckon she'll be my friend no more."

"But you're *her* friend whether she likes it or not. So much of a friend that you'd even hurt her rather than let her hurt someone else. That's something, in my book."

At that moment, Mike Fink and Armor-of-God came up to him. "Sing us that song you thought up in jail, Alvin!"

At once several others clamored for the song—it was that kind of festive occasion.

"If Alvin won't sing it, Arthur Stuart knows it!" somebody said, and then there was Arthur tugging at his arm and Alvin joined in singing with him. Most of the jury was still there to hear the last verse:

> *I trusted justice not to fail.*
> *The jury did me proud.*
> *Tomorrow I will hit the trail*
> *And sing my hiking song so loud*
> *It's like to start a gale!*

Everybody laughed and clapped. Even Miss Larner smiled, and as Alvin looked at her he knew that this was the moment, now or never. "I got another verse that I never sung to anybody before, but I want to sing it now," he said. They all hushed up again to hear:

> *Now swiftly from this place I'll fly,*
> *And underneath my boots*
> *A thousand lands will pass me by,*
> *Until we choose to put down roots,*
> *My lady love and I.*

He looked at Margaret with all the meaning he could put in his face, and everybody hooted and clapped. "I love you, Margaret Larner," he said. "I asked you before, but I'll say it again now. We're about to journey together for a ways, and I can't think of a good reason why it can't be our honeymoon journey. Let me be your husband, Margaret. Everything good that's in me belongs to you, if you'll have me."

She looked flustered. "You're embarrassing me, Alvin," she murmured.

Alvin leaned close and spoke into her ear. "I know we got separate work to do, once we leave the weavers' house. I know we got long journeys apart."

She held his face between her hands. "You don't know what you might meet on that road. What woman you might meet and love better than me."

Alvin felt a stab of dread. Was this something she had seen with her torchy knack? Or merely the worry any woman might feel? Well, it was *his* future, wasn't it? And even if she saw the possibility of him loving somebody else, that didn't mean he had to let it come true.

He wrapped his long arms around her waist and drew her close, and spoke softly. "You see things in the future that I can't see. Let me ask you like an ordinary man, and you answer me like a woman that knows only the past and the present. Let my promise to you now keep watch over the future."

She was about to raise another objection, when he kissed her lightly on the lips. "If you're my wife, then whatever there is in the future, I can bear it, and I'll do my best to help you bear it too. The judge is right here. Let me begin my life of new freedom with you."

For a moment, her eyes looked heavy and sad, as if she saw some awful pain and suffering in his future. Or was it in her own?

Then she shook it off as if it was just the shadow of a cloud passing over her and now the sun was back. Or as if she had decided to live a certain life, no matter what the cost of it, and now would no longer dread what couldn't be helped. She smiled, and tears ran down her cheeks. "You don't know what you're doing, Alvin, but I'm proud and glad to have your love, and I'll be your wife."

Alvin turned to face the others, and in a loud voice he cried, "She said yes! Judge! Somebody stop the judge from leaving! He's got him one more job to do!" While Peggy went off to find her father and drag him back so he could give her away properly, Verily Cooper fetched the judge.

On the way over to where Alvin waited, the judge put a kindly arm across Verily's back. "My lad, you have a keen mind, a lawyer's mind, and I approve of that. But there's something about you that sets a fellow's teeth on edge."

"If I knew what it was, sir, you may be sure that I'd stop."

"Took me a while to figure it out. And I don't know what you can do about it. What makes folks mad at you right from the start is you sound so damnably English and educated and fine."

Verily grinned, then answered in the vernacular accent he had grown up with, the one he had spent so many years trying to lose. "You mean, sir, that if I talks like a common feller, I'll be more likable?"

The judge whooped with laughter. "That's what I mean, lad, though I don't know as how *that* accent is much better!"

And with that they reached the spot where the wedding party was assembled. Horace stood beside his daughter, and Arthur Stuart was there as Alvin's best man.

The judge turned to Sheriff Doggly. "Do the banns, my good sir."

Po Doggly at once cried out, "Is there a body here so foolish as to claim there's any impediment to the marriage of this pair of good and godly citizens?" He turned to the judge. "Not a soul as I can see, Judge."

So Alvin and Peggy were married, Horace Guester on one side, Arthur Stuart on the other, all standing there in the open on the grounds of the smithy where Alvin had served his prenticehood. Just up the hill was the springhouse where Peggy had lived in disguise as a schoolteacher; the very springhouse where twenty-two years before, as a five-year-old girl, she had seen the heartfires of a family struggling across the Hatrack River in flood, and in the womb of the mother of that family there was a baby with a heartfire so bright it dazzled her, the like of which she'd never seen before or since. She ran, then, ran down this hill, ran to this smithy, got Makepeace Smith and the other men gathered there to race to the river and save the family. All of it began here, within sight of this place. And now she was married to him. Married to the boy whose heartfire shone like the brightest star in her memory, and in all her life since then.

There was dancing that night at Horace's roadhouse, you can bet, and Alvin had to sing his song five more times, and the last verse thrice each time through. And that night he carried his Margaret—his now, and he was hers—in those strong blacksmith's arms up the stairs to the room where Margaret herself had been conceived twenty-eight years before. He was awkward and they both were shy and it didn't help that half the town was charivareeing outside the roadhouse halfway till dawn, but they were man and wife, made one flesh as they had so long been one heart even though she had tried to deny it and he had tried to live without her. Never mind that she had seen his grave in her mind, and herself and their children standing by it, weeping. That scene was possible in every wedding night; and at least there would be children; at least there would be a loving widow to grieve him; at least there would be memory of this night, instead of regretful loneliness. And in the morning, when they awoke, they were not quite so shy, not quite so awkward, and he said such things to her as made her feel more beautiful than anyone who had ever lived before, and more beloved, and I don't know who would dare to say that in that moment it wasn't the pure truth.

18

JOURNEYS

Two days later they were ready to light out. They made no secret about the carriage Armor-of-God hired in Wheelwright, ready to take them off the ferry as soon as they crossed the Hio. That would be enough to decoy the stupid ones. As for the clever ones, well, Mike Fink had his own plan, and even Margaret allowed as how it might well work.

Friends came to the roadhouse all that evening to bid goodbye. Alvin and Peggy and Arthur were well known to

792 • *Orson Scott Card*

them all; Armor-of-God had a few friends here, from business traveling; and Verily had made some new friends, having been the spokesman for the winning side in a highly emotional trial. If Mike Fink had local friends, they weren't the sort to show up in Horace Guester's roadhouse; as Mike confided to Verily Cooper, his friends were most of them the very men Alvin's enemies had hired to kill him and take the plow once he got out on the road tomorrow.

When the last soul had left, Horace embraced his daughter and his new son-in-law and the adopted son he had helped to raise, shook hands with Verily, Armor, and Mike, and then went about as he always did, dousing the candles, putting the night log on the fire, checking to make sure all was secure. As he did, Measure helped the travelers make their way, lightly burdened, quietly down the stairs and out the back, finding the path with only the faintest sliver of moon. Even at that, they walked at first toward the privy, so that anyone casually glancing wouldn't think a thing amiss, unless they noticed the satchel or bag each one carried. Meantime, Measure kept watch, in case someone else was thinking to snatch Alvin that night while he was relieving himself. He kept watch even though Peggy Larner—or was it Goody Smith now?—assured him that not a soul was watching the back of the house.

"All my teaching is in your hands now, Measure," Alvin whispered as he was about to step off the back porch into the night. "I leave you behind this time again, but you know that we set out on the real journey together as true companions, and always will be to the end."

Measure heard him, and wondered if Peggy maybe whispered to him something she had seen in his heartfire, that Measure worried lest Alvin forget how much Measure loved him and wanted to be on this journey by his side. But no,

Alvin didn't need Peggy to tell him he had a brother who was more loyal than life and more sure than death. Alvin kissed his brother's cheek and was gone, the last to go.

They met up again in the woods behind the privy. Alvin went about among them, calming them with soft words, touching them, and each time he touched them they could hear it just a little clearer, a kind of soft humming, or was it the soughing of the wind, or the call of a far-off bird too faint to hear, or perhaps a distant coyote mumbling in its sleep, or the soft scurry of squirrel feet on a tree on the next rise? It was a kind of music, and finally it didn't matter what it was that produced the sound, they fell into the rhythm of it, all holding each other's hands, and at the head of the line, Alvin. They moved swift and sure, keeping step to the music, sliding easily among the trees, making few sounds, saying nothing, marveling at how they could have walked past these woods before and never guessed that such a clear and well-marked path was here; except when they looked back, there was no path, only the underbrush closed off again, for the path was made by Alvin's progress in the midst of the greensong, and behind his party the forest relaxed back into its ordinary shape.

They came to the river, where Po Doggly waited, watching over two boats. "Mind you," he whispered, "I'm not sheriff tonight. I'm only doing what Horace and I done so many times in the past, long before I had me a badge— helping folks as ought to be free get safe across the river." Po and Alvin rowed one of them and Mike and Verily the other, for though he was unaccustomed to such labor, no wooden oar would ever leave a blister on Verily's hands. Silently they moved out across the Hio. Only when they got to the middle did anyone speak. Peggy, controlling the tiller, whispered to Alvin, "Can we talk a little now?"

"Soft and low," said Alvin. "And no laughing."

How had he known she was about to laugh? "We passed a dozen of them as we walked through the woods, all of them asleep, waiting for first light. But there's none on the opposite shore, except the heartfire we're looking for."

Alvin nodded, and gave a thumbs up to the men in the other boat.

They skirted the shore on the Appalachee side for about a quarter mile before coming to the landing site they looked for. Once it had been a putting-in place for flatboats, before the Red fog on the Mizzipy and the new railroad lines slowed and then stopped most of the flatboat traffic. Now an elderly couple lived there mostly from fishing and an orchard that still produced, poorly, but enough for their needs.

Dr. Whitley Physicker was waiting in the front yard of that house with his carriage and four saddled horses; he had insisted on buying or lending them himself, and refused any thought of reimbursement. He also paid the old folks who lived there for the annoyance of having visitors arrive so late at night.

He had a man with him—Arthur Stuart recognized him at once and called him by name. John Binder smiled shyly and shook hands all around, as did Whitley Physicker. "I'm not much for rowing, at my age," Dr. Physicker explained. "So John, being as trustworthy a man as ever there was, agreed to come along, asking no questions. I suppose all the questions he *didn't* ask are answered now."

Binder smiled and chuckled. "Reckon so, all but one. I heard about how you was teaching folks about Makery away out there in Vigor Church, and I hoped you might teach some of it here. Now you're going."

Alvin reassured him. "My brother is holed up in the road-house. Nobody's to know he's there, but if you go to Horace Guester and tell him I sent you, he'll let you go up and talk to Measure. There's a hard tale he'll have to tell you—"

"I know about the curse."

"Well good," said Alvin. "Cause once that's done, he can teach you just what I was teaching in Vigor Church."

Po Doggly and John Binder pushed the boats off the shore before the others were even mounted on their horses or properly seated in the carriage; Whitley Physicker waved from Binder's boat. Alvin shook hands with the old couple, who had got up from their beds to see them off. Then he climbed up into the front seat of the carriage with Margaret; Verily and Arthur sat behind. Armor and Mike rode two of the horses; Verily's horse and the horse that Alvin and Arthur would ride together were tied to the back of the carriage.

As they were about to leave, Mike brought his horse— stamping and fuming, since Mike was a sturdy load and not much of a horseman—beside the carriage and said to Alvin, "Well this plan worked too well! I was looking forward to scaring some poor thug half to death before the night was through!"

Peggy leaned over from the other side of the front seat and said, "You'll get your wish about a mile up the road. There's two fellows there who saw Dr. Physicker's carriage come here this afternoon and wondered what he was doing with four horses tied behind. They're just keeping watch on the road, but even if they don't stop us, they'll give the alarm and then we'll be chased instead of getting away clean."

"Don't kill them, Mike," said Alvin.

"I won't unless they make me," said Mike. "Don't worry, I ain't loose with other folks' lives no more." He rode to Armor, gave him the reins, and said, "Here, bring this girl along with you. I do better on my feet for this kind of work." Then he dismounted and took off running.

Near as I can gather from Mike Fink's tale of the event—and you got to understand that a fellow who wants his story to be truthful has to allow for a lot of brag before deciding what's true in a tale of Mike Fink's heroic exploits—those two smarter-than-normal thugs was dozing while sitting with their backs to opposite sides of the same stump when all of a sudden they both felt their arms pretty near wrenched right out of their sockets and then they were dragged around, grabbed by the collars, and smacked together so hard their noses bled and they saw stars.

"You're lucky I took me a vow of nonviolence," said Mike Fink, "or you'd be suffering some pain right now."

Since they were already suffering something pretty excruciating, they didn't want to find out what this night-wandering fellow thought of as pain. Instead, they obeyed him and held very still as he tied their hands to a couple of lengths of rope, so that the one man's right hand was tied on one end of a rope that held the other man's left, with about two feet of rope between them; and the same with their other two hands. Then Fink made them kneel, picked up a huge log, and laid it down across the two lengths of rope that joined them. What he could lift alone they couldn't lift together. They just knelt there as if they were praying to the log, their hands too far apart even to dream of untying their bonds.

"Next time you want gold," said Fink, "you ought to get yourself a pick and shovel and dig for it, stead of lying in wait in the night for some innocent fellow to come by and get himself robbed and killed."

"We wasn't going to rob nobody," burbled one of the men.

"It's a sure thing you wasn't," said Fink, "cause any man ever wants to get at Alvin Smith has to go through me, and I make a better wall than window, I'll tell you that right now."

Then he jogged back to the road, waved to the others, and waited for them to come alongside so he could mount his horse. In a couple of minutes it was done, and they rode briskly south along a lacework of roads that would completely bypass Wheelwright—including the fancy carriage waiting all day empty by the river, until Horace Guester crossed over, got in the carriage, and used it to shop for groceries in the big-city market that was Wheelwright's pride and joy. That's when the ruffians knew they had been fooled. Oh, some of them lit out in search of Alvin's group, but they had a whole day's head start, or nearly so, and not a one of them found anything except a couple of men kneeling before a log with their butts in the air.

ALL THE WAY to the coast, Calvin expected to be accosted by Napoleon's troops, the carriage blown to bits with grapeshot or set afire or some other grisly end. Why he expected Napoleon to be ungrateful he didn't know. Perhaps it was simply a feeling of general unease. Here he was, not yet twenty years old, and already he had moved through the salons of London and Paris, had spent hours alone discussing a thousand different things with the most powerful man in the world, had learned as many of the secrets of that powerful man as he was likely ever to tell, spoke French if not fluently then competently, and through it all had remained aloof, untouched, his life's dream unchanged. He was a Maker, far more so than Alvin, who remained at the rough frontier of a crude upstart country that couldn't properly call itself a nation; who had Alvin known, except other homespun types like himself? Yet Calvin felt vaguely afraid at the thought of going back to America. Something was trying to stop him. Something didn't want him to go.

"It is nerves," said Honoré. "You will face your brother. You know now that he is a provincial clown, but still he remains your nemesis, the stick against which you must measure yourself. Also you are traveling with me, and you are constantly aware of the need to make a good impression."

"And why would I need to impress *you*, Honoré?"

"Because I am going to write you into a story someday, my friend. Remember that the ultimate power is mine. You may decide what you will do in this life, up to the point. But I will decide what others think of you, and not just now but long after you're dead."

"If anyone still reads your novels," said Calvin.

"You don't understand, my dear bumpkin. Whether they read my novels or not, my judgment of your life will stand. These things take on a life of their own. No one remembers the original source, or cares either."

"So people will only remember what you say about me—and you they won't remember at all."

Honoré chuckled. "Oh, I don't know about that, Calvin. I intend to be memorable. But then, do I care whether I'm remembered? I think not. I have lived without the affection of my own mother; why should I crave the affection of strangers not yet born?"

"It's not whether you're remembered," said Calvin. "It's whether you changed the world."

"And the first change I will make is: They must remember me!" Honoré's voice was so loud that the coachman slid open the panel and inquired whether they wanted something from him. "More speed," cried Honoré, "and softer bumps. Oh, and when the horses relieve themselves: Less odor."

The coachman growled and closed the panel shut.

"Don't you intend to change the world?" asked Calvin.

"Change it? A paltry project, smacking of weak ambition and much self-contempt. Your brother wants to build a city. You want to tear it down before his eyes. *I* am the one with vision, Calvin. I intend to *create* a world. A world more fascinating, engrossing, spellbinding, intricate, beautiful, and real than this world."

"You're going to outdo God?"

"He spent far too much time on geology and botany. For him, Adam was an afterthought—oh, by the way, is man found upon the Earth? I shall not make that mistake. I will concentrate on people, and slip the science into the cracks."

"The difference is that your people will all be confined to tiny black marks on paper," said Calvin.

"My people will be more real than these shallow creatures God has made! I, too, will make them in my own image—only taller—and mine will have more palpable reality, more inner life, more connection to the living world around them than these mud-covered peasants or the calculating courtiers of the palace or the swaggering soldiers and bragging businessmen who keep Paris under their thumbs."

"Instead of worrying about the emperor stopping us, perhaps I should worry about lightning striking us," said Calvin.

It was meant as a joke, but Honoré did not smile. "Calvin, if God was going to strike you dead for anything, you'd already be dead by now. I don't pretend to know whether God exists, but I'll tell you this—the old man is doddering now! The old fellow talks rough but it's all a memory. He hasn't the stuff anymore! He can't stop us! Oh, maybe he can write us out of his will, but we'll make our own fortune and let the old boy stand back lest he be splashed when we hurtle by!"

"Do you ever have even a moment of self-doubt?"

"None," said Honoré. "I live in the constant certainty of failure, and the constant certainty of genius. It is a species of madness, but greatness is not possible without it. Your problem, Calvin, is that you never really question yourself about anything. However you feel, that's the right way to feel, and so you feel that way and everything else better get out of your way. Whereas I endeavor to change my feelings because my feelings are always wrong. For instance, when approaching a woman you lust after, the foolish man acts out his feelings and clutches at an inviting breast or makes some fell invitation that gets him slapped and keeps him from the best parties for the rest of the year. But the wise man looks the woman in the eye and serenades her about her astonishing beauty and her great wisdom and his own inadequacy to explain to her how much she deserves her place in the exact center of the universe. No woman can resist this, Calvin, or if she can, she's not worth having."

The carriage came to a stop.

Honoré flung open the door. "Smell the air!"

"Rotting fish," said Calvin.

"The coast! I wonder if I shall throw up, and if I do, whether the sea air will have affected the color and consistency of my vomitus."

Calvin ignored his deliberately crude banter as he reached up for their bags. He well knew that Honoré was only crude when he didn't much respect his company; when with aristocrats, Honoré never uttered anything but bon mots and epigrams. For the young novelist to speak that way to Calvin was a sign, not so much of intimacy, but of disrespect.

When they found an appropriate ship bound for Canada, Calvin showed the captain the letter Napoleon had given him. Contrary to his worst fears, after seeing a production of a newly revised and prettied-up script of *Hamlet* in London, the letter did not instruct the captain to kill Calvin and Honoré at once—though there was no guarantee that the fellow didn't have orders to strangle them and pitch them into the sea when they were out of sight of land.

Why am I so afraid?

"So the Emperor's treasurer will reimburse me for all expenses out of the treasury when I come back?"

"That's the plan," said Honoré. "But here, my friend, I know how ungenerous these imperial officials can be. Take this."

He handed the captain a sheaf of franc notes. Calvin was astonished. "All these weeks you've pretended to be poor and up to your ears in debt."

"I *am* poor! I *am* in debt. If I didn't owe money, why would I ever steel myself to write? No, I simply borrowed the price of my passage from my mother *and* my father— they never talk, so they'll never find out—and from two of my publishers, promising each of them a completely exclusive book about my travels in America."

"You borrowed to pay our passage, knowing all along that the Emperor would pay it?"

"A man has to have spending money, or he's not a man," said Honoré. "I have a wad of it, with which I have every intention of being generous with you, so I hope you won't condemn my methods."

"You're not terribly honest, are you?" said Calvin, half appalled, half admiring.

"You shock me, you hurt me, you offend me, I challenge you to a duel and then take sick with pneumonia so that I can't meet you, but I urge you to go ahead without me. Keep in mind that *because* I had that money, the captain will now invite us into his cabin for dinner every night of the voyage. And in answer to your question, I am perfectly honest when I am creating something, but otherwise words are mere tools designed to extract what I need from the pockets or bank accounts of those who currently but temporarily possess it. Calvin, you've been too long among the Puritans. And I have been too long among the Hypocrites."

* * *

IT WAS PEGGY who found the turnoff to Chapman Valley, found it easily though there was no sign and she was coming this time from the other direction. She and Alvin left the others with the carriage under the now-leafless oak out in front of the weavers' house. For Peggy, coming to this place now was both thrilling and embarrassing. What would they think of the way things had turned out since they set her on this present road?

Then, just as she raised her hand to knock on the door, she remembered something.

"Alvin," she said. "It slipped my mind, but something Becca said when I was here a few months ago—"

"If it slipped your mind, then it was supposed to slip your mind."

"You and Calvin. You need to reclaim Calvin, find him and reclaim him before he turns completely against the work you're doing."

Alvin shook his head. "Becca doesn't know everything."

"And what does that mean?"

"What makes you think Calvin wasn't already the enemy of our work before he was born?"

"That's not possible," said Peggy. "Babies are born innocent and pure."

"Or steeped in original sin? Those are the choices? I can't believe that you of all people believe either idea, you who put your hands on the womb and see the futures in the baby's heartfire. The child is already himself then, the good and bad, ready to step into the world and make of himself whatever he wants most to be."

She squinted at him. "Why is it that when we're alone, talking of something serious, you don't sound so much the country bumpkin?"

"Because maybe I learned everything you taught me,

only I also learned that I don't want to lose touch with the common people," said Alvin. "They're the ones who are going to build the city with me. Their language is my native language—why should I forget it, just because I learned another? How many educated folks do you think are going to come away from their fine homes and educated friends and roll up their sleeves to make something with their own hands?"

"I don't want to knock on this door," said Peggy. "My life changes when I come into this place."

"You don't have to knock," said Alvin. He reached out and turned the knob. The door opened.

When he made as if to step inside, Peggy took his arm. "Alvin, you can't just walk in here!"

"If the door wasn't locked, then I can walk in," said Alvin. "Don't you understand what this place is? This is the place where things are as they must be. Not like the world out there, the world you see in the heartfires, the world of things that can be. And not like the world inside my head, the world as it might be. And not like the world as it was first conceived in the mind of God, which is the world as it should be."

She watched him step over the threshold. There was no alarum in the house, nor even a sound of life. She followed him. Young as he was, this man she had watched over from his infancy, this man whose heart she knew more intimately than her own, he could still surprise her by what he did of a sudden without thought, because he simply knew it was right and had to be this way.

The endless cloth still lay folded in piles, linked each to each, winding over furniture, through halls, up and down stairs. They stepped over the spans and reaches of it. "No dust," said Peggy. "I didn't notice that the first time. There's no dust on the cloth."

"Good housekeepers here?" asked Alvin.

"They dust all this cloth?"

"Or maybe there's simply no passage of time within the cloth. Always and forever it exists in that one present moment in which the shuttlecock flew from side to side."

As he said these words, they began to hear the shuttlecock. Someone must have opened a door.

"Becca?" called Peggy.

They followed the sound through the house to the ancient cabin at the house's heart, where an open door led into the room with the loom. But to Peggy's surprise, it wasn't Becca seated there. It was the boy. Her nephew, the one who had dreamed of this. With practiced skill he drove the shuttlecock back and forth.

"Is Becca . . ." Peggy couldn't bring herself to ask about the weaver's death.

"Naw," said the boy. "We changed the rules a little here. No more pointless sacrifice. You done that, you know. Came here as a judge—well, your judgment was heeded. I take my shift for a while, and she can go out a little."

"So is it you we talk to now?" asked Alvin.

"Depends on what you want. I don't know nothing about nothing, so if you want answers, I don't think I'm it."

"I want to use the door that leads to Ta-Kumsaw."

"Who?" the boy asked.

"Your uncle Isaac," said Peggy.

"Oh, sure." He nodded with his head. "It's that one."

Alvin strode toward it.

"You ever used one of these doors before?" asked the boy.

"No," said Alvin.

"Well then ain't you the stupid one, heading right for it like it was some ordinary door."

"What's different? I know it leads to the Red lands. I

know it leads to the house where Ta-Kumsaw's daughter weaves the lives of the Reds of the west."

"Here's the tricky part. When you pass through the door, you can't have no part of yourself touching anything here but air. You can't brush up against the doorjamb. You can't let a foot linger on the floor. It's not a step through the door, it's a leap."

"And what happens if some part of me *does* touch?"

"Then that part of this place drags you down just a little, slows you, lowers you, and so instead of you passing through the door in one smooth motion, you go through in a couple of pieces. Ain't nobody can put you together after that, Mr. Maker."

Peggy was appalled. "I never realized it was so dangerous."

"Breathing's dangerous too," said the boy, "if'n you breathe in something to make you sick." He grinned. "I saw you two get all twined up together here. Congratulations."

"Thanks," said Alvin.

"So what do they call you now, judge woman?" the boy asked Peggy. "Goody Smith?"

"Most still call me Peggy Larner. Only they say Miz Larner now, and not Miss."

"I call her Margaret," said Alvin.

"I reckon you'll really be married when she starts to think of herself by the name you call her, instead of the name her parents called her by." He winked at Peggy. "Thanks for getting me my job. My sisters are glad, too, they had nightmares, I'll tell you. There ain't no love of the loom in them." He turned back to Alvin. "So are you going or what?"

At that moment the door flew open and a tied-up bundle flew through it.

"Uh-oh," said the boy. "Best turn your back. Becca's

coming through, and she travels stark nekkid, seeing as how women's clothing can't fit through that door without touching."

Alvin turned his back, and so did Peggy, though unlike Alvin she cheated and allowed herself to watch anyway. It was not Becca who came through the door first, however. It was Ta-Kumsaw, a man Peggy had never met, though she had seen him often enough in Alvin's heartfire. He was not naked, but rather clothed in buckskins that clung tightly to his body. He saw them standing there and grunted. "Boy Renegado comes back to see the most dangerous Red man who ever lived."

"Howdy, Ta-Kumsaw," said Alvin.

"Hi, Isaac," said the boy. "I warned him about the door like you said."

"Good boy," said Ta-Kumsaw. He turned his back on them then, just in time for Becca to leap through the door wearing only thin and clinging underwear. He gathered her at once into his arms. Then together they untied the bundle and unfolded it into a dress, which she drew down over her head. "All right," said Ta-Kumsaw. "She's dressed enough for a White woman now."

Alvin turned around and greeted her. There were hand-shakes, and even a hug between women. They talked about what had happened in Hatrack River over the past few months, and then Alvin explained his errand.

Ta-Kumsaw showed no emotion. "I don't know what my brother will say. He keeps his own counsel."

"Does he rule there in the west?" asked Alvin.

"Rule? That's not how we do things. There are many tribes, and in each tribe many wise men. My brother is one of the greatest of them, everyone agrees to that. But he doesn't make law just by deciding what it should be. We don't do anything as foolish as you do, electing one president and concentrating too much power in his hands. It was good enough when good men held the office, but always when you create an office that a man can lay hands on, an evil man will someday lay hands on it."

"Which is going to happen on New Year's day when Harrison—"

Ta-Kumsaw glowered. "Never say that name, that unbearable name."

"Not saying it won't make him go away."

"It will keep his evil out of this house," said Ta-Kumsaw. "Away from the people I love."

In the meantime, Becca had finished dressing. She came to the boy and bumped him with her hip. "Move over, stubby-fingers. That's my loom you're tangling."

"Tightest weave ever," the boy retorted. "People will always know which spots I wove."

Becca settled onto the chair and then began to make the shuttlecock dance. The whole music of the loom changed, the rhythm of it, the song. "You came for a purpose, Maker? The door's still open for you. Do what you came to do."

For the first time Peggy really looked at the door, trying to see what lay beyond it; and what lay beyond was nothing. Not blackness, but not daylight either. Just . . . nothing. Her eyes couldn't look at it; her gaze kept shifting away.

"Alvin," she said. "Are you sure you want to—"

He kissed her. "I love it when you worry about me."

She smiled and kissed him back. As he took off his cap and his boots, and his long coat that might flap against the doorjamb, he couldn't see how she reached into the small box she kept in a pocket of her skirt; how she held the last scrap of his birth caul between her fingers and then watched his heartfire, ready to spring into action the moment he needed her, to use his power to heal him even if he, in some dire extremity, could not or dared not or would not use it himself.

He ran for the door, leapt toward it left-foot-first, his right foot leaving the ground before any part of him broke the plane of the door. He sailed through with his head ducked down; he missed the top of the door by an inch.

"I don't like it when people leap through all spread out like that," said Ta-Kumsaw. "Better to spring from both feet at once, and curl up into a ball as you go."

"You athletic men can do that," said Becca. "But I can't see myself hitting the floor like that and rolling. Besides, you leap half the time yourself."

"I'm not as tall as Alvin," said Ta-Kumsaw. He turned to Peggy. "He grew to be very tall."

But Peggy didn't answer him.

"She's watching his heartfire," said Becca. "Best leave her alone till he comes back."

ALVIN TUMBLED AND fell when he hit the floor on the other side; he sprawled into a pile of cloth and heard the sound of laughter. He got up and looked around. Another cabin, but a newish one, and the girl at the loom was scarcely older than he was. She was a mixup like Arthur, only half-Red instead of half-Black, and the combination of Ta-Kumsaw and Becca was becoming in her.

"Howdy, Alvin," she said. He had expected her voice to sound like Ta-Kumsaw's and Tenskwa-Tawa's, accented when she spoke in English, but she spoke like Becca, a bit old-fashioned sounding but like a native speaker of the tongue.

"Howdy," he said.

"You sure came through like a ton of bricks," she said.

"Made a mess of the piles of cloth here."

"Don't fret," she said. "That's why they're there. Papa always smacks into them when he comes through like a cannonball."

With that he ran out of conversation, and so did she, so he stood there watching as she ran her loom.

"Go find Tenskwa-Tawa. He's waiting for you."

Alvin had heard so much about the fog on the Mizzipy that he had halfway got it into his head that the whole of the western lands was covered with fog. When he opened the cabin and stepped outside, though, he found that far from being foggy, the sky was so clear it felt like he could see clear into heaven in broad daylight. There were high mountains looming to the east, and he could see them so crisp and clear that he felt as though he could trace the crevices in the bare granite near the top, or count the leaves on the oak trees halfway up their craggy flanks. The cabin stood at the brow of a hill separating two valleys, both of which contained lakes. The one to the north was huge, the far reaches of it invisible because of the curve of the Earth, not because of any haze or thickness of the air; the lake to the south was smaller, but it was even more beautiful, shining like a blue jewel in the cold sunlight of late autumn.

"The snow is late," said a voice behind him.

Alvin turned. "Shining Man," he said, the name slipping from his lips before he could think.

"And you are the man who learned how to be a man when he was a boy," said Tenskwa-Tawa.

They embraced. The wind whistled around them. When they parted, Alvin glanced around again. "This is a pretty exposed place to build a cabin," he said.

"Had to be here," said Tenskwa-Tawa. "The valley to the south is Timpa-Nogos. Holy ground, where there can be no houses and no wars. The valley to the north is grazing land, where the deer can be hunted by families that run out of food in the winter. No houses either. Don't worry. Inside a weaver's house is always warm." He smiled. "I'm glad to see you."

Alvin wasn't sure if he could remember Tenskwa-Tawa ever smiling before. "You're happy here?"

"Happy?" Tenskwa-Tawa's face went placid again. "I feel as though I stand with one foot on this earth and the other foot in the place where my people wait for me."

"Not all died that day at Tippy-Canoe," said Alvin. "You still have people here."

"They also stand with one foot in one place, one foot in the other." He glanced toward a canyon that led up into a gap between the impossibly high mountains. "They live in a high mountain valley. The snow is late this year, and they're glad of that, unless it means poor water for next year, and a poor crop. That's our life now, Alvin Maker. We used to live in a place where water leapt out of the ground wherever you struck it with a stick."

"But the air is clear. You can see forever."

Tenskwa-Tawa put his fingers to Alvin's lips. "No man sees forever. But some men see farther. Last winter I rode a tower of water into the sky over the holy lake Timpa-Nogos. I saw many things. I saw you come here. I heard the news you told me and the question you asked me."

"And did you hear your answer?"

"First you must make my vision come true," said Tenskwa-Tawa.

So Alvin told him about Harrison being elected president by bragging about his bloody hands, and how they wondered if Tenskwa-Tawa might release the people of Vigor Church from their curse, so they could leave their homes, those as wanted to, and become part of the Crystal City when Alvin started to build it. "Was that what you heard me ask you?"

"Yes," said Tenskwa-Tawa.

"And what was your answer?"

"I didn't see my answer," said Tenskwa-Tawa. "So I have had all these months to think of what it was. In all these months, my people who died on that grassy slope have walked before my eyes in my sleep. I have seen their blood again and again flow down the grass and turn the Tippy-Canoe Creek red. I have seen the faces of the children and babies. I knew them all by name, and I still remember all the names and all the faces. Each one I see in the dream, I ask them, Do you forgive these White murderers? Do you understand their rage and will you let me take your blood from their hands?"

Tenskwa-Tawa paused. Alvin waited, too. One did not rush a shaman as he told of his dreams.

"Every night I have had this dream until finally last night the last of them came before me and I asked my question."

Again, a silence. Again, Alvin waited patiently. Not patiently the way a White man waits, showing his patience by looking around or moving his fingers or doing something else to mark the passage of time. Alvin waited with a Red man's patience, as if this moment were to be savored in itself, as if the suspense of waiting was in itself an experience to be marked and remembered.

"If even one of them had said, I do not forgive them, do not lift the curse, then I would not lift the curse," said Tenskwa-Tawa. "If even one baby had said, I do not forgive them for taking away my days of running like a deer through the meadows, I would not lift the curse. If even one mother had said, I do not forgive them for the baby that was in my womb when I died, who never saw the light of day with its beautiful eyes, I would not lift the curse. If even one father had said, The anger still runs hot in my heart, and if you lift the curse I will still have some hatred left unavenged, then I would not lift the curse."

Tears flowed down Alvin's face, for he knew the answer now, and he could not imagine himself ever being so good that even in death he could forgive those who had done such a terrible thing to him and his family.

"I also asked the living," said Tenskwa-Tawa. "Those who lost father and mother, brother and sister, uncle and aunt, child and friend, teacher and helper, hunting companion, and wife, and husband. If even one of these living ones had said, I cannot forgive them yet, Tenskwa-Tawa, I would not lift the curse."

Then he fell silent one last time. This time the silence lasted and lasted. The sun had been at noon when Alvin arrived; it was touching the tops of the mountains to the west when at last Tenskwa-Tawa moved again, nodding his head. Like Alvin, he, too, had wept, and then had waited long enough for the tears to dry, and then had wept again, all without changing the expression on his face, all without moving a muscle of his body as the two of them sat facing each other in the tall dry autumn grass, in the cold dry autumn wind. Now he opened his mouth and spoke again. "I have lifted the curse," he said.

Alvin embraced his old teacher. It was not what a Red man would have done, but Alvin had acted Red all afternoon, and so Tenskwa-Tawa accepted the gesture and even returned it. Touched by the Red Prophet's hands, his cheek against the old man's hair, the old man's face against his shoulder, Alvin remembered that once he had thought of asking Tenskwa-Tawa to strengthen the curse on Harrison, to stop him from misusing his bloody hands. It made him ashamed. If the dead could forgive, should not the living? Harrison would find his own way through life, and his own path to death. Judgment would have to come, if it came at all, from someone wiser than Alvin.

When they arose from the grass, Tenskwa-Tawa looked north toward the larger lake. "Look, a man is coming."

Alvin saw where he was looking. Not far off, a man was jogging lightly along a path through the head-high grass. Not running in the Red man's way, but like a White man, and not a young one. His hatless bald head glinted momentarily in the sunset.

"That ain't Taleswapper, is it?" asked Alvin.

"The Sho-sho-nay invited him to come and trade stories with them," said Tenskwa-Tawa.

Instead of asking more questions, Alvin waited with Tenskwa-Tawa until Taleswapper came up the long steep path. He was out of breath when he arrived, as might have been expected. But as Alvin sent his doodlebug through Taleswapper's body, he was surprised at the old man's excellent health. They greeted each other warmly, and Alvin told him the news. Taleswapper smiled at Tenskwa-Tawa. "Your people are better than you thought they were," he said.

"Or more forgetful," said Tenskwa-Tawa ruefully.

"I'm glad I happened to be here, to hear this news," said Taleswapper. "If you're going back through the weaver's house, I'd like to go with you."

WHEN ALVIN AND Taleswapper returned to Becca's cabin within the heart of the weaver's house, it had been dark for two hours. Ta-Kumsaw had gone outside and invited Peggy's and Alvin's friends to come in and eat with his family. Becca's sister and her daughters and her son joined them; they ate a stew of bison meat, Red man's food cooked the White man's way, a compromise like so much else in this house. Ta-Kumsaw had introduced himself by the name of Isaac Weaver, and Peggy was careful to call him by no other name.

Alvin and Taleswapper found them all lying on their bed-rolls on the floor of the parlor, except for Peggy, who was sitting on a chair, listening as Verily Cooper told them tales of his life in England, and all the subterfuges he had gone through in order to conceal his knack from everyone. She turned to face the door before her husband and their old friend came through it; the others also turned, so all eyes were on them. They knew at once from the joy on Alvin's face what Tenskwa-Tawa's answer had been.

"I want to ride out tonight and tell them," said Armor-of-God. "I want them to know the good news right *now*."

"Too dark," said Ta-Kumsaw, who came in from the kitchen where he had been helping his sister-in-law wash the dishes from supper.

"There's no more rules, now, the curse is lifted free and clear," said Alvin. "But he asks that we do something all the same. That everyone who used to be under the curse gather their family together once a year, on the anniversary of the massacre at Tippy-Canoe, and on that day eat no food, but instead tell the story as it used to be told to all strangers who came through Vigor Church. Once a year, our children and our children's children, forever. He asks that we do that, but there'll be no punishment if we don't. No punishment except that our children will forget, and when they forget, there's always the chance that it might happen again."

"I'll tell them that too," said Armor. "They'll all take a vow to do that, you can be sure, Alvin." He turned to Ta-Kumsaw. "You can tell your brother that for me when next you see him, that they'll all take that vow."

Ta-Kumsaw grunted. "So much for calling myself Isaac in order to conceal from you who I really am."

"We've met before," said Armor, "and even if we hadn't, I know a great leader when I see one, and I knew who it was Alvin came to see."

"You talk too much, Armor-of-God, like all White men," said Ta-Kumsaw. "But at least what you say isn't always stupid."

Armor nodded and smiled to acknowledge the compliment.

Alvin and Peggy were given a bedroom and a fine bed, which Peggy suspected was Ta-Kumsaw's and Becca's own. The others slept on the floor in the parlor—slept as best they could, which wasn't well, what with all the excitement and the way Mike Fink snored so loud and the way Armor had to get up to pee about three times an hour it seemed like, till Peggy heard the activity, woke Alvin up, and Alvin *did* something with his doodlebug inside Armor's body so he didn't feel like his bladder was about to bust all the time. When morning came the men in the parlor slept a little late, and woke to the smell of a country breakfast, with biscuits and gravy and slabs of salted ham fried with potatoes.

Then it was time for parting. Armor-of-God was like an eager horse himself, stamping and snorting till they finally told him to go *on*. He mounted and rode out of Chapman Valley, waving his hat and whooping like those damn fools on election night the week before.

Alvin's and Peggy's parting was harder. She and Taleswapper would take Whitley Physicker's carriage and drive it to the next town of any size, where she'd hire another carriage and Taleswapper would drive this one north to Hatrack River to return it to the good doctor. From there Peggy intended to go to Philadelphia for a while. "I hope that I might turn some hearts against Harrison's plans, if I'm there where Congress meets. He's only going to be president, not king, not emperor—he has to win the consent of Congress to do anything, and perhaps there's still hope." But Alvin knew from her voice that she had little hope, that she knew already along what dark roads Harrison would lead the country.

Alvin felt nearly as bleak about his own prospects. "Tenskwa-Tawa couldn't tell me a thing about how to make the Crystal City, except to say a thing I already knew: The Maker is a part of what he Makes."

"So . . . you will search," said Peggy, "and I will search."

What neither of them said, because both of them knew that they both knew, was that there was a child growing already in Margaret's womb; a girl. Each of them could calculate nine months as well as the other.

"Where will you be next August?" asked Alvin.

"Wherever I am, I'll make quite sure you know about it."

"And wherever you are, I'll make quite sure I'm there."

"I think the name should be Becca," said Peggy.

"I was thinking to call her after you. Call her Little Peggy."

Peggy smiled. "Becca Margaret, then?"

Alvin smiled back, and kissed her. "People talk about fools counting chickens before they hatch. That's nothing. We name them."

He helped her up into the carriage, beside Taleswapper, who already had the reins in hand. Arthur Stuart led Alvin's horse to him, and as he mounted, the boy said, "We made up a song about us last night, while you two was upstairs!"

"A song?" said Alvin. "Let's hear it then."

"We made it up like as if it was you singing it," said Arthur Stuart. "Come on, you all got to sing! And at the end I made up a chorus all by myself, I made up the last part *alone* without *no help* from *nobody*."

Alvin reached down and hauled the boy up behind him. Arthur Stuart's arms went around his middle. "Come on," the boy shouted. "Let's all sing."

As they began the song, Alvin reached down and took hold of the harness of the carriage's lead horse, starting the parade up the road leading out of Chapman Valley.

A young man startin' on his own
Must leave his home so fair.
Better not go wand'rin' all alone
Or you might get eaten by a bear!

I'm wise enough to heed that song,
But who'll make up my pair?
If I choose my boon companion wrong
Then I might get eaten by a bear!

I'll take a certain mixup lad—
He's small, but does his share—
And I'll watch him close, cause I'd be sad
If the boy got eaten by a bear!

I'll take along this barrister
With lofty learned air,
And I'll make of him a forester
So he won't get eaten by a bear!

Behold this noble river rat
With brag so fine and rare!
He's as dangerous as a mountain cat—
He will not get eaten by a bear!

Now off we go, where'er we please.
We're heroes, so we dare
To defy mosquitoes, wasps, and fleas,
And we won't get eaten by a bear!

They reached the main road and Peggy turned right, heading north, while the men took their horses south. She waved from the driver's seat, but did not look back. Alvin stopped to watch her, just for a moment, just for a lingering moment, as Arthur Stuart behind him shouted, "Now I get to sing the last part that I made up all by myself! I get to!"

"So sing it," said Alvin.

So Arthur Stuart sang.

> *Grizzly bear, grizzly bear,*
> *Run and hide, you sizzly bear!*
> *We'll take away your coat of hair*
> *And roast you in your underwear!*

Alvin laughed till tears streamed down his face.

19

PHILADELPHIA

When Calvin's and Honoré's ship arrived in New Amsterdam, the newspapers were full of chat about the inauguration, which was only a week away in Philadelphia. Calvin remembered Harrison's name at once—how many times had he listened to the tale of the massacre at Tippy-Canoe? He remembered meeting the bloody-handed bum on the streets of New Amsterdam, and told the tale to Honoré.

"So you created him."

"I helped him make the best of his limited possibilities," said Calvin.

"No, no," said Honoré. "You are too modest. This man created himself as a monster who killed people for political gain. Then this Red prophet destroyed him with a curse. Then, from the hopeless ruin of his life, you turned his path upward again. Calvin, you finally impress me. You have achieved, in life, that infinite power which is usually reserved to the novelist."

"The power to use up enormous amounts of paper and ink to no avail?"

"The power to make people's lives take the most illogical turns. Parents, for instance, have no such power. They can help their children along, or, more likely, shatter their lives as someone's mother once did with her casual adultery even as she abandoned her child to the tender mercies of the boarding school. But such parents have no power then to heal the child they have injured. Having brought the child low, they cannot raise the child up. But *I* can bring a man low, then raise him up, then bring him low again, all with a stroke of the pen."

"And so can I," said Calvin thoughtfully.

"Well, to a degree," said Honoré. "To be honest, however, you did not bring him low, and now, having raised him up, I doubt you can bring him low again. The man has been elected president, even if his domain consists primarily of trees and tree-dwelling beasts."

"There's several million people in the United States," said Calvin.

"It was to them that I referred," said Honoré.

The challenge was too much for Calvin to resist. Could he bring down the president of the United States? How would he do it? This time there could be no scornful words that would provoke him into self-destruction, as Calvin's words had helped the man resurrect himself from shameful oblivion. But then, Calvin had learned to do much more subtle things than mere talk in the many months since then. It would be a challenge. It was almost a dare.

"Let's go to Philadelphia," said Calvin. "For the inauguration."

Honoré was perfectly happy to board the train and go along. He was amused by the size and newness of the tiny towns that Americans referred to as "cities," and Calvin constantly had to watch out for him as he practiced his feeble English with the kind of rough American who was likely to pick up the little Frenchman and toss him into a river. Honoré, armed only with an ornate cane he had purchased from a fellow-voyager, had fearlessly walked through the most wretched immigrant districts of New Amsterdam and now of Philadelphia. "These men aren't characters in novels," said Calvin, more than once. "If they break your neck, it'll really be broken!"

"Then you'll have to fix me, my talented knackish friend." He said the word *knackish* in English, though truth to tell no one would have understood the word but Calvin himself.

"There's no such word as *knackish* in the English language," Calvin said.

"There is now," said Honoré, "because I put it there."

As Calvin awaited the inauguration, he considered many possible plans. Nothing with mere words would do the job. Harrison's election had been so openly based on lies that it was hard to imagine how anything could now be revealed about Harrison that would shock or disappoint anyone. When the people elected a president like this one, who ran a campaign like the one he ran, it was hard to imagine what kind of scandal might bring him down.

Besides, Calvin's knack was now way beyond words. He wanted to get inside Harrison's body and do some mischief. He remembered Napoleon and how he suffered from the gout; he toyed with the idea of giving Harrison some debilitating condition. Regretfully he concluded that this was beyond his power, to fine-tune such a thing so that it would cause pain without killing. No doubt Calvin would have to wait around to watch, to make sure that whatever he did wasn't cured. And besides, pain wouldn't bring Harrison low any more than gout had stopped Napoleon from fulfilling all his ambitions.

Pain without killing. Why had he put such a ridiculous limitation on himself? There was no reason not to kill Harrison. Hadn't the man ordered the death of Calvin's own brother Measure? Hadn't he slaughtered all those Reds and caused all of Calvin's family and neighbors to be under a curse for most of Calvin's life? Nothing brought a man lower than dying. Six feet under the ground, that was as low as a body ever got.

The day of the inauguration, the first day of the new year, was bitterly cold, and as Harrison walked through the streets of Philadelphia to the temporary stand where he would take the oath in front of several thousand spectators, it began to snow. Proudly he refused even to put on a hat—what was cold weather to a man from the west?—and when he reached the platform to give his speech, Calvin was delighted to see that the new president's throat was already sore, his chest already somewhat congested. It was really a simple matter of Calvin to send his doodling bug inside the chest of White Murderer Harrison and encourage the little animals inside his lungs to grow, to multiply, to spread throughout his body. Harrison, you're going to be one very, very sick man.

The speech lasted an hour, and Harrison didn't cut out a single word, though by the end he was coughing thickly into his handkerchief after every sentence. "Philadelphia is colder to hell," Honoré said in his feeble English as they finally left the square. "And your President he is one dammit long talker." Then, in French, Honoré asked, "Did I say it right? Did I swear properly?"

"Like a stevedore," said Calvin. "Like a river rat. I was proud of you."

"I was proud of you too," said Honoré. "You looked so serious, I thought maybe you were paying attention to his speech. Then I thought, No, the lad is using his powers. So I hoped you might sever his head as he stood there and make it roll down splat on his speech. Let him put his hands on *that* to take his oath of office."

"That would have been a memorable inauguration," said Calvin.

"But it wouldn't be good for you to take another man's life," said Honoré. "All joking aside, my friend, it isn't good for a man to get a taste for blood."

"My brother Alvin killed a man," said Calvin. "He killed a man who needed killing, and nobody said boo to him about it."

"Dangerous for him, but perhaps more dangerous for you," said Honoré. "Because you are already filled with hate—I say this not as criticism, it's one of the things I find most attractive about you—you are filled with hate, and so it is dangerous for you to open the faucet of murder. That is a stream you may not be able to damp."

"Not to worry," said Calvin.

They lingered in Philadelphia for several more weeks, as Harrison's bad cold turned into pneumonia. He struggled on, being something of a tough old nut, but in the end he died, scarcely a month after his inauguration, having never been healthy enough even to name a cabinet.

This being the first time a president of the United States had died in office, there was some unresolved ambiguity in the Constitution about whether the vice-president merely acted as president or actually took the office. Andrew Jackson neatly resolved the issue by walking into Congress and placing his hand on the Bible they kept there as a reminder of all the virtues they worked so hard to get the voters to believe they possessed. In a loud voice he took the oath of office in front of all of them, daring them to deny him the right to do so. There were jokes about "His Accidency the President" for a while, but Jackson wasn't a man to be trifled with. All of Harrison's cronies found themselves with sore backsides from bouncing down the steps of the George Washington Building where the executive branch of the government had its offices. Whatever Harrison had planned for America would never happen now, or at least not in the way that he had planned it. Jackson was in nobody's pocket but his own.

Calvin and Honoré agreed that they had done a great service for the nation. "Though my part of it was very small," said Honoré. "A mere word. A suggestion." Calvin knew, however, that in his own heart Honoré undoubtedly took credit for the whole thing, or at least for everything beneficial that resulted from it. That knowledge scarcely bothered Calvin, though. Nothing really bothered him now, for his power had been confirmed in his own heart. *I brought down a president and no one knew that I did it. Nothing messy or awkward like Alvin's killing of that Finder with his own bare hands. I learned more than the honing of my knack on the continent. I acquired finesse. Alvin will never have that, crude frontiersman that he is and always will be.*

How easy it had been. Easy and free of risk. There was a man who needed to die, and all it took was a little maneuvering in his lungs and it was done. Well, that plus a few adjustments as the man lay in his sickbed in the presidential mansion. It wouldn't do to have his body fight off the infection and recover, would it? But I never had to touch him. Never even had to speak to him. Didn't even have to get ink on my fingers, like poor Honoré, whose characters never really breathe despite all his skill, and so never really die.

Calvin allowed himself, on the last night he and Honoré spent in Philadelphia, to lie in bed imagining Alvin's death. A slow agonizing death from some miserable disease like lockjaw. I could do that, thought Calvin.

Then he thought, No I couldn't, and went to sleep.